Raves for Phil Rickman's
CURFEW . . .

CURFEW

PHIL RICKMAN

BERKLEY BOOKS, NEW YORK

Previously published in the U.K. as *Crybbe*.

CURFEW

A Berkley Book / published by arrangement with
the author

PRINTING HISTORY
G. P. Putnam's Sons edition / July 1993
Berkley edition / August 1994

ISBN: 0-425-14334-1

BERKLEY®
Berkley Books are published by The Berkley Publishing Group,
200 Madison Avenue, New York, New York 10016.
BERKLEY and the "B" design
are trademarks belonging to Berkley Publishing Corporation.

PRINTED IN THE UNITED STATES OF AMERICA

10 9 8 7 6 5 4

In memory of
JOACHIM "LUPO" WOLF,
a genuine New Age healer,
who partly inspired this book.

Acknowledgments

Crybbe is physically very similar to several towns along the middle section of the Welsh border. It's as close to Offa's Dyke as Knighton and, like Presteigne, it has its own curfew. However, neither of these towns shares Crybbe's basic problems and the people are rather friendlier . . . so don't be afraid to call in and spend some money.

It should also be noted that Crybbe Court was built around the same time—and to a similar design—as Monaughty, a former monastery grange now being very carefully restored by Douglas Blane, who was good enough to show us around.

An enormous number of people have been very helpful during the writing of this book.

They include, in alphabetical order: Dr. Viv Davies, Mike Eatock, Alan Edwards, Dr. Ashley Fraser, Nigel Fullerton, Tony Geraghty, John Hollis, Dave Howes, The Reverend Geraint Hughes, the Amazing Arthur Hyde, Alun Lenny, Ralph Parsons, Nicola Rolinson, Edna Williams and Robin Williamson.

Thanks particularly to Carol Rickman and Bill Scott-Kerr for deeply perceptive editing.

And to Anna and Colin Haycraft for . . . well, they know . . .

The spirit-path theory of ley-lines is explored extensively in *Symbolic Landscapes* by Paul Devereux (pub: Gothic Image), who was decent enough to discuss his conclusions with me, well ahead of the book's publication.

And finally, for anyone who suspects the amount of electricity failure experienced in Crybbe is a gross exaggeration, during the period of writing—just over a year—there were over twenty power cuts in the otherwise-civilized area where we live, not thirty miles from the Border. This was quite normal. Thanks a lot, South Wales Electricity, you've been an inspiration.

prologue

"Beyond the fields we know." That, according to the Edwardian fantasist Lord Dunsany, was where we'd find an enchanted country.

Dunsany was wrong. The magic is in those same fields. And we don't know them at all.

J. M. POWYS,
The Old Golden Land

In Crybbe, night did not fall.

Night rose.

It welled out of the bitter brown earth caged in brambles in the neglected wood beyond the churchyard, swarming up the trees until they turned black and began to absorb the sky.

Collecting the shadows of graves, the night seeped out of the churchyard and across the vicarage lawn, where Murray Beech stood, knowing he was the wrong vicar for this parish but not knowing there couldn't be a right one.

Murray, with a certain distaste, was wondering how you went about an exorcism.

In the center of the town, patches of night gathered like damp about the roots of timber-framed buildings. They'd been turned into shops now, and offices and flats, but they still shambled around the square like sad old drunks.

Puddles of night stained the boots of Jack Preece, plodding across the cobbles to toll the curfew bell from the parish church, as he did every night and would go on doing until—as, being a farmer, he expected—arthritis got him and young Jonathon took over.

When Jack went to ring the old bell, he walked alone. Nobody else on the streets, the town holding its breath, even the sagging old buildings seeming to tense their timbers.

Nobody went into the Cock; nobody came out. Same with the Lamb down the street.

Tradition.

What other reason could there be?

Minnie Seagrove, sixty-three, a widow, had no doubts at all where the night began.

It began in that thing they called the Tump.

She could see it from the big front window of her bungalow on the Ludlow road. Nobody else could see it better.

Not that she wanted to. Ugly great lumps like this were ten a penny in the North and the Midlands where Mrs. Seagrove had lived. Only, in those areas, they were known as industrial spoil-heaps and were gradually removed in landscaping and reclamation schemes.

However, this thing, this Tump, wouldn't be going anywhere. It was protected. It was an Ancient Monument—supposed to have been a prehistoric burial mound originally, and then, in the Middle Ages, there might have been a castle on top, although there were no stones there anymore.

Mrs. Seagrove didn't see the point in preserving just a big, unpleasant hump with a few trees on top. It was obviously not natural, and if it was left to her, the council would be hiring Gomer Parry with his bulldozers and his diggers to get rid of it.

Because that might also get rid of the black thing that ran down from the mound in the twilight and scared the life out of Minnie Seagrove.

All right, she'd say to herself, I know, I know . . . I could simply draw the curtains, switch on the telly, and forget all about it. After all, I never noticed it—not once—when Frank was alive. But then, there didn't seem to be so many power cuts when Frank was alive.

How it came about, she was watching telly one night, coming up to *News on Ten,* and the power went off, and so she automatically went across to the window to see if the lights were on across the river, in the town.

And that was when she first saw it.

Horrible. Really horrible. It was . . . well, it was like the night itself bounding down from the Tump and rushing off, hungry, into the fields.

But why can't you just stop looking? Why can't you stay well away from that window when it's going dark?

I don't know.

That's the really frightening thing. I don't know.

Yes, I do.

It's because I can feel when it's there. No matter what I'm doing, what's on telly or the radio or what I'm reading, ever since I first dashed to the window during that power cut, I always know when it's on its way down from the mound. Without even going to the window, I *know* when it's there.

And the reason I look—the reason I *have* to look, even though it scares me half to death—is that I have to know, I have to be sure *that it isn't coming this way.*

Crybbe: a small onetime market town within sight of Offa's Dyke, the earthwork raised in the Dark Ages to separate England from Wales.

A town like a dozen others on either side of the border; less distinctive than most.

Except that here, the night rose.

part one

✠ ════════════════════════════════════

Some persons have super-normal powers not of a magitien, but of a peculiar and scientific qualitie.

DR. JOHN DEE,
Letter to Lord Burghley, 1574

�֍————————————————————————————

Sometime—and please, God, make it soon—they were going to have to sell this place. And on evenings like this, when the sky sagged and the bricks of the houses across the street were the color of dried blood, Fay would consider how they'd have to bait the trap.

On a fresh page of the spiral-bound notepad, she wrote:

> FOR SALE
>
> Bijou cottage in small, historic town amid spectacular Welsh border scenery. Close to all amenities, yet with lovely open views to rear, across pastoral countryside towards Offa's Dyke. Reasonably priced at . . .

. . . what? You couldn't make it too cheap or they'd be suspicious—and with good reason.

She'd suggest to her dad that they place the ad in the *Sunday Times* or the *Observer,* under "rural property." These were the columns guaranteed to penetrate the London suburbs, where the dreamers lived.

They probably wouldn't have heard of Crybbe. But it did sound appealing, didn't it? Cozy and tucked away. Or, alternatively, rather mysterious, if that was what you were looking for.

Fay found herself glancing at the bookshelves. Full of illusions. She saw the misty green spine of *Walking the Welsh Marches.* The enigmatic *Old Straight Track* by Alfred Watkins. And the worst offender: J. M. Powys's *The Old Golden Land,* which suggested that the border country was full of "secret doorways," through which you could penetrate "ancient mysteries." And lots of pictures taken through lenses coated with Vaseline and wishful-thinking.

She would really hate doing this to somebody, selling the house and perpetuating the myth. But not as much as she'd hate having to stay here. And you couldn't let your conscience run away with your life, could you?

Anyway, there were some people—like, say, the Newsomes—who rather deserved what this town was doing to them.

"Off to the pub," the canon called merrily from the hall. "Fay, can you hear me? I said, I'm off to the boozer."

"OK, Dad."

"Spot of social intercourse."

"You'll be lucky." Fay watched him stride past the window toward the town square. The old devil still looked deceptively fit for someone who, ever so slowly, was going mad.

He would put on a wonderful performance for the prospective purchasers, always assuming they caught him on one of his better days. That Santa Claus beard and the matching twinkle. They'd love him. More important, they'd trust him, the poor sods.

But before she could unleash this ample bundle of ecclesiastical charm on the public, there was just one minor difficulty to overcome.

The canon didn't appear to want to leave Crybbe. Ever.

This was the central problem in Fay's life. This was what kept her awake at night.

Christ, how *could* he? He didn't tramp the hills, wasn't much interested in peregrine falcons or otters or bog orchids. How, for God's sake, could he bear to go on living in this no-hope town now that the woman who'd brought him here had been dead for nearly a year?

His mind was congealing, like a fried egg on a cold morning. The specialists had confirmed it, and at first Fay had refused to believe them. Although once you knew, the signs were pretty obvious.

And decay was infectious. Fay realized she herself had somehow passed that age when you could no longer fool yourself that you were looking younger than you felt.

She took a deep breath. This was not like her at all.

On the table in front of her lay a small, flat, square box containing fifteen minutes' worth of tape she'd recorded that morning. On the box was written in pencil

Henry Kettle, dowser.

Later, Fay would create from the tape about six minutes of
radio. To do this she would draw the curtains, switch on the
Anglepoise lamp and the Revox editing machine, and forget she
was in Crybbe.

It was what kept her sane.

She wondered what kind of reaction she'd get if she told it
like it was to the perusers of the property columns.

Fay picked up the pencil and wrote on the pad:

> FOR SALE
> Faded terraced house in godforsaken
> backwater somewhere in damp
> no man's land long disowned by both
> Wales and England.
> Fully modernized—in 1960.
> Depressingly close to bunch of run-down shops,
> selling nothing in particular.
> Backing on to infertile hill country,
> full of dour farming types and pompous
> retired bank managers from Luton.
> No serious offer ignored.

In fact, she added, we'd tear your bloody hand off . . .

 two

Close up, she was like a dark, crooked finger pushing out of the
earth, beckoning him into the brambles.

When he looked back from the entrance to the field, she'd
shriveled into something more sinister: a bent and twisted old
woman. A crippled crone.

Or maybe just the broken stump of a fence post. Maybe
only that.

She hadn't been visible from here at all until, earlier that day,

Mr. Kettle had put on his thick gloves and pulled away the brambles, then pruned the hedge around her so that she stood naked, not even a covering of moss.

Now he'd brought Goff to see his discovery, and he should have felt a bit proud, but he didn't. All the time he'd been cutting away the undergrowth something had been pulling at him, saying, *Leave it be, Henry, you're doing no good here.*

But this was his job, and this stone was what showed he'd earned his money. It made a nonsense of the whole business if he didn't reveal the only real evidence that proved the line was there, falling sure as a shadow across the field, dead straight, between two youngish oak trees and . . .

"See that gate?"

"The metal gate?"

"Aye, but he's likely replaced generations of wooden ones," Mr. Kettle said, his voice rolling easy now, like the hills around them. Even without the final proof he'd have been confident of this one. Wonderful feeling it was, when you looked up and everything in the landscape—every hill and every tree, every hedge, every gateway—suddenly smiled at you and nodded and said you were right, you done it again, boy.

Like shaking hands with God.

Happening again, so suddenly like this, everything dove-tailing, it had taken his mind off the doubts, and he'd been asking himself: how can there be anything wrong, when it all falls together so neatly.

He indicated the gate again. "Prob'ly the cattle chose the spot, you following me?"

"Because they'd always go out that way! Out of the field, right?"

"You're learning." Though it was still warmish, Mr. Kettle wore a heavy tweed suit. He carried what once had been a medical bag of scuffed black leather, softened with age. The tools of the trade in there, the forked twigs and the wire rods and the pendulums. But the tools weren't important; they just made the clients feel better about paying good money to a walking old wives' tale like him.

Max Goff had a white suit, a Panama hat, and the remains of an Aussie accent. For a long time Mr. Kettle had found it hard to take him seriously, all the daft stuff he came out with about wells of sacred power and arteries of healing energy and such.

The New Age—he kept on about that. Mr. Kettle had heard it all before. Twenty years ago they were knocking on his door in their Indian caftans and headbands, following him out to stone circles, like Mitchell's Fold up in Shropshire, where they'd sit smoking long, bendy cigarettes and having visions, in between pawing each other. Now it was a man in a white suit with a big, powerful motorcar, but it was the same old thing.

Many, many times he'd explained to people that what he did was basically about *science*. Wonderful, yes—even after all these years the thrill was there all right. But it was a natural thing. Nothing psychic about dowsing.

"Now look *up* from the gate," said Mr. Kettle.

"Yeah, that . . . church steeple, you mean?"

"No, no, before that. Side of that bit of a hedge."

"Oh . . . that thing."

The old girl was about a hundred yards down the field, separated from the hedge now, blackened against the light, no more than three feet tall. But she was there, that was the point. In the right place.

"Yes," Mr. Kettle said. *"That* thing."

It was no good, he didn't like her. Even if she'd proved him right he didn't like the feeling coming off her, the smell that you could smell from a good distance, although not really.

"Is it a tree stump?" And then, "Hey, you're kidding, it can't be!" The little eyes suddenly sparking. He'd be ruthless and probably devious in his business, this feller, but he had this enthusiastic innocence about him that you couldn't altogether dislike.

"Jeez," Goff said. "I thought they'd all gone!"

"Why don't you go over and have a look at 'er?" Mr. Kettle put down his bag and sat on it under the hedge and patted the grass so that Arnold, his dog, would sit down, too. And they both sat and watched this bulky, bearded bloke making his ungainly way across the tufted meadow. Impatient, stumbling, because he'd thought they'd all gone, the old stones of Crybbe.

Mr. Kettle, too, had believed they'd all gone, until this morning when they'd finally let him into the field for the first time and he'd located the line and walked slowly along it, letting it talk to him, a low murmur.

And then the tone had altered, strengthened, calling out to him, the way they did. "I'm here, Henry, the only standing stone left standing within a mile of Crybbe."

Or vibrations to that effect. As megaliths went, she wasn't impressive, but she hadn't lost her voice. Not a voice he liked, though; he felt it was high and keening and traveled on a thin, dry wind.

But it proved he hadn't lost his capacity to receive. The *faculty.*

"Still there, then, Arnold. Every time I goes out I reckon it isn't bound to work anymore." He scratched the dog's head. "But it's still there, boy."

The only conclusion Mr. Kettle could reach about why this stone had survived was that there must've been wood here and the thing had been buried in brambles. And if they'd noticed her at all, they, like Goff, might have thought it was just an old tree stump.

He could see the figure in the white suit bending over the stone and then walking all around, contemplating the thing from different angles, as if hoping she'd speak to him. Which, of course, she wouldn't because if Goff had possessed the *faculty* there'd have been no reason to send for Henry Kettle.

An odd customer, this Goff, and no mistake. Most of the people who consulted dowsers—that is, actually paid them—had good practical reasons. Usually farmers looking for a water supply for their stock. Or occasionally people who'd lost something. And now and then those afflicted by rheumatics, or worse, because they'd got a bad spring under the house.

"Why am I still thinking he's trouble then, Arnie?"

The dog considered the question, looked serious.

Well, hell, he didn't *want* to think that. Not at all, because this Goff was the first person who'd ever paid him to go ley-hunting.

"Mr. Kettle," he'd said, coming straight to the point, which Mr. Kettle liked, "I've been advised that this used to be quite a center for prehistoric remains, and I wanna know, basically, what happened to them. Can you find out where they used to be? The old stones? The burial mounds? And I'm told you can kind of detect ley-lines, too, yeah?"

"Well," Mr. Kettle had said carefully, "I know what you mean. It do sometimes seem they fall into straight lines, the old monuments."

"No need to be coy with me, Mr. Kettle. I'm not afraid to call a ley-line a ley-line."

Now this had, at first, been a joy, this survey, this ley-hunt. Bit of an eye opener. To say the least.

Until . . .

One morning, knowing there had to have been a stone in a particular place in Big Meadow and then digging about and finding part of it buried nearby, Mr. Kettle had got a feeling that something about this was not regular. In most areas, old stones were lost gradually, over centuries, plucked out at random, when exasperation at the damage done to a plow or a harrow had finally overcome the farmer's inbred superstition.

But at Crybbe, he was sure, it had been systematic.

Like a purge.

Mr. Kettle's excitement was dampened then by a bad feeling that just wouldn't go away. When he dug up the stone he thought he could smell it—something faintly putrid, as if he'd unearthed a dead sheep.

And, as a man who lived by his feelings, he wondered if he ought to say something. About the purge on the stones. About the history of the Court—John Dee, Black Michael, and the hangings. And about the legends, which traveled parallel to history and sometimes, if you could decode them, told you far more about what had really happened than the fusty old documents in the county archives.

Mr. Kettle, who kept his own records, was getting more and more interested in Crybbe—wishing, though, that he didn't have to be. Wishing he could ignore it. Detecting a problem here, a serious long-term problem, and wishing he could turn his back on it.

But, as the problem was likely to remain long after he'd gone, he'd taken steps to pass on his fears. With a feller like this Max Goff blundering about the place, there should always be somebody who knew about these things—somebody trustworthy—to keep an eye open.

He supposed he ought to warn Goff, but the thought of "something sinister" would probably only make the place more appealing.

"And, anyway, you can't tell these New Age types anything, can you, Arnold?" Mr. Kettle was scratching the dog's head again. "No, you can't, boy."

*   *   *

Ten minutes later Goff was back, puffing, the flush in his cheeks making his close-mown beard seem even redder. Excitement coming off him like steam.

"Mr. Kettle, let me get this right. According to your calculations, this is line B, right?"

"That's correct."

"And by following this line, as you dowsed it, we suddenly come across what could be the only remaining stone in the alignment. Is it exactly where you figured it'd be?"

"Well . . ." Mr. Kettle got to his feet and picked up his bag. Max Goff eyed it.

"Got the rods in there? Can we dowse the line some more, maybe find another stone?"

No, we bloody can't, Mr. Kettle thought. You might as well ask, how about if we grabs hold of this electric cable to see if he's live?

He saw, to his dismay, that Goff was looking at him in some kind of awe; he'd found a new guru. It was not a role Mr. Kettle fancied. "Getting late," he said. "I ought to be away. Don't like driving in the dark these days."

"When can you come again?"

"Look," Mr. Kettle said. "I'm an old man. I likes my fireside and my books. And besides, you got it all now. You know where they all are. Or used to be."

This Goff was a man whose success in business had convinced him that if you knew a source, knowledge and experience could be bought like . . . what would this feller buy? . . . cocaine? Mr. Kettle, who still read two newspapers every day, knew a bit about Max Goff and the kind of world he came from.

"Maybe your role in this is only just beginning," Goff said. "How about I send a car for you next time?"

Money was no object for this bugger. Made his first million by the time he was twenty-seven, Mr. Kettle had read, by starting his own record company. Epidemic, it was called. And it had spread like one. Now it was international magazines and book publishing.

"Well," Mr. Kettle said. "Isn't much more as I can tell you, anyway. You've got the maps. Nothing more to be found, even if you excavates, I reckon."

"Hmmm." Goff was making a show of being unconvinced, as they followed what Mr. Kettle now thought of, wrote of in his journal—but never spoke of—as the Dark Road, the Thoroughfare of the Dead. Returning at dusk, back into Crybbe, a town which had loitered since the Middle Ages, and probably before, in the area where England hardened into Wales.

On the very border.

three

It was the seventh bell they always rang, for the curfew.

Almost rang itself these days. Seventeen years Jack had been doing it. Didn't need to think much about it anymore. Went regular as his own heartbeat.

The bell clanged above him.

Jack let the rope slide back through his hands.

Seventy-three.

His hands closed again around the rope.

Seventy-four.

He hadn't been counting. At any point during the ringing Jack could tell you what number he was on. His arms knew. His stomach knew.

One hundred times every night. Starting at ten o'clock. Newcomers to the town, they'd asked him, "Don't you find it spooky, going up there, through that graveyard, up all those narrow stone steps, with the church all dark, and the bell ropes just hanging there?"

"Don't think about it," Jack would say. And it was true; he didn't.

There were eight bells in the tower, and that was reckoned to be a good peal for this part of the country.

For weddings, sometimes in the old days, they'd all be going. Even fairly recently—though not anymore—it had been known for some snooty bride from Off to bring in a handful of bell-

ringers from her own parish for the big day. This had only
been permitted for weddings, sometimes. On Sundays, never.
And not Christmas. Not even Easter.

And also, every few years some bearded clown in a sports
jacket would pass through. And then the church or the town
council would get a letter from the secretary of some group of
nutters that traveled the country ringing other people's bells.

The town council would say no.

Occasionally—this was the worst problem—there'd be somebody like Colonel Croston who'd moved in from Hereford,
where he was reckoned to have been in the SAS. He liked to
keep fit. Jogged around the place.

And rang bells, as a hobby.

He'd been a pain in the neck at first, had Colonel Croston.
"No bell-ringers apart from you, Jack? That's appalling. Look,
you leave this one to me."

Jack Preece remembered the Colonel putting up posters invit-
ing all able-bodied folk to come to the church one Friday night
and learn the ropes. "Give me six months. Guarantee I'll knock
them into shape."

Jack had gone along himself because he didn't like the thought
of youngsters running up and down the stone steps and swinging
on his ropes.

When the two of them had been waiting around for nearly
an hour he let the despondent Colonel take him for a drink.
"Doesn't deserve these bells, Jack, this town."

"Aye, aye," Jack had said noncommittally, and had permitted
Colonel Croston to buy him a large brandy.

He hadn't bothered to tell the Colonel that even he only knew
how to ring the curfew using the seventh bell. Well, no point in
buggering with the others, see, was there? No point in making
a show. They could have pulled the other bells down and sold
them off for scrap, far as Jack Preece was concerned.

Anyhow, what they'd done now, to save a lot of bother and
pestering was to take down all the ropes. Except, of course, the
one that rang the seventh bell.

Some nights, Jack would be real knackered after a day's
dipping, or shearing, or lambing. He'd stagger up them steps,
hurting all over his body, dying for a pint and aching for his
bed. Some nights he'd grab hold of that rope just to stop himself
falling over.

Still the hundred would be done. And done on time.

And it was on nights like this that Jack felt sometimes he was helped. Felt the belfry was kind of aglow, and other hands were pulling on the rope beside his own.

Spooky?

Well, he didn't think about it. Where was the point in that?

Mr. Kettle and Max Goff walked slowly into the town over a river bridge with old brick walls which badly need pointing, the river flat and sullen below. Past a pub, the Cock, with flaky paintwork and walls that had once been whitewashed but now looked gray and unwashed.

A dark, smoky, secretive little town. There was still an afterglow on the fields, but the town was already embracing the night.

Henry Kettle didn't claim to understand the people of Crybbe. They weren't hostile and they weren't friendly. They kept their heads down, that was all you could say about them. A local historian had once told him this was how towns and villages on the border always used to be. If there was any cross-border conflict between the English and the Welsh, they never took sides openly until it was clear which was going to win. Also, towns of no importance were less likely to be attacked and burned.

So keeping their heads down had got to be a way of life.

Tourists must turn up sometimes. By accident, probably. Mr. Kettle reckoned most of them wouldn't even bother to park. Sure the buildings were ancient enough, but they weren't painted and polished up like the timber-frame villages on the Hereford black-and-white trail. Nothing here that said "visit me" with any enthusiasm, because there was no sense of pride.

From the church tower, above the cobbled square, a lone bell was clanging dolefully into the musty dusk. It was the only sound there was.

"What's that?" Goff demanded.

"Only the curfew."

Goff stopped on the cobbles, his smile a great gash. "Hey, really . . . ? This is a real curfew, like in the old days?"

"No," Mr. Kettle said. "Not really. That's to say, people are no longer required to be off the streets by nightfall. Just tradition nowadays. The Preece family, it is, performs the duty.

One of 'em goes up the belfry, God knows how many steps, every night, summer and winter; nine-thirty, or is it ten?"

He looked up at the church clock, but it was too dark to make out where its hands were pointing. He was sure there used to be a light on that clock. "Hundred times it rings, anyway."

"Might only be a tradition, but there's still nobody on the streets," Max Goff observed. "Is there?"

"That's 'cause they're all in the pubs," said Mr. Kettle. "No, what it is, there's some old trust fund arranges for the bell to be rung. The Preeces get grazing rights on a few acres of land in return for keeping up the custom. Passed down, father to son, for four hundred-odd years. Being farmers, they always has plenty sons."

They stood in the square until the ringing stopped.

"Crazy," Goff said, shaking his big head in delight. "Cray-zee. This is the first night I've spent here, y'know? I've always stayed in Hereford. It's magic, Mr. Kettle. Hey, we still on the line?"

"I suppose we must be. Aye, see the little marker by there?"

A stone no more than a foot high, not much more than a bump in the cobbles. Goff squatted next to it and held his palms over it, as though he expected it to be hot or to light up or something. The dog, Arnold, watched, his head on one side, as if puzzled by a human being who went down on all fours to sniff the places where dogs had pissed.

Two middle-aged women walked across the square talking in low voices. They stopped talking as they walked past Goff, but didn't look at him, nor Mr. Kettle, nor each other.

Then they went rigid, because suddenly Arnold's head was back and he was howling.

"Jeez!" Goff sprang up. The two women turned, and Mr. Kettle felt he was getting a very dark, warning look, the women's faces shadowed almost to black.

"Arnold!" With some difficulty—beginning to think he must have a bad spring under his own house, the way his rheumatism had been playing up lately—Mr. Kettle got down on his knees and pulled the dog to him. "Sorry, ladies."

The women didn't speak, stood there a moment then turned and walked away quickly as the howling subsided because Mr. Kettle had a hand clamped around Arnold's jaws. "Daft bugger, Arnold."

"Why'd it do that?" Goff asked, without much interest.

"I wish I knew, Mr. Goff."

He unclamped the dog's jaws, and Arnold gave him a reproachful glance and then shook his head.

"OK?" Goff said, feet planted firmly on the cobbles, legs splayed, quite relaxed. Wasn't getting it, was he? Wasn't feeling the resistance? Didn't realize he was among the descendants of the people who'd pulled down the stones.

Goff was just a big white blob in the dim square. Mr. Kettle walked to where their cars were parked in a little lot behind the church overhung with yew trees. His own car was a dusty VW Estate. Goff had a Ferrari.

"Can I say something?" Henry Kettle had been thinking about this for the past fifteen minutes or so. He didn't much like Goff, but he was a kindly old chap who wanted at least to put out a steadying hand.

"Of course."

Mr. Kettle stood uneasily in the semidark. "These places . . . " he began, and sucked in his lips, trying to concentrate. Trying to get it right.

"I suppose what I'm trying to say is places like this, they—how can I put it?—they invites a kind of *obsession.*" He fell silent, watching the buildings in the square hunching together as the night took over.

A harsh laugh came out of Goff. "Is that it?" he asked, rudely.

Mr. Kettle unlocked his car door and opened it for Arnold. "Yes," he said, half surprised because he'd thought he was going to say more. "Yes, I suppose that *is* it."

"Mr. Kettle." Goff took a steep breath. "Perhaps I oughta explain. This place . . . I mean, look around . . . it's remote, half forgotten, run-down. For centuries its people lived from the land, right? But now agriculture's in decline, it doesn't provide extra jobs anymore, and there's nothing here to replace it. This town's in deep shit, Mr. Kettle."

Mr. Kettle couldn't argue with that; he didn't say anything. Watched Max Goff spread his hands, Messiah-style.

"And yet, in prehistory, this was obviously a sacred place," Goff said. "We have this network of megalithic sites—a dozen or so standing stones, suggestions of a circle or a henge. And the Tump, of course. Strong indications that this was a major focus of the Earth force. A center of terrestrial energy, yeah? You see any signs of that energy now?"

"People pulled the stones out," Mr. Kettle said.

"Precisely. And what happened? They lost touch with it."

"Lost touch with what?"

"With the life force, Mr. Kettle! Listen, give me your opinion on this. Whaddaya think would happen if . . . ?"

Max Goff walked right up to Mr. Kettle in the ill-lit square and looked down at him, lowering his voice as if he were about to offer him a tip for the stock market. Mr. Kettle felt most uneasy. He was getting the dead-sheep smell.

"Whadda *you* think would happen," Goff whispered, "if we were to put the stones *back?*"

Well, Mr. Kettle thought, that depends. Depends on the true nature of leys, about which we *know* nothing, only speculate endlessly. Depends whether they're forgotten arteries of what you New Age fellers like to call the Life Force. Or whether they're something else, like paths of the dead.

But all he said was, "I don't know, Mr. Goff. I wouldn't like to say."

four

How old was the box, then?

Warren Preece reckoned it was at least as old as the paneling in the farmhouse hall, which was estimated to be just about the oldest part of the house. So that made it sixteenth century or so.

He was into something here, all right. And the great thing, the really fucking great thing about this was that no other bastard knew about it. Lived in this house all his life, but he'd never had cause to poke about in the chimney before—well, you wouldn't, would you?—until that morning, when his old man had shouted, "Put that bloody guitar down, Warren, and get off your arse and hold this torch, boy."

Piss off, Warren had spat under his breath, but he'd done it, knowing what a bastard the old man could be when a job wasn't going right.

Then, standing in the fireplace, shining the torch up the chimney—the old man on a stepladder struggling to pull this crumbling brick out—a bloody great lump of old cement had fallen away and broken up and some of the dust had gone in Warren's eye.

"You clumsy bastard, Dad!" Warren fell back, dropping the torch, ramming a knuckle into his weeping eye, hearing masonry crumbling where he'd staggered and kicked out. If he made it to college without being registered disabled through living in this broken-down pile of historic crap, it'd be a real achievement.

"Come on, Warren, don't mess about! I need that light."

"I'm f . . . Hang on, Dad, I can't flaming see." Hunched in the fireplace, scraping at his gritty, watery eye.

And it was then, while picking up the torch—flashing it on and off to make sure the bulb hadn't broken when he'd dropped it—that Warren found this little tunnel.

It was no more than a deepish recess in the side wall of the fireplace, about eighteen inches off the ground. Which would have put it on a level with the top of the dog grate, when they'd had one. Must have been where he'd kicked back with his heel, hacking off a cob of sixteenth-century grunge.

Warren shone the light into the recess and saw what looked like carving. Put a hand inside, felt about.

"Hey, this was . . . "

"Warren! What you bloody doing down there, boy?"

Quickly he shoved bits of brick into the opening, ramming them tight with the heel of his trainer. Then shone the torch back up the chimney for the old man pretty damn fast.

In fact, for the rest of the day he'd been a very willing laborer—"You stay there, Dad, I'll get it." "Want me to mix the cement down here and pass it up, Dad?" "Cuppa tea, Dad?" Anything so the old man'd get the job done and bugger off out of the way.

The old man had been surprised and pleased, grinning through a faceful of soot, patting Warren on the shoulder. "We done a good job there, boy. He won't set on fire again, that ole chimney. Fancy a pint?"

He'd never said that before. Well, not to Warren. Most nights, sometimes with Jonathon, he just went off to the Cock without a word.

So Warren, too, was surprised and almost pleased. But wasn't going for no pint with the old man tonight. No way.

"Told Tessa I'd be round, Dad. Sorry."

The old man looked quite relieved. Warren had watched him tramping off up the track, eager to wash the dust out of his throat. So eager he hadn't bothered to clean up the mess in the hearth and so hadn't noticed anything he shouldn't.

Stupid git.

Warren got himself a can of Black Label from the fridge and went back to the fireplace to pull out them old bricks.

He'd got the box out, was squatting on the hearth, dusting it off, when he heard Jonathon's car. He'd tucked the box under his arm—bloody heavy, it was, too—and got it out through the back door and around the back of the barn, where he'd hidden it in the bottom of an old water-barrel.

And gone up to his room and waited for Jonathon to piss off.

The way he saw it, you didn't seal up an oak box like this and stash it away in a secret compartment in the chimney unless there was something pretty damn valuable inside. And, as he'd discovered, just about anything a bit old was valuable these days.

Warren had a mate, a guy who got rid of stuff, no questions asked. He could be looking at big money here on the box alone. It was in good shape, this box, sealed up warm and dry for centuries. Warren looked at the box and saw a new amplifier for the band. He looked harder and saw this secondhand Stratocaster guitar. Felt the Strat hanging low around his hip, its neck slippery with sweat.

The curfew bell was tolling in the distance. His dad had sunk a swift pint and plodded off up the tower to do his nightly duty, silly old bugger.

"Why do you keep on doing that, Dad? Don't pay, do it? And no bugger takes any notice 'part from setting their watches."

"Tradition, boy. Your granddad did it for over thirty years. And when I gets too rheumaticky to climb them steps, Jonathon'll do it, right, son?"

Jonathon nodding. He was always "son," whereas Warren

was "the boy." Said something, that did.

What it said was that Jonathon, the eldest son, was going to get the farm. Well, OK, if Jonathon wanted to wallow in shit, shag sheep all his life, well, fair enough.

Warren didn't give a toss about going to college in Hereford either, except that was where the other guys in the band lived.

But Crybbe—he could hardly believe this—was where Max Goff was going to be.

Max Goff, of Epidemic Records.

He'd seen him. Been watching him for days. Somehow Max Goff had to hear the band. Because this band was real good, he could feel it. This band fucking *cooked*.

The box was in one of the sheds on the old workbench now. He'd rigged up an old lambing light to work by, realizing this was going to be a delicate operation. Didn't want to damage the box, see, because it could be worth a couple of hundred on its own.

Now. He had a few tools set out on the bench: hammer, screwdriver, chisel, Stanley knife. Precision stuff, this.

Warren grinned.

OK, if it came to it, he *would* have to damage it, because he hadn't got all bloody night. But better to go in from underneath than cut the lid, which had a bit of a carving on it—nothing fancy, like, nothing clever, just some rough symbols. Looked like *they'd* been done with a Stanley knife. A sixteenth-century Stanley knife. Warren had to laugh.

Around about then, Crybbe had another power cut, although Warren Preece, working in the shed with a lambing light, wasn't affected at all.

But Fay Morrison was furious.

She'd always preferred to do her editing at night, especially on the days when she was producing complete programs. There'd just be her and the tape machine under a desk lamp. And then, when the tape was cut together, she would switch off the lamp and sit back, perhaps with a coffee, and play it through in the cozy darkness. Only a red pilot light and the soft green glow of the level meters, the gentle swish of the leader tape gliding past the heads.

Magic.

This was what made radio so much more satisfying than

television. The intimacy of moments like this. And the fact that you could do all the creative work on your own, only going into a studio for the final mix.

Fay really missed all that. Hadn't imagined she'd miss it *so much.*

Tonight, she'd waited until her father had wandered off to the pub for his nightly whiskey and his bar supper. And then she'd gone into her office, which used to be Grace Legge's sitting room.

And still was, really, in the daytime. But at night you could switch off the G-plan furnishing and the fifties fireplace, and the front room of Number 8, Bell Street, Crybbe, became more tolerable, with only a secondhand Revox visible in the circle of light from the Anglepoise.

Fay had a package to edit for Offa's Dyke Radio. Only a six-minute piece to be slotted into somebody else's afternoon chat-and-disk show on what was arguably the worst local shoe-string station in the country.

But it was still radio, wasn't it? After a fashion.

And this morning, doing her contribution for a series on—yawn, yawn—"people with unusual hobbies," Fay had actually got *interested* in something. For a start, he was ever such a nice old chap—most of the people around here, far from being quaint rural characters, were about as appealing as dried pars-nips.

And he'd actually been happy to talk to her, which was also a first. Until she'd come here, Fay had encountered very few people who didn't want to be on the radio: no cameras, no lights, and no need to change your shirt or have your hair done. But in this area, people would make excuses—"Oh, I'm too busy, call again sometime." Or simply refuse—"I don't want to *be* on the wireless"—as if, by collecting their voices on tape, you were going to take their souls away.

Yes, it was *that* primitive sometimes.

Or so she felt.

But the water-diviner, or dowser, had been different and Fay had been fascinated to learn how it was done. Nothing, appar-ently, to do with the hazel twig, as such. Simply a faculty you developed through practice, nothing as airy-fairy as "intuition."

And it definitely was *not psychic.*

He kept emphasizing that, scrutinizing her a bit warily as she stood there, in her T-shirt and jeans, wishing she'd brought a sweater and a wind-muff for the microphone. It had been a bit breezy in that field, even if tomorrow was Midsummer Day.

"Do you think *I* could do it, Henry?" she'd asked, on tape. You always asked this question, sounding as if it had just occurred to you. There would then follow an amusing couple of minutes of your attempting to do whatever it was and, of course, failing dismally.

"You could have a try," he'd said, playing along. And so she'd taken the forked twig in both hands. "Hold it quite firmly, so it doesn't slip, but don't grip it too hard. And, above all, *relax . . .* "

"OK," she'd heard herself say through the speaker. And that was when the power went off.

"Bloody *hell!*" Fay stormed to the window to see if the other houses in the street were off. Which they were.

It was the fourth power cut in a month.

"I don't believe it!"

OK, you could imagine that on some distant rock in the Hebrides, even today, there would be quite a few times when the power got waylaid on its way from the mainland.

But this was close to the epicenter of Britain. There were no high mountains. And they were not in the middle of an electric storm.

There was a bump and the sound of two empty spools clattering on the floor.

"Pushkin, is that you?"

Grace's cats got everywhere.

Fay decided she didn't like this room very much in the absolute dark.

She felt along the wall for the tape-recorder plug, removed it, and went to bed.

Warren should have known.

Sixteenth-century lock. Not as if it was Chubb's finest, was it? Stanley knife into the groove, sliding it around a bit, that was all it took. Then the screwdriver pushed into the gap. Hit it just once with the palm of his hand.

It didn't exactly fly open, the box. Well, it wouldn't, would it? Being as how it had turned out to be lead-lined.

Fucking lead! No wonder it was so heavy. Good job he hadn't

tried to cut into it through the bottom.

Course that lead lining was a bit of a disappointment. Warren had been hoping the box weighed so much because it was full of gold coins or something of that order. Lead, even antique lead, was worth bugger all, he was pretty sure of that.

Funny smell.

Well, not that funny. Old, it smelled old and musty. He moved the lambing light closer, poked a finger in.

Cloth, it was. Some sort of old fabric, grayish. Better be a bit careful here, bloody old thing might disintegrate.

On the other hand, he couldn't afford to waste any time. His old man—who wasn't much of a drinker—might even now be on his way back from the church. He might, of course, have called back round the pub for one with Jonathon and his mates. (If Warren was in the pub with *his* mates and the old man came in, he'd turn his stool around, pretend he hadn't seen him, but Jonathon would call him over, buy him a pint; that was the kind of smarmy git Jonathon was.) But most likely he'd come home, getting a few early nights in before haymaking time and dipping and all that rural shit.

And as he came up the track he'd see the light in the shed.

Warren pulled the lamp down, away from the shed window. He couldn't see much through the glass, with its thick covering of cobwebs full of dust and dead insects, except that it was very nearly dark and there was a mist.

He was feeling cold now, wanting to get it over with and go back to the house. It was going to be no big deal, anyway. Old papers probably. Some long-dead bugger's last will and testament.

He prodded the cloth stuff with the end of the Stanley knife and then dug the blade in a bit and used the knife to pull the fabric out of the box in one lump.

What was underneath the cloth was whitish and yellowish, like brittle old paper or parchment crumpled up.

He gave it a prod.

And the Stanley knife dropped out of Warren's fingers—fingers that had gone suddenly numb.

"Aaaa . . . "

Warren caught his breath, voice gone into a choke.

The knife fell into the box and made this horrible little chinking noise.

five

Mr. Kettle raised a hand to Goff as he drove away. He was thinking, well, *somebody* had to buy the Court. Better this rich, flashy bugger—surely—than a family man with a cozy wife and perhaps a daughter or two, with horses for the stables and things to lose. Good things. Peace of mind. *Balance* of mind.

He left the town on the Ludlow road which would take him past the Court. It wouldn't be Goff's only home. Well, he'd move in and stride around for a while, barking orders to battalions of workmen, changing this and restoring that in the hope it would give the house some personality, a bit of atmosphere. And then he'd get tired of the struggle and go back to London, and the Court would become a weekend home, then an every-other-weekend home, then a holiday home, then just an investment.

Then he'd sell it.

And the process would begin all over again.

Dead ahead of him at this point, the Court crouched like an animal behind the Tump. The Tump was a mound which at some stage may or may not have had a castle on top. Trees sprouted from it now and brambles choked the slopes. The Tump was a field away from the road, about two hundred yards, and there was a wall around it.

Arnold whined once and crept into the back seat, where he lay down.

Behind the wall, the Tump loomed black against the dull, smoky dregs of the dusk. All the more visible because there were no lights anywhere. Nothing. Had there been a power cut?

It had always been obvious to Mr. Kettle that whether or not the Tump had once had a castle on it, before that—long, long before that—it had been a burial place of some importance. He'd been up there but found no sign of its having been excavated. Which was not that unusual; mounds like this were ten a penny in the Marches.

The business of the stones. *That* was unusual.

What *would* happen if he put them back, the same stones where you could find them, substitutes where they'd vanished entirely? Well, probably nothing. Nothing would happen. That was what Mr. Kettle told himself as he drove in the direction of the Tump along a road which vaguely followed the ley he'd marked on the Ordinance Survey map as "line B." The mound, of course, was on the line.

He was relieved when the road swung away from the ley and the shadow of the Tump moved over from the windshield to the side window. Now, why was that? *Why* was he relieved?

He slowed for the final bend before the town sign and glanced in the mirror, seeing in the dimness the dog's intelligent eyes, wide, bright and anxious.

"He don't know really what he's takin' on, Arn," Mr. Kettle said, his voice softening as it always did when he and the dog were alone.

He put out his left hand to switch on the headlights. Towns ended very abruptly in these parts. Full streetlighting and then, in the blink of an eye, you were into the countryside, where different rules applied. But tonight there were no lights; it was all one.

People said sometimes that the Court must be haunted, whatever that meant. Atmospherics, usually. The couple of times he'd been in there it had been cold and gloomy and had this miserable, uncared-for kind of feeling. In Mr. Kettle's experience, so-called haunted houses were not normally like that—they could be quite bright and cheerful in the daytime, except for those cold bits. There were always cold bits.

But what was wrong with the Court was more fundamental. It was a dead spot. Nothing *psychic,* though, you understand? Just nothing thrived there. Indeed, he couldn't figure out why it hadn't been abandoned and left to rot centuries ago, long before it had become a "listed" building, deemed to be of historic interest.

Arnold sprang up on the back seat and growled.

"And what's up with you now?"

The dog had his front paws on the back of Mr. Kettle's seat, his furry head against his master's cheek, lips curled back, showing his teeth, white and feral in the gloom.

Mr. Kettle tried to follow Arnie's gaze, thinking maybe the dog had caught sight of a badger ambling out of the hedge. But all he could see was the yellow of the headlights thrown back at him.

He rubbed at the windshield. "Bugger me, Arn, that mist's come down quick tonight, boy."

But there was nothing moving in the mist. No noise, no lights, no badgers, not even tree shapes.

Only the Tump.

He was up in the highest field now, but at the bottom end by the wood, the lambing light at his feet, the grass wet and cold, the sweat on him mingling with the mist, the spade handle clammy with it. He didn't care; he'd never felt like this before.

Warren scraped the earth into the hole and pulled the turf back over it, slamming it down with the spade, jumping on it, getting it tight so nobody would know. Not that anybody came here; only the sheep, and the old man once or twice a year.

Beneath the turf and the soil and the clay was the old box, buried good and deep, with the Stanley knife still inside it. It seemed right, somehow, to leave the knife in the box.

Or it seemed *not* right to put his hand in the box and take the knife out.

Not with the other hand in there.

"Where did that come from?"

The dog snarled.

The Tump was off-center in the mist. But it shouldn't have been there at all because he'd passed it, he must have, couple of minutes ago at least.

"Now just you sit down, you daft dog." And then he looked up at the Tump and said suddenly, softly, "You're not right, are you?"

And at that moment Arnold was thrown to the floor, as, without warning, the car lurched off to the right, the steering wheel spinning away so fiercely it burned the palms of Mr. Kettle's hands when he tried to hold it.

"Oh no you don't, you bugger." Addressing, through his teeth, neither the dog, nor the car, for he should have been half expecting this, bloody old fool. Wrenching at the wheel, as the black mound rose up full in the windshield.

From behind his seat, the dog's growl built to a yelp of terror.

"I know, I'm sorry!" Cursing the part of him which responded to nonsense like this; mad as hell at his bloody old, slowing body which no longer seemed to have the strength to loose it out.

Arnold cringed on the floor next to the back seat, shivering and panting. Then Mr. Kettle felt the bumps and heard the clumps under the car, and knew what must have happened.

"We're in the bloody field!"

Common land. Unfenced. Flat and well-drained enough where it met the road to offer no obstacles to car wheels.

No obstacles at all, until you got to the humps and ridges. And then the wall.

They said the wall, which almost encircled the mound, had been built centuries ago of stones taken from the old castle foundations. It was not high—maybe five feet—but it was a very thick wall, and as strong and resistant as ever it'd been. He'd never thought about this before, but why would they build a wall around it?

Behind the wall, the Tump bulged and glowered and Mr. Kettle's faculty started leaping and bounding the way his body hadn't managed to in thirty years.

The wild senses were rising up, leaving the body hobbling behind and the old car trundling across the field, going its own sweet way.

And something in Henry Kettle, something he used to be able to control, locking into the Tump's wavelength with a long, almost grateful shudder. As if it was going home.

"Oh Christ, Arnold," said Mr. Kettle. "Oh Christ."

Knowing it for the first time. Why they must have built a wall around it. Knowing a lot of things about the stones and the leys . . .

Knowing all this as the car went over a ridge in the field—maybe one of the old ramparts when it had been a castle—and began to go downhill, and faster.

Nothing *psychic* here. Understand *that*.

Stamping down on the brake—frantic now—but the car going even faster, ripping through the field like a tank. A muffled bump-clank, bump-clank, then the rending of metal and the car plowing on like a wounded animal, roaring and farting.

In the windshield, the trees on the Tump were crowding out of the mist, a tangle of black and writhing branches, spewing like entrails from a slashed gut, the centermost trees suddenly flung apart as if blown by a gale, as if the wind was bursting out and over the mound like a fountain of air.

And he could see it. *He could see the wind* . . .

And as it rushed down, it took the form . . .

Nothing psychic, nothing psychic, nothing . . .

of a huge black thing, a dog . . . hound . . . bounding down the mound and leaping at the car, an amber hunger smoking in eyes that outshone the headlights because . . .

" . . . you're bloody *evil* . . . "

And Arnold screaming from behind. Not barking, not whimpering, but making the most piteously distressed and upsetting noise he'd ever been forced to hear.

And all the time thinking—the words themselves forming in his head and echoing there—I've seen it. It was there. *I've seen Black Michael's Hound.*

And when the illusion of the wind and the thing it carried had gone he saw the headlight beams were full of stone.

Nothing to be done. Bloody old fool, he thought sadly, and suddenly it seemed he had all the time there was to ponder the situation and realize he hadn't touched the brake pedal, not once. The car having automatic transmission—only two pedals—what had happened was his foot had plunged down hard, time and time again, on the other one.

The accelerator.

Well, he did try to pull the stupid foot off, but his knee had locked and he saw through the windshield that the thick, solid stone wall was being hurled at him by the night, and the night would not miss.

There was a hollow silence in the car and that seemed to last a *very* long time, and Mr. Kettle could feel Arnold, his faithful dog somewhere close to him, quiet now. But his eyes'd be resigned, no light in them anymore.

Mr. Kettle put out a hand to pat Arnold but probably did not reach him before the impact killed both headlamps and there was no light anywhere and no sound except, from afar, the keening song of the old stone.

                              *   *   *

A few minutes later the electricity was restored. Bulbs flared briefly, stuttered, died, and then came back to what passed, in Crybbe, for life.

Business had not been interrupted in either of the two bars at the Cock, where, through past experience, a generator was always on hand. When the lights revived, closing time had come and gone, and so had most of the customers.

Few people in the houses around the town realized the power was back, and the wavering ambience of oil lamps, Tilley lamps and candles could be seen behind curtained windows.

One electric light blinked back on and would remain needlessly on until morning.

This was the Anglepoise lamp on Fay Morrison's editing table. She'd unplugged the tape machine before going to bed but forgotten about the lamp. All through the night it craned its neck over her desk diary and a spiral-bound notepad, the one which often served, unintentionally, as a personal diary, especially when she was feeling angry and hopeless.

Across the page, in deeply indented frustration, the pencil lettering said,

              . . . we'd tear your bloody hand off . . .

part two

❄ ❄ ═══════════════════════════════════════

Although I have been able to divine water and do other simple things of that kind for many years . . . I had not thought that this faculty might be related to the formation of ghosts.

T. C. LETHBRIDGE,
Ghost and Divining Rod (1963)

✤ ————————————————————————

one

*"No, no . . . don't hold him like that. Not so tightly. You're like
a nervous kiddie riding a bike."*

"Oh, sorry. Like this?"

*"Better. Don't think of him as an implement—he's an exten-
sion of your arms. Be comfortable."*

"I think I've got it. What do I do now?"

*"Just walk across towards the tree—and don't be so ner-
vous, girl."*

"Well, I've never done it before, Henry. I'm a virgin."

She thought, shall I leave that?

Nah. Maria will only chop it. She'll think I'm trying to be
clever. Too clever for Offa's Dyke Radio, God forbid.

Fay marked it up with a white Chinagraph pencil, sliced out
just over a foot of tape with a razor-blade cutter, spliced the
ends, ran the tape again.

Crunch, crunch. Rustle, rustle.

"All right, now, Fay, ask yourself the question."

*"Huh? Oh, er . . . is . . . Is There Any Water Under Here?
I feel a bit daft, to be honest, Henry. And there's . . . nothing . . . happening. Obviously haven't got your natural aptitude,
if that's the word."*

*"Course you have, girl. Anybody can do it as really wants to.
It's not magic. Look, shall I help you?"*

"Yes, please."

"Right, now, we'll do it again. Like this."

"Oh, you're putting your hands . . . "

*"Over yours, yes. Now relax, and we'll walk the same path
and ask ourselves the same question."*

"OK. Here we go. Is There Any . . . ? Fucking hell, Henry!"

Laughter.

"Caught you by surprise, did it?"

"You could say that."

Pause.

"Look, Henry, do you think we could do that bit again, so I can moderate my response?"

Fay marked the tape. Fast forwarded until she heard herself say, "OK, Take Two," made another white mark after that and picked up the razor blade.

Shame really. Never as good second time around. All the spontaneity gone. "Whoops" had been the best she could manage the second time, when the forked hazel twig had flipped up dramatically, almost turning a somersault in her hands, nearly dislodging the microphone from under her arm.

"Whoops". . . . not good enough. She started to splice the ends of the tape together, wondering if she had time to go into a field with the Uher and do a quick "Gosh, wow, good heavens, I never expected that," and splice it in at the appropriate point.

The phone rang.

"Yes, what?" The damn roll of editing tape was stuck to her hands and now the receiver.

"Fay Morrison?"

"Yes, sorry, you caught me . . . "

"This is James Barlow in the newsroom."

"Which newsroom?" Fay demanded, being awkward because the voice somehow reminded her of her ex-husband, who always called people by their full names.

"Offa's Dyke Radio, Fay." No, not really like Guy. Too young. A cynical, world-weary twenty-two or thereabouts. James Barlow, she hadn't dealt with him before.

"Sorry, I was editing a piece. I've got tape stuck to my fingers."

"Fay, Maria says she commissioned a package from you about Henry Kettle, the water-diviner chap."

"Dowser, yes."

"Pardon?"

"Water-diviner, James, is not an adequate term for what he does. He divines all kinds of things. Electric cables, foundations of old buildings, dead bodies . . . "

"Yeah, well, he obviously wasn't much good at divining stone walls. Have you done the piece?"

"That's what I'm . . . "

" 'Cause, if you could let us have it this morning . . . "

"It's not for News," Fay explained. "It's a soft piece for Maria. For Alan Thingy's show. Six and a half minutes of me learning how to dowse." Fay ripped the tape from the receiver and threw the roll on the editing table. "What did you mean about stone walls?"

"Tut-tut. Don't you have police contacts down there, Fay? Henry Kettle drove into one last night. Splat."

The room seemed to shift as if it was on trestles like the editing table. The table and the Revox suddenly looked so incongruous here—the room out of the 1960s, gray-tiled fireplace, G-plan chairs, lumpy settee with satin covers. Still Grace Legge's room, still in mourning.

"What?" Fay said.

"Must've been well pissed," said James Barlow, with relish. "Straight across a bloody field and into this massive wall. Splat. Actually they're speculating, did he have a heart attack? So we're putting together a little piece on him, and your stuff . . . "

"Excuse me, James, but is he . . . ?"

" . . . would go quite nicely. We'll stitch it together here, but you'll still get paid, obviously. Yes, he is. Oh, yes. Very much so, I'm told. Splat, you know?"

"Yes," Fay said numbly.

"Can you send it from the Unattended, say by eleven?"

"Yes."

"Send the lot, we'll chop out a suitable clip. Bye now."

Fay switched the machine back on. Now it no longer mattered, Take Two didn't sound quite so embarrassing.

" . . . whoops! Gosh, Henry, that's amazing, the twig's flipped right over. If your hands hadn't been there, I'd've . . . "

A dead man said, "Dropped it, I reckon. Well, there you are then, Fay, you've found your first well. Can likely make yourself a bob or two now."

"I don't think so, somehow. Tell me, what exactly was happening there? You must have given it some thought over the years."

"Well . . . it's nothing to do with the rod, for a start. It's in you, see. You're letting yourself connect with what's out there and all the things that have ever been out there. I don't know, sounds a bit cranky. You're, how can I say . . . you're reminding your body that it's just part of everything else that's going on, you following me? Never been very good at explaining it, I just does it . . . You can mess about with this, can't you, Fay, make *it sound sensible? Feller from the BBC interviewed me once. He...*"

"*Yes, don't worry, it'll be fine. Now, what I think you're saying is that, in this hi-tech age, man no longer feels the need to be in tune with his environment.*"

"*Well, aye, that's about it. Life don't depend on it anymore, do he?*"

"*I suppose not. But look, Henry, what if...?*"

She stopped the tape, cut it off after "Life don't depend on it anymore." Why give them the lot when they'd only use forty seconds?

Anyway, the next bit wasn't usable. She'd asked him about this job he was doing for Max Goff and he'd stepped smartly back, waving his arms, motioning at her to switch the tape off. Saying that it would all come out sooner or later. "Don't press me, girl, all right?"

Later, he'd said, "Not being funny, see. Only it's not turned out as simple as I thought it was going to be. Something I don't quite understand. Not yet, anyway."

She hadn't pressed him. Very unprofessional of her. She had, after all, only approached Henry Kettle about doing six minutes for the "people with unusual hobbies" spot because she'd heard Max Goff had brought him to Crybbe and it was her job to find out what Goff himself was doing here.

But she'd ended up liking Henry Kettle, and actually liking somebody was sometimes incompatible with the job. So now nobody would know what he'd been doing for Goff unless Goff himself chose to disclose it.

Fay sat down, she and the room both in mourning now. He'd been a great character, had Henry, he'd leave a gap.

But if you had to go, maybe Splat wasn't a bad exit line at the age of—what was he, eighty-seven? Still driving his own car, too. Fay thought about her dad and the sports cars he'd had. He'd prefer Splat to arterial strangulation anytime.

Talking of the devil, she caught sight of him then through the window, strolling back toward the cottage with *The Guardian* under his arm, looking at ladies' legs and beaming through his big, snowy beard at people on either side—even though, in Crybbe, people never seemed to beam back.

The cottage fronted directly onto the street, no garden. Canon Alex Peters pushed straight into the office. He wasn't beaming now. He was clearly annoyed about something.

"Don't they just bloody love it?"

"Love what?" Fay joined some red leader to the end of the tape, deliberately not looking up, determined not to be a congregation.

"A tragedy. Death, failure—'specially if it's one of the dreaded People from Off."

"What are you on about, Dad?"

"That's what they say, 'From Off. Oh, he's from Off.' I've calculated that 'Off' means anywhere more than forty miles away. Anywhere nearer, they say, 'Oh, he's from Leominster' or 'He's from Llandrindod Wells.' Which are places not near enough to be local, but not far enough away to be 'Off.' "

"You're bonkers, Dad." Fay spun back the finished tape.

"Anyway, this poor sod was apparently from Kington or somewhere, which is the middle category. Not local but not 'Off.' So they're quite content that he's dead but not as happy as they'd be if he was from, say, Kent."

It clicked.

"You're talking about Henry Kettle."

"Who?"

"Henry Kettle. The dowser I interviewed yesterday morning."

"Oh God," Canon Peters said. *"That's* who it was. I'm sorry, Fay, I didn't connect, I . . . "

"Never mind," Fay said soothingly. Sometimes, on his good days, you were inclined to forget.

Her father, who'd been about to sit down, was instantly back on his feet. "Now look . . . It's got nothing to with Dr. Alphonse sodding Alzheimer."

"Alois."

"What?"

"Alois Alzheimer. Anyway, you haven't got Alzheimer's disease."

The canon waved a dismissive hand. "Alzheimer is easier to say than arteriosclerotic dementia, when you're going gaga." He took off his pink cotton jacket. "Nothing to do with that, anyway. Always failed to make connections. Always putting my sodding foot in it."

"Yes, Dad."

"And stop being so bloody considerate."

"All right then. Belt up, you old bugger, while I finish this tape."

"That's better." The canon slung his jacket over the back of the armchair, slumped down, glared grimly at *The Guardian*.

Fay labeled the tape and boxed it. She stood back and pulled down her T-shirt, pushed fingers through her tawny hair, asking him, "Where was it, then? Where did it happen?"

Canon Peters lowered his paper. "Behind the old Court. You know the tumulus round the back, you can see it from the Ludlow road? Got a wall round it? That's what he hit."

"But—hang on—that wall's a bloody mile off the road."

"Couple of hundred yards, actually."

"But still . . . I mean, he'd have to drive across an entire field, for Christ's sake." When James Barlow had said something about Mr. Kettle crossing a field she'd imagined some kind of extended grass-verge. "Somebody said maybe he'd had a heart attack, so I was thinking he'd just gone out of control, hit a wall not far off the road. Not, you know, embarked on a cross-country endurance course."

"Perhaps," speculated the canon, "he offed himself."

"Rubbish. I was with him yesterday morning, he was fine. Not the suicidal type, anyway. And if you're going to do yourself in, there have to be rather more foolproof ways than that."

"Nine out of ten suicides, somebody says that. There's always an easier way. He was probably just confused. I can sympathize."

"Any witnesses?" Above the tiled fireplace, opposite the window, was a mirror in a Victorian-style gilt frame. Fay inspected her face in it and decided that, for a walk to the studio, it would get by.

Canon Peters said, "Witnesses? In Crybbe?"

"Sorry, I wasn't thinking."

"Wouldn't have known myself if I hadn't spotted all the police activity, so I grilled the newsagent. Apparently it must have happened last night, but he wasn't found until this morning."

"Oh God, there's no chance he might have been still alive, lying there all night . . . ?"

"Shouldn't think so. Head took most of it, I gather, I didn't go to look. A local milkman, it was, who spotted the wreckage and presumably said to himself, 'Well, well, what a mess,' and then wondered if perhaps he ought not to call Wynford, the copper. No hurry, though, because . . . "

"He wasn't local," said Fay.

"Precisely."

Fay said it for the second time this week. "Why don't you get the hell out of this town, Dad? You're never going to feel you belong."

"I like it here."

"It irritates the hell out of you!"

"I know, but it's rather interesting. In an anthropological sort of way." His beard twitched. She knew she wasn't getting the whole story. What was he hiding, and why?

Fay frowned, wondering if he'd seen the spoof FOR SALE notice she'd scribbled out during a ten-minute burst of depression last night. She said tentatively, "Grace wouldn't want you to stay. You know that."

"Now look, young Fay." Canon Peters leaned forward in the chair, a deceptive innocence in the wide blue eyes which had wowed widows in a dozen parishes. "More to the point, there's absolutely no need for *you* to hang around. You know my methods. No problem at all to find some lonely old totty among the immigrant population to cater for my whims. In fact, you're probably cramping my style."

He raised *The Guardian* high so that all she could see was his fluffy white hair, like the bobble on an old-fashioned ski hat.

"Anyway," he mumbled. "Early stages yet. Could be months before I'm a dribbling old cabbage."

"Dad, I'll . . . !" The phone rang. "Yes, what . . . ? Oh. Mrs. Seagrove."

All she needed.

"Serves you right," rumbled the canon from the depths of *The Guardian.*

"I saw it again, Mrs. Morrison. Last night. When the power was off."

"Oh," Fay said, as kindly as she could manage. "Did you?"

"I can't bear it anymore, Mrs. Morrison."

Fay didn't bother to ask her how she could see a huge coal-black beast when all the lights were out; she'd say she just *could.* She was one of the aforementioned lonely old Midland immigrant widows in a pretty cottage on the edge of town. One of the people who rang local reporters because they needed someone to make a cup of tea for.

"I'm at the end of my tether, Mrs. Morrison. I'm going out of my mind. You wouldn't think anything as black as that could glow, would you? I'm shivering now, just remembering it."

In other places they rang the police for help. But in Crybbe the police was Sergeant Wynford Wiley and nobody wanted to make a cup of tea for him.

"I've tried to explain, Mrs. Seagrove. It's a fascinating . . . "

"It's not fascinating, my love, it's terrifying. It's no joke. It's frightening me out of my mind. I can't sleep."

"But there's nothing I can do unless you're prepared to talk about it on tape. I only work for the radio, and unless we can hear your voice . . . "

"Why can't you just *say* someone's seen it without saying who I am or where I live?"

"Because . . . because that's not the way radio works. We have to hear a voice. Look," Fay said, "I really would like to do the story. Perhaps you could find someone else who's seen it and would be prepared to talk about it and have it recorded."

Mrs. Seagrove said bitterly, "They all know about it. Mrs. Francis at the post office, Mr. Preece. They won't admit it. They won't talk about it. I've tried telling the vicar; he just listens and he smiles, I don't think he even believes in God, that vicar. Perhaps if you came round this afternoon, we could . . . "

"I'm sorry," Fay said, "I've got several jobs on the go at the moment."

"Ho, ho," said *The Guardian.*

"Look," Fay said. "Think about it. It's quite easy and informal, you know. Just me and a portable recorder, and if you make any fluffs we can keep doing it again until you've got it right."

"Well, perhaps if you came round we could . . . "

"*Not* unless you're prepared to talk about it on tape," Fay said firmly.

"I'll think about it," Mrs. Seagrove said.

Fay put the phone down. Of course, she felt sorry for the lady. And ghost stories always went down well with producers, even if the eyewitnesses were dismissed as loonies. Local radio *needed* loonies; how else, for instance, could you sustain phone-in programs in an area like this?

But ghost stories where nobody would go on the record as having seen the apparition were nonstarters. On that same basis, Fay thought ruefully, a lot of stories had been nonstarters in Crybbe.

two

The windshield was in splinters. There was blood on some of them, dried now. And there were other bits, pink and glistening like mince on a butcher's tray, which Max Goff didn't want to know about.

"What are you saying here?" he demanded irritably. "You're saying it's a fucking *omen?*"

He looked up at the hills shouldering their way out of the morning mist, the sun still offstage, just.

He turned and gazed at the Tump. A prosaic, lumpen word for the mystic mound, the branches of the trees on its summit still entwined with tendrils of mist.

A thing so ancient, so haunted, yet so benign. Yeah, well, *he* believed in omens, but . . .

There was some kind of awful creaking, tearing sound as the tow truck hauled the car out of the wall. A heavy crump and a rattle as the VW's shattered front end came down on the turf, its radiator ripped off, car intestines hanging out.

Max Goff winced. Beside him, Rachel Wade, his personal assistant, was saying in her deep voice, "Don't be silly." Spreading out her hands in that superior, pained, half-pitying way she had. "All I'm saying is it's not exactly an *auspicious* start, is it?"

Goff stared coldly at Rachel in her shiny, new Barbour coat and a silk scarf. Knowing how much he'd depended on her judgment in the past, but knowing equally that this was an area where she was well out of her depth. A situation where the smooth bitch couldn't be relied upon to get it right. No way.

She didn't, of course, want him to go through with it. Nobody whose opinion was worth more than shit had been exactly encouraging, but Rachel was subtler than most of them. She hadn't said a word about the nylon sheets in their room at the Cock. Had made no comment about the coffee at breakfast being instant. Just sat there, languid and elegant and at ease, refusing everything they offered her with a professional smile. Yeah, OK, under normal circumstances Goff himself would have insisted on different sheets and ground coffee and some kind of muesli instead of Rice Krispies. But he might need the Cock again.

Actually, he might need to buy it.

He'd been pondering this possibility, deciding not to discuss it with Ms. Wade just yet, when the local Plod had turned up, waiting respectfully in the lobby until he'd finished his Nescafé, then asking, "Are you Mr. Goff, sir? Mr. *Max* Goff?" as if they didn't recognize him.

The body had been taken away by the time they got to the scene. Max Goff only hoped the poor old bastard had at least one surviving relative. He didn't really feel like identifying the Kettle corpse in some seedy white-tiled mortuary where the atmosphere was heavy with obnoxious smells and bodily gases.

If it came to that, Rachel could do it. She'd hired Kettle originally. And nothing ever fazed Rachel, just as nothing ever blew her mind—there was even something suspiciously nonchalant about her orgasms.

"Right, Tom," somebody shouted, and the tow truck started across the field, the broken car on its back, a smashed coffin on an open hearse.

Then the truck stopped for some reason.

And, in that moment, the sun came out of the mist and the land was suddenly aglow and throbbing with life force.

And Goff remembered what day this was.

He turned toward the light, head back, eyes closing and the palms of his hands opening outward to receive the burgeoning energy.

I am here. At the zenith of the year. I am in a state of total submission.

"It's the solstice," he whispered. "I'd forgotten."

"Oh," said the uncommitted Rachel Wade. "Super."

As if guided, Max Goff turned back to the open field, opened his eyes and saw . . .

. . . reflected, quite perfectly, in the rear window of Henry Kettle's smashed-up old Volkswagen on the back of the truck he saw the venerable mound, the Tump at Crybbe Court, and the sun above it like a holy lamp.

And the connection was formed.

Revelation.

The truck started up again, moved off toward the road.

Goff pointed urgently at the mound, talking rapidly, forefinger stabbing at the air between him and Rachel. "Listen, when they built these things, the old Bronze Age guys, they'd, you know, consecrate them, according to their religion, right?"

Rachel Wade looked at him, expressionless.

"What they'd do is, they'd sacrifice somebody. I mean, the remains have been found, sacrifices, not burials—they have ways of telling the difference, right?"

Rachel freed a few strands of pale hair from the collar of her Barbour, flicked them back.

"And sometimes, right," Goff surged on, "at very important sites, the high priest himself would be sacrificed. Without resistance. Willingly, yeah?"

Rachel said, "How would they know that?"

"Know what?"

" 'A,' that he died willingly. And 'b,' that the fragments of bones or whatever belonged to a high priest?"

Goff was annoyed. "Jeez, they *know*, OK? Doesn't matter how, I'm not a flaming archaeologist. But what it meant was, the sacrifice would put the seal on the sanctity of the place. The dead priest would live on as its guardian. For all time, right?"

A police sergeant came over, the same one who'd fetched them from the Cock. Big moon-faced guy, didn't strike Goff as being all that bright. "We'd just like you to make a statement, if you would, sir."

"Everything Max Goff does is a Statement," Goff told him and grinned. "Who was it wrote that?"

"Time out," said Rachel automatically and a little wearily. "August 1990."

The police sergeant didn't get it. "You appear to have been the last person to see Mr. Kettle alive, sir. You'll probably be called to give evidence to that effect at the inquest."

"Shit," Goff said. "How . . . ? No, that's OK. That's fine. I'll join you back at the house. Ten minutes, right?"

"If you wouldn't mind, sir."

"Point I was making," Goff said, impatiently turning his back on the departing policeman, "is that Henry Kettle was about as close as you could find to a kind of high priest these days. Guy in tune with the earth and its spirit, responding to its deeper impulses. Shamanic, yeah?" Closing his eyes, he felt the holy light of the solstice on his face. Carried on talking with his eyes squeezed tightly shut. Talking to himself really, letting his thoughts unravel, the connections forming.

"So Henry Kettle—how old was the guy? Eighty-five? How long did he have to go, anyway? So, OK, we have this old man, the shaman, homing in, a dead straight line across the field—straight at the mound, the Tump, right—and . . . "

Goff opened his eyes suddenly and fully, and was dazzled by radiant blobs of orange and blue spinning from the top of the mound.

" . . . and . . . whoomp!" He clapped his big hands violently together.

Smiling hugely at Rachel Wade. "Listen, what I'm saying is, we're not looking at some bad omen here. It's a positive thing. Like the high priest going almost willingly to his death, like sacrificing himself all over again to put his life energy into my project. Whoomp!"

Rachel said, "That's really sick, Max." But Goff was looking up at the mound with a new pride, not listening.

"I bet if we mark out those tire tracks across that field we'll find they correspond exactly to line B."

"Line B?"

"The fucking ley-line, Rachel."

"Max, that's . . . "

Goff looked hard at Rachel. She shut up.

Jesus, she thought.

Whoomp.

three

"Bit for level, Fay."

"OK, here we go . . . "

Mr. Kettle said, *" . . . All right then, we know there's got to be water yereabouts . . . "*

"OK, that's fine, Fay . . . I'm rolling. Go in five."

She wound back, set the tape running, and took the cans off her ears, leaving them around her neck so she'd hear the engineer call out if he ran into problems.

Leaning back in the metal-framed typist's chair, she thought, God, I've been shunted into some seedy sidings in my time, but this . . .

. . . was the Crybbe Unattended Studio.

Ten feet long and six feet wide. Walls that closed in on you like the sides of a packing case. A tape machine on a metal stand. A square mahogany table with a microphone next to a small console with buttons that lit up. And the chair. And no windows, just a central light and two little red lights—one above the door outside to warn people to keep away in case whoever was inside happened to be broadcasting live to the scattered homesteads of the Welsh Marches.

This studio used to be the gents' lavatories at the back of the Cock, before they'd built new ones inside the main building. Then some planning wizard at Offa's Dyke Radio had presumably stuck a plastic marker into the map and said without great enthusiasm: Crybbe—well, yeah, OK, not much of a place, but it's almost exactly halfway up the border and within a couple miles of the Dyke itself . . . about as central as we'll get.

Then they'd have contacted the Marches Development Board, who'd have told them: No problem, we can offer you a purpose-built broadcasting center on our new Kington Road Industrial Estate at an annual rent of only . . .

At which point the planning wizard would have panicked and assured them that all that was required was a little room to accommodate reporters and interviewees (one at a time) and for sending tape down a land-line to Offa's Dyke main studios. All self-operated. No staff, no technicians. Very discreet. You walk in, you switch on, and a sound engineer records your every word from fifty miles away.

Which was how they'd ended up with the former gents' at the Cock. A tired, brick building with a worn slate roof, at the end of a narrow passageway past the trash cans.

The original white tiles with worrying brown stains had gone now. Or at least were hidden behind the black acoustic screening which formed a little soundproof module inside the building.

But sometimes, especially early in the morning, Fay would swear she could smell . . .

"That's lovely, Fay, thanks very much."

"Thanks, Barry," Fay told the microphone on the desk. All engineers were called Barry.

"It's Elton, actually," he said. "Hang on, Gavin's here, he'd like a word."

Elton. Jesus, nobody in this country who was called Elton could possibly be over twenty-one. Even the damned engineers at Offa's Dyke were fresh out of engineering school.

Gavin Ashpole came on the line, the station's news editor, an undeveloped rasp, unsure of whether it was supposed to sound thrusting or laid-back. He wanted to know if Fay was any closer to an interview with Max Goff about his plans for Crybbe Court. Or at least some sort of statement. "I mean, is it going to be a recording studio, or what? We going to have famous rock stars helicoptering in? We need to know, and we need to know *before* we read about it in the bloody papers."

"No, listen, I told you, his PA insists he doesn't want any publicity yet, but . . . "

Calm down, woman, don't rise to it.

"But when he's got things together," Fay finished lamely, "she says they'll tell me first. I . . . I've no reason to think she's bullshitting."

"Why can't you doorstep him? Just turn up. Put the fucker on the spot."

"Look, isn't it better to try and stay on the right side of the guy? There could be a lot of mileage in this one for us, in . . . in the future." Hesitating because "in the future" she wasn't going to be here, was she?

Absolutely no way she could tell him about the late Henry Kettle being hired by Goff to do some dowsing around the Court. Partly because she hadn't been able to persuade Mr. Kettle to tell her what he was supposed to be looking for. And partly because loony Gavin Ashpole would start wondering how he could implicate the famous Goff in Henry's death.

"I don't know, Fay." Ashpole switching to the Experienced News Editor's pensive drawl. "I'm not into all this pussyfooting about. We're gonna lose out, here. Listen, try him again, yeah? If you don't get anywhere, we'll have to, you know, reconsider things."

He meant if she didn't get him an interview soon they'd send in some flash kid from the newsroom to show her how it was done. Nasty little sod, Gavin Ashpole. All of twenty-four. Career to carve.

You've got to stop this, Fay warned herself, as the line went dead. You're becoming seriously obsessed with age. Good God, woman, you're not *old.*

Just older than almost everybody else connected with Offa's Dyke Radio. Which, OK, was not exactly *old* old, but . . .

What it is, she thought, your whole life's been out of sync, that's the problem. Goes back to having a father who was already into his fifties when you were conceived. Discovering your dad is slightly older than most other kids' granddads.

And yet, when you are not yet in your teens, it emerges that your mother is threatening to divorce your aged father because of *his* infidelity.

Fay shook her head, playing with the buttons on the studio tape machine. He'd given up the other woman, narrowly escaping public disgrace. Eight years later he was a widower.

Fast forward over that. Too painful.

Whizz on through another never-mind-how-many years and there you are, recovering from your own misguided marriage to a grade-A dickhead, pursuing your first serious career—as a radio producer, in London—and, yes, almost starting to enjoy yourself . . . when, out of the blue, your old father rings to invite you to his wedding in . . .

"Sorry, where did you say . . . ?"

"C-R-Y-B-B-E."

"Where the hell is that, Dad? Also, more to the point, who the hell is Grace?"

And then—bloody hell!—before he can reply, you remember.

"Oh my God, Grace was the woman who'd have been cited in Mum's petition! Grace Legge. She must be . . . "

"Sixty-two. And not terribly well, I'm afraid, Fay. Money-wise, too, she's not in such a healthy position. So I'm doing the decent thing. Twenty years too late, you might say . . . "

"I might not say anything coherent for ages, Dad. I'm bloody speechless."

"Anyway, I've sort of moved in with her. This little terraced cottage she's got in Crybbe, which is where she was born. You go to Hereford and then you sort of turn right and just, er, just carry on, as it were."

"And what about your own house? Who's taking care of that?"

"Woodstock? Oh, I, er, I had to sell it. Didn't get a lot, actually, the way the market is, but . . . "

"Just a minute, Dad. Am I really hearing this? You sold that bloody wonderful house? Are you going senile?"

Not an enormously tactful question, with hindsight.

"No option, my dear. Had to have the readies for . . . for private treatment for Grace and, er, things. Which goes—I know, you don't have to tell me—goes against everything I've always stood for, so don't spread it around. But she's really not awfully well, and I feel sort of . . . "

"Sort of guilty as hell."

"Yes, I suppose. Sort of. Fay, would you object awfully to drifting out here and giving me away, as it were? Very quiet, of course. Very discreet. No dog collars."

This is—when?—eleven months ago?

The wedding is not an entirely convivial occasion. At the time, Grace Legge, getting married in a wheelchair, has approximately four months to live, and she knows it.

When you return to a damp and leafless late-autumnal Crybbe for the funeral, you notice the changes in your dad. Changes which a brain scan will reveal to be the onset of a form of dementia caused by hardening of the arteries. Sometimes insufficient blood is getting to his brain. The bottom line is that it's going to get worse.

The dementia is still intermittent, but he can hardly be left on his own. He won't come to London—"Grace's cats and things,

I promised." And he won't have a housekeeper—"Never had to pay a woman for washing my socks and I don't plan to start now. Wash my own."

Fay sighed deeply. Cut to Controller's office, Christmas Eve. "Fay, it's not rational. Why don't you take a week off and think about it? I know if it was *my* father he'd have to sell up and get himself a flat in town if he was expecting me to keep an eye on him."

"This is just it, he *doesn't* expect me to. He's an independent old sod."

"All right. Let's say you do go to this place. How are you supposed to make a living?"

"Well, I've done a bit of scouting around. This new outfit, Offa's Dyke Radio . . ."

"Local radio? *Independent* local radio? Here today and . . . Oh, Fay, come on, don't do this to yourself."

"I thought maybe I could freelance for them on a bread-and-butter basis. They've got an unattended studio actually in Crybbe, which is a stroke of luck. And the local guy they had, he's moved on, and so they're on the lookout for a new contributor. I've had a chat with the editor there, and he sounded quite enthusiastic."

"I bet he did."

"And maybe I could do the odd program for you, if freelancing for a local independent as well doesn't break some ancient BBC law."

"I'm sure that's not an insurmountable problem, but . . ."

"I know, I know. I'm far too young to be retiring to the country."

"And far too good, actually."

"You've never said that before."

"You might have asked for more money."

Typical bloody BBC.

Fay spun back the Henry Kettle tape—why couldn't you rewind your life like that?—and let herself out, throwing the studio into darkness with the master switch by the door. But the spools were still spinning in her head.

She locked up and set off with a forced briskness up the alley, an ancient passageway, smoked brick walls with a skeleton of years-blackened beams. Sometimes cobwebs hung down and

got in your hair. She wasn't overfond of this alley. There were
always used condoms underfoot; sometimes the concrete flags
were slippery with them. In winter they were frozen, like milky
ice-pops.

She emerged into the center of Crybbe as the clock in the
church tower was chiming eleven. Getting to eleven sounded
like a big effort for the mechanism; you could hear the strain.

There were lots of deep shadows, even though the sun was
high, because the crooked brick and timbered buildings slouched
together, like down-and-outs sharing a cigarette. Picturesque and
moody in the evening, sometimes. In the daytime, run-down,
shabby.

People were shopping in the square, mainly for essentials.
The shops in Crybbe specialized in the items families ran out
of in between weekly trips to the supermarkets in Hereford or
Leominster. In Crybbe, prices were high and stocks low. These
were long-established shops, run by local people: the grocer, the
pharmacist, the hardware and farming suppliers.

Other long-established businesses had, like Henry Kettle, gone
to the wall. And been replaced by a new type of store.

Like The Gallery, run by Hereward and Jocasta Newsome,
from Surrey, specializing in the works of border landscape
artists. In the window, Fay saw three linked watercolors of the
Tump at different times of day, the ancient mound appearing to
hover in the dawn mist, then solid in the sunlight and then stark
and black against an orange sky. A buff card underneath said, in
careful copperplate:

THE TUMP—a triptych, by Darwyn Hall.
Price: £975.

Wow. A steal. Fay wondered how they kept the place open.
She walked on, past a little, scruffy pub, the Lamb, past Middle Marches Crafts, which seemed to be a greeting-card shop
this week. And then the Crybbe Pottery, which specialized in
chunky earthenware Gothic houses that lit up when you plugged
them in but didn't give out enough light by which to do anything
except look at them and despair.

"Morning, Mr. Preece," she said to the town mayor, a small
man with a face like a battered wallet, full of pouches and
creases.

" 'Ow're you," Mr. Preece intoned and walked on without a second glance.

It had been a couple of months before Fay had realized that "How are you" was not, in these parts, a question and therefore did not require a reply on the lines of "I'm fine, Mr. Preece, how are *you?*" or, "Quite honestly, Mr. Preece, since you ask, I'm becoming moderately pissed off with trying to communicate with the dead."

Brain-dead, anyway, most of them in this town. Nobody ever seemed to get excited. Or to question anything. Nobody ever organized petitions to the council demanding children's playgrounds or leisure centers. Women never giggled together on street corners.

Fay stopped in the street, then, and had what amounted to a panic attack.

She saw the spools on the great tape deck of life, and the one on the right was fat with tape and the one on the left was down to its last half inch. Another quarter of a century had wound past her eyes, and she saw a sprightly, red-faced little woman in sensible clothes returning from the Crybbe Unattended, another masterpiece gone down the line for the youngsters in the newsroom to chuckle over. *Poor old Fay, all those years looking after her dad, feeding him by hand, constantly washing his underpants . . . Think we'd better send young Jason over to check this one out?*

And the buildings in the town hunched a little deeper into their foundations and nodded their mottled roofs.

'Ow're you, they creaked. *'Ow're you.*

Fay came out of the passageway shivering in the sun, tingling with an electric depression, and she thought she was hearing howling, and she thought that was in her head, too, along with the insistent, urgent question: how am I going to persuade him to turn his back on this dismal, accepting little town, where Grace Legge has left him her cottage, her cats, and a burden of guilt dating back twenty years? How can I reach him before he becomes impervious to rational argument?

Then she realized the howling was real. A dog, not too far away. A real snout-upturned, ears-back, baying-at-the-moon job.

Fay stopped. Even in the middle of a sunny morning it was a most unearthly sound.

She'd been about to turn away from the town center into the huddle of streets where Grace's house was. Curious, she followed the howling instead and almost walked into the big blue back of Police Sergeant Wynford Wiley.

He was standing facing the police station and a woman. Who was hissing at him. Who was half his size, sharp-faced, red-faced, sixtyish, back arched like a cornered cat.

"What you want me to do?" Wynford was yelling, face like an Edam cheese. "Shoot 'im, is it?"

"I don't care what you do," the woman screeched. "But I'm telling you this ... *I don't like it.*" She looked wildly and irrationally distressed. She was vibrating. "You'll get it stopped!"

The dog howled again, an eerie spiral. The woman seized the policeman's arm as if she wanted to tear it off. Fay had never seen anyone so close to hysteria in Crybbe, where emotions were private, like bank accounts.

"Whose dog is it?" Fay said.

They both turned and stared at her and she thought, Sure, I know, none of my business, I'm from Off.

The ululation came again, and the sky seemed to shimmer in sympathy.

"I said, whose dog is it?"

four

From a wicker basket in the pantry Mrs. Preece took the fattest onion she could find. She crumbled away its brittle outer layer until the onion was pale green and moist in the palm of her hand.

She sat the onion in a saucer.

"Stuff and nonsense," commented Jimmy Preece, the mayor of Crybbe. The sort of thing most of the local men would say in such situations.

With a certain ceremony, as if it were a steaming Christmas

pudding, Mrs. Preece carried the onion on its saucer into the parlor, Jimmy following her.

She placed it on top of the television set. She said nothing. "A funny woman, you are," Jimmy Preece said gruffly, but not without affection.

Mrs. Preece made no reply, her mouth set in a thin line, white hair pulled back and coiled tight.

They both heard the click of the garden gate, and Jimmy went to the window and peered through the gap in his delphiniums.

Mrs. Preece spoke. "Is it *him?*"

Jimmy Preece nodded.

"I'm going to the shop," Mrs. Preece said. "I'll go out the back way. Likely he'll have gone when I get back."

What she meant was she wouldn't come back until he was good and gone.

Jocasta Newsome, a spiky lady, said in a parched and bitter voice, "It isn't working, is it? Even *you* have to admit that now?"

"I don't know what you mean." Her husband was pretending he didn't care. He was making a picture frame in pine, two ends carefully locked into a wood vise to form a corner. The truth was he cared desperately, about lots of things.

"You," Jocasta said. "Me. It. Everything." She was wearing a black woolen dress and a heavy golden shawl fastened with a Celtic brooch at her shoulder.

"Go away." Hereward started flicking sawdust from his tidy beard. "If all you can be is negative, go away."

On the workbench between them lay the immediate cause of this particular confrontation: the electricity bill. He'd let sawdust go all over that deliberately. "We'll query it," Hereward had stated masterfully. "Yes," Jocasta had replied, "but what if it's correct? How long can we go on paying bills like that?"

The worst of it was, they couldn't even rely on a constant supply. He'd never known so many power cuts. "One of the problems of living in a rural area, I'm afraid," the electricity official had told him smugly, when he complained. "Strong winds bring down the power lines, thunder and lightning, cows rubbing themselves against the posts, birds flying into . . . "

"I'm trying to run a business here!"

"So are the farmers, Mr., ah, Newsome. But they've seen the

problems at first hand, up on the hills. So *they,* you see, they
realize what we're up against."

Oh yes, very clever. What he was saying to Hereward, rec-
ognizing his accent, was, You people, you come here expecting
everything to be as smooth as Surrey. If you really want to be
accepted in the countryside you'd better keep your head down
and your mouth shut, got it?

Hereward growled and Jocasta, thinking he was growling at
her, looked across at him in his new blue overalls, standing by
his new wooden vise, and there was a glaze of contempt over
her sulky eyes.

"The rural craftsman," she observed acidly. "At his bench.
You're really rather pathetic."

"I'm trying to rescue the situation," Hereward snarled through
clamped teeth, "you stupid bitch."

Jocasta looked away, walked out, slammed the studio door.

And in the vise, the newly constructed corner of Hereward's
first frame fell symbolically apart.

Hereward sank to his knees.

Very deliberately, he picked up the two lengths of molded
wood and set about realigning them. He would not be beaten.
He would not give up.

And he would not let her disdain get to him. If they couldn't
sell enough original works of art they would, for a limited
period, sell a number of selected prints at reasonable prices.
And the prices would be kept reasonable because he would
make the frames himself. Dammit, he *did* know what he was
doing.

And he *had* recognized that there would be problems getting a
new gallery accepted in a lesser-known area. Obviously, places
like Crybbe had fewer tourists—all right, *far* fewer. But those
who came were the *right sort* of tourists. The intelligent, child-
less couples who didn't need beaches, and the cultured newly
retired people with time to construct the quality of life they'd
always promised themselves.

Slowly but emphatically, The Gallery would build a reputation among the discerning. They would travel from as far away
as Shrewsbury and Cheltenham and even Oxford and London.
And The Gallery would expand, and then other specialist dealers
would join them, and pretty soon it would be Crybbe for fine art,
the way it was Hay-on-Wye for books.

"Of course, it took time," he would say at dinner parties. "Good Lord, I remember, in the early days, when, to save money, one actually made one's own frames . . . "

"Festival, is it?" Jimmy Preece's eyes were like screwheads countersunk into old mahogany. "We never had no festival before."

"Precisely the point, Mr. Mayor." Max Goff tried to smile sincerely and reassuringly, but he knew from hundreds of press photos that it always came out wide and flashy, like car radiators in the 'sixties.

"No." Mr. Preece shook his head slowly, as if they were discussing water-skiing or first-division football, things which, transparently, were not part of the Crybbe scene. "Not round yere."

Goff leaned forward. He'd given a lot of thought to how he'd sell this thing to the townsfolk. A festival. A celebration of natural potential. Except this festival would last all year round. This festival would absorb the whole town. It would re-create Crybbe.

"The point is, Mr. Mayor . . . You got so much to be festive *about.*" Go on, ask me what the hell you got to be festive about.

The mayor just nodded. Jeez.

"Let me explain, OK?" White-suited Goff was feeling well out of place in this cramped little parlor, where everything was brown and mottled and shrunken-looking, from the beams in the ceiling, to the carpet, to Jimmy Preece himself. But he had to crack this one; getting the mayor on his side would save a hell of a lot of time.

"OK," Goff said calmly. "Let's start with the basics. How much you heard about me?"

Jimmy Preece smiled slyly down at his feet, encased in heavy, well-polished working boots with nearly as many ancient cracks as his face.

Goff flashed the teeth again. "Never trust newspapers, Mr. Mayor. The more money you make, the more the c . . . the more they're out to nail you. 'Specially if you've made it in an operation like mine. Which, as I'm sure you know, is the music business, the recording industry."

"I've heard that."

"Sex, drugs, and rock and roll, eh?"

"I wouldn't know about those things."

"Nor would I, Mr. Mayor," Goff lied. "Only been on the business side. A business. Like any other. And I'm not denying it's been highly successful for me. I'm a rich man."

Goff paused.

"And now I want to put something back. Into the world, if you like. But, more specifically . . . into Crybbe."

Mr. Preece didn't even blink.

"Because you have a very special town here, Mr. Mayor. Only this town, it's forgotten just how special it is."

Come on, you old bastard. Ask me *why* it's so flaming special.

Goff waited, keeping his cool. Very commendably, he thought, under the circumstances. Then, after a while, Jimmy Preece made his considered response.

"Well, well," he said. And was silent again.

Max Goff felt his nails penetrate the brown vinyl chair-arms. "I don't mean to be insulting here, Mr. Mayor," he said loudly, with a big, wide, shiny smile—a 1961 Cadillac of a smile. "But you have to face the fact that this little town is in *deep shit.*"

He let the words—and the smile—shimmer in the room.

"Terminally depressed," he said. "Economically sterile."

Still the mayor said nothing. But his eyes shifted sideways like the eyes of a ventriloquist's doll, and Goff knew he was at last getting through.

"OK." He pulled onto his knee a green canvas bag. "I'm gonna lay it all down for you."

Yeah, there it was. A hint of anxiety.

"Even a century ago," Goff stared the old guy straight in the eyes, "this town was home to over five thousand people. How many's it got now?"

Mr. Preece looked into the fireplace. Breathed in as if about to answer, and then breathed out without a word.

"I'll tell you. At the last census, there were two thousand, nine hundred and sixty-four. This is in the town itself; I'm not including the outlying farms."

From the canvas bag, Goff took a pad of recycled paper, opened it. Began to read the figures. "Crybbe once had a grammar school and two primary schools. It's now down to a single primary and the older kids get bussed to a secondary school eight miles away, yeah?"

Mr. Preece nodded slowly and then carried on nodding as if his head was working loose.

"Even as recently as 1968," Goff said, "there were four policemen in Crybbe. How many now?"

Mr. Preece's lips started to shape a word and then went slack again as Goff zapped him with more statistics. "Back in the fifties, there were three grocer's shops, two butcher's, couple of chemist's, and there was . . . "

Mr. Preece almost yelled, "Where you gettin' all this from?" But Goff was coming at him like a train now, and there was no stopping him.

" . . . a regular assize court earlier this century, and now what? Not even petty sessions anymore. No justices, no magistrates. Used to be a self-sufficient local authority, covering a wide area from Crybbe and employing over seventy people. Now there's your town council. Not much more than a local advisory body that employs precisely one person part-time—that's Mrs. Byford, the clerk who takes the notes at your meetings."

"Look, what . . . what's all this about?" Jimmy Preece was shrinking back into his chair, Goff leaning farther toward him with every point he made, but deciding it was time to cool things a little.

"Bottom line, Mr. Mayor, is you got a slowly aging population and nothing to offer the young to keep them here. Even the outsiders are mostly retired folk. Crybbe's already climbed into its own coffin and it's just about to pull down the lid."

Goff sat back, putting away his papers, leaving Jimmy Preece, Mayor of Crybbe, looking as tired and wasted as his town. "Mr. Mayor, how about you call a public meeting? Crybbe and me, we need to talk."

In the gallery itself—*her* place—Jocasta Newsome was starting to function. At last. God, she'd thought it was never going to begin. She walked quickly across the quarry-tiled floor—tap, tap, tap of the high heels, echoing from wall to wall in the high-roofed former chapel, a smart brisk sound she loved.

"Look, let me show you this. It's something actually quite special."

"No, really." The customer raised a hand and a faint smile. "*This* is what I came for."

"Oh, but . . . " Jocasta fell silent, realizing that a £1,000 sale was about to go through without recourse to the skills honed to a fine edge during her decade in International Marketing. She pulled herself together, smiled, and patted the hinged frame of the triptych. "It *is* rather super, though, isn't it?"

"Actually," the customer said, turning her back on the triple image of the Tump, "I think it's absolutely dreadful."

"Oh." Jocasta was genuinely thrown by this, because the customer was undoubtedly the *right kind:* Barbour, silk scarf, and that offhand, isn't-life-tedious sort of poise she'd always rather envied.

The woman revived her faint smile. "I'm sorry, I didn't mean to be rude. My boss thinks it's wonderful, and that's all that matters. I suppose it's the subject I'm not terribly taken with. It's only a large heap of soil, after all."

Jocasta mentally adjusted the woman's standing; she had a boss. Dare she ask who he was? "I'll pa . . . I'll have it packaged for you."

"Oh, don't bother, I'll just toss it in the back of the Jeep. Haven't far to go."

How far exactly? Jocasta asked silently, directing a powerful ray of naked curiosity at the woman. It usually worked.

The door closed behind him. Max Goff stood a moment on the sunlit step, Crybbe laid out before him.

Jimmy Preece's retirement cottage was a fitting place for the mayor to live, at the entrance to the narrow road off the little square, the one which led eventually to the Court—Jimmy Preece being the head of the family which had lived at Court Farm since sixteen-something at least.

It was fitting also for the mayor because it was at the top of the town, with the church of St. Michael on the right. And you could see the buildings—eighteenth, seventeenth century and earlier—staggering, gently inebriated, down the hill to the river, with its three-arched bridge.

From up here Goff could easily discern the medieval street-pattern—almost unchanged, he figured. The newer buildings—the school, the council housing and the small industrial estate—had been tacked on and could, no doubt, just as easily be flicked away.

It was bloody perfect.

Unspoiled.

And this was precisely *because* it was not a wealthy town, because it was down on its luck and had been for a long, long time. Because it was not linked to the trunk roads between Wales and the Midlands and was not convenient, never would be. No use at all for commuting to anywhere.

And yet, beneath this town, the dragon slumbered.

She was going to ring Darwyn Hall, the artist, immediately, but Hereward walked in, still wearing his artisan's outfit and carrying a mug of coffee. The mug was one of the misshapen brown things they'd felt obliged to buy from the Crybbe Pottery.

"Who was that?"

Jocasta was sitting at her desk in the corner of the gallery, putting the check away. It was a customized company check, the word *Epidemic* faded across it like a watermark. "A sale, of course," she said nonchalantly.

"Good God." Hereward looked around to see which of the pictures had gone. "Picking it up later, are they?"

"You should be looking in the window." Jocasta just couldn't hold her cool any longer, and an awful smirk of delight was spreading over her face like strawberry jam.

"You're joking," Hereward said, stunned. He strode to the window and threw back the shutters. "Good grief!" He turned back to Jocasta. "Full price?"

"This is not a bloody discount store, darling."

"Stone me," said Hereward. "The triptych. Just like that? I mean, who . . . ?"

Jocasta waited a second or two, adjusted the Celtic brooch at her shoulder, and then casually hit him with the big one.

"Max Goff."

"Gosh." Hereward put down his cup. "So it's true, then. He *has* bought the Court."

"Sent his personal assistant to collect it," Jocasta said. "Rachel Wade."

"This is far from bad news," Hereward said slowly. "In fact, this could be the turning point."

Mrs. Preece waited across the square with her shopping bag until she saw the large man in the white suit stride out past the delphiniums. He didn't, she noticed, close the garden gate behind him. She watched him get into his fancy black car and didn't go across to the house until she couldn't even hear its noise anymore.

Jimmy was still sitting in the parlor staring at the wall.

Mrs. Preece put down her shopping bag and reached over Jimmy to the top of the television set, where the onion was sitting in its saucer.

"You'll be late for your drink," she said.

"I'm not going today. I 'ave to talk to the clerk before she goes back to the library."

"What was he after?" demanded Mrs. Preece, standing there holding the saucer with the onion on it.

"He wants us to call a public meeting."

"Oh, he does, does he? And who's he to ask for a public meeting?"

"An interferer," Jimmy Preece said. "That's what he is."

Mrs. Preece said nothing.

"I don't like interferers," Jimmy Preece said.

There was nothing his wife could say to that. She walked through to the kitchen, holding the saucer before her at arm's length as if what it had on it was not a peeled onion but a dead rat.

In the kitchen she got out a meat skewer, a big one, nearly a foot long, and speared the onion, the sharp point slipping easily into its soft, moist, white flesh.

Then she took it across to the Rayburn and opened the door to the fire compartment. With a quick stab and a shiver—partly of revulsion, partly satisfaction—she thrust the onion into the flames and slammed the door, hard.

five

"This may seem an odd question," the vicar of Crybbe said after a good deal of hesitation, "but have you ever performed an exorcism?"

The question hung in the air for quite a while.

Sunk into his armchair in Grace's former sitting room, Canon Alex Peters peered vaguely into the thick soup of his past. *Had* he done an exorcism? Buggered if he could remember.

The sun was so bright now—at least *suggestive* of warmth—that Alex had stripped down to his washed-out Kate Bush T-shirt, the letters in "Bush" stretched to twice the size of those in "Kate" by the considerable belly he'd put on since the doctor had ordered him to give up jogging. On his knees was a fiendish-looking black tomcat which Grace had named after some famous Russian. Chekhov? Dostoevsky? Buggered if he could remember that either.

"Ah, sorry, Murray. Yes, exorcism. Mmm."

What should he say? East Anglia? Perhaps when he was in charge of one of those huge, terrifying, flint churches in Suffolk . . . Needed to be a bit careful here.

"Ah! I'll tell you what it was, Murray—going back a good many years this. Wasn't the full bell, book, and candle routine, as I remember. More of a quickie, bless-this-house operation. Actually, I think I made it up as I went along."

The Reverend Murray Beech raised an eyebrow.

Alex said, "Well, you know the sort of thing . . . 'I have reason to believe there's an unquiet spirit on the premises, so, in the name of the management, I suggest you leave these decent folk alone and push off back where you came from, there's a good chap.' "

The Reverend Murray Beech did not smile.

"Expect I dramatized it a bit," Alex said. "But that's what it boiled down to. Seemed to work, as I recall. Don't remember any come-backs, anyway. Why d'you ask?"

Although he wore the regulation-issue black shirt and clerical collar, rather than a Kate Bush T-shirt, young Murray Beech didn't seem like a real vicar to Alex. More like the ambitious deputy head of some inner-city comprehensive school. He was on the edge of one of Grace's G-plan dining chairs, looking vaguely unhappy about the can of lager Alex had put unceremoniously into his hand.

"You see, the way you put it then," Murray said carefully, as though he were formulating a point at a conference, "makes it seem as if . . . you knew at the time . . . that you were only going through the motions."   •

"Well, that's probably true, old chap. But who knows what we do when we go through the motions?" A sunbeam stroked Alex's knees; the cat shifted a little to make the most of it. "Do I understand, Murray, that someone has invited you to perform an exorcism?"

"This appears to be the general idea," the vicar said uncomfortably. "The central dilemma is, as you know, I'm not into sham. Too much of that in the church."

"Absolutely, old chap."

"You see, my problem is . . . "

"Oh, I think I know what your problem is." Perhaps, Alex thought, it used to be my problem too, to an extent. How sure of our ground we are, when we're young ministers. "For instance, Murray, if I were to ask you what you consider to be the biggest evils in the world today, you'd say . . . ?"

"Inequality. Racism. Destruction of the planet due to unassuageable . . . I'm not going to say capitalism; let's call it greed." He eyed *The Guardian* on Alex's chair arm. "Surely you'd agree with that?"

"Course, dear boy. Right on the nose. Look, Tolstoy, would you mind not sharpening your claws on my inner thigh, there's a good cat. So who wants you to do this exorcism?"

"Difficult." Murray smiled without humor. "Difficult situation. It's a teenager. Lives with the grandparents. Thinks there's some sort of"—his mouth pursed in distaste—"disruptive etheric intrusion. In the house."

"Poltergeist, eh? What have the grandparents got to say?"

"That's the difficulty. I'm not supposed to speak to them. This . . . person is rather embarrassed about the whole thing. Having read somewhere that so-called poltergeists are often caused by, or attracted to, a disturbed adolescent. You know that theory?"

"Rampant hormones overflowing. Smart boy. In my day, of course, the vicar would just have told him to stop jerking off and the thing would go away."

Murray said, "It's a girl."

"Oh."

"She wants me to go along when her grandparents are out and deal with this alleged presence."

"Oh dear." Alex opened his can of Heineken with a snap. "You're right, my boy, it *is* a difficult one. Erm . . . " He looked across at Murray, all cropped hair, tight mouth, and steely efficiency. "Do you suppose this youngster might have something of a . . . *crush* on you?" Well, it wasn't entirely beyond the bounds of possibility; there were some pretty warped kids around these days.

"Oh, I don't think it's that, Alex. That would be comparatively easy to deal with."

"Glad you think so. What have you said to her, then?"

"We had a long discussion about the problems and insecurities of the postpubescent period. Made more difficult in this case because she has no parents to go to—mother dead, father in the merchant navy. You see, I don't want to fail the kid. Because, you know, so few people in this town ever actually come to me for help. Especially with anything of a nonmaterial nature—i.e., anything that doesn't involve opening rummage sales. It's obvious most of them find me an institutional irrelevance most of the time."

"Wouldn't say that, old chap."

"Wouldn't you? Oh, certainly, they're always there on Sunday. Well, enough of them, anyway. So no congregation problems, as such, but . . . "

"That's what it's all about, old son. That's the core of it. Bums on pews."

"Is it? Is that what you think?" The dining chair creaked as Murray hunched forward, chin thrusting. "Have you ever looked out over *your* parishioners and seen all the animation, all the commitment, of a doctor's waiting room or a bus queue?"

Alex nodded. "They're not *expressive* people in this town, I grant you. Perhaps a chap like you ought to be working in a more happening situation, as they say."

Murray clearly thought so too. But Alex could see the difficulty. He'd been lucky to get a parish this size at his age, still in his twenties. Could be a key step on the way to the bishop's palace before he turned forty if he made the right impression.

They heard footsteps on the path, a key in the front door. "Ah, here's Fay. Look, Murray, why don't we ask *her* about your problem? Used to be a teenage girl herself not awfully long ago."

"No!" Murray Beech jerked on the edge of his dining chair. "Not a word, if you don't mind, Alex. I don't want this turned into a joke on the radio."

"Good God, Murray, I hardly think . . . "

"Please."

"OK, if that's how you'd prefer it. I say, what's wrong with old Chekhov?"

The cat had leapt onto the chair back next to Alex's shoulder, looking even less at ease than the vicar of Crybbe.

"Dad," Fay called from the hall. "You haven't got Rasputin in there, have you? If you have, just hold on to him." There was a patter of paws. "We may have a minor integration problem."

The cat hissed in Alex's ear.

"I must go," Murray Beech said, putting the unopened can of lager on top of Grace's little nest of tables.

The door opened and a dog came in, followed by Fay. The dog was straining on the end of a clothesline. It was a rather bizarre dog. Black and white, the size of a sheepdog. But with a terrier's stance and enormous ears, like a donkey's.

The dog ignored Rasputin but sniffed suspiciously at Murray Beech, as the vicar came to his feet.

"Sorry about this, Dad," Fay said. "But you and Rasputin'll have to make allowances, show a little charity. Oh, hullo, Murray, I'm quite glad you're here."

The dog ambled over to Alex. "He's had a bereavement," Fay said. "Listen, Murray, do you know Mrs. Byford?"

Halfway to the door, the vicar stiffened. "The Old Police House?"

"That's the one, yes. Is she all right?"

"I'm sorry . . . What do you mean, 'all right'?"

Alex, patting the dog, observed how inhibited Murray Beech became when Fay was around. Partly, he thought, because of what she did for a living and partly, no doubt, because he couldn't help fancying the arse off her. Open to that kind of thing now, too, since his engagement had gone down the toilet.

"This Mrs. Byford," Fay said, "was throwing the most amazing fit. He"—looking at the dog—"was howling in his cell at the cop shop, and Mrs. Byford was reacting as if it was the four-minute warning or something. Really going for Wynford, the copper. 'Get it stopped! I'm not having it! I don't like it!' Way over the top."

"Perhaps he simply feels she has a right to peace and quiet," Murray said tightly.

"Living next to the cop shop? Drunks getting hauled in on a Saturday night? What the hell does she know about peace and quiet?"

Murray shrugged. "I'm sorry, I have to go. I'll talk to you again, Alex."

"Yes, call anytime, old chap."

When the vicar had gone, Fay said, "Creep."

"No, just a duck out of water," Alex said, stroking the rigid Rasputin. "He'd be far more at home in Birmingham, preaching peaceful coexistence with Islam. Who's your extraordinary friend?"

"Um, yes. I'm sorry to spring him on you, but it all happened very quickly, what with this loopy woman—definitely something wrong with her." Fay knelt down and detached the clothesline from the dog's collar. "He's called Arnold. He was Henry Kettle's dog. He seems to have been in the car when it crashed. Must have got out through a window afterwards. They found him this morning, sitting by the wreckage like the Greyfriars Bobby. Breaks your heart, doesn't it?"

Arnold rested his chin for just a moment on Alex's knee. There was a savage hiss from Rasputin. "Poor old chap," Alex said. He thought the dog had strangely kind eyes. "But he can't stay here."

Arnold glanced at Rasputin with disinterest, then padded away. Fay said, "I was afraid, to be honest, of what Wynford might have done to shut him up."

"Oh, surely not."

"I don't know, the police round here are . . . different. Wynford had him in this concrete coal-shed kind of place. Hard floor, no windows, no basket or anything. A metal bucket to drink out of. Barbaric. So I thought, that's it, he's not staying here. Then

Wynford and I had this terrific battle."

"Oh dear," Alex said. "Poor chap."

" 'Oh, we has to let the RSPCA deal with it. We has to abide
by the Procedures.' 'Bollocks,' I said. 'Send the RSPCA round
to see me.' "

"No contest," Alex said.

"Listen, that guy is seriously weird. His features are too small
for his head and they never alter. So I just opened the shed
door and walked off, and the dog followed me. Wynford's left
standing there, face getting redder and redder, like a pumpkin
with a light inside on Halloween."

Arnold was pottering around the room, sniffing uncertainly,
huge ears pricked.

"It's remarkable really, he doesn't seem to have been injured
at all, though I don't suppose bruises would show up on a dog.
Psychologically, though . . . "

"Yes, it's a damn shame. But, Fay . . . "

" . . . psychologically, he could be in pieces."

"But he can't stay here, Fay." Alex sat up, trying to look
authoritative. "Grace would have a fit. She wasn't at all fond
of dogs. And neither's old Rasputin."

"Dad"—Fay was wearing *that* expression—"Grace is *bloody
dead.* Anyway . . . " She squatted down beside Arnold and cra-
dled his black and white snout in her hands. Long black whis-
kers came out between her fingers. "If he goes, I go too."

Canon Alex Peters took a long swig of cold Heineken.

"Splendid," he said.

  six

People kept looking at her.

This was not usual. Normally, on these streets, even if you
were greeted—"Oow're you"—you were not looked at. You
were observed, your presence was noted, but you were not
directly examined.

Maybe, she thought, it was the dog. Maybe they recognized the late Henry Kettle's dog. Or maybe they'd never before seen a dog on the end of a thin, red, plastic-covered clothesline that the person on the other end was now wishing she hadn't adapted because, every time the dog tugged at the makeshift lead, her right hand received what could turn out to be third-degree burns.

"Arnold, for Christ's sake . . . "

With Henry Kettle he'd appeared ultradocile, really laid-back. Now he was like some loony puppy, pulling in all directions, wanting to go nowhere, needing to go anywhere. And fast.

You had to make allowances. He was disoriented. He'd had a bereavement. In fact, the worst thing that could happen to a one-man dog had happened to Arnold. So allowances definitely were called for. And one of the people who was going to have to make them was Canon Alex Peters. In Fay's experience all this cat-and-dog incompatibility business was grossly exaggerated. Even Rasputin would, in time, come around.

But another animal was another root in Crybbe. *And you don't want that, Fay, you don't want any roots in Crybbe.*

Bill Davies, the butcher, walked past with fresh blood on his apron, and he stared at them.

Fay was fed up with this. She stared back. Bill Davies looked away.

Maybe they were all afflicted with this obsession about dogs fouling pavements. She'd have to buy one of those poop-scoop things. On the other hand, did that kind of obsession really seem like Crybbe, where apathy ruled?

"For God's sake, Arnie, make up your mind." They'd come to the square, and he seemed to want to turn back. He circled miserably around, dragging the clothesline and winding it around the legs of a woman bending over the tailgate of a Range Rover, shoving something in the back.

"Oh hell, I'm really sorry. Look, if you can stand still, I'll disentangle you. I'm very sorry."

"No problem," the woman said, looking quite amused. She was the first person who hadn't stared at them, which meant she must be from Off.

Of course she was—she was Max Goff's personal assistant, Ms. Coolly Efficient.

"We're not used to each other," Fay explained. "It's Henry

Kettle's sheepdog, the poor chap who . . . I'm looking after him."

"Oh, yes." Rachel Wade stepped out of the loop of clothes-line. "You're from the radio."

"We all have a living to make," Fay said, and then, making the most of the encounter, "Look, can I talk to you sometime? I'm being hassled by my boss to find out what's happening to the Court." That hurt, referring to Gavin Ashpole as a boss, which he wasn't and was never going to be.

"Sure," Rachel said, surprising her.

"When?"

"Now, if you like. We could go over to the Court. Max is out seeing people."

"Great."

"Hop in then," Rachel said. But Arnold didn't want to. In the end Fay had to pick him up and dump him on the back seat, where he flattened himself into the leather and panted and trembled.

"Sorry about this." Fay climbed into the passenger seat. "He's—not surprisingly—more than a bit paranoid. He was in Henry's car when it . . . you know."

"Oh dear, poor dog. I didn't know about that." Rachel Wade started the engine. "It's rather a mystery, isn't it. About old Kettle. Do you think he'd been drinking?"

"I didn't know him very well. I think a heart attack or a stroke or something seems more likely, don't you?"

"He was a nice old man." Rachel swung the Range Rover off the square into the street that wriggled down past the church, the graveyard on the right, a few cottages on the left. The street narrowed and entered a wood, where the late-afternoon sun was filtered away and the colors faded almost to gray. "I don't believe all that dowsing stuff. But he was a nice old man."

"Don't you? I thought . . . "

"Oh, *Max* does. Max believes it. Good God, yes. However, I don't get paid to share his wilder obsessions. Well, *he* thinks I do . . . " Rachel exhaled a short, throaty laugh.

They came out of the wood. A track to the left was barred by a gate with a metal sign: COURT FARM. Where the Preeces farmed. Jack, son of Jimmy, the mayor, and Jack's two sons. Fay had seen Jack once, slinking almost furtively out of the church, his nightly duty accomplished.

"And what exactly is Mr. Goff's obsession with the Court?"

"I'll show you in a minute," Rachel said affably.

This was too easy. Fay was suspicious. She watched Rachel Wade driving with a languid economy of movement, like people drove in films, only you knew they weren't in real, moving vehicles. This was the kind of woman who could change a wheel and make it look like a ballet. Made you despair.

Rachel said, "Is that your father, the old clergyman? Or your grandfather or something?"

"Father. You've met him?"

"In the Cock. We got into conversation after my lighter fell off the bar and he picked it up." Rachel smiled. "In fact, if he'd been considerably younger, I'd almost have thought . . . "

Fay nodded wryly. "The old knocking-the-lighter-off-the-bar routine. Then he carries out a detailed survey of your legs while he's picking it up. He's harmless. I think."

"He's certainly a character." Rachel pulled up in a walled courtyard amid heaps of sand and builders' rubble. Before them random gray-brown stones were settled around deep-set mullioned windows and a dusty oak door was half open.

Fay took a breath.

"Crybbe Court," Rachel said. "But don't get too excited." She snapped on the hand brake. "Leave the dog in the car; he won't like it. Nobody does, really, apart from historians, and even they get depressed at the state of it."

Fay wondered what had made her think it was going to be mellow and warm-toned like a country house on a Christmas card.

"It's old," she said.

"Elizabethan."

She felt cold and folded her bare arms. Outside, it was a fairly pleasant midsummer's day; in here, stark and grim as dankest February.

Somehow, she'd imagined rich drapes and tapestries and polished paneling. Probably because the only homes of a similar period she'd visited had been stately homes or National Trust properties, everything exuding the dull sheen of age and wealth, divided from the masses by brass railings and velvet ropes.

In Crybbe Court these days, it seemed, only the rats were rich.

The room was large, stone-floored and low-ceilinged, and apparently fortified against the sun. The only direct light was from three small, high-set windows, not much more than slits. Bare blue sky through crossed iron bars.

Fay said, "I suppose it's logical when you think about it, the period and everything, but I didn't imagine it would be quite so . . ."

She became aware of a narrow, stone staircase spiraling into a vagueness of cold light hanging from above like a sheet draped over a banister.

" 'Ghastly,' " Rachel said, "is, I think, the word you're groping for. Let's go upstairs. It's possibly a little less oppressive."

The spiral staircase opened into a large chamber with mullioned windows set in two walls. Bars of dusty sunshine fell short of meeting in the middle. It had originally been the main family living room, Rachel explained. "Also, I'm told, the place where the local high sheriff, a man named Wort, held out against the local populace who'd arrived to lynch him. Have you heard that story?"

"I've heard the name, but not the story."

"Oh, well, he was a local tyrant back in the sixteenth century. Known as Black Michael. Hanged men for petty crimes after allowing their wives to appeal to his better nature, if you see what I mean. Also said to have experimented on people before they died, in much the same way as the Nazis did."

"Charming."

"In the end, the local people decided they'd had enough."

"What? The townsfolk of Crybbe actually rebelled? What did they do, write 'Wort Must Go' on the lavatory wall?"

"Probably, for the first ten years of atrocities. But in the end they really did come out to lynch him, all gathered out there in the courtyard, threatening to burn the place down with him in it if he didn't come out."

"And did he?"

"No," said Rachel. "He went into the attic and hanged himself from the same rafters from which he'd hanged his offenders."

"And naturally," Fay said, "he haunts the place."

"Well, no," Rachel said. "He doesn't, actually. No stories to that effect anyway. And when Mr. Kettle toured the house, he said it was completely dead. As in vacant. Unpresenced, or however you care to put it. Max was terribly disappointed. He had to console himself with the thought of the hound bounding across his path one night."

"What?"

"Black Michael's Hound. Nobody ever sees Michael, but there is a legend about his dog. A big, black, Baskerville-type creature said to haunt the lanes on the edge of town. It comes down from the Tump."

Fay thought at once of the old lady who kept telephoning her, Mrs. Seagrove. "I didn't know about that."

Rachel looked at her, as if surprised anybody should *want* to know about it.

"When was it last seen?" Fay asked.

"Who knows. The book Max found the story in was published, I think, in the fifties. One of those 'Legends of the Border' collections. The more recent ones don't seem to have bothered with it."

Fay wondered if it would help Mrs. Seagrove to know about the legend. Probably scare her even more. Or maybe Mrs. Seagrove *did* know about it and had either invented or imagined her own sighting, which would explain everything. The problem with old ladies was you could never be quite sure of their state of mind, especially the ones who lived alone.

She asked bravely, "Are we going up to the attic, then?"

"Certainly not," Rachel said firmly. "For one thing, it's not terribly safe. The floor's pretty badly rotted away up there and Max isn't insured against people breaking their necks. Unless they've been hanged."

Fay shivered and smiled and looked around. "Well," she said. "It could be wonderful, I suppose. If it was done up."

"With a million pounds or so spent on it, perhaps." Rachel prodded with a shoe and sent a piece of plaster skating across the dusty wooden floor. "I can think of better things you could do with a million pounds."

"Has it been like this since—you know—Tudor times?"

"Good God, no. At various times . . . I mean, in the past century alone, it's been a private school, a hotel . . . even an actual dwelling place again. If we had a torch you'd see bits of wiring and the ruins of bathrooms. But nothing's ever lasted long. It was built as an Elizabethan house, and that, in essence, is what it keeps reverting to."

"And now?"

"No big secret. Max is a New Age billionaire with a Dream."

"You don't sound very impressed."

Rachel stood in the center of the room and spread her hands. "Oh God . . . He wants to be King Arthur. He wants to set up his Round Table with all kinds of dowsers and geomancers and spiritual healers and other ghastly cranks. He's been quietly infiltrating them into the town over the past year. And there'll be some kind of Max Goff Foundation, on a drip feed from Epidemic, hopefully with the blessing of the Charity Commissioners. And people will get ludicrous grants to go off and search for their own pet Holy Grails."

"Sounds quite exciting," said Fay, but Rachel looked gloomy and rolled her eyes, her hands sunk deep into the pockets of her Barbour.

"Money down the drain," she said.

"What's a . . . a geomancer?"

"It's some sort of spiritual chartered surveyor. Someone who works out where it's best to live to stay in harmony with the Earth Spirit, whatever that is, to protect yourself and your family against Evil Forces. Need I go on?"

There were passages leading off the big room, and Fay took one and found herself in a dark little bedchamber. It was the first room she'd seen that was actually furnished. There was an old chest under the pathetically inadequate window and a very small four-poster bed.

"Like a four-poster cot, isn't it?" Rachel had drifted in after her. "People were smaller in those days."

It was no more than five feet high and not much longer, with very thick posts and an oak headboard with a recessed ledge. On the ledge was a pewter candle holder with a candle stub in it. The drapes were some kind of cumbersome brocade, thick as tarpaulin and heavy with grease.

"It seems they'd leap into bed," Rachel said, "and draw all the curtains tight. And then blow out their candle. Having first read a passage from the Bible—you see there's space on the ledge for a Bible. Because they just *knew* that on the other side of the curtains, the evil spirits would be hovering *en masse*. Cozy, isn't it?"

"Claustrophobic." Fay had never liked four-posters.

"However, if you want a *real* scare . . . " Rachel held out a box of matches. " . . . light the candle and look in the chest."

She stood there holding the matchbox, not much more than another shadow in the dim, grimy bedchamber, only a crease in her Barbour at the elbow catching the light. The coat's dull waxen surface looked right for the period, and Fay had the alarming sensation that the dingy room was dragging them back into its own dark era. Was Rachel smiling? Fay couldn't see her face.

She found herself accepting the matchbox.

"Go on," Rachel said. "Light the candle."

"OK." She tried not to sound hesitant, asking herself, You aren't *nervous*, are you, Fay?

No, she decided. Just bloody cold. It might have occurred to me to wonder why she was wearing a Barbour on Midsummer Day. And she might have warned me about the temperature in this place.

She reached beyond the post at the bedhead and pulled the candle holder from the recess. Struck a match. Saw the candle tray was full of dead flies and bluebottles. Turned it upside down, but not all of them fell out.

Yuk. Fay lit the candle.

Shadows bounced.

"The chest under the window?"

She could see Rachel Wade's face now, in the candlelight, and it *wasn't* smiling. "Look," Rachel said, "forget it. Come on. I was only joking."

"No you weren't." Fay smelled wax, from the candle and from Rachel's coat perhaps. "I'd better open the blasted thing before this candle burns away."

Rachel Wade shrugged. Fay crossed to the window, which left only a smear of light across the top of the chest. Obviously not Elizabethan, this chest; it had black lettering stamped across its lid and was carelessly bound with green-painted metal strips.

Fay lifted the lid and lowered the candle.

She recoiled at once. "Oh," she said.

"Sorry."

"What is it?"

Its eye sockets were black and two upper teeth were thin and curved. A small cobweb hung between them. The mouth was stretched wide in a fossilized shriek.

"It's a cat, isn't it? A mummified cat?"

"Tiddles. Max calls it Tiddles."

"Cute," Fay said and shuddered.

"Not very. It was found in the rafters. It may have been walled up there alive."

"God."

"Practical geomancy," Rachel said. "The spirit of the cat acts, apparently, as a guardian. They found half a horse behind the kitchen wall. Come on, let's go."

seven

Asleep in his armchair, Canon Alex Peters dreamed he was asleep in his armchair. Tucked up in a soft blanket of sunbeams, he awoke in time to watch the wall dissolve.

It began with the fireplace. He was aware that Grace's dreadful see-through clock and the gilt-framed mirror were fading, while the black, sooty hole of the fireplace itself was getting bigger.

Gradually, the hole took over, becoming darker and wider and then spreading up through the mantelpiece, almost as far as the ceiling, until the whole chimney breast dissolved into a black passageway.

There formed a filigree of yellowish light, and then, dimly at first, Grace appeared in the passageway. Standing there, quite still.

"What happened to your wheelchair?" Alex asked. He was glad, of course, to see her back on her feet.

"No you're not," Grace said. Her lips did not move when she spoke, but her body became brighter, as if the spiderweb of lights was inside her, like glowing veins. "You were glad when I died, and you'll be glad to know I'm still dead."

"That's not true," protested Alex. But you couldn't lie to the dead, and he knew it.

Grace turned her back on him and began to walk away along
the passage. Alex struggled to get up, desperate to explain.
But the chair wouldn't let him. He shouted to the spindly,
diminishing figure. "Grace, look, don't go, give me a hand,
would you?"

The chair held him in a leathery grip.

"Grace!" Alex screamed. "Grace, don't go! I want to
explain!"

Just once, Grace glanced back at him over her shoulder, and
there was a pitying smile on her face, with perhaps a shadow
of malice.

Max Goff did not, of course, have any immediate plans to live
in Crybbe Court itself, Rachel Wade said. Good *God*, no.

Well, perhaps one day. When it was fully restored.

"You mean," Fay said as they walked out into the sunlight,
"restored to what it would've been like if the Elizabethans had
had full central heating and ten-speaker stereos."

"You're getting the general picture," Rachel confirmed, and
showed her the place where Max actually would be living within
the next week or so.

It was an L-shaped stone stable block behind the house.
It already had been gutted, plumbed, and wired, and a giant
plate-glass window had been inserted into a solid stone wall
to open up a new and spectacular view of the hills from what
would be the living room.

At least, the view *would* have been spectacular if it hadn't
been semiobscured by a green mound, like an inverted pudding
basin or a giant helmet.

"His beloved Tump," Rachel said. And there wasn't much
affection there, Fay thought, either for the mound or for Max
Goff.

"Is it a burial mound or a—what d'you call it—castle
mound . . . motte?"

"Probably both. Either way it's pretty unsightly, like an over-
grown dump. And decidedly creepy by moonlight. I mean, who
wants to stare out at a grave? Whoever built this place had the
right idea, I think, by putting a blank stable wall in front so it
wouldn't frighten the horses."

Fay realized the Court itself was built in a hollow, and the
Tump was on slightly higher ground, so that it seemed, from

here, higher than it actually was. It loomed. The stone wall which surrounded it had partly fallen down on this side, revealing the mesh of dense bushes and brambles at the base of the mound.

"Poor Mr. Kettle," Fay said, reminded by the wall.

Rachel fingered a strand of pale hair, the nearest she'd come, in Fay's presence, to a nervous gesture. "The bitter irony is that Max plans to move that wall. He calls it a nineteenth-century abomination. Some experts think it's older than that and should be preserved, but he'll get his way, of course, in the end."

Rachel stepped on a piece of soft plaster and ground it into the newly boarded floor.

"He always does," she said.

It was clear now to Fay that this was not the same Rachel Wade who, a week ago, had briskly swept her down the steps of the Cock with vague promises of an interview with Goff when his plans were in shape. Sure, on that occasion, she'd had a tape recorder over her shoulder. But even if she'd carried one today, she felt, Rachel's attitude would not have been markedly different.

Something had changed.

Fay said cautiously, "So when is he going to talk to me? On tape."

"Leave it with me," Rachel said. "I'll fix it." She spread her arms to usher Fay back toward the wooden framework evidently destined to be a doorway.

"I hate having to ask this sort of question." Fay stopped at the entrance. "But he isn't going to be talking to anyone else, is he, first?"

"Not if I can help it. Listen, we've been walking around this place for the last forty-five minutes, and I've forgotten your name."

"Fay. Fay Morrison."

"Would you like a job, Fay?"

"Huh?"

"Quite ludicrous salary. Seductively fast company car. Lots of foreign travel."

Fay stared at her.

"Expense account," Rachel said. "Untold fringe benefits." She'd turned her back on the big window. From the far end of the room, the hills had been squeezed out of the picture; the window was full of Tump.

"How long have you been doing this?" Fay asked. "As Goff's PA."

"Nearly four years now. I think I've done rather well on the whole. Although the physical demands are not too arduous. Max's bisexuality goes in alternating phases. During his DC periods he can leave you alone for months."

The gray eyes were calm and candid.

"Jesus Christ," Fay said.

"Oh, don't get me wrong—I don't mind *that*. I almost became an actress, anyway. And with Max, there's rarely anything terribly tiring. And never anything particularly *bizarre*. Well, except for the crystals, and he only ever tried that once. And anyway, one always has to weigh these things against the benefits. No, it's just . . . "

Rachel dug her fists deep into the pockets of her Barbour until Fay could see the knuckles outlined in the shiny, waxed fabric.

" . . . It's just I don't think I can go through with it *here*," Rachel said. "Do you know what I mean?"

Grace Legge came here to die, Dad came to go slowly loopy, and I came to watch.

"Yes," Fay said bleakly, "I know *exactly* what you mean. I'm beginning to realize how hard it is to get anything positive to take off here."

She'd read somewhere that nobody could say for certain where the name Crybbe came from. It was obviously a corruption of the Welsh, and there were two possible derivations:

crib—the crest of a hill (which seemed topographically unlikely, because the town was in a valley),

or

crybachu—to wither.

"It appeals to him, you know," Rachel said. "The fact that failure is so deeply ingrained here. Brings out the crusader in him. He's going to free the place from centuries of bucolic apathy."

"The first story Offa's Dyke got me to cover," Fay remembered, "was the opening of a new factory on the industrial estate. Quite a lively little setup producing chunky colored sandals—in fact I'm wearing a pair, see? They were providing eight local jobs and the Marches Development Board were predicting it'd be twenty before the end of the year."

"Closed down, didn't it? Was it last week?"

"I'd have ordered another pair if I'd known," Fay said.

They stared at each other, almost comically glum, then Rachel tossed back her ash-blond hair and strode determinedly through to the room which would soon be a kitchen.

"Come on, let's get out of here, he'll be back soon." She picked up two tumblers from the draining surface next to the new sink, and Fay followed her outside, where she dug a bottle of sparkling wine from the silt in the bottom of an old sheep trough—"My private cellar."

And then they collected a grateful Arnold from the Range Rover and wandered off across the field, down the valley to the river, where you could sit on the bank fifty yards from the three-arched bridge and probably not see the Court anymore, or even the Tump.

On the way down the field Fay looked over her shoulder to watch the Tump disappearing and saw a man among the trees on its summit. He was quite still, obviously watching them.

"Rachel, who's that?"

"Where?"

"On the Tump. I don't think it's Goff."

Rachel turned around and made no pretense of not staring.

"It's Humble," she said. "Max's minder. He loves it here. He used to be a gamekeeper. He prowls the woods all the time, supposedly organizing security. I think he snares rabbits and things."

"*Very* Green Party, I must say," Fay said.

"Max's principles tend to get overlooked where Humble's concerned. I think he sometimes serves the need that occasionally arises in Max for, er, rough boys."

"I think I'm sorry I asked," said Fay.

Alex awoke.

There was pressure on his chest. When he was able to open his eyes just a little, with considerable difficulty, he looked into blackness.

Oh Lord, he thought, I've actually entered the dark place. I'm in there with Grace.

Yet he was still in the armchair. The chair was refusing to let go of him. It had closed around him like an iron lung or something. He was a prisoner in the chair and in the dark, and there was a pressure on his chest.

"Grace?" he said feebly. "Grace?"

The darkness moved. The darkness was making a soft, rhythmic noise, like a motorboat in the distance.

Alex opened his eyes fully and stared into luminous amber-green, watchful eyes. He chuckled; the darkness was only a big, black cat.

"Ras . . . Ras . . . " he whispered weakly, trying to think of the creature's name.

The cat stood up on his chest.

"Rastus!" Alex said triumphantly. "Hullo, Rastus. You know, for a minute, I thought . . . Oh, never mind, you wouldn't understand."

He wondered if it was teatime yet. The clock said . . . what? Couldn't make out if it was four o'clock or five. Around four, Grace always liked a pot of tea and perhaps a small slice of Dundee cake. She'd be most annoyed if he'd slept through teatime.

Fay, on the other hand, preferred a late meal. Women were so contrary. It generally saved a lot of argument if he ate with them both.

Alex chuckled again. No wonder he was getting fat.

Rachel put the bottle in the river and took off her Barbour. "I'll be thirty-six in January."

"Happens to us all," Fay said.

"I was . . . very much on top of the situation when I took the job. Nothing could touch me, you know? I was chief press officer at Virgin, and he headhunted me. He said, name your price, so I doubled my salary and he said, OK, it's yours—can you believe that?"

She handed Fay the glasses, pulled the bottle out of the water, and shot the cork at the bridge. It fell short, and they watched it bobbing downstream. "Does that count as pollution?" Rachel wondered.

"Why was Goff so attracted to Crybbe?"

Rachel poured wine until it fizzed to the brim of both tumblers. "Magic."

"Magic," Fay repeated in a flat voice.

"Earth magic."

"You mean ley-lines?"

"You know what all that's about? I mean, don't be ashamed, it's all speculation anyway."

"Tell me what it means in the Crybbe context."

"OK, well, presumably you know about Alfred Watkins who came up with the theory, back in the 1920s. Lived in Hereford, did most of his research in these hills. Had the notion, and set out to prove it, that prehistoric sacred monuments—standing stones, stone circles, burial mounds, all this—were arranged in straight lines. Just route markers, he thought originally, on straight roads."

"I've got his book, *The Old Straight Track.*"

"Right. So you know that where four or five sites fell into a straight line, he'd call it a ley, apparently because a lot of the places where these configurations occurred had names ending in l-e-y, OK?"

"Like Crybbe?"

Rachel grinned. "Well, he didn't know about Crybbe, or he'd probably have called them Crybbe-lines. You read through Watkins's book, you won't find a single mention of Crybbe."

"I know. I looked. I was quite disappointed."

"Because, apart from the Tump, there's nothing to see. However, it seems there used to be bloody dozens of standing stones and things around here at one time, which disappeared over the centuries. Farmers used to rip them out because they got in the way of plowing and whatever else farmers do."

Rachel waved a dismissive hand to emphasize the general tedium of agriculture. "Anyway, there are places in Britain where lots of ley-lines converge, ancient sacred sites shooting out in all directions. Which, obviously, suggests these places were of some great sacred significance, or places of power."

"Stonehenge?"

"Sure. And Glastonbury Tor. And Avebury. St. Michael's Mount in Cornwall. And other places you've probably never heard of."

"But not Crybbe. You're really not going to tell me Crybbe was ever sacred to anybody."

Rachel swallowed a mouthful of wine and wiped her mouth with a deliberately graceless gesture before topping up her glass. "Down on your knees, woman, I'm afraid you're on holy ground."

The bridge carried the main road into town, and behind it Fay could see chimneys and the church tower. Wooded hills—a mixture of broadleaf and conifer—tumbled down on three sides. From anywhere at a distance, Crybbe looked quite picturesque.

"So how come there aren't busloads of pilgrims clogging the roads, then? How come this is close to being Britain's ultimate backwater?"

"Because the inhabitants are a bunch of hicks who can't recognize a good tourist gimmick when they get one on a plate. I mean, they did rip out the bloody stones in the first place. That's why Max brought in Henry Kettle. He had to know where the stones used to be."

"Henry divines the spots!"

"Sure. He pinpoints the location, then what you do is stick a pole in the ground at the exact spot. And if you're as rich and self-indulgent as Max Goff, what you do next is have lots of lovely new stones cut to size and planted out in the fields. Prehistoric landscape-gardening on a grand scale."

"Gosh." Fay was picturing a huge, wild rock-garden, with daffodils growing around the standing stones in the spring. Crybbe suddenly a little town in a magic circle. "I think that sounds rather a nice thing to do . . . don't you? I mean, bizarre, but nice, somehow."

"Except it's not quite as easy as it sounds," Rachel said. "And it's going to cause trouble. Within a couple of weeks Kettle'd discovered the probable sites of nearly thirty prehistoric stones, couple of burial mounds, not to mention a holy well."

"Wow."

"And fewer than a quarter of the sites are on the eight and a half acres of land which Max bought with the Court, so if he's going to restore Stone Age Crybbe he's got to negotiate with a lot of farmers."

"Ah. Mercenary devils, farmers."

"And awkward sods, in many cases."

"True. So how's he going to handle it?"

"He wants to hold a big public meeting to tell the people how he plans to revitalize their town. I mean, obviously you've got the considerable economic benefits of tourism—look how many foreign trippers flock to Avebury. But also—unwisely in my view—he's going to explain all the esoteric stuff. What ley-lines are really all about, and what they can do for the town."

"Energy lines," Fay said. "I've also read that other book, *The Old Golden Land.*"

"By J. M. Powys, distant descendant of the great mystical writer, John Cowper Powys. Max loves that book. Coincidentally—or not, perhaps—he's just bought the company which published it. So he owns it now, and he likes to think he owns J. M. Powys . . . for whom He Has Plans."

"He's coming here?"

"If he knows what's good for him. He'll have plenty of like-minded idiots for company. There are already nine New Age people living in the town in properties craftily acquired by Max over the past few months. Alternative healers, herbalists, astrologers."

"Can't say I've noticed them," Fay admitted.

"That's because some of them look quite normal. Only *they* know they are the human transmitters of the New Energy about to flow into Crybbe."

"The idea being that ley-lines mark out some kind of force field, channels of energy, which Bronze Age people knew how to tap in to. Is that right?"

"The Great Life Force, Fay. And so, naturally, re-siting the stones will bring new life flowing back into Crybbe. Max reckons—well, he hasn't worked it out for himself, he's been told by lots of so-called experts—that Crybbe is only in the depressed state it is today because all the stones have gone. So if you put them back, it'll be like connecting the town for the first time to the national grid. The whole place will sort of light up."

Fay thought about this. "It sounds rather wonderful."

"If you like that kind of fairy tale."

"Is it?"

"Oh, well, sure, what does it matter if it's true or not, it'll bring in the crowds, be an economic boost, a psychological panacea, create a few jobs. But you see, Fay, I *know* this guy." Rachel held up the bottle, but Fay shook her head and Rachel poured what remained into her tumbler. "I don't think I can stand to watch him being baronial at Crybbe Court, with his entourage of fringe scientists and magicians and minstrels and sundry jesters."

"Is that the central point, at which all these ley-lines are supposed to meet? The Court? Or is it the church?"

"The Tump," Rachel said. "It's the Tump. It's not a center, it's a sort of axis. The lines come off it in a fan shape. The Tump is like this great power station. Get the idea? I mean, really, isn't it just the biggest load of old rhubarb you ever heard?"

Rachel brought an arm from behind her head and lobbed the empty wine bottle into the air. Arnold tensed, about to spring after it, until he saw where it was going.

There was a satisfying splash.

"Now surely," Rachel said, "that's *got* to be pollution."

❧ _____ *eight*

Fay walked back to the cottage, for Arnold's sake and to clear her head, although she hadn't drunk all that much wine—not compared to Rachel, anyway. Arnold, however, looked as if he'd been drinking heavily, veering from side to side on his tautened clothesline. He was hopeless.

Goff had not returned when they arrived back at the Court. She'd left Rachel carrying the triptych into the stable block, where it was to be double-locked into a storeroom. Nearly a thousand quid's worth of less-than-fine art. Hereward and Jocasta Newsome would, for once, have good reason to appear appallingly smug.

"Whichever way you look at it, Arnie," Fay said reflectively, "our friend Goff is making waves in Crybbe."

No bad thing, either.

Could she understand the guy's obsession? Well, yes, she could. A man who'd made his first million marketing anarchic punk-rock records in the mid-seventies. Waking up in the nineties to find himself sitting on a heap of money in a wilderness of his own creation. All the cars and yachts and supertoys he'd ever want and nothing to nurture the soul.

Not exactly a quantum leap, was it, from there to the New Age dream?

And, the more she thought about it, the proposed mystical liberation of an obscure Welsh border town from years of economic decay was a story that deserved a bigger audience than it was ever going to reach through Offa's Dyke Radio.

In fact, this could be the moment to approach her old chums at the BBC. How about a forty-five-minute radio documentary chronicling Goff's scheme to turn Crybbe into a New Age Camelot? She could hear a sequence in her head, lots of echoey footsteps and tinkly music, the moaning of men and machinery as massive megaliths were maneuvered into position. It sounded good.

On the other hand, she had an arrangement with Offa's Dyke, and the little shit Ashpole would want first bite at every snippet that came out of the Goff camp.

. . . or we'll have to, you know, reconsider things . . .

Little turd.

And while Radio Four was the interesting option, a chance to prove she could still make national-quality programs, Offa's Dyke was bread and butter. Of course, if there was a prospect of getting out of Crybbe and back to London or Manchester or Bristol in the foreseeable future, she could make the BBC program and bollocks to O.D.

She passed the farm entrance and followed Arnold and the road into the wood, where the sudden darkness brought with it a wave of loneliness and resentment toward her dad. Why did the old bugger have to stay out here? All that nonsense about his having to sell the house in Woodstock to pay for Grace's treatment.

Somehow, Dad, Fay thought, all your money's gone down the drain. And tonight, the close of what appeared to have been one of his better days, seemed as good a time as any to make him tell her precisely how it had happened.

A bush moved.

It happened on the edge of her vision, just as she'd passed it, and she thought, it's the wind, then realized there was none.

Arnold growled.

Fay froze. "Who's that?"

Bloody hell, the phantom flasher of Crybbe. Well, there had to be one. Fay laughed. Nervously.

There was also Black Michael's Hound.

You wouldn't think anything as black as that could glow, would you?

Thank you, Mrs. Seagrove.

There was a snigger. An involuntary cry was snatched from Fay, and then he was off. She saw him vanish behind a tree, then reappear, moving in a crouch, like a spider, up the field, in the direction of the farm, an unidentifiable shadow. Perhaps it was that man Humble, Goff's minder.

"Have a nice wank, did we?" Fay called after him. But it wasn't funny, and that was why her voice cracked. She was discovering that back alleys in the city, full of potato-chip wrappings and broken glass, could sometimes be less scary than a placid sylvan lane at sunset.

Because there was the feeling, somehow, that if it *did* happen here, it would be worse.

Hereward Newsome couldn't wait to get home to tell his wife what he'd learned in the Cock.

Hereward went off to what he described to visitors as "my local hostelry" perhaps two nights a week and stayed for maybe an hour. He considered a local hostelry was one of those things a man ought to have when he lived in the country, if he was to communicate with the locals on their own level.

"Why bother?" demanded Jocasta, who made a point of never going with him to the Cock. "Why on earth should I learn about sheep and pigs? Why can't the locals learn about fine art and communicate with us on *our* level?"

"Because it's their town," Hereward had reasoned. "Pigs and sheep have been their way of life for centuries, and now the industry is in crisis and they feel their whole *raison d'être* is threatened. We should show them we understand."

And he did his best. He'd started reading everything he could find in *The Guardian* about sheep subsidies and the Common Agricultural Policy so he could carry on a respectable discussion with the farmers in the public bar. He'd commiserate with them about the latest EC regulations and they'd say, "Well, well," or "Sure t'be," in their quiet, contemplative tones and permit him to buy them another couple of pints of Ansell's Bitter.

However, he was always happier if Colonel Croston was in there, or even old Canon Peters. He might not have much in common with either of them, but at least it would be a two-way conversation.

Tonight, however, he'd found common ground . . . in a big way.

Lights were coming on in the farmhouse as Hereward parked the 2CV neatly at the edge of the slice of rough grass he called "the paddock." There was a Volvo Estate in the garage, but he never took that into town unless there were paintings to be shifted.

"It's me, darling." Hereward hammered on the stable door at the side of the farmhouse. He kept telling her there was no need to lock it; that was the beauty of the countryside. But every other week she'd point out something in the paper about some woman getting raped in her cottage or a bank manager held to ransom in his rural retreat. "But not in *this* area," Hereward would say, looking pained.

Even though she'd have recognized his voice, Jocasta opened only the top half of the door so she could see his face and be sure he wasn't accompanied by some thug with a shotgun at his back.

"It *is* me," Hereward said patiently, when his wife finally let him in. "Listen, darling, what did I say about the turning point?"

"Coffee?" Jocasta said. Hereward frowned. When she was solicitous on his return from the pub it usually meant she'd just concluded an absurdly lengthy phone call to her sister in Normandy. Tonight, though, he'd let it pass.

"Sorry," Jocasta said, plugging in the percolator. "Turning point? You mean Goff?"

"You remember I told you about that guy Daniel Osborne, the homeopath? Who moved into a cottage in Bridge Street? With his wife, the acupuncturist? Now I learn that next door but one to him—this is quite extraordinary—there's a hypnotherapist who specializes in that . . . what d'you call it when they try to take people back into previous lives?"

"Regression." Jocasta turned toward him. He thought she looked awfully alluring when her eyes were shining. He had her full attention.

"The fact is . . . " Hereward was smiling broadly. "There're lots of them. And we didn't know it. All kinds of progressive, alternative practitioners and New Age experts. In Crybbe."

"You're serious?"

"Look, I've just had this from Dan Osborne himself; they can talk about it now. Seems Max Goff's been secretly buying property in town for months and either selling it at a very reasonable price or renting it to, you know, the *right* people. What we're getting here are the seeds of a truly progressive alternative community. That is, no . . . no . . . "

"Riffraff," Jocasta said crisply. "Hippies."

"If you must. In fact, it's the sort of setup that . . . well . . . the Prince of Wales would support."

"There's got to be a catch," Jocasta said, ever cautious. "It seems remarkable that we haven't heard about it before."

"Darling, everybody's been ultradiscreet. I mean, they don't look any different from your ordinary incomers, and there's always been a big population turnover in this area. Look, here's an example. You remember the gray-haired woman, very neat, very well-dressed, who was in The Gallery looking at paintings a couple of days ago. Who do you think that was?"

"Shirley MacLaine."

"Jean Wendle," said Hereward.

"Who?"

"The spiritual healer! She used to be a barrister or something and gave it up when she realized she had the gift."

"Oh." Jocasta digested this. "Are you saying Crybbe's going to be known for this sort of thing? With lots of . . . "

"Tourists! Upmarket *thinking* tourists! The kind that don't even like to be called tourists. It's going to be like Glastonbury here—only better. It'll be . . . *internationally famous.*"

"Well," said Jocasta, "if what you say is true, it's really quite annoying nobody told us. We might have sold up and moved out, not realizing. And it's still going to take time . . . "

"Darling," Hereward said, "if Goff can pull off something like this under our very noses, the man is a magician."

The solemnity of the curfew bell lay over the shadowed square by the time Fay and Arnold came back into town, and she found herself counting the clangs, getting louder as they neared the church.

Fifty-seven, fifty-eight, fifty-nine . . .

There was something faintly eerie about the curfew. Was she imagining it, or did people make a practice of staying off the streets while it was actually being rung, even if they came out afterward? She stood staring at the steps in front of the Cock, willing somebody to walk in or out to prove her wrong.

Nobody did. Nobody was walking on the street. There was no traffic. No children played. No dogs barked. Only the bell and the cawing of crows, like a distorted echo.

Seventy-three, seventy-four, seventy-five . . .

Every evening the curfew would begin at precisely ten o'clock. You could set your watch by it, and people often did.

How the custom had survived was not entirely inexplicable. There'd been a bequest by one Percy Weale, a local wool merchant and do-gooder back in the sixteenth century. He'd left land and money to build Crybbe School and also a further twelve acres in trust to the Preece family and their descendants on condition that the curfew bell be rung nightly to safeguard "the moral and spiritual welfare" of the townsfolk.

Should the Preece family die off or neglect the task, then the land must be rented out and the money used to pay a bell-ringer. But even in times of plague or war, it was said, the curfew bell had never been silenced.

Because hanging on to those twelve acres would be a matter of pride for the Preeces. Also economics. Fay was learning that farmers in these parts would do almost anything to hold what land they had and would lay in wait for neighboring death or misfortune to grab more. When a farm was sold, the neighbors swooped like buzzards, snatching up acreage on every side, often leaving a lone farmhouse marooned in the middle, condemned either to dereliction or sumptuous restoration by city folk in search of a rural retreat. The Newsomes lived in one, with a quarter acre of their own surrounded on all sides by other people's property.

Ninety-eight, ninety-nine. One hundred. Although the sun's last lurid light was spread like orange marmalade across the hills, the town center wore a somber gown of deep shadows.

Fay noticed Arnold's clothesline had gone slack.

He was sitting on the cracked cobbles, staring up at the church tower, now overhung with florid cloud. As Fay watched him, his nose went up and, with a mournful intensity, he began to howl.

As the howl rose, pure as the curfew's final peal, with whose dwindling it mingled in the twilit air, Fay was aware of doors

opening in the houses between the shops and the pubs on the
little square.

No lights came on. Nobody came out. Arnold howled three
times, then sat there, looking confusedly from side to side, as
if unsure he'd been responsible for the disturbance.

Fay could feel the stares coming at her from inside the shadowed portals in the square, and the air seemed denser, as if
focused hostility were some kind of thickening agent, clotting
the atmosphere itself.

She felt she was being pressed backward into the church wall
by a powerful surge of heavy-duty disapproval.

Then someone, a female voice, screeched out, *"You'll get that
dog out of yere!"*

And the doors began quietly to close, one by one, in muted
clicks and snaps.

By which time Fay was down on her knees, clutching Arnold
to her breast, squeezing his ridiculous ears, warming her bare
arms in his fur.

Finding she was trembling.

Jack Preece came out of the church and walked away in the
direction of the Cock, without looking at them.

nine

Grace's house was just an ordinary cottage in a terraced row
which, for some reason, began in stone and ended in brick.
Fay could pick it out easily because it was the only one in
the row with a hanging basket over the front door. As hanging
baskets went, this one wasn't subtle; she kept it bursting with
large, vulgar blooms and watered them assiduously because this
hanging basket was a symbol of something she was trying to say
to Crybbe.

There was no light and no sound from inside, and she thought
at first there must have been another blasted power cut. Then a

light blinked on and off next door, and she heard a television from somewhere.

"He's gone to the pub," she told Arnold. Most nights her dad would stroll over to the Cock for a couple of whiskeys and one of their greasy bar-snacks.

She would wait up for him. Because tonight they were going to have this thing out.

And by the end of the week, no argument, there was going to be a For Sale sign next to the hanging basket. And she would start work on the Goff documentary, which Radio Four were *definitely* going to commission. And Offa's Dyke Radio, the Voice of the Marches, could start looking for another stringer to justify the Crybbe Unattended.

But when Fay marched into the office, she found a note on her editing table informing her that Canon Alex Peters had escaped to bed.

> Not feeling terrifically well, to be honest. Having an early night, OK? So if you must have that dog in the house, keep the bugger quiet!

Fay smiled—she knew he'd come around—then frowned at the postscript.

> Oh yes, Guy rang. Wants you to ring him back.

Bloody Guy. Did she really need this on top of everything?

She turned the note over in case there was an addendum, *re* Guy. Eight years ago, her dad had been the only person with the perception to warn her off, everyone else having congratulated her, in some kind of awe, before they'd even met Guy in the flesh—one friend (you never forgot remarks like this) saying, *"You ... You and Guy Morrison?"*

Never mind. All in the past. Especially Guy.

No regrets?

You had to be kidding.

Except he *would* keep phoning. As if she were just another one of his contacts—*Oh, hey, listen, I'm going to be in your part of the world next week. Buy you a drink?*

Fay sat down at the editing table. Rachel had drunk most of the wine with no discernible effects, while Fay consumed less

than a third of the bottle and now the room was sliding about.
In the light from the Anglepoise it still looked very Grace, this
room: H-shaped tiled fireplace and, above it, an oval mirror
in a thick gilt frame. On the mantelpiece was a clock with a
glass case revealing a mechanism which looked like a pair of
swinging testicles in brass.

This room—the whole house—was frozen in time, in a none-
too-stylish era. Round about the time, in fact, when Fay's dad
had split up with Grace and returned to her mother. It was as if
Grace had given up after that—certainly she hadn't married until
the canon had come back into her life. She seemed to have lived
quietly in Crybbe with her sister, until the sister died. Worked
quietly in the library.

A quiet woman. A Crybbe woman. As Fay understood it,
she'd been working in Hereford, for the diocese, when she'd
had her fling with Alex.

"How could she come back here?" Fay said aloud, and picked
up the phone to call Guy. Then put it back. She'd caught sight
of Arnold, who was looking up at her in his unassuming way,
one ear pricked, the other flopped over.

"Arnold, I'm sorry . . . What do you feel like for dinner?"

He may have wagged his tail, but she couldn't be sure, it was
that kind of tail.

The kitchen had knotty-pine cupboards and pink-veined
imitation-marble countertops, one of which bore her dad's
beloved microwave. Arnold accepted stewed steak from a
can, served on one of Grace's best china plates. When he'd
finished, Fay let him out in the small back garden, where it was
almost fully dark. There was no sign of Rasputin or Pushkin, his
lieutenant. They'd be out hunting in the endless fields beyond
the garden fence.

And in this pursuit they were obviously not alone. Somewhere out there a lightball bobbed, possibly following the line of
a hedge which was said to mark the old border between Wales
and England. (Nobody in this town ever spoke of being English
or Welsh because, at various times in its undistinguished history, Crybbe had been in both countries.)

Fay watched the light for several minutes, listening. Illegal
badger-digging was, she'd heard, one of the less-publicized
local recreations. Nasty, vicious, cruel. But nobody had ever
been prosecuted locally. She'd often wondered how Sergeant

Wynford Wiley would react if she rang him up one night and directed him to a spot where it was actually taking place: spurts of squealing, scuffling, and snuffling as the terriers were sent into the soil to rip the badgers from their sett. There was a man who kept a pack of terriers on a farm two or three miles away, ostensibly for hunting foxes. Fay wished she could nail the swine.

But she suspected that, even if it was three o'clock in the morning when she rang, Wynford would claim a prior appointment.

The countryside. Where so many pastimes were sour and furtive. And tolerated.

Arnold trotted in from the garden.

Fay was very tired. She laid out a thick mat under her editing table and folded an old blanket on top. "I don't know what you're used to, Arnold, but the management will listen sympathetically to any complaints in the morning."

Arnold sat quietly next to the mat. Apart from the episode in the square, he hadn't seemed a very demonstrative dog.

Fay brought him a bowl of water. "I'm going to shut you in, Arnold. Because of the cats. OK?"

She scribbled a note to pin on the door, telling her father not to go into the office, if, as happened occasionally, he couldn't sleep and came down. *And don't let any CATS in there!*

Then she went to bed.

She never put on the bedroom light; the room looked squalid enough by daylight. It was almost as claustrophobic as the Crybbe Unattended Studio, and its wallpaper had faded to brown. Fay would have redecorated the place, but she wasn't staying, was she?

They weren't staying.

The bathroom had been modernized, with characteristic taste. A bath, shower, and washbasin in livid pink and black.

Fay washed.

She looked in the mirror as she wiped the face people had been amazed at Guy Morrison falling for.

Guy used to say she should spell her name F-e-y, because she looked like a naughty elf. It had seemed like a kind of compliment at the time—she used to be naive like that. Especially where Guy was concerned.

And she wasn't going to waste any time speculating about
what Guy might want, because the answer was no.

Snapping off the bathroom light, she found her way back
to bed by the diffused rays of the midsummer moon—very
nearly full, but trapped like a big silver pickled onion in a
cloud sandwich.

She lay awake for a long time in her single divan, thinking
about the curfew and the furtive figure in the hedge, about
Henry Kettle and Arnold and the wall. Splat.

Horrible.

How did it happen? There'd be a postmortem, forensic tests,
and an inquest, but only Arnold would ever really know, and
he was only a dog.

" . . . *You'll get that dog out of yere . . .* "

Very sympathetic people in Crybbe. Very caring. Wonderful,
warmhearted country folk.

Miserable bastards.

Eventually, Fay fell asleep with the moon in her eyes. She
awoke briefly and saw it, all the clouds gone, and she remembered that sleeping with direct moonlight on your face was
supposed to send you mad. She giggled at that and went back
to sleep and dreamed a midsummer night's dream in which she
was lying in bed and Arnold was howling downstairs.

Oh *no!*

Fay flung the covers aside and sat up in bed.

Arnold's howling seemed to filter up from below, like slivers
of light coming up through the cracks in the floorboards. It
probably would be even louder from the canon's bedroom,
which was directly over the office.

She got out of bed and crept to the top of the stairs, hissing,
"Shut it, Arnold, for God's sake!"

Barefooted, Fay moved downstairs. It was bloody chilly for a
midsummer's night, especially when you were wearing nothing
but a long T-shirt with several holes in it.

At the bottom of the stairs she stopped and turned back,
picking up what she hoped was the sound of her dad's snoring.
She ran a hand over the wall in search of the light switch, but
when she found it and pressed, nothing happened. Everything
Hereward Newsome had ever said about those cretins at the
electricity company was dead right.

When she opened the office door, Arnold shot out and she caught him and he leapt into her arms and licked her face. "Don't try and get round me," she whispered. "You are *not* sleeping on my bed."

But when she carried him back into the office, he whimpered and jumped out of her arms and she went back and found him standing by the front door, ears down, tail down, quivering.

"Oh, Arnold . . . "

Did dogs have nightmares? Had he been reliving last night: an almighty crunch, an explosion of glass, his master's head in a shower of blood?

"I know, Arnold." Patting him. "I know." His coat felt matted, almost damp. Did dogs sweat?

Christ, he couldn't be bleeding, could he? She picked him up and lugged him back into the office, automatically flipping the light switch by the door.

Damn! Damn! Damn!

"Arnold!" He'd squirmed out of her arms again and run away into the hall.

Fay clutched helplessly at the air. Torch . . . Candle . . . Anything. God, it was cold. Moonlight was sprinkled over the room, like frost. The light twinkled on the twisting testicular mechanism of the clock on the mantelpiece, fingered the mirror's ornate, gilt frame, quietly highlighting everything that was part of *then,* while the now things, the trestle editing table and the Revox, were screened by shadow. As though in another dimension.

Everything was utterly still.

Get me, she thought, out of here. Out of this sad, forsaken house, out of this fossilized town.

Then a sudden, most unearthly sound uncurled from the fireplace. Like a baby's cry of joy, but also, she thought, startled and shivering, also like an owl descending delightedly on its prey.

It came again and it sang with an unholy pleasure and she saw Rasputin sitting massively in the hearth like an Egyptian temple cat on a sarcophagus.

Rasputin's emerald eyes suddenly flared, and he sprang.

Fay gasped and went backward, clutching at the wall, involuntarily closing her eyes against imagined flashing claws.

But the huge cat was not coming at her.

When she looked again, he'd landed solidly in a beam of pallid moonlight on the varnished mahogany arm of the fireside chair, and he was purring.

In the chair Grace Legge sat rigidly, her brittle teeth bared in a dead smile and eyes as white and cold as the moon.

part three

part three

A car's steering wheel, like a dowsing rod, is designed to amplify small movements of the driver's hands; so a reflex twitch in someone who slips unconsciously into a dowsing mode would be enough to send a car travelling at a fair speed into an uncontrollable spin.

TOM GRAVES,
Needles of Stone

one

Memory is circling like a silent helicopter over these soft, green fields, strung together with laces of bright river. It's a warm day in June or July, a Friday—the day you heard they'd sold the paperback rights to The Old Golden Land.

Directly below, throwing a shadow like a giant sundial at three o'clock, is the Bottle Stone.

It's about five feet tall and four thousand years old. Nobody seems to know whether erosion or some damage long ago left it shaped like a beer bottle, or whether it was always like that.

It seems now—looking down, looking back—to be as black as its shadow. But there's an amber haze—Memory may have created this, or maybe not—around the stone. Also around the people.

Six of them, mostly young, early twenties. They're sharing a very expensive picnic. You paid for it. You led them on a raid to this posh high-street deli, then the wine shop. And then you all piled into a couple of cars—old Henry Kettle too, although he says he'd rather have a cheese sandwich than all these fancy bits and pieces—and you came out here because it was the nearest known ancient site, an obvious place to celebrate.

Memory hovers. It's trying to filter the conversation to find out who started it, who raised the question of the Bottle Stone Legend.

No good. The voices slip and fade like a radio between stations, and it's all too long ago. The first part you really remember is when Andy says . . . that there's a special chant, known to all the local children.

> *Johnny goes round the Bottle Stone,*
> *The Bottle Stone, the Bottle Stone,*
> *Johnny goes round the Bottle Stone,*
> *And he goes round ONCE.*

And the Big Mac went round and round the toilet bowl, and Joe Powys watched it and felt queasy.

He'd walked back to the Centre in a hurry and picked up the mail. He hadn't looked at the mail, even though it seemed unusually profuse. Just ran into the shop and dumped it on the counter. Then he'd gone into the lavatory and thrown up.

The Big Mac had been everything they'd promised it would be. Well, big, anyway. Never having eaten—or even seen at close hand—a Big Mac before, he'd decided on impulse this morning that he should go out and grab one for breakfast. It would be one more meaningful gesture that said, Listen, I am an ordinary guy, OK?

Not a crank. Not a prophet. Not a hippie. No closer to the earth than any of you. See—I can actually eat bits of dead cow minced up and glued together.

But his stomach wasn't ready to process the message.

He washed his hands, stared gloomily at himself in the mirror. He actually looked quite cheerful, despite the prematurely gray hair. He had a vision of himself in this same mirror in ten years' time, when the gray would no longer be so premature. In fact, did it look so *obviously* premature now?

He flushed the toilet again. Felt better. Went through to the kitchen and made himself a couple of slices of thick toast.

Fifteen minutes before he had to open the shop. He put the plate on the counter and ate, examining the mail.

There was a turquoise letter from America. It might have been his U.S. agent announcing proposals for a new paperback reprint of *The Old Golden Land.*

It wasn't; maybe he was glad.

"Dear J.M.," the letter began.

Laurel, from Connecticut, where she was newly married to this bloke who ran a chain of roadside wholefood diners. Laurel: his latest—and probably his last—earth-mysteries groupie, once lured spellbound to *The Old Golden Land.* Writing to ask for a copy of his latest book.

What latest book?

Then there was an unsolicited shrink-wrapped catalogue from a business-equipment firm. It dealt in computers, copiers, fax machines. The catalogue was addressed to

The Managing Director,
J.M. Powys Ltd.,
Watkins Street, Hereford

In the head office of J. M. Powys Ltd., the managing director choked on a toast crumb. The head office was a three-room flat in an eighteenth-century former brewery, now shared by an alternative health clinic and Trackways—the Alfred Watkins Centre. The business equipment amounted to a twenty-five-year-old Olivetti portable, with a backspace that didn't.

Powys didn't even open three catalogues from firms with names like Crucible Crafts and Saturnalia Supplies, no doubt offering special deals on bulk orders of joss sticks, talismans, tarot packs, and cassette tapes of boring New Age music simulating the birth of the universe on two synthesizers and a drum machine.

The New Age at the door again. Once, he'd had a letter duplicated, a copy sent off to every loony New Age rip-off supplier soliciting Trackways' patronage.

It said:

This centre is dedicated to the memory and ideas of Alfred Watkins, of Hereford, who discovered the ley system—the way ancient people in Britain aligned their sacred places to fit into the landscape.

Alfred Watkins was an archaeologist, antiquarian, photographer, inventor, miller, and brewer. He doesn't appear, however, to have shown any marked interest in ritual magic, Zen, yoga, reincarnation, rebirthing, primal therapy, shiatsu, or t'ai chi.

So piss off.

He'd realized when he sent it that Alfred Watkins's work, had he lived another fifty years, might have touched on several of these subjects. Perhaps the old guy would have been at the heart of the New Age movement and a member of the Green Party.

The recipients of the circular obviously realized this, too, and kept on sending catalogues, knowing that sooner or later Joe Powys was going to give in and fill up Trackways with New

Age giftware to join the solitary box of "healing crystals" under the counter.

Because if he didn't, the way business was going, Trackways would be closing down within the year.

There were only two envelopes left now. One was made from what looked like high-quality vellum which he'd never have recognized as recycled paper if it hadn't said so on the back, prominently.

A single word was embossed in the top left-hand corner of the envelope.

EPIDEMIC

Powys finished his toast, went to wash his hands, came back, and turned the envelope over a couple of times before he opened it. It contained a letter which didn't mess around.

Dear J. M. Powys,
    As you may have learned, Dolmen Books, publishers of The Old Golden Land, *have now been acquired by the Epidemic Group.*

Shit, Powys thought, I didn't know that.

I am writing to you on behalf of the Group Chairman,

Max Goff, Powys thought, aghast. I've been acquired by Max bloody Goff.

Mr. Max Goff, who has long been an admirer of your work and would like to meet you to discuss a proposition.

. . . And from what I've heard of Max Goff's propositions to personable young blokes such as myself . . .

We should therefore like to invite you to a small reception at the Cock Inn, Crybbe,

. . . I may have to invent a prior engagement . . .

*on Friday, 29 June at 12:30 P.M. I'm sorry it's such short
notice, but the acquisition of Dolmen was only confirmed
this week and I obtained your address only this morning.*
*   Please contact me if you have any queries.*
*   Please contact me anyway.*

                                        Yours sincerely,
                                        Rachel Wade,
                                        PA to Max Goff

Powys sat and looked around the shop for a while, thinking
about this.

He could see on the shelves, among the dozens of earth-
mysteries books by Alfred Watkins and his successors, the
spine of the deluxe hardback edition of *The Old Golden Land*
and about half a dozen paperback copies, including the garish
American edition with the Day-Glo Stonehenge.

On the counter in front of Powys was a token display stand:
dowsing rods and pendula. Mr. Watkins might have been able
to dowse, but he didn't have anything to say in his books about
"energy dowsing." Or indeed about earth energies of any kind.

But all that was academic; the dowsing kits were selling well.
Soon you wouldn't be able to visit a stone circle without finding
some studious duo slowly circumnavigating the site, dangling
their pendulum and saying "Wow" every so often.

Under the counter, because Powys hadn't had the nerve to
put them on sale, was the box of "healing" crystals which
Annie—his new assistant with the Egyptian amulet—had persuaded him to buy. "Got to embrace the New Age, Joe, and let
the New Age embrace you. Mr. Watkins wants you to let the
New Age in, I can feel it. Sometimes I even think I can see
him standing over there by the door. He's holding his hat and
he's smiling."

Wow!

Powys reached into the crystals box and helped himself to a
handful of Sodalite (for emotional stability and the treatment of
stress-related conditions).

Max Goff, he thought.

Max Goff!

Clutching the crystals, he discovered he was holding in his

other hand a small, creased, white envelope, the last item of
mail.

> Mr. J. Powys,
> The Alfred Watkins Centre,
> Hereford

Handwritten, not too steadily. Inside, a single sheet of lined
blue notepaper.

> *Cwm Draenog,*
> *Titley,*
> *Kington*

Dear Mr. Powys,
   *If you have not already heard I am sorry to have to
inform you of the death of my neighbor Mr. H. Kettle.*

What . . . ?

*He was killed in a road accident in Crybbe where he was
working and did not suffer.*

Jesus Christ!

*Mr. Kettle left an envelope with me to be opened after his
death in which he stated what he wanted to happen to his
possessions as he did not trust solicitors. The house and
all the contents is to be sold and the money sent to his
daughter in Canada but he wants you to have his papers
and his dowsing rods. If you would like to come to the
house I am in most of the time and will let you into Mr.
Kettle's house.*

> *Yours faithfully,*
> *Gwen Whitney (Mrs.)*

J. M. Powys put down the letter. He ought to have opened
the shop ten minutes ago.
   The Sodalite crystals (emotional stability and the treatment of
stress-related conditions) began to dribble through his fingers
and roll across the wooden counter.

two

Rachel noticed that Denzil George, owner of the Cock, had several shaving cuts this morning. He'd obviously overslept, unused, no doubt, to rising early to prepare an 8 A.M. breakfast for his guests. What a torpid town this was.

"Parcel come for you," Denzil said, placing a small package by Max's elbow.

"Thanks." Max tossed it to Rachel.

"No stamp," Rachel noticed. "Obviously delivered by hand."

"Better open it," Max said, digging into some of the muesli he'd had delivered to the pub.

Rachel uncovered a tape cassette and a note. "Who's Warren Preece?"

Max looked up.

"He's sent you a tape of his band."

"Delivered by hand, huh?" Max put down his spoon thoughtfully. "I dunno any Warren Preece, but the surname has a certain familiar ring. Maybe you should find out more, Rach."

"Yes," Rachel said, pushing back her chair. "I'll ask the landlord."

The Anglicans' *Book of Common Prayer* had nothing to say about exorcising spirits of the dead.

The Reverend Murray Beech knew this and was grateful for it. But he was leafing through the prayer book anyway, seeking inspiration.

Murray was following the advice of Alex Peters and attempting to compile for himself a convincing prayer to deliver in an allegedly haunted house.

He came across the words *Peace be to this house and to all that dwell in it.* This actually appeared under the order for The Visitation of the Sick, but Murray made a note of it anyway. Surely, with an alleged "haunting"—Murray recoiled from the word in embarrassment—what you were supposedly dealing with was a sick property, contaminated by some form of so-called "psychic" radiation, although, in *his* "exorcism"—oh, God—the prayers would be aimed at the troubled souls of the living. In his view, the health of a property could be affected only by the attitude and the state of mind of the current inhabitants, *not* by any residual guilt or distress from, ah, previous residents.

He looked around his own room—the neat bookshelves, the filing cabinets, the office desk with metal legs at which he sat, the clean, white walls—feeling a twinge of pain as he remembered the walls being painted by Kirsty exactly a fortnight before she'd said, "I'm sorry, Murray. This isn't what I want."

Murray looked quickly back at the prayer book, turned over a page, came upon the following entreaty:

> *Oh Lord, look down from heaven, behold, visit and relieve this thy servant . . . defend him from the danger of the enemy.*

He breathed heavily down his nose. He abhorred words like "enemy." The duty of the Church was to teach not opposition, but understanding.

He was equally uncomfortable with the next and final part of the prayer book before the psalms began.

A COMMINATION
or
Denouncing of God's Anger and Judgements
against Sinners.

The first page ended on an uncompromising note.

> *Cursed are the unmerciful, fornicators and adulterers, covetous persons, idolaters, slanderers, drunkards and extortioners.*

"Not many of us left *un*cursed," Murray muttered.

The curse of the modern minister's life, in his opinion, was the video-hire shop. Infinitely more alluring to teenagers than the church. And full of lurid epics in which members of the

clergy in bloodied cassocks wielded metal crucifixes with which
to combat scaly entities from Hell.

One result of this was that a few people seemed to think they
should summon the vicar in the same way they'd call in the
exterminator to deal with their dampness and their rats.

The telephone bleeped. "I'll ring you when they're out,"
she'd told him. He hadn't replied. At the time, he was considering going to her grandparents and explaining his dilemma.
But he'd concluded this would not only be a cop-out, it would
be wrong. Because she'd come to him in confidence and she
was no longer a minor. She was eighteen and would be leaving
school in two or three weeks.

Murray closed *The Book of Common Prayer* and picked up
the phone. "Vicarage."

"They're out," Tessa said.

Barry, the overweight osteopath from upstairs, was between
patients, eating a sandwich—herbal pâté on whole wheat.

"I've been taken over by Max Goff," said Powys, discon-
solate.

"Dolmen has, yeah, I read that. He can't do you any harm,
though, can he? You're out of print, aren't you?"

"Between impressions," Powys corrected him. "Barry, are
you really proposing to realign somebody's slipped disk with
hands covered in soya margarine?"

"Beats olive oil. And cheaper. Hey, Mandy says she saw you
coming out of McDonald's this morning."

"Couldn't have been me."

"That's what I thought," Barry said dubiously.

"Anyway," Powys said, "Goff wants to see me. In Crybbe."

"I thought you were going to say 'in the nude' for a minute,"
said Barry, wiping his hands on his smock. "No, from what I
hear he's surrounding himself with people sharing his own deep
commitment to the New Age movement. If it's this lunch in
Crybbe on Friday, several people I know have been invited and
nobody's turning him down, because if he likes you, he invites
you to join his Crybbe community, which means—listen to
this—that you get offered a place to live, on very advantageous
terms. And all kinds of fringe benefits."

"Why aren't you there, then?"

"Bastard's already got an osteopath," Barry said. "Gerry

Moffat. You believe that? He could have had me, but he went for Moffat. Moffat!"

"Who else?"

"Dan Osborne, the homeopath, he's moved in already. Superior bastard. Paula Stirling. Robin Holland. Oh, and that little French aromatherapist who was in Bromyard, remember her?"

"I can still smell her. Listen, do these people know what Max Goff *is?*"

"Used to be, Joe. Used to be. This is the new user-friendly, ozone-fresh Max Goff. Play your cards right and he'll let you feel his aura."

"I wouldn't feel his aura with asbestos gloves," said Powys.

"And he's got some pretty heavy mystical types as well," said Barry. "Jean Wendle, the spiritual healer, some guy who's reckoned to be Britain's biggest tarot hotshot, and Andy Boulton-Trow. All converging on the New Age Mecca."

"Andy?" Powys said. "Andy's involved in this?"

"And there's a single kid," says Andy, "moving round the stone, very slowly at first, while all the other kids are sitting in a circle, clapping their hands, doing the chant. And by the time they finish the chant, he's back where he started. Got to be a 'he,' it doesn't work for girls."

Andy Boulton-Trow, lean and languid, lying back in the grass, spearing a quail's egg from the jar beside him. His voice is deep and lazy, like a stroked cello.

"And then he goes round again . . . only this time it's just ever-so-slightly faster . . .

> *"Johnny goes round the Bottle Stone*
> *. . . and he goes round TWICE.*

"And they keep on repeating it. And it gets faster and faster, building up the momentum, and the kid's got to move faster each time to maintain the pace.

> *"Johnny goes round the Bottle Stone*
> *. . . and he goes round THRICE.*
> *. . . goes round FOUR times.*
> *. . . FIVE times.*

"And how long do they keep it up?" Rose asks. She's looking radiantly happy today (this memory is agony). "How many times . . . ?"

"Oh." There's a gleam in Andy's eye. "Thirteen. Thirteen times."

"Must be jolly dizzy by then," one of the others says—Ben Corby's girlfriend, Fiona Something.

"Ex-act-ly." Andy drags out the word for emphasis. "The kid's completely confused. He's not thinking properly. And it's then that his mates all leap on him and, before he knows what's happening, they hustle him across to the fairy hill. Over there . . . see it?"

"Not much of a hill," Rose observes.

"Fairies are not very big," you tell her. "You could fit a couple of dozen on there."

Andy says, "So they lie him facedown on the fairy hill . . . and that's when it happens . . . "

"What?" you ask. "What happens?"

"Whatever happens," says Henry Kettle, searching in the cardboard picnic box for something uncomplicated and British, "it's all in the mind, and it don't do anybody any good, meddling with that old nonsense."

"Oh yeah," Barry, the osteopath, said. "Andy's right at the center of things. As was old Henry Kettle. I suppose you heard about that."

"Just now," Powys said. He hadn't planned to mention Henry. "I had a letter from his neighbor to say he was dead. I don't know what happened, do you?"

"Have to wait for the *Hereford Times* for the full story, but apparently it said on the local radio that his car went off the road and plowed into a wall around Crybbe Tump. I don't know that area too well, but . . . "

"Crybbe Tump? He hit the wall around Crybbe Tump?"

"Killed instantly. Bloody shame. I liked old Henry. He helped you with the book, didn't he?"

Powys nodded.

"The buzz is," said Barry, "that Henry was doing some dowsing for Max Goff."

"Dowsing what?"

Barry shrugged. "Whatever he'd been doing, he was on his
way home when it happened. There was a power cut at the
time, don't know whether the street lamps were off, that may
have thrown him. Bloody shame."

"A power cut," said Powys.

"That significant?"

"Just a thought." Powys shook his head, his mind whizzing
off at a peculiar tangent, like a faulty firework.

 three

Fay woke late. She'd lain awake until dawn, eyes open to the
bedroom ceiling, Arnold a lump of solid heat alongside her on
the bed.

It was nearly nine before she came downstairs. Outside it was
raining. The rain on the window was the only sound. There was
no mail on the mat, no sign of the canon.

The door to the office was closed, as she'd left it last night.
The note to her father still pinned to it. *And don't let any CATS
in there!*

Rasputin.

He must still be in the office.

She opened the door but did not go in.

"Rasputin," she called. A morning croak in her voice—that
was all it was. Really.

But she could not bring herself to go back into that room,
not yet, though Arnold didn't seem worried. She left the door
ajar, went through to the kitchen, let the dog out in the back
garden.

When she turned back to the kitchen, Rasputin and Pushkin
were both in the opposite corner, waiting by their bowls. Fay
opened a can of Felix. The two cats looked plump and harmless.
Perhaps it really *had* been just a horrific dream, conditioned by
her own desperation.

She forked out a heap of cat food, straightened up.

"Right," she said decisively and marched out of the kitchen and into the hall, where she tore the note off the office door and hit the door with the flat of her hand so that it was thrown wide.

She walked in, eyes sweeping the room like searchlights. She saw the Revox, two spools leaning against it. Her desk diary open. Her father's note, about Guy's phone call. She raised her eyes to the H-shaped fireplace and the mantelpiece, to the see-through clock with the mechanism like a pair of balls still jerking obscenely from side to side.

The fireside chair was empty, its scatter cushions plumped out. If someone had been sitting in it the cushions would have been flattened.

Unless, of course, that person had tidily shaken them out and . . .

Oh, come on!

She made herself cross to the mirror and look into it at her own face.

The first shock was the incredible childlike fear she saw in her eyes.

The second was the other face. She whirled around in alarm.

The canon was standing in the doorway. He wore pajamas. His feet were bare. His hair was standing up in spikes, his beard sprayed out in all directions, like a snowstorm. His bewildered blue eyes were wide and unfocused.

He stared at Fay as if she were an intruder. Then the eyes relaxed into recognition.

"Morning, Grace," he said.

While Max drove, Rachel took the cassette box from her shoulder bag.

"OK?"

"Go ahead," Max said.

Rachel slipped the tape into the player and studied the plastic box. The band's name was typed in capitals across the plain label: FATAL ACCIDENT. She wrinkled her nose.

Drums and bass guitar blundered out of the speakers. Rachel lowered the volume a little. By the time the first track was over, they were parked at the back of the Court, next to the stable block, where builders were busy.

Rain slashed the windshield.

Max turned up the sound to compensate. He was smiling faintly. They sat in the Range Rover for two more tracks. The only words Rachel could make out on the last one were "goin' down on me," repeated what seemed like a few dozen times. She consulted the inside of the label; the song was called "Goin' Down on Me."

"That's the lot," she said neutrally. "There's only three numbers." Remembering where the Max Goff Story had begun, in the punk-rock era of the mid-seventies, she didn't add "thankfully."

Max began to laugh.

Rachel ejected the tape, saying nothing.

"Jeez," Max said. "Was that shit, or was that shit?"

Rachel breathed out. For a couple of minutes there, watching him smiling, she'd thought he might actually be enjoying it.

"You want me to post it down to Tommy, get him to send it back in a fortnight with the customary slip?"

"What . . . ?" Max twisted to face her. "You want us to give the official piss-off to Mayor Preece's flaming grandson?"

"But if you tell him it's good you'll have to do something with it, won't you?"

Max shrugged. "So be it. One single . . . not on Epidemic, of course. Coupla grand written off against tax . . ."

Then he thumped the top of the dashboard. "No, hey, listen, I'll tell you what we do—you send this kid a letter saying we think the band has promise, we think it's a . . . an interesting sound, right? But we're not sure any of these three tracks is quite strong enough to release as a debut single, so can we hear a few more? That'll buy some time—maybe the band'll split before they can get the material together. How's that sound to you?"

"It sounds devious," Rachel said.

"Of course it does, Rach. Do it tonight. I mean, shit, don't get me wrong—they're no worse than say, The Damned, in '77. But it was fresh then, iconoclastic."

"It was shit then, too."

"Yeah, maybe," Max conceded. "But it was necessary. It blew away the sterile pretensions from when the seventies went bad. But now we're picking up from the sixties, and we won't make the same mistakes."

"No," Rachel said, in neutral again.

A heavy flatbed truck crunched in beside them. The rain had washed a layer of thick, gray dust from the door of the cab and Rachel could make out the words " . . . aendy Quarry, New Radnor."

"Hey . . . " Max said slowly. "If this is what I think it is . . . " He threw his door open, stepped down into the rain in his white suit, and was back inside a minute, excited, raindrops twinkling in his beard.

"It *is,* Rach. The first stones have arrived. The Old Stones of Crybbe, Mark Two."

"Oh," said Rachel, pulling up the collar of her Barbour for the run to the stables. "Good."

But Goff, Panama hat jammed over his ears, made her watch while the stones were unloaded, pointing out things.

"Different sizes, right? Even where they'd vanished entirely, Kettle was able to figure out how tall they'd been."

"Using his pendulum, I suppose."

"Of course, what we're seeing here gives an exaggerated idea of what they'll look like *in situ.* Half of the length'll be under the soil. Maybe more than half. Like giant acupuncture needles in the earth."

"Who's going to advise you about these things now Mr. Kettle's dead?" Rachel wondered as men in donkey jackets and orange slickers moved around, making preparations to get the gray and glistening monoliths down from the truck. One stone had to be at least fifteen feet long.

"And how do you know it's the right kind of stone?" Things were moving too fast for Rachel now. Max was an awesome phenomenon when he had the hots for something.

"Yeah, well, obviously, Kettle was good—and he knew the terrain. But Andy Boulton-Trow's been studying standing stones for nearly twenty years. Been working with a geologist these past few weeks, matching samples. They checked out maybe a dozen quarries before he was satisfied, and if he's satisfied, I'm satisfied."

A clang came from the back of the truck, a gasp of hydraulics. Somebody swore. Max called out sharply, "Hey, listen, be careful, yeah? I want you guys to handle those stones like you're dealing with radioactive flaming isotopes."

He said to Rachel, "Andy's moving up here, end of the week. He's gonna supervise planting stones on our land. Then we'll bring the farmers up here, show 'em what it looks like, and go into negotiations. Hey, you had a call from J. M. Powys yet?"

"He'll only have got my letter this morning, Max."

"Give him until lunchtime, then call him. I want Powys. I don't care what he costs."

The customer was short and fat and bald. He wore denims, a shaggy beard and an earring.

"You're J. M. Powys, right?"

Teacher, Powys thought. Or maybe the maverick in some local government planning department.

"You are, man. Don't deny it. I recognize you from the picture on the cover. You've gone gray, that's all."

Powys spread his arms submissively.

"Hey listen, man, that was a hell of a book, *The Old Golden Land.*"

"Thanks," Powys said.

"So what are you doing here, running a shop? Why aren't you writing more? Got to be ten years since *Golden Land.*"

"Even longer," Powys said. "More like twelve."

You could count on at least one of these a week, more in summer. Sometimes they were women. Sometimes, in the early days of the Watkins Centre, friendships had developed from such encounters. *The Old Golden Land* had hit the market at the right time, the time of the great mass exodus from the cities, couples in their thirties in search of meaning and purpose.

People were very kind when they found out who he was. Usually they bought something from the shop, often a paperback of the book for him to sign. Most times he felt guilty. Guilty that he hadn't followed through; guilty that he'd written the thing in the first place and misled everybody.

"I did that one that takes a new look at Watkins's original leys," he offered, a bit pathetically. *"Backtrack."*

The bald, bearded guy waved it away. "Disappointing, if you don't mind me saying so, J.M. No magic."

"Wasn't really meant to be magical," Powys said. "The idea was just to walk the leys and see if they were as obvious now as when Watkins discovered them."

"Yeah, and you found some of them to be distinctly dodgy. That's not what we want, is it?"

Powys laughed.

"Well, it's not, is it? People pouring scorn on the whole idea, your archaeologists and so on, and here's J. M. Powys defecting to the Establishment viewpoint."

"Not exactly. What I feel is, we might have been a bit premature in explaining them as marking out channels of earth energy. Why not—because they connect so many burial mounds and funerary sites, even churchyards—why not simply paths of the dead . . . ?"

The customer stepped back from the dowsing display he'd been fingering. He looked shocked.

"Paths of the dead?" he said. "Paths of the dead? What kind of negative stuff is that?"

Halfway through the door, he turned around. "You *sure* you're J. M. Powys?"

"Fay?"

"Oh. Hullo, Guy."

"You didn't return my call."

"No, I didn't, did I? Well, Dad's having one of his difficult days."

"He sounded fine last night."

"Well, he isn't now," Fay said testily. Maybe he thought she was making it all up about the canon going batty. Maybe she ought to produce medical evidence.

"No. I'm sorry. It must be difficult for you."

"Oh, please, not the sympathy. What do you want, Guy?"

"I want to help you, Fay."

No comment.

"I'd like to put some money in your purse."

Fay began to smolder. Purses were carried by little women.

"As you may know, I'm currently on attachment to BBC Wales as senior producer, features and documentaries."

Guy had been an on-the-road TV reporter when she'd first known him. Then a regional anchorman. And then, when he'd realized there'd be rather less security in on-screen situations after he passed forty or so, he'd switched to the production side. Much safer; lots of corners to hide in at cutback time.

"And I've got quite a nice little project on the go on your patch," Guy said. "Two fifty-minute-ers for the network."

"Congratulations." But suddenly Fay was thinking hard. It couldn't be . . .

Guy said, "Max Goff? You know what Max Goff's setting up?"

Shit!

"He's developing a conscience in his middle years and putting millions into New Age research. Anyway, he's bought this wonderful Elizabethan pile not far from you, which he plans to restore."

"And where did you hear about this, Guy?"

"Oh . . . contacts. As I say, we'll be doing two programs. One showing how he goes about . . . what he's going to do. How the locals feel about him, this sort of thing. And the second one, a few months later, examining what he's achieved. Or not, as the case may be. Good, hmm?"

"Fascinating." The *bastard*. How the hell had he pulled it off? "And you've got it to yourself, have you?"

"Absolutely. It means Goff will have this one reliable outlet to get his ideas across in an intelligent way."

Fay seethed.

No Radio Four documentary. Not even any exclusive insider stuff for Offa's Dyke. So much for Rachel Wade and her promises. All the time, they'd been negotiating with her ex-husband—obviously aware of the connection, keeping quiet, leading her along so she wouldn't blow the story too soon.

"So what I was thinking, Fay, is . . . Clearly we're not going to be around the whole time. We need somebody to keep an eye on developments locally and let us know if there's anything we should be looking at. I was thinking perhaps a little retainer for you—I can work it through the budget, we producers have full financial control now of a production, which means . . . ."

Black mist came down. The smug, scheming, patronizing *bastard*.

When Fay started listening again, Guy was saying, " . . . would have offered you the official researcher's contract, but one of Max Goff's conditions is that we use the author of some trashy book which seems to have inspired him. Goff wants this chap to be the official chronicler of the Crybbe project and some sort of editorial adviser on the programs. Of course, that's just a formality, I can soon lose him along the way . . . "

Fay put the phone down.

Screwed again.

The clock ticked. Arnold lay by her feet under the table. The chair where, in her mind, the smug, spectral Grace Legge had sat was now piled high with box files. Nothing could sit in it now, even in her imagination.

Fay picked up the phone again and—deliberate, cold, precise—punched out the number of the Offa's Dyke Radio news desk.

"Gavin Ashpole, please. Oh, it *is* you. It's Fay Morrison. Listen. I can do a piece for the lunchtime news. Explaining exactly what Max Goff intends to do in Crybbe."

She listened to Ashpole asking all the obvious questions.

"Oh yes," she said. *"Impeccable* sources."

Fay put down the phone, picked up the pad, and began to write.

four

The police station was at the southern end of the town center, just before the road sloped down to the three-arched river bridge. Attached to the station was the old police house. Murray Beech strode boldly to the front door and rapped loudly with the knocker, standing back and looking around for someone he might say hello to.

He very much wanted to be seen. Did not want anyone to think there was anything remotely surreptitious about this visit. Indeed, he'd been hoping Police Sergeant Wynford Wiley would be visible through the police-station window so he could wave to him. But he was not. Nobody was there.

As a last resort Murray had been round to Alex Peters's house, hoping to persuade the old man to come with him as adviser, witness, and . . . well, chaperon. There'd been no sign of Alex or his daughter, no answer to his knocks.

But Murray didn't have to knock twice on the door of the old police house. She must have been waiting behind it.

"Good afternoon, Tessa," he said loudly, putting on his most clergymanly voice.

Tessa Byford looked at him in silence. Eighteen. Dark-haired, dark-eyed, pale-faced. Often seen leather-jacketed on street corners with the likes of Warren Preece.

But not an unintelligent girl. A talented artist, he'd heard. And more confident than most local girls. Born here, but brought up in Liverpool until her mother died and her father dumped her on his parents in Crybbe so he could go back to sea.

Murray could understand why she'd never forgiven her father for this.

He thought: sullen, resentful, and eighteen. Prime poltergeist fodder . . . if you accept the tenets of parapsychology.

About which Murray, of course, kept an open mind.

He smiled. "Well," he said, "I'm here."

Tessa Byford did not smile back. Without a word, she led him into a small, dark sitting room, entirely dominated by an oppressive Victorian sideboard, ornate as a pulpit, with many stages, canopies, and overhangs.

Murray felt it was dominating him, too. He was immediately uncomfortable. The room seemed overcrowded, with the sideboard and the two of them standing there awkwardly, an unmarried clergyman and a teenage girl. It hit him then, the folly of what he was doing. He should never have come.

She looked down over his dark suit.

"You've not brought any holy water, have you?"

Murray managed a weak smile. "Let's see how we get on, shall we?"

It occurred to him that, while she might be an adult now, this was not actually her house. He'd allowed himself to be lured into somebody else's house.

"You should've brought holy water," she said sulkily.

Murray tried to relax. His plan was merely to talk to the girl, say a helpful prayer, and then leave. He found a straight-backed dining chair and sat on it squarely—always felt foolish sinking into someone's soft fireside furniture, felt it diminished him.

"I still wish your grandparents were here."

"Gone shopping," she said, still standing. "In Hereford. Won't be back until tonight. I only stayed to wait for you. I was going to give you another five minutes. Wouldn't stay here on me own. Not anymore."

Why did he think she was lying?

"I wish you'd felt able to discuss this with them."

She shook her head firmly. "Can't. You just can't." Her thin lips went tight, her deep-set eyes stony with the certainty of it.

"Have you tried?"

Tessa's lips twisted. "Me gran . . . says people who are daft enough to think they've seen a ghost ought to keep it to themselves."

"So you have tried to talk to her about it."

Tessa, grimacing, went through the motions of wiping something nasty off her hands.

Murray tried to understand but couldn't. Neither Mrs. Byford nor her husband appeared to him to be particularly religious. They came to church, if not every week. He'd watched them praying, as he did all his parishioners from time to time, but detected no great piety there. Just going through the motions, lip movements, like the rest of them. A ritual as meaningless as Sunday lunch, and rather less palatable.

There was no Bible on the shelf, no books of any kind, just white china above a small television set. No pictures of Christ on the wall, no framed religious texts.

And yet the room itself stank of repression, as if the people who lived here were the narrowest type of religious fundamentalists.

Tessa was standing there expressionless, watching him. The next move was his. Because he was trying so hard not to be, he was painfully aware of her breasts under what, in his own teenage days, had been known as a tank top.

"I know what you're thinking," she said, and Murray sucked in a sharp breath. "But I'm not," she said. "I'm not imagining any of it. You don't imagine things being thrown at you in the bathroom, even if . . . "

Her lips clamped and she looked down at her feet.

"If what?" Murray said.

"Show you," Tessa mumbled.

Murray felt sweat under his white clerical collar. He stood up, feeling suddenly out of his depth, and followed Tessa Byford into the hall and up the narrow stairs.

* * *

"All right, Fay?"

"I don't know."

She was going hot and cold. Maybe succumbing to one of those awful summer bugs.

All she needed.

"Give me a minute . . . Elton. I want to make a few adjustments to the script."

"OK, no hurry. I've got a couple of pieces to finish. Come back to you in five minutes, OK?"

"Fine," Fay said, "fine."

She took off the headphones and leaned back in the studio chair, breathing in and out a couple of times. Outside it was still raining and not exactly warm; in here, she felt clammy, sticky. She pulled her T-shirt out of her jeans and flapped it about a bit.

The air in here was always stale. There should be air conditioning. The Crybbe Unattended itself was probably a serious infringement of the Factories Act or whatever it was called these days.

And the walls of the studio seemed to be closer every time she came in.

That was psychological, of course. Hallucinatory, just like . . .

She slammed a door in her mind on the icy Grace Legge smile, just as she'd slammed the office door last night before stumbling upstairs after the dog. She wondered how she was ever going to go into that room again after dark. She certainly wouldn't leave the dog in there again at night.

How primitive life had become.

"Fay!" A tinny voice rattling in the headphones on the table. She put them on.

Ashpole.

"Fay, tell me again what he's doing . . . "

"Goff?"

She told him again about the New Age research center, about the dowsers and the healers. She didn't mention the plan to reinstate the stones. She was going to hold that back—another day, another dollar.

"No rock stars, then."

"What?"

"All a bit of a disappointment, isn't it, really," Ashpole said.

"Is it?" Fay was gripping the edge of the table. Just let him start . . .

"Nutty stuff. New age. Old hippies. Big yawn. Some people'll be interested, I suppose. When can we talk to the great man in person?"

"Goff? I'm working on it."

That was a laugh. Some chance now. *I'll ask my ex-husband, he owns all the broadcasting rights.* God, God, God!

"Hmm," Ashpole said, "maybe we should—"

Without even a warning tremor, Fay erupted. "Oh sure! Send a *real* reporter down to doorstep him! Why don't you do that? Get him to claim on tape that he's the son of God and he's going to save the fucking world!"

She tore off the headphones and hurled them at the wall, stood up so violently she knocked the chair over. Stood with her back to the wall, panting, tears of outrage bubbling up.

What was happening to her?

"See that mirror?"

She was pointing at a cracked circular shaving mirror in a metal frame.

"It flew off the window ledge," Tessa Byford said. "That's how it got the crack. Course, they accused me of knocking it off."

"How can you be sure you didn't?"

It was a very cramped bathroom. Murray moved up against the sink trying not to brush against the girl.

Ludicrous. He felt completely and utterly ludicrous; he was suffocating with embarrassment.

"Look," she said, oblivious of his agony, "I just opened the door and it flew off at me. And other things. Shaving brush, toothpaste. But it was the mirror that started it. I had to look in the mirror."

"It could have been a draft, Tessa." Appalled at how strangled his voice sounded.

"It wasn't a bloody draft!"

"All right, calm down. Please."

"And when I picked it up, the mirror, there was blood in the crack."

"Your blood?"

"No!"

"Whose, then?"

"The old man's."

"Your grandfather?"

"No, the old man! He used to live here. I saw him. I could see him in the mirror."

"You're saying he's dead, this old man?"

"What do *you* think?" Tessa said, losing patience with him. Tension rising. The girl was disturbed. This was not what the Church should be doing. This was psychiatric country.

"And you think you saw his face in the mirror."

"And other mirrors." She sighed. "Always in mirrors."

"Tessa, listen to me. When you first told me all about this you said you thought it was a poltergeist and you thought it was happening because you were at that age when . . . when . . . But you're eighteen. You're not an adolescent anymore."

"No."

He saw something moving in her dark eyes, and there was a little dab of perspiration above her top lip. Murray began to feel soiled and sordid. She said softly—and almost euphorically, he thought later—"His throat was cut. When I saw him in the mirror, he'd cut his throat. Put his razor through the artery. That was where the blood . . . "

Murray swallowed. There was an overpowering smell of bleach.

"Would you mind," he said, "if we went back downstairs?"

When the studio phone rang it was Gavin Ashpole being soft-spoken and understanding. They all knew these days that if a woman flared up uncharacteristically it had to be a spot of premenstrual tension. Tact and consideration were called for.

"So, when you're ready, love," Ashpole said amiably, "just give us the fifty-second voice-piece. And then you can play it by ear with Goff. I mean, don't *worry* about it—long as nobody gets him first, I'll be happy. Must go, the other phone, thanks, Fay."

She shouldn't have exploded like that. Most unprofessional.

Fay put on the headphones, adjusted the mike on its stand.

"Ow!"

Bloody thing was hot.

Surely that wasn't possible with a microphone, even if there was an electrical fault. She didn't touch it again but looked round the back, following the flex to where it plugged into the console. Nothing amiss.

And there was nothing to come unscrewed on this mike. It was a standard American-made Electrovoice, about six and a half inches long, gunmetal gray with a bulb bit enlarging the end, like . . .

Well, like a penis, actually.

Fay put out a finger, touched the tip, giggled.

Sex-starved cow. Pull yourself together.

"You ready now, Fay?"

"Oh yes, I'm ready, Elton. I really am."

"Bit for level, then . . . "

She picked up the script, which would take up the story from the newsreader's link.

"It's widely known," Fay enunciated clearly into the microphone, "that Max Goff has been involved in setting up a charitable trust to . . . "

"Yeah, fine. Go in five."

Fay composed herself. Not easy in this heat. The T-shirt was sticking to her again. Have to put in a complaint. Four, three, two . . .

"It's widely known that Max Goff has been involved in setting up a charitable trust to finance so-called New Age ventures—such as alternative healing techniques and the promotion of Green awareness.

"He's also interested in fringe science and the investigation of ley-lines, which are supposed to link standing stones, Bronze Age burial mounds, and other ancient sites across the landscape . . . "

Most times, when you were putting in a voice-piece—especially if, like this, it wasn't live—you weren't really aware of the sense of it anymore. Only the pattern of the words, the balance, the cadence and the flow. It was conversational and yet completely artificial. Automatic-pilot stuff after a while. Easy to see how some radio continuity announcers simply fell in love with their own voices.

"The project will be based at sixteenth-century Crybbe Court, for which Mr. Goff is believed to have paid in excess of half a million pounds.

"It's expected to be a major boost to the local economy, with . . . "

"Whoah, whoah," Elton shouted in the headphones. "What are you doing, Fay?"

"What?"

"You're distorting."

"Huh?"

"How close are you to the mike?"

"I . . ."

Fay tasted metal.

"Oh . . . !"

Her eyes widened, a movement went through her, like an earth tremor along a fault line. Her hands thrust the microphone away, revolted.

The mike fell out of its stand and over the end of the table where it dangled on its flex. Fay sat there wiping the back of a hand over her lips.

"What the hell . . . ?" said the voice in the headphones. "Fay? Fay, are you there?"

"O Lord, we humbly beseech you, look down upon us with compassion . . . "

Eyes tensely closed, Murray was trying to concentrate. He could still smell bleach from the bathroom, although they were downstairs again now, in the sitting room that was full of repressed emotions, deep-frozen. In the shadow of the vast pulpit-sideboard.

Churchlike. More churchlike, anyway, than a bathroom.

But the Church was not a building. *He,* in this dark little parlor, at this moment, was the Church.

(Two feet away . . . an eighteen-year-old girl in holed jeans and a straining tank top. A girl he didn't think he liked very much anymore. A girl with a glistening dab of sweat over her upper lip.)

And, because there was nothing to help him in *The Book of Common Prayer,* he must improvise.

" . . . look down with compassion, Lord, on our foolish fancies and fantasies. Lift from this house the burden of primitive superstition. Hold up your holy light and guide us away from the darkened recesses of our unconscious minds . . . "

His voice came back at him in a way he'd never experienced before in prayer. Not like in church, the words spinning away, over the congregation and up into the rafters. Or muted, behind bedside screens, against the chatter and rattle and bustle of a hospital ward.

Here, in a room too crowded with still, silent things for an echo, it all sounded as slick and as shallow as he rather suspected it was. He was stricken with isolation—feeling exposed and raw, as if his veneer of priestly strength was bubbling and melting like thin paint under a blowtorch.

Murray ran a damp finger around the inside of his clerical collar. He realized in horror that the only ghost under exorcism in this house was his own undefined, amorphous faith.

As if something was stealing that faith, feeding from it.

His collar felt like a shackle; he wanted to tear it off.

He knew he had to get out of here. Knowing this, while hearing his voice, intoning the meaningless litany.

"Bring us, Lord, safely from the captivity of our bodies and the more insidious snare of our baser thoughts. Lead us—"

Her voice sliced through his.

"I think it likes you, Vicar," Tessa said sweetly.

His eyes opened to a white glare. The girl was holding the cracked shaving mirror at waist level, like a spotlight, and when she tilted the mirror, he saw in it the quivering, flickering image of a cowering man in a dark suit and a clerical collar—the man gazing down at his hands, clasping his rearing penis in helpless remorse, in a tortured parody of prayer.

Murray screamed and fled.

A few moments later, when he tumbled half sobbing, half retching into the street, he could hear her laughter. He stood with his back to a lamppost, sob-breathing through his mouth. He looked down and felt his fly; the zip was fully fastened.

He felt violated. Physically and spiritually naked and shamed.

A door slammed behind him, and he *still* thought he could hear her laughing. At intervals. As if whatever had got into her was sharing the fun.

five

"The bitch doesn't get in here again. Not ever. Under any circumstances. You understand?"

Max was pulsing with rage. Rachel had seen it before, but not often.

Offa's Dyke Radio had run the item on its lunchtime bulletin—from which, Rachel had been told, the story had been picked up by a local freelance hack and relayed to the London papers. Several of which had now called Epidemic's press office to check it out.

And Goff's secretary in London had phoned Goff in time for him to catch the offending Offa's Dyke item on the five o'clock news.

"That report . . . from Fay Morrison, our reporter in Crybbe," the newsreader had said unnecessarily at the end.

"Fay Morrison? Guy Morrison?" Goff said.

Rachel shook her head. "Hardly likely."

"Yeah," Goff accepted. And then he spelled it out for her again, just in case she hadn't absorbed his subtext. When he wanted the world to know about something, he released the information in his own good time. *He* released it.

"So from now on, you don't talk to *anybody*. You don't even *think* about the Project in public, you got that?"

"Maybe," Rachel said, offhand, tempting fate, "you should fire me."

"Don't be fucking ridiculous," Max snapped, and stormed out of the stable block to collect his bags from the Cock. He was driving back to London tonight, thank God, and wouldn't be returning until Friday morning, for the lunch party.

When she could no longer hear the Ferrari arrogantly clearing its throat for the open road, Rachel Wade rang Fay, feeling more than a little aggrieved.

They shouted at each other for several minutes before Rachel made a sudden connection and said slowly, "You mean Guy Morrison is your *ex-husband?*"

"He didn't tell you? Well, of course, he wouldn't. Where's the kudos in having been married to me?"

Rachel said, thoughtlessly, "He's really quite a hunk, isn't he?"

A small silence, then Fay said, "Hunk of shit, actually."

"Max was right," Rachel said. "You're being a bitch. You did the radio piece as a small act of vengeance because your ex had pushed your nose out."

"Now look . . . "

"No, *you* look. Guy's programs wouldn't have affected anything. You'd still have had the stories for Offa's Dyke Radio, *and* you'd have had them first. I do actually keep my promises."

Fay sighed and told her that the truth was she was hoping to do a full program. For Radio Four. However, with a TV documentary scheduled, that now looked like a nonstarter.

"So I was cutting my losses, I suppose. I really didn't think it'd come back on you. Well . . . I suppose I didn't really think at all. I overreacted. Keep overreacting these days, I'm afraid. I'm sorry."

"I'm sorry, too," Rachel said, "but I have to tell you you've burned your boats. Max has decreed that you should be banned from his estate forever."

"I see."

"I can try and explain, but he isn't known for changing his mind about this kind of thing. Why should he? He *is* the deity in these parts."

In the photograph over the counter, Alfred Watkins wore pince-nez and looked solemn. If there were any pictures of him smiling, Powys thought, they must be filed away in some family album; smiling was not a public act in those days for a leading local businessman and a magistrate. It was perhaps just as well—Alfred Watkins needed his dignity today more than ever.

"Don't forget," Powys said, "he'll be watching you. Any joss sticks get lit, he'll be very unhappy."

"No he won't," Annie said. Annie with the Egyptian amulet, still living in 1971, before the husband and the four kids. "He fancies me, I can tell by the way he smiles."

"He never smiles."

"He smiles at *me*," Annie said. "OK, no joss sticks. If you're not back by tomorrow I'll open at nine, after I get rid of the kids."

"I'm only going to Kington."

"You're going back to the Old Golden Land," Annie said, half smiling. He'd shown her the letter from Henry's neighbor, Mrs. Whitney. "Admit it, you're going back."

"What happens?" Andy says. "Well, you go around the stone thirteen times and then you lie on the fairy hill and you get the vision. You see into the future, or maybe just into yourself. According to the legend, John Bottle went round the stone and when he lay on the mound he went down and down until he entered the great hall of the Fairy Queen with whom he naturally fell in love. It was so wonderful down there that he didn't want to leave. But they sent him back, and when he returned to the real world he became a great seer and prophet.

"Of course . . . "—Andy ate a black olive—" . . . he could never settle in the mundane world, and he knew that one day he'd have to go back . . . "

Powys drove his nine-year-old Mini out of the city, turning off before the Wye bridge.

In essence, Alfred Watkins had been right about the existence of leys. Powys felt this strongly. And Henry Kettle had been better than anybody at finding where the old tracks ran, by means of dowsing.

"After all these years," he'd said once to Powys, "I still don't know what they are. But I know they're there. And I know that sometimes, when you're standing on one, it can affect you. Affect your balance, like. Give you delusions sometimes, like as if you've had a few too many. Nothing *psychic,* mind, nothing like that. But they do *interfere* with you. Sometimes."

They might interfere with you when you were walking along them, with or without your dowsing rods. Or when you were driving along a stretch of road which happened—as many did—to follow one of the old lines. Many accident blackspots had been found to be places where leys crossed.

Coincidence.

Of course. And you could go crazy avoiding stretches of road just because they happened to align with local churches and standing stones. Nobody really went that far.

Certainly not Henry. Who, you would have thought, was too experienced a dowser ever to be caught out that way.

But when an experienced dowser crashed into a wall around an ancient burial mound, it demanded the kind of investigation the police would never conduct.

He didn't expect to find anything. But Henry Kettle was his friend. He was touched and grateful that Henry had bequeathed to him his papers—perhaps the famous journal that nobody had ever seen. And the rods, of course, don't forget the rods. (Why should he leave his rods to a man who couldn't dowse?)

Powys left Hereford by King's Acre and headed toward the Welsh border, where the sun hung low in the sky. During his lunch break, he'd spent half an hour with the Ordnance Survey maps of Hereford and eastern Radnorshire. He'd drawn a circle around the blob on the edge of the town of Crybbe where it said:

The Tump
(mound)

He'd taken a twelve-inch Perspex ruler and put one end over the circle and then, holding the end down with one finger, moved the ruler in an arc, making little pencil marks as he went along, whenever he came upon an ancient site. When the ruler had covered three hundred and sixty degrees he took it away and examined all the marks, haphazard as circles and crosses on a football-pool coupon.

And stared into the map like a fortune-teller into a crystal ball or the bottom of a teacup. Waiting for a meaningful image or a pattern to form among the mesh of roads and paths and contour lines . . . mound, circle, stone, church, earthwork, moat, holy well . . .

But from a ley-hunter's point of view, it was all very disappointing.

There was a large number of old stones and mounds all along the Welsh border, but the Tump didn't seem to align with any of them. The nearest possible ancient site was Crybbe parish church, less than a mile away. He looked it up in Pevsner's *Buildings* and established that it was certainly pre-Reformation—always a strong indication that it had been built on a pre-Christian site.

But when he drew a line from the Tump to the church and then continued it for several miles, he found it didn't cross any other mounds, churches, or standing stones. Not even a crossroads or a hilltop cairn.

The ley system, which appeared to cover almost the whole of Britain and could be detected in many parts of the world, seemed to have avoided Crybbe.

"Bloody strange," Powys had said aloud, giving up.

What the hell was there for Henry Kettle to dowse in Crybbe? Why had Max Goff chosen the place as a New Age center?

Powys came into the straggling village of Pembridge, where the age-warped black-and-whites seemed to hang over the street instead of trees. Driving down toward Kington and the border, he felt a nervousness edging in, like a foreign station on the radio at night. He rarely came this way. Too many memories. Or maybe only one long memory, twisted with grief.

Fiona, Ben's girlfriend, laughing and burrowing in one of the bags for the bottle of champagne. "Better open this now, warm shampoo's so yucky."

Ben holding up a fresh-from-the-publisher copy of the book. On the cover, a symbolic golden pentagram is shining on a hillside. In the foreground, against a late-sunset sky, a few stars sprinkled in the corners, is the jagged silhouette of a single standing stone. Across the top, the title, The Old Golden Land. Below the stone, in clean white lettering, the author's name, J. M. Powys.

And below that it says, With photographs by Rose Hart.

Rose looks at you, and her eyes are bright enough to burn through the years, and now the pain almost dissolves the memory.

Ben saying, "A toast, then . . . "

But Andy is raising a hand. "There remains one small formality."

Everybody looking at him.

"I think Joe ought to present himself to the Earth Spirit in the time-honored fashion."

Forget it, you think. No way.

"I mean go round the Bottle Stone. Thirteen times."

Fiona clapping her hands. "Oh, yes. Do go round the stone, Joe."

six

Henry's place was the end of a Welsh longhouse, divided into three cottages. The other two had been knocked into one, and Mrs. Gwen Whitney lived there with her husband.

Powys arrived there around eight-thirty, driving through deep wells of shadow. Remembering Henry coming out to meet him one evening around this time, his dog, Alf, dancing up to the car.

That night, twelve years ago, Powys pleading with Henry: "Come on . . . it's as much your book as mine. *The Old Golden Land* by Henry Kettle and Joe Powys."

"Don't be daft, boy. You writes, I dowses. That's the way of it. Besides, there's all that funny stuff in there—I might not agree with some of that. You know me, *nothing psychic*. When I stop thinking of this as science . . . well, I don't know where I'll be."

And an hour or so later: "But, Henry, at the very least . . . "

"And don't you start offering me money! What do I want any more money for, with the wife gone and the daughter doing more than well for herself in Canada? You go ahead, boy. Just don't connect me with any of it, or I'll have to disown you, see."

Silence now. The late sun turning the cottage windows to tinfoil. No dog leaping out at the car.

Mrs. Whitney opened her door as he walked across.

"Mr. Powys." A heavy woman in a big, flowery frock. Smiling that sad, sympathetic smile which came easily to the faces of country women, always on nodding terms with death.

"You remember me?"

"Not changed, have you? Anyway, it's not so long."

"Twelve years. And I've gone gray."

"Is it so long? Good gracious. Would you like some tea?"

"Thank you. Not too late, am I?"

"Not for you, Mr. Powys. I remember one night, must have

been four in the morning when we finally heard your car go from here."

"Sorry about that. We had a lot to talk about."

"Oh, he could talk, Mr. Kettle could. When he wanted to." Mrs. Whitney led him into her kitchen. "I think it looks nice gray," she said.

Later, they stood in Henry's cell-like living room, insulated by thousands of books, many of them old and probably valuable, although you wouldn't have thought it from the way they were wedged into the shelves, some upside down, some back to front. On a small cast-iron mantel shelf, over the Parkray, were a few deformed lumps of wood. Local sculpture, Henry called it. He'd keep them on the mantelpiece until he found more interesting ones in the hedgerows, then use the old ones for the fire.

Mrs. Whitney handed Powys a battered old medical bag. "This was in the car with him. Police brought it back."

A thought tumbled into Powys's head as he took the bag. "What about Alf?"

"Oh, old Alf died a couple of years back. He got another dog—Arnold. Funny-looking thing. I says, 'You're too old for another dog, Mr. Kettle.' 'Give me a reason to keep on living,' he says. Always said he couldn't work without a dog at his side. Arnold, he was in the car with Mr. Kettle, too. He wasn't killed. A lady's looking after him in Crybbe. She'll have her hands full. Year or so with Mr. Kettle, they forgot they was supposed to be dogs."

Powys smiled.

"Daft about animals, Mr. Kettle was. He's left half his money—I didn't put this in the letter—half his money's going to a dogs' shelter over the other side of Hereford. Daughter won't like that."

"Henry knew what he was doing," Powys said. "What's going to happen to the house?"

"She'll sell it. She won't come back, that one. She'll sell it and it'll go to some folks from Off, who'll put a new kitchen in and one of them fancy conservatories. They'll likely stop a couple of years, and then there'll be some more folks from Off. I don't mind them, myself, they never does no harm, in general."

Powys opened the medical bag. The contents were in compartments, like valuable scientific equipment. Two remodeled wire coat-hangers with rubber grips.

Mrs. Whitney said, "There's a what-d'you-call-it, pendulum thing in a pocket in the lid."

"I know," Powys said. "I remember."

"Mr. Kettle had his old dowsing records in . . . you know, them office things."

"Box files."

"Aye, box files. Must be half a dozen of them. And there's this I found by his bed."

It was a huge old black-bound business ledger, thick as a Bible. He opened it at random.

> . . . and in the middle meadow I detected the foundations of an old house from about the fifteenth century. I got so engrossed in this I forgot all about finding the well . . .

He could hear Henry chuckling as he wrote in black ink with his old fountain pen, edge to edge, ignoring the red and black rules and margins.

He turned to the beginning and saw the first entry had been made nearly twenty years earlier. Out of four or five hundred pages, there were barely ten left unfilled. End of an era.

Powys closed the ledger and held it, with reverence, in both hands.

"His journal. I doubt if anybody else has ever seen it."

"Well, you take it away," said Mrs. Whitney. "Sometimes I had the feeling some of them things Mr. Kettle was doing were—how shall I say?—not quite Christian."

"Science, Mrs. Whitney. He was always very particular about that."

"Funny sort of science," Mrs. Whitney said. "There's a letter, too, only gave it to me last week."

A pale-blue envelope, "J. M. Powys" handwritten in black ink.

"Oh, he was a nice old chap," Mrs. Whitney said. "But, with all respect for the departed, he'd have been the first to admit as he was more'n a bit cracked."

For Fay, there would be no secret pleasure anymore in editing tape in the office at night, within the circle of Anglepoise light, a soft glow from the Revox level-meters, and all the rest in shadow.

For none of what dwelt beyond the light could now be assumed to be simply shadow. Once these things had started happening to your mind, you couldn't trust anything anymore.

That evening, she and the canon watched television in what used to be Grace's dining room at the rear of the house and was now their own sitting room. Two bars of the electric fire were on—never guess it was summer, would you?

Arnold lay next to Alex on Grace's enormous chintzy sofa. The dog did not howl, not once, although Fay saw him stiffen with the distant roll of the curfew. He'd be sleeping upstairs again tonight.

She watched Alex watching TV and sent him mind messages. We have to talk, Dad. We can't go on here. There's nothing left. There never was anything, you ought to realize that now.

Alex carried on placidly watching some dismal old black-and-white weepie on Channel Four.

Fay said, at one point, "Dad?"

"Mmmm?"

Alex kept his eyes on the screen, where Stewart Granger was at a crucial point in his wooing of Jean Simmons.

"Dad, would you . . . " Fay gave up, "care for some tea? Or cocoa?"

"Cocoa. Wonderful. You know, at one time, people used to say I had more than a passing resemblance to old Granger."

"Really?" Fay couldn't see it herself.

"Came in quite useful once or twice."

"I bet it did."

Fay got up to make the cocoa, feeling more pale and wan than Jean Simmons looked in black and white. In one day she'd hung up on Guy, betrayed Rachel, demolished relations with Goff before she'd even met him. And caught herself about to give a blowjob to a microphone in the privacy of the Crybbe Unattended Studio.

What I need, she thought, is to plug myself into a ley-line, and she smiled to herself—a despairing kind of smile—at the absurdity of it all.

The box files wouldn't all fit in the trunk of the Mini. Three had to be wedged on the back seat, with the doctor's bag.

But the ledger, the dowsing journal of Henry Kettle, was on the passenger seat where Powys could see it, Henry's letter on top.

Just past the Kington roundabout he gave in, pulled onto the side of the road and, in the thinning light, he opened the letter.

Dear Joe,

I'm doing this now, while I feel the way I do. If it all sorts itself out you'll probably never read this letter. None of it will make much sense to you at first and if it never does make any sense it means my fears will be groundless.

What it comes down to is I've been working out at Crybbe for a chap called Max Goff who's bought Crybbe Court.

The nature of the job is dowsing some old alignments where the stones and such have all gone years ago, and it's been giving me the shivers, quite honestly, that whole place. Don't get me wrong, there's nothing psychic or any of that old rubbish, but it's not right and as far as I can work out it's a long-term kind of thing. I intend to keep an eye on the situation in the weeks and months and, God willing, the years ahead and keep on revising my notes, but I'm not getting any younger and you could go anytime at my age and I feel as how I ought to inform somebody. You have had some daft ideas in your time but you're a good boy basically and the only person I can think of who I can trust not to dismiss this out of hand as an old fool's ramblings.

God knows, I'm not infallible and I could be wrong and I don't even know as yet the nature of what's up in Crybbe, only I get the feeling it's long-term, and I'd like to think there was somebody who could keep an eye on what that Goff's up to.

Now my daughter, we've grown apart, no kidding myself anymore. She's out in Canada and she's VERY WELL OFF. So I've written to my solicitor in Hereford informing him that as well as all the papers my house is to be left to you. Consider it as a token of my confidence.

Yours sincerely,
H. Kettle
(Henry)

"God almighty," Powys said.

He could see lights coming on in Kington, through the trees. On the other side of the road, darkening hills. Somewhere, on the other side of the hills, Crybbe.

Leaving him the house was ridiculous. He'd probably changed his mind by now, anyway.

But the letter was dated 19 June.

Only two days before Henry's death.

Powys opened the ledger at the last completed page. It also was dated 19 June.

> *Quite a successful day. Located three more old stones. One of them would be eleven feet above the ground, which would make it quite rare for the Crybbe area, the nearest one as high as that being down near Crickhowell. I have been over this twice to make sure. It is very peculiar that there should have been so many big stones in such a small area. I tried to date this big one, but all I could come up with was 1593 when it was destroyed. It seemed certain to me that this was done quite deliberately, the whole thing taken out and broken up. This was all quite systematic, like the burning down of monasteries during the Reformation.*
>
> *What intrigues me is how this Goff could have obtained the information about there having been stones here when even I had never heard of them. Sometimes I feel quite excited by all this, it is undoubtedly the most remarkable discovery of prehistoric remains in this country for many years, even if the archaeologists will never accept it. At other times, however, I do get quite a bad feeling that something here is not right, although I cannot put my finger on it. I have always disliked the Tump for some reason. Some places are naturally negative, although perhaps "natural" is not the word I want. The Welsh border is a very funny place, but I am sure there is a good scientific explanation.*

The last entry. Neatly dated and a line drawn under it. Two days later Henry Kettle was lying dead in his car under Crybbe Tump.

It was dark when Powys got back to Hereford. He lugged the box files up the stairs to his little flat above Trackways and left

them in the middle of the floor, unopened. It would take months
to explore that lot.

But he was committed now.

He went down to the shop and put on the lights. From
his photograph, Alfred Watkins frowned down on the counter.
Powys could see why: Annie had put the box of "healing"
crystals on display.

He wrote out a note and left it wedged under the crystals
box.

> *Dear Annie,*
>   *Please hold fort until whenever. I'll call you. Don't light
> too many joss-sticks.*

Feeling a need to explain, he added,

> *Gone to Crybbe.*
> *P.S. Don't get the wrong idea. It might be old, but it's not
> golden.*

When he put out the lights in the shop, he noticed the answering machine winking red.

A woman's low, resonant voice.

"J. M. Powys, this is Rachel Wade at Crybbe Court. I wanted
to remind you about Friday. I'd be grateful if you could call
back on Crybbe 689, which is the Cock Hotel, or 563, our new
office at Crybbe Court. Leave a message if I'm not around.
Things are a little chaotic at present, but we'd very much like to
hear from you. If you can't make it on Friday, we could arrange
another day. Just please call me."

"I'll be there," Powys said to the machine. "OK?"

He went upstairs to bed and couldn't sleep. He'd seen Henry
barely half a dozen times in the past ten years. If the old guy
really had left him his house to underline his feelings about
Crybbe, then they had to be more than passing fears.

"What have you dumped on me, Henry?" he kept asking the
ceiling. And when he fell asleep he dreamed about the Bottle
Stone.

seven

The following day was overcast, the sky straining with rain that never seemed to fall. After breakfast, Jimmy Preece, gnarled old mayor of Crybbe, went to see his son.

He found Jack tinkering with the tractor in the farmyard, his eldest grandson, Jonathon, looking on, shaking his head.

"Always the same," Jack grunted. "Just when you need it. Mornin', Father."

"I been telling him," Jonathon said. "Get a new one. False economy. This thing gets us through haymaking, I'll be very surprised indeed."

Jimmy Preece shook his head, then he nodded, so that neither of them would be sure which one he was agreeing with.

"Got to take an overview," said Jonathon, this year's chairman of the Crybbe and District Young Farmers' Club. "Going from day to day don't work anymore."

"Break off a minute, will you?" Jimmy said. "Come in the 'ouse. I want a bit of advice."

He knew that'd get them. Jack straightened up, tossed his wrench into the metal toolbox, and walked off without a word, across the farmyard to the back door. "Warren!" he roared. "Put that bloody guitar down and make some tea."

In the kitchen, waiting for the kettle to boil, Warren whipped the letter out of his back pocket and read it through again. He'd thought at first it might have been Peter, the drummer, playing one of his jokes. But where would Peter have got hold of paper with the Epidemic letterhead?

Dear Mr. Preece,
  Thank you for sending us the cassette of FATAL ACCI-
DENT, which I return.
  Max Goff has listened with interest to your songs and
believes there could be considerable potential here . . .

It was signed by this Rachel Wade, the snooty tart Warren had seen driving Max Goff around. It had to be genuine.

Well, fuck, what had he got to be surprised about? Max Goff hadn't got where he was today without he could spot a good band when he heard one.

Have to get working, then. Have to get a few more numbers together. Get on the phone to the boys, soon as the old man and bloody Jonathon were out of the way.

Warren took their tea. They were sprawled around the big living room, granddad getting his knackered old pipe out. Looked like the start of a long session, and the phone was in the same room. Warren was nearly grinding his teeth in frustration.

Stuff this, he'd walk into town and use the phone booth by the post office. He left the tray of mugs on a stool and cleared out quick, before the old man could come up with some filthy old job for him.

Out in the hallway, though, he stopped, having second thoughts. Warren liked to know about things. He tramped loudly to the main door, kicked it shut, then crept quietly back and stood by the living-room door, listening.

And soon he was bloody glad he had.

Fay had decided that what she must do, for a start, was get her dad out of the town for a few hours so she could talk to him. *Really* talk.

It seemed ridiculous that she couldn't do this in the house, but that was how it was. Often, in Crybbe, you simply couldn't seem to approach things directly. There were whole periods when everything you tried to do or say was somehow deflected.

In the same way, she felt the place smothered your natural curiosity, made the urge to find out—the act of wanting to *know*—seem just too much trouble.

It wasn't that the air was in any way soporific, she thought, unlocking the Fiesta. Not like the famous country air was supposed to be, or the dreamy blue ozone at the seaside that sent you drifting off at night on waves of healthy contentment.

Here, it was as if the atmosphere itself was feeding off you, quietly extracting your vital juices, sapping your mental energy, so that you crawled into bed and lay there like a dried-out husk.

Had the air done this to the people? Or had the people done it to the air?

Or was it just her, living with an old man whose mind was seizing up.

Fay gave him a blast on the horn. Come on, Dad, you're not changing your mind now.

In the local paper she'd found a story about people in a village fifteen miles away receiving some kind of conservation award for adopting their local railway station, planting flowers on the embankments, that kind of thing. Ashpole had agreed it would probably make a nice little soft package. End-of-the-program stuff, keep it down to four minutes max.

From the back seat, Arnold barked. It was a gruff, throaty bark, and his jaws clamped down on it as soon as it was out. It was the first one Fay had ever heard him produce. He must be settling in. She leaned over and ruffled his big ears, pleased.

Alex emerged by the front door at last. It had been far from easy persuading him to come with her, even though he did seem much better today, more aware.

He sat with his hands on his lap as she drove them out of town, on the Welsh side. "Hope you know a decent pub over there, my child."

"We'll find one."

The sky was brightening as she drove into the hills, the border roads unraveling through featureless forestry, then open fields with sheep, a few cows, sparse sprinklings of cottages, farm buildings, and bungalows.

The little railway station was on the single-track Heart of Wales line, which went on to Shrewsbury. It wasn't much more than a halt, with a wooden bench and a waiting room the size of a bus shelter.

Fay had arranged to meet the secretary of this enthusiastic committee which existed to defend the unprofitable line against what seemed to be a constant threat of imminent closure by British Rail. He turned out to be a genial guy and a good talker, and he'd brought along a couple of villagers who spent their weekends sprucing up the station surrounds, planting bulbs. They were friendly and self-deprecating.

In Crybbe it would have to have been the newcomers who took the job on. But Crybbe didn't have a station, anyway. Only B roads.

Interviews done, she stood for a moment at the edge of the line, looking out toward the hills and thinking what a quiet, serene place this actually was. Untampered with. All the old patterns still apparent.

A buzzard glided overhead, then banked off like a World War II fighter, flashing the white blotches under its wings.

She thought, It's me. All this is wonderful. It isn't mean and tight and stifling at all. I'm just a sour bitch who thinks she's had a raw deal, and I'm blaming the poor bloody border country.

Alex was in the car, white beard brushing his *Guardian* as he read, still managing without glasses at pushing ninety. He was wearing a baggy cardigan over his Kate Bush T-shirt. Fay thought suddenly, I wish I knew him better.

". . . and Mrs. Wozencraft's cottage—old Jessie Wozencraft—that's his as well, he's bought that."

"Good luck to him," Jonathon said. "Old place is near enough falling down."

"That's not the point, Jonathon," said Jack Preece. "Point your granddad's makin' is . . . "

"Oh, I know what he's sayin'—and he's dead right. What bloody use is an acupuncturist in Crybbe?"

"What do they do, anyway?"

"They sticks needles in you, to cure things."

"Wouldn't stick any in me, boy. I hates them injections."

"It don't matter what they does!" Warren heard his granddad thumping the chair arm. "It's the principle. Retired folk I don't mind so much, give 'em a bit of bird-watchin' and a library book and they don't bother nobody, and they always dies after a few years anyway. What *I* object to is these clever-arsed fellers as wants to *change* things to what they thinks they should be, if you know what I'm sayin'. Everything pretty-pretty and no huntin' the little furry animals. And no jobs either, 'cause factories spoils the view."

"Market forces, Granddad. You can't do nothin' about market forces."

"Nine properties 'e's had so far, I counted. Nine! Everything for sale within a mile of town, he's bought it."

"Many as that, eh?"

Warren didn't like the way this conversation was going. He fingered the crisp Epidemic notepaper in his pocket.

Jonathon said, "Well, nobody else'd've bought 'em, would they? Not with interest rates the way they are. All right, it's speculation . . . "

"It's not just speculation, Jonathon. There's a purpose to it, and it's not right. You heard that woman on the wireless. New Age and psychic powers. I don't know nothin' about any of it and I don't want to, and I don't want *him* doin' it yere."

"Woken a lot of people up to it, that bit on the radio," Jack said. "Everybody talkin' about it in the Cock last night, the post office this morning. Lot of people's worried it's going to bring the hippies in."

"What are any of 'em but hippies? Quack healers, fortune-tellers . . . "

"Who is she, Father? Somebody said it was that girl who lives with 'er dad, the old feller with the beard."

"Fay Morrison," Granddad said. "Nice enough girl. Comes to council meetings."

"Tidy piece," Jonathon said.

Warren knew who they meant. Seen her the other night, coming back from the Court with that dog. Followed her behind the hedge. Spying, most likely, she was, nosy cow.

"I admit I never wanted 'em to put that radio studio in," his granddad said. "But if it 'adn't been for this girl nobody'd've believed it. They years it on the wireless, it brings it 'ome to 'em, isn't it?" Warren heard the old feller sucking on his pipe. "Ah, but he's a crafty bugger, that Goff. Comes to my door tryin' to get round me, all the things he's goin' to do for the town. Get the mayor on his side, first—tactics, see."

"Well, we can't stop him. Can't block market forces, Grand-dad."

"We can stop him takin' our town off us to serve his whims!"

"And how're we supposed to do that?"

"He wants a public meeting, we'll give him one."

"What are you sayin' here, Father? Give him a rough time? Let him know he isn't wanted?"

Behind the door, Warren began to seethe. This was fucking typical. Here was Max Goff, biggest bloody independent record producer in the country, on the verge of signing Fatal Accident to Epidemic. And these stick-in-the-mud bastards were scheming to get rid of them.

Jonathon was saying, "See them stones he had delivered? Bloody great stones, dozens of 'em."

"Building stone?"

"No, just great big stones. Huge buggers. Like Stonehenge, that kind."

Things went quiet, then Warren heard his granddad say, "He's overSteppin' the mark. He's got to be stopped."

Warren wanted to strangle the old git. He wanted to strangle all three of them. Also that fucking radio woman who'd let it all out and stirred things up. The one who shouted after him through the hedge that night, called him a jerkoff.

Every pub they'd tried had stopped serving lunch at two o'clock—so much for all-day opening—and so they'd wound up at this Little Chef, which didn't please him. "Bloody cooking by numbers. Two onion rings, thirty-seven chips. All this and alcohol-free lager, too. And these bloody girls invariably saying, 'Was it all right for you?' as if they're just putting their knickers back on."

"At least they're there when you want them," Fay said, getting back on the A49. "Would you like to see Ludlow?"

"Like to go home, actually."

"God almighty! What is it about that place?"

"Left my pills there."

"I know you did. But luckily, *I* brought them. What's your next excuse?"

Alex growled. "Wish I'd had a son."

"Instead of me, huh?"

"Sons don't try to manage you."

"Dad, I want to talk to you."

"Oh God."

"Was that the first time Guy rang, the other night?"

"Hard to say, my dear. Once I put the phone down I tend to forget all about him. He may have rung earlier. Does it really matter?"

"I don't mean just that night. Has he rung any other time when I've been out?"

"Can't remember. Suppose he could have done. I didn't think you cared."

"I don't. It's just Guy's coming down to make a documentary about Max Goff, and I was wondering how he found out there was something interesting going on. I know you tend to absorb local gossip like a sponge and then somebody squeezes you a bit and it all comes out, and then you forget it was ever there."

"You think I told him?"

"Did you?"

"Did I? God knows. Say anything to get rid of him. Does it matter?"

Fay glanced in her side mirror, then trod on the brakes and pulled violently to the side of the road. "Of course it bloody matters!"

"I think you're overwrought, my child. You're young. You need a bit of excitement. Bit of stimulation. Country life doesn't suit you."

"Crybbe doesn't suit me."

"So why not simply . . . ?"

She said carefully, "Dad. You may be right. There may be nothing at all wrong with Crybbe. But, yes, I think it's time I left. And I think it's time *you* left. You've no reason to stay. You've no roots there, no real friends there."

He said sadly, "Oh, I have."

He wasn't looking at her. He was looking straight out at the A49, trucks chugging past.

"Who? Murray Beech? He'll be off, first chance of a bigger parish. He's got nothing to thank Crybbe for—his fiancée didn't hang around, did she?"

"No," Alex said. "Not Murray."

"Who, then?"

He didn't reply.

Fay fiddled with the keys in the ignition. Alex talked to everybody, old vicars never changed. A friend to everyone, essence of the job. But how many did he really know?

"What are you saying, Dad?"

"Grace," he whispered, and Fay saw the beginning of tears in his old blue eyes.

She put a hand on his arm. "Dad?"

"Don't ask me about this, Fay," Alex said. "Please. Just take me home."

eight

�֍ ────────────────────────────────────

On top of the Tump it all came clear.

You could see over the roofs of the stables and Crybbe Court itself, which was sunk into a shallow dip. And there, only just showing above the trees, was the church tower. But then, the trees hadn't always been so high—or even there at all.

The church was at the high point of the town, the main street sloping down to the river. From here you couldn't see the street or the river—but you *could* see the fields on the opposite bank, rising into hills thickened now with forestry. And at one time, before the introduction of the voracious Sitka Spruce from Alaska, that might have been bare hillside, and there would have been other markers to pick up the line.

Joe Powys looked all around him and saw how clearly the Tump had been positioned to dominate the town, even the church, and draw in the landscape like the corners of a hand-kerchief.

That old feeling again, of being inside an ancient mechanism. At the center of the wheel.

Identifying the line took an act of imagination because there were no markers anymore. But Henry Kettle had discovered where upright stones had once been aligned to guide the eye from the Tump to the distant horizons.

But there was something about it that Henry Kettle didn't like.

Powys moved away from the highest point and stood next to a twisted hawthorn tree. The sky was a tense, luminous gray, swollen like a great water-filled balloon, and he felt that if it came down low enough to be pricked by the tree's topmost thorns, he'd be drowned.

It was his own fault. Places like this could ensnare your mind, and your thoughts became tangled up with the most primitive instincts, old fears lying hidden in the undergrowth like trailing brambles.

As quickly as he could, but still very carefully, Powys came down from the Tump, climbed over the wall, and didn't look back until he was well into the field, heading toward the road, where he'd left the Mini. Halfway across the field, there was a bumpy rise, and it was here that he found the hubcap.

He sat on a hummock with the disk on his knee. It was muddy and badly rusted, but he could still make out the symbol in the center—two letters: VW.

"Still the same car, then, Henry. How old is it now? Twenty-two, twenty-three?"

Holding Henry's hubcap, Powys looked back at the Tump.

I have always disliked the Tump for some reason. Some places are naturally negative.

Powys thought, Sinister bloody thing that must once have appeared as alien as a gasworks or a nuclear reactor. He looked down at the wall, realizing that the section he'd climbed over was just a few yards from the part where the stonework was so obviously scraped, but hadn't collapsed because it was too hard for that. Harder than the rusting heap of twenty-year-old tin Henry Kettle drove.

From the foot of the wall, shards of broken glass glimmered like dew in the trodden-down grass.

Christ, Henry, how could this happen?

Henry, can you hear me?

Although perhaps "natural" is not the word I want . . . But I am sure there is a good scientific explanation.

You misled us, Henry. Nothing psychic, you kept saying. We should have realized it was just a dirty word to you, a word for phony mediums and fortune-tellers at the end of the pier. "Ancient science" was your term, because it didn't sound cranky.

He could see the tracks now, grass flattened, lumps of turf wrenched out. The field was unfenced and the car must have cut across it diagonally, plowing straight on instead of following a sharpish left-hand bend in the road.

Powys left the metal disk on the hummock and scrambled up to the road, collecting a hard look from a man driving a Land Rover pulling a trailer.

Now, if Henry was driving out of town, he'd be pointing straight at the Tump, then the road curved away, then it was directed toward the Tump again, very briefly, then came the left-hand bend and you were away into the hills.

But Henry never made the left-hand bend. The car left the road, taking him into the field. He might not have noticed what he'd done at first, if it was dark. And then the field went quite suddenly into this slope, and . . . crunch.

Not so farfetched at all, really. There'd be an accidental-death verdict and nobody would delve any deeper. All the rest was folklore.

He went back into the field, walked down toward the Tump, skirting its walled-in base, not knowing what he was hoping for anymore.

Come on, Henry. Give us a sign.

It began to rain. He ran to a clump of trees to shelter and to watch the Tump, massive, ancient, glowering through the downpour, as magnificently mysterious as the Great Pyramid.

Powys turned away and wandered among the trees, emerging on the other side into a clearing beside a building of gray-brown stones.

Crybbe Court?

No, not the Court itself, the stable block—now seriously renovated, he saw. There was an enormous oblong of glass set in the wall—a huge picture window, facing the Tump.

Behind the building he could see the corner of a forecourt, where two men stood in the rain looking down on four long, gray, jagged stones.

Powys stiffened.

One of the men was dark and thin and was talking to the other man in a voice which, had Powys been able to hear it, would probably have reminded him of a stroked cello.

"Least you can do, mate," Andy tells you. "Look at all the money the book's going to make. Think of it as a kind of appeasement of the Earth Spirit."

Fiona claps her hands. "Oh, go on, Joe. We'll all sit here and chant and clap."

"Bastards." You look at Rose, who smiles sympathetically. Reluctantly you stand up, and everybody cheers.

Well, everybody except Henry. "Don't wanna play about with these old things." Quaint old Herefordshire countryman.

Andy leaning on an elbow. "I thought you weren't superstitious, Henry. Ancient science and all that. Nothing psychic."

"Aye, well, electricity's science too, but you wouldn't wanna go sticking your fingers up a plug socket."

Thankful for his advice, you make as if to sit down.

"Not got the bottle for it, Joe?"

Ben starts clapping very slowly, and the others—except Henry—pick up the rhythm. "Joey goes round the Bottle Stone, the Bottle Stone, the Bottle Stone . . . "

Crybbe was forty-five minutes away. Minor roads all the way once they'd left the A49. Neither of them spoke; Fay was thinking hard, bringing something into focus. Something utterly repellent that she hadn't, up to now, allowed herself to contemplate for longer than a few seconds.

A woman in a cold miasma, frigid, rigid, utterly still. Not breathing. *Past* breathing . . . long past.

She looked in the driving mirror, and there was Arnold, the dog, sitting upright on the back seat; their eyes met in the mirror.

"You saw her, Arnold. You saw *something.* But did *I?"*

Did I see the ghost of Grace Legge?

Ghost. Spirit of the dead. And yet that image, the Grace thing, surely was without spirit. Static. Frozen. And the white eyes and that horrible smile with those little, thin fish-teeth.

That was her. Her teeth. Tiny little teeth, and lots of them, discolored, brittle. The memory you always carried away, of Grace's fixed smile, with all those little teeth.

She'd been nothing to Fay, just dad's Other Woman. No, not exactly nothing. Twenty years ago, she'd been something on the negative side of nothing. Somebody Fay had blamed—to herself, for she'd never spoken of it, not to anyone—for her mother's death. And she'd blamed her father, too. Perhaps this was why, even now, she could not quite love him—terrible admission.

She had, naturally, tried hard for both of them when she came down for the wedding. Water under the bridge. An old man's fumbling attempts to make amends and a very sick woman who deserved what bit of happiness remained for her.

Perhaps her dad thought he'd killed them both. Both his wives.

Compassion rising, Fay glanced sideways at Alex, sitting there with his old green cardigan unbuttoned and ATE USH in fading lettering across his chest.

What this was about—*had* to be—was that he, too, had seen something in the night.

And what must that be like for an old man who could no longer trust his own mind or even his memories? If she wasn't sure what she'd seen—or even if she'd seen anything—what must it be like for him?

Fay clutched the steering wheel tightly, and goose pimples rippled up both arms.

That's why you can't leave, Dad. You've seen something that none of your clerical experience could ever prepare you for. You're afraid that somehow she's still there, in the house you shared.

And you're not going to walk out on her again.

Henry Kettle had written,

It is very peculiar that there should have been so many big stones in such a small area.

Long after Andy and the other man had walked away, Powys still stood silently under the dripping trees, staring in fascination at the recumbent stones in the corner of the courtyard.

Megaliths.

And Andy Boulton-Trow, whom Powys hadn't seen for twelve years. Designer of the cover of *The Old Golden Land*. Painter of stones, sculptor of stones, collector of stone lore.

The stones lay there, gleaming with fresh rain. Old stones, or new stones? Did it matter; one stone was as old as another.

Stones didn't speak to him the way they spoke to Henry Kettle, but he was getting the idea. Max Goff, presumably, intended to place new stones in the spots identified by Henry.

And the obvious man to select and shape the stones—an act of love—was Andy Boulton-Trow, who knew more about the nature of megaliths than anyone in Europe. Powys had met Andy at art college, to which Andy had come *after* university to learn about painting and sculpture . . . with specific regard to stone.

From beyond the courtyard, he heard an engine start, a vehicle moving away.

Then all was quiet; even the rain had ceased.

Powys slid from the trees and made his way around the side of the stone stable-building to the corner of the courtyard where the stones lay.

*   *   *

Fay drove into Crybbe from the Ludlow road. The windshield wipers squeaked as the rain eased off.

She thought, We're never going to be able to talk about this, are we, Dad? Not for as long as you live.

She stopped in front of the house to let him out. "Thank you," he said, not looking at her. "It's been . . . a pleasant day, hasn't it?"

"I'll put the car away. You stay here, Arnold."

She backed the car into the entry, a little tunnel affair in the terrace, parking too close to the wall; there was only just room to squeeze out. "Come on, Arnold."

Alex was waiting for them at the back door. His face was grave but his blue eyes were flecked—as they often were now—with a flickering confusion.

"Got the tea on, Dad?"

"Fay . . . I . . . "

He turned and went into the kitchen. The kettle was not even plugged in.

"Fay . . . "

"Dad?"

He walked through the kitchen, into the hall, Fay following, Arnold trotting behind. At the door of the office, Grace's sitting room, he stood to one side to let Fay pass.

"I'm so sorry," he said.

At first she couldn't see what he meant. The clock was still ticking away on the mantelpiece, the fireside chair still piled high with box files.

"The back door was open," Alex said. "Forced."

She saw.

They must have used a sledgehammer or a heavy ax because it was a tough machine, with a metal top.

"Why?" Fay felt ravaged. Cold and hollow and hurting like a rape victim. "For God's sake, *why?*"

Her beloved Revox—nighttime comfort with its swishing spools and soft-glowing level-meters—had been smashed to pieces, disemboweled.

A few hundred yards of tape had been unspooled and mixed up with the innards, and the detritus was splattered over the floor like a mound of spaghetti.

nine

The women who had, in recent years, been powerfully attracted to Joe Powys had tended to wear long, hand-dyed skirts and shapeless woollies. Sometimes they had frizzy hair and sometimes long, tangled hair. Sometimes they were big-breasted earth-mother types and sometimes small-boned and delicate like Arthur Rackham fairies.

Sometimes, when Powys fantasized—which was worryingly rarely, these days—he imagined having, as he put it to himself, a bit of smooth. Someone scented. Someone who shaved her armpits. Someone who would actually refuse to trek across three miles of moorland to find some tiny, ruined stone circle you practically had to dig out of the heather. Someone you could never imagine standing in the middle of this half-submerged circle and breathing, "Oh, I mean, gosh, can't you feel it . . . can't you feel that primal force?"

The woman facing him now, he could tell, was the kind who'd rather see Stonehenge itself as a blur in the window of a fast car heading toward a costly dinner in Salisbury.

But even if she'd been wearing a homemade ankle-length skirt with a hemline of mud, clumpy sandals, and big wooden earrings, he would, at this moment, have been more than grateful to see her.

She said, "I think you could let him go now, Humble. He really doesn't look very dangerous."

"Find out who he is first," said the hard-faced bastard with a grip like a monkey wrench, the guy he'd first seen frowning at him through the window of a Land Rover when he was checking out the Tump.

He made Powys bend over the vehicle's high hood, which tossed another pain ball into his stomach.

This man had punched him in the guts with a considered precision and such penetration that he was seriously worried about internal bleeding.

"Ta very much." Deftly removing Powys's wallet from the inside pocket of his muddied jacket. Not a local accent; this was London.

"If this is a mugging," Powys said awkwardly, face squashed into the hood, "you could be . . . "

"Fucking shut it." His nose crunched into the metal, Powys felt blood come.

"Don't even twitch, pal, OK?"

"Mmmph."

"Right, then, I'm going to have a little butcher's through here, see what you got by way of ID, all right?"

"Humble, if you don't let him go I'm going to call the police."

"Rachel, you do your job, I do mine. Our friend here don't want that. Ask him. Ask him what he was doing on private property. Ain't a poacher. Ain't got the bottle."

He cringed, expecting Humble to tap him in the guts again to prove his point. But the pressure eased and he was allowed to stand. His nose felt wet, but he didn't think it was broken. He looked at the woman, who must be close to his own age, had light, midlength hair and calm eyes. "I'm sorry," she said. "Humble's used to dealing with the more urban type of trespasser."

"Trespasser?" Powys wiped off some blood with the back of a hand. "Now, look . . . You tell this bloody psycho . . . " He stopped. What could she tell him? He wondered where Andy Boulton-Trow had vanished to.

"All right now are we?" Dipping into Powys's wallet, Humble smiled with the lower half of a face which had all the personality of a mousetrap. He pulled out a plastic-covered driver's license and handed it to the woman. She took it from him reluctantly. Opened it out. Gave a little gasp.

"Oh dear," she said.

"Yeah, don't tell me. One of Max's bits of fluff." Humble smirked. "In which case, no problems, he'll have been enjoying himself."

Rachel closed the license and held out her hand for the wallet. Very carefully she put the license back, then she handed the wallet to Powys.

"Not entirely accurate, Humble," she said. "And when he hears about this, Max, I suspect, is going to have you strung up by the balls."

                    *   *   *

Police Sergeant Wynford Wiley was shaking his great turnip
head. "Mindless."

"Mindless?" said Fay. "You think it's *mindless?*"

"We always prided ourselves," Wynford said, thick blue legs
astride the wreckage. "Never suffered from no vandalism in this
town. Not to any great extent, anyhow."

Only vandalism by neglect, Fay thought dully. She wondered
why she'd bothered to call the police now. Wynford was just so
sinister—like one of those mean-eyed, redneck police chiefs you
saw in moody American movies set in semiderelict one-street
wooden towns in the Midwest.

"Think somebody would've seen 'em, though." The gap
narrowed between Wynford's little round eyes. "Course, Mrs.
Lloyd next door, deaf as a post, see. Knock on the door, she
don't answer. You got to put your face up to the window."

Fay imagined Wynford's face, flattened by glass. Give the
poor old girl a heart attack.

He said, "Scene-of-crime boy'll be over later, with his box
of tricks. I'll knock on a few doors along the street, see what
I can turn up."

He paused in the doorway, looked back at the wreckage.

"Mindless," he said.

Fay turned to her dad for support, but Alex, gazing down his
beard at the Revox ruins, had nothing to say.

"Doesn't it strike you as odd," Fay said clinically, "that this
tornado of savagery appears somehow to have focused itself on
one single item? I'm no criminologist, but I've witnessed my
share of antisocial behavior, and this, Sergeant, is *not* what I'd
call mindless. Psychopathic, perhaps, but mindless in the sense
of randomly destructive, no."

Wynford's big, round face was changing color. Nobody, she
thought, contradicts Chief Wiley on his own manor.

"What you sayin' 'ere, then? Somebody wants to stop you
broadcastin'? That it?"

"It's possible. Isn't it?"

"And *is* it gonner stop you broadcastin'?"

"Well, no, as it happens. I . . . I've got a portable tape recorder I do all my interviews on, and I can edit down at the studio
in town, there's a machine there. But would they know that?"

"Listen." Wynford was now wearing an expression which might have been intended to convey kindness. Fay shuddered. "He—they—just came in and smashed up the most expensive thing they could find. Then, could be as 'e was disturbed—or *thought* 'e was gonna be disturbed, maybe 'e years somebody walkin' past . . . "

"Maybe he wasn't disturbed at all," Fay said. "Maybe he just left because he'd achieved what he set out to do."

"I think you're watchin' too much telly."

"Can't very well watch too much TV in Crybbe. The power's never on for longer than three hours at a stretch."

Wynford turned his back on her, opened the office door. Arnold walked in, saw Wynford, and growled.

"See you've still got that dog. Didn't leave 'im in the 'ouse, then, when you went out?"

"What? Oh. No, he came with us," Fay said. "What happened with the RSPCA, by the way? Does anybody want to claim him?"

"No. I reckon 'e's yours now. If 'e stays."

"How do you mean?"

"Well. If 'e don't take off, like."

He was wearing such a weird smile that Fay pursued him to the front door. "I don't understand."

Wynford shrugged awkwardly. "Well, you might wake up one day, see, and . . . 'e'll be . . . well, 'e won't be around anymore."

Fay felt menaced. "Meaning what? Come on . . . what are you saying?"

Wynford's face went blank. "I'll go and talk to some neighbors," he said, and he went.

"Dad," Fay said, "I've said this before, but there's something very wrong with that guy."

"Sorry, my dear?" Alex looked up. His eyes were like floss.

"Sit down, Dad, you've had a shock."

"I'm fine," Alex said. "Fine. If there's nothing I can do here, I'll probably have an early night."

Fay watched the policeman walk past the window, imagined him peering through it with his face squashed against the glass, like a robber in a stocking mask.

She recoiled, stared at the gutted hulk of the Revox, a bizarre idea growing in her head like a strange hybrid plant.

She turned to Arnold, who was standing placidly in the doorway gazing up, for some reason, at Alex, his tail well down.

"Christ," Fay said.

Something had occurred to her that was so shatteringly preposterous that . . .

"Dad, I have to go out."

"OK," Alex said.

. . . if she didn't satisfy herself that it was completely crazy, she wasn't going to get any sleep tonight.

"You go and walk off your anger," Alex said. "You'll feel better."

"Something . . . " Fay looked around for Arnold's plastic clothesline. "Dad, I've just got to check this out. I mean, it's so . . . " Fay shook her head helplessly. "I'll be back, OK?"

She took J. M. Powys to her room at the Cock. The big room on the first floor that she shared with Max. But Max was in London.

The owner, Denzil, watched them go up. J. M. Powys looked, to say the least, disheveled, but Denzil made no comment. Rachel suspected that if she organized an orgy for thirty participants, Denzil would have no complaints as long as they all bought drinks in the bar to take up with them.

Rachel closed the bedroom door. The room was laden with dark beams and evening shadows. She switched a light on.

So this was J. M. Powys. Not what she'd imagined, not at all.

"Don't take this wrong, but I thought you'd be older."

"I think I am older." He tried to smile; it came out lopsided. There was drying blood around his mouth. His curly hair was entirely gray.

"Er, is there a bathroom?"

"Across the passage," Rachel said. "The *en-suite* revolution hasn't happened in Crybbe yet. Possibly next century. Here, let me look . . . Take your jacket off."

It was certainly an old jacket. The once-white T-shirt underneath it was stiff with mud and blood.

Gently, Rachel prized the T-shirt out of his jeans. His stomach looked like a sky with a storm coming on. "Nasty. That man is a liability."

"I've never . . . " Powys winced, "been beaten up by a New

Age thug before. It doesn't feel a lot different, actually."

Rachel said, "Humble has his uses in London and New York, but . . . Just move over to the light, would you . . . I really don't like the way he's going native; I caught him laying snares the other day. Look, Mr. Powys, I don't know what I can do for bruising, apart from apologize profusely and buy you dinner. Not that you'll thank me for that, unless you're into cholesterol in the basket."

"I don't mind that. I had a Big Mac the other day."

He sounded almost proud. Perhaps J. M. Powys was as loony as his book, after all.

Addressing the fireplace, Alex said, "Why? You've always been so house-proud. Why do this?"

He mustn't touch anything. Fingerprints. Couldn't even tidy the place up a bit until they'd looked for fingerprints. Waste of time, all that. They wouldn't have Grace on their files.

Alex started to cry.

"Why can't you two get on together?"

A tangled ball of black, unspooled tape rustled as he caught it with his shoe. Like the tape, the thoughts in his head were in hopeless, flimsy coils and, like the tape, could never be rewound.

All the way up the High Street, Fay kept her eyes on the gutter.

She saw half a dozen cigarette ends. A crumpled potato-chip packet and a candy wrapper. Two ring-pulls from beer cans. And a bus ticket issued by Marches Motors, the only firm which ran through Crybbe—twice a week, if you were lucky.

But neither in the gutter nor up against the walls did she find what she was looking for.

When Arnold stopped to cock his leg up against a lamppost, Fay stopped, too, and examined the bottom of the post for old splash marks.

There were none that she could see, and Arnold didn't hang around. He was off in a hurry, straining on the clothesline as he always did on the street. She'd have to get him a lead tomorrow.

Now *there* was a point. Fay steered Arnold past Middle Marches Crafts and the worn sign of the Crybbe Pottery, which her dad said was about to close down. There was a hardware shop around the corner.

Hereward Newsome was emerging from The Gallery. "Oh, hi, Fay. Out on a story?"

"You're working late."

"We're rearranging the main gallery. Making more picture space. Time to expand, I think, now the town's taking off."

"Is it?"

"God, yes, you must have noticed that. Lots of new faces about. Whatever you think of Max Goff, he's going to put this place on the map at last. I've been talking to the marketing director of the Marches Development Board—they're terribly excited. I should have a word with him sometime; they're very keen to talk about it."

"I will. Thanks. Hereward, look, you haven't got a dog, have you?"

"Mmm? No. Jocasta had it in mind to buy a Rottweiler once—she gets a little nervous at night. Be good deal more nervous with a Rottweiler around, I said. Hah. Managed to talk her out of that one, thank God."

"Do you know anybody who *has* got one?"

"A Rottweiler?"

"No, any sort of dog."

"Er . . . God, is that the time? No, it's not something I tend to notice, who has what kind of dog. Look, pop in sometime; there's a chap—artist—called Emmanuel Walters. Going to be very fashionable. You might like to do an interview with him about the exhibition we're planning. Couple of days before we open, would that be possible? Give you a ring, OK?"

She nodded and smiled wanly, and Hereward Newsome walked rapidly away along the shadowed street, long strides, shoulders back, confident.

Fay dragged Arnold around the corner to the hardware shop. As in all the other shops in Crybbe, there was never a light left on at night, but at least it had two big windows—through which, in turn, she peered, looking for one of those circular stands you always saw in shops like this, a carousel of dog leashes, chains, and collars.

There wasn't one.

No, of course there wasn't. Wouldn't be, would there? Nor

would there be cans of dog food or bags of Bonios.

The streets were empty and silent. As they would be, coming up to curfew time, everybody paying lip service to a tradition which had been meaningless for centuries. She was starting to work it out, why there was this artificial kind of tension in the air: nobody came out of anywhere for about three minutes either side of the curfew.

Except for the newcomers.

"Fay. Excuse me."

Like Murray Beech.

Walking across the road from the church, one hand raised, collar gleaming in the dusk.

"Could I have a word?"

When he reached her, she was quite shocked at how gaunt he appeared. The normally neatly chiseled face looked suddenly jagged, the eyes seemed to glare. Maybe it was the light.

Fay reined Arnold in. There was a sense of unreality, of her and the dog and the vicar in a glass case in the town center, public exhibits. And all the curtains parting behind the darkened windows.

Sod this. *Sod it!*

"Murray," she said quite loudly, very deliberately, "just answer me one question."

He looked apprehensive. (In Crybbe, every question was a threat.)

Fay said, "Do you know anybody with a dog?" The words resounded around the square.

The vicar stared at her and his head jerked back, as if she'd got him penned up in a corner with her microphone at his throat.

"Anybody," Fay persisted. "Any kind of dog. Anybody in Crybbe?"

"Look, it was about that I . . . "

"Because I've been scouring the gutters for dog turds and I can't find any."

"You . . . ?"

"Not one. Not a single bloody dog turd. Surprise you, does it? No dog turds in the streets of Crybbe?"

Fay became aware that she was coiling and uncoiling the clothesline around her fingers, entwining them until the plastic flex bit into the skin. She must look as mad as Murray did.

She felt her face was aflame and her hair standing on end. She felt she was burning up in the center of Crybbe, spontaneous emotional combustion in the tense minutes before the curfew's clang.

"No dog turds, Murray. No dog leashes in the shops. No . . . " The sensation of going publicly insane brought tears to her eyes. "No rubber bones . . . "

Murray pulled himself together. Or perhaps, Fay thought, in comparison with me it just looks as though he's together.

"Go home, Fay," he said.

"Yes," Fay said, "I will."

With Arnold tight to her legs, she turned away and began to walk back in the direction she'd come along the silent street. It was nearly dark now, but there were no lights in any of the houses.

Because people would be watching at the windows. The woman, the vicar, and the dog. A tableau. A little public drama.

She turned back. "It's true, though, isn't it? Apart from Arnold here, there aren't any dogs in Crybbe."

"I don't know," Murray said. It was obvious the idea had never occurred to him. "But . . . well, it's hardly likely, is it?" She couldn't see his face anymore, only his white collar, luminous like a cyclist's armband.

"Oh yes," Fay said, "it's likely. Anything's likely in this town."

"Yes, well . . . I'll just . . . I'll just say what I've been asked to say before . . . before you go."

There came a heavy metallic creak from the church tower. The bell swinging back.

And . . . *clanggg!*

It had never sounded so loud. The peal hit the street like a flash of hard, yellow light.

Arnold sat down in the road and his head went back.

Fay saw him and fell on her knees with both hands around his snout.

As the first peal died, Murray Beech said, "I've been asked . . . to tell you to keep the dog off the streets."

"What?"

"Especially at . . . curfew time. People don't . . . they don't like it."

Rage rippled through Fay. She looked up into the vicar's angular, desperate face.

"What?"

Her hands unclasped. She came slowly to her feet.

She watched as Arnold swallowed, shook his head once, and then quivered with the vibration from the tower as the great bell swung back.

Clangggg!

Arnold's first howl seemed to rise and meet the peal in the air above the square with an awful chemistry.

"Who?" Fay said quietly.

"Go home!" the vicar hissed urgently. "Take the thing away."

"Who told you to tell me?"

There was a shiver in the night, the creak of the bell hauled back.

Fay shrieked, *"Who told you, you bastard?"*

The bell pealed again, like sheet lightning. Arnold howled. The old buildings seemed to clutch each other in the shadows. And she was hearing the muffled clatter of his footsteps before she was aware that Murray Beech was running away across the square, as if Hell was about to be let loose in Crybbe.

ten

"You really didn't have to go to all this trouble," J. M. Powys said. "Chicken in the basket would have been fine."

Rachel said, "Care to send down for some?"

"Forget it." He was remembering how she'd massaged the bruises on his stomach with her lips. What happened? How did this come about?

The room, overlooking the cobbled square, bulged from the Cock's aged frame above an entryway. Once, they'd heard footsteps on the stones directly underneath.

Lights shone blearily from town houses, and the room's leaded windows dropped a faint trellis on the sheets.

They lay in complete silence for a long time before he turned to her and said, "Er . . . well . . ."

"Don't look at *me*," Rachel said. "I certainly didn't intend it to happen. I know I'm hardly the person to claim she isn't a whore, but we didn't even know each other until a couple of hours ago. And I'm not actually promiscuous. Most of the time these days I can take it or leave it."

It had been the curfew which had seemed to shatter the idyll. They'd fallen apart, Powys feeling bewildered, Rachel looking almost perturbed.

He didn't even remember getting into bed. They hadn't drunk anything or smoked anything, and it was not yet ten-thirty. He'd quite fancied her, certainly, but there'd been other things on his mind. Like serious pain.

He thought she was smiling. It *felt* like she was smiling. In her deep and opulent voice, she said, "Perhaps we should think of it as one of those whirlwind passions."

"Well, I'm glad you're not annoyed," said Powys. He couldn't remember much until the curfew, crashing like an alarm clock hauling him out of a hot dream. "That curfew," he said. "Kind of eerie, don't you think? Did you hear a dog howling at the same time at one point? Or was that me?"

"No, it was a dog, all right. Really rather spooky, J.M."

"Why do people keep calling me J.M.?"

"It sounds classier than Joseph Miles."

He remembered circumstances in which she'd seen his driver's license. Suddenly his stomach was hurting again.

"Tell me," she said. "Are you really a descendant of John Cowper Powys?"

"I wouldn't entirely rule it out." To take his mind off the pain, he flicked aside a few strands of fine, fair hair to admire the curve of her long neck. "Hey, look, what would Max Goff say if he found out I'd been in his bed with his . . . ?"

His . . . what, exactly?

"Don't worry about that; he'd be honored. I'm only a minion; you're his inspiration. But he isn't going to find out." Rachel turned her face toward him. "I won't even tell him you were trespassing on his property."

"I wasn't trespassing. It was what you might call an exploratory tour."

"Quite," said Rachel. "You were snooping."

"Well, probably. Look, I really am sorry about . . . "

"J.M., I'm not a virgin. The unwritten part of my job description includes ensuring that the boss goes to sleep fully relaxed."

"What?" He was shocked.

"Routine," Rachel said dismissively. "Like winding up an alarm clock."

"Stone me." He found this impressively cool and candid. And rather sad. He felt a faintly surprising tenderness coming on.

"I must say," Rachel said, "I was genuinely surprised to find out who you were. I was rather expecting J. M. Powys to be a vague, if benevolent, old cove in a woolly hat and half-moon glasses. By the way, I think your book's a dreadful sham. Do you mind?"

"Golden Land?" He started to smile. He'd been right about Rachel. "Why do you think that? No, I don't mind at all. I don't bruise as easily as a cursory examination might suggest."

"Well, let's not talk about that now."

"No, go on. Talk about it."

"Really?" Rachel faced him across the bed, not touching. "OK. Well, the central premise, if I have this right, is that there's a hidden link between us and the earth, a link known to our remote ancestors, but which we've forgotten about."

"The psychic umbilicus." As time went on, Powys had grown less and less convinced he'd written this crap.

"And, by going to the various ancient shrines, stone circles, holy wells, places like that, we can unblock the doorways and find our way back, as it were, into the Old Golden Land. Which seems to be your metaphor, or whatever, for this kind of harmony with the environment, feeling a part of one's surroundings. Us and the earth feeding each other?"

Powys nodded. "What's wrong with it so far?"

"Nothing at all," Rachel said. "Perfectly commendable. Except it's translated itself into all these old hippies staggering about with their dowsing rods and holding up their hands and feeling the Earth Spirit. I mean—let's be realistic about this—if these are the people with the keys to the cosmos, then God help us."

Powys was impressed. "I think you could be my ideal woman."

"Jesus," said Rachel. "You really *are* mixed up."

After a minute or two, he said, "I got a lot of it wildly wrong. It was nearly thirteen years ago, that book. I was too young to write it. I'd like to do it again. Or better still, I'd like not to have done it in the first place."

"It's a bit late for that," Rachel said. "You do realize you're largely responsible for Max's very costly fantasies?"

"What does that mean?"

"It means he's going to be the first king of the Old Golden Land, and he wants you to be the Royal Scribe and tell the world about it."

"Oh, my God. You think I should disappear?"

Rachel pulled his left hand to her breast. "Not just yet. If you really have found the flaws in your own arguments, I can't help wondering if you might not be the one person who can bring him to his senses."

Jocasta Newsome didn't know which was worse: spending a night in with Hereward or being alone.

She thought about lighting a fire, but, like most aspects of country life, it had lost its magic.

Could she ever have imagined there'd come a time when a log fire in an open fireplace would not only fail to induce a small romantic thrill but would actually have become a drag? In the end, she'd been forced to admit that logs were messy, time-consuming, and not even very warm. The only one who got overheated was Hereward, chopping away and coming in covered with sweat—nearly as damp as most of his logs, which were so full of sap that when you threw them on the fire they just sat there for hours and hissed at you.

And the Aga, of course. Very attractive, very prestigious for dinner parties. But it wasn't made to run all the radiators one needed for a barn like this. If they wanted proper oil-fired central heating, they'd have to install a boiler—electric heating was, of course, out of the question with all the power cuts and Hereward turning white when the quarterly bill arrived.

It had now become Jocasta's ambition to make sufficient money out of The Gallery to sell it and acquire premises somewhere civilized. With or without Hereward, but preferably without.

This morning Rachel Wade had phoned to say Max Goff had

been terribly pleased with the Tump triptych. And would they please look out for more pictures of ancient sites. Or any local landscapes by local artists.

Local artists! There were none. Even Darwyn Hall was Birmingham-born.

This afternoon, just before closing time—after school, presumably—another "local" artist had called in. A girl of seventeen or eighteen. An odd, dark, solemn girl. Would they like to put on an exhibition of her drawings?

Well, God forbid it should ever come to that. Children's drawings!

The girl's portfolio was now propped against the antique pine dresser in the kitchen—"Yes, of course we'll *look* at them, my dear, but our artists do tend to be experienced professionals, you know."

She'd let Hereward examine them when he returned from his weekly attempt to become accepted in the public bar of the Cock by proving he could be as boring as the natives. If they only knew how far ahead of them in the boredom stakes he really was, he'd never have to buy his own drinks again.

Jocasta stretched like a leopard on the sofa.

She herself was bored out of her mind. Farmers were said to shag sheep in these hills. Maybe she should go out and find a ram.

"Sex magic." Rachel was telling Powys the sordid story of her life as Goff's overpaid PA. "That was the other thing that almost pushed me over the edge."

"Isn't all sex magic?" Thinking, particularly, of tonight.

"Certainly not," said Rachel.

"Yeah, I know. I do know what you're talking about. Aleister Crowley, all that stuff?"

Rachel said, "Fortunately, it didn't last. Though Crowley was about the same build as Max, Max couldn't summon Crowley's stamina. Not too pleasant while it lasted, though. Lots of dressing up and ritual undressing. The idea appeared to be to build up the power and then direct it at the moment of orgasm. He was the Great Beast, I was . . . "

"The Scarlet Woman?" Powys vaguely remembered Crowley's autobiography, remembered not finishing it.

"Terribly tawdry," Rachel said. "Needless to say, it didn't

work—or I presume it didn't. Point is, Max isn't a wicked man, it's just a case of what you might call Bored Billionaire Syndrome. You've got all the money you'll ever want, all the women and all the boys. But you're not . . . quite . . . God."

"What can one do about this minor shortfall?"

Rachel said, "He's doing it."

And Powys nodded, resigned, as she told him about Goff's plans to restore the prehistoric legacy of Crybbe. "Crybbe's Max's psychic doorway. His entrance to your Old Golden Land."

"As identified by Henry Kettle."

"And how reliable was *he?* Is dowsing for real?"

"It was in Henry's case. Henry was red hot."

"The modern equivalent of the Stone Age shaman."

"Who said that?"

"Max."

"Figures," Powys said. He sighed. "Last night I went round to Henry's house to pick up his papers, his journal. Apparently he wanted me to have them. Anyway, it was pretty clear Henry had a few misgivings about what Goff was asking him to do—well, not so much that as what he was finding. He didn't like the Tump."

"*I* don't like the Tump," Rachel said.

"And leys—we don't really know anything about leys. All this energy-lines stuff is what people *want* to believe. Henry was quite impatient with the New Agers and their designer dowsing rods. He used to say we shouldn't mess with it until we knew exactly what we were messing *with.*"

Powys watched the lattice of light on the bedspread. "A more plausible theory says leys are spiritual paths to holy shrines, along which the spirits of the ancestors could also travel. Evidence shows a lot of psychic activity at places where leys cross, as well as mental disturbance, imbalance."

"Obviously the place to bring out the best in Max," Rachel said dryly. "Excuse me, J.M., I need a pee."

In the end, Jocasta had gone ahead and lit a fire, for what it was worth. The logs fizzed, the flames were pale yellow, and the smoke seeped feebly between them, as she lay on the sheepskin rug enjoying, in a desultory way, a favorite fantasy involving the Prince of Wales in his polo outfit.

There was a crack from the logs and something stung her leg. Jocasta screamed and leapt up. A smell of burning—flesh probably—made her beat her hands against her thigh in a panic.

She switched on a table lamp with a green and yellow Tiffany shade and stood next to it, examining her leg.

Nothing visible, except a tiny smudge, Jocasta licked a finger and wiped it away, pulled down her skirt, and was swamped by a sudden mud tide of self-disgust.

From the living-room window she could see the lights of the town through the trees at the end of the paddock. The paddock itself was like a black pond. She fetched from the kitchen the portfolio of drawings brought in by the girl. If the kid was any good at all, she might sell them very cheaply. Not in the gallery itself, of course, but in the small gift section they were setting up in a little room at the side.

Jocasta sat on the sofa and opened the portfolio by the light of the Tiffany lamp.

At first she was simply surprised. She'd expected landscapes and she'd expected an immature hesitancy of touch.

So the things that surprised her were the strength and vigor of the drawings in India ink, spatters and blotches used for effect, boldly controlled in the manner of Gerald Scarfe and Ralph Steadman.

And the fact that they were not landscapes, but interiors with figures.

An old man shaving.

The eyes, wide open, magnified in a shaving mirror to alarming effect. The chin tilted, the throat uplifted to the razor.

A tumbler on a window ledge collecting the blood.

At first she was simply surprised.

Then the shock set in. The realization, with a rush of bile to the throat, of what was depicted in the drawing. She tore her gaze away, covering the drawing, in horror, with her hands.

Then the lights went out.

Through the window, she saw that the lights of the whole town had gone out, too.

Jocasta didn't move. She was sitting there on the sofa staring into the sputtering half-dead logs in the grate, but seeing, swimming in her mind, the image of the thing on her knee, still covered by her hands, an old man cutting his own throat with a razor.

She thought she was sweating at first.

Under her hands the paper felt wet and sticky and, like the sap oozing from the green logs on the open fire, something warm seemed to be fizzing and bubbling between her fingers.

Jocasta let the portfolio fall to the floor and shriveled back into the sofa, almost sick with revulsion.

J. M. Powys stood by the window, bare feet on bare boards. Looking down on the street, at a few customers emerging from the main entrance of the Cock directly below. The last he saw before all the lights went out was a couple of men stumbling on the steps and clutching at each other, obviously drunk but not conspicuously merry.

He'd been here several times, but never at night. Never heard the curfew before. And now, as if the curfew had been a warning that the town would close down in precisely one hour, somebody had switched off the lights.

Such coincidences were not uncommon on the border.

He remembered manufacturing the phrase "The Celtic Twilight Zone" as the title for Chapter Six of *Golden Land*.

The border country—any border country—has a special quality. Two cultures merging, two types of landscape, an atmosphere of change and uncertainty. In such places, it used to be said, the veil between this world and others is especially thin. Border country: a transition zone . . . a psychic departure lounge . . .

Rachel returned, slipped out of the robe, joined him at the window, naked. The moon was out now, and her slender body was like a silver statuette.

"You get used to it," Rachel said, "living in Crybbe."

"The electricity?"

"It seems we're on the end of a power line, or something. So whenever there's a problem elsewhere it trips a switch and the whole valley goes off. Something like that. It'll be back on in a few minutes, probably."

Powys put out a hand to her, then held back and put the hand on the cool window ledge. Things to sort out first, before he allowed himself to forget.

"Henry Kettle," he said. "His car went out of control and crashed into the wall around the Tump. Freak accident. What did Goff have to say about that?"

Rachel said, "You don't want to hear that. Come back to bed, J.M."

They did go back to bed. But she told him anyway.

"The nearest thing to a Stone Age shaman. I mentioned that."

She lay in the crook of his arm, his hand cupped under a breast.

Powys said, "Nobody knows a thing about Stone Age shamans or what they did."

"Maybe it was Bronze Age."

"Them either."

"Max said they would sometimes sacrifice themselves or allow themselves to be sacrificed to honor the Earth Spirit or some such nonsense."

"Theory," Powys said.

"He said it must have been like that with Henry Kettle. Getting old. Knew he was on borrowed time. So he . . . consciously or subconsciously, he decided to end it all and put his life energy into Max's project. Max was standing there looking at the wreckage of Kettle's car. 'Whoomp!' he kept saying. 'Whoomp!' And clapping his hands."

"OK, you've convinced me," Powys said. "This guy's pissing in the dark, and he has to be stopped before it goes all over everybody."

Arnold whimpered. Fay awoke, feeling the dog trembling against her leg.

Although the bedroom light was out, she knew somehow that *all* the lights were out.

Knew also that in the office below, the little front room that had been Grace Legge's sitting room, *she* was in residence. Pottering about, dusting the china and the clock. The empty grin, eye sockets of pale light.

And would she see, through those resentful, dead sockets, the hulk of the wrecked Revox and the fragments of its innards sprayed across the room?

Or was that not a part of her twilit existence?

Oh, please . . . Fay clutched Arnold.
Probably there was nothing down there.
Nothing.
Probably.

part four

part four

Most of the natives once stood in superstitious awe of the ancient standing stones which are dotted up and down Radnorshire. Even today there are farmers who prefer to leave the hay uncut which grows round such stones, and some people avoid them at night as they would a graveyard.

W. H. HOWSE,
History of Radnorshire

Around midmorning, Fay picked up the phone and sat there for several minutes, holding it to her ear, staring across the office, at nothing. The scene-of-crime officer had just left, a young detective with a metal case. Lots of prints on the Revox and the desk, but they'd probably turn out to be her own and her father's, the SOCO had said cheerfully, fingerprinting them both. Everybody was a bit of a pro these days. He blamed television.

Fay held the phone at arm's length as it started making the continuous whine that told you you'd knocked it off its rest. She looked into the mouthpiece. The SOCO had fingerprinted that as well.

She tapped the button to get the dial tone back. Could she really make this call?

. . . And what's the story, Fay?

It's very bizarre, Gavin. The fact is, I've discovered there are no dogs in Crybbe.

No dogs in Crybbe.

None at all. That is, except one.

Just the one.

Yes, mine. That's how I found out.

I see. And how come there are no dogs in Crybbe, Fay?

Because they howl at the curfew bell, Gavin. People don't like that.

That figures. But if there are no dogs in Crybbe, how do you know they howl at the curfew?

Well, I don't. I'm assuming that's the case, because Arnold howls at it. That's Arnold, my dog. Least, I think he's my dog.

Yes, well, thank you very much, Fay. Look, this illness your old man's got. This dementia. Anything hereditary there, by any chance?

"Oh *God!*"

Fay crashed the phone down.

Arnold lay at her feet, an ungainly black and white thing with monster ears and big, expressive eyes.

The only dog in Crybbe.

This morning, Fay had gone out soon after dawn into an intermittent drizzle. She'd followed a milkman, at whom no dogs had barked no matter how carelessly he clanked his bottles. She'd followed a postman, whose trousers were unfrayed and who whistled as he walked up garden paths to drop letters through letter boxes and onto doormats, where they lay unmolested by dogs.

She'd walked down by the river, where there was a small stretch of parkland with swings for the children and no signs warning dog owners not to allow their nonexistent pets to foul the play area.

Finally, at around eight-fifteen, she'd approached a group of teenagers waiting for the bus to take them to the secondary school nine miles away.

"Does any of you have a dog?"

The kids looked at each other. Some of them grinned, some shrugged, and some just looked stupid.

"You know me, I'm a reporter. I work for Offa's Dyke Radio. I need to borrow a dog for an item I'm doing. Can any of you help me?"

"What kind of dog you want?"

"Any kind of dog. Doberman . . . Chihuahua . . . giant, wire-haired poodle."

"My sister, she had a dog once."

"What happened to it?"

"Ran away, I think."

"We 'ad a dog, we did."

"Where's it now?"

"Ran off."

"I was your dog, *I'd* run off," another kid said, and the first kid punched him on the shoulder.

"Listen, what about farm dogs? Mr. Preece, has he got a sheepdog?"

"Got one o' them Bobcats."

"What?"

"Like a little go-kart thing with four-wheel drive. Goes over hills. You got one o' them, you don't need no sheepdog, see."

"Yes," Fay had said. "I think I see."

She didn't see at all.

* * *

Powys left Crybbe before seven and was back before ten, a changed man.

He wore a suit which was relatively uncreased. His shoes were polished, his hair brushed. He was freshly shaven.

He parked his nine-year-old Mini well out of sight, in the old cattle market behind the square, and walked across to the Cock, carrying a plausible-looking black folder under his arm.

Taking Rachel's advice.

"Don't let him see you like that. You have to meet his image of J. M. Powys, so if you can't look older, at least look smarter. Don't let him see the car; he mustn't think you need the money—he's always suspicious of people who aren't rich. And you don't know anything about his plans."

"Isn't Humble, the New Age minder, going to tell him he caught me nosing around?"

"I think not."

He entered the low-ceilinged lobby of the Cock, where all the furniture was varnished so thickly that you could hardly tell one piece from another. It was like sitting in a tray of dark chocolates left on a radiator. Powys wedged himself into what he assumed to be an oak settle, to wait for Rachel.

Guy Morrison would be here, she'd told him, starting work on a documentary. He'd once worked with Guy on a series of three-minute silly-season items on Ancient Mysteries of the West for a Bristol-based regional magazine program—J. M. Powys hired as the regular "expert interviewee." His clearest memory was of the day he'd suggested they look beyond the obvious. Taking Guy down to Dartmoor to see a newly discovered stone row believed to be oriented to the rising moon. He remembered the TV reporter looking down with disdain at the ragged line of stones, none more than eighteen inches high, barely below the level of his hand-stitched hiking boots. "Let's move on," Guy had said, affronted. "I'm not doing a piece-to-camera in front of *that.*"

Presently, the Cock's taciturn owner, Denzil George, emerged from some sanctum and glanced across. He displayed no sign of recognition. Still been in bed, presumably, when Powys was sliding out of a side door into the alley just after six-thirty this morning.

" . . . do for you?" Denzil said heavily. Powys thought of some shambling medieval innkeeper, black-jowled, scowling, lumpen-browed.

"Nothing at all, thanks, mate. I'm waiting for . . . ah, this lady, I think."

Rachel had appeared on the stairs, sleek in a dark-blue business suit. "Mr. Powys?"

"Good morning. Am I too early?"

"Only a little. We're terribly glad you were able to make it. Mr. George, I'm taking Mr. Powys along to the Court, so if Mr. Goff calls in, tell him we've gone on ahead, will you? And lunch as arranged, OK?"

Rachel tossed a brilliant smile at the owner, and Denzil stumped back into his lair, where Powys imagined him breakfasting on a whole loaf of bread without slicing it.

"Very svelte," said Rachel, surveying Powys on the steps outside.

"You're surprised, aren't you? You thought I probably hadn't worn a suit since the seventies. You thought it was going to be the wide lapels and the kipper tie."

"Had a momentary fear of flares, then decided you were too young," Rachel said flatteringly. "Come along, J.M."

A few minutes later he was admiring her thighs pistoning in and out of the dark skirt, as she drove the Range Rover, impatiently pumping the clutch, long fingers carelessly crooked around the wheel.

"We're going to the Court?"

"Couple of hours before they all arrive. I thought you'd like to see the setup, or lack of one."

She drove directly across the square and then thrust the vehicle into a narrow fork beside the church. Powys remembered coming out of this lane last night in the same seat, nursing his nose, feeling foolish.

The nose still hurt. But this morning, he thought, with a kind of wonder, he was feeling more . . . well, more focused than he had in years.

And he wanted to know more about Rachel.

She swung the Range Rover between stone gateposts, briefing him about today's lunch. "Informal gathering of the people at the core of the venture. New Age luminaries. A few supportive locals—newcomers, mostly. And Max's advisers."

"Andy Boulton-Trow?"

Rachel parked in the courtyard. "Of course, you know him."

"All earth-mysteries people know each other. Andy—we were at art college together, which is where *The Old Golden Land* started. Both got into mystical landscapes. Auras around stone circles, Samuel Palmer moons over burial mounds on the Downs. Andy was a mature student, he'd already been to university."

"He seems a very deep guy. Laid-back."

"I suppose so," said Powys.

"Max says Boulton-Trow's knowledge of stones and prehistoric shamanic rituals is second to none."

"Yeah, possibly."

"But you wrote the book," Rachel said.

Powys smiled. "And professes to despise commercial books on earth mysteries. Comes from not needing the money."

"Private income?"

"Inherited wealth. Something like that. Never discussed it."

Rachel said, "And who's Rose Hart?"

"She took the pictures for the book," Powys said quietly.

Rachel made no move to get out of the vehicle.

"There were four of us," Powys said, looking straight through the windshield. "Sometimes five. Andy and me and Rose, who was studying photography, and Ben Corby, who thought of the title—comes from an old Incredible String Band song—and sold the idea to a publisher."

He paused. "Rose was my girlfriend. She's dead."

"Don't talk about it if you don't want to," Rachel said. "Come and look at the crumbling pile before the others arrive."

Rachel had keys to the Court. One was so big it made her bag bulge. "Watch where you're stepping when we go in. It's dark."

Not too dark to find Rachel's lips.

"Thanks," he said quietly.

Rachel didn't move. The house was silent around them.

Back from the town, around midmorning, Fay came in quietly through the kitchen door; Arnold didn't bark. He was shut in the kitchen with Rasputin, who was glaring at him from a chair. Arnold seemed glad to see her; he wagged his tail and planted his front paws on her sweater.

"Good boy," Fay said.

Then she heard the wailing. A sound which clutched at her like pleading fingers.

Dad?

"Stay there," she hissed. "Stay."

Wailing. The only word for it. Not the sound of a man in physical pain, not illness, not injury.

She moved quietly into the hallway. The office door, two yards away, was ajar. Little was visible through the gap; the curtains were drawn, as they might be, she thought, in a room where a corpse is laid out.

Her movements stiff with dread, Fay removed her shoes, padded to the door, and peeped in.

In the office, in the dead woman's sitting room, the drawn curtains screening him from the street, Canon Alex Peters was sobbing his old heart out.

He was on his knees, bent over the slender wooden arm of the fireside chair in which Grace Legge had seemed to materialize. His head was bowed in his arms and his ample shoulders trembled like a clifftop before an avalanche.

Fay just stood there. She ought to know what to do, how to react, but she didn't. She'd never known her dad to cry before. When he'd displayed emotions, they were always healthy, masculine emotions. Bluff, strong, kindly stuff.

In fact, not emotions at all really. Because most of the time Alex, like many clergymen, was an actor in a lot of little one-man playlets put on for the sick, the bereaved, and the hopeless.

He'd be mortified if he thought she'd seen him like this. Fay crept back across the hall. It was so unbearably sad. So sad and so crazy.

So unhealthy.

So desperately wrong.

She moved silently back into the kitchen and attached Arnold's clothesline to his collar. "Let's go for a walk," she whispered. "Come back in an hour and make a lot of noise."

As she slowly turned the back-door handle, a trailing moan echoed from the office.

"I will," Alex sobbed. "I'll get rid of her. I'll make her go."

His quavering voice rose and swelled and seemed to fill the

whole house. A voice that, if heard in church, would freeze a congregation to its pews, cried out, "Just—please—don't hurt her!"

Fay walked away from this, quickly.

two

✤ ─────────────────────────────────────

There really was a rope dangling from the steepest part of the roof. Powys could just about reach its frayed end.

"Careful," Rachel warned. "You'll fall into the pit."

The rope felt dry and stiff. "This is a touch of black humor?"

"Well, it's obviously not the original rope, J.M. Somebody probably put it there to hold on to, while doing repairs or something. Creepy up here, though, isn't it?"

The attic was vast. There were small stabs of blinding daylight here and there, signifying holes in the roof or missing slates. Underfoot, jagged gaps through which you could see the boarded floor of the room beneath.

"I don't know why I brought you up here, really," Rachel said. "I usually avoid this bit—*not* that I'm superstitious."

She was spotlit by two thin beams from roof gaps. He remembered her standing next to him, naked, in the window last night, pale, slim, silvery. She'd brought a small flashlight, and he shone it to the upper extremity of the rope, where it was tied around a beam.

"How many poor bastards did the Hanging Sheriff dispose of up here?"

"Hard to say, he was only sheriff for a year. But you could be hanged for most things in those days. Stealing cattle or sheep, picking your nose in church . . . "

"That's how Wort got his rocks off, do you think? Watching people dangle?"

Rachel wrinkled her nose in distaste. "They say he was obsessed with what you might call the mechanics of mortality, what happens the moment the spirit leaves the body. Him and his friend, John Dee."

"Not *the* John Dee?"

"The guy who was Elizabeth I's astrologer. His old family home's along the valley."

"Of course it is," said Powys, remembering. "It's a farm now. I went over there when I was doing *Golden Land.* Somebody told me Dee had been into ancient sites and dowsing."

"Well, he must have been into hanging, too," Rachel said. "If he was a mate of Michael Wort's."

A jet of wind flew across the attic with a thin whine like a distant baby's crying. The rope started to sway, very slowly.

Powys said, "He was certainly into magic, but back in the sixteenth century magic and science were filed in the same drawer."

He put out a hand to stop the rope swinging. He didn't like this rope with its dangling strands—somehow more disturbing than if there'd been an actual noose on the end. A sense of something recently severed.

"Anyway," said Rachel, "the last hanging up here was Wort's own. There was some sort of peasants' revolt in the town, and one night they all gathered outside wielding flaming torches and threatening to burn the place down unless he came out."

"We know you're in there . . . " Powys said flippantly, still holding the rope, not feeling at all flippant.

"So he shuffled up here and offed himself. That's one story. Another says there was a secret tunnel linking this place with Crybbe church and he escaped."

"Where was he buried?"

"I don't know," Rachel said. "I never really thought about it. Probably at some crossroads with a stake through his heart, wouldn't you think? Naturally, they say he haunts the place—or rather his dog does."

"This place?"

"The town. The outskirts. The quiet lanes at sunset. Over the years, according to Max, people have claimed to come face-to-face with this big black dog with glowing eyes. And then they die, of course. Like in *The Hound of the Baskervilles.*"

Powys took his hand away from the rope, and it began to swing again, very gently.

"Rachel, luv," he said, "can you hear voices?"

"Shit." Rachel moved to the stairs. "Nobody was supposed to be here for another hour."

She went swiftly down the steps, Powys following, not wanting to be left alone up here, where Rachel believed the only danger was the unstable floor. Blessed are the skeptics. For they shall be oblivious of the numinous layers, largely unaffected by the dreary density of places, unbowed by the deadweight of ancient horror. Lucky bastards.

While people like me, he thought, would no more come up here alone than pop into a working abattoir to shelter from the rain.

Only a short way down the stairs, Rachel disappeared.

Powys shone the torch down the twisting stone steps. The beam just reached to the great oak door at the bottom.

"Rachel!" He felt panic in his throat, like sandpaper. There was a creak to his left; he spun around and the beam found a shadowed alcove he hadn't noticed on the way up here.

Suddenly, white light blasted him and he hid his eyes behind an arm.

"This," Rachel said, from somewhere, "is the only part of the house I really like."

"What's known as a prospect chamber."

The window directly facing them, almost floor to ceiling, was without glass. In fact, it wasn't really a window, simply a gap between two ivy-matted gables. A rusting iron bar was cemented into the gap at chest height.

The prospect chamber was tiny, too small for any furniture. But it had a view.

Powys's eyes widened.

He saw they were directly above the cobbled forecourt. Then there were the two gateposts and then the straight road through the wood. Over the tops of the trees he could see the weathercock on the church tower.

Without the wood, the town would be at his feet.

And everything—the gateway, the road, the church—was in a dead straight line.

He'd seen this view before.

In fact, if he turned and looked over his shoulder . . .

He *did* turn and looked only into blackness.

But if he could see through the walls of the house, what he would see behind him, following the same dead straight line . . . would be the Tump.

"Is this opening as old as the house?"

"I presume so," Rachel said. "Spectacular, isn't it?"

"Which means Wort had it built. Maybe *this* is why John Dee came here, nothing to do with the bloody hangings. Rachel, have you ever actually *seen* a ley-line?"

"This?"

"It's textbook. In fact . . . " He leaned across the iron bar, not pushing it because it didn't look too steady. "This is the strongest evidence I've seen that the ley system was recognized in Elizabethan times. We know that John Dee occasionally came back to his old home and during those times he studied dowsing and investigated old churches and castle sites. He called it, in his records and his letters, treasure hunting. But what kind of treasure, Rachel? You know, what I think . . . "

He stopped. There were the voices again.

"Humble," Rachel said. "And somebody else."

Powys's stomach contracted painfully.

"I don't think Humble actually got round to apologizing to you, did he?" said Rachel.

"I owe him one."

"Don't even contemplate it. He's a very nasty person. Ah, they were waiting for Max."

The black Ferrari hit the gravel with an emphatic crunch. Humble stepped out and opened the driver's door. Andy Boulton-Trow was with him.

"I don't like the company he keeps either," Powys said.

"Humble? Or Boulton-Trow?"

"Either."

Rachel said, "Is there something I don't know about you and Boulton-Trow?"

> *Joey goes round the Bottle Stone,*
> *The Bottle Stone, the Bottle Stone,*
> *Joey goes round the Bottle Stone,*
> *And he goes round . . .*

"Hold it!"
They all look at Andy.

"It's widdershins," he says.

"What?" says Ben.

"Widdershins. Anticlockwise. You're going round the wrong way, Joe."

"Why?"

"Because that's what you have to do. I was watching a bunch of kids. It's traditional. Widdershins, OK?"

You shrug, but you aren't entirely happy about this. Old Henry Kettle gets up, turns his back, and walks off, down toward the river.

"OK," Ben says. "Start again."

Sod it. Only a game. You start to tramp slowly around the stone. There's a smile on your face because what you're thinking about is how much you love Rose and how glad you are that they managed to get her name on the cover.

And he goes round . . . ONCE.

When Guy came to the door, Fay simply pretended there was nobody in, knowing it had to be her ex-husband calling in on the way to his lunch date with Max Goff and his cohorts.

Knowing, also, that if Guy was in the mood he was arrogant enough to have lined her up as today's emergency standby leg-over. *Fay, hi! (Long time, no bonk!)*

Behind the bathroom door she clenched her fists.

There was a second ring.

Fay sat on the toilet with the lid down. The lid was still topped by one of Grace's dinky little light-green Candlewick loo-mats.

Grace. Her dad thought that Grace Legge, dead, had smashed the Revox. Somehow. It was insane. And there was no way they could talk about it.

There was no third ring.

Arnold sat at Fay's feet and wagged his tail. He never reacted to the doorbell.

Only the curfew bell.

"Arnold," Fay said, "do you want to talk about this?"

Arnold looked at her with sorrowful eyes. Even when his tail was wagging his eyes were sorrowful.

She held his muzzle between her hands. She couldn't remember ever feeling so confused, so helpless. So completely wiped out.

The phone rang in the office. Fay drifted down to answer it, not in any hurry. She wished she'd put on the answering machine, but the thing had been disabled so many times by power cuts that she'd almost abandoned it.

"Hello."

There was a hollow silence at the other end.

"Yes. Hello."

"Mrs. Morrison?" A local accent. Male.

"Yes. Who's that?"

"Mrs. Morrison, you been told."

"Have I? Told what?"

"So this is your last warning, Mrs. Morrison. You 'ave till weekend."

"To do what?"

But, of course, she knew.

"And what if I don't?" Fay said grimly. "What if I say I have no intention of even considering getting rid of the dog? Especially as nobody seems prepared to explain what the hell all this is about?"

"You been told," the voice said. "And that's it."

three

✥ ————————————————————————————

Gomer Parry did plant hire.

He operated from an old wartime aircraft hangar up the valley, outside the village where he lived. In this hangar he had two trucks, the heaviest tractor in the country, a big JCB, and a small JCB and these two bulldozers.

You didn't hire the equipment; what you hired was Gomer Parry, a tough little bloke with mad, gray hair and wire-rimmed glasses.

Been a farmer for nearly twenty years before the magic of plant hire had changed his life. Sold most of his land to buy the old hangar and the machinery. Gomer Parry: sixty-four now, and he never looked back.

Gomer could knock buildings down and make new roads through the forestry. He could dig you a septic tank and a leaching field that soaked away even in Radnorshire clay. And during bad winters, the highways authority always hired him as a snowplow.

This was the only time other people recognized the truly heroic nature of his job. They'd pour out of their homes, dozens of them, as he busted through the last snowdrift to liberate some remote hamlet that'd been cut off for a fortnight. Big cheers. Mug of tea. Glass of Scotch. Good old Gomer.

But last winter had been a mild winter. Bugger all snow anywhere. And only Gomer saw the heroic side of the other things he did.

A few months ago he'd done this broadcast about the perils of digging drainage ditches and such. Explaining it to that little girl from the local radio. How, for him, it was like a military exercise—although not modern military; more like in these epic films where the knight gets into his armor, which is so heavy he has to be winched onto his horse. It was in these terms that Gomer Parry spoke on the radio of his life at the controls of the JCB.

Probably gave the listeners a good laugh. Certainly didn't bring him any more work. He couldn't remember a worse year, the local farmers—his regular clients—tighter than ever. Constipated buggers sitting there waiting for a laxative from Brussels. Farmers wouldn't fart these days unless they got an EC grant for it.

So Gomer Parry, feeling the pinch, had been very near excited when he had a phone call from Edgar Humble.

He'd played darts with Edgar Humble in the public bar at the Lamb in Crybbe. Edgar didn't say much, which was unusual for a Londoner; he just kept beating you at darts. But Gomer knew who employed him, and that was why he was very near excited when he got the call, because from what he'd heard here was a bloke who was going to need plenty of plant hire.

"Knock walls down, can you?" Edgar Humble asked.

"What kind of walls?"

"Stone wall. Victorian, I'd say. Thick, solid. Five, six feet high. Couple of feet thick in places. Too much for yer?"

Gomer had almost laughed down the phone. "Put it this way,"

he said. "If I'd been in business round Jericho way, all those years ago, they wouldn't have needed no bloody trumpets."

"Max," Rachel said, "this is J.M. Powys."

Max Goff put on his Panama hat. Bizarre, Powys thought. Eccentric. But not crazy. Those are not crazy eyes.

Goff looked at Powys for a good while. He had a beard like red Velcro. "How long you been here?"

"Since last night," Powys said steadily. "I stayed at the Cock."

"Yeah? Shit hole, huh? I hope you put it on my tab." Goff grinned at last and stuck out a stubby hand. "Hi, J.M. Welcome to Crybbe. Welcome to the Old Golden Land."

Powys took the hand. Goff's grip was flaccid. Powys said, "You think this is the Old Golden Land?"

The countryside was colorless. Mist was still draped around the Court like grimy lace curtains.

"Not yet," Goff said. "But it will be. Listen, if I'd known you were here I'd've driven back last night."

"That's OK. Ms. Wade was looking after me."

Rachel was standing behind Goff in the courtyard. Powys deliberately didn't look at her. Neither, he noticed, did her boss, the man who overpaid her for little extras.

Goff jerked his Velcro chin at the two men at his side. "This is Edgar Humble, my head of security."

"Mr. Humble," Powys said tightly.

"And Andy Boulton-Trow, who of course you know, yeah?"

Andy wore a white shirt and black jeans. Close up, he looked even thinner than he'd been twelve years ago. You could see the bones flexing in his face as he smiled. It was a quick, wide smile.

It made Powys feel cold.

"Joe."

"Andy," he said quietly.

"Long time, my friend." Andy's hair, once shoulder-length, was shaven right to the skull, and he was growing a beard. It would be black.

They hadn't met since Rose's funeral.

Goff said, "Now Henry Kettle's gone, Andy's my chief adviser in the Crybbe project. Andy knows stones."

Chief adviser. Jesus.

There was a big difference between Andy Boulton-Trow and

Henry Kettle. What it came down to was: Henry would have
said, don't mess with electricity until you know what you're
doing. Andy would say, sure, just hold these two wires and
then bring them together when I give you the nod, OK?

"So you lost Henry," Powys said.

Andy dropped the smile.

"Tragic," Goff said. "There's gonna be a Henry Kettle memorial."

A memorial. Well, that was all right, then. That made up for
everything.

"We haven't decided yet where it's gonna go."

"But somewhere prominent," Andy said.

Powys didn't say a thing.

"J.M.," Goff said, "we need to talk, you and I. At length. I
have a proposition. Hell, we all know each other, I'll spell out
the basics. I want you to write me a sequel to *Golden Land* for
Dolmen. I want it to be the Crybbe story. The—hey, what about
this?—The *New* Golden Land."

Goff beamed and looked around, Powys thought, for applause.

"What I'm talking here, J.M., is a substantial advance and
the quality republication in under a year's time of the original
Golden Land, to pave the way. Revise it if you like. New
pictures. In color. Whatever."

Sure. Scrap Rose's pictures, Powys thought dully. Get better ones.

"And there's a place for you here."

"A place?"

"A place to live. A beautiful house with a view of the river.
Part of the deal. Rachel will take you there after we eat."

"Mr. Goff . . . " He wondered why people kept giving him
houses.

"Max."

"I have a place already. I run a little shop in Hereford called
Trackways, which . . . "

"I know," said Goff.

" . . . which is more than a shop. Which is a kind of museum
to Alfred Watkins as well, the only one of its kind in Hereford,
which . . . "

"But it doesn't *need* to be in Hereford," Goff said. "And it
doesn't have to be a little shop. Come over here."

He led Powys to a corner of the courtyard and pointed across the field behind the stables, about a hundred yards from the Tump, where the trees began to thicken into the wood.

"As befits the stature of the man, the Watkins Centre needs to be a major development in, let's say, an eighteenth-century barn."

On the edge of the wood was a massive, tumbledown barn complex, beams and spars poking out of it like components of a badly assembled dinosaur skeleton.

"Place needs to be big enough to house a huge collection of Watkins's photographs and ley-maps, and scores of original paintings of ancient sites. And it needs to be here. In Crybbe."

Powys felt like a cartoon character who'd been flattened by a steamroller and become a two-dimensional mat.

Lowering his voice, Goff said, "I know your situation, J.M. I know you put all the money from *Golden Land* into Trackways, and I know how difficult it must be keeping Trackways afloat."

He clapped Powys on the back. "Think about it, yeah?"

Goff strolled back to the silent group of three standing next to the Ferrari. "Rach, there's been a slight change of plan. We have lunch at two, we spend the afternoon in discussion groups, then we assemble, early evening, at the Tump."

Powys saw part of a cobweb from the attic floating free from a padded shoulder of Rachel's blue business suit.

"The Tump?"

"A ceremony," Goff said. "To launch the project. We're gonna knock down the wall around the Tump. Maybe that's where Mr. Kettle's memorial should be. We're gonna finish what he began. We're gonna liberate the Tump."

Andy Boulton-Trow nodded.

Goff grinned massively. "It's the beginning," he said. "Come on, let's get back to the Cock, see who shows up."

From the top of the farmyard there was a fine view of the river and the Welsh hills behind. But Jimmy Preece and his son Jack were looking, for once, the other way, up toward the Court. This was a view Jack had been conditioned, over the years, to avoid—as if, when he emerged from the farmyard gates, he was to wear an imaginary patch over his right eye.

This afternoon a great black cloud hung over the Tump.

Below it, the bulldozer was bright yellow.

"Gomer Parry's," Jack said.

"Sure t'be," Jimmy said. "And only one reason 'e's down there."

"So what you gonner do, Father?"

"No choice, Jack. I shall 'ave to 'ave a word with 'im when 'e gets back."

The two men stood in silence for over a minute.

Then Jack mumbled, almost to himself. "Sometimes . . . sometimes I wonders, well, so what? What if 'e *do* come down, that ole wall? An' the ole bell . . . what if 'e *don't* get rung some nights?"

Jimmy Preece was too certain of his son even to reply. Jack was like him. Jonathon was like Jack. And Warren—well, Warren was only a second son, so it didn't matter anyway, about Warren.

The mayor was about to walk away, back into town, when he heard Jack saying,

" . . . And the ole box. If the ole box is gone, do it matter?"

Jimmy Preece stopped and turned and walked back very slowly to where Jack stood, a bigger man than Jimmy, habitually in dark-green overalls.

"The ole box?"

"I don't know, Father, 'e's gone. Maybe. Might've gone. Hard to say, isn't it, without pulling the whole wall out?"

Jimmy Preece said, "Can't 'ave gone, Jack. Sometimes them ole bricks subside. I told you, anyway, leave 'im alone, that ole box. Keep 'im walled up. Tell Jonathon when 'e's thirty and married. Never tell Warren."

"Found some bits of plaster and stuff in the fireplace," Jack said. "Poked about a bit and the bricks fell out the cavity."

"Put 'em back, block 'em up."

"That's what I was doin'. Cavity, though, see, cavity was empty, Father."

"That case, you got a job to do, Jack. You get in there and find where the box's fallen to, then you put 'im back on the ledge and you seals the bugger up proper. And another thing, Jack, you get that dog seen to. Last night . . . "

"I know. Yeard 'im from the belfry even. I phoned 'er up. I give 'er till weekend."

"This is the weekend," said Jimmy Preece. "Get Jonathon to do it."

Jack Preece looked down at his boots. "Gets to me sometimes, Father, that's all. Why us?"

He walked off without saying goodbye, because none of the
Preeces ever said goodbye to each other; only " 'Ow're you" on
Christmas morning.

four

❖ ───

The one time Rachel had seen Guy Morrison, at a preliminary
meeting with Max in London, he'd been wearing a lightweight
suit with sunglasses in the breast pocket and carrying a briefcase
and a mobile phone.

Today, Guy was in director mode. He wore denims and a
leather pouch, like a holster, on his belt. He had blond hair
and craggy features. A TV man from central casting, Rachel
thought. At his shoulder stood a dumpy, stern-faced girl with
straight black hair and a waterproof clipboard.

Hustling J.M. off to the Cock, Goff had told Rachel over
his shoulder, "Morrison wants to do a few exterior shots of
the Court with nobody about. Stick around till he shows, Rach,
keep an eye on him."

"Who is this, Catrin?" Guy Morrison asked the black-haired
girl in Rachel's hearing. "Remind me."

"Guy, this is Rachel Wade, Max's PA." Catrin's accent had
a clipped sibilance Rachel identified as northwest Wales.

"Of course, yes."

Rachel offered him a languid hand. "We've spoken on the
phone."

Guy Morrison took the hand and held it limply for an extra
moment, looking steadily, unsmiling, into her eyes. "You're
almost everything your voice implied, Rachel Wade."

"Good," said Rachel, with a tight, tired smile.

Guy Morrison dropped Rachel's hand, stepped back, looked
around the courtyard, then up into the sky again, where clouds
and mist still formed a damp canopy.

He frowned. "I wanted some GVs today. Establishing shots. But this weather's not conducive. At all. So I've told the crew, Rachel Wade, to set up in that stable place. Acceptable to you, yes?"

"Fine."

"Because what I thought I'd do after lunch is bang off a brief opening interview with Max Goff. Background of sawing and rubble everywhere. Traces of sawdust on the white suit, emphasizing the hands-on approach. May not use it, but I'm not happy unless there's something in the can on Day One."

"You'd better see how he feels about that."

Guy Morrison nodded and turned away. She watched him pace the courtyard, looking up at the hills fading into mist and at the Court itself, gray and spectral in its small hollow, like an old galleon half sunk into a mud flat.

When they arrived back at the Cock, close to 1 P.M., a car was being parked on the square, close to the steps: a silver-gray Ford Escort with an Offa's Dyke Radio sticker on its windshield.

The driver got out and came over.

"Rachel, is it? Could I just have a word?"

Guy Morrison, peering at the car sticker and registering it was only local radio, went ahead, up the steps, with his assistant.

"I'm from Offa's Dyke Radio. We carried a report yesterday without checking the details with you."

Rachel had never seen this person before. He was a short-ish, muscular man, about twenty-five, with a half-grown mustache.

"Word reached me you weren't happy about what went out, and I just want you to know I've looked into it. Gavin Ashpole. News Editor. You'll be seeing more of me."

"Good," said Rachel dismissively. "Now if . . . "

"Problem is, we've been using a freelance, Fay Morrison, in Crybbe, but it hasn't been working out."

"Apart from this one instance," Rachel said, "I don't think . . . "

"So, from now on, any *major* stories in this area, we're going to handle direct. What Mr. Goff's doing amounts to a major story, naturally, so if there's anything you want to say, anything you want to get out on Offa's Dyke Radio, you call me direct. Here's my card."

"Thank you."

"In fact—this is off the record—we're considering putting a staff reporter into Crybbe. Especially if your thing takes off and the population starts to expand."

"Really."

"In which case"—Ashpole spread his hands, palms down in a flat, cutting movement—"we'd simply stop using Morrison altogether."

"I see," Rachel said.

What an appalling little creep, she thought.

Over a bland buffet lunch—carnivores catered for, but strictly no smoking—Max Goff explained his plan to publish, in perhaps two years' time, *The Book of Crybbe*.

"Gonna be an illustrated record of the project," said Goff. He paused and looked into his audience. "And a blueprint for the Third Millennium."

Warm applause. They'd needed extra tables in the dining room at the Cock.

Goff said, "I've asked J. M. Powys to write the book. Because his work remains, to my mind, the most inspiring evocation of a country still able to make contact with its inner self."

Powys smiled modestly. The magical, mystical J. M. Powys. Too old, he thought miserably, to become someone else. Too young not to want to.

About forty people were there, some from London and elsewhere, to hear about the project and consider getting involved. Thin, earnest men in clean jeans and sneakers and women in long skirts and symbolic New Age jewelry. Powys didn't know most of them. But he felt, dispiritedly, that he'd met them all before.

There was a delicate-looking tarot reader called Ivory with a wife old enough to be his mother and big enough to be his minder. A feminist astrologer called Oona Jopson, in whose charts, apparently, Virgo was a man. She had cropped hair and a small ring through her nose.

After Goff sat down, Powys listened idly to the chat. He heard an experimental hypnotist talking about regression. "I've got an absolute queue of clients, mostly, you know, from London, but what I'd really like is to get more of the *local* people on the couch . . . "

Apart from Andy Boulton-Trow, the only person he'd actually encountered before was the spiritual healer, Jean Wendle, from Edinburgh, who was older than the rest, gray-haired with penetrating eyes.

"This really your scene, Jean?"

"This? Heaven forbid. Crybbe, though . . . Crybbe's interesting."

"You reckon?"

"Well, goodness, Joe, you said it. If you hadn't revealed what a psychically charged area this was, none of us would be here at all, would we?"

"You're very cruel."

She narrowed her eyes. "Come round one night. We can discuss it. Anyway . . . " She smiled at him. "How are things now?"

He looked around the room for Rachel, couldn't see her.

"I think things are finally looking up," he said.

Later, Goff took him into a corner of the dining room and lowered his voice.

"Confidentially," he said, "I need somebody who understands these matters to make sure this arsehole Morrison doesn't screw up. Part of the deal, he uses you as script consultant. No J. M. Powys, no documentary. J. M. Powys disagrees with anything, it doesn't go out."

"That'll be fun."

Goff put a hand on Powys's arm. "Hey, you know when I first knew I had to have you write the book?"

Powys smiled vacantly, beyond embarrassment.

"See, when I first came to Crybbe, the very first day I was here, I look around and suddenly I can see this about the border country being a spiritual departure lounge. I'm standing down by the river, looking over the town to the hills of England on one side and the hills of Wales on the other. And that other phrase of yours, about the Celtic Twilight Zone, I'm hearing that, and I'm thinking, yeah, this is it. The departure lounge. It just needs a refuel, right? You know what I'm getting at here? You can feel it in this room right now. All these people, all reaching out."

"Maybe they're reaching out for different things."

"Ah shit, J.M., it's all one thing. *You* know that. Down to generating energy and throwing it out. What you put out you get back, threefold. Jeez, pretty soon, this town is gonna *glow.*"

*   *   *

"Seems to me there are things you need to work out, Joe," Andy Boulton-Trow said. "Maybe this is the place to do it."

Those lazy, knowing, dark-brown eyes gazing into your head again, after all these years. I can see your inner self, and it's a mess, man.

Andy was probably Goff's role-model New Ager. He had the glow. Like he'd slowed his metabolism to the point where he was simply too laid-back to be affected by the aging process.

"Let's talk," Andy said, and they took their wineglasses into the small, shabby residents' lounge just off the dining room.

Andy lounged back on a moth-eaten sofa, both feet on a battered coffee table. Somehow, he made it look like the lotus position.

He said, "Never got over it, did you?"

Powys rolled his wineglass between his hands, looking down into it.

"I mean Rose," Andy said.

"It was a long time ago. You get over everything in time."

Andy shook his head. "You're still full of shit, Joe, you know that?"

"Look," Powys said reasonably, trying to be as cool as Andy. "We both know I should never have gone round the Bottle Stone. And certainly not backwards."

"Bottle Stone?" Andy said.

"And certainly not backwards. I should have told you to piss off."

"I'm not getting you," Andy said.

"What I saw was . . . " Powys felt pain like powdered glass behind his eyes. "What I saw was happening to *me,* not Rose."

"You had some kind of premonition? About Rose?"

"I told you about it."

Andy shrugged. "You had a premonition about Rose. But you didn't act on it, huh?"

"It was *me.*"

"You failed to interpret. That's a shame, Joe. You had a warning, you didn't react, and that's what's eating you up. Perhaps you've come here to find some manner of redemption."

Andy shook his head with a kind of laid-back compassion.

*   *   *

If it was a big job, Gomer Parry worked with his nephew, Nev.
Today Nev had just followed him up in the van and they'd got
the smaller bulldozer down from the truck, and then Nev had
pushed off.

No need for a second man. Piece of piss, this one.

Unless, of course, they wanted him to take out the whole
bloody mound.

Gomer chuckled. He could do that too, if it came to it.

He was sitting in the cab of the truck, listening to Glenn Miller
on his Walkman. The bulldozer was in the field, fueled up,
waiting. Not far away was a van with a couple of loudspeakers
on its roof, such as you saw on the street at election time. Funny
job this. Had to be on site at one o'clock to receive his precise
instructions. Seemed some middle bit had to come out first.
Make a big thing of it, Edgar Humble had said. A spectacle.
No complaints there; Gomer liked a bit of spectacle.

With the Walkman on, he didn't hear any banging on the
cab door. It was the vibrations told him somebody was trying
to attract his attention.

He took off the lightweight headphones, half turned, and saw
an old checked cap with a square patch on the crown, where a
tear had been mended. Gomer, who was a connoisseur of caps,
recognized it at once and opened his door.

"Jim."

"What you doin' yere, Gomer?" the mayor, Jimmy Preece,
asked him bluntly.

"I been hired by that Goff," Gomer said proudly. "He wants
that bloody wall taken out, he does."

"Does he. Does he indeed."

"Some'ing wrong with that, Jim? You puttin' a bid in for the
stone? Want me to go careful, is it?"

Jimmy Preece took off his cap and scratched his head. Even
though it was still drizzling, he didn't put the cap back on but
rolled it up tighter and tighter with both hands.

"I don't want you doin' it at all, Gomer," he said. "I want
that wall left up."

"Oh aye?" Gomer said sarcastically. "Belongs to you, that
wall, is it?"

The mayor's eyes were watery as raw eggs. "You're not
allowed, take it from me, Gomer, that's a fact. Been there

for centuries, that wall. He'll have a protection order on 'im, sure to."

"Balls," said Gomer. "I was told he was Victorian, no older'n that."

"Well, you was told wrong, Gomer. See, I don't want no argument about this. No bad feeling. Just want you to know that we, that is, me and Jack and several other prominent citizens of this area, includin' several farmers and civic leaders, would prefer it if the wall stayed up."

Gomer couldn't believe it.

"Just 'ang on, Jim, so's I gets this right. You're sayin' if I falls that thing, then . . . "

Jimmy Preece tightened his old lips until his mouth looked like a complicated railway junction.

"You bloody well knowed why I was yere, di'n't you?" said Gomer. "You knowed exac'ly."

"I been invited," the mayor said sadly. "That Goff, 'e phone me up and invited me to watch. Silly bugger."

"So what you're sayin', if I brings him down, that wall, you'll . . . "

"I'm not sayin' nothin'," the mayor said firmly. "I got no authority to order you about, and I don't intend . . . "

"Oh no, Jim, you're only bloody threatenin' me! You're sayin' if I starts workin' for Goff, then I don't get no work nowhere else around yere. Right?"

Gomer leveled a grimy forefinger at the mayor. "You bloody stay there! Don't you bloody move! I'll get a witness, an' you can say it again in front of 'im."

The mayor said calmly, "You won't find no witnesses in this town as'll say I threatened you, Gomer, 'cause I 'aven't. You can do what the hell you likes for Mr. Goff."

" 'Cept pull that wall down, eh?"

" 'Cept pull that wall down," the mayor agreed.

five

"What have you got to lose?" Rachel had asked him, and he wondered about this.

The cottage was on a little grassy ridge, overlooking the river. Rachel told him Max had been so taken with the little place he'd thought of spending nights here himself until work on the stable block was finished. But, with extra builders, overtime, bonuses, it looked as if the stables would be habitable within the next few days. And Max had to spend a long weekend in London, anyway.

"So it's yours," Rachel said. "If you want it."

It had only four rooms. Kitchen, bathroom, bedroom, and this small, square living room, with a panoramic, double-glazed view downstream.

"A writer's dream," Rachel said noncommittally.

"Furnished, too," Powys said.

"It was a second home. The first thing Max's agent did was to acquire a list of local holiday homes and write to the owners offering disproportionate sums for a complete deal, basic furniture included. Just over a third of them said yes within two days—boredom setting in, wouldn't it be nice to have one in Cornwall instead? Then, out of the blue, here's Fairy Godfather Goff with a sack of cash."

"And you say he's in London for the weekend?"

"That's the plan," Rachel said. "But—you may be glad to hear, or not—I'm staying."

Powys kissed her.

"Mmm. I'm staying because there's a public meeting to organize for next week. The people of Crybbe come face-to-face with their savior for the first time and learn what the New Age has to offer *them.*"

"Should be illuminating. You think any of them know what New Age means?"

"J.M., even *I* don't know what it means. Do you?"

"All I was thinking, if it involves having big stones planted in their gardens, country folk can be a tiny bit superstitious. Especially stones their ancestors already got rid of once."

Rachel perched on the edge of a little Jotul wood-burning stove. She licked a forefinger and made the motions of counting out paper money. "Rarely fails," she said. "And if they're really superstitious, they can always move out and sell Max the farm for . . ."

"A suitably disproportionate sum," said Powys. "It's another world, isn't it? So, er, you'll be on your own this weekend."

Rachel moved a hip. She was wearing tight wine-colored jeans and a white blouse. "Max suggests I move out of the Cock and into the stables."

"But nobody'll be there to know one way or the other, will they?" Powys had been quite taken with the reproduction brass bed upstairs.

"There's Humble, in his caravan. He doesn't like me."

"Does he like anybody?"

"Debatable," said Rachel.

"I'm sure we can work something out. What's the rent on this place, by the way?"

"I think it's part of the advance against royalties. There'll be an agreement for you to sign. This gives you a small—small to Max, but not necessarily to you—lump sum as well. If you don't finish *The Book of Crybbe* he gets the cottage back. He also reserves the right to install standing stones or other ritual artifacts on your lawn."

"Rachel, luv, help me. What do I do?"

"My advice? Take it, but ask for a bigger lump sum. He won't double-cross you. He's a very determined man. This town does *not* know what's hit it. Not yet. I'd feel better if you were here as some sort of fifth column. He'll listen to you."

Powys shook his head, bemused.

Perhaps you've come here to find some manner of redemption.

Perhaps.

All he had to do was make one phone call and Annie would dive on the chance of taking over Trackways for an unspecified period. Just her and Alfred Watkins and an ever-broadening selection of New Age trivia. It might even start making a reasonable profit.

Rachel said, "One more thing. If you'd like a word processor, please specify the make and model, to match your existing software."

Powys thought about this, chin in hands, patched elbow on the pine dining table. "New ribbon for the Olivetti."

When they reached the Tump, they split up, for the sake of appearances. It was 7 P.M. The rain was holding off, but the evening was very still and close, the sky hanging low, looking for trouble.

Rachel looked around and saw quite a big semicircle of people, many more than had been at the lunch.

Word had got around that something was going to happen. Word very soon got around in this town, she'd found.

"What's going on, Ms. Wade?" Jocasta Newsome was posing dramatically against the lowering sky in a glistening new ankle-length Barbour, conspicuously more expensive than Rachel's.

"Max is going to get rid of the wall around the Tump."

"Oh," said Jocasta, disappointed. "That's all?"

"It's a major symbolic gesture," Rachel said patiently.

"Is that a television camera?"

"They're making a documentary about Max."

"Oh." Jocasta brightened. "That's, er . . . oh, Guy Morrison, isn't it? I think he's rather good, don't you?"

"Yes, excellent," Rachel said absently. "Excuse me."

She'd seen Fay on the edge of the field, with the dog still on the end of a clothesline. Fay looked forlorn in a royal-blue raincoat that was too long for her. She wore no makeup and her hair was damp and flattened.

"I know," she said. "Don't tell me. He's here."

"Do you mean Guy? Or the Offa's Dyke man?"

Fay raised both eyebrows. "Surrounded, am I?"

"I'm sorry about this, Fay, I really am."

"They rang me," Fay said. "Offa's Dyke rang and said, don't bother with it, we're covered. I think they're trying to edge me out."

"Ashpole's a tedious little man."

"Poisonous," Fay said.

"Fay, look, perhaps there's something . . . " If she could somehow turn Max around, fix it so he'd just talk to Fay. Most unlikely.

"Not your problem, Rachel, if I can't function here. Tempted to blame it on the town, but that's the easy answer, isn't it?" Fay grinned. "If you really want to do something, I suppose you could suggest Ashpole might get some terrific actuality of the wall coming down if he stood directly beneath it . . . "

She wound the end of the clothesline more firmly around her hand. "Come on, Arnold, we'll go down by the river."

Max Goff was on the summit of the Tump. He had a microphone on a long lead. The dripping trees were gathered around him.

Crouched under a bush, Guy Morrison's cameraman was shooting Goff from a low angle. It would look very dramatic, this apparition in white against the deep-gray sky and the black trees. On his knees next to Goff, as if in worship, Guy's soundman held a two-foot boom mike encased in a wind barrier like a giant furry caterpillar.

There were two big speakers on the roof of a van at the foot of the mound.

"This has been a dramatic and tragic week," said Goff.

"Yeah, not too bad for level," the soundman said.

"It fucking better be, pal," the assembly heard. "I'm not saying it again."

Behind the speaker van, Powys smiled.

Guy Morrison said, "I'm not pleased with him, Joe. He dropped this on me without any warning at all. A spontaneous idea, he said. He's got to learn that if he wants spontaneity we have *got* to know about it in advance."

I have always disliked the Tump for some reason.

Powys thought, What does the wall mean, Henry? Why is there a wall around it?

He scrambled across the field, away from the crowd, unable to shake the feeling that perhaps getting rid of the wall was not the best thing to do—but wondering whether this feeling had been conditioned by Henry's misgivings about the mound.

Halfway across the field he saw the hubcap from Henry's Volkswagen, glinting in a bed of thistles. It reminded him that his own car was still parked alongside the road at the end of this field.

Henry's journal was in the car.

Bloody stupid thing to do. Anybody could have nicked the car, gone off with the journal.

Behind him Goff's voice boomed out of the speakers. "I'm glad-ad that-at so many of you were able to come today-ay."

Powys moved swiftly through wet grass toward the road. He reached it at a point about fifty yards from the roadside. The white Mini was there; it looked OK.

"Is that your car?"

A lone bungalow of flesh-colored bricks squatted next to the roadside, and at the end of its short drive stood a stocky, elderly woman in a sweater and a tartan skirt, an ensemble which spelled out: new arrival.

"Yes, it is," Powys said, taking out his keys to prove it; unlocking the trunk.

"You arrived just in time, dear, I was about to report it to the police."

"Yes, I'm sorry, I got delayed."

Actually, I was beaten up and then went to bed with a woman I'd never seen before but whose voice I'd heard on my answering machine, but you don't want to hear about all that.

Henry Kettle's journal lay where he'd left it, on top of the spare tire.

"What's going on over there?" She had a Midlands accent.

"They're pulling down the wall around the mound."

"Why are they doing that?"

Did she really want to know this? "Well, because it's a bit ugly. And out of period with the Tump. That's what they say."

"I'll tell you one thing, dear, that wall's never as ugly as the thing in the middle. I don't like that thing, I don't at all. My husband, he used to say, when he was alive, he used to say he'd seen prettier spoil-heaps."

"He had a point," Powys said, opening the driver's door.

"I'm on me own now, dear. It frightens me, the things that go on. I'd leave tomorrow, but I wouldn't anywhere near get our money back on this place, not the way the market is. It wouldn't buy me a maisonette in Dudley."

Powys closed the car door and walked over.

"What did you mean, it frightens you?"

"You from the local paper, dear?"

"No, I'm . . ."

A shopkeeper.

"I'm a writer. My name's Joe Powys."

"I've never heard of you, my love, but don't take it to heart. Mrs. Seagrove, Minnie Seagrove. Would you like a cup of tea? I'm always making tea for people in that lay-by. Truck drivers, all sorts."

"I won't put you to that kind of trouble," said Powys. "But I would like to know what, specifically, frightens you about that mound?"

Mrs. Seagrove smiled coyly. "You'll think I'm daft. That girl from the local radio thinks I'm daft. I ring her sometimes, when it gets on top of me, the things that go on."

"What things are those? I'll tell you honestly, Mrs. Seagrove, I'm the last person who's going to think you're daft."

Following the river, Fay walked Arnold down the field, toward the bridge, close to where she and Rachel had gone with the bottle of wine on a sunny afternoon that seemed like weeks and weeks ago.

It was one of Fay's "thinking" walks. She wanted, as someone once said, to be alone.

Before leaving, she'd pored over some of the books in her small "local" collection—Howse's *History of Radnorshire,* Ella Mary Leather's *The Folklore of Herefordshire,* Jacqueline Simpson's *The Folklore of the Welsh Border.* Not quite sure what she was looking for.

Anything to do with dogs, really. Dogs and bells.

There'd been separate entries on both. Two books referred to the Crybbe curfew, one of only a handful still sounded in British towns—purely tradition—with two of them along the Welsh border. There was all the usual stuff about the bequest of Percy Weale, wealthy sixteenth-century wool merchant, to safeguard the moral welfare of the town. One book briefly mentioned the Preece family as custodian of the tradition.

Fay untied Arnold's clothesline. He snuffled around on the riverbank, going quite close to the water but never getting his paws wet. Interested in something. Perhaps there were otters. The river looked fat, well-fed by rain.

Not raining now, but it probably would before nightfall, the clouds moving in together like a street gang, heavy with menace.

It was only since coming to Crybbe that Fay had begun to regard intangibles like the sky, the atmosphere, climatic changes as . . . what? Manifestations of the earth's mood?

Or something more personal. Like when a mist seemed to cling to you, throwing out nebulous tentacles, as if you and it . . . as if it *knew* you.

And the atmosphere hereabouts—threatening or blandly indifferent—was not an expression of the earth's mood so much as . . . She stopped and stared across the darkening river at the huddle of Crybbe.

Not the earth's mood, but . . . the *town's* mood.

This thought came at the same moment as the shot.

Fay whirled.

The riverside field was empty, the clouds united overhead, thick and solid as a gravestone. There were no more shots and no echo, as if the atmosphere had absorbed the shock, like a cushion.

Everything still, the field unruffled, except for a patch of black and white—and now red—that pulsed and throbbed maybe twenty yards from Fay.

"Arnold?" she said faintly. "Arnold?"

six

From where Rachel was standing, Max Goff, arms folded, resembled an enormous white mushroom on the Tump.

In tones which, roughed by the speakers, didn't sound as reverent as they were perhaps intended to, Goff paid a brief tribute to Henry Kettle, said to be among the three finest dowsers in the country, killed when his car crashed into the obscene Victorian wall built around this very mound.

"No way we can know what went through Mr. Kettle's head in those final moments. But I guess there was a kind of tragic poetry to his death."

Rachel closed her eyes in anguish.

"And his death . . . began a minor but significant preliminary task which I intend to complete today."

Max paused, looked down at his feet, looked up again. The cameraman could be seen zooming in tight on his face.

"The Victorians had scant respect for their heritage. They regarded our most ancient burial mounds as unsightly heaps which could be plundered at will in search of treasure. And to emphasize what they believed to be their dominance over the landscape and over history itself, they liked to build walls around things. Maybe they had a sense of the awesome terrestrial energy accumulating here. Maybe they felt threatened. Maybe they wanted to contain it."

Or maybe they didn't fool themselves it even existed, Rachel thought cynically.

"But whatever their intention," Goff began to raise his voice, "this wall remains a denial. A denial of the Earth Spirit."

He lifted an arm, fist clenched.

"And this wall has to come down as a first symbolic act in the regeneration of Crybbe."

People clapped. That is, Rachel noticed, members of the New Age community clapped, raggedly.

"Only it won't be coming down today," Humble said.

Rachel's eyes snapped open.

"We got a problem, Rachel. This is Mr. Parry. The bulldozer man."

A little man in wire-rimmed glasses stuck out a speckled brown hand. "Gomer Parry Plant Hire."

"How do you do," said Rachel suspiciously. "Shouldn't you be down there with your machinery?"

"Ah, well. Bit of a miscalculation, see," said Gomer Parry. "What it needs is a bigger bulldozer. See, even if I hits him high as I can reach, that wall, he'll crash back on me, sure to. Dangerous, see."

"Dangerous," Rachel repeated, unbelieving.

"Oh hell, aye."

"OK. So if it needs a bigger bulldozer," Rachel said carefully, "then get a bigger bulldozer."

"That," said Gomer Parry, "is, I'm afraid, the biggest one I got. Other thing is I got no insurance to cover all these people watchin'."

Rachel said, very slowly, "Oh . . . shit."

"Well, nobody said it was goin' to be a bloody circus," said Gomer Parry.

Goff stood there, on the top of the Tump, still and white; monarch of the Old Golden Land.

He was waiting.

He came across the field in loose, easy strides, the twelve-gauge under his arm, barrel pointing down. He wore a brown waterproof jacket and green Wellingtons.

It was darker now. Still a while from sundown, but the sun hadn't figured much around here in a long time.

"Sorry, miss." Cursory as a traffic warden who'd just handed you a ticket. "Shouldn't 'ave let 'im chase sheep, should you?"

"*What?*"

It was only afterward she realized what he'd said. Fay, on her knees, blood on her jeans, from Arnold.

The dog lay in the grass, bleeding. He whined and twitched and throbbed.

"Move back, miss. Please."

And she did. Thinking it had all been a horrible mistake and he was going to help her.

But when she shuffled back in the grass, almost overbalancing, he strolled across and stood over the dog, casually leveling his gun at the pulsating heap.

Fay gasped and threw herself forward, on top of Arnold, feeling herself trembling violently, like in a fever, and the dog hot, wet and sticky under her breasts.

"Now don't be silly, miss. 'E's done for, see. Move away, let me finish 'im off."

"Go *away!*" Fay screamed. "Fuck off!" Eyes squeezed closed, lying over Arnold. The dog gave a little cry and a wheeze, like a balloon going down.

"Oh no," Fay sobbed. "No, please . . . "

Lying across the dog, face in the grass, blind anger—*hatred*—rising.

They both saw the dog fall, not far from the river, a blur of blood. The woman running, collapsing to her knees. Then the man wandering casually across the field.

"The bastard. Who is he?"

"Jonathon Preece," Mrs. Seagrove said, white-faced, clinging to her gate. "From Court Farm."

"What the hell's he think he's doing?"

"I wish I could run," Mrs. Seagrove said, her voice quaking with rage and shock. "I'd have that gun off him. Look . . . " She clutched his arm. "What's he doing now, Joe? He's going to shoot her, he's going to shoot the girl as well!"

Incredibly, it did look like it. She'd thrown herself over the dog. The man was standing over them, the gun pointing downward.

"Do you know her?"

"Too far away to tell, Joe." Mrs. Seagrove began to wring her hands. "Oh, I hate them. I hate them. They're primitive. They're a law unto themselves."

"Right." Powys was moving toward the field. Common land, he was thinking, common land.

"Shall I call the police?"

"Only if I don't come back," Powys said, shocked at how this sounded. For real. Jesus.

He slipped and scrambled to his feet with yellow mud on his gray suit. "Shit." Called back, "What did you say his name was?"

"For God's sake, be careful. Preece, Jonathon Preece."

"Right. You stay there, Mrs. Seagrove. Get ready to phone." Jesus, he thought, realizing he was trembling, what kind of place *is* this?

Guy Morrison was about to tear his hair. This was a two-camera job and he only had one. How was he supposed to shoot Goff *and* the destruction of the wall with one camera?

What this needed was a shot of the bulldozer crashing through, with a shower of stone, and a cut to Goff's triumphant face as he savored the moment from his eyrie on the Tump. It would be a meaningful sequence, close to the top of the first program, maybe even under the titles.

But how was he supposed to get that with one crew? If he'd known about this beforehand, he'd have hired a local news cameraman as backup—Griggs, for instance. But he *didn't* know about it in advance because this arrogant, fat bastard was playing his cards too close to his chest.

At least the delay was a breathing space.

"Which you want to go for, then?" the cameraman, Larry

Ember, asked him, pulling his tripod out of the mud close to the summit of the mound.

Guy pushed angry, stiffened fingers through his blond hair. "Whichever we go for, it'll be wrong," he said uncharacteristically. "Look, if we set up next to Goff, how much of the bulldozer stuff do you reckon you can shoot from here?"

"Useless," Larry Ember said. "You're shooting a wall collapsing, you got to be under the thing, like it's tumbling towards you. Even then, with one camera, you're not going to get much."

"Maybe we can fake it afterwards. Get the chap to knock down another section of wall round the back or something. We've got no choice, I need to get his reactions."

"Could always ask *him* to fake it afterwards."

"Perhaps not," said Guy.

"Fucking cold up here," Larry said. "What kind of summer is this?"

A swirling breeze—well, more than a breeze—had set the trees rattling around them.

"Going to fucking rain, too, in a minute." Larry Ember looked up at a sky like the inside of a rotten potato. "We should have had lights up here. I told you we needed an electrician as well. You can't cut fucking costs on a job like this."

"I didn't *know* it was going to happen," Guy hissed. "Did I? I thought it was going to be a couple of talking heads and a few GVs."

Goff lurched over, white jacket flapping in the wind. "Some flaming cock-up here. Switch that damn thing off for now, Guy, will you?"

"You the producer, or is he?" the cameraman wondered provocatively.

"Go along with him. For now." Guy had gone red. His dumpy, serious-faced assistant, Catrin Jones, squeezed his arm encouragingly. Guy knew she'd been in love with him for some time.

Below them, the speakers on the van began to crackle. Goff's voice came out fractured. " . . . et . . . chel Wade . . . up here. Get Rach . . . ade . . . up here NOW."

Catrin zipped up her fleecy body-warmer. "It's a funny thing . . . "

"Nothing," snapped Guy, "about this is funny."

"No, I mean it's so cold and windy up here and down

there . . . nothing." She waved a hand toward the crowd below—
some people drifting away now. "No wind at all, nobody's hair
is blowing or anything."

"OK." Guy prodded Larry Ember's left shoulder, bellowed
down his ear. "Executive decision. Let's get down there. Take
a chance, shoot it from below."

" . . . ucking sticks gonna blow over." Larry clutched his camera as the wind buffeted the tripod. The wind seemed to be coming from *underneath.* Catrin's clipboard was suddenly snatched
from her hands and wafted upward with a wild scattering of
white paper, like birds disturbed.

She squealed. "Oh *no!"* Clawing frantically at the air.

"Leave it!" Guy said.

"It's the shot list!"

"Just let it go!"

Five yards away, Goff was shrieking into the microphone, to
no effect. The sound had gone completely.

" . . . king weird, this setup." Larry's words snatched into the
swirling wind.

"One more shot!" Guy screaming down the cameraman's ear
again. "Get Goff. Get him *now!"*

Goff's arms were flailing, the wide lapels of his white jacket
whipped across his chin, the trees roaring around him, the sky
black. He was out of control.

Guy wanted this.

Powys edged round the field, concealed—he hoped—by gorse
bushes and broom, then crossed it diagonally, approaching the
man, Jonathon Preece, from behind, as quietly as he could. Feeling himself quivering: outrage and apprehension. He could see
the woman lying not quite flat, spread across the dog, looking
up now at Preece.

Heard her harsh whisper. " . . . done, you bastard?"

"I'm allowed," Preece said with, Powys thought, surprising
belligerence, the shotgun under his arm, barrel unbroken. "If a
dog's threatening sheep . . . "

"There *are* no bloody sheep!"

"There is in that next field," he insisted. "Up there, 'e was.
I seen 'im before. We 'ad four lambs killed up there t'other
week."

"You're lying! This dog wasn't even here last week."

"If a farmer got reason to think . . . " Waving his arms for emphasis, the gun moving about under one.

"You going to shoot *me* now?"

Jonathon Preece looked down at the gun under his arm and stepped back a pace or two. Powys froze, only three or four yards behind him now. Preece bent down, watching the woman all the time, and laid the shotgun on the grass to one side.

"See. I put 'im down now, the ole gun. You go 'ome. Nothing you can do." A bit defensive now. "I'm within my legal rights, you ask Wynford Wiley. Can't be 'elped. No place for dogs, sheep country."

The woman didn't move. Powys saw a tumble of tawny hair over a blue nylon raincoat.

A curious thing happened then. Although it was way past 9 P.M. and the sky was deep gray—no trace of sunlight for hours—a shadow fell across the field like an iron bar.

And down it, like a gust of breath through a blowpipe, came a harsh wind.

"What's he doing? What *is* he doing?"

Rachel couldn't believe it. Max was jumping up and down on the summit of the mound, his white jacket swirling around him, his white trousers flapping, as if he was trying to keep his balance, struggling to stay on his feet.

"Look like 'e's been caught in a hurricane," Gomer Parry observed.

But there was no wind. The trees behind Goff on the Tump appeared quite motionless, while Goff himself was dancing like a marionette with a hyperactive child wielding the strings.

He's just angry, Rachel thought. Out of his mind with rage because the wall isn't collapsing and the PA system's broken down. Teach him to hire local firms for a job like this.

She was aware, on the edge of her vision, of Andy Boulton-Trow in his white shirt and his tight, black jeans looking up at the dancing bear on the mound. Andy's beard-shadowed face was solemn and watchful, then it split into a grin and he started shaking his head.

He saw Jonathon Preece look up in sudden alarm as the shaft of wind made a channel of black water across the river, from bank to bank.

There was a strangled yelp from the woman or the dog or both, but he couldn't hear either of them clearly because of the wind.

It came like a hard gasp of breath.

Bad breath.

The wind smelled foul. And as Powys, choking, reeled away from it, his sense rebelled and the whole scene seemed to go into negative for a moment, so that the sky was white and the grass was red and the river gleamed a nauseous yellow.

He stumbled, eyes streaming, a roaring in his ears.

And when the noise faded and the halitosis wind died and his vision began to clear, Joe Powys found he was holding the twelve-gauge shotgun.

It was heavier than he expected, and he stumbled, almost dropping it. He gripped it firmly in both hands, straightened up.

Jonathon Preece roared, "Who the 'ell . . . ?" Powys saw his face for the first time—raw pink cheeks. Age maybe twenty-two or -three.

"Steady, pal."

"You give me that gun, mister!"

"Advise me, Jonathon." Powys pointed the shotgun in the general direction of Jonathon Preece's groin. "I've never used one of these before. Do I have to pull the two triggers to blow both your balls off, or is one enough?"

He was gratified to see fear flit, fast as an insect, across Jonathon Preece's eyes. "I don't know who you are, mister, but this is none of your business."

Powys felt himself grinning. In his right hand, the barrel of the twelve-gauge was comfortably warm, like radiator pipes. The stock fitted into his armpit, firm as a crutch.

"You watch it, mister. Ole thing'll go off."

"Yes," Powys said.

He raised the barrel, so that it was pointing into Jonathon's chest.

"You put 'im down. Be sensible!"

His finger under the trigger guard, so firm. He thought, This man deserves what's coming to him. This man needs to die. He felt a hard thud of certainty in his chest. An acute satisfaction, the flexing of an unknown muscle.

He drank in the dusk like rough ale, closed his eyes, and squeezed.

"Nnnn . . . oooo."

Saw, in slow motion, the chest of Jonathon Preece exploding, the air bright with blood, a butcher shop's cascade.

A tiny, feeble noise. He turned. The woman in the blue raincoat was up on her knees now, breathing hard. The tiny, feeble noise came out of the lump of sodden fur exposed on the grass.

"Arnie!" She looked up at Powys; he saw tear-stained, blood-blotched cheeks, clear green eyes, and a lot of mud. "Oh God, he's hanging on. Can you help me?"

Powys's mouth was so dry he couldn't speak.

Jonathon Preece screamed. "You got no bloody sense? Gimme that gun!"

"I . . ."

"Please," the woman begged.

"Gimme it!" The farmer took a step forward.

From out of the town's serrated silhouette came the first sonorous stroke of the curfew.

Powys looked down in horror at the gun. It felt suddenly very cold in his hands.

"Gimme . . . "

"Get it yourself," Powys said, backing away, far enough away from Jonathon Preece, in this light, to remain unsure of what was happening until he heard the splash.

When the gun hit the water, Powys saw Mrs. Seagrove hurrying down the bank toward them and then he saw Jonathon Preece's purpling face and became aware, for the first time, as the farmer advanced on him with bunched fists, that Jonathon Preece was bigger than he was. As well as being younger and fitter and, at this point, far angrier.

"You fuckin' done it now, mister. Antique, that gun is. Three generations of my family 'ad that gun."

Powys shrugged, palms up, backing off. He felt loose, very tired suddenly. "Yeah, well . . . not too deep just there . . . Jonathan. Be OK. When it dries out."

Preece's head swiveled—Mrs. Seagrove coming quickly toward them, red-faced, out of breath—and he stopped, uncertain.

Mrs. Seagrove stood there in her sweater and her plaid skirt, breathing hard, eventually managing to gasp, "Did you see it? *Did you . . . ?*"

Powys looked at her, then at Jonathon Preece, who had turned
to the river and was glaring out. The river looked stagnant.
Preece hesitated, stared savagely into the drab water, started
to say something and then didn't.

"Please," the woman said from the grass.

It began to rain, big drops you could see individually against
the hard sky.

Powys pulled off his jacket and knelt down. The dog's eyes
were wide open, flanks pulsating. Powys didn't know what to
do.

The dog squirmed, blood oozed.

Powys laid the jacket down. "Put him on this." He slid
both hands beneath the dog. "Gently. We'll get him to a vet.
You . . . you never know your luck."

In the river now, almost up to the tops of his Wellingtons,
Jonathon Preece bellowed, "I know your face, mister. I'll 'ave
you!"

"Oh, piss off," Powys said, weary of him. He heard Mrs.
Seagrove wailing, "You must've seen it. It was coming right
at you. It went *through* you."

seven

Jean Wendle was living in a narrow town house on the square.
Inside, it was already quite dark. She put on a reading lamp. Its
parchment shade made the room mellow. Gold lettering on the
book spines, the warm brass of a coal scuttle in the hearth. It
reminded Alex of his first curate's house in Oxfordshire, before
he'd been promoted into an endless series of vast, unheatable
vicarages and rectories. She'd certainly brought the warmth of
her personality into the place.

Jean Wendle made him sit in a smoker's bow chair, his
back to the fireplace, with its Chinese screen, facing a plain,
whitewashed wall.

"Some days," Alex said, "it seems fine. I mean there might be nothing wrong. Or perhaps that, in itself, is an illusion. Perhaps I think I'm all right and everybody else sees me as stark, staring . . . "

"Shush." Touch of Scottish in her voice; he liked that. "Don't tell me. Don't tell me anything about it. Let me find out for myself."

Yes, he really rather fancied her. Sixtyish. Short, gray hair. Still quite a neat little body—pliable, no visible stiffening. Sort of retired gym-mistress look about her. And nice mobile lips.

Cool fingers on his forehead. Moving from side to side, finding the right spot. Then quite still.

And quite sexy. Would he have let himself in for this if he hadn't fancied her a bit?

Not a chance.

"Don't talk," she said.

"I wasn't talking."

"Well, don't think so loudly. Not for a moment or two. Just relax."

Taken him a few days to arrive at the cool hands of Jean Wendle. Well, a few nights—tentative approaches in the pub. Not a word to Fay. Definitely not a word to Grace.

And why shouldn't he? What was there to lose? The GP in Crybbe was a miserable beggar—hadn't been much use to poor old Grace, had he? Drugs. Always drugs. Drugs that made you sleepy, drugs that made you sick. And at the end of the day . . .

Gradually, he and reality would go their separate ways. Rather appealing in one sense—what did reality have to commend it these days? But not exactly a picnic for anyone looking after him. Alex knew what happened to people who lost their minds. It sometimes seemed that half his parishioners had been geriatrics. They remembered having a wash this morning, when it was really days ago. They peed in the wardrobe, by mistake.

Fay, now—that child was suffering a severe case of misplaced loyalty. If he couldn't get rid of her, it was his solid intention to pop himself off while he could still count on getting the procedure right. She'd thank him for it one day. Better all around, though, if he could make it look like an accident. Fall off the bridge or something.

Would have been a pity, though, with all these alternative

healing characters roaming around, not to give it a try first. What was there to lose?

The first chap he'd been to, Osborne, had not been all that encouraging. Almost as depressing as the doc. Alex got the feeling old age was not what the New Age was about.

And all this "like cures like" stuff. A drop of this, a drop of that. Little vials of colorless liquid, touch of the medieval apothecary.

"How long before it starts to work?"

"You mustn't expect dramatic results, Alex," Osborne told him. "You see, holistic medicine, by definition, is about improving the health of the whole person. Everything is interconnected. Obviously, the older one is, the more set in its ways the body is, therefore the longer . . . " He must have seen the expression in Alex's eyes. "Look, my wife's an acupuncturist, perhaps that might be more what you . . . "

"All those bloody needles. No, thanks."

"It isn't painful, Alex."

"Pain? I don't mind pain!"

Just the image of himself lying there, an overstuffed pincushion.

This kind of healing was a good deal more dignified, if you concentrated on those cool hands and didn't think too hard about what was supposedly going on in the spirit world.

He'd grilled her, naturally.

"Dr. Chi? Dr. bloody Chi? You don't *look* like a nutter, Wendy. How can you seriously believe you're working under the supervision of some long-dead Chinky quack?"

"My name's Jean," she'd corrected him softly.

"Dr. Chi!" Alex draining his Scotch. "God save us."

"Do you really want to know about this, Alex, or are you just going to be superior, narrow-minded, chauvinistic, and insulting?"

"Was I? Hmmph. Sorry. Old age. Senile dementia."

"Are you really old enough to be senile, Alex? What are you, seventy?"

"I'm certainly way past flattery, Wendy. Way past eighty, too. Go on, tell me about this Peking pox doctor from the Ming dynasty."

He'd forced himself to listen patiently while she told him about Dr. Chi, who, she said, she'd once actually seen—as a white, glowing, egg-shaped thing.

"The name is significant. Dr. Chi. *Chi* is the Oriental life force. Perhaps that's the name I've subconsciously given him. I don't know if I'm dealing with a doctor from the Ming dynasty, the T'ang dynasty, or whenever. He doesn't speak to me all singsong, like a waiter serving chicken chow mein. All I know is there's a healing force and I call him Dr. Chi. Perhaps he never was a human doctor at all, or perhaps he's something that last worked through a Chinese physician. I'm not clever enough to understand these things. I'm content to be a channel. Good gracious, don't you believe in miracles, Alex? Isn't that the orthodox Anglican way anymore?"

Regarding the Anglican Church, he wasn't entirely sure what he believed anymore.

Powys found the page, ran his finger down the column headed "Veterinary Surgeons." "OK, D. L. Harris. Crybbe three-nine-four."

Mrs. Seagrove dialed the number and handed him the phone.

The woman in the bloodstained blue raincoat sat in the hall. The dog lay on Powys's jacket on the woman's knee, panting.

"Have a cup of tea while you're waiting," Mrs. Seagrove said.

She shook her head. "No. Thank you. We may have to take him somewhere."

The number rang for nearly half a minute before a woman answered.

"Yes."

"Mr. Harris there, please?"

"What's it about?" Local accent.

"We've got a very badly injured dog. Could you tell me where to bring it?"

A silence.

"Dog, you say?" Shrill. As if he'd said giraffe or something.

"He's been shot."

"I'm sorry," the woman said, flat-voiced. "But Mr. Harris is out."

"Will he be long? Is there another vet?"

"Sorry." Cool, terse. "We can't help you."

A crackle; the line broke.

"I don't believe it," Powys said. "She said the vet was out, I asked when he'd be back or was there anyone else, and she said she couldn't help me. Can you believe that? This was a vet's, for God's sake."

"Wrong," Fay Morrison said bitterly. "This was a *Crybbe* vet's."

"What the fuck was happening up there?" Max Goff lay on his bed in his room at the Cock.

"You tell me," said Andy Boulton-Trow.

"I never felt so high. Like, at first I was really angry, really furious at the inefficiency. Why weren't they bringing the flaming wall down, why was nothing happening, why was the sound failing?"

"And then?"

"Then I felt the power. The energy. I never felt anything so heavy before. It took off the top of my skull. That ever happen to you?"

"Once or twice," Andy said.

"Come to London with me," Goff said. "Stay at my place."

"I have things to do here."

"Then I'll stay here. We'll stay in this room. You got things to teach me, I realize this now. We'll stay here. I'll get rid of Ms. Wade. I'll send *her* back to London."

Andy placed a hand on Max's knee.

"You go back to London, Max. There's such a thing as too much too soon. You'll get there. You'll make it."

Andy didn't move his hand. Max shivered.

"Took off the top of my skull. And then the curfew started."

"Yes," Andy said. "The curfew."

"I don't think I like that curfew," Jean Wendle said, pouring Earl Grey, after the treatment. "I don't know whether it's the bell or what it represents. I don't like restrictions."

"Oh, quite," Alex said. "Couldn't stand it if it was a *real* curfew. But as a bit of picturesque traditional nonsense, it's all right, isn't it?"

"I think it is a real curfew, in some way," Jean said. "I don't know why I think that. Well, yes, I do—people *do* stay off the streets while it's being rung, have you noticed that? But I think there's something else. A hundred times a night is an awfully big tradition."

"I suppose so."

Alex would give her the benefit of the doubt on anything tonight. He didn't remember when he'd last felt so relaxed, so much at peace. And him a priest. Best not to go into the implications of all this.

"It's a very odd little town," Jean said. She drew gold-dusted velvet curtains over a deep Georgian window.

"Aren't they all."

"No, they aren't. This is. There are—how can I put it?—pockets of strange energy in this town. All over the place. People see things, too, although few will ever admit it."

"See things?" Alex was wary.

"Manifestations. Light effects. Ghosts."

"Hmm," said Alex. "Good cup of tea."

"Being on the border is a lot to do with it. When we make a frontier . . . when we split something physically asunder in the landscape, especially when we build something like Offa's Dyke to emphasize it, we create an area of psychic disturbance that doesn't go away."

Alex stirred his tea, wishing she'd talk about something else.

Jean said, "Do you think they've taken on more than they can handle? Max Goff and the New Age people?"

"I thought you were one of them."

"I like to keep a certain distance," Jean said. "I like to watch. Can they control it, I wonder? Or is it too volatile for them?"

"Oh, we can't control anything," Alex said. "That's something everybody learns sooner or later. Least of all control ourselves."

It was well after midnight by the time they came out of the vet's.

Without Arnold.

"I couldn't stand the way he was looking at me," Fay said. "It's not been his week, has it? He's in a car crash, sees his master die. Saved from the clutches of the Crybbe constabulary, finds he's become a kind of pariah in the town. Then he gets shot."

The Mini had been parked for over two hours on a double yellow line outside the vet's surgery in Leominster, fifteen miles from Crybbe. The nearest one from which they'd managed to get a response. The vet handling night calls had been understanding but had made no comments either way about the wisdom of farmers shooting dogs alleged to be worrying sheep.

The vet had said Arnold would probably live. "Just don't expect him to be as good as new with all that lead inside him."

One of the back legs had taken most of it. Bones had been broken. The vet had seemed a bit despondent about that leg. Fay had spent half an hour holding Arnold at different angles while the vet examined what he could, removing shotgun pellets. He might have to operate, he said, and got Fay to sign a paper relating to responsibility if Arnold died under anesthetic.

Now Fay and Powys were standing on the pavement, unwinding. It was very quiet in Leominster, the other side of midnight. No menace here, Fay thought.

J. M. Powys was shaking out his jacket. It was scarcely identifiable as a jacket anymore. It looked as if someone had faced a firing squad in it.

"Oh God," Fay said. "I'm so sorry."

J. M. Powys dangled the jacket from an index finger and looked quite amused. J. M. Powys. Bloody hell. "It's hard to believe you're J. M. Powys. I thought you'd be . . . "

"Dead."

"Well, not quite."

"That lady, Mrs. Seagrove. She called you Mrs. Morrison. You're not Guy's wife, are you?"

"No," Fay said. "Not anymore."

She explained, leaning on an elderly Mini in a quiet street in Leominster, lights going out around them. Explained quite a few things. Talking too much, the way you did when you'd been through something traumatic. Only realizing she was shooting her mouth off when she heard herself saying, "I've got to get out of that place, or I'm going to implode. Or maybe I'll just kill somebody."

She pulled both palms down her cheeks. Shook her hair, like a dog. "What am I going on about? Not your problem. Thanks for everything you've done. I shall buy you a new jacket."

"I don't want a new jacket." Powys opened the car door. "I like them full of patches and sewn-up bits."

He drove carefully out of the town, dipping the headlights politely when they met another vehicle. They didn't meet many. The lights sometimes flashed briefly into the eyes of rabbits sitting in the hedgerows. Once, J. M. Powys had to brake for a badger scampering—that was really the word, she'd have expected badgers to lumber—across the road and into a wood.

Fay realized she hadn't phoned her dad. He'd be worried. Or he wouldn't, depending on his state of mind tonight. Too late now.

"Arnold!" Powys said suddenly, breaking five minutes of slightly sleepy silence.

"What?"

"Arnold. Not Henry Kettle's dog? You aren't the person who's looking after Henry's dog?"

"And not making an awfully good job of it, so far."

"Stone me," said Powys. "Sometimes coincidence just seems to crowd you into corners."

"Especially in Crybbe," Fay said. She wished she was traveling through the night to somewhere else. Virtually anywhere else, actually.

The bones were very white in the torchlight. There were also some parchment-colored bits, skin or sinew, gristle.

"Ah," Tessa said, less than awed. "I know what that is."

Warren was miffed. How the fuck could she know anything about it?

"Yeah," Warren said. "It's a hand."

"It's a Hand of Glory."

"What you talking about?"

"A dead man's hand."

"Well, that's bloody obvious, isn't it?"

"A hanged man's hand," Tessa said.

Warren squatted down next to her. The spade lay on the grass, next to a neat pile of earth and the square of turf, set carefully to one side so it could be replaced.

"Which means it's got magic powers," Tessa said. "Where'd you find it?"

"Around."

"All right, *don't* tell me! What's that Stanley knife doing in there?"

"Well, I . . . " Buggered if he was going to tell her he'd been scared to put his hand in and take the knife out. "I'm seeing what effect it 'as on it. You know, like you puts an old razor blade under a cardboard pyramid and it comes out sharp again.

New Age, that." Warren cackled. "I'm learnin' all about this New Age, now, see. 'Ow'd you know that?"

"Know what?"

" 'Bout it being a hanged man's hand."

"I think I'd like to draw it," Tessa said. "Maybe I'll come up here again."

"No." It was *his* hand. "Keep diggin' it up, the ground'll get messed up and somebody else might find it."

"They won't. Do you know why you brought it here, Warren?"

"Good a place as any."

Tessa smiled.

"What you done with them other drawings, the old feller?"

"Got fed up with him," Tessa said. "Passed him on."

"Who to?"

"Dunno where he might end up," Tessa said mysteriously. "Part of the fun." She smiled and fitted a forefinger down the front of Warren's jeans and drew him toward her, across the old box.

"Let's do it here . . . do *it* . . . by the box. Leave it open, see what happens."

"Prob'ly come crawlin' out an' pinch your bum," Warren said slyly. "Anyway, it's too late now for that."

Tessa took her finger out of Warren's jeans. "I waited for you."

"Had a job to do."

"What was so important?"

"You'll find out," Warren said.

Tessa reached out and touched a white knucklebone.

"Cold," she said. "It's nice and cold."

"It was cold in the river, too," Warren said.

Rachel lay in the brass bed. When he slid in gratefully beside her, she awoke.

"J.M.?"

"I couldn't put a light on. The power's off again."

He'd lit up Bell Street with the headlights, watching the small figure in bloodstained blue nylon walking to her door. When she was safely inside, he drove back into the lightless main street, where all the windows were blind eyes. Then down the hill and over the bridge. A tight right turn, and there was the perfect little riverside cottage. He'd almost expected it not to be there, like a dream cottage.

The presence of Rachel in the bed reinforced a sense of home. Before she could ask, he told her where he'd been, poured it all out, the whole bizarre episode.

"Arnold?" Rachel sat up in the darkness. "Jonathon Preece shot Arnold?"

He told her about the shotgun, how he'd come to pick it up from the grass.

"I really wanted to kill him. I thought I *had* killed him at one point. I could feel myself pulling the triggers, both triggers, and then his chest . . . It was as if time had skipped a beat, and I'd already shot him."

"You're overtired," Rachel said.

"Then the dog—Arnold—whimpered, and I was back in the second before I did it. Arnold was Henry Kettle's dog."

"I know."

"You don't know how badly I wanted to kill that guy."

"This doesn't seem like you, J.M."

"No," Powys said. "It didn't."

There was a window opposite the bed. Across the river, he saw a few sparse lights coming on, like candles on a cake.

"Power's back."

"And you're a hero, J.M.," Rachel said, molding her body into his. "Although you'll be a marked man in Crybbe if anyone finds out."

part five

✤✤✤✤✤

You won't need to worry and you won't have to cry
Over in the old golden land.

ROBIN WILLIAMSON,
From the album *Wee Tam and the Big Huge*

one

"No, don't move 'im yet, Gomer."

Jack Preece ambled across the field to where Gomer Parry and his nephew, Nev, were preparing to get the bulldozer back on the truck.

"Don't speak to me, Jack." Gomer didn't turn around. "Embarrassed? Humiliated, more like!"

"Aye, well, I'm sorry, Gomer."

"Sorry? You bloody should be sorry, Jack Preece. Never before have Gomer Parry Plant Hire failed to carry out a contract. Never! I should 'ave told your dad where 'e could stick 'is . . ."

"Only, see, the district council's 'avin' a bit o' trouble on the new landfill site over Brynglas," Jack Preece said. "Need of an extra bulldozer, quickish, like. Three days' work, sure t'be."

Gomer Parry turned shrewd eyes on Jack Preece, standing in the damp old field, between downpours, his back to the Tump and the famous wall—still intact, except for the bits of masonry dislodged when old Kettle had his crash.

"Reckon you can do it, Gomer?"

Gomer shot him a penetrating look through his wire-rimmed glasses. "Something goin' on yere, Jack. Don't know what it is, but there's something."

"Aye, well," Jack Preece said, eyes averted. "No need to worry about your reputation, Gomer, anyway. You'll be all right. We looks after our own, isn't it."

He started to walk away, then turned back. "You seen Jonathon about?"

"Not lately," Gomer said.

"Boy didn't come 'ome last night."

"Only young once, Jack," said Gomer.

"Aye," said Jack. "Sure t'be."

* * *

Powys drove back to Hereford, loaded up a couple of suitcases, a box of books, his Olivetti, and two reams of paper.

"Aha," said Barry, the osteopath from upstairs. "Ensnared! He's got you. I knew he would. What was the deciding factor, Powys? The money?"

Powys shook his head.

"The women?"

Powys said, "Just hold that door open for me, would you?"

"I knew it! It's the Summer of Love in Crybbe. You always were a sucker for a cheesecloth cleavage."

"Barry," said Powys, "don't you have somebody's spine to trample on?"

"Good luck, Joe," Annie said wistfully.

"What d'you mean 'good luck'?" He'd noticed the crystals had been joined on the counter by a small display of astrological amulets in copper. Where the hell had she found those?

"You're going back," Annie said.

"I am not 'going back.' "

Annie and Barry smiled knowingly to each other.

During the return drive it rained. It rained harder the nearer he got to Crybbe. Powys did some thinking, images wafting across his mind with the rhythm of the windshield wipers.

Seriously unseasonal rain was throwing the river over the banks like rumpled bedclothes. He saw an image of a shotgun getting slowly pushed downstream, its barrels clogged with corrosive silt. Unless Jonathon had managed to retrieve it. Would he ever find out? And would Jonathon report him to the police?

Unlikely. He hoped. Well, it was a question of image: the farmer who let a townie in a suit pinch his gun and toss it in the river. They'd love that in the saloon bar of the Cock; it would go down in the folk history of the town.

Rachel was spending the morning at the Court, organizing workmen putting finishing touches to the stable block. He thought of going to see Mrs. Seagrove.

He carried his suitcases into the cottage. It was a good cottage, a better home than his flat. It had wonderful views over the river—slopping and frothing feverishly, after hours of heavy rain.

He couldn't stay here for long though. Not on false pretenses. There was no way he was going to write the New Age Gospel According to Goff.

And the sequence by the river last night kept replaying itself. The feeling of the warm gun, the knowledge that he was not only capable of killing but *wanted* to kill. The bar of shadow across the grass and the river, all the way from the Tump, where Henry Kettle died.

And Arnold, Henry Kettle's dog. A dowser's dog, Henry used to say, isn't like other dogs.

It wasn't raining anymore. Through the large window in the living room, he saw the clouds had shifted like furniture pushed to the corners of the room, leaving a square of light. Fifty yards away, the river, denied its conquest of the meadow, slurped sulkily at its banks. On the other side of the river, in a semidistant field—probably Goff's land—Powys saw two tiny figures, one holding a couple of tall poles.

He thought, The dodmen. Alfred Watkins's term for the prehistoric surveyors who had planned out the leys, erecting standing stones and earthworks at strategic points. The surveyors would, Watkins imagined, have held up poles to find out where tall stones would be visible as waymarkers. Now modern dodmen were at work, re-creating prehistoric Crybbe in precisely the way it was presumed to have been done four thousand or so years ago.

From here, Powys couldn't even make out whether they were dodmen or dodwomen. But he was prepared to bet one of them would be Andy Boulton-Trow.

Calm, laid-back, omniscient old Andy.

I think Joe ought to present himself to the Earth Spirit in the time-honored fashion . . .

. . . the very least you can do, mate . . .

. . . think of it as a kind of appeasement.

Now Andy was personally supervising the operation to open up the town of Crybbe to the Earth Spirit.

On past experience of this irresponsible bastard, did that sound like good news?

"I think," Hereward Newsome said, almost shaking with triumph, "that I've cracked it."

"You saw him?"

"He's gone back to London. I saw Rachel Wade. She said go ahead."

Hereward took off his jacket, hung it over the back of the antique-pine rocking chair by the Aga, sat down, and began to roll up his shirtsleeves. "But we need to move fast."

"Why?" If Jocasta wasn't as ecstatic as she might have been, this was because Hereward's news had eclipsed her own small coup.

"I mean a buying trip. To the West Country, I'd suggest, and pronto. There's Ernest Wilding at Street, Devereux in Penzance, Sally Gold in Totnes, Melanie Dufort in . . . where is it now, someplace near Frome? All specializing in megalith paintings—or they were. And there have to be more. What happened to the Ruralists? Where's Inshaw these days?"

"Not far from here, I heard."

"Oh." He stood up. "Anyway, I'm going to make some calls now. Strike while Goff's hot. If we go down there this weekend, fetch a few back to put in front of him on Tuesday when he comes back."

Hereward paced the kitchen. Any second now, Jocasta thought, he'll start rubbing his hands. Still, it *was* good news.

"You ought to see his proposed exhibition hall. Rachel showed me this huge barn he's going to rebuild. It'll be a sort of interpretive center for prehistoric Crybbe and the whole earth-mysteries thing. He's looking for maybe seventy paintings. *Seventy!* Darling, if we can provide *half* of those, we're talking . . . let's be vulgar, if we can get the kind of stuff he wants, we're talking megabucks."

"Why can't we go *next* weekend?"

"Look . . . so we close the gallery for a day. What have we got to lose, with Goff out of town? And the way things have been, can we afford to delay?"

"Hereward!" God, he was so irritating. "What about Emmanuel Walters?"

"Oh." Hereward sat down. "It's Sunday, isn't it?"

"Ye-es," Jocasta said, exasperated, "it is. And it's a bloody good job one of us is efficient." Adding nonchalantly, "I've even arranged a celebrity to open the exhibition."

"Oh yes?"

Jocasta's lips cemented into a hard line. Even if it was a member of the Royal Family it wouldn't impress Hereward at the moment, still on his Max Goff high.

"It's Guy Morrison."

"Oh. Er, super. Didn't he used to be . . . ?"

"He's producing and presenting the documentary the BBC are doing on Max Goff and Crybbe. He seems very pleasant. He agreed at once. I think he's at rather a loose end. He's spending the weekend here, getting to know the town. Getting to know the people who count."

"Not much use coming to The Gallery, then." Hereward guffawed insensitively.

Jocasta scowled. That was *it*. "I know," she said, "why don't you go to the West Country on your own. I'll stay behind and handle the private view."

"Yes, I suppose it makes sense."

Jocasta knew it made no sense at all. Good old Hereward, always anxious to be accepted by artists as a friend, someone who understood the creative process, would spend hundreds of pounds more than she would. But at least she'd get rid of him for a couple of days. Increasingly, Jocasta had been thinking back with nostalgia to the days when they'd had separate jobs and only met for a couple of hours in the evening.

Hereward said—a formality, she thought—"Will you be all right on your own?"

Just for a minute she thought about last night and those drawings and the sticky feeling on her hands which had proved, when the lights came on, to be no more than perspiration.

"I shall be fine," she said.

Mrs. Seagrove brought him tea in one of her best china cups—as distinct, she pointed out, from the mugs she took out to the truck drivers in the roadside.

"I thought I'd seen the last of you, Joe. How's the doggie?"

"We think he's going to be OK."

"That's good." She was wearing today a plaid skirt of a different tartan. "I'm not Scottish," she said. "Frank and I used to go up there every autumn, and we'd visit these woolen mills."

There was a picture of Frank on the sideboard. He was beaming and holding up a fish which might have been a trout.

"He was thrilled when we got this place, so near the river. He joined the angling club. It was a shame. Turned out to be not a very good river for fishing. And the problem was, Joe, Frank could see the river, but I could only see *that*."

She sat with her back to the big, horizontal window with its panoramic view across the river to the woods and, of course, the Tump.

"About that . . . " Powys said.

"I thought you'd come about that." Mrs. Seagrove held her teacup on her kilted knees, flat and steady as a good coffee table. "Well, I'm glad somebody's interested. Mrs. Morrison's always too busy. Unless I want to talk about it on the radio, she says. Well, I said, would you make a spectacle of yourself on the wireless?"

"Last night, you said something was coming at us. From the Tump?"

"People are fascinated by these things. I'm not. Are you, Joe?"

"Well, I used to be. Still am, in a way, but they worry me now."

"Quite right. I'm not interested, I've never been interested."

"It nearly always happens to people who are not interested," said Powys.

"I think I know when it comes now, what time, so I draw the curtains and turn the telly up, but some nights I just have to go and look, just to get it out of the way. I'm scared to death, Joe, but I look, just to get it out of the way."

"And what time is it?"

"Usually after nine o'clock and before they ring that bell in the church. Not always. It's early sometimes, almost full daylight—although it goes dark all of a sudden, kind of thing, like as if it's bringing its own darkness, do you know what I mean? And just once—it was that night the poor man crashed his car—just once, it was later, about half-tennish. Just that once."

Powys said, "It's a dog, isn't it? A big, black dog."

"Yes, dear," said Mrs. Seagrove very quietly. "Yes, it is."

"How often have you . . . ?"

"Seven or eight times, I've seen it. It always goes the same way. Coming from the . . . the mound thing."

"Down from the mound, or out of the mound?"

"I couldn't honestly say, dear. One second it's not there, the next it is, kind of thing. I'm psychic, I suppose. I never wanted to be psychic, not like this."

"Is it—I'm sorry to ask all these questions—but is it obviously a dog? It couldn't be anything else?"

"You ask as many questions as you like, dear. I've been finding out about you, I rang a friend of mine at the library in Dudley. No, that's an interesting point you make there—is it really a dog? Well, I like dogs. I wouldn't be frightened of a dog, would I? Even a ghost dog—naturally, it'd be a shock, the first time you saw it, kind of thing, but no, I don't think I'd be frightened. Oh dear, I wish you *hadn't* asked me that now, it's disturbed me, that has, Joe."

"I'm sorry."

"I don't want to stay here. I'd be off tomorrow, but how much would I get for this, even if I managed to sell it?"

"If you really wanted to go quickly," Powys said, "I think I could find you a buyer. You'd get a good price, too."

"Not you?"

"Good God, no, not me. I couldn't afford it, even if . . . Look, leave it with me for a day or two."

"I don't know what to say, dear." Mrs. Seagrove's eyes were shining. "In a way, I'd feel bad about somebody having this place. But they might not be psychic, mightn't they?"

"Or they might be quite interested."

"Oh no," she said. "Nobody's interested in evil, are they?"

two

Guy dropped by.

She opened the back door, thinking it was the milkman come for his money, as was usual on a Saturday.

"Fay. Hi."

"Oh, my God."

She wouldn't have chosen to say that, but Guy seemed pleased at the reaction. Perhaps he saw it as an urgent suppression of instinctive desire.

"Thought I'd drop by, as I had some time on my hands." Incandescent smile. "Spending the weekend here, getting acclimatized."

New crowns, Fay spotted. Good ones, of course.

"Crew's gone back, but I've been invited to open some shitty art exhibition tomorrow night. Must be a bit short on celebrities in these parts if they want *me.* " Guy laughed.

Still a master of double-edged false modesty, Fay thought, wishing she'd changed, combed her hair, applied some rudimentary makeup.

And then despising herself utterly for wishing all that.

"Come in, Guy. Dad's gone for a walk; he'll be devastated to have missed you."

"How is he?" Guy stepped into the hall and looked closely at everything, simulating enormous interest in the chipped cream paintwork, the wallpaper with its faded autumn leaves, the nylon carpet beneath his hand-stitched, buffed, brown shoes.

He wore a short, olive, leather jacket, soft as a very expensive wallet.

"We used to have some fascinating chats, your father and I, when I was in Religious Programs."

"I expect he learned quite a lot," Fay said, going through to the kitchen.

"That was how I swung the Crybbe thing, you know. It cut plenty of ice with Max Goff, me being an ex–religious affairs producer. Indicated a certain sensitivity of touch and an essentially serious outlook. Nothing crude, no juvenile piss-taking."

"Tea or coffee?" Fay said. "Why did you leave Religious Programs, anyway? Seemed like a good, safe earner to me. Just about the only situation where you can work in television and still get to heaven."

"Well, you know, Fay, there came a time when it was clear that Guy Morrison had said all he needed to say about religion. Is it ground coffee or instant?"

"Would I offer you instant coffee, Guy?"

"I don't like to make presumptions about people's financial positions," Guy said sensitively.

"We're fine."

"I did tell you, didn't I, that I'd probably have brought you in as researcher, except for this J. M. Powys problem?"

"Thanks, but I doubt I'd've had time, anyway. Pretty busy, really." The handle came off the cup she was holding—that'd teach her to lie twice.

"He was foisted on me, Fay. Nothing I could do."

"I met him last night. Seemed a nice bloke."

Just before lunch, J. M. Powys had phoned to ask how Arnold was. Comfortable, Fay had said, having been on the phone to the vet as early as was reasonable. Stable. As well as can be expected.

Guy crinkled his mouth. "One-book wonder, J. M. Powys. A spent force."

Must be a nice bloke if Guy despises him, Fay thought. She began to filter the coffee in silence.

Eventually, Guy, sitting at the kitchen table, said, "Long time since we met face-to-face, Fay. Three years? Four?"

"At least." Physically, he'd hardly changed at all. Perhaps the odd characterful crease, like the superb-quality leather of his jacket. Pretty soon, she thought in dismay, he'll be looking too comparatively young ever to have been married to me.

Guy said, "You're looking . . . er, good, Fay."

What a bastard. She made a point of not replying in kind.

Guy said, "Quite often, you know—increasingly, in fact—I find myself wondering why we ever split up."

"Didn't it have something to do with you screwing your production assistant?"

Guy waved a dismissive hand. "Trivial, trivial stuff. I was young, she threw herself at me. You know that. I'm essentially a pretty faithful sort of person. No, what we had . . ." He pushed Grace's G-plan dining chair away from the table and leaned back, throwing his left ankle over his right knee and catching it deftly with his right hand. He obviously couldn't quite remember what they'd had.

"I often wish we'd had children, Fay."

Oh hell.

Guy's intermittent live-in girlfriend had apparently proved to be barren. Fay remembered him moaning about this to her one night on the phone. She remembered thinking at the time that infertility was a very useful attribute for an intermittent live-in girlfriend to have. But Guy was at the age when he wanted there to be little Morrisons.

"I'm at the Cock."

"What?"

"The Cock Hotel," Guy said. "It's an appalling place."

"Dreadful," Fay said, pouring his coffee.

"I think I'm going to have to make other arrangements when we start shooting in earnest."

"I should."

"Can you think of anywhere?"

"Hasn't Goff offered you accommodation?"

"Nothing suitable, apparently. He says. Though we do have special requirements—meals at all hours."

Sore point, obviously.

"Still," Fay said cheerfully. "I've heard he's going to buy the Cock, turn it into a New Age Holiday Inn or something."

She brought her coffee and sat down opposite him. If anything, he was even more handsome these days. It had once been terribly flattering to be courted by Guy Morrison. And expectedly painless to become divorced from him.

"I've changed, you know, Fay."

"Hardly at all, I'd've said."

"Oh, looks . . . that's not what it's all about. Never was, was it?"

Of course not, she thought. However, in your case, what else is there to get excited about?

"And you're obviously just as arrogant," she said brightly.

"Confidence, Fay," he said patiently. "Not arrogance. If you don't continually display confidence in this business, people think you're . . . "

"A spent force? Like J. M. Powys?"

"Something like that. I should have held on to you," he said softly, a frond of blond hair falling appealingly to an eyebrow. "You kept me balanced. I was terribly insecure, you know, that's why . . . "

"Oh, for God's sake, Guy, you were never insecure in your life. This is *me* you're giving all this bullshit to. Let's drop this subject, shall we?"

He looked hurt. But not *very* hurt.

"How did you get on yesterday?" Fay asked him, to change direction. "They never managed to pull the wall down, did they?"

"Don't ask," Guy said, meaning "ask."

"All went wrong, then?" This was probably the reason Guy was here. He was in urgent need of consolation.

"I've just been looking at the rushes."

"What, you've been back to Cardiff?"

"No, no, I sent Larry to a video shop in Leominster last night to transfer the stuff to VHS so I could whiz through it at the Cock. When he came back, he said, 'You're not going to like this,' and cleared off quick. I've just found out why. Good grief, Fay, talk about a wasted exercise. First, there's bloody Goff—plans a stunt like that and doesn't tell me until it's too late to hire a second crew, and then . . . "

"But it didn't happen, anyway. The wall's still there."

"I know, but we had what ought to have been terrific footage of Goff going apeshit on top of the Tump, when the sound system packed in and the bulldozer chap said he couldn't do it. But the light must've been worse than I thought or Larry hadn't done a white-balance or something—he denies that, of course, but he would, wouldn't he?"

"What, it didn't come out?" Fay, who'd never worked in television, knew next to nothing about the technicalities of it. "I thought this Betacam stuff didn't need much light."

"Probably something wrong with the camera, Larry claims. First this big black thing shoots across the frame, and then all the color's haywire. By God, if there's any human error to blame in Cardiff, somebody's job could be on the line over this."

"But not yours, of course," said Fay. "Hold on a minute, Guy." She was listening to a vague scraping noise. "It's Dad. He can't get his key in the door."

Fay dashed into the hall, closing the kitchen door behind her and opening the front door. The canon almost fell over the threshold, poking his key at her eye.

"Thank God." Fay caught his arm, whispered in his ear, "Come and rescue me, Dad. Guy's here, and he's in a very maudlin mood."

"Who?" He was out of breath.

"Guy, you remember Guy. We used to be married once. I've got this awful feeling he's working up to asking me to have his baby."

A blurred film had set across the canon's eyes. He shook his head, stood still a moment, breathing hard, then straightened up. "Yes," he said. "Fay. Something you need to know."

"Take your time."

"Tape recorder. Get your tape recorder." His eyes cleared, focused. "There's been an accident. A death. Everybody's talking about it. I'll tell you where to go."

"There'll be no delay," the dodman said. "We start tonight."

"Don't you need planning permission?" Powys asked.

The dodman only smiled.

As expected, he'd turned out to be Andy Boulton-Trow with
a mobile phone and a map in a transparent plastic folder.

"There are six we can put in immediately. Either on Max's
land around the Court or on bits of ground he's been able
to buy. Not a bad start. You're getting one, did you know
that?"

"Thanks a bunch."

"The top of your little acre, where it meets the road. See?"
Andy held out his plastic-covered photocopy of Henry's map.
"Right there."

It was a large-scale OS blowup. The former location of each
stone was marked by a dot inside a circle and the penciled
initials H.K.

They were standing in Crybbe's main street, just above the
police station, looking down toward the bridge. Two of Andy's
dodmen were making their way across, carrying white sighting
poles. Powys asked him how long it had been going on, all this
planning and surveying and buying up the land.

"Months. Nearly a year, all told. But it's all come to a head
very rapidly. In some curious way, I think Henry's death fired
Max into orbit. Henry's done the legwork; now it was down to
Max to pull it all together. There are more than fifty workmen
on the project now. Stables'll be finished by Monday, ready for
a start on the Court itself next week. First half-dozen stones in
place by tomorrow night. That's moving, Joe."

"No, he doesn't piss about, does he?"

"All that remains is to persuade the remaining few diehards
either to sell their land or accept a stone on it. Hence Tuesday's
public meeting. A formality, I'd guess. He'll have bought them
off by then. Agent's out there now, negotiating. Farmers will do
anything these days to stay afloat. Caravan sites, wind farms,
you name it. They take what comes. Most of them have no
choice."

Powys wondered if you could stop people planting a standing
stone close to where you lived, perhaps diverting some kind of
energy through your house. How would a court make a ruling
on something which had never been proved to exist?

"It seems amazing," he said, "that there were so many stones
around here and every single one of them's been ripped out."

"Except for one Henry found. Little bent old stone under a
hedge."

"Do you think they destroyed them because they were superstitious?"

Andy shrugged.

"Because you'd think, if they were superstitious, they'd have been *scared* to pull them out, wouldn't you?"

"People in these parts," Andy said, "who knows how their minds work?"

Powys looked up the street toward the church tower. "There's a major ley, isn't there, coming from the Tump, through the Court, then the church, right through the town to the hills?"

"Line one." Andy held out the plan.

"I was up in the prospect chamber at the Court. It might have been constructed to sight along that ley."

"Might have been?"

"You think it was?"

"Yes. I think so." Andy's black beard was making rapid progress, concealing the bones of his face. You couldn't tell what he was thinking anymore.

"John Dee," Powys said. "John Dee was a friend of Michael Wort's, right? Or, at least, he seems to have known him. We know John Dee was investigating earth mysteries in the 1580s, or thereabouts. Is it possible Dee was educating Wort and that they built the prospect chamber as a sort of observatory?"

"To observe what?"

"I don't know. Whatever they believed happened along that ley."

Two cars came out of the square at speed, one a police car. Obviously together, they passed over the bridge and turned right not far beyond Powys's cottage.

"Took their time," Andy observed.

"What's happening?"

"Body found in the river," Andy said without interest. "That's why we had to stop work down there. They get very excited. Not many floaters in Crybbe. Yes, I think you could be close to it. But perhaps it was Wort who initiated Dee into the secret, have you considered that? He was a remarkable man, you know."

But suddenly Powys was not too concerned about which of them had initiated the other.

It was quiet again in the street. The cars had vanished down a track leading to the riverbank.

* * *

Fay's fingers were weak and fumbling. For the first time, she
had difficulty working the Uher's simple piano-key controls.

Nobody had even covered him up.

She'd expected screens of some kind, a police cordon like
there always were in cities. You couldn't get near. She'd never
seen a drowned man before, in all his sodden glory.

Nobody had even thrown a coat over him, or a blanket.
They'd simply tossed him on the bank, limp and leaking. Skin
blue—crimped, corrugated. Eyes wide open—dead as a cod on
a slab. Livid tongue poking out of the froth around his lips and
nostrils.

Tossed on the bank. Like somebody's catch.

Gomer's catch, in this case.

Gomer Parry, who'd found the body, was only too happy to
give her what he described as an exclusive interview. He told
her how he'd come to check on his bulldozer, which was over
there in Jack Preece's field, awaiting its removal to the council's
Brynglas landfill site on Monday, when he'd spotted this thing
caught up in branches not far from the bank.

" 'E'd not been in long," Gomer said knowledgeably. "Several reasons I got for sayin' that. Number one—no bloatin'.
Takes . . . oh, maybe a week for the ole gases to build up inside,
and then out 'e comes, all blown up like a life jacket. Also,
see—point number two—if 'e'd been in there long . . . fishes
woulda been at 'im."

Gomer made obscene little pincer movements with clawed
fingers and thumb and then pointed into the river, no longer
in flood, but still brown and churning, bearing broken branches
downstream.

They'd been frozen to the fringe of a silent group of local
people on the wet riverbank. They were half a mile from the
bridge, on the bend before the river moved across the Crybbe
Court land, flowing within two hundred yards of the Tump.

"Current brings 'em in to the side yere, right on the bend, see,"
Gomer said. "Then they gets entangled in them ole branches
and the floodwater goes down, and there 'e is, high an' dry.
They've 'ad quite a few yere, over the years. Always the same
spot."

Gomer sat down on a damp tree stump, his back to the body,
got out a battered square tin and began to roll himself a cigarette.

"Nibbled to the bone, some of 'em are," he said, with unseemly relish. "So I reckon, if I was to put a time on it, I'd say 'e's been in there less than a day."

Fay thought she knew exactly how long he'd been in there. Approximately twenty hours. Oh God, this was dreadful. This was indescribably awful. Her fingers went rapidly up and down with the zip of her blue raincoat.

"Now, you notice that wrinkling on 'is face," Gomer said. "Well, see, that's what you calls the 'washerwoman's 'ands' effect."

"Gomer!" The color of Sergeant Wynford Wiley's face was approaching magenta as he loomed over the little man in wire-framed glasses.

"When your wealth of forensic knowledge is required," Wynford said, "we shall send for you. Meanwhile, all this is totally *sub joodicee* until after the inquest. And *you* should know that," he snapped at Fay.

"Look, Wynford," Fay snapped back, to beat the tremor out of her voice. "*Sub judice* applies to court cases, not inquests. Nobody's on trial at an inquest."

Really know how to make friends, don't I? she thought as Wynford bent his face to hers. He didn't speak until he was sure he had her full attention. Then, very slowly and explicitly, he said, "We don't like *clever people* round yere, Mrs. Morrison."

Then he straightened up, turned his back on her, and walked away.

"Fat bastard." Gomer bit on his skinny, handcrafted cigarette. "You got all that, what I said?"

"Yes," Fay said. "But he's right. I won't be able to use most of it, not because it's *sub judice,* but because we don't go to town on the gruesome stuff. Especially when relatives might be listening."

Christ, how could she go through the motions of reporting this story, knowing what she knew? Knowing, if not exactly how, then at least why it had happened.

There was a little crowd around the body, including its father, Jack Preece, and its younger brother, Warren Preece. Jack Preece's face was as gray as the clouds. He looked up from the corpse very steadily, as if he knew what he would see next and the significance of it.

And what he saw next was Fay. His tired, hopeless, brown
eyes met hers and held them. It was harder to face than a
curse.

She thought, *He knows everything.* And she dragged her gaze
away and looked wildly around her, but there was nobody to
run to for comfort and nowhere to hide from Jonathon Preece's
dead eyes and the eyes of his father, which held the weight of
a sorrow she knew she could only partly comprehend.

three

Not one person had appeared to recognize Guy Morrison. Twice
today he'd circuited this dreary town, and nobody had done more
than glance at him with, he was forced to admit, a barely cursory
interest.

Guy liked to be recognized. He needed to be recognized. He
was insecure, he readily admitted this. Everyone he knew in
television was insecure; it was a deeply neurotic business. And
it was a visual medium—so if people started to pass you in the
street without a second, sidelong glance, without nudging their
companions, then it wouldn't be too long before the program
controller failed to recognize you in the lift.

Altogether, a legitimate cause for anxiety.

And Fay had depressed him. Living like a spinster, watching
her father coming unraveled, in the kind of conditions Guy
remembered from his childhood—remembered only in black-
and-white, like grainy old television. He couldn't understand
why Fay had failed to throw herself at him, sobbing, "Take
me away from all this," instead of bustling off with her Uher
over her shoulder in pursuit of a local news item that would be
unlikely to make even a filler paragraph in tomorrow's Sunday
papers.

Guy, rather than attempt to construct a conversation with the
canon, had claimed to be overdue for another appointment, and

thus had ended up making his second despondent tour of the town center.

Country towns were not supposed to be like this. Country towns were supposed to have tea shops and flower stalls and Saturday markets from which fat, friendly Women's Institute ladies sold jars of homemade jam and chutney sealed by grease-proof paper and rubber bands.

Without a crew, without Catrin and her clipboard, and without even a hint of recognition from the public, Guy felt a sudden sense of acute isolation. He'd never been anywhere quite like this before—a town which seemed to have had all the life sucked out of it, bloodless people walking past, sagging like puppets whose strings had been snipped.

He was almost inclined to cancel his room at the Cock and race back home to Cardiff.

Instead, in the gloomy late afternoon, as it began to rain again, he found himself strolling incuriously into The Gallery, where he and Jocasta Newsome would soon recognize a mutual need.

Outside, Powys had found some logs for the Jotul stove. They were damp, but he managed to get the stove going and stacked a couple of dozen logs on each side of it to dry out.

He couldn't remember bleaker weather at the end of June.

His cases stood unpacked by the window. On the ledge, a blank sheet of paper was wound into the Olivetti.

Life itself seemed very temporary tonight.

Just before seven, a grim-faced Rachel arrived, soaked. She tossed her dripping coat on the floor.

"Coffee, J.M. I need coffee. With something in it." She collapsed onto the hard orange sofa, flung her head back, closing her eyes. "I suppose you've heard?"

Powys said, "They found a body in the river."

"What are you going to do, J.M.?"

"Do they know what happened?"

"I don't think so. They haven't questioned anyone except the father and Gomer Parry."

Powys went into the little kitchen to look for coffee and called back, "Have they found the gun?"

"Not so far as I know," Rachel said. "Perhaps Jonathon Preece didn't find it either. Perhaps the place where you threw it was deeper than you thought. Humble, who seems to know what he's talking about, says there are all kinds of unexpected potholes in the riverbed. He says nobody in their right mind would attempt to wade across, even in a dry summer, when the water level's low."

"Humble?" Powys's voice had an edge of panic.

"He volunteered the information. In passing. I wasn't stupid enough to ask him. I feigned disinterest."

Not a difficult act, he accepted, for Rachel.

He returned with two mugs and a bottle of Bell's whiskey. "I can't find any coffee, but I found this in a cupboard." He poured whiskey into a mug and handed it to Rachel. "Can't find any glasses either."

Rachel drank deeply and didn't cough or choke.

Powys said, "What do you think I ought to do?"

Rachel held the mug in both hands and stretched out her long legs to the stove in a vain quest for heat. "I think we should wait for Fay. She's going to come here after she's filled her scrupulously objective story about the drowning tragedy at Crybbe."

"That won't be easy. What's she going to say?"

"It seems," said Rachel, "that minor flooding at Crybbe has claimed its first victim."

She looked tired. There were dark smudges on her narrow face. "Just hope they don't find the gun. I don't know what water does to fingerprints, do you?"

As the second stroke of the curfew hit the reverberation of the first, clean and hard, Warren Preece tossed his used condom, well-filled, into the alley and zipped up his jeans.

"Close," he said. "But I reckon I can improve on it if I puts my mind to it."

Tessa Byford was leaning back against the brick wall of the Crybbe Unattended Studio, still panting a little. "You're confident tonight."

"Yeah." The trick, he'd learned (he'd learned it from Tessa, but he'd allowed himself to forget this) was to time it so you came in the split second before the bell crashed. Tonight he'd lost his load a good five seconds before the first bong. Still near as buggery took the top of his head off, though—always did here—but it could be better.

Warren got a special kick out of thinking of his old man up the tower, waiting to pull on the rope while he, Warren, was down here bonking his brains out. Dead on time again tonight: nothing would come between Jack Preece and that bell, not even his favorite son drying out in some police morgue.

"Ask not," Warren intoned, "for whom the ole bell tolls. It tolls tonight, ladies and gen'lemen, for Jonathon Preece, of Court Farm, Crybbe."

He giggled.

There was a snap of white—Tessa pulling up her knickers.

Warren said, "I been feeling—just lately, like—as if I'm the only guy in this town, the only one who's really alive sorter thing. The only walkin' corpse in the graveyard. Bleeargh!"

Warren wiggled his hands and rolled his eyes.

Written two new songs, he had, in the past couple of days. Red-hot stuff, too. Didn't know he had it in him—how *much* he had in him. He reckoned Max Goff's tape would be ready in a couple of weeks. Goff was going to be real blown away by this next one.

"What would you have done, Warren, if that woman hadn't come out of the studio before we got started? Or if she'd come out in the middle?"

"Woulder made no difference. Or I coulda saved some for 'er, couldn't I? Takin' a chance, she is, comin' yere this time o' night. An' she wouldn't say a word, see, 'cause I seen what 'appened by the river, 'ow they killed poor Jonathon. Poor Jonathon!"

Warren started to grin. "Oh, you should've seen 'im, Tess. Lyin' there with 'is tongue out. Just about as wet and slimy as what 'e was when 'e was alive. I couldn't 'ardly keep a straight face. And—you got to laugh, see—fucking Young Farmers' . . ."

Warren *did* laugh. He placed both hands flat on the brick wall and almost beat his head into it with laughing.

" . . . fuckin' Young Farmers' needs a new chairman now, isn't it? Oh, shit, what a bloody crisis!"

"You going to volunteer, Warren?"

"No." Warren wiped his streaming eyes with the back of a hand. "I'm goin' into the plant hire business." He went into another cackle. "I'm gonner hot-wire me a bulldozer."

She was the kind of woman who, in normal circumstances, he would have taken care to avoid, like sunstroke. She was vain, pretentious, snobbish and too bony in the places where one needed it least.

But these were not normal circumstances. On a wet Saturday evening in Crybbe, Jocasta Newsome was almost exotic.

Guy had her on the hearthrug, where damp logs spat the occasional spark into his buttocks.

She was tasty.

And grateful. Guy loved people to be grateful for him. She was voracious in a carefree sort of way, as if all kinds of pent-up emotions were being expelled. She laughed a lot; he made her laugh, even with comments and questions that were not intended to be funny.

Like, "And your husband—is he an artist?"

Jocasta squealed in delight and ground a pelvic bone painfully into his stomach.

Guy said, just checking, "You're sure there's no chance he'll be back tonight?"

"Tonight," said Jocasta, "Hereward will be in one of those awful restaurants where the candles on the tables are stuck in wine bottles and some unshaven student is hunched up in the corner fumbling with a guitar. He'll be holding forth at length to a bunch of artists about the beauty of Crybbe and how well in he is with the local yokels. He'll be telling them all about his close friend Max Goff and the wonderful experiment in which he, Hereward, is playing a pivotal role. The artists will drink bottle after bottle of disgusting wine paid for, of course, by Hereward and they'll think, 'What a sucker, what an absolutely God-sent idiot.' And they'll be mentally doubling their prices."

Jocasta propped herself up on one arm, her nipples rather redder than the feebly smoldering logs in the grate.

"Oh yes," she assured him. "We are utterly alone and likely to remain so for two whole, wonderful days. How long have *you* got, Guy? Inches and inches, if I'm any judge. Oh my God, what am I saying?"

The thought of *two whole days* of Jocasta Newsome didn't lift Guy to quite the same heights. He reached for his trousers.

Dismay disfigured her. "What are you doing? I didn't mean . . . "

"Just going to the loo, if you could direct me. Guy Morrison never goes anywhere without trousers. Not the kind of risk one takes."

"Oh." Jocasta relaxed. "Yes. We're having a downstairs cloakroom made, but it isn't quite . . . Up the stairs, turn left, and there's a bathroom directly facing you at the end of the passage. Don't be long, will you?"

Mercifully, she didn't qualify the final entreaty with another dreadful *double entendre.*

Guy slithered into his trousers and set off barefoot up the stairs, slightly worried now. Happily married women were fine. *Un*happily married women were worse than unattached women. They clutched you as if you were a life belt. They were seldom afraid of word getting out about you and them. And while it might be all right for pop stars, scandal was rarely helpful to the careers of responsible producer-presenters in Features and Documentaries.

Bare-chested on the stairs, he shivered. The walls had been stripped to the stonework. Too rugged for Guy Morrison. He probably wouldn't come here again. He decided he'd open the exhibition tomorrow night and slide quietly away. A one-night stand was OK, but a two-night stand carried just a hint of commitment.

The lights went out.

"Oh, blast!" he heard from the drawing room.

"What's happened?"

"Power cut," Jocasta shouted. "Happens all the time. Take it slowly and you'll be OK. When you get to the bathroom you'll find a torch on top of the cabinet."

Guy stubbed his toe on the top banister post and tried not to cry out.

But he found his way to the bathroom quite easily because of a certain greasy phosphorescence oozing out of the crack between the door and its frame.

"Funny sort of power cut," he said, not thinking at all.

"Police say there are no suspicious circumstances, but they still can't explain how Mr. Preece, whose family has been farming in the area for over four hundred years, came to be in the river."

"That report," the Offa's Dyke news anchor said, *"from Fay Morrison in Crybbe. Now Sport, and for Hereford United . . . "*

Fay switched off Powys's radio.

It was thirty-three minutes past ten and almost totally dark.

"Must've been awkward for you." J. M. Powys rammed a freshly dried log into the Jotul and slammed the iron door on it.

Fay, in a black sweat suit, was cross-legged on the hearth, by the stove.

"Not really," she said. "In cases like this you're not expected to probe too hard. If it'd been a child, I'd be spending most of the night talking to worried mothers about why the council needed to fence off the river. Then tomorrow, this being Crybbe, I'd have to explain to Ashpole why the worried mothers were refusing to be interviewed on tape. But in a case like this, it's just assumed he killed himself. Be an open verdict. Unless . . . "

"Unless they find the gun." Powys switched on a green-shaded table lamp. Rachel drew the curtains against the night and the rain and the river.

Fay said, "If anybody had any suspicions, we'd have heard from the police by now. All the same, Jack Preece . . . "

"His father," Powys said.

"Yes. Jack Preece knows. I could see it in his eyes when we were down by the river, with the body."

"Knows what?"

"I think he knows Jonathon had gone out to shoot Arnold."

Rachel sat down on the sofa. "What makes you . . . ?"

"Just a minute. Hang on." Powys stood up. "You say Jonathon *had gone out to shoot Arnold.* You're saying he'd deliberately targeted Arnold?"

Fay nodded.

"Do I get the feeling there's a history to this?"

Fay swallowed. "If I tell you this, you're going to switch to small talk for a few minutes and then look for an excuse to get rid of me. It's so weird."

"Fay." Powys spread his arms. "I'm the bloke who wrote *The Old Golden Land.* Nothing's too weird."

There was a longish silence. Then the green-shaded table lamp went out.

"Bugger," Rachel said.

"OK," Fay said slowly. "You can't see my face now, and I won't be able to see the incredulity on yours."

She took a long breath. She told them about dogs in Crybbe.

"How long have you known this?" Powys asked.

"Only a day or so. I should be doing a story on it, shouldn't I? A town with no dogs? Jesus, it's not common, is it? But life here is so much like a bad dream, I'm sure if I sold it to the papers, when all the reporters arrived to check it out, there'd be dogs everywhere, shelves full of Chum at the grocer's, poop-scoops at the ironmonger's, posters for the Crybbe and District Annual Dog Show . . . "

She was glad they couldn't see the helpless tears in her eyes.

"I can't *trust* myself here," Fay said, fighting to keep the tears out of her voice. "I can't trust myself to perceive anything correctly. Too much has happened."

"Have you thought about why it could be?" Powys asked, a soft, accepting voice in the darkness. "Why no dogs?"

"Sure I've thought about it—in between thinking about my dad going bonkers, about holding on to my job, about somebody breaking in and smashing up my tape machine, about being arrested for manslaughter, about living with a gho . . . about lots of things. I'm sorry, I'm not very rational tonight."

"So what you're saying is"—Rachel's *very* rational voice— "that, because you wouldn't get rid of Arnold, Jonathon Preece deliberately set out to shoot him?"

"I had a phone call. An anonymous call. Get rid of him by this weekend, or . . . "

"Or he'd be shot?"

"There was no specified threat. Just a warning. I think Jack Preece was the caller. Therefore, it seems likely he sent Jonathon out with the gun."

She heard Powys fumbling with the stove and its iron door was flung wide, letting a stuttering red and yellow firelight into the room.

His face looked much younger in the firelight. "If this is right about no dogs—I'm sorry, Fay, if you say there are no dogs, I believe you—we could be looking at the key to something here."

"You're the expert," Fay said.

"There aren't any experts. This is the one area in which nobody's an expert."

"If all dogs howl at the curfew," Rachel said logically, "why don't they just get rid of the curfew? It's not as if it's a major tourist attraction. Not as if they even draw attention to it. It just happens, it's just continued, without much being said. OK, there's this story about the legacy of land to the Preeces, but is anybody really going to take that away if the curfew stops?"

"I don't think for one minute," said Powys, "that that's the real reason for the curfew."

Fay sat up, interested. "So what *is* the real reason?"

"If we knew that, we'd know the secret of Crybbe."

"You think there's something to know? You think there's a good reason why the place is as miserable as sin?"

"There's something. Fay, how did you come to get Henry's dog. I mean, did you know him well?"

"Hardly at all. I'd done an interview with him on the day he died."

"That's interesting. What sort of an interview? What was it about?"

"Er . . . dowsing. I wanted to know what he was doing in Crybbe, but it was obvious he didn't want to talk about that, so . . . Anyway, it was never used."

"Have you still got the tape?"

"I imagine so. If you want to hear it, come down to the studio sometime. Up the covered alley behind the Cock."

"Tomorrow morning?"

"Nine o'clock?"

"Fine."

"And about Arnold, I got him from the police because it was obvious nobody else was going to. He was howling away in full daylight, and I'm pretty sure now that if I hadn't taken him, he'd have been dead. They'd have killed him. Before nightfall. Before the curfew."

The torchlight shone in Jocasta's eyes.

"It's me," Guy said. "Look . . . "

"Yes, I know. Come here, I'm cold."

"I haven't been," said Guy. "I couldn't go."

"I don't understand—you've got the torch."

"Jocasta," Guy hissed urgently, closing the drawing-room door quietly behind him. "For Christ's sake, why didn't you tell me we weren't alone?"

Jocasta felt *very* cold. She began to tremble, crawled to the sofa, and scrabbled for her dress.

"Who is he?" Guy demanded. She couldn't see him, only the torch. "Is he your father?"

Jocasta tried to speak and couldn't. She tried to stand up, tried to step into her dress, got her legs tangled, fell back on the rug.

"I waited," Guy said. "But he didn't come out."

Jocasta, squatting on the rug in the torch circle, struggled vainly to zip up her dress. No eager fingers to help her now.

"What the hell's going on, Jocasta?"

She found her voice, but didn't recognize it. "My father," she said slowly, "is in Chiswick. My husband, Hereward, is somewhere in Somerset. There is nobody here. Nobody here but us, Guy."

A log shifted in the grate, sending up a yellow spark shower, like a cheap firework.

"Then who the fuck was that old man in the bathroom? Having a shave, for crying out loud, with a . . . with a . . ." His voice faltered. "With a cut-throat razor."

The improbability of the scenario seemed to occur to him at last.

"How could I see him? How could I see him when all the lights . . . ?"

Guy's voice went quiet. "He was a strange kind of yellow," he said unsteadily. "A very feeble shade of yellow."

The torchlight wavered as he advanced on the sofa. "Where are my clothes? I'm getting out of here."

"*No!*" Jocasta leapt at him, clutching the arm which held the torch. He dropped it. It lay on the floor, its beam directed into the fireplace. The logs looked dead and gray in the strong, white light.

"Don't go," Jocasta implored. "You can't go. You can't leave me. For God's sake, don't leave me here with . . . with . . ."

four

The following morning, Sunday, just before 9 A.M., there was a sudden burst of sunlight, a splash of dripping yellow in a washed-out, watercolor sky.

The light looked to be directly over the Tump, the trees on its sides and summit massing menacingly around the watery orb. It was, Rachel thought, as if a green-gloved hand had reached out from the foliage, snatched the emergent sun, and crunched it like an egg.

"I think we should call the police," she said.

"Why?" said Humble. "Whoever done it saved us a job."

The Tump squatted under the sun, fat and smug. You could almost think the Tump was the culprit—as if the great mound had taken a deep breath, pulled in its girth, and then let go, bellying out and crumbling the wall before it.

Then Rachel had seen the bulldozer, still wedged in the rubble.

"And there's Gomer Parry," she said. "What's he going to say?"

"Proves him wrong, dunnit? He reckoned the machine wouldn't go frew the wall."

"Without the wall collapsing on it. Which it has."

A chunk of wall about fifteen feet wide had been smashed in or wrenched out and then the bulldozer plunged in again. Clearly an amateur job, but the spot had been well-chosen. It would leave a jagged gap directly under the huge picture window in the stable block.

"All we do about Gomer, we just pay him off," Humble said. He was unshaven. He wore a black motorcycle jacket. Half an hour ago he'd rung J. M. Powys's riverside cottage. "Put Rachel on." She'd been quite shocked, didn't see how he could possibly have known about her and J.M.

It meant Max would know by now. Max would not be particularly annoyed that she was with J. M. Powys, but she'd done it without clearing it with him first—*that* was the serious offense.

Time to move on, Rachel decided abruptly. The façade's crumbling. Time to negotiate a settlement.

"I think the bulldozer's damaged," she said. "Look at the way the blade thing is twisted."

"Couple of thou' should see Gomer right. See, Rachel, you bring in the Old Bill, you're causing unnecessary hassle. Somebody might get the idea we paid him to do it. Max would not like that."

"Him? You sound as if you know who did it."

"Yeah, well, I got my suspicions."

"Would you like to share them?"

"I keep my eyes open," Humble said.

"Not much you don't know, is there, Humble?"

Humble smirked. "Not much, Rachel. Not much."

The metal plate on the door said, *When red light is showing, do not attempt to enter.*

The red light was on.

Not sure what to do, Powys walked around the dull, brick building which had once been a lavatory. When he arrived back at the door he was holding up a foot.

"Oh shit, what's this?"

Making a face, Powys scraped off the used condom against a corner of the wall.

She was watching him in some amusement from the studio door, open now, the red light still on.

"Sorry, should have warned you. You'll never pick up a dog turd in this town, but French letters . . . an all-too-common hazard. Especially just here."

Powys looked around and counted five of the things, shriveling into the gravel. "Favorite place," Fay said. "The grunts and squeals can be quite disconcerting when you arrive here in the dark."

"Maybe it's the red light gets them going." Powys looked up at the sign. " 'Do not attempt to enter.' Obviously nobody takes much notice of that."

"Come in," said Fay.

He followed her into the little building and looked around. "Incredible. A radio studio in Crybbe."

"Geographically convenient." Fay was unpacking two reels of quarter-inch tape. "It's certainly not a reflection of the importance of the town."

She set the tape rolling. "I won't waste time. This is one bit. Henry Kettle's dowsing master class."

"OK. Here we go. Is there any . . . ? Fucking hell, Henry!"

"Caught you by surprise, did it?"

Powys grinned. "Bit like sex, isn't it. The first time. Did the earth move for you?"

"Certainly did when he put his hands over mine. The rod just sort of flipped over. I did wonder afterwards if he was *making* it happen. Just to get it over with, get me off his back. He was obviously very busy. But I can be quite persistent, I suppose."

He thought she probably could. She looked very nice this morning, in a dark skirt and a glittery kind of top.

She noticed him studying the ensemble. "I'm going to church afterwards." Pushing the buttons on the tape machine and flipping the controls on the console. "Then I've got to go and pick up Arnold from the vet's."

"He's OK?"

"Actually the vet said on the phone that I might get a bit of a shock when I saw him, but there was nothing to worry about. Have you ever been inside the church?"

He shook his head. "But you're a regular churchgoer, I suppose. With your dad in the business."

"Oh hell, nothing to do with that. And I'm not, actually. What it is, Dad tells me Murray—that's the vicar—is doing his sermon on the New Age Phenomenon in Our Midst. I'll probably get a story out of it. Murray's a very mixed-up person. The town's damaged him, I think."

"You think this town damages people?"

"It's damaged me," said Fay. "Listen, this is the bit. Obviously, what I was really interested in was what Henry Kettle was doing for Goff, and at one point I asked him, straight out."

" . . . So, tell me, Henry, you're obviously in the middle of a major dowsing operation here in Crybbe. What exactly does that involve?"

"Oh, I . . . Oh dear. Look, switch that thing off a minute, will you?"

"He was waving his arms about, the way people do when you ask them a question they can't answer."

"And did you switch off?"

"I did, I'm afraid," Fay said. "Sometimes you flip the pause button a couple of times to make it look as if you have and then record the lot, but I was starting to like him. 'Don't press me, girl,' he kept saying."

"Did he say anything to indicate he was bothered, or upset by what he was finding?"

"I think he did, and it must be on the other tape." Fay spun all the way back and pulled the reel off the deck. "Hold this a minute, would you, er . . . sorry, I don't actually know what the J.M. stands for."

"Joe."

"Joe Powys. Mmm. It's a whole different person. Now, Joe Powys, some answers." She had her fists on her hips, the second reel clutched in one. "Who killed Henry Kettle?"

"Ah," he said.

"You don't think it was an accident at all, do you?"

"Well," he said, "I don't think it's who killed him so much as *what* killed him. I'm sure nobody tampered with his brakes or anything."

"So you think it might be something, shall we say . . . supernatural? And *don't* say it depends what I mean by supernatural."

"How about you put the tape on, then we'll talk about it?"

"And you went to see Mrs. Seagrove again, didn't you?"

"We loonies have to stick together."

"So you *did* go to talk about the black dog . . . OK, OK, I'll put the tape on."

She dragged the yellow leader tape past the heads, set it running on fast forward, stopped it. "Somewhere around here, I think. I'd caught up with Henry in the wood between the Court and the church. I'd come straight from another job and I still had about half a tape left, so I just ran it off, walking along with Henry. When you're putting a package together you need lots of spare atmos and stuff."

"Atmos?"

"Ambient sounds. Birdsong, wind in the trees. Also, I needed bits of him trudging along doing his dowsing bit. Radio's nearly as much of a fake as telly, you reshape it afterwards, rearrange sentences, manufacture pauses for effect—using spare ambience. So here's Henry in the wood. I hope."

"That's curious. That is curious."

"That's it. Hang on a minute, Joe, I'll find the start. OK, here we go . . . "

" . . . *keep you a minute, Fay, just something I need to look at. Bear with me."*

"That's OK, Mr. Kettle. Can I call you Henry during the interview? Makes it more informal."

"You please yourself, girl. Call me a daft old bugger if you like."

Powys felt almost tearful. Every time someone like Henry died, the world faded a shade further into neutral.

"Well, bugger—don't mind me, Fay, talking to myself. That's curious. That is curious. If I didn't know better, I'd almost be inclined to think it wasn't an old stone at all. Funny old business . . . Just when you think you've come across everything, you find something that don't . . . quite . . . add up. Come on, then, Fay, let's do your bit of radio, only we'll go somewhere else if you don't mind . . . "

Powys said, "Can you just play that bit again?"

" . . . *almost be inclined to think it wasn't an* old *stone at all . . . "*

"That's the bit." There was a parallel here, something from Henry's journal. "Fay, where was this, can you show me? Have you time before church?"

"We'll have to be a bit quick, Joe," Fay said, rewinding.

Murray Beech watched his sermon rolling out of the printer with barely an hour to go before the service. Normally he worked at least three weeks in advance, storing the sermons on computer disk. This one had been completed only last night, at great personal risk—Murray had twice lost entire scripts due to power cuts.

But the electricity rarely failed in the morning, and the printer whizzed it out without interruption.

Certain claims have already been made for the effects of this so-called New Awakening . . .

Why am I doing this? he asked himself.

Because it's what they want to hear, he answered shamefully. Never imagined it would come to this. What harm were they causing, these innocent cranks with their ley-lines and their healing rays?

Ironically, Murray had come to Crybbe aware of the need for tolerance with country folk, their local customs, their herbal remedies. But it had proved to be a myth. Country people, *real* country people weren't like this, not in Crybbe anyway, where he'd never been offered a herbal remedy or even a pot of homemade jam. And where the only custom was the curfew, an unsmiling ritual, performed without comment.

On a metal bookshelf sat the three-volume set of Kilvert's diary, given to him by Kirsty when he told her he was leaving Brighton to become a vicar in the border country.

"Just like Kilvert!" She'd been thrilled. He'd never heard of Kilvert, so she'd bought him the collected diaries, the record (expressively written, if you liked that sort of thing) of a young Victorian clergyman's life, mainly in the village of Clyro, about twenty miles from Crybbe. Kilvert had found rich colors in nature and in the people around him. He'd also found warmth and friends, even if he did have a rather disturbing predilection for young girls.

Murray's stomach tightened; he was thinking of dark-eyed Tessa, a sweat dab over her lips.

Loneliness.

Loneliness had brought him to this.

I've no friends here.

Kirsty had spent a week in Crybbe, long enough to convince her this was not the border country beloved of Francis Kilvert.

"You once said you'd follow me anywhere my calling took me. Africa . . . South America . . . "

"But not Crybbe, Murray. I'd die. I'd wither."

She'd given him Kilvert's diary for his birthday two years ago.

Exactly two years ago. Today was his birthday.

"Is there *no* chance of your finding a living down here, Murray?" his mother had asked this morning, on the phone.

They'd been proud, of course, as he had, when he'd been given Crybbe—such a large parish, such a young man.

Nobody else wanted it.

No homemade jam. No Women's Institute. No welcome at the primary school. No harvest supper. No bell-ringers. No friends. No wife.

He could, of course, have betrayed the inert, moribund villagers by siding openly with the New Age community, who at least sought some kind of spirituality, albeit misguided. He would, perhaps, have made friends, of a sort, among them.

But he knew his role as priest was to support his parishioners, even if they did not support him, apart from token mute appearance at his services. Even if they did not deserve him.

Murray was disgusted with himself for thinking that.

Loneliness. Loneliness had brought him to this.

The only way either of them knew into the wood was through the Court grounds. When they arrived there in Fay's Fiesta, Rachel was outside the stables with one of the interior designers, a small, completely bald man she introduced as Simon.

"What this place is about," Simon was saying, "is drama. Drama and spectacle."

Powys didn't even have to go inside to see what he meant. The original stable doors had been replaced with huge portals of plate glass, through which you could look down into a kind of theater, the kitchen and dining room walled off from a single cavernous room, the length of the building, ending in a wide, wooden desk, its back to the huge picture window.

And the Tump.

When Max was sitting at his desk, he would be directly under the mound. From the top of the room it would look as if the great tumulus with its wavy trees was growing out of his head.

Especially now that . . .

"What happened to the wall?"

Rachel grimaced. "Person or persons unknown came in the night to do Max a big favor, using Gomer Parry's bulldozer. I'm sure Humble knows who it was; he tends to be out there in the small hours, killing things. But Humble isn't saying."

The attack on the wall, the opening up of the stable block, with glass at either end . . . the formation of a conduit between the Tump and Crybbe.

Powys looked at it through Goff's eyes: a stream of healing energy—deep blue—surging through the stables, through the Court itself, through the wood to the church and then into the town.

Equally, though, you could see the Tump as a huge malignant tumor, assisted at last to spread its black cells and bring secondary cancers to Crybbe, a town already old and moldering.

"Natural drama," Simon, the designer, said. "Great."

*   *   *

In the center of the wood was a huge hole, newly dug, around five feet deep.

"Must be destined for a big one," Powys said. "And they're making sure it's going to be visible."

Fay looked around in horror. "There was a bit of a clearing when I was here with Henry, but nothing . . . nothing like this."

The immediate area was strewn with chainsaw carnage. Stumps of slaughtered trees, heaps of wet ash where branches had been burned.

Looking back the way they'd come, Powys could see the roof of the Court. "I reckon most of this wood's going to disappear. They want to open up the view from the prospect chamber, reconnect the town with the Court—and the Tump."

"But you can't just chop down a whole wood!" Fay glared at Rachel, who backed off, holding up both hands.

"Listen, I know nothing about this. This is Boulton-Trow's province."

"Aren't trees like this protected?"

"I should imagine so," said Rachel. "But it's hardly an imprisonable offense. You can take out injunctions to prevent people chopping down individual trees, but once they're gone, they're gone, and if you do it quietly, well . . . "

"Like starting from the middle and working outwards," Powys said. "I don't know how old this wood is, but the indication from the prospect chamber is that at the end of the sixteenth century it wasn't here at all. I reckon it was planted not to give the Court more privacy but so the townsfolk couldn't see the Court. So they could pretend it wasn't there. Just as the stable block was put in to block the Court off from the Tump. They were scared of something."

He was balancing on the edge of the hole, looking down. "So, Fay, this is where Henry discovered there'd been a stone."

"I think so. Must be."

"And yet he had the feeling the stone that stood here wasn't an *old* stone."

"That's what he seemed to be saying." Fay was more concerned about the wholesale destruction of the wood. "And these are supposed to be bloody *New Age* people!" She peered through what remained of the trees. "Can I get to the church this way?"

"Sure," Rachel said. "Five minutes' walk. There's a footpath, newly widened. Goes past a redbrick heap called Keeper's Cottage, which is where Boulton-Trow's living."

"He lives here?" Powys said, surprised. "In the wood?"

"Yes, and rather him than me. Go past it, anyway, Fay, and you're in the churchyard in no time."

"Thanks." Fay pulled a bunch of keys from her bag. "Do me a favor, Joe, I've got to catch Murray's blasted sermon. Could you bring my car round to the church when you've finished here? It's got the Uher in the back. I'll need to interview him afterwards."

She vanished into the bushes. Like an elf, he thought.

"I came to a decision this morning," Rachel said.

She sat down on a tree stump. "I'm going to quit."

"Good. I mean, that's terrific. You're wasted on that fat plonker."

"I'm becoming peripheral anyway. Max doesn't listen to me anymore. He's getting so fanatical I don't think there's anything you or I can do to stop him. Also, he's entering one of his DC phases. He's besotted with Boulton-Trow."

"Andy? Is it reciprocated?"

"You know the guy better than me, J.M."

"He's an opportunist."

"There you are, then."

He watched her, pale and graceful in this arboreal charnel house. She brushed a stray hair out of one eye.

He said, "When will you tell him?"

"Probably after his public meeting on Tuesday."

"That's marvelous, Rachel. You won't regret it. Coming to church?"

Rachel stood up. "Oh gosh, far too busy. Least I can do is make sure his stable block's ready for him. Besides, I'm not a churchy person. I'm one of those who think it's a waste of Sunday—what do you call that, an atheist or an agnostic?"

He put an arm around her waist. "You call it a smug bitch."

He grinned, happy for her.

five

"And let's pray now," Murray Beech said, head bowed, "for the soul of our brother Jonathon Preece . . ."

Kneeling in a back pew, Fay tensed.

" . . . taken so suddenly from the heart of the agricultural community he served so energetically. Those of us who knew Jonathon—and can there be any here who did not?—will always remember his tireless commitment to the Young Farmers' movement and, through this, to the revival of an industry in which his family has labored for over four hundred years."

Powys slid the Uher into the empty pew next to Fay and slipped in after it. Fay kept on looking directly ahead, over the prayer-book ledge, seeing, near the front of the church, the heads of Jack Preece and Jimmy Preece. One of the few places you ever saw these heads uncapped.

"And we pray, too," Murray intoned passionlessly, "for the Preece family in its time of sorrow and loss . . ."

Fay saw young Warren Preece, head nodding rhythmically now and then, as if connected to some invisible Walkman.

Saw Mrs. Preece, Jimmy's wife, hands clasped in prayer. Expecting to see a damp tissue crumpled in her palm. But Mrs. Preece, seen side-on, looked as dry-eyed and stern as her husband. They seemed to have their eyes open as they prayed—if indeed they *were* praying.

Looking around, Fay found that everyone's were open, everyone she could see.

Crybbe: a place where emotions were buried as deep as the dead.

Wisely, perhaps, Murray didn't make a big deal of it. He went into the Lord's Prayer and didn't mention Jonathon Preece again.

Fay relaxed.

What had she expected? A denunciation from the pulpit? All heads turned in mute accusation?

Whatever, she breathed again. And became aware of the significance of something she must surely have noticed already: the presence of her father, on the end of a pew two rows in front of her and Powys.

The canon went to church every Sunday, sometimes attending both the morning and evening services. He sat near the front and sang loudly—"Bit of moral support for young Murray; boy needs all the backup he can get."

So what was he doing farther back, a couple of rows behind the nearest fully occupied pew? Could it be something to do with there being only one other person on Alex's pew and this person being at the same end of the pew as Alex? And being a woman?

"Bloody hell," said Fay to herself. "He's found a woman."

Guy Morrison woke up into the grayness of . . . 5 A.M., 5:30?

He found his watch on the bedside table.

It told him the time was 11:15.

For crying out loud! He turned over and found he was alone in a king-size bed of antique pine, in a pink-washed room with large beams in the ceiling and a view, through small square panes, of misty hills. He'd never seen this view before.

Guy lay down again, regulating his breathing.

He saw a door then, and a glimpse of mauve tiles told him it led to an *en suite* bathroom, which put him in mind of another bathroom, full of seeping yellow.

With a momentary clenching of stomach muscles, *everything* came back.

He remembered peeing on his shoes in the dark paddock because she wouldn't let him return to that bathroom—not that he needed much persuading.

He remembered them staying in the kitchen for a long time, drinking coffee—him not talking much and not listening much either, after she'd been gushing like a broken fire hydrant for an hour or so—until it was nearly light and she'd decided it was safe to go to bed. This bed. He remembered waking up periodically to find her hanging on to him in her fitful, unquiet sleep and wondering how he could ever have found her so attractive.

Guy pushed back the quilt to find he was naked, and he couldn't see his clothes anywhere. If he went downstairs like this it would be just his luck to find the vicar and the entire bloody Women's Institute having morning coffee in the drawing room.

He went into the *en suite* bathroom, looked at himself in the mirror, and was horrified at the state of his hair and the growth of his beard, detecting a distressing amount of gray and white stubble. He looked around for something to shave with—normally, he used a state-of-the-art rechargeable twice a day—and could find only a primitive kind of safety razor.

Remembering, at this point, the old man with the cut-throat razor in the other bathroom. And hours later in the well-lit kitchen, thrusting aside his fourth cup of coffee, asking her directly, "Are you telling me it was a *ghost?*"

He'd once done a documentary about ghosts. They were, the program had suggested, nature's holograms. Something like that. You might get images of the dead; you could just as easily have images of the living. When the phenomenon was eventually understood it would be no more frightening than a mirage.

This one was frightening, he supposed, only briefly, in retrospect. What had he really felt when he saw the glow around the door and then walked into the bathroom and the old man had looked up and met his eyes? Fear, or a kind of fascination?

Did this old man have eyes? He must have had. Guy couldn't recall his features. Only a figure bent over the washbasin, shaving. The image, perhaps, of a man who had lived in this house for many years and perhaps shaved thousands of times in that very basin—well, perhaps not that actual basin, but certainly in the room. And this mundane, everyday ritual had imprinted itself on the atmosphere.

The apparition was frightening, Guy decided, because it happened at night during a power cut. Also, because he was feeling a few misgivings about what he'd got himself into and was perhaps a little jittery anyway.

Guy shaved with the razor, his first wet shave in years, and cut himself twice, quite noticeably—no pieces-to-camera for *him* for a couple of days. Perhaps this chap didn't have an electric shaver because he couldn't rely on one, with all the power cuts they apparently had. Jocasta had gone on and on last night about the power cuts and the exorbitant electricity bills. How living in the country wasn't a simple life at all and certainly not cheap. How she couldn't get out of here fast enough. How her poor husband was weak and naive beyond comprehension.

Guy didn't like the sound of that bit at all, much preferred screwing happily married women whose only need was a touch of glamour in their lives.

The true horror of the night, now he thought about it, had been the hours he'd spent with a furrow-faced Jocasta in the kitchen afterward, listening to her whining on and on.

"Guy, where are you?"

He looked around the bathroom door and saw her standing by the bed. She wore a floor-length Japanese silk dressing gown and fresh makeup. Façade fully restored. She must have spent an hour or so in here before he was awake.

"Good morning, Jocasta." Guy stepped naked and smiling into the bedroom, forgetting about the two cuts on his face, stanched by small pieces of soft toilet tissue. Perhaps . . . Perhaps he could afford to give her just one more . . .

But she didn't look at him in any meaningful way. "Please get dressed," Jocasta said crisply. "I want to show you something."

Guy's smile vanished.

"Your clothes are in Bedroom Two, across the passage. Coffee and croissants in ten minutes."

And Jocasta swished away, leaving him most offended. Women did not turn their backs and swish away from Guy Morrison.

When he arrived in the kitchen nearly twenty minutes later, he was fully dressed, right up to his olive leather jacket, and fully aware again of who he was. He accepted coffee but declined a croissant. He must, he said, be off. Perhaps she could give him a time for the exhibition opening, keeping it as tight as possible because he had quite a few people to see.

Jocasta pushed a large folder toward him across the kitchen table. "I'd be glad," she said, "if you could take a look at these."

"Look, I *am* rather pushed—"

"It won't take a minute." She was very composed this morning, probably embarrassed as hell about last night's tearful sequence. He opened the folder in a deliberately cursory fashion. What the hell was all this about? Was he expected to *buy* something?

The drawing was pen-and-ink. The face was inspecting itself in a mirror. Every wrinkle on the face—and there were many—was deeply etched. The eyes were sunken, the cheeks hollow, the nose bulbous.

Guy inhaled sharply. He looked up at Jocasta in her Japanese dressing gown, could tell she was working hard to hide her feelings, holding a mask over her anticipation. Anticipation and something else. Something altogether less healthy.

He looked down at the drawing again. He felt a deep suspicion and a growing alarm.

"Is this some sort of joke?"

"Is it him?" Jocasta asked.

"I don't know what you mean. Who did these?"

"Is it *him?*"

Of course it was him. It was either him or Guy was going mad. His deep suspicion was suddenly drenched in cold confusion and a bitter, acrid dread.

"Look at the next one."

All the sensation had left his fingers. He watched them, as if they were someone else's fingers, lifting the first drawing, laying it to one side, facedown on the table.

He didn't understand.

A moment earlier, he saw, the old man had slashed his throat. The open razor had fallen from one spasmed hand—it was drawn in midair, floating a fraction of an inch below a finger and thumb—while the fingers of the other hand were pushing into the opened throat itself, as if trying to hold the slit tubes together, to block the tunnels of blood.

The blood was black ink, blotch upon blotch, spread joyously, as if the pen nib was a substitute for the cut-throat razor.

Guy thrust the drawing aside, came raggedly to his feet. He stumbled to the sink and threw up what seemed like half a gallon of sour coffee.

It was not the drawing, he thought as he retched. It was the knowledge of what, if he'd stayed a moment longer in the bathroom last night, he would have seen.

He wiped his mouth with the back of a hand, saw Jocasta watching him in distaste, knew exactly what she was thinking: that perhaps all men were as pathetic as her husband.

"I'm sorry," Guy said. He washed his hands and his face, snatched a handful of kitchen towel to wipe them. No, dammit, he wasn't sorry at all.

"I think you owe me an explanation," he said coldly.

*   *   *

Murray Beech leaned out of his pulpit, hands gripping its edges, as if he were sitting up in the bath.

"And what," he demanded, "*is* this so-called New Age? Can there be any true meaning in a concept quite so vague?"

He paused.

"The New Age," he said heavily.

He glared out into the church—late-medieval and not much altered. "Some of you may remember a popular song, 'This is the Dawning of the Age of Aquarius.' "

"He's going to knock it, then," Powys whispered to Fay.

"Well, of course he's going to knock it," Fay said, out of the side of her mouth. "That's why I'm here."

The Uher sat on the pew at her side, its spools turning, the microphone wedged between two prayer books on the ledge. She was recording the sermon for her own reference. She wouldn't get anything of broadcast quality at this range and she hadn't got permission anyway. She'd talk to him on tape afterward, throw his own words back at him and see how he reacted.

" 'Harmony and Understanding,' " Murray quoted. " 'Sympathy and Trust Abounding.' "

Alien concepts in Crybbe, Fay thought cynically. The vicar's words must be settling on this comatose congregation with all the weight of ash flakes from a distant bonfire.

Caught in white light from a small Gothic window set high in the nave, Murray Beech—light-brown hair slicked flat, metallic features firmly set—was looking about fifteen years older than his age. A man with problems.

Fay's dad shuffled and coughed. He didn't know she was here.

Who was this woman, then? Slim and small-boned, she wore a wide-brimmed brown felt hat which concealed her hair and neck.

The vicar announced there would be a public meeting in Crybbe on Tuesday night, when the members of this congregation would be asked to consider the merits of the New Age movement and decide to what extent they would allow it to infiltrate their lives.

Now, he had no wish to condemn the obviously sincere people who offered what appeared to be rather scenic shortcuts to their own idea of heaven. Indeed, it might be argued that any kind of spirituality was better than none at all.

The canon coughed again; the woman next to him was very still. Almost . . . almost *too* still.

"We have a choice," said Murray. "We can pray for the strength and the will to confront the reality of a world defiled by starvation, injustice, and inequality—a world crying out for basic Christian charity.

"Or," he said, with the smallest twist of his lips, "we can sidestep reality and amuse ourselves in what we might call the Cosmic Fairground."

Everyone alive moved a little, Fay thought, watching the woman. Even sleeping people moved.

No. Not here. You can't follow him here. Not into church.

Murray hauled himself farther up in his pulpit, raised his voice.

"How appealing! How appealing it must seem to live in a little world where, if we're sick, we can pass off the health services and the medical advances of the past hundred years as irrelevant and call instead upon the power of . . . healing crystals."

Powys smiled.

But Fay had stiffened, feeling the tiny hairs rising on her bare arms. Her father's face was turned toward the pulpit. He had never glanced at the woman by his side. Fay thought, I can see her, *but can he?*

" . . . a little world, where, if we feel we are suffering a certain starvation of the soul, we need not give up our Sunday mornings to come to church. Because all we need to do is to go for a stroll along the nearest ley-line and expose ourselves to these famous cosmic rays."

Fay heard him as if from afar. She was looking at her father. And at the woman. *Neat, small-boned, wide-brimmed hat concealing her hair and neck. And unnaturally still.*

The church was darkening around Fay. The muted colors had drained out of the congregation. Everything was black and white and gray. Nobody moved. Murray Beech, flickering like an ancient movie, black and white in his surplice, was gesturing in the pulpit, but she couldn't hear him anymore.

She stared hard, projecting her fear and—surprised at its strength—her uncontrollable resentment. Until she felt herself lifting from the pew, aware of a sudden concern in the eyes of Joe Powys, his hand reaching out for her from a long, long way

away, but not touching. Fay rising on a malign wave while, at
the same time, very slowly, the woman sitting next to her father
began, for the first time, to move.

Began, very slowly, to turn her head.

And Fay was suddenly up on her feet in the silent church,
shrieking aloud, "How dare you? Get out! How dare you come
in here!"

Gripping the prayer-book shelf so hard that it creaked.

"Why?" Fay screamed. "Why can't you just get on with your
death and leave him alone?"

Then everybody was turning around, but Fay was out of the
church door, and running.

six

When the Mercedes Estate carrying Simon and his three young
assistants had vanished into the lane, Rachel watched Andy
Boulton-Trow, stripped to the waist, supervising the loading of
three long stones into the back of a truck. There was a small
digger in the back, too, one of those you could hire to landscape
your own garden.

"Last ones," Andy said, jabbing a thumb at the stones. He'd
acquired, very rapidly, an impressive black beard, somehow
hardening his narrow jaw.

Rachel said, "The others are in?"

"The ones that are safe to put in, without arousing complaints from the landowners. We've got a nice one here for
your friend Joe."

He didn't, she noticed, put any kind of stress on the words
"your friend."

"And then I'm pushing off for a day or two," Andy said,
stretching.

"Is Max aware of this?"

"I really don't know, Rachel."

She wondered if perhaps he was pushing off somewhere *with* Max. "A very heavy guy," Max had said once. "He knows all the options."

Whereas J.M. had implied that while Andy knew as much about earth mysteries as anybody could reasonably be expected to, it was unwise to trust him too far. "He takes risks, especially when the potential fall guy is someone else."

The implication being that he, J. M. Powys, had once been the fall guy. One day, away from here, he would tell her about this.

"What's going on over there?" Rachel had seen a cluster of men emerging from the rear entrance of the Court. Two of them carried a rotting plank which they hurled on a heap of rubbish in a corner of the courtyard.

"Big clean-out," Andy said. "Before the renovation proper begins. All the junk from upstairs—the detritus of the various attempts to modernize the Court, anything not in period—has to go. Didn't Max tell you?"

"I think he mentioned something," Rachel said uncomfortably. He hadn't, of course. Increasingly, things had been happening around her without any kind of consultation.

Like the appropriation of Gomer Parry's bulldozer in the night?

Max liked to live dangerously; she didn't. She was deeply glad to be leaving his employ.

"Make a good bonfire," Andy Boulton-Trow said, nodding at the pile of rubbish. "Maybe we should organize one for Lammas or something. A cleansing."

He stretched his lithe body into the truck. "Have fun," he said.

Powys raced out of the church, clutching the Uher by its strap. She'd left it there, on the pew, still recording, with a motor hum and a hiss of turning spools.

He scanned the churchyard, but she was gone. He ran to the gate, looked both ways, thought he could hear running footsteps, but there was nobody in sight. He glanced over his shoulder and saw a white-bearded, dog-collared old man in the church entrance, also looking from side to side.

Her father. Both of them looking for Fay.

Powys stabbed vaguely at the Uher's piano-key controls until the hum and hiss ceased with a final whir. Then he slung the machine over his shoulder, stuck the microphone in his pocket and set off toward Bell Street. Or would she have gone to the studio?

Making an outburst in church was a clear sign of instability. People who made outbursts in church were usually basket cases.

Except in Crybbe. Leaping up and screaming, Powys thought, was surely a perfectly natural reaction to the miasma of almost anesthetized lack of interest emanating from that congregation.

Bloody weird, though, what she'd said.

Why can't you just get on with your death and leave him alone?

Bloody weird.

As he came to the corner of Bell Street, he almost lost a foot to a familiar red Ford Fiesta, shrieking around the corner in low gear, crunching over the curb.

The driver saw him, and the Fiesta squeaked and stalled. The passenger door flew open and bumped the Uher, and the driver called out, "Get in!"

Powys climbed in and sat with the Uher on his knee. "You left this in the church," he said.

"Thanks." Fay started the engine and the car spurted into the square.

"Your father . . . "

"Fuck my father," she snapped, and she didn't speak again until they passed the town boundary and there were open hills all around and a rush of cold air through the side windows, the glass on both sides wound down to its limits.

Fay breathed out hard and thrust her small body back into the seat, the Fiesta going like a rocket down a lane originally created for horses.

"Got to be something awry," she said remotely, "when the most newsworthy item on the tape is the reporter having hysterics."

Powys said, "When's visiting time at the vet's, then?"

She turned toward him. "You want to come?"

"I've got a choice? Watch the road, for Christ's sake!"

She said, "You want me to talk about it, I suppose."

"Up to you."

"Well," she said, "I suppose if I can talk about it to anybody, I can talk about it to you. Don't suppose I'll be telling you anything you haven't heard before."

"That's right," Powys said. "I'm an accredited crank. And I'll be a dead crank if you don't . . ."

"Yet so cynical." Fay slowed down. "You didn't used to be cynical. Unless that wide-eyed, wow-man-what-a-mindblower feel to *The Old Golden Land* was a put-on."

"Well," he said, "the lighthearted element kind of dissipated." He closed his eyes and the past tumbled down to him, like a rock slide.

> *Joey goes round the Bottle Stone*
> *And he goes round ONCE.*

> *What's happening is you're developing a link with the stone, in an umbilical kind of way. You're feeling every step you take, bare feet connecting sensuously with the warm, grassy skin of the earth. And all the while the terrestrial magnetism—let's imagine it exists—is seeping up through the soles of your feet . . .*

> *And he goes round TWICE.*

Stop it.

He rubbed his eyes. "That *was* your dad, was it, with the white beard? Rachel told me about him. She said he was, er, something of a fun guy for his age."

"He was always fun," Fay said. "That was the problem. Clergymen aren't supposed to have that much fun."

Powys watched her drive, *not* like Rachel. She bumped the gears, rode the clutch, and went too fast around blind bends.

He tried to watch the landscape. "Nothing like this where I grew up. Love at first sight, when I came down here."

"Where was that? Where you came from."

"Up north. Very industrialized part. A long bus ride to the nearest cow. Every square yard, for as far as you could see, built on for about the fourth time. Where we lived they'd eradicated grass like a disease. It's quite nice now, if you like Georgian-style semis with concrete barbecue pits."

Fay said, "I grew up in old vicarages and rectories, in little villages with thatched houses. And Oxford for a time."

"Deprived childhood, huh?"

"There's more than one kind," Fay said. "Not many ley-lines where you came from, I suppose."

"You just had to work harder to find them," Powys said, stiffening as Fay clipped the hedge to avoid an oncoming truck.

"Bloody loony."

Could she, he wondered, really be referring to the innocent truck driver?

"How long has he known Jean Wendle?"

"Who?"

"Your dad. He was sitting next to Jean Wendle. In church."

After a moment, Fay trod on the brakes. The Fiesta was almost in the middle of the road. The driver of a BMW behind them blasted his horn and revved in righteous rage.

"What?"

She didn't seem to notice the middle-aged, suit-and-tie-clad BMW driver thrusting up two furious fingers as he roared past.

"Jean Wendle," Powys said. "The healer."

Fay gripped the wheel tightly with both hands, threw her head back, and moaned.

"Oh God, Joe. That was Jean Wendle?"

"It was."

Fay unclipped her seat belt.

"Would you mind taking over, before I kill us both? I think I've made the most awful fool of myself."

Alex had given Murray Beech the usual can of Heineken, and this time Murray had snapped it open and drunk silently and gratefully.

"You heard my sermon," Murray said. They were in the living room at the back of the house in Bell Street. The vicar was slumped in an armchair. He looked worn out.

"And you heard my daughter, I suppose," Alex said.

"What was the matter with her?"

"You tell me, old boy." Alex had once been chaplain to a rehabilitation center for drug addicts; Murray reminded him of the new arrivals, lank-haired, gray-skinned, eyes like mud.

"What did you think of my sermon?"

"Good try," Alex said. "Full marks for effort. Couple of Brownie points, perhaps, from the town council. Then again, perhaps not. What d'you want me to say? You and I both know that this fellow Goff's congregation's going to be a bloody sight more dedicated than yours."

"Sour grapes, eh?"

"You said it, old chap."

"I don't know what to do," Murray said, desolate.

Alex sighed.

"I could be good at this job," Murray said. "Anywhere else, I could be really good. I'm a good organizer, a good administrator. I *like* organizing things, running the parish affairs, setting up discussion groups, counseling sessions. I've got ideas. I can get things done."

"Archdeacon material, if ever I saw it."

"Don't laugh at me, Alex."

"Sorry."

"You see, I did what I thought was right in the context of my position in Crybbe. The sermon, I mean. I expected people to come up to me outside. You know . . . Well said, Vicar, all this. I thought I was echoing their own thoughts. I know they don't like what's happening at the Court."

"How d'you know that?"

"Not from listening to them talk, that's for certain. They don't even seem to talk to each other. No chit-chit, no street-corner gossip. Do you think that's natural? Nobody said a word to me today. I was standing there holding out a hand, thanks for coming, nice to see you, hope you're feeling better now, the usual patter. And some of them were taking my hand limply, as if I was offering them a sandwich at the fête. Then they'd nod and trudge off without a word. No reaction in church either except for Fay's outburst and the boy, Warren Preece, who was staring at me with the most astonishing malevolence in his eyes."

"Which boy's that?"

"Warren Preece? The mayor's grandson, the younger brother of the chap who drowned in the river. Looking at me as if he blamed me for his brother's death."

"Doesn't make much sense, Murray."

"Didn't to me, either. I tried to ignore it. Perhaps it was nothing to do with his brother. He's a friend of the girl, Tessa Byford. You remember I asked you about exorcism."

"Oh. Yes. How did that go?"

"You haven't heard anything, then?"

"Nothing at all, old chap. Didn't it go well?"

"You're sure you haven't heard anything? You wouldn't lie, to save my feelings?"

"Sod off, Murray, I'm a Christian."

Murray said, "That girl's seriously disturbed. Tessa Byford. The Old Police House. I think I'm talking about evil, Alex. I think I was in the presence of evil. I think she invited me in to flourish something in my face. As if to say, this is what you're up against, now what are you going to do?"

"And what did you do?"

"I ran away," Murray said starkly. "I got the hell out of there, and I haven't been back, and I'm scared stiff of meeting her in the street or a shop because I think I'd run away again."

"Oh dear," Alex said.

Murray leaned his head back into the chair and closed and opened his eyes twice, flexing his jaw.

Alex said, "I seem to remember asking you what you thought were the world's greatest evils."

"I expect I said inequality, the Tory government, or something. Now I'd have to say I've seen real evil and it was in the eyes of a schoolgirl. And now, I don't know, in a boy of eighteen or nineteen. What does that say about *me?*"

"Perhaps it says you've grown up," Alex said. "Or that you've been watching those X-rated videos again. I don't know either. I've been fudging the bloody issue for years, and now I'm too old and clapped out to do anything about it. Perhaps, you know, this is one of those places where we meet it head-on."

"Crybbe?"

"Just thinking of something Wendy said. May look like a hemorrhoid in the arsehole of the world, but the quiet places are often the real battlegrounds. Some of these New Age johnnies are actually not so far off-beam when you talk to them. You come across Wendy?"

Murray looked blank.

"Strict Presbyterian upbringing," Alex said. "No nonsense. Yet she apparently cures people of cancer and shingles and things with the help of an egg-shaped Oriental blob called Dr. Chi. Now, I ask you . . . But it's all terminology, isn't it. Dr. Chi, Jesus Christ, Allah, E.T. . . . There's a positive and a negative, and whatever all this energy is, well, perhaps we can

color it with our hearts. Pass me another beer, Murray, I don't
think I'm helping you at all."

"I thought you weren't supposed to drink."

"Sod that," said Alex. "Look at me. Do I seem sick? Do I
seem irrational?"

"Far from it. In fact, if you don't mind my saying, I've never
known you so lucid."

"Well, there you are, you see. Dr. Chi. Little Chink's a bloody
wonder. And there's you trying to drive his intermediary out of
town. We think we're so smart, Murray, but we're just pupils
in a spiritual kindergarten."

"I think I'm cracking up," Murray said.

"Perhaps you need to consult old Dr. Chi as well. I can
arrange an appointment."

Murray stood up very quickly and headed for the door. "Don't
joke about this, Alex. Just don't joke."

"Was I?" Alex asked him innocently. "Was I joking, do you
think?"

seven

"But . . ."

Well, she couldn't say she hadn't been warned.

The vet, an elderly, stooping man in a cardigan, said there'd
been quite a concentration of shotgun pellets in the dog's rear
end.

"Fairly close range, you see. Must have been. If he'd moved a
bit faster, the shot would have missed him altogether. I got some
of them out, and some will work to the surface in time. But he'll
always be carrying a few around. Like an old soldier."

Arnold was lying on a folded blanket, his huge ears fully
extended. His tail bobbed when Fay and Joe appeared. His left
haunch had been shaved to the base of the tail. The skin was
vivid pink, the stitching bright blue.

"But he's only got three legs," Fay said.

"I did try to save it, Mrs. Morrison, but so much bone was smashed it would have been enormously complicated and left him in a lot of pain, probably for life. It's quite unusual for the damage to be so concentrated. But then, dogs that are shot are usually killed."

"He's a survivor," Fay said.

Arnold was not feeling sorry for himself, this was clear. He thumped his tail against his folded brown blanket and tried to get up. Fell down again, but he tried. Fay rushed to pat him to stop him trying again.

"Never discourage him from standing up," the vet said. "He'll be walking soon, after a fashion. Managed a few steps in the garden this morning. Falls over a lot, but he gets up again. He's young enough to handle it with aplomb, I think. Be cocking his stump against lampposts in no time. Need a lot of attention and careful supervision when he's outside, for a while. But he'll be fine. Some people can't cope with it, you know. They have the dog put down. It's kinder, they say. Kinder to them, they mean."

With a stab of shame, Fay found herself thinking then about her father.

"And there's one thing," the vet said. "He won't be considered much of a danger to sheep now. I can't see this particular farmer coming after him again."

"Most unlikely," Powys agreed.

There must have been twenty or thirty people around the Court this afternoon, pulling things down, turning out buildings like drawers. And this was a Sunday; every one of them, no doubt, on double-time. Money no object.

The Crybbe project seemed to have taken on a life of its own. Everything was happening unbelievably quickly, three or four months' work done inside a week. As if Max knew he had to seize the place, stage a coup before bureaucracy could be cranked into action against him.

And it was happening all around Rachel, as if she wasn't there. Had Max ordered her to stay behind here just to make this point?

Max's own energy seemed to be pumped entirely into his project, as if he didn't have an empire to run. Even from London, directing people and money to Crybbe.

Because, unknown to its hundreds of employees, this was now the spiritual center of the Epidemic Group. Crybbe. The Court.

The Tump.

She'd caught sight of a specimen of his proposed new logo: a big green mound with trees on it. In Max's vision, all the power of Epidemic—the recording companies, the publishing houses, the high-street shops—would emanate from the Tump.

On a wall in the stable there was a map of the town with every building marked. The ones owned by Epidemic and now inhabited—or soon to be—by alternative people had been shaded red. She'd counted them; there were thirty-five properties, far more than Max was publicly admitting. Far more than even she had known about.

She tried to imagine the town as the alternative capital of Britain, with thousands of people flooding in to take part in seminars, follow the ley-lines with picnic lunches, consult mystics and healers. People in search of a spiritual recharge or a miracle cure.

A kind of New Age Lourdes.

Crybbe?

Rachel shook her head and wandered across the courtyard, head down, hands deep in the pockets of her Barbour. Couldn't wait to get rid of this greasy bloody Barbour for good.

She arrived at the burgeoning rubbish pile, which would soon consist of the entire non-Tudor contents of the Court. Leftovers from four centuries. Reminders of the times when the Court's other incarnations had been a private school (failed), a hotel (failed), even a billet, she'd been told, for American servicemen during World War II.

It was a shame; a lot of the stuff they were throwing out would be quite useful to some people and some of it valuable. A darkwood table, scratched but serviceable. A wardrobe which was probably Victorian and would sell, cleaned up, for several hundred quid in any antique shop. Peanuts to Max.

Money to burn. Hardly New Age. What happened to recycling?

The pile was over twelve feet high. Filthy carpets which, unrolled, would probably turn out to be Indian. A rocking chair.

A couple of chests, one thick with varnish, the other newer, bound with green-painted metal strips, black lettering across its lid; you couldn't make out what it said.

Rachel looked hard at the second chest. Where had she seen it before?

Good Lord! She ran to the chest and pulled up its lid. They couldn't do this . . .

But they had.

Exposed to full daylight, Tiddles, the mummified cat, looked forlorn, a wisp of a thing, his eye sockets full of dust, one of his saber teeth broken, probably in transit to the heap.

Tiddles, the guardian. Evicted.

She looked up at the Court, its lower windows mainly boarded up, the upper ones too small to give any indication of what was going on inside.

One thing she knew. Tiddles might not be Tudor—seventeenth century, somebody had suggested—but he was part of that place. He would have to go back.

Goes round FOUR times.

The earth force (assume it exists) rising up through the soles of your feet, a kind of liquid light. Up into your legs and then, into the body itself, the solar plexus, the first major energy centre. Feel it forming into a pulsing ball of warm, white light, while the chant goes on, the rhythmic clapping . . .

And he goes round FIVE times.

"Powys, I need to tell you . . . "

"Sorry?"

"Are you OK, Powys?"

"Yes, sorry, I was . . . "

Powys driving Fay's Fiesta through a delirium of damp trees, their foliage burgeoning over the road. Fay sitting in the passenger seat with Arnold on the blanket on her knee, fondling the dog's disproportionately large ears.

"Powys, I need to tell you why I went berserk in church."

He said nothing. She seemed a good deal more relaxed now; something had obviously resolved itself.

"Have you ever seen a ghost?"

He shook his head. "Terrible admission, isn't it? My belief in ghosts is founded entirely on hearsay."

"Who exactly is Jean Wendle?"

"She's a spiritual healer. One of the more convincing ones. Nice woman. Used to be a lawyer. Barrister. Or an advocate, as they say in Scotland. Very high-octane. Then she found she could heal people, so she gave up the law to devote her life to it. They were about to make her a judge at the time. It caused . . . uproar in legal circles."

"Oh!"

"You remember now?"

"Yes. It was in the papers, wasn't it? How long's she been in Crybbe?"

"As I understand it," he said, "she was one of the first of Goff's big-name signings. Rachel says Max wanted to put her into this old rectory he's bought, a couple of miles outside town. But she insisted on being at the heart of things, so she's living in a town house on the square."

"I didn't know she knew my father."

"Jean gets to know everybody. Unobtrusively."

"She was sitting so still," Fay said. "In church. So very still."

"She slows her breathing sometimes. She's a bit uncanny. She . . . intuits things. Absorbs atmospheres and interprets what's really going on. I'm impressed by Jean. Scares me a bit, too, I must admit."

"Scared me," Fay said, "in church. I thought I was seeing Dad's late wife." She paused. "Again," she said.

They were coming into Crybbe. Powys slowed for the thirty-m.p.h. speed limit.

"You said . . . *late* wife?"

"She was called Grace Legge. The house we live in was hers. She died last year. I saw her last week."

"Bloody hell, Fay."

"I'd never seen one before. You know how it is—you've read about ghosts, you've seen the films, you've interviewed people who swear they've seen one. But you don't . . . quite . . . believe they exist."

"Except in people's minds," he said.

"Yes." Fay ran her fingers deep into Arnold's warm fur. "I don't recommend the experience. You know what they say about the flesh creeping? The spine feeling chilled? Grace was ghastly, dead. What's the time?"

"Ten past five."

"We haven't eaten," Fay remembered. "No wonder I'm shooting my mouth off. Light-headed. You coming in for something, Powys? Omelet? Sandwich? I'm afraid Dad'll be there, so forget everything I said about Grace."

"Thanks, but I ought to find Rachel."

Powys pulled up at the bottom of Bell Street, took out the keys, and passed them to Fay.

Arnold tried to stand up on Fay's knee. "Hang on," Powys said. He went around to open Fay's door and she handed Arnold to him while she got out and shook off the dog hairs.

As Powys handed Arnold back, as gently as he could, Fay looked him hard in the eyes. Serious, almost severe.

"If you've got any sense, Joe Powys," she said, "you'll piss off out of Crybbe pronto and take Rachel with you. She's gold. She's the only person I know around here who's got her act together. Come on, Arnie, I'm afraid we're home."

"What about you? Strikes me you need to get out more urgently than any of us."

"Why? Because I'm losing my marbles like Dad?"

And like me? he wondered, walking down the street toward the river.

And immediately twelve years fell away and he was going around the stone again.

Round and round. Mesmeric. Tribal.

Widdershins, widdershins . . . against the sun, against nature . . .

. . . And he goes round SEVEN times . . .

Powys stood on the bridge and threw up his hands, warding it off, wiping it away, but the atmosphere was thick with it. He could feel Memory's helicopter beating the air above his head with great sweeping, buffeting strokes. It had never been so powerful. He was standing upright on the bridge, but his mind was ducking and crouching, cowering. He looked around for somewhere to run to, but it was all around him.

. . . EIGHT times . . .

Fluidity of movement, breathing changing rhythm. Something else breathing for you, running beside you . . . widdershins, widdershins . . . and doing your breathing.

. . . NINE . . .

Can't stop. Can't stop.
Out of your hands now.
Widdershins, widdershins.

. . . TEN . . .

Below you, the tiny figure running around the stone.
Widdershins . . . all wrong.
Below. The stone and the running figure.
Widdershins.
All wrong.

. . . ELEVEN . . .

And the ball of light rising up hard, bright, glowing, pulsing . . . into the chest.
Widdershins.
Engulfing your heart, but it's no longer warm, and it's bursting, with a shocking rush into your head, where it's . . .
WIDDERSHINS!

He was inside the running figure now, pounding across the bridge and into the short gravel drive of the little black and white riverside cottage.

Powys flung himself onto the long-unmown lawn, soft and damp and full of buttercups and dandelions.

He lay on his stomach with his face into the grass, his eyes closed and the cool vegetation pressed into the sockets. Kept rubbing it in until it was a green mush and not so cool anymore.

"You're going back," Annie had said.

Back to the Old Golden Land. Back—he'd told himself—to find out what had happened to Henry Kettle. Back—they said behind his back—to find redemption.

The cold in his stomach told him he was back, but that there was no redemption to be found here.

He opened his eyes and blinked and then the screaming started to come out of him like aural vomit, for at the top edge of the little ridge on which the cottage stood, something black and alien thrust out of the grass.

The stone was only five feet tall but looked taller because of the prominence of its position.

Its base was fat and solidly planted in the earth. It maintained its girth until, three feet above the ground, it tapered into a neck, presenting the illusion of a large black beer bottle.

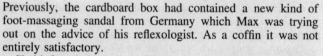

eight

Previously, the cardboard box had contained a new kind of foot-massaging sandal from Germany which Max was trying out on the advice of his reflexologist. As a coffin it was not entirely satisfactory.

She'd found the box in Max's bedroom, which was built into the eaves over the far end of the long room where his desk stood. The four-poster bed, facing the mound, had deep-gray drapes. Max had not spent a single night here yet, but it seemed to Rachel that the atmosphere in the room was already fetid with tension and a lingering sense of suffocated longing. Rachel thought of the nights of the Great Beast and the Scarlet Woman and was sickened and ashamed. She'd snatched the shoe box and fled.

The box was necessary. There was no way she could carry Tiddles's chest up to the attic on her own. As she knelt in the yard by the rubbish pile, she was worried the mummified cat would come apart or disintegrate while being transferred from the chest. He felt as light as wads of dust under an old sofa.

"Poor little devil," Rachel said. "You certainly haven't much energy left to put into Max's project."

Returning Tiddles to his sentry post in the Court would, she decided, be her last meaningful task in Crybbe.

And she didn't want witnesses.

For over an hour Tiddles lay in his box on the kitchen table in the stables while Rachel waited for the workmen to finish clearing the Court. It was after 7 A.M.; still she could hear them inside, while a van waited in the courtyard.

At nearly 8 P.M., she threw on her Barbour, picked up the shoe box, marched purposefully across to the Court's main entrance, and hauled open the dusty oak door.

There was a clang from above. A thump. The sound of a large piece of furniture being hurled to the floor.

What were they *doing* up there? And who exactly were they? Not—judging by the quality of the stuff they'd tossed out—a knowledgeable antique dealer among them. Rachel decided it was time to throw *them* out.

Or time, at least, to establish the identity of the smart-arse who was deciding so arbitrarily which items of furniture to discard.

With the shoe box under her arm, she went in.

"Hello . . . Excuse me!"

Her voice seemed to go nowhere, as if she was shouting into a wind tunnel.

The Court was so full of noise. Ceiling-shaking bangs and crashes, as if the entire building was being torn apart. Yet no one had come out of here in at least a couple of hours and the rubbish pile was no higher than it had been when she'd found the cat's wooden chest.

"HELLO!"

She looked around. Half-light floated feebly through the high-level slits and barely reached the stone floor.

Rachel followed the sounds and stormed up the spiral stone staircase.

"Excuse me." Calling out as she neared the first floor. "I need to lock this place up for the night, so if you could give me some idea how long you're going to be . . . "

She stepped out into the main chamber, where families had lived and where the Hanging Sheriff, Sir Michael Wort, had held out against the rebel hordes.

"Oh," Rachel said.

She was alone.

The weak evening light washed through two mullioned windows, but the shadows were taking over now.

Well, she certainly wasn't going to play hide-and-seek with a bunch of silly buggers getting paid well to clean the place out before morning. She had half a mind to lock them in. Except the keys were in her bag, in the stables.

There was a double crash from above and the sound of glass shattering.

"What the hell . . . ?"

Rachel bounded angrily up the next spiral. Didn't they know how easily they could kill themselves up there, or bring half the ceiling down? Had nobody warned them about the state of the floor?

The heavy door to the attic was ajar. They'd been given keys, then. That bastard Max must have had another set made without even telling her. She thrust through the arched doorway, past the alcove concealing the entrance to the prospect chamber. Up toward the attic.

It was only when she was halfway up the steps that it occurred to her that among the bangs and the crashes there'd been no laughter, none of the usual banter of men working together, no shouted directions, no oaths, no . . .

No voices at all.

And now she was standing here, on the last stairway, far above her blades of light through broken slates, and it was absolutely silent.

"What," Rachel demanded, "is going on?"

What was more disquieting than this sudden inexplicable cessation of bangs and crashes was the hairline crack she detected in her own voice. She cleared her throat and gave it more vehemence.

"Come on, I haven't got all night. Where are you?"

Rachel did not remember ever being superstitious. She did not believe in good luck, bad luck, heaven, hell, psychic forces, or the secret power of ley-lines. She found the whole New Age concept not only essentially unsound but, for the most part, very tedious indeed.

Yet—and for the first time—she found the place not just gloomy in a sad, uncared-for kind of way, but in the sense of being oppressive. And yes, OK, eerie. She admitted to herself that she didn't want to go so far into the attic that she might see the rope hanging from the ceiling, even though she knew it could not be a very old rope.

But this was a side issue. Something to be acknowledged and perhaps examined later with a raising of eyebrows and a glass of whiskey beside the Jotul stove in J. M. Powys's riverside retreat.

For here and for now, there was only one serious, legitimate fear: a fear of the kind of men who, on hearing a woman calling out to them and coming up the stairs, would stop what they were doing, slide into the shadows, and keep very, very quiet.

Until this woman appeared at the top of the steps, with nothing to defend her except a dead cat in a shoe box.

So no way was she going all the way to the top.

Rachel studied her breathing, set her lips in a firm line, tossed back her hair, and began to descend the spiral stairway. If the men in the attic were unaware of the instability of the floor and the danger to themselves, that was their business. They were presumably well-insured.

If they fell, they fell. She hadn't been hired as caretaker of Britain's least-stately home, and she wasn't prepared to tolerate being pissed around any longer. Tomorrow—perhaps even tonight—she would phone Max in London and inform him that she had quit. As of now.

As she descended the twisted stairway it began to grow darker. When she reached the bottom, she found out why. The door sealing off the prospect chamber and the attic must have swung closed behind her, cutting off the light from the first-floor hallway.

She pushed it with the flat of her hand.

It didn't move.

She put the shoe box on the stairs and pushed hard with both hands.

It was an oak door, four inches thick, and it did not move.

Well, it might have jammed.

"Look, would somebody mind helping me with this door?"

No response.

Or—oh, God, can I really credit this?—the bastards might have locked her in.

It was important to hold on to her anger.

"When I get out of here," Rachel said suddenly, icily, without thinking, "you can consider yourselves officially fired."

Which, on reflection, was a pretty stupid thing to say. They'd never let her out. She tried again.

"Now look, don't be stupid. It's very dangerous up here. The floor's full of holes, you know that. And I haven't got a torch."

She threw her weight against the door, half expecting somebody to have quietly unlocked it so that it opened suddenly and she went tumbling down the stairs. Such was the mentality of people like this.

But all that happened was she hurt her shoulder.

"Look, would you mind letting me out?"

She stopped suddenly and leaned back against a wall, breathing hard, an awful thought occurring to her.

What if Humble was behind this?

Suppose, as she would normally have expected, the workmen had actually cleared off hours ago. Who, after all, really worked until eight on a Sunday evening? Certainly not the kind of unskilled vandals who'd been let loose in here.

What, then, if it had been Humble who had come up here and made a lot of noise to lure her inside? He'd never liked her, and he knew she didn't like him. He might think she was putting the knife in for him with Max. Maybe Max had found out what Humble had done to J.M. that night. Maybe Humble's job was on the line, and he thought she was responsible.

But if Humble was behind this he would have needed an accomplice. One of them up here to make all the racket, one to lock the door after she'd gone through.

Which still meant that someone was up here with her now, on this side of the locked door. Keeping very, very quiet.

Rachel spun around.

It was so dark with the door closed that she could hardly see as far as the twist in the staircase which took it to the attic. Anything could be around that bend, not six feet away.

"Humble!"

Not much authority left in her voice, nor much anger. She was a woman alone in the darkness of a decaying old house, with a man who intended her harm.

"Humble, listen . . . whichever side of the door you are . . . I don't know why you're doing this. I wish you'd tell me, so we can have it out. But if it's anything to do with what happened the other night with J. M. Powys, I want you to know that I haven't said anything to Max and I don't intend to. A mistake is a mistake. Humble, can you hear me?"

The door didn't have a handle, only a lock. She bent down and tried to look into the keyhole, to see if there was a key in the other side.

She couldn't tell one way or the other; it was too dark. Her own keys were in her bag, on the kitchen table.

"Humble, look, if you've heard what I said, just unlock the door and I'll give you time to get out of the building. I don't want any unpleasantness because . . ."

Oh, what the hell did it matter now?

" . . . because I'm handing in my notice tomorrow. I've got another job. In London. You won't have to deal with me again. Did you hear that? Do you understand what I'm saying? Humble!"

Rachel beat her fists on the oak door until she felt the skin break.

She had grown cold. She wrapped her Barbour around her and sat down on a stone stair next to the cardboard coffin and listened hard.

Nothing. She couldn't even hear the birds singing outside, where there was light.

But from the attic, clearly not far beyond the top of the spiral stairway, came a single, sharp, triumphant bump.

He remembered . . . TWELVE . . . spiraling down out of the sky, seeing the stone thickening and quivering and throbbing, the haze around it like a dense, toxic cloud. At which point Memory went into negative, the fields turned purple, the river black. Everything went black.

He didn't remember the scramble of feet, all four of them rushing the new author, J. M. Powys, picking him up, carrying him to the so-called fairy mound and dumping him facedown on its grassy flank with shrieks of laughter.

He was only able to construct this scene from what Ben Corby had told him years later.

From Ben's story, he'd tried to form an image of Rose, but he couldn't be sure whether she was laughing, too, or whether she'd stopped short, her face clouding, feeling premonition like a small tap on the shoulder from a cold, stiff hand.

Every time he pushed himself into replaying the scene in his head, he forced Rose to be laughing when they dumped him on the mound. He always put the laugh on freeze-frame and then pulled the plug. So that he could climb out of it without breaking down.

Powys stood in the neutrality of a sunless summer evening and put both hands on the Bottle Stone—at its shoulders, where it began to taper into the neck—and pushed hard.

It was solid. A proper job, as Henry Kettle would have said. Probably several feet of the thing underground, the earth compressed around it, a few rocks in there maybe. Tufts of long grass embedded at the base. It might have been here for four thousand years. You could dig for three hours and it would still be erect.

It needed a JCB to get it out.

But first he had to force himself to touch it, to walk all around it (only not widdershins, *never* widdershins). This stone, a cunningly hewn replica of something which had speared his dreams for twelve years.

He also reserves the right, Rachel had said, *to install standing stones or other ritual artifacts on your lawn.*

All down to Andy Boulton-Trow. He could imagine Andy's unholy delight at finding, among Goff's collection of newly quarried megaliths, one roughly (not roughly, *exactly*) the size and shape of the Bottle Stone.

Or maybe, knowing that Powys was coming to Crybbe, he'd actually had one cut to shape and then planted it in a spot that would emphasize the correlation of the stone and the river, re-creating the fateful scene of twelve years ago.

Rough therapy? Or another of Andy's little experiments?

Fifty yards away, the brown river churned like a turbulence of worms toward the bridge.

* * *

The canon was angry.

"And you didn't tell me. You didn't even *tell* me."

They'd taken one of the big cushions from the sofa in what was now their living room, at the rear of the house, and put it on the rug in front of the fire, and then put the three-legged dog on the cushion.

Arnold didn't object to this at all, but something in Alex had clearly snapped.

"It's got to stop, Fay. It isn't helping. In fact, it's making things a good deal worse."

"I'm sorry. I didn't want to get you all worked up."

"Well, I *am* worked up. Even though it was young Preece and he's dead. Divine retribution, if you ask me."

"That's not a very Christian thing to say, Dad."

"Listen, my child." Alex, kneeling on the rug, waved a menacing forefinger. "Don't you ever presume to tell *me* what's Christian."

He went down on his hands, face-to-face with Arnold. "Poor little perisher. Shouldn't be allowed out with you, Fay, the way you get up people's noses."

"Oh, I get up people's noses, do I?"

"If you got up noses for a living, you couldn't do a better job. Coming here with your superior Radio Four attitude—'Oh dear, have to work for the little local radio station, never mind, at least there's no need to take it seriously . . . ' "

"Now just a minute, Dad . . . "

" ' . . . Oh, God, how am I expected to do any decent interviews with people who're too thick to string three coherent sentences together?' "

The canon clambered awkwardly to his feet and then dumped himself into an armchair he'd battered into shape over several months. He swung around, as if the chair was a gun turret, training on her a hard, blue glare. A once-familiar glare under which she used to crumble.

"You," he said, "were never going to adapt to their way of life, because it was the *wrong* way to do things, because they keep their heads down and don't parade in front of the council offices with placards if they don't get their bins emptied."

"Dad, I'm supposed to be a reporter . . . "

"And when this fat fellow—what's his name? . . . Goff—when this meddling lunatic arrives with his monumentally crazy scheme to turn the place on its head . . . Well, guess who can't get along with him *either*. Why, it's Miss Sophisticated Fay Peters, late of Radio Four! And she won't get back to London where she belongs . . . "

"Dad, you know bloody well . . . "

" . . . because she has this astonishing notion that her dilapidated old dad won't be able to manage without her! Jesus *Christ!*"

Alex slumped into silence.

Fay couldn't speak either. If this was Jean Wendle's doing, it was remarkable. Lucid, cogent, powerful, clear-eyed. He might have been ten years younger and in total control of himself.

She was shaken. He was right, of course, even if there was a lot he didn't know.

Or maybe there were things he did know.

When she did finally manage to utter something, it wasn't what she'd had in mind to come out with at all.

"Dad," she heard this pathetic little-girl voice saying, close to tears. "Dad, why is Grace haunting us?"

Warren never even saw his granddad until the old bugger was on him.

He was out by the Tump, thinking how much bigger it looked now from the side where the wall had been ripped out. Old thing could breathe now.

Big, fat mound. Like a giant tit.

Gomer'd carted his bulldozer away, moaning it'd cost over two thousand quid to repair it; Warren thought that was a load of old crap, Gomer trying it on. Who gave a shit, anyway? Standing here, Warren felt again the raw, wild power he'd first experienced the night he buried the old box. He would've been in town, up the alley, shagging the arse off Tessa, except she'd wanted to go to this art exhibition, could you believe that?

He'd left the old man at home, drinking. Never used to drink at home. Gone to pieces since Jonathon drowned, the elder son, the heir.

Warren was the heir now. They'd have to give the bloody old farm to him. You had to laugh, sometimes.

Jonathon was being planted on Wednesday. An inquest would be opened tomorrow. Warren had wanted to go along with the old man, who had to give evidence that the stiff really was Jonathon Preece. But they said after he'd done that, it'd be adjourned for a few weeks, so they'd have a long wait before they heard all the interesting stuff from the pathologist who'd cut Jonathon up on the slab.

After the inquest had been opened, the body'd be released for burial, but the old man said they wouldn't be having it back at the house. Another disappointment for Warren, who'd planned to come down in the night and look under the shroud at all the stitches where the pathologist had put Jonathon's guts back.

From behind, the hand came down on Warren's shoulder like a bird's claw.

"What you doin' yere, boy?"

Warren would've turned around and slugged him, if he hadn't recognized the voice.

" 'Ow're you, Granddad."

"I said, what you doin' yere?"

"I come for a walk, like. Free country, innit?"

"Come with me, boy, I want a word with you."

"Sorry, Granddad, got no time, see. Got to meet somebody down the town."

The old git looked real weird tonight. Skeletal. Skin hanging loose over his bones. Powerful grip he had, though, and he used it now on Warren's arm, above the elbow, digging into the muscle.

"Ow! Bloody gedoff, you old . . . Where we goin'?"

Jimmy Preece pulled him all the way to the edge of the field, well away from the Tump and the hole where the wall had been—pointing at this gap now, saying in a hard, rough voice,

"You know anythin' about that, boy?"

"What you on about?"

"You know what I'm on about." The old bugger's eyes were twin glowworms, burrowed deep in his frazzled face. "The feller as nicked Gomer's bulldozer and rammed it through that wall. You know him, boy?"

"I never . . . I swear to God!"

Next thing Warren knew, he was on his back in the grass, half stunned. The old git'd knocked him clean off his feet with one massive swipe across the face.

"Never use the name of God in sight of that thing again, you understand me, boy?"

Warren lay there, felt like his face was afire and his brains were loose. "You mad ole . . . you got no right . . . "

His granddad put out a hand and helped him to his feet.

"Sorry, boy. Nerves is all shot, see, what with Jonathon and now this."

Warren backed off. Stood with a hand over his blazing cheek.

"Warren, you and me got to talk."

"That's what you calls it, is it?"

His granddad took his cap off, scratched his head, replaced the cap.

"Jonathon dyin', see, that changes things. With Jonathon around, didn't matter if you went through your life without knowin' nothin'. Your dad, 'e's the first Preece 'ad less than three children. Weren't 'is fault your mam left 'im, but that's besides the point. I only 'ad two sisters, but if anythin'd 'appened to me, they'd have done it, no arguments."

"What you on about?"

"The bell, Warren."

"Oh, that ole thing. Stuff that."

"You what, boy?"

"Stuff it. I done some thinkin' about that. You can all get bloody stuffed, you think I'm ever gonna take over that bell from Dad. Jonathon might've been mug enough, but I couldn't give a fucking shit, you wanna know the truth, Granddad. My future's not round yere, see. I'm a musician."

"Music?" The old feller spat hard, once. Spat right there on the grass. "Music? Pah!"

Warren backed off, felt his face contorting. His finger was out and pointing at the old bastard's sucked-in face.

"You know *nothin',*" Warren snarled. "You wanner know about my music, you ask Max Goff. 'E's gonner sign me, see. 'E's gonner sign the band. So you can do what you like. You can fuckin' disinherit me . . . you can keep your run-down farm. And you can take your bell and you can shove it, Granddad. I couldn't care less."

His granddad went quiet, standing there, face as gray as the clouds.

"I shouldn't worry," Warren sneered. "One o' them newcomers'll take it on. That Colonel Croston, 'e's keen on bells."

"No! The Preeces done it through plague and droughts and wartime when ringing bells was an offense. But we done it, boy, 'cause it's got to be done, see. Got to be."

The old feller near desperation. Touch of the pleading there now. Stuff him.

"I don't wanner talk to you no more, Granddad. You're not all bloody there, you ask me."

"Warren, there's things . . ."

"Oh yeah, there's things I don't know! Always, ever since I was so 'igh, people been tellin' me there's things I don't know. Maybe I don't wanner know, maybe . . . What's up with you now?"

His granddad was looking past him at something that caused his mouth to open a crack, bit of dribble out the side, false teeth jiggling about. Disgusting.

He turned and began to walk back toward the road, toward the town, Warren slinking half a dozen paces behind. When the gap between them was wide enough, Warren turned and saw what looked like the sunset reflected in one of the top windows of the old house, just below the roofline.

Except there wasn't any sun, so it couldn't be a sunset.

Warren shrugged.

ten

The smell happened first.

It happened quite suddenly, as if in the cracking of a rotten egg. The smell and with it the light. Elements of the same change.

The smell was filthy. Sulfur, and something cesspit putrid.

The light came in oily yellows, the yellow of candles made of animal fat and the yellow of pus from a wound gone bad. The light came from no particular direction but glistened on the stone walls like lard.

Rachel shrank from the walls, but she couldn't get away from the stairs. Where she crouched, it was no longer dry and dusty but wet, warm, and slick, like phlegm. She touched a stone step just once, and something unpleasant came off on her fingers. She tried to wipe them on the oak door, but that also was coated with a thick, cheesy grease, gritty here and there with what felt like fly corpses.

Rachel pulled the hand away in disgust, wiped it on her Barbour, knowing she could no longer bring herself to beat on this door. Her fists were sore and peeling, anyway, and if there were people out there they weren't going to help her. Perhaps they were waiting for the cool, superior, professional woman to break down, to shriek and sob and plead.

"I can't stand this," she said aloud. "I shall be sick."

Which couldn't make the atmosphere any more fetid.

But if I was a woman with any imagination, she thought, I would be very, very frightened.

For the Court, always so drab and dusty and derelict—gloomy, but no more menacing than an empty warehouse—had swollen into a basic sort of life.

Ludicrous. A grotesque self-delusion. But that was what it felt like. Flickerings of things. Presences in the shadows. The smell itself was like the house's own foul breath.

She began to breathe hard herself. Broke out in a coughing fit. Then tried to breathe slowly and selectively, keeping her mouth closed, because the air was so rancid that when she took it in, there gathered at the back of her throat a richly cloying, raw-meat taste like sweating, sweet salami. Rachel—suffocating, closing her mouth, closing her eyes, trying to close down all her senses; trying, above all, not to hear—thought, I need air. I need light. I need to walk up these few steps.

I need the prospect chamber.

Soft, fresh evening air. Gentle evening light.

The prospect chamber. Eight, ten steps away.

But I can't move from here. I can't move because of . . .

. . . those taunting sounds from the darkness above.

Sometimes soft, rustling like satin. Sometimes loud as a foundry overhead. And then stopping for a period of tense, ominous quiet—until it begins again, louder and closer. Then distant again. I am here, I am there, I can be anywhere I choose in an instant because I'm not hu . . .

Shut up! Shut up!

It's what he *wants* you to think.

Creaks. Thrustings. What might have been hollow footsteps on wood, flat footsteps on stone. On stone steps.

He's coming down!

Stopping just before the bend, not six feet away from where she crouched, holding her arms around herself, beginning to shiver.

Pull yourself together. Someone is trying to terrify you. It's only another person. You can handle people; you always could. You are cool and controlled; you can be remote, haughty, off-hand, intimidating. You are flexible. You can be dominant, or compliant, at will.

All you have to do is stride up there and face whoever it is.

Yes, but *that's* what he wants.

And what if you go up there and there's . . .

Nothing.

Nothing but the dark.

"Help me!" Rachel was screaming out seconds later, her voice, always so calm and deep, now parched and bitter with anger and despair. "Hum . . . ble! Andy! Anybody! Please!"

Then, in a soft and aching whisper, she said, "J.M.?"

And her eyes filled uncontrollably with tears. When I get out of here, I'm going to get us both away. Tonight. That's a promise.

If I get out of here. If I ever get to breathe the sweet night air.

God help me, Rachel thought, but I'm not going to scream anymore. When she'd screamed, the scream had come up from her stomach, like bile.

When she looked down at herself she saw that her Barbour's waxy surface gleamed sickly yellow like the walls. She wanted to take it off, but she didn't like the cold. She'd never liked the cold.

She wanted to remove her shoes, so as to move more quietly up the stairs toward the prospect chamber, but the thought of that ooze between her toes . . .

She closed her eyes. Closed her eyes and opened them, and

rose, picking up the cardboard box containing the dead cat, the
guardian.

"Come on, Tiddles," Rachel said, wiping the tears away.

She wished the appalling sounds would begin again, if only to
muffle her footsteps.

They did not. Silence woven as thick as a tapestry hung over
the stairs, which were visible only because of the phosphorescence which seemed to move with her, not so much lighting the
way as holding her close, in a thick and stifling miasma.

When she looked back there was merely an oily blackness
behind her, in the place near the door where she had crouched.

Rachel couldn't remember a nightmare this bad. She was
sweating in the clammy Barbour which seemed to have become
part of this place, as if the yellow light steaming from the
walls was revaporizing on the wax of the coat in clusters of
tiny bubbles.

She came to the bend in the stairs.

All she had to do was follow the spiral.

To her left would be the alcove concealing the door to the prospect chamber. Above her—how far above her she couldn't tell
because there was no light and she could not remember—would
be the attic.

Better not to think about the attic. Shut it out.

*I don't go into the attic. I'm not superstitious, I just don't go
into the attic . . .*

Two steps.

Two steps to the alcove and the prospect chamber and light
and air. She could stand in the opening and shout and scream
and *somebody* would have to hear her.

Oh, please. Please don't let the door be locked.

Rachel made it to the second step and was about to fall into the
alcove, throw herself at the door to the prospect chamber . . .

This is the only part of the house I like.

. . . when—to a shattering chorus of harsh clangs and
grinding, strangled creaks, a malfunctioning clock mechanism
amplified a thousand times—the greasy darkness shredded
before her like a rotting curtain, revealing the attic all lit
up in bilious yellow, except for the quivering shadow of
the rope hanging from the apex of the roof, turning slowly,
stretched taut.

By something palely shining, the source of all the light, noosed and squirming.

It was not far off 10 P.M., the night sidling in, when Powys drove the Mini between the gateposts of the Court and became instantly aware of the Tump behind the house.

He could not see the Tump, but he saw for the first time that the trees towering over the Court from behind were the trees growing out of its summit.

Once you knew this you could almost see the shadow of the great mound outlined in the Elizabethan stonework of the Court itself; the Tump and house fused into a single . . .

. . . entity.

Even as he had that thought, something flared in the house, and then went out, like a light bulb which explodes the second it's switched on. He saw a momentary afterglow in one of the small windows immediately below the eaves.

Maybe Andy's in there. Maybe I can wait behind the door until he comes out. And then I'll start hitting him.

Powys accelerated, drove around the house to the courtyard, parked in front of the stable block, next to the Range Rover—felt a pang of gratitude when he spotted that, longing to see Rachel again.

The stable door was unlocked; he went in.

"Rachel?"

The place was dim; although it probably faced west, there was little light left in the sky. From here, at the top of the long room, now sectionalized, you looked down toward the big picture window and the gray and smoky Tump.

"Rachel, luv, you in there?"

Maybe the light, way up in the house, had been her, with a torch. *I don't like that. It may not frighten her up there, but it scares the crap out of me.*

And why had the torch gone out?

"Rachel!"

He looked around for light switches, found a panel of them behind the door, pressed everything. Concealed lighting came on everywhere without a blink.

On the kitchen table was a scattering of magazines. New Age stuff. And a black leather bag, open. Rachel's bag.

He went outside again, anxiety setting in with the dusk. He

looked across at the Court. Soon the sky and the stone would meld and the house would be an amorphous thing balanced on the edge of the night.

Powys moved to the rear entrance, trying not to crunch gravel. He pushed the door, but it didn't give. Locked.

He didn't waste time with it, but followed the walls of the house around to the front and almost cried out when something big and black reared up in his path.

It didn't move. It was a massive rubbish pile, except many of the items on it didn't look like rubbish to Powys, even in this light. Near the top of the heap was an enormous double wardrobe, Victorian Gothic, its top corner projecting sharply out of the pile, as if in protest.

This time Powys tried the front door, and found that it, too, was locked.

He looked back along the dead-straight drive into the wood, listening to the silence. No birds left to sing.

Directly above him, he knew, would be the prospect chamber, set into the highest eaves, the house's only orifice when the doors were locked and barred.

Powys stepped back from the door and shouted as loud as he could up in the direction of the chamber's hidden maw.

"Rachel!"

A moment in a void.

Then he saw a glowing filament of sporadic pale-yellow zig-zagging the length of the eaves, like very feeble lightning.

He heard a scream so high and wild it might have been an animal on the brink of violent death in the woods.

And then a chasm opened under all his senses.

You land with a breathtaking thump on the fairy mound, not hearing the laughter, only aware of the pit beneath you, an endless lift shaft. You're falling, down and down and down, faster and faster, a tiny point of white light far below you . . . a point of light, which gets no larger the farther you fall because what it is . . . is the light reflecting from a spearhead, dirty and speckled with rust, as you can see quite clearly in the long moments before you feel the tearing agony, watching the spear's shaft disappearing into your stomach in an explosion of blood.

*   *   *

"Noooooooooo!"

He staggered frantically but uselessly about, trying to position himself below her, as she plummeted from the prospect chamber like a shot bird, the Barbour billowing out, waxy wings against the leaden sky.

But she crashed down in the only place he could not hope to throw himself in her path, and he actually heard her neck break as it connected with the projecting corner of a Victorian Gothic wardrobe of old, dark wood.

Something came after her—a small, gray-brown wisp of a thing.

part six

❋❋❋❋❋❋❋

. . . In many such cases it has been suspected that there was an unconscious human medium, commonly an emotionally disturbed adolescent, at the root of the manifestations. If these effects can be produced unconsciously, it is reasonable to suppose that people can learn to produce them by will. Indeed, in traditional societies young people who have evident talents for promoting outbreaks of psychical phenomena are marked out as future shamans . . .

JOHN MICHELL,
The New View Over Atlantis

Monday morning and, over the dregs of an early breakfast, Fay finally found out the truth about her father, Grace, and the house. And wound up wishing, in a way, that she'd remained ignorant, for in ignorance there was always hope.

It was not unknown for Alex to be up for an early breakfast—on one best-forgotten occasion five or six weeks ago he'd been clanking around in the kitchen at 5 A.M. and, when his swollen-eyed daughter had appeared in the doorway, had admonished her for going out and not leaving him any supper.

No, it hadn't made any sense—except in terms of the quantity of blood reaching her dad's brain—and Fay was resigned to it. With a cold, damp apprehension, she'd accepted there would come a time when it might be necessary to change the locks on the front door and deprive him of a key so he wouldn't go out wandering the streets in the early hours in search of a pub or a woman or something.

However, there were still times—like last night—when it might almost be in remission.

But last night—*Dad, why is Grace haunting us?*—they'd parted uncomfortably, Alex mumbling, "Talk about it in the morning." The prospect of his remembering had seemed so remote that even Fay had expunged it from her memory.

Then this morning, she'd come down just before eight, and there was her dad fishing a slice of bread out of the toaster with a bent fork and making unflattering observations about the quality of Taiwanese workmanship.

"Been remiss," he'd mumbled. "Shouldn't have tried to cover up."

"So you burnt the toast again," Fay said. "No big deal, Dad."

"No—*Grace,* you stupid child. I'm trying to say I should have told you about Grace."

"Oh."

And out it all came, for the first time, as if the blood supply to his brain had suddenly tripled, making him more cogent, more aware of his own defects than she could ever remember. This Wendle woman . . . was it conceivable she'd pulled off some astonishing medical coup here?

"Grace . . . " Alex said. "This lady with whom I'd had a small dalliance over twenty years earlier, she rather more serious about it than I. I mean, she really wasn't my type at all, not like your mother. Grace was a very proper sort of woman, prissy some might say."

"I never liked to say it myself, Dad."

"Such a sheltered life, you see, here in Crybbe. And then the secretarial job with the diocese. I think—God help me—I think she really believed that having an affair with a clergyman was somewhat less sinful than having a less . . . er, less physical relationship with a layman."

"Nearer my God to thee," Fay said wryly.

"Quite. She was quite *unbearably* understanding when . . . when your mother found out and threatened to get us all, via the divorce courts, into the *News of the World*. Tricky period. Things were quite hairy for a while. But, there we are, it ended surprisingly amicably. Quite touching, really, at the time."

Fay said, "You mean she accepted her martyrdom gracefully, as it were, to save your precious career."

Alex lowered his eyebrows. "Quite," he said gruffly. "Of course, I felt sorry for Grace and we kept in contact—in an entirely platonic way—for many years."

"Even when Mum was alive?"

"Platonically, Fay, platonically. Came back to Crybbe to live with her sister, as you know, then she died, and Grace was alone, a very aloof, proper little spinster in a tidy little house. Terribly sad. Do you think I might have another . . . ?"

"I'll pour it."

"Thank you. And then, of course, I had the letter from young Duncan Christie at the cathedral, just happening to mention Grace was in a pretty depressed state. Not too well, sister recently dead. Feeling pretty sorry for herself, and with reason. Never been quite the same since . . . you know. Well . . . "

"You've told me this bit. A chance for you to make amends."

"Nemesis, you see. I *had* ruined the poor woman's life, after all."

"That might be questionable."

Alex shook his head, in a rare gloomy mood. "And, well, I just happened to turn up there one day, just passing through, you know. And I just happened to stay. So, after all these years, Miss Legge finally becomes Mrs. Peters—or, as she liked to put it, Mrs. *Canon* Peters. And Alex resigns himself to a year or two of ministering to this rather severe elderly lady, incurably ill and incurably set in her ways—odd, really, she seemed much older than me, although she was twenty-odd years younger."

"Yes, but . . . "

"I know. I'm coming to it. Woodstock. Why didn't I sell this place when Grace died and go back to Woodstock?"

"The very question I've been trying to ask you for months, Dad."

"Er . . . Yes." Alex slurped milk into his coffee. Fay looked up as hard rainspots hit the window. The dried-blood bricks of the houses across the street gleamed drably.

"You see, there are things you don't know about Woodstock. Like the fact that it, er . . . well, it wasn't mine to sell, actually."

Fay closed her eyes.

"Still belonged to Charlie Wharton. I may have conveyed the impression I'd bought it off him. Fact is, I was only sort of keeping it warm for his retirement, and I was surviving rather longer than either of us had envisaged. And they were about to boot him out of the bishop's palace, you see, so he was pretty anxious to have the place back. In fact, I, er, well, I might have been facing a spot of legal action to remove me if I hadn't cleared off when I did. To be honest."

Might have guessed, Fay thought. Might have bloody guessed.

"So what it comes down to," she said, smiling icily, "is that you were rather more anxious to move in with Grace than she was to have you."

"Well. Until I, er, raised the possibility of marriage."

Fay nodded, still smiling.

"Problem is, as you know, money and I have never got along terribly well together. Ladies, horses, unwise investments . . . "

Alex stirred his coffee. The rain came down harder. Fay noticed a damp patch near the kitchen ceiling. It was getting bigger.

"Dad," she said, "you are a total, unmitigated shit."

Alex went on stirring his coffee and didn't deny it.

Fay went to wash the breakfast dishes, digesting the information and its significance: that her father was not a wealthy man, that his total assets amounted to little more than a very small terraced cottage in a back street in Crybbe. A cottage which, even if sold to, say, Max Goff, would hardly pay a year's rent on a basement room in Battersea.

She wondered what kind of pension he'd got. And if he had debts she knew nothing about.

So much to think about that it seemed silly even to raise the issue. However . . .

"You've seen her, haven't you? Since she died, you've been seeing her."

"Oh, Fay." Alex rubbed his eyes. "This part's so difficult. The past few months—such a blur. I don't know what I've done, what I've seen. These past couple of days . . . It's as though I'm waking up. Wendy perhaps, I don't know."

"You know what I'm talking about, though. Let's not piss about here, Dad. Grace's ghost."

She shivered, just saying the words, Grace's empty fish-smile in her mind.

"I . . . This really is hard. Especially for me, as a priest. All my life . . . so many anomalies. So many things one can't encompass within the scriptural parameters. That business in Y Groes a year or two ago. And now young Murray and his evil children."

"You haven't told me about *that.*"

"Sworn to silence, child. And, you see, there's always a rational explanation, always a psychological answer. Murray pushing ahead with his career in the blissful certainty that a clergyman can operate more effectively if he *doesn't* believe."

"Sod Murray, Dad . . . Grace."

"You don't have to bring me back to the bloody point. I'm not rambling."

"Sorry."

"All right. So I'm guilty of whatever crime it might be to smooth things out for two elderly folk in a bit of a mess. The problem is, when Grace popped her clogs rather sooner than expected, my overwhelming reaction, I'm sorry to say, was one of relief. There we are. Truth out. I'd got a roof over my head and she wasn't under it anymore. How's that for a Christian attitude?"

"Not so deplorable."

"It may not seem deplorable to you, wretched child, but I wanted to suffer. I *needed* to suffer. I'd been getting away with things all my life, and here I was again landing on my feet."

Fay thought, Christ, what's he saying? Is he saying that, in his dislocated mental condition, he *created* Grace's ghost, a resentful avenging presence to remind him of his sins?

"And you," Alex said. "Why the devil did *you* have to come back and look after me? I didn't want to inflict myself on you. Prissy little Grace didn't want you in her house."

The crux of it. He might be able to project Grace, like a gruesome magic-lantern slide on his own dusty mental screen.

But you can't make me see her, Dad. You can't do that.

How could she tell him what she'd seen? (Did I really see it? *Did* I see it?) What would *that* do for his remission?

"OK, Dad," she said. "Drink your coffee. I understand. Look, I've missed the news now."

Fay switched on the Panasonic radio on the kitchen window-ledge. She had indeed missed the news and had to listen to a couple of minutes of sport before the headlines were repeated.

"And to recap on today's main story: In Crybbe, police are investigating the death of a personal assistant to billionaire businessman Max Goff. The dead woman, thirty-five-year-old Rachel Wade, appeared to have fallen from a high window in historic Crybbe Court. This is Offa's Dyke Radio News. Next bulletin: ten o'clock."

For long, long seconds, Fay didn't move at all. Stood frozen at the sink, a damp dishcloth hanging from one hand.

The kitchen clock, two minutes fast, said 9:17.

Alex, sliding his chair back, getting to his feet, said, "How come you didn't pick that one up, Fay?"

"I normally make the police calls before you get up," Fay said numbly. "We had breakfast instead. Offa's Dyke has an early reporter, in at half past five."

"Ah." Alex brought his coffee cup to the sink. "Expect you'll be off to find out what happened." He looked up, his beard pure white in the dull morning. "You all right, Fay? How well did you know this woman?"

"Fine, Dad," said Fay. "No, I . . . I didn't know her *very* well. Excuse me."

Arnold struggled to his feet to follow her out of the room, fell over again. Fay picked him up and carried him into the office, her face buried in his fur.

As she put him down on the fireside chair, she caught a glimpse of her own face in the gilt-framed mirror, a face as pale as dead Grace.

Fay picked up the phone, called the Information Room at Divisional HQ.

"Not much we can tell you, I'm afraid."

"It was an accident, though?"

"All I can say is, investigations are proceeding."

"You mean, it might *not* have been an accident?"

"Hang on a minute," the police voice said, then she heard, "Yes, sir, it's Fay Morrison from Offa's Dyke. Sure, just a sec. Mrs. Morrison, the duty inspector would like a word."

"Good morning, Mrs. Morrison, Inspector Waring here. I wonder if you'd be good enough to pop into the police station at Crybbe, see the chief inspector."

"Why?"

"Just a few things you might be able to clear up for us."

"Like what?"

"I think I'd rather the chief told you that, if you don't mind."

"Oh, come on," said Fay. "Off the record."

A moment's hesitation, then, "All right, off the record, we've a chap helping with inquiries, Joseph Miles Powys. Says he was with you yesterday."

"What?"

"Would you mind, Mrs. Morrison, just popping into the station? They won't keep you long."

"I'm . . . I'm on my way," Fay said.

two

In his room at the Cock, Guy awoke at nine-thirty.

He'd come back here for a good night's sleep, but it hadn't been one, and he awoke realizing why.

He blinked warily at the overcast, off-white morning. At his suitcase on the floor by the dressing-table. At the wardrobe door agape, exposing his leather jacket on a hanger.

And, finally, at the portfolio against the wall next to the door. Especially at that.

He should never have slept with those drawings in the room. In the practical light of morning, Guy knew he should have left the portfolio in his car. Or, better still, dumped them back at The Gallery after his abortive attempt to quiz the girl.

On his way to the bathroom, he picked up the portfolio and left it propped up in the passage, hoping somebody would nick the thing. It was still there when he returned after a pee and a very quick wash—he didn't like spending too long in bathrooms anymore, even by daylight.

Back in his room, Guy burrowed in his suitcase for his rechargeable shaver. He shaved, bending down to the dressing-table mirror, wondering about Jocasta, what kind of night she'd had.

Well, yes, he'd felt bad about Jocasta, in a way, especially when she'd clutched at his arm, pleading, "One more night—just one night. Hereward'll be back tomorrow. Guy, I can't . . . I *can't* spend a night there alone."

"Look," he'd argued reasonably. "Why not lock yourself in your, er, suite? You don't have to go near that bathroom, do you? I promise you, I'll find out about this, I'll tackle the girl again tomorrow."

"You won't," Jocasta had wailed. "Your crew'll be back and you'll spend all day filming and you'll forget all about me. I've been very stupid, I know . . . but please, can't you just . . . ?"

"No!"

Jocasta had sniffed and wandered back into The Gallery, leaving him alone on the street with the stiff-backed portfolio under his arm.

Dammit, he'd done what he could. Opened her poxy exhibition, been charming to the invited guests, none of whom—it seemed to Guy—could get away fast enough.

And he'd tried to get at the girl, the damned girl in black with the cruel, dark eyes.

"There she is!" Jocasta grabbing his arm in front of everybody, hissing at him and writhing like an anaconda.

"Where? Who?"

"The one who brought those drawings in."

"You invited her?"

"Of course I didn't. She's just turned up. Guy, we've got to make her tell us what it's all about."

"We? We have?"

The girl had spoken to nobody, just wandered around inspecting paintings, wearing a faintly superior, supercilious expression—as well she might, he'd conceded, given the standard of work on show: the artist, Emmanuel somebody or other, apparently specializing in brownish *pointilliste* studies of derelict farmyards.

To Guy, the girl looked far too mature and aware to be still at school.

Jocasta pushing the portfolio at him—"Please . . . talk to her. She'll be impressed by you. She won't dare lie."

But the girl didn't seem even to have heard of Guy Morrison, which didn't make her any more endearing. Add to this the dark-eyed unfriendly face—and the attitude.

"I was very interested," Guy began smoothly, "in the drawings you gave Mrs. Newsome. The ones in this folder."

"I don't know anything about them."

"That's interesting. She tells me you asked her to try and sell them for you."

"Don't know what you're on about. She's crazy, that woman. You know she's on Valium and stuff, don't you?"

"Are you saying you didn't do these drawings? In which case, who did?"

"Why don't you get lost, blondie," Tessa Byford said loudly, sweet as lemon, "you're really not my type."

She turned away from Guy Morrison and melted into the

"crowd"—a dozen or so people looking uncomfortable, feeding each other canapés and surface-chat. Except for one very thin woman with stretched, yellow-white skin, standing alone and smiling vacuously at Guy, with small needle-teeth.

Guy smiled back, but she didn't acknowledge him, and he went outside with the portfolio under his arm, to be followed by the faintly tipsy, hysterical Jocasta.

"No!" he'd said firmly. "Do you understand? No!"

Which was how he'd come to walk away still holding the portfolio, feeling angry and confused. Needing a good night's sleep so he could think this thing out. The girl had obviously known about the ghost of the old man haunting the Newsomes' house. Had given Jocasta the drawings in a calculated attempt to terrify her.

But why? What had the girl got against Jocasta? Was there something Guy didn't know?

In the privacy of his room he'd thought of examining the drawings in some detail, but he found he didn't want to take them out of their folder. The whole business seemed less frightening now than distasteful.

Not the sort of thing Guy Morrison needed while shooting an important documentary.

He didn't need the dreams either.

Last night Guy had dreamed he was back on the rug in front of the fire, where Jocasta straddled him, swinging her hips tantalizingly above his straining loins.

"Yes, yes . . ." Guy urged in the dream, but she held herself just a fraction of an inch away so he could feel the heat of her but not the touch of her skin.

"Please," he moaned. "Please come down."

Her face was above his; she seemed to be floating, both hands in the air. He felt her pubic hair brush the tip of his . . .

"Come . . . down . . . on me."

"No!" Jocasta said calmly.

"Oh please! Please . . . I can't, I can't . . . *I can't hold on!*"

He tried to put his arms around her neck to pull her down on him, but his arms went right through her, as though she had no substance.

He dreamed then—the way you did sometimes—that he woke up, still feeling alarmingly excited. He was in his room at the Cock and he could still feel her presence above him, her bodily musk in his nostrils. He moaned and breathed in deeply.

And almost choked.

She smelled foul.

A decaying, rancid smell that filled up his throat and turned the sweat on his body to frost, and when he opened his eyes he stared into the whitened, skeletal face of the woman from The Gallery with the little needle-teeth.

He really woke up then, in a genuine cold sweat.

No more nights alone in the Cock, Guy Morrison decided. Tonight . . . well, tonight would have to be a very special night for his adoring production assistant, Catrin Jones.

The lesser of several evils.

Chief inspectors were getting younger. This one was a kind of Murray Beech in blue; steely-eyed, freshly shaven although he may have been up most of the night.

"Yes," she said. "We'd been to pick up my dog from the vet's. I . . . I needed somebody to drive the car so I could keep the dog on my knee."

"No," she said. "No, I haven't known him long. Just a couple of days, in fact. In this job you get to know people quite well quite quickly."

Don't ask what was wrong with the dog, she pleaded silently. *It has nothing whatsoever to do with this. Nothing.*

"We got back . . . I suppose it would have been shortly before seven. Yes, he drove back. The last I saw of him, he was walking home . . . to the cottage he was living in. Max Goff had commissioned him to write a book about Crybbe."

"Miss Wade?" she said, "Yes, I . . . got on very well with her. I suppose we had similar backgrounds."

"Rose?" she said later. "Rose who . . . ?"

"Rose Hart," replied Chief Inspector William Hughes, a high-flier from Off. "Have you heard of her?"

"No . . . Oh, wait a minute. Photographs by Rose Hart. On the cover of *The Old Golden Land,* it said 'Photographs by Rose Hart.' Is that who you mean?"

"You don't know anything about her? You never met?"

"No . . . What's the connection here?"

"Mrs. Morrison, I have to be intrusive. What's your relationship with Joseph Miles Powys?"

"What?"

"Were you sleeping with him?"

"What . . . ?"

"I'm sorry, I have to ask this."

"Of course I wasn't bloody sleeping with him. I'd only known the bloke a couple of days."

"And how long had he known Miss Wade?"

"Oh." Fay leaned back in the metal chair in the bare little room. There was a table and two other metal chairs; the chief inspector in one, Wynford Wiley in the other. Fat, florid, red-necked Wynford Wiley, with a suggestion of a smile on his tiny lips.

"I see what you mean," Fay conceded quietly.

"Two days? Three days? Four perhaps?"

"Yes, OK. It was what you might call a whirlwind romance."

"Quite normal for some people, Mrs. Morrison."

"Yes, but Rachel wasn't . . . "

"No?"

"No. Listen. Perhaps relationships do form quickly when . . . when you aren't happy."

"She . . . She wasn't happy working for Max Goff, no. She wasn't happy about what he was doing in Crybbe. She thought he was pouring money down the drain. The thing is . . . it wasn't too easy to quit; she was being paid an awful lot of money as Goff's PA."

The way you babbled under interrogation, no matter how smooth you thought you were at handling people.

"How unhappy would you say she was?"

"Look," Fay said, rallying. "I think it's time you made it clear what kind of investigation this is. What do you suspect? Suicide? Or what?"

"Or what?" repeated the chief inspector.

"Or murder, I suppose," Fay said.

"What do *you* think it was?"

"I don't know the circumstances. Are you trying to say—I mean, is this the bottom line? Powys pushed poor Rachel out of the window because she found out he was having it off with me? I mean, bloody hell, come *on* . . . "

"It wasn't a window, Mrs. Morrison. It was something called the prospect chamber. Do you know it?"

"No. That is . . . I've heard of it."

"Did you go out again last night, after Mr. Powys had brought you home?"

"No."

"Is there anybody who can . . . ?"

"My father."

"I understand he's not been very well, Mrs. Morrison. I believe he gets a bit confused."

"Oh God, Hughes, do you get a kick out of this?"

"It's my job, Mrs. Morrison."

"Still, what have I got to complain about? It'll sound interesting on the radio tonight, won't it?"

Wynford Wiley grinned, which wasn't pleasant. "Which radio you gonner 'ave it on, Mrs. Morrison?"

He looked down at his big hands. Hands like inflated rubber gloves, twirling a pen.

"Only I yeard Offa's Dyke Radio wasn't too happy with you lately, see. Just what I yeard, like."

Hughes said, "Mrs. Morrison, do you know what happened to Rose Hart?"

Fay shook her head slowly.

The chief inspector consulted a file on the table in front of him.

"Twelve years ago," he said, "Rose Hart and Joe Powys were sharing a flat in Bristol. It was a Victorian building in a not very pleasant area of town, and Mr. Powys told the inquest they were hoping to move somewhere else."

"Inquest?" Fay said faintly.

"At the rear of the house was an overgrown area which couldn't really be called a garden. One afternoon Joe Powys went up to London to see his publisher—this is what he told the inquest. When he got back he couldn't find Rose anywhere, but a window was wide open in the flat—this is the fourth floor."

"Oh no," Fay said.

"Joe told the coroner he dashed downstairs and out the back, and there she was. Rose Hart."

Fay brought a hand to her mouth. There *was* such a thing as coincidence. Wasn't there?

"The verdict was accidental death. Nobody quite believed that, everybody thought she'd killed herself, but coroners tend to be kind. When there's room for doubt, when there isn't a note . . ."

"That's very sad," Fay said.

"It certainly was, Mrs. Morrison. Half buried in this over-grown patch at the back of this building in Bristol, where they lived, there were these old railings."

"Jesus," Fay whispered.

"They had spikes, rusty iron spikes. Three of them went through Miss Hart. One deeply into the abdominal area, where she was carrying what was thought to be Mr. Powys's baby."

Fay said nothing.

"Very messy," Hughes said.

three

People were flinging themselves out of windows to the ground, and the gray masonry was cracking up around them.

The single bolt of lightning had caused a great jagged cleft in the tower. Fire and smoke spewed out.

"What's this one mean?" Guy Morrison asked.

Adam Ivory didn't look up. His wife whispered, "This card is simply called The Tower. Or sometimes The Tower Struck by Lightning. It signifies a cataclysm."

"Is that good or bad?" Guy was not greatly inspired by the tarot. What he'd really been after was a crystal-ball type of clairvoyant. One could do things with crystal balls televisually. He supposed it might be possible to match up some of these images with local scenes, but it would be a bit contrived.

"What I mean is, are we talking about something cataclysmi-cally wonderful, or what?"

"It can be either way," Hilary Ivory said. She was older and bigger than her husband; her hair was startlingly white. "Good or evil. A catharsis or simply a disaster, with everything in ruins. It depends on the spread."

The cameraman, Larry Ember, looked up from his view-finder, the Sony still rolling. His expression said, How long you want me to hold this bloody shot?

Guy made small circles with a forefinger to signify Larry should keep it running. Initially this was to have been no more than wallpaper—images of New Age folk doing what they did. But then he'd persuaded Adam Ivory, who called himself a tarotist, to try and read the future of the Crybbe project.

Guy had managed to convince him that this was being shot with Goff's full approval and would in no way threaten the Ivorys' tenure of this comfortable little town-center apartment. It occurred to him that the opportunity of relocating to form part of a like-minded community in Crybbe had been something of a godsend for Adam and Hilary; the tarot trade couldn't have been very lucrative in Mold.

Ivory had agreed to be recorded on VT while doing his reading but had stipulated there was to be no moving around, no setting up different angles, no zooming in or out, or anything which might affect his concentration.

Larry had done a bit of snorting and face-pulling at this. Cameramen weren't overconcerned about public relations, and it was evident to Guy that this cameraman thought this interviewee was a snotty little twerp.

Guy Morrison would not have disagreed completely, but in the absence of a crystal-ball person, this might be the best he'd get in the general area of divination.

The camera had been rolling for nearly seven minutes, and for the last four the shot had been entirely static: Adam Ivory—who wore a suit and looked more like a dapper, trainee accountant than a clairvoyant—intent on the spread of nine cards, the last of which was The Tower.

Little gaily dressed puppet figures hurling themselves to the ground.

Guy thought of Rachel Wade. An unfortunate incident. It would bring regional news crews into Crybbe, if they weren't here already. Trespassers on his property.

"Adam, are you going to tell us what the cards are indicating?" Guy asked softly.

Silence.

Larry Ember, who'd been a working cameraman when Guy was still at public school, stepped back from his tripod, the camera still running.

He looked straight at his director, the way cameramen did,

conveying the message, You're supposed to be in charge, mate, what are you going to do about this fucking mess?

Then, turning away from Guy, Larry lit a cigarette.

Hilary Ivory was on him in seconds, furiously pointing at her husband and shaking her hair into a blizzard. Guy tensed, just praying she didn't snatch the cigarette out of Larry's fingers; he'd once known a film-unit cameraman who'd hit a woman in the face for less than that.

Adam Ivory himself rescued the situation. He moved. Larry bent over his camera again.

Ivory's movement amounted to taking off his glasses, cleaning the lenses on the edge of the black tablecloth and putting the glasses back on again.

He resumed his study of the cards, and Larry's shoulders slumped in disgust.

Time, Guy realized, was passing. Goff was coming back, he'd heard, in the wake of this Rachel Wade business.

His eyes were drawn back to The Tower. It would be inexcusably tasteless to cut from shots of policemen and the upstairs window at the Court to these little puppet-figures tumbling from a graystone tower struck by a bolt of lightning. Pity.

Adam Ivory looked up suddenly, eyes large and watery behind the rimless glasses.

The soundman's boom mike came up between Ivory's legs, fortunately out of sight.

"Forget it," Ivory croaked. "Scrap it."

"Scrap it?" Guy said. *"Scrap it?"*

He didn't believe this.

"I'm sorry," Ivory said. "It isn't working. I don't think it's ... It's not reliable. The cards obviously don't like this situation. I should never have agreed to do a reading in front of a TV camera. As well as ... "

He fell silent, staring hard at the cards, as if hoping they'd rearranged themselves.

"As what?" Guy said, trying to control his temper. "As well as what?"

"Other negative influences." Ivory glanced nervously at the glowering cameraman and glanced quickly away. "The balance is so easily affected."

Guy said carefully, "Mr. Ivory, are you trying to say the cards were ... the prediction was unfavorable?"

The camera was still running. Guy very deliberately walked around to Ivory's side of the table and peered over his shoulder at the cards. He saw Death. He saw The Devil.

"I am not . . . "

Ivory swept the nine cards together in a heap. Guy noticed his fingertips were white.

" . . . trying to say . . . "

He snatched his hands away, as if the cards were tainted.

" . . . anything."

And pushed both hands underneath his thighs on the chair, looking like a scared but peevish schoolboy.

Larry Ember shot half a minute of this, then switched off and slid the camera from its tripod. "Fucking jerkoff," he muttered.

Hilary Ivory went to her husband, looking concerned in a motherly way.

A single tarot card fell over the edge of the table. Guy picked it up. It was The Hanged Man.

He put it carefully on the table, faceup in front of Ivory.

"What's this one mean?"

"It's very complicated," Hilary said. "The little man's hanging upside down by his foot, so it's got nothing to do with hanging, as such."

"Look, would you please leave?" the tarotist almost shrieked, his face sweating like shrink-wrapped cheese under the TV lights. "I . . . I don't feel well."

Larry Ember lit another cigarette.

"No," Mr. Preece said, "I won't."

He and his wife had not been inhospitable. Catrin Jones, Guy's production assistant, had been given the second-best chair and a cup of milky instant coffee.

"But you see . . . " She didn't know where to begin. The blanket refusal was not at all what she'd expected, even though she conceded it had been a difficult week for Mr. Preece, with the drowning of his grandson and everything.

"Biscuit?" offered the mayor.

"Oh no, thank you."

Catrin wondered why there was an onion in a saucer on top of the television.

"Because what we were thinking," she said rapidly, "is that it would be far better to talk to you in advance of tomorrow night's public meeting rather than afterwards at this stage, because . . ."

"You *are* talkin' to me," said the mayor simply.

"On camera, Mr. Preece," Catrin said. "On camera."

"I'm not going to change my mind. I'm keeping my powder dry."

"Oh, but, you see, you won't be giving anything away because it won't be screened for months!" Catrin's voice growing shrill and wildly querulous. "And it's not a great ordeal anymore being on television. We could shoot you outside the house so there wouldn't be any need for lights, and as well as being terrifically gifted, Guy Morrison is well-known for being a very understanding, *caring* sort of producer."

"That's as may be," Mr. Preece said. "All I'm sayin' is I don't 'ave to be on telly if I don't want to be, and I *don't.*"

"But you will be during tomorrow night's meeting. What's the difference?"

"I doubt that very much."

"Mr. Preece, you are supposed to be chairing the meeting."

"Aye, but as *you* won't be allowed in with that equipment, it makes no odds, do it?"

Catrin, outraged, sat straight up in her chair. "But it's a *public* meeting! Anybody can go in. It's all arranged with Max Goff!"

"Max Goff?" Mr. Preece's leathery jowls wobbled angrily. "Max Goff isn't running this town *yet,* young woman. And if I says there's no telly, there's no telly. Police Sergeant Wynford Wiley will be in attendance, and any attempts to smuggle cameras in there will be dealt with very severely."

"But . . . " Catrin was close to tears. She had never before encountered anyone less than delighted and slightly awed at the possibility of being interviewed by Guy Morrison.

" 'Ave another cup of coffee," said the mayor.

What he kept seeing was not Rachel plunging out of the sky. Not the willowy, silvery body broken on the rubbish pile.

He would not think of that—not here, in this grim Victorian police station. If he thought of that he'd weep; he wasn't going to indulge in that kind of luxury, not here.

No, what he kept seeing was the gray-brown thing, falling like smoke.

He'd seen it again as he waited for the police. It lay where it had landed, three or four yards from the pile, light as the fluff which collected in a vacuum cleaner.

I've seen them before, Powys thought now. In museums, in glass cases, labeled: *remains of a mummified cat found in the rafters, believed to have been a charm against evil.*

The cat had fallen to the ground *after* Rachel.

He hadn't told them that.

"And you heard her scream, did you?"

"She cried out. Before she fell."

"She wasn't screaming as she fell?"

"I don't think so. I mean, no, she wasn't . . . "

"Didn't that strike you as odd?"

"Nothing struck me at the time, except the sheer bloody horror of it."

Telling it four times at least. How he'd attacked the rubbish heap, frantically hurling things aside to reach her.

Lifting her head. Staring into her face, eyes open so wide that you could almost believe . . . until you felt the deadweight, saw—last desperate hopes corroding in your hands—the angle of the head to the shoulders.

Staring stricken into her face, and the curfew bell began to toll, a distant death knell.

" . . . can we return to this point about the door, Mr. Powys. You say you tried the rear door to the courtyard and found it locked. You couldn't budge it."

"No. It was locked. I put my full weight against it."

"Then how do you explain why, when we arrived, this door was not only unlocked but was, in fact, ajar?"

"I can't explain that. Unless there was someone else in there with Rachel."

"Someone other than you . . . "

"Look, I've told you, I . . . "

They'd gone over his statement several times last night and then said OK, thank you very much, you can go home now, Mr. Powys, but we'll undoubtedly want to talk to you again.

But he knew, as he tried to sleep back at the cottage, that they were out there, watching the place, making sure he didn't go anywhere.

And it was no real surprise when the knock came on the door at 8 A.M., and the car was waiting—a car, to take him less than a quarter of a mile across the bridge to the police station.

"You didn't tell us, Mr. Powys, that this wasn't exactly a new experience for you. You didn't tell us about Rose."

So who had?

Somebody had.

He sat on the metal chair, alone in the interview room, wishing he still smoked. He could hear them conversing in the passage outside, but not what they were saying.

"So you went to Leominster with Fay Morrison?"

"Yes."

"Attractive woman, Mrs. Morrison."

"Yes."

"What was wrong with the dog?"

"He had a badly injured leg."

This could lead back to Jonathon Preece in no time at all. Holistic police-work. Everything interconnected.

Joseph Miles Powys, I am arresting you on suspicion of the murders of Jonathon Preece, Rachel Wade, and Rose Hart. You don't have to say anything, but anything you do say . . .

Perhaps I *should* confess, he thought, looking up to the single, small, high window and seeing a hesitant sun in the white sky, wobbling nervously like the yolk of a lightly poached egg.

Maybe I did it. Maybe I killed her, as surely as if I'd been standing behind her in the prospect chamber, with both hands outstretched.

He thought, If I start believing that, we're all finished. So he went back to thinking about the cat.

four

The sun was out for the first time in ages, but hanging around unsurely like a new kid in the school doorway.

Fay walked aimlessly up the hill from the police station toward the town square and the Cock, pausing by the railings

alongside the few steps to its door. Even a weak sun was not
kind to this building; its bricks needed pointing, its timbers
looked like old railway sleepers.

The Cock didn't even have a sign, as you might have imagined, with a bright painting of a proud rooster crowing joyfully
from the henhouse roof. But, knowing Crybbe, would you *really*
imagine a sign like that?

And anyway, whoever said the name referred to that kind
of cock? A far more appropriate emblem for this town, Fay
thought, would be a decidedly limp penis.

Crybbe. *Crybachu* (to wither).

Fay looked down the alley toward the brick building housing
the Crybbe Unattended Studio and wondered if she'd ever get
in there again. They were obviously handling the Rachel Wade
story themselves; nobody had even attempted to contact her.

I need the money, Fay realized suddenly. I need an income.
I need a job. Why are they doing this to me?

She thought of Joe Powys—I think *I've* got problems—helping the police with their inquiries. Quite legitimately, by the
sound of it.

Rachel Wade . . . the dead woman, Rachel Wade.

He couldn't have . . . surely. She liked Joe. He seemed so
normal, for the author of a seminal New Age treatise.

Well, comparatively normal.

Oh God, what was happening?

She didn't notice the door open quietly in a narrow town
house to the left of the Cock, didn't hear the footsteps. When
she turned her head, the woman was standing next to her,
looking across the square to the church.

"Good morning, Fay."

Fay was too startled, momentarily, to reply. She'd never seen
this woman before, a woman nearly as small as she was, perhaps
a quarter of a century older.

Well, never seen the *face* before.

"Jean Wendle?" Fay said.

"I am."

Last seen in a hat, sitting very still, impersonating the ghost
of Grace Legge.

"May I perhaps offer you a coffee?" Jean Wendle said.

*   *   *

Catrin Jones knew Guy would be furious about the mayor's ban on cameras at tomorrow's public meeting.

She also knew from experience that when bad news was brought to him Guy had a tendency to take it out on the messenger.

The need to salvage something from the morning had brought her to this subdued, secluded house opposite the church, at the entrance to the shaded lane leading down to Crybbe Court.

"I'd be delighted to help you, any way I can," said Graham Jarrett, hypnotherapist, small, silver-haired, late fifties.

"I was thinking perhaps this, what is it, recession . . . ?"

"Regression."

It was very quiet and peaceful in the house, with many heavy velvet curtains. Catrin could imagine people here falling easily into hypnosis.

"Yes. Regression," she said. "This is . . . past lives?"

"Well, we don't like to talk necessarily in terms of past lives," Graham Jarrett said, matter-of-fact, like a customer-friendly bank manager. "But sometimes, when taken back under hypnosis to an area of time prior to their birth, people do seem to acquire different personalities and memories of events they couldn't be expected to have detailed knowledge of."

"Fantastic," Catrin said.

"I certainly wouldn't be averse to having you film a session, if the client was in agreement."

"That would be excellent," Catrin said.

"But I have to warn you that many of them do prefer it to be private."

"Oh, listen, my producer—Guy Morrison—is a wonderfully reassuring man. They would have nothing to worry about with Guy."

"Perhaps he would like to be regressed himself?" said Graham Jarrett with a meaningful smile.

"Oh. Well . . . "

"Or you, perhaps?"

"Me?"

"Think about it," Graham Jarrett said lightly.

Fay sat in the wooden bow-chair. Jean Wendle was on the edge of a huge, floppy sofa with both hands around a mug of coffee. She wore a white cashmere sweater and pink canvas trousers.

"I heard it on the news," she said. "About poor Rachel Wade."

"Yes," Fay said, wondering if she'd also heard about Powys helping with inquiries.

"It's a crumbling old place, the Court. What was she doing there at that time of night?"

"I don't know. I've only heard the news, too. I'll expect I'll be finding out. All I know is . . . "

Oh, what the hell, the woman was supposed to have been a lawyer, wasn't she? Maybe she could help.

"All I know is, the police aren't convinced it was an accident. Joe Powys apparently saw her fall and called the police. They're kind of holding him on suspicion."

A sunbeam licked one gilt handle of a big Chinese vase with an umbrella in it, then crept across the carpet to the tip of Jean Wendle's moccasins.

"Oh dear," Jean said.

Fay told her how things had been between Joe and Rachel, in case she wasn't aware of that. She described her own interrogation by the police. What they'd told her about Rose.

"Can they hold him, do you think?"

"It doesn't sound as if they have any evidence to speak of," Jean said. "They can't convict on a coincidence. They also have to ask themselves why this man should engineer the death of his lover in the same way that a previous girlfriend died and then immediately report it as an accident—knowing that the police would sooner or later learn about the earlier misfortune. I wonder how they found out about that so quickly. Did Joe tell them himself, I wonder? Do you mind if I smoke?"

Fay shook her head. Jean went across to the Georgian table, put down her coffee mug, lifted the lid on an antique writing box, found a thin cigar and a cheap, disposable lighter. She picked up a small, silver ashtray and brought everything back to the sofa.

"It could be, of course, that the police are looking at possible psychiatric angles."

Fay was thrown.

Yes, I'm an accredited crank, Joe had said. Had said several times, variations on the same self-deprecating theme.

"You're saying they think he's possibly a psychopath who's

into pushing women out of upstairs windows. And—I don't
know—subconsciously he's seeking help and that's why he
called the police after he'd done it?"

Jean shrugged. "Who knows how the police around here
think? Perhaps they'll do some checks with Bristol police to
find out if he really was in London the afternoon Rose died.
If they arrest him, he'll need a solicitor. Until they decide what
they're going to do, I don't think there's anything *we* can do.
Meanwhile . . . "

Jean Wendle turned serious, quizzical eyes on Fay.

"Tell me about yesterday. In the church. Tell me what that
was all about."

Fay sighed. It seemed so long ago. And, in retrospect, so
foolish. Also, it said too much about her state of mind that even
when Jean had turned in the pew to look at her, she was still
seeing somebody else.

"It's very silly," she said. "I thought you were Grace
Legge—that's my father's late wife."

Jean Wendle nodded, showed no surprise at all. "You've been
seeing this woman?"

"Once. I think. I mean, how can anyone say for sure? They
don't really exist, do they, only in our minds."

"That depends."

"On what we mean by 'existing,' I suppose. Well, all I
can say is that, whatever it was, I'm not anxious to see it
again."

Jean smiled. She was, Fay thought, the sort of woman—sharp,
poised—you wouldn't mind being like when you were older.
That is, you wouldn't mind so much being older if you were
this relaxed.

"I don't quite know what came over me. You were just so
completely still that the thought occurred to me that there was
nobody at all sitting next to Dad, but *I* was seeing Grace."

Jean said, "The time you really did see her—when you saw
whatever it was you saw—where was this?"

"In the house. In the office, which used to be her 'best'
room. The room that, when she was alive, I suppose she thought
of as her sacred place—so neat and perfect because nobody
really used it. Maybe she thought this room had been violated
by my desk and the equipment and everything. Or maybe I
thought she'd be angry and so I conjured up this fantasy . . . "

"You don't think that for one minute," Jean said.

"No," Fay admitted. "All right, I don't think that."

"Then please, only tell me what you *do* think. And stop looking at me as though you're wondering what I might change you into."

"Miss Wendle . . . "

"Jean."

"Jean. Look, I'm sorry, but it gets you like this after a while, Crybbe. I've been here nearly a year, and it gets to you."

"You mean you can't relate to the people here. You don't understand what makes them tick."

"Do you?"

"Well, I think . . . " Jean lit the cigar at last. "People talk a lot about energy. Energy lines, ley-lines. Trying to explain it scientifically. Makes them seem less like cranks if they're talking about earth energies and life forces."

She inhaled deeply, blew out a lot of blue smoke.

"The pronouncements of New Age folk are wrapped up in so much glossy jargon. Concealing massive ignorance."

"What are you doing in Crybbe, then, if you think it's all bullshit?"

"Oh, it isn't *all* bullshit, not by any means. And at least they're searching. Trying to reach out, as it were. Which itself generates energy. In fascinating contrast to the natives, who appear to be consciously trying not to expend any at all. And perhaps to the electricity company, who can't seem to summon sufficient to see us through an entire day."

"I'm sorry. What are you saying?"

"I'm saying that perhaps the people of this town are as they are because they've known for generations what a psychically unstable area this is, and most people—sadly, in my view—are afraid to confront the supernatural and all it implies. For instance, I should be very surprised if you were the only person who was seeing the shades of the dead in this town."

Fay shivered slightly at that. *The shades of the dead . . .* It sounded almost beautiful. But Grace wasn't.

"I try to avoid letting anything get touched by the dead hand of science or indeed pseudoscience," Jean said. "But let's suppose that in certain places certain forms of energy collect.

Our friend Joe Powys says in his book that the border country
is . . . Have you read it?"

"The psychic departure lounge."

"Yes, and poor Henry Kettle, the dowser, couldn't abide such
terminology because he was really awfully superstitious and
terrified of admitting it."

"Nothing psychic."

Jean waved her cigar. "A terrible old humbug, may he rest
in light. Henry, of course, was just about as psychic as anyone
can get. Anyway, your ghost. Grace. Did she speak?"

"Not a word."

"And she didn't move?"

"No."

"Harmless, then."

"I'm so glad," Fay said skeptically.

"Can I explain?"

"Please do."

"OK, if we stick to our scientific terminology, then pockets
of energy can accumulate in certain volatile areas, and in such
areas, the spirits of the dead, usually in a most rudimentary
form, may appear. Like a flash of static electricity. And they
go out just as quickly. Or you'll get sounds. Or smells."

"The scent of fresh-cut lilies or something."

"Or fresh shit," Jean said harshly. "It depends."

"I'm sorry. I wasn't flippant when it was happening to me."

"I doubt you were," Jean said. "All right, sights or sounds or
smells—or tastes even. Rarely anything simultaneous, because
there's rarely sufficient energy to support it. If there was a
massive accumulation of it, then one might have a complete
sensory experience."

"I only saw her. And it was cold. It went cold."

"Energy loss," Jean said. "Quite normal. So, if I may give you
some advice, if you should see your Grace again, blink a couple
of times . . . and she'll be gone. She can't talk to you, she can't
see you; there's no brain activity there. Entirely harmless."

"Not pleasant, though," Fay said, reluctant to admit feeling
better about the idea of Grace as a mindless hologram.

"No," Jean said, "the image of a dead person is rarely pleasant, but it's not as much of a problem as these damned power
cuts."

"You really think that's connected?"

"Oh, it has to be. Psychic activity causes all kinds of electrical anomalies. Voltage overloads, or whatever they call them. Sometimes people will find they have terrific electricity bills they can't explain, and the electricity people will come along and check the meters and the feeds, and they'll say, 'We're awfully sorry, madam, but you must have consumed it, our equipment cannot lie.' The truth is the householders may not have used it, but *something* has."

Fay remembered poor Hereward Newsome and his astronomical bills.

"But your wee ghost," Jean said, "is the least of your problems here. Sporadic psychic activity on that level isn't enough to cause power fluctuations on the Crybbe scale. Whatever's happening, there's much more that needs to be explained before you can get close to it."

"You've been very reassuring," Fay said. "Thank you. I'm also very impressed with what you're doing for Dad. He's almost his old self again. I mean, do you really think there's any hope of . . . ?"

"I never discuss my patients," Jean said severely.

By the time Fay left Jean Wendle's house, the sun had vanished behind an enormous black rain cloud and she hurried down the street to make it home before the rain began.

She saw Guy across the square, followed by his cameraman with the camera clamped to his shoulder and a tripod under his arm. Guy made as if to cross the road toward her, but Fay raised a hand in passing greeting and hurried on. She couldn't face Guy this morning.

"Fay," someone said quietly.

She turned her head and then stopped.

Blink a couple of times, Jean Wendle had advised, but this apparition didn't disappear.

"Joe," she said.

He looked terrible, bags under hopeless eyes, hair like cigarette ash.

"They had to let me go," he said. "Insufficient evidence."

Fay said nothing.

"Can we talk?"

"Maybe it's not a good time," Fay heard herself say. "I don't think you killed Rachel, let's just leave it at that for now."

Which was the last thing she wanted to do. She bit her upper lip.

"They had you in, presumably," he said.

"Yes."

"And they told you about Rose."

"Yes."

"And that's why you don't want to talk about it."

"Look," Fay said. "I've lost the only real friend I had in this town, I *desperately* want to talk about it, I just . . . "

"It wasn't an accident," Powys said.

"What?"

"It wasn't an accident. After she fell, something else came out."

"What are you saying?"

"A cat."

Fay looked at him. There was something seriously abnormal about all this. About Joe Powys, too.

"I don't mean a live cat. This one's been dead for centuries."

"Tiddles," Fay said faintly, getting a picture of black eye sockets and long saber teeth.

And her. *She* was becoming abnormal. She had to get out of here.

"Cats that've been dead for hundreds of years don't hurl themselves three stories to the ground while somebody puts on a light show under the eaves."

"Hallucination," Fay said.

"No."

Fay thought about Jean Wendle and the energy anomalies, about Grace, about the curfew and the howling and the town with no dogs.

Joe said, "Can you spare the rest of the day?"

No! she wanted to shriek, and then to push past him and run away down the street and keep running.

"I might have a job. I have to go home and talk to my father and check the answering machine."

"If it turns out you're free, can I pick you up? Say, twenty minutes?"

"I . . . "

Would that be entirely safe? she wanted to ask. Am I going to be all right as long as I stay away from open windows?

"All right," she said.

five

"They said, Don't leave town. Or words to that effect."

Joe Powys floored the accelerator.

"Fuck them," he said.

Fay tried to smile.

They'd left Crybbe on a road she wasn't too familiar with, the road into Wales by way of Radnor Forest, which didn't seem to be a forest at all but a range of hills.

He hadn't said where they were going.

She didn't care. She felt apart from it all, in a listless kind of dream state. She was watching a movie about a woman who was out for a drive with a murderer. But in films like this, the woman had no reason to suspect the man was a murderer, only the viewers knew that; they'd seen him kill, she hadn't.

The woman in this particular movie had a black and white three-legged dog on her knee. Must be one of those experimental, surrealist epics.

The car moved out of an avenue of trees into a spread of open, sheep-strewn hills with steep, wooded sides and hardly any houses.

Before they left she'd written a note for her dad, fed the cats, and listened to the answering machine, which said,

"Hi, Fay, this is James Barlow from Offa's Dyke. Just to say we understand Max Goff's coming back to Crybbe and he'll probably be holding a press conference around four this afternoon, following this Rachel Wade business. But don't worry about it, Gavin says to tell you he'll be going over there himself . . . "

So I'm free, Fay thought bitterly. Free as a bloody bird.

As if he were watching the same movie, Powys said, "If I killed her, why would I report it?"

"Why did you?"

"Had to get an ambulance. There might have been a chance."

"Did she . . . ? Oh God, did she die instantly?"

"I heard it, you know, snap. Her neck."

She thought his voice was going to snap, too, and tried not to react. "What were you doing there, anyway? How come you happened to be under the window when she fell?"

"Still don't know how much of that was coincidence. Don't know if she saw me. If she was trying to attract my attention and fell against the bar. But she didn't call out to me. She just screamed. As if she was screaming at something inside the house."

"And couldn't she get out? The house was locked up with her in it?"

"It was locked when I tried the doors. It wasn't when the police got there. So they say. Work that one out."

"So she was killed by somebody in the house . . . *If* she was killed. Humble?"

"Well, they didn't like each other. But that doesn't explain the light. Doesn't really explain the cat either."

"Maybe Rachel was holding the cat, for some reason, and it took longer to reach the ground because there was no weight left in it. Joe, I have to ask you this . . . What exactly were you doing at the Court?"

"Told the cops I was looking for Rachel. I think I was really looking for Andy. Oh God . . . " He sighed. "What happened was he'd planted a stone outside the cottage, an exact replica of a thing that's been hanging over me for years."

"A stone?"

"The Bottle Stone. Do you want to know this? It'll be the first time I've talked about it to anybody. Apart from the people there."

"Do you want to tell me?"

"I don't know . . . OK. Yeah."

He fell silent.

"What do you want?" Fay said. "A drumroll?"

"Sorry. OK. It goes back over twelve years. To the Moot."

"The Moot," Fay said solemnly.

"It's organized every year by *The Ley-Hunter* magazine. It's a gathering of earth-mysteries freaks from all over the place. We meet every year in a different town to discuss the latest theories and walk the local leys."

"I bet you all have dowsing rods and woolly hats."

"You've been to one?"

Fay laughed. It sounded very strange, laughter, today.

"This particular year," Powys said, "it was in Hereford. Birth-place of Alfred Watkins. Everybody was amazed there wasn't a statue—nothing at all in the town to commemorate him, which is how I came to establish Trackways a couple of years later. But, anyway, all the big names in earth mysteries were there. And we were all there too. Rose and me. Andy. Ben Corby, who was at college with us, bit of a wheeler-dealer, the guy who actually managed to sell *Golden Land* to a publisher. And Henry Kettle, of course. We knew there was a deal coming through, and on the Monday morning after the Moot, before we all set off for home, Ben rang the publishers and learned they'd sold the paperback rights for ten thousand quid."

Powys smiled. "Bloody fortune. Well, it was a nice day, so we decided, Rose and I, to invite the others—the people who'd been in on the book from the beginning—to come out for a celebratory picnic. We wondered where we could go within reach of Hereford. Then Andy said, 'Listen,' he said, 'I know this place . . . ' "

She looked out through the side window of the Mini. She didn't recognize the country. One hill made a kind of plateau. She counted along the top—like tiny ornaments on a green baize mantelpiece—three mounds, little tumps. A thin river was woven into the wide valley bottom.

Powys was dizzily swiveling his head. "Somewhere here . . . "

The third mound had a cleft in it, like an upturned vulva.

"Yes," he said. "Yes." He hit the brakes, pulled onto the side of the road. "It was down there."

"The Bottle Stone?"

Powys nodded.

"Let me get this right," Fay said. "This . . . legend, whatever it was . . . "

"It's a common enough ritual, I've found out since. It can be a stone or a statue or even a tree—yew trees are favorites for it. You walk around it, usually anticlockwise, a specific number of times—thirteen isn't uncommon. And then you have an experience, a vision or whatever. There's a church in south Herefordshire where, if you do it, you're supposed to see the Devil."

"But you didn't see anything like that?"

"No, just this sensation of plunging into a pit and becoming . . . impaled. And there was nothing ethereal about it, I can feel it now, ripping through the tissue, blood spurting out . . . "

"Yes, thank you, I get the picture."

"But it happened to *me*. That was the point. No indication of any danger to Rose."

"Was she unhappy?"

"Not at all. That day at the Bottle Stone, she was *very* happy. That's what's so agonizing. I've had twelve years to get over it . . . I can't. If I could make sense of it . . . but I can't."

"And it was . . . how long, before . . . she fell?"

"Not quite two weeks. OK, thirteen days."

"Hmm." Fay's fingers were entwined in the fur around Arnold's ears. "Was . . . was she unhappy at all afterwards? I mean, pregnant women . . . "

"It was at a very early stage. I don't even know if it had been officially confirmed."

"She hadn't told you?"

Powys shook his head. "The postmortem report—that was the first I knew about it."

"So this experience you had on the so-called fairy mound . . . What are your feelings about that? Do you feel you were being given a warning, that there was something you should have realized?"

Powys said, "You're interviewing me, aren't you? I can spot the inflection."

"Oh God, I'm sorry, Joe. Force of habit. How about if I try and make the questions less articulate?"

"No, carry on. At least it's more civilized than the cops. No, it didn't make any sense. Any more than the average nightmare."

"And you told Rose."

"No."

"Why not?"

"Because it had been such a nice day up to then. Because the future looked so bright. Because I didn't want to cast a pall. I just said when they dumped me on the mound I must have fainted. I said I was very dizzy. I did tell Andy about it after . . . after Rose died."

"And what did he say?"

"He said I should have told Rose."

"That was tactful of him."

"And what do *you* think, Fay? What do you think I should have done?"

"What about Henry Kettle? What did *he* say?"

"He wanted nothing to do with it. He used to say this kind of thing was like putting your fingers in a plug socket."

Fay glanced at him quickly, uneasily, over Arnold's ears. Was it possible that Joe Powys was indeed insane? Or, worse perhaps, was it possible he was *sane?*

He was hunched over the steering wheel. "Oh, Fay, how could I have killed Rachel?"

He looked at her. "I'm not saying I was in love with her. We'd only known each other a couple of days, but . . . "

She looked up into the hills, all the little tumps laid out neatly.

He said, "Think Arnold can manage a walk?"

Arnold struggled to his feet on Fay's knee.

"He obviously thinks so," Fay said. "Come on, then. Let's go and find the Bottle Stone."

Max began to breathe hard.

It was astonishing.

"Take me over again, Mel," Max said. "Then maybe we'll get Guy Morrison and his crew to come up with you. We have to have pictures of this. For the record."

He leaned forward, thoughts of Rachel's death blown away by all this magic.

Melvyn, his helicopter pilot, took them over the town again, making a wide sweep of the valley. Max counted six standing stones—first time around he'd missed the one by J. M. Powys's cottage near the river.

He couldn't believe it. A week ago Crybbe was scattered . . . random, like somebody'd crapped it out and walked away. Now it had form and subtle harmonies, like a crystal. It had been earthed.

He could spot, clear as if it had been blasted in with a giant aerosol paint-spray, the main line coming off the Tump. It cut through the Court, cleaved a path through the woods until it came to a small clearing, and in the center of this clearing, surrounded by tree stumps and chain-sawed branches, there was a tall stone, thin and sharp as a nail from up here.

Lucky he owned the wood. Lucky, also, that nobody in Crybbe seemed to give a shit about tree conservation.

Nice work, Andy.

Andy. Such a plain and simple user-friendly name. But the thought of Andy made him shiver, and he liked to shiver.

The line eased out of the wood, across the graveyard, and sliced into the church, clean down the center of the tower. Then it plowed across the square and hit this building.

Which building?

"Go in a bit, Mel."

The helicopter banked, and Max looked back. Shit, it was the Cock, he'd never realized the line cut through the pub . . . the pub he'd known intuitively he had to buy. Maybe, sleeping there in that crummy room, he'd picked up the flow. These things happened when you were keyed in to the system.

His thoughts came back to Rachel. Who, for once, had not been keyed in. Who hadn't known how to handle country people. Who hadn't believed in the Crybbe project, hadn't believed in much.

Should he feel any kind of guilt here? Leaving her to handle things while he was in London, knowing she was out of sympathy with the whole deal?

"OK, Max?"

"Yeah, sure, Mel. Take us in."

Thrown out on the fucking rubbish heap—like the Court itself didn't want anybody in there hostile to the project. Rough justice. Jeez.

Was this fanciful, or what?

What he'd do, he'd have some kind of memorial to Rachel fashioned in stone. A plaque on a gate or a stile along the ley-walk, well away from the Court. Couldn't have people staring up at the prospect chamber—"Yeah, this was where that woman took a dive, just here."

But accidents were bad news. First thing, he'd need to have that crossbar replaced, arrange things so the whole room was sealed off until it was fully safe.

They cleared the river and headed back over the town toward the Court. The other leys were not so obvious as the big one down the middle; this was because fewer than half the new stones were in place, several farmers refusing to give permission until after the public meeting. Or, more likely, they were

holding out to see how keen he was, how much he was prepared
to pay. Yeah, he could relate to that.

Cars in the courtyard. People waiting for him. Press conference scheduled for 5 P.M.

He looked at his Rolex. It was 11:15. Time to find out precisely what had happened. Talk to the police before he faced
the newsmen and the TV crews, whose main question would
be this:

Mr. Goff, this is obviously a terrible thing to happen. It must
surely have overshadowed your project here?

The press were just so flaming predictable.

Arnold was in fact moving remarkably well. "He doesn't think
he's disabled," Fay said. "He just thinks he's unique."

They climbed over a stile. Arnold managed to get under it
without too much difficulty. She picked him up for a while,
carried on walking across the field with the dog in her arms.
The few sheep ignored them.

The sky was full of veined clouds, yellow at the edges, like
wedges of ancient Stilton cheese.

Powys had watched Fay wander down the field and at one
point Memory, vibrating on its helipad, turned her into Rose in
a long white frock and a wide straw hat, very French Impres-
sionist.

He blinked and Rose was Fay again, in light-blue jeans and
a Greenpeace T-shirt.

She put Arnold down. He fell over and got up again.

Fay stopped and turned to him.

"Where is it, then?"

He said faintly, "It isn't here."

"I thought perhaps there was something wrong with my eyes,"
Fay said.

"I don't understand it. This was the field. There's the river,
see. The hills are right. There's the farmhouse, just through
those trees."

Fay didn't say a word.

"You think I'm bonkers, don't you?"

"Scheduled ancient monuments don't just disappear," she
said. "Do they?"

six

One of the women who cleaned the church was paid to come into the vicarage on weekdays to prepare Murray's lunch. He rarely saw her do it, especially in summer; it would just be there on a couple of dishes, under plastic wrap. Variations on a cold-meat salad and a piece of fruit pie with whipped cream. She never asked if he enjoyed it or if there was something he would prefer.

He lifted up a corner of the plastic wrap, saw a whitish, glistening smudge of something.

Mayonnaise. He knew it could only be mayonnaise.

But still Murray retched and pushed the plate away. This had been happening increasingly, of late—he'd scraped the lunch untouched into the garbage. He never seemed to miss it afterward, rarely felt hunger, although he knew he was losing weight and even he could see his face was gaunt and full of long shadows. Pretty soon, he thought sourly, there would be rumors going around that he had AIDS.

Next week he might let it be known that he was interested in a move. He would see how he felt.

Today was not the day to do anything hasty.

Today he'd left the vicarage as usual, before eight, and walked the fifty yards to the church. Where he'd found what he'd found.

The church door had not been damaged because it was never locked. Nothing had been torn or overturned. Only the cupboard in the vestry, where the communion wine and the chalice were kept, had been forced.

Murray had heard of cases where centuries-old stained glass had been smashed or, in the case of Catholic churches, plaster statues pounded to fragments. Swastikas spray-painted on the altar cloth. Defecation in the aisle.

Nothing so unsubtle here.

What was missing was that element of frenzy, of uncontrolled

savagery. This was what had unnerved him, made him look over
his shoulder down the silent nave.

Candles—his own Christmas candles—had been left burning
on the altar, two of them, one so far gone that it was no more
than a wick in a tiny pool of liquid wax. Between the candles
stood the communion chalice, not empty.

What was in the bottom of the cup was not mayonnaise.

Murray had looked inside once, then turned away with a
short, whispered, outraged prayer—it might have been a prayer
or it might have been a curse; either way it was out of character.
His reserve had been cracked.

With distaste, he'd placed the chalice on the stone floor,
remembering too late about fingerprints but knowing even then
that he would not be calling in the police, because that was all
they'd done.

And it was enough.

It was inherently worse than any orgy of spray paint and
destruction. The single small, symbolic act, profoundly personal, almost tidy. Appalling in its implication, but nothing in
itself, simply not worth reporting to the police and thus alerting
the newspapers and Fay Morrison.

"They always ask you," he remembered a colleague with an
urban parish complaining, "if you suspect Satanism. What are
you supposed to say? It's certainly more than antisocial behavior, but do you really want some spotty little vandal strutting
around thinking he's the Prince of Darkness?"

But this, he thought—staring down at his plastic-wrapped
lunch, suddenly nauseous and unsteady—this is another gesture
to *me*. It's saying, Come out. Come out, "priest," come out
and fight.

However, as he'd thought while rinsing out the chalice this
morning, *this* can hardly be linked to Tessa Byford, can it?

Murray had thrown away the candles, performed a small,
lonely service of reconsecration over the chalice, and decided
to keep the outrage to himself. By the time the Monday cleaner
came in at ten, there had been no sign of intrusion.

As for the small cupboard in the vestry—he would unscrew
it from the wall himself and take it to an ironmonger's in
Leominster, explaining how he'd had to force the lock after
being stupid enough to lose the key. Silly me. Ha ha.

Impractical souls, vicars. Absentminded, too.

Just *how* absentminded he was becoming was brought dramatically home to him when the doorbell rang just before two o'clock and he parted the lace curtains to see a hearse parked in front of the house with a coffin in the back.

It had slipped his mind completely. But, even so, wasn't it at least a day too early?

"Ah, Mr. Beech," the undertaker said cheerfully. "Got Jonathon Preece for you."

"Yes, of course."

"Funeral's Wednesday afternoon, so it's just the two nights in the church, is it?"

"Yes, I . . . I wasn't expecting him so soon. I thought, with the postmortem . . . "

"Aye, we took him for that first thing this morning and collected him afterwards."

"Oh. But didn't you have things to, er . . . ?"

"No, we cleaned him up beforehand, Mr. Beech. If there's no embalming involved, it's a quick turnover. Right then, top of the aisle, is it? Bottom of the steps before the altar, that's where we usually . . . "

"Yes, fine. I'll . . . "

"Now you just leave it to us, Mr. Beech. We know our way around. We'll make him comfortable."

"In that case," Jean Wendle said firmly, "do you mind if I come in and wait? If that wouldn't be disturbing you."

A refusal would be impossible. This was a deliberate, uncompromising foot-in-the-door situation, it having occurred to Jean that if she took it easy, she might actually get more out of the wife.

Mrs. Preece took half a step back. With no pretense of not being reluctant, she held the cottage door open just wide enough for Jean to slide inside. There were roses around the door, which was nice, which showed somebody cared. Or *had* cared.

"Thank you."

The first thing Jean noticed in the parlor was a fresh onion on a saucer on top of the television.

She was fascinated. She hadn't seen this in years.

Mrs. Preece actually had hair like an onion, coiled into a tight, white bun, and everything else about her was closed up just as tight.

She looked unlikely to offer her guest a cup of tea.

"I do realize things must be very difficult for you at present," Jean said. "If there is anything I can do . . . "

Mrs. Preece snorted.

Jean smiled at her. "The reason I'm here, the public meeting will be upon us tomorrow evening and I felt there were one or two things I should like to know in advance."

"If you're yere as a spy for Mr. Max Goff," Mrs. Preece said bluntly, "then there's no need to dress it up."

Jean was not unpleasantly surprised.

"Do you know, Mrs. Preece," she said, being equally blunt, "this is the first experience I've ever had of an indigenous Crybbe person coming right out with something, instead of first skirting furtively around the issue."

"Maybe you been talking to the wrong people," said Mrs. Preece.

"And who, would you say, are the 'wrong' people? By the way, I wouldn't waste that nice onion on me."

"I *beg* your pardon."

"Just don't tell me," Jean said levelly, "that the onion on the saucer is there to absorb paint smells or germs. You put it there to attract any unwelcome emanations from people you don't want in your house. And when they've gone you quietly dispose of the onion. Will you be getting rid of it when I leave, Mrs. Preece?"

Mrs. Preece, face reddening, looked down at her clumpy brown shoes.

"Or am I flattering myself?" Jean said.

"I don't know what you're talking about."

"Och, away with you, Mrs. Preece. I'm no one of your London innocents."

"You're none of you innocent," Mrs. Preece cried. "You're all as guilty as, as . . . " Her voice dropped. "As guilty as sin."

"Of what?" Jean asked gently.

Mrs. Preece shook her head. "You're not getting me going; I'm not stupid. You must know as you're doing no good for this town."

"And why is that, Mrs. Preece? Do you mind if I sit down?"

And before Mrs. Preece could argue, Jean had slipped into the mayor's fireside chair.

"Because it seems to me, you see, that all the new people love

Crybbe just exactly the way it is, Mrs. Preece. They would hate anything to happen to the local traditions. In fact, that's why I'm here. I was hoping your husband could tell me a wee bit about the curfew."

Mrs. Preece turned away.

"I'm also compiling a small history of the town and its folk-lore," Jean said.

"Nothing to tell," Mrs. Preece said eventually. "Nothing that's not written down already."

"I don't think so. I think there is a remarkable amount to tell which has never been written down."

Mrs. Preece stood over Jean. She wore a large, striped apron, like a butcher's. Discernible anxiety in her eyes now.

"Tell *me* about it, Mrs. Preece. Tell me about the ritual which your husband's family has maintained so selflessly for so many centuries."

"Just a bequest," the mayor's wife said. "That's all. A bequest of land a long time ago in the sixteenth century. Depending on the bell to be rung every night."

"This is codswallop," Jean Wendle said. "This is a smoke-screen."

"Well, we 'ave the documents to prove it!" Mrs. Preece was getting angry. "That's how much it's codswallop!"

"Oh, I'm sure you do. But the real reason for the curfew, is it not, is to protect the town from . . . well, let's call it the Black Dog."

Mrs. Preece's face froze like a stopped clock.

Into the silence came lazy footsteps on the path.

"Be my husband back." Very visibly relieved.

Damnation, Jean almost said aloud. So close.

But it wasn't the mayor. A thin, streaky-haired youth with an earring shambled in without knocking.

"All right, Gran? I come to tell you . . . "

"You stay outside with them boots, Warren!"

"Too late, Gran." The youth was in the living room now, giving Jean Wendle the once-over with his narrow eyes.

Ah, she thought. The surviving grandson. Interesting.

"Hello," Jean said. "So you're Warren."

" 'S right, yeah." From his earring hung a tiny silvery death's-head.

"I was very sorry to hear about your brother."

Warren blew out his mouth and nodded. "Aye, well, one o' them things, isn't it. Anyway, Gran, message from the old . . . from Dad. All it is—they brought Jonathon back and 'e's in the church."

"I see," said Mrs. Preece quietly. "Thank you, Warren."

"In 'is coffin," said Warren.

Jean observed that the boy was somewhat less than grief-stricken.

"Lid's on, like," Warren said.

Jean thought he sounded disappointed.

"But 'e's not screwed down, see, so if you wanna go'n 'ave a quick look at 'im, there's no problem."

"No, I don't think I shall," his grandmother said, "thank you, Warren." Tiny tears were sparkling in her eyes.

"If you're worried the ole lid might be a bit 'eavy for you, Gran," Warren said considerately, "I don't mind goin' along with you. I got half an hour or so to spare before I got to leave." He turned to Jean. "I got this band, see. We practices most Monday and Wednesday nights."

Mrs. Preece said, her voice high and tight, "No, *thank you,* Warren."

Warren watched his grandmother's reaction with his head on one side. This boy, Jean registered with considerable interest, is trying not to laugh.

"See, it's no problem, Gran," Warren said slowly and slyly. " 'Cause I've already 'ad 'im off once, see, that ole lid."

He stood with his hands on narrow hips encased in tight, leather trousers, and his lips were just the merest twist away from a smirk.

Jean had been listening to the tension in the air in the small, brown living room, humming and then singing, dangerously off-key, sending out invisible wires that quickly tautened and then, finally, snapped.

"Get out!" Mrs. Preece's big face suddenly buckled. "GET OUT!"

She turned to Jean, breathing rapidly. "And you as well, if you please."

Jean stood up and moved quietly to the door. "I'm really very sorry, Mrs. Preece."

"Things is not right," Mrs. Preece said, sniffing hard. "Things is far from right. And no you're not. None of you's sorry."

*   *   *

They'd stopped for coffee but hadn't eaten, couldn't face it.

Fay still felt a bit sick and more than a bit alone. She badly needed someone she could rely on, and Joe Powys no longer seemed like the one. But while she felt slightly betrayed, she was also sorry for him. He looked even more lost than she felt.

"All I can think of," he said, driving listlessly back to Crybbe, "is that the stone near the cottage is the actual one—the Bottle Stone."

"You mean he had it dug up under cover of darkness and . . . "

"Sounds crazy, doesn't it?"

"I'm afraid it does, Joe. Why would Boulton-Trow want to do that, anyway?"

"Well, he knows that was the worst thing that ever happened to me, and . . . "

"And he wanted to bring it all back by confronting you with the stone again? That would make him . . . well, you know . . . quite evil. I can't imagine . . . "

"I'm sorry. I'm asking too much of you. Maybe I ought to stay out of your way for a while."

Fay looked at him hopelessly. "Maybe we'll take some time and think about things. See what we can come up with."

She decided she'd go, after all, to Goff's press conference, in a private capacity, just to listen. See what questions other people raised and how they were answered.

"I don't think we *have* much time," Joe Powys said. "I really don't."

"Why? I mean . . . before what?"

"I don't know," he said.

He looked broken.

Alone again, Mrs. Preece shut herself in the living room, fell into her husband's sunken old chair, and began to cry bitterly, her white hair spooling free of its bun, strands getting glued by the tears to her mottled cheeks.

When the telephone rang, she ignored it and it stopped.

After some minutes Mrs. Preece got up from the chair, went to the mirror, and tried to piece together her bun without looking at her face.

Out of the corner of her right eye she saw the onion in its saucer on top of the television set.

Then Mrs. Preece let out a scream so harsh and ragged it felt as though the skin was being scoured from the back of her throat.

The onion, fresh this morning, was as black as burnt cork.

seven

Goff said, "As you say, Gavin, it's been a hell of a blow, obviously cast a pall over things here. Rachel'd been with me nearly four years. She was the best PA I ever had. But you ask if it's gonna dampen my enthusiasm for what we're doing here . . . I have to say no, of course it isn't. What we have here is too important for Crybbe . . . and for the human race."

Gavin Ashpole, of Offa's Dyke Radio, nodded sympathetically.

At the back, behind everybody, Fay groaned. Nobody noticed her, not even Guy.

There were about a dozen reporters and two TV crews in the stable block, everybody asking what Fay thought were excruciatingly banal questions.

But, OK, what else *could* they ask? What did they have to build on? If it hadn't involved Max Goff, all this sad little episode would have been worth was a couple of paragraphs in the local paper and an Offa's Dyke one-day wonder. A small, insignificant, accidental death.

OK, Goff didn't want the residue of anything negative hanging on him or the Crybbe project. But if Rachel had been here, she'd have talked him out of this minicircus; it wasn't worth a press conference, which would only draw the wrong kind of attention.

But then, if Rachel had been here . . . Fay felt the clutch of sorrow in her breast and something else less definable but close to anxiety.

Joe had said, "Got to sort this out. I'm going to find him."

"Boulton-Trow? Is that wise?"

"I want to take a look at this place he's got in the wood."

"I saw it. Yesterday, when I took the shortcut to church. It might be better inside, but it looks like a hovel."

"We'll find out."

"I didn't like it. I didn't like the feel of the place."

Joe had shrugged. She'd felt torn. On one hand, yes, he really ought to sort this thing out, even if it meant facing up to his own delusions. On the other hand, well, OK, she was scared for him.

"You go to your press conference," he'd said, touched her arm hesitantly, and then walked away, head down, across the square toward the churchyard.

So here she was, sitting a few yards behind Guy's stocky, aggressive-looking cameraman, Guy standing next to him, occasionally whispering instructions. The chairs had been laid out in three rows in the middle tier of the stable block, so that the assembled hacks were slightly higher than Goff.

And yet, somehow, he appeared to be looking down on them.

Goff was at his desk, his back to the window and the Tump, as if this was his personal power source.

"Max," one of the hacks said, "Barry Speake, *Evening News*. Can I ask you what kind of feedback you're getting from the local community here? I mean, what's the local response to your plans to introduce what must seem to a lot of ordinary people to be rather bizarre ideas, all this ley-lines and astrology and stuff?"

Goff gave him both rows of teeth. "Think it's bizarre, do you, Barry?"

"I'm not saying *I* think it's bizarre, Max, but . . . "

"But you think simple country folk are too unsophisticated to grasp the concept. Isn't that a little patronizing, Barry?"

There was a little buzz of laughter.

"No, but hold on." Goff raised a hand. "There's a serious point to be made here. We call this New Age, and, sure, it's new to us. But folks here in Crybbe have an instinctive understanding of what it's about because this place has important traditions, what you might call a direct line to the source . . . Something

I'd ask the author J. M. Powys to elaborate on, if he were here . . . Yeah, lady at the back."

Fay stood up. "Mr. Goff, you're obviously spending a lot of money here in Crybbe . . . "

"Yeah, just don't ask me for the figures."

Muted laughter.

Fay said, "As my colleague tried to suggest, it *is* what many people would consider a slightly bizarre idea, attempting to rebuild the town's prehistoric heritage, putting back all these stones, for instance. What I'd like to know is . . . *why Crybbe?* Who told you about this place? Who told you about the stones? Who said it would be the right place for what you had in mind?"

Goff's little eyes narrowed. He was wearing, unusually, a dark suit today. Out of respect for the dead Rachel? Or his image.

"Who exactly are you?" he said. "Which paper you from?"

"Fay Morrison." Adding, "Freelance," with a defiant glance at Ashpole.

"Yeah, I thought so."

He'd never actually seen her before. He was certainly making up for that now, little eyes never wavering.

"I'm not sure how relevant your question is today," Goff said. "But, yeah, on the issue of how we came to be doing what we're doing here, well, we've been kicking this idea around for a year or two. I've had advisers and people looking . . . "

"What kind of advisers? Who exactly?" The questions were coming out without forethought; she was firing blind. In fact, what the hell was she doing? She hadn't planned to say a word, just sit there and listen.

Goff looked pained. "Ms. Morrison, I don't see . . . Yeah, OK . . . I have many friends and associates in what's become known as the New Age movement—let me say, I don't like that term, it's been devalued, trivialized, right? But, yeah, it was suggested to me that if I was looking for a location which was not only geophysically and archaeologically suited to research into forgotten landscape patterns and configurations but was also suited—shall we say atmospherically—to research into human spiritual potential, then Crybbe fitted the bill."

He produced a modest, philanthropic sort of smile. "And it was also clearly a little down on its luck. In need of the economic boost our center could give it. So I came along and looked around, and I . . . Well, that answer your question?"

"Was it the late Henry Kettle? Did he suggest you come here?"

"No, I sought advice from Henry Kettle, in a very small way, at a later stage. We were already committed to Crybbe by then. What are you getting at here?"

Goff leaned back in his leather rock-and-swivel chair. He was alone at the desk, although Humble and a couple of people she didn't recognize were seated a few yards away. Fay didn't think Andy Boulton-Trow was among them.

"Well," she said, still on her feet, "Henry Kettle was, of course, the *first* person to die in an accident here, wasn't he?"

"Aw now, hey," Goff said.

Several reporters turned their heads to look at Fay. Maybe some of them hadn't heard about Henry. He was hardly a national figure, except in earth-mysteries circles. His death had been a minor local story; his connection with Goff had not been general knowledge, still wasn't, outside Crybbe.

It occurred to her that what she'd inadvertently done here was set the more lurid papers up with a possible Curse of Crybbe story. She imagined Rachel Wade looking down on the scene from wherever she was, rolling her eyes and passing a hand across her brow in pained disbelief.

Fay started to feel just a little foolish. Gavin Ashpole, sitting well away from her, was smirking discreetly into his lap.

She knew Goff had to make a move here.

He did. He gave the hacks a confidential smile.

"Yeah, take a good look," he said, extending a hand toward Fay. "This is Ms. Fay Morrison."

More heads turned. Guy's, not surprisingly, was one of the few which didn't.

"Ms. Morrison," drawled Goff, "is a small-time freelance reporter who earns a crust here in town by stirring up stories nobody else can quite see."

Some bastard laughed.

"Unfair," Fay said, starting to sweat. "Henry Kettle . . . "

"Henry Kettle"—Goff changed effortlessly to a higher gear—"was a very elderly man who died when his car went out of control, probably due to a stroke or a heart attack. We'll no doubt find out what happened when the inquest is held.

Meantime, I—and any right-thinking, rational person—would certainly take a dim view of any sensation-mongering attempt to make something out of the fact that my company had paid him a few pounds to do a few odd jobs. I think suggesting any link between the death of Henry Kettle in a car accident and Rachel Wade in a fall is in extremely poor taste, indicating a lamentable lack of professionalism—and a certain desperation perhaps—in any self-styled journalist who raised it."

Goff relaxed, knowing how good he was at this. Fay, who'd never been much of an orator, lapsed, red-faced, into a very lonely silence.

"Now," Goff said, not looking at her, "if there are no further questions, I have ten minutes to do any TV and radio interviews outside."

The heads had turned away from Fay. She'd lost it.

"You don't do yourself any favors, do you, Fay?" Ashpole said dryly, out of the side of his mouth, passing her on the way out, not even looking at her.

"I suppose," Guy Morrison said, "you'd know about all the suicides around here, wouldn't you?"

Seven P.M. The only other customer in the public bar at the Cock was this large man, the local police sergeant, Wynford somebody. He was leaning on the bar with a pint, obviously relieved at unloading the two Divisional CID men who'd spent the day in town in connection with this Rachel Wade business.

Guy was feeling relieved, too. His heart had dropped when Max Goff had approached him immediately after the conclusion of the appalling press conference—Guy expecting to be held responsible for his wayward ex-wife and, at the very least, warned to keep her out of Goff's way in the future.

But all Goff wanted was for the crew to get some aerial pictures of Crybbe from his helicopter, so that was OK. Guy had sent Catrin Jones up with Larry and escaped to the pub. Sooner or later he'd be forced to have a discreet word with Goff and explain where things stood between him and Fay—i.e., that she was an insane bitch and he'd had a lucky escape.

Meanwhile, there was this business of the suicide and the haunting. This was upsetting him. He wouldn't be able to concentrate fully until it was out of the way, because Guy Morrison didn't like things he didn't understand.

He waited for Wynford's reaction. He'd got into suicides by suggesting that perhaps Rachel Wade had killed herself. Would they ever really know?

Guy Morrison was an expert at manipulating conversation, but Wynford didn't react at all.

As if he hadn't noticed the silence, Guy said, "Doesn't do a place's reputation any good, I suppose, being connected with a suicide. I was talking to that woman who runs The Gallery. It seems her house is allegedly haunted by a chap who offed himself."

Wynford didn't look up from his beer, but he spoke at last. "You been misinformed, my friend."

"I don't mean anything recent," Guy said. "This probably goes back a good while. Talking about the same place, are we? Heavily renovated stone farmhouse, about half a mile out of town on the Hereford road?"

"Yes, yes," Wynford said. "The ole Thomas farm."

"Well, as I said, it could be going back quite a while. I mean, anytime this century, I suppose, maybe earlier."

How long had there been cutthroat razors anyway? he wondered. Hundreds of years, probably.

"Bit of a romancer, that woman, you ask me," Wynford said. "From Off, see."

Meaning a newcomer, Guy supposed. It was an interesting fact that he personally was never regarded as a stranger in areas where he was recognized from television. If they'd seen you on the box, you'd been in their living rooms, so you weren't an intruder.

Except, perhaps, here in Crybbe.

"No, look," Guy said, "this happened in the bathroom. Oldish chap. Cut his own throat with one of those old-fashioned open razors."

Wynford licked his cherub's lips, his eyes frosted with suspicion.

"What's wrong?" Guy asked.

"Somebody tell you to ask me about this, did they?"

"No," Guy said. "Of course not."

"You sure?"

"Look, Sergeant, what's the problem here?"

Wynford had a drink of beer. "No problem, sir."

"No, you *do* . . . " Guy was about to accuse him of knowing something about this but keeping it to himself.

He looked into the little inscrutable features in the middle of the big melon face and knew he'd be wasting his time.

Wynford swallowed a lot of beer, wiped his mouth. His face was very red. He's on the defensive, Guy thought, and he doesn't like that.

He was right. Wynford looked at him for the first time. "Somebody said you was married to that Fay? Or is it you just got the same name?"

"No, it's true, I'm afraid. We were married for . . . what? Nearly three years, I suppose."

Wynford smiled conspiratorially, a sinister sight. "Good between the sheets, was she?"

What an appalling person. Guy, who didn't like people asking *him* questions unless they were about his television work, looked at his watch and claimed he was late for a shoot. And, actually, they had got something arranged for later; Catrin had set up one of those regressive-hypnotist chaps and agreed to be the subject.

Should be entertaining. Perhaps in some past life she'd actually been someone interesting. He wondered, as he strolled into the square, what crime she could have committed to get landed with the persona of Catrin Jones.

In the Crybbe Unattended Studio, Gavin Ashpole sniffed.

He knew the place used to be a toilet, but that wasn't what he could smell.

This was a musky, perfumed smell, and the odd thing was that Gavin wasn't sure he could actually smell it at all. It was just *there*.

Probably because Fay Morrison used this studio for an hour or so every day.

There were a few of her scripts on the spike in the outer room. All handwritten, big and bold in turquoise ink.

Gavin picked up the phone and sniffed the mouthpiece. Sweating comfortably, cooling in his running suit. Gavin was a fitness freak, kept a bag in the back of his car with his jogging gear and his sneakers inside. Any spare half hour or so he'd get changed, go for a run. Tuned your body, tuned your mind, and other people could sense it, too. You were projecting creative energy, dynamism.

He'd got an hour's running in tonight. Been up into the hills. Felt good. In control of himself and his destiny. Within a year he'd either be managing editor of Offa's Dyke or he'd have moved on.

Unlike Fay Morrison, who was over the hill and going down the other side fast. Left to him, the station would never have agreed to use her stuff. She was unreliable, awkward to deal with. And obviously unbalanced.

Bloody sexy, though.

The thought hit him surprisingly hard, a muscular pulse, where you noticed it.

He hadn't really considered her on this level before. She was older than he was. She'd had a lot more experience on radio, and although she never mentioned that, it was always there in the background, making her sound superior.

And she was a nutter. Not rational. Not objective as a reporter.

He'd see the boss tomorrow and explain precisely what had happened at Goff's press conference. She's doing us a lot of damage, he'd say. If she's put Max Goff's back up, who else is she antagonizing? No need to say anything to her or put anything in writing, just fade her out. Use less and less of her material until she stops bothering to send any. Then we'll put somebody else in.

Gavin attached a length of red leader to the end of his tape. It hadn't taken much editing, just a forty-second clip for the morning.

He rang the newsroom to tell them he was ready to send, put on the headphones, waited for the news studio to come through on the line.

He felt Fay in the headphones. She'd worn them over that dark-blond hair.

Sexy bitch.

He stretched his legs under the desk, feeling the calf muscles tighten and relax, imagining her in here with him, in this tiny little studio, not big enough for two, you'd be touching one another all the time.

Projecting forward to tomorrow night. He was back in Crybbe covering the public meeting, the big confrontation between Goff and the town councilors. Fay had followed him in here, apologizing for her behavior, saying she'd been worrying about her father, letting it take her mind off her work, couldn't handle things anymore, couldn't he see that?

He could see *her* now, kneeling down by the side of his chair, looking up at him.

Got to help me, Gavin.

Why should I help you?

I like muscular men, Gavin. Hard men. Fit men. *That's* how you can help me, Gavin.

He put his hands out, one each side of her head, gripped her roughly by the hair.

Her lips parted.

"Gavin!"

"Huh?"

"We've been calling out for five minutes."

"You couldn't have been," Gavin rasped into the microphone. He was sweating like a bloody pig.

"We could certainly hear you panting, mate. What were you doing exactly?"

"Very funny, Elton. I've been for a run. Six miles. You going to take some level or not?"

"Go ahead, I'm rolling. Hope you're going to clean up in there afterwards, Gavin."

Angrily, Gavin snapped the switch, set his tape turning. This was another little clever dick who'd be looking for a new job when he was managing editor.

He took his hand out of his running-suit trousers, put it on the desk below the mike and watched it shaking as if it wasn't his hand at all.

�֎ ————————————————————————

eight

On reflection, maybe chopping holes in this particular wood wasn't such a crime. It was not a pleasant wood. Something Powys hadn't consciously taken in when they were here yesterday and Fay had been so incensed about the slaughter of the trees, and Rachel had . . .

No. He didn't like the wood.

And it was uncared for. Too many trees, overcrowded. Trees which had died left to rot, strangled by ivy and creepers, their white limbs sticking out like the crow-picked bones of sheep, while sickly saplings fought for the soil in between the corpses.

The wood was a buffer zone between the Tump and the town, and some of what would otherwise have reached the town had been absorbed by the wood, which was why it had such a bad feel and why people probably kept out.

And perhaps why Andy Boulton-Trow had chosen to live here.

Until you reached the clearing, the path was the only sign that anyone had been in this wood for years. It was too narrow for vehicles; a horse could make it, just about. But nobody with a car would want Keeper's Cottage.

It was redbrick, probably 1920s, small and mean with little square windows, looked as if it had only one bedroom upstairs. It was in a part of the wood where conifers—Alaskan Spruce or something—had choked out all the hardwoods, crowding in like giant weeds, blinding Keeper's Cottage to the daylight.

A sterile place. No birds, no visible wildlife. Hardly the pick of Goff's properties. Hardly the type of dwelling for a Boulton-Trow. Even the gardeners whom he assumed certain Boulton-Trows would employ wouldn't be reduced to this.

The door had been painted green. Once. A long time ago.

Powys knocked.

No answer. Unsurprising. Nobody in his right mind would want to spend too much time in Keeper's Cottage.

OK, either he isn't here or he is, and keeping quiet.

Powys felt old sorrow and new sorrow fermenting into fury. He called out, "Andy!"

No answer.

"Andy, I want to talk."

Not even an echo.

Powys walked around the cottage. It had no garden, no outbuildings, only a rough brick-built shelter for logs. The shelter was coming to pieces; most of the bricks were loose and crumbling.

So he helped himself to one. A brick. And he went to the back of the house, away from the path, and he hefted the brick, thoughtfully, from hand to hand for a moment or two before hurling it at one of the back windows.

A whole pane vanished.

Powys slipped a hand inside and opened the window.

Dementia, Alex thought, was an insidiously cunning ailment. It crept up on you with the style of a pickpocket, striking while your attention was diverted.

One didn't wake up in the morning and think, Hello, I'm feeling a bit demented today, better put the trousers on back to front and spray shaving foam on the toothbrush. No, the attitude of the intelligent man—saying, Look, it's been diagnosed, it's there, so I'm going to have to watch myself jolly carefully—was less effective than one might expect.

And the problem with this type of dementia—furred arteries not always letting the lift go all the way to the penthouse, as it were—was that the condition could be at its most insidiously dangerous when you were feeling fine.

Today he'd felt fine, but he wasn't going to be fooled.

"Keep calm, at all times," Jean Wendle had said. "Learn how to observe yourself and your actions. Be detached, watch yourself without involvement. I'll show you how to do this, don't worry. But for now, just keep calm."

Which wasn't easy when you lived with someone like Fay, who'd made a career out of putting people on the spot.

She'd come in just after six and put together rather a nice salad with prawns and other items she obviously hadn't bought in Crybbe. Bottle of white wine, too.

And then, over coffee . . .

"Dad, we didn't get a chance to finish our conversation this morning."

"Didn't we?"

"You're feeling OK, aren't you?"

"Not too bad."

"Because I want to get something sorted out."

God preserve me from this child, Alex thought. Always has to get everything sorted out.

"The business of the Revox. You remember? The vandalism?"

"Of course I remember. The tape recorder, yes."

"Well, they haven't actually pulled anybody in for it yet."

"Haven't they?"

"And perhaps you don't think they ever will."

"Well, with that fat fellow in charge of the investigation, I must say, I'm not overoptimistic."

"No, no. Regardless of Wynford, you don't really think . . . "

"Fay," Alex said, "how do you know what I think or what I don't think? And what gives you . . . ?"

"Because I heard you talking to Grace."

"Oh," said Alex. He had been about to take a sip of coffee; he didn't.

Fay was waiting.

"Well, you know," Alex said, switching to autopilot, "I've often had parishioners—old people—who talked to their dead husbands and wives all the time. Nothing unusual about it, Fay. It brought them comfort, they didn't feel so alone anymore. Perfectly natural kind of therapy."

"Dad?"

"Yes?"

"Has Grace brought *you* comfort?"

Alex glared with resentment into his daughter's green eyes.

"Why did you think it was Grace who smashed up the Revox?"

He started to laugh, uneasily. "She's dead."

"That's right."

Alex said, "Look, time's getting on. I've a treatment booked for eight."

"With Jean? What's she charging you, out of interest?"

"Nothing at all. So far, that is. I, er, gave her a basic outline of the financial position and she suggested I should leave her the fee in my will."

"Very accommodating. Perhaps you could make a similar arrangement regarding your tab at the Cock. Now, to return to my question . . . "

Alex stood up. "Let me think about this one, would you, Fay?"

How could he tell her his real fears about this? Well, of *course* dead people couldn't destroy property on that scale. Even poltergeists only tossed a few books around. Even if dead people felt a great antipathy to someone in their house, it was only living people who were capable of an act of such gross violence.

But perhaps dead people were capable of making living people do their dirty work.

Did I? he asked himself as he walked up Bell Street. Was it *me?*

Alex felt terribly hot and confused. Just wanted to feel the cool hands again.

The microphone was in the way. Jarrett had it on a bracket-thing attached to the ceiling so that it craned over the couch like an old-fashioned dentist's drill.

Guy said, rather impatiently, "What do we need that thing for, anyway, if we're recording the whole session on VT?"

"I understand that, Guy," Jarrett said, "but *I* need it. I keep a record of everything. Also, it acts as a focus for the subject. I'm using the microphone in the same way as hypnotists used to swing their watches on a chain."

"OK," Guy said, "I'll go with that. We'll do some shots of the mike, make it swim before our eyes. OK, Larry?"

"No problem, I'll do it afterwards, come in over Catrin's shoulder. We OK with the lights?"

Guy looked at Graham Jarrett, small and tidy in a maroon cardigan, silver-haired and just a tiny bit camp. Graham Jarrett said, "One light may actually assist us if it isn't directly in her eyes, because we'll all be thrown into shadow and Catrin will be in her own little world. Can you make do with one, say that big one?"

"I don't see why not," Guy said, gratified, remembering the hassle he'd had with Adam Ivory. Nice to know some New Age people could live with television.

Jarrett arranged a tartan traveling rug over the couch and

patted a cushion. "OK then, Catrin, lie down and make yourself comfortable. I want you to be fully relaxed, so have a good wriggle about . . . Where's your favorite beach . . . somewhere on the Med? West Indies?"

"Porth Dinllaen," Catrin said patriotically. "On the Lleyn, in north Wales."

Guy turned away, concealing a snigger.

Jarrett adjusted the mike, switched on a cassette machine on a metal table on wheels, like a drinks cart. "OK, can we try it with the lights?"

Guy signaled to the lighting man, and Catrin's face was suddenly lit up, he thought, like a fat Madonna on a Christmas card. There was a tiny black personal microphone clipped into a fold of her navy-blue jumper.

"Right, Catrin," Jarrett said softly. "It's a soft, warm after-noon. You're on the beach . . . "

"Hang on," Tom, the soundman, said. "Let's have some level. Say something, Catrin. Tell us what you had for lunch."

It was another twenty minutes or so before everyone was satisfied. Guy watched Jarrett taking off Catrin's shoes and draping another traveling rug over her stumpy legs, just below the knees. No bad thing; Catrin's legs wouldn't add a great deal to the picture. Only wished he'd known about this far enough in advance to have set up someone more photogenic. He thought, with some amazement, back to this morning, when the night terrors had persuaded him that he ought to invite Catrin to share his room tonight. He shuddered. Thank heaven he hadn't said anything to her.

"OK," said Jarrett. "It's very warm, not too hot, just pleasant. Perhaps you can hear the sea lapping at the sand in the distance. And if you look up, why, there's the sun . . . "

The big light shone steadily down.

"Happy, Catrin?"

Catrin nodded, her lips plumped up into a little smile.

"But I don't want you to look at the sun, Catrin, I'd like you to look at the microphone. You must be quite comfortable with microphones, working for the BBC . . . "

Guy, watching her intently, didn't notice her go under, or slide into a hypnotic trance or whatever they did. Nothing about her seemed to change, as Jarrett took her back to previous holidays when she was a child. He almost thought she was putting it on when she began to burble in a little-girl sort of voice, about her parents and her sister and paddling in the sea and seeing a big jellyfish—lapsing into Welsh at one point, her first language.

She would fake it, he knew; she wouldn't want to let him down.

But then Catrin started coming out with stuff that nobody in her right mind would fake.

Hard against the streaming evening light, Jack Preece took the tractor into the top meadow and he could tell the old thing was going to fail him, that poor Jonathon had been right when he said it was a false economy.

Nobody had open tractors like this anymore. Tractors had changed. Tractors nowadays were like Gomer Parry's plant-hire equipment, big shiny things.

Jack had sworn this old thing was going to see them through the haymaking, which would mean he could put off the investment until next year, maybe check out what was available secondhand.

But Jonathon had been right. False economy. Especially if it failed him in the middle of the haymaking and he had to hire one from Gomer to finish off.

Jonathon had been right, and he'd tell him so tonight, the least he could do.

Jack hadn't been in yet to see his son's coffin; couldn't face it. Couldn't face people seeing him walking into the church, the bloody vicar there, with his bank-manager face and his phony words of comfort. The bloody vicar who didn't know the score, couldn't know the way things were, couldn't be any help whatever.

But that was how vicars had to be in this town, Father said. Don't want no holy-roller types in Crybbe. Just go through the motions, do the baptisms and the burials, keep their noses out and *don't change nothing . . . don't break the routine.*

And Jack wouldn't break *his* routine. He'd go into the church as usual tonight to ring the old bell, and he'd go just a bit earlier—but not so much earlier as anybody'd notice—so he could spend five minutes alone in there, in the near-dark, with his dead son.

Jack urged the tractor up the long pitch, and the engine farted and spluttered like an old drunk. If it couldn't handle the pitch on its own anymore then it was going to be bugger-all use pulling a trailer for the haymaking and he'd be going to Gomer for help—at a price.

He'd be going to Warren, too, for help with the haymaking this time, and the price there was a good deal heavier. All these years, watching Warren growing up and growing away, watching him slinking away from the farm like a fox. Jack thinking it didn't matter so much, only one son could inherit—only enough income from this farm to support one—and if the other one moved away, found something else, well, that could only help the situation. But now Jack needed Warren and Warren knew that, and that was bad because there was a streak of something in Warren that Jack didn't like, always been there but never so clear as it was now.

"Come on, then." Jack talking to the tractor like she was an old horse. Be better off with an old horse, when you thought about it.

"Come on!"

Could be tricky if she stalled near the top of the pitch and rolled back. Jack was ready for this happening, always a cautious man, never had a tractor turn over on him yet, nor even close to it.

"Go on!"

Bad times for the Preeces.

Not that there'd ever been good times, but you didn't expect that. You held on; if you could hold on, you were all right. Farming wasn't about good times.

He'd be fifty-five next birthday, of an age to start taking it a bit easy. No chance of that now.

He saw himself going into the church to ring the bell in less than two hours' time, and Jonathon lying there in his box. What could he say?

You was right, son, was all he'd mumble. You was right about the ole tractor.

When what he really wanted to say—to scream—was, *You stupid bugger, boy . . . all you had to do was shoot the bloody dog and you winds up . . . bloody drowned!*

Father always said, You gotter keep a 'old on your feelin's, Jack, that's the main thing. You let your feelin's go, you're out of control, see, and it's not for a Preece to lose control, we aren't *privileged* to lose control.

Bugger you, Father! Is that all there is? Is that all there'll ever be? We stands there in our fields of rock and clay, in the endless drizzle with our caps pulled down so we don't see to the horizon, so we don't look at the ole Tump, so we never asks, *why us?*

Tears exploded into Jack's eyes just as he neared the top of the pitch and through the blur he saw a great big shadow, size of a man, rising up sheer in front of him. He didn't think; he trod hard on the brake, the engine stalled, and then he was staring into the peeling gray-green paint on the radiator as the tractor's nose was jerked up hard like the head of a ringed bull.

The old thing, the tractor, gave a helpless, heart-tearing moan, like a stricken old woman in a geriatric ward, and the great wheels locked and Jack was thrown into the air.

He heard a faraway earth-shaking bump, like a blast at a quarry miles away, and he figured this must be him landing somewhere. Not long after that, he heard a grinding and a rending of metal, and when he looked down he couldn't see his legs, and when he looked up he could only see the big black shadow.

It was very much like a *hand,* this shadow, a big clawing black hand coming out of the field, out of the stiff, ripe grass, on a curling wrist of smoke.

As he stared at it, not wanting to believe in it, it began to fade away at the edges, just like everything else.

nine

Although her eyes were fully open, she wasn't looking at anything in the room, not even at the microphone suspended six inches above her lips. There was a sheen on her face, which might have been caused by the heat from the single TV light. The only other light in the draped and velvety room was a very dinky Tiffany-shaded table lamp in the corner behind Guy Morrison and the camera crew.

GRAHAM JARRETT: "Can you describe your surroundings? Can you tell me where you are?"
CATRIN JONES: "I am in my bedchamber. In my bed."

They understood she was called Jane. She only giggled when they asked for her second name. But strangely, after a few minutes, Guy Morrison had no difficulty in believing in her. She spoke, of course, with Catrin's voice, although the accent had softened as if a different accent was trying to impose itself, and the inflection was altered. This was not Catrin, not any Catrin he knew.

JARRETT: "Is it night?"
CATRIN: "It is dark."
JARRETT: "So why aren't you asleep?"
CATRIN: "I ache too much."
JARRETT: "Are you not well?"
CATRIN: "I'm aching inside."
JARRETT: "You mean you're unhappy about something?"
CATRIN (sounding distressed): "I'm aching inside . . . inside." (Long pause and a mixture of wriggles, half-smiles, and soft moans.) "My sheriff's been to take his pleasure."

Strewth. This really was not shrill, plump, chapel-raised Catrin, from Bangor.
Also, Guy realized, watching Catrin licking her lips suggestively, it was suddenly not usable footage.

CATRIN: "He watches me. Sometimes he comes in the night and I can see him and he watches me. I awake. The room . . . so cold . . . He is here . . . uurgh . . . he's . . . His eyes. His eyes in the darkness. Only his . . . eyes . . . aglow."

Catrin was rolling from side to side, breathing in snorts. The tartan rug slipped from her legs. She dragged her skirt up to her waist and spread her legs.

CATRIN (screaming): "Is that what you've come to see?"

*   *   *

"Wonderful," Alex murmured. "I think this is the only thing I live for these days."

The cool hands.

"You," Jean Wendle said, "are an old humbug."

"That's Dr. Chi's diagnosis, is it?"

"Shush."

"Hmmph."

After the treatment, Jean made coffee but refused to let Alex have any whiskey in his. "Time you took yourself in hand," she said.

"No chance of *you* taking me in hand, I suppose?"

Jean smiled.

"This dementia of yours," she said, sitting next to him on the sofa. "When I said the other night that you should relax and observe yourself, I think I was teaching my grandmother to suck eggs. I think you almost constantly observe yourself. I think you have a level of self-knowledge far beyond most of the so-called mystics in this town."

"Oh, I'm just a bumbling old cleric," Alex said modestly.

"This . . . condition of yours. Unlike, say, Alzheimer's, it's far from a constant condition. Sometimes the blood flow to the brain is close to normal, is that right? I mean, like now, at this particular moment, there is no apparent problem."

"I don't know about that," Alex said. "Some people would say consulting someone who communes with a long-dead Chinese quack is a sure sign of advancing senility. Oh hell . . . I'm sorry, Wendy, I've sheltered so long behind not taking anything seriously."

"It's Jean."

"Yes, of course. I . . . I want to say you've made a profound difference to me. I haven't felt so well in a long time. I feel I'm part of things again. That make sense?"

"When precisely did you first suspect there was something wrong with your general health?"

"Oh . . . I suppose it would be not long after poor old Grace died. Feeling a bit sorry for myself. I'd had a spot of angina, nothing life-threatening, as they say, but my morale . . . "

"Because Grace had died?"

Alex sat back, said, "You scare me, Wendy. Bit too perceptive for comfort. Yes, I was low because of the guilt I was feeling at being initially really rather relieved that she'd popped off."

He paused for a reaction but didn't get one.

Jean stood up, went away, and returned, looking resigned, with a bottle of Bell's whiskey. "Perhaps you can start taking yourself in hand tomorrow."

"God bless you, my dear." Alex diluted his coffee with a good half-inch of Scotch.

A silence. Alex thought he could hear a distant siren sound, like a police car or an ambulance.

"I gather you've been talking to my daughter."

Jean rested a hand lightly on his thigh. "I don't think she knows quite what to make of you."

Alex looked at Jean's hand, not daring to hope. "And what about you, Wendy? Do you . . . ?"

The siren grew louder. Jean stood up and went across to the deep Georgian window.

She looked back at him over a shoulder, her little bum tight in pale-blue satin trousers. Coquettish? Dare he describe that look as *coquettish?*

"Oh, I think I can make something of you," Jean said.

"Fire Service."

"Hello, it's Fay Morrison from, er . . . from Offa's Dyke Radio. Can you tell me what's happening in Crybbe? Where's the fire?"

"You've been very quick, my girl. I don't think they've even got there yet. It isn't a fire. It's a tractor accident. Tractor turned over, one person trapped. The location is Top Meadow, Court Farm. One machine. No more details yet, I'm afraid."

"Court Farm? Bloody hell!" Fay reached for the Uher. "Thanks a lot." She put the phone down. "What do you want to do, Arnie? You coming, or are you going to wait here for Dad?"

Thinking, What if he's here on his own when the curfew starts? Who's going to keep him quiet?

Arnold was lying under what used to be an editing table before somebody smashed the Revox. He was obviously finding it easier to lie down than sit. He wagged his tail.

"OK, then, you can come. Need any help?"

Arnold stood up very carefully, shook himself and fell over. Stood up again, seemed to be grinning, like he often did.

Before leaving the office she forced herself, as she always did now, to look back from the doorway to the fireplace, the mantelpiece with its testicular clock, the armchair where the ghost of Grace Legge had materialized.

She tried to avoid this room now, after dark.

She wished she could talk to Joe Powys.

Preferably on the ground? Away from any windows?

Don't be stupid.

She looked at the clock and saw it was nearly nine and realized she was worried about Joe and had been for over an hour; that was why she was sitting over the phone.

She'd never once worried about Guy. Guy was always OK. In any difficult situation Guy would either find a way out or simply walk away from it as if it had never happened to him. Whereas Joe was vulnerable because, as anybody who'd read his book could deduce, he was a professional believer. Present him with a crackpot theory and he'd make it sound sensible—which was what made him so useful to Max Goff.

She hadn't heard from him since he'd told her he was going to look for Andy Boulton-Trow.

Joe was like a child in a dark bedroom where there's a monster in the wardrobe and a dwarf behind the dressing table and the lampshade is a human head on a string and every deep shadow is alive, and he was out there now in a town full of deep, deep shadows.

JARRETT: "Do you live in a house?"

CATRIN: "At the inn. We all live at the inn. Me and my sisters and my father. My father is the . . . "

JARRETT: "The licensee? The landlord?"

CATRIN (*contemptuously*): "*He'll* never be a lord."

JARRETT: "And what's the name of the inn?"

CATRIN: "The Bull. There's another inn called the Lamb, where Robert lived."

JARRETT: "Robert? Who is Robert?"

CATRIN: "My man. He's hanged now. The sheriff hanged him."

JARRETT: "Jane, can I ask you this? The sheriff had
your . . . Robert . . . hanged. And now he sleeps with you?
Is that what you're saying?"

CATRIN *(laughing, tears on her face):* "He doesn't sleep
much!"

Guy was transfixed. Something astonishing was happening
here. No way had Catrin the imagination to conjure stuff like
this.

Unless Jarrett had broken through the inhibitions to a deeper
layer of the girl . . . perhaps this was the *real* Catrin.

But what about all the Crybbe references? Was it even conceivable that his production assistant was the reincarnation of
a woman who had lived in this same town in the reign of
Elizabeth I?

Guy didn't understand; he was at a disadvantage; he hated that.

Approximately fifteen minutes later he began to hate the
situation even more. Jarrett had brought the character, Jane,
several years forward in an attempt to discover how long the
sheriff's exploitation of her had continued, and the responses
were becoming garbled.

CATRIN: "But I am the best of us all, he says, and he will
never leave me, never . . . never. I'm stroking his beard,
his hard, black beard. Never leave me . . . never, never,
NEVER!"

JARRETT: "Jane, please listen . . . "

CATRIN: "I'll come down . . . I'll come down on you."

Catrin began to giggle and to roll her head again. She started
to ignore Jarrett's questions. He looked vaguely puzzled by this
and left her alone to squirm about for a few minutes. Larry
Ember took the opportunity to change the tape and his camera
battery.

Then Catrin blinked, as if trying to focus on something, the
giggling slowly drying up.

And her lips went into a pout.

CATRIN *(with a new authority):* "Come here. I'm cold."

Her voice had changed again. It was affected now, and petu-
lant. And very English.

CATRIN: "Come on! For Christ's sake, Guy!"

Guy froze. Larry looked up from his viewfinder, the camera still rolling.

CATRIN: "We are utterly alone and likely to remain so for two whole, wonderful days. How long have *you* got? Inches and inches, if I'm any judge."

A profound chill spread through Guy.

CATRIN: "There's a bathroom directly facing you at the end of the passage."

Catrin smiled. Guy thought he was going to scream.

CATRIN: "Don't be long, will you?"

Guy Morrison strode erratically into camera range, dragging a wire, nearly bringing the light down.
"Fucking hell, Guy," Larry Ember yelled.
Guy ignored him, shook his shoe out of the lamp wire, clutched at Graham Jarrett's cardigan. "Wake her up. For Christ's sake, man, wake her up!"

ten

It was cold in the wood.
Still, he waited.
The words in his pocket, scribbled in the pages of a pocket diary, kept appearing in his mind, as though the lines were rippling across a computer screen.

Alle the nyte came strange noyses and lytes and the dogges howled in the yarde and when he vysyted me in myne chamber he apered lyke a clowde and a yellow cullor in the aire.

By nine-thirty, the air was singing with tension, as if great pylons were carrying buzzing, sizzling power cables across the darkening sky.

Joe Powys was standing by the new stone in the clearing, around the center of the wood, a hundred yards or so from Keeper's Cottage.

This stone, narrow, like a sharpened bone, would be on the line from the Tump, through the Court to the church.

At either end of the clearing, undergrowth had been hacked away to form the beginning of a track. Or to reinstate an old one. He knew all about this track now. This was the legendary secret passage between the Court and Crybbe church, along which Sir Michael Wort was said to have escaped.

Like most legends, it was a literal interpretation of something more complex.

Something suggested by the notes he'd found in Keeper's Cottage, which had turned out to be a primitive kind of schoolhouse.

Primitive in that there was no electricity, only candles, and it was not very clean. It smelled of candles and mold . . . and paint.

There was a mattress and a quilt. Andy (or someone) had slept here. Like a monk might sleep in a little whitewashed cell with no worldly possessions. Or a rich philanthropist might feel the need to live like a squatter for a while to restructure his consciousness.

Or a modern man might have a need, somehow, to shed centuries . . .

. . . tolde me he woulde come at nyte in hys spyryte, by the olde roade.

These were Andy's own notes, handwritten; Powys had discovered them in the only modern luxury item to be found in Keeper's Cottage—absurdly, a black leather Filofax.

The Filofax had been kept in what once might have been a bread oven inside the stone open fireplace, which suggested this hovel was rather older than it appeared from the outside.

Upstairs, Powys had found a single room with a skylight, which appeared to be used as an artist's studio. There was a table with brushes and palettes on it and colored inks and a large assortment of paints, oil and acrylic.

There was turpentine and linseed oil and other dilutants in tightly corked medicine bottles. He uncorked one and sniffed incautiously.

It was urine.

Another one looked like blood.

Eye of newt, he thought, toe of frog.

Christ.

This room, with its skylight, was the only well-lit area of the house; all the windows in the sides of the building were screened by dense conifers.

There was a work in progress on an easel—a canvas under-painted in black and yellow ocher. Shapes of buildings and a figure.

He decided not to sniff the painting.

There were two chairs up here, just as there were two down-stairs. Andy and a lover.

Or a pupil.

He didn't know quite why he thought that. Maybe it was because someone else had been doing what he himself was doing—copying out pages of material from the Filofax. In the bread oven had been a small pile of loose-leaf pages with writing on them in a different hand—bold, big letters. A schoolboy hand. Or a schoolgirl. There was also a paperback book on Elizabethan magic, with pages marked. He'd read one—and immediately put the book into his pocket, to study later.

The Filofax had contained about thirty loose-leaf pages of closely written notes, together with hand-drawn plans and maps. Powys had sat down at the table with the artist's materials on it, a rough-hewn item of rustic garden furniture. He'd copied everything out as carefully as he could, including the maps and plans, some of which made sense, some of which didn't.

He could have stolen the Filofax; that would have been simpler.

But he suspected that what he held here was something like what the old magicians called a *grimoire,* a book of magical

secrets, a Book of Shadows. It belonged only to one person.
To anyone else—if you believed in all this, which he was
rather afraid he did—it could be as insidiously dangerous as
a radioactive isotope.

So what you did, you copied it out.

He stopped copying at one stage, his wrist aching, a distant
siren sounding in his head like the beginning of a migraine.

"What the hell am I doing?"

I mean, am I out of my mind?

He'd crossed again into the Old Golden Land, where everything answered to its own peculiar and archaic logic.

So, by candlelight, he'd gone on copying material from the
Filofax into the blank pages of a slim blue book of his own
with photographs of stones and mounds in it and maps of Britain
networked with irregular thin black lines. Embossed gold letters
on the cover spelled out "The Ley-Hunter's Diary 1993." They
sent him one every year; he carried it around, the way you did,
but this was the first time he'd ever actually written in one.

It took him a long time.

And if Andy had come back, caught him at it?

So what? The bastard had more explaining to do than he did.

He was scared, though. You couldn't not be, in this environment. Not if you were inclined to believe it worked.

As he wrote, he started to understand. Not all of it, but
enough. Enough to convince him that the original source of
some of these notes was probably Dr. John Dee, astrologer
to Elizabeth I. That Dee, who lived along the valley, who
was not psychic but studied people who were, had been the
recipient of the visit from the man who came "at nyte in hys
spyryte."

And that the visitor was Michael Wort, High Sheriff of
Radnorshire.

And you can prove that?

Of course not. What does that matter? *I* believe it.

But you're not rational, Powys. You're a certifiable crank.

He'd put the Filofax back into the bread oven, wishing there
was somewhere to wash his hands, and climbed out through the
window again, walking away into the dusk, the wood a gloomy,
treacherous place now, spiked with fallen branches and bramble
tentacles.

The night coming on, and he didn't feel so certain of his ability to deal with this, this . . .

  diabolical sorcerie.

This phrase appeared several times in the text.

Standing, now, by the stone, feeling the tension like an impending thunderstorm, only denser. And the feeling that when the storm broke and the rain crashed down, the rain would be black and afterward the earth would not be cleansed and purified but in some way poisoned.

Acid rain of the soul.

He moved a few feet away from the stone, stood behind a thick old oak tree bound with vines and creepers. The logic of the Old Golden Land told him that right next to the stone was not the place to be when the storm broke.

It also told him that the ringing of the curfew every night was some kind of climax and if he wanted to get a feel of what was going on, he ought to stay near that stone for . . . what?

He stretched his arm toward the sky to see his watch.

For less than half an hour.

He was frightened, though, and really wanted to creep back through the wood to the nearest lights.

So he thought about Henry Kettle and he thought about Rachel. And found himself thinking about Fay, too.

She sped through the shadowed streets, Arnold on the passenger seat.

Not the other son—what was his name? . . . Warren—not him, surely.

She could hear her own report: *The accident came only a week after Warren's brother, Jonathon, was tragically drowned in the swollen river near his home . . .*

The usual reporter's moral conflict taking place in her head. Better for the Preece family if it was someone else. Better for the media if it was another Preece—Double Disaster for Tragic Farm Family.

Better for her, in truth, if she was away from Offa's Dyke Radio, which was clearly in the process of ditching her anyway. And away from Crybbe also, which went without saying.

Headlights on, she dropped into the lane beside the church. Nothing like other people's troubles to take your mind off your own.

Other, brighter headlights met hers just before the turning to Court Farm, and she swung into the shoulder as the ambulance rocketed out and its siren warbled into life.

Still alive, anyway. But that could mean anything.

Fay drove into the track. She'd never been to Court Farm before.

Firemen were standing around the yard, and there was a policeman, one of Wynford's three constables. Fay ignored him; she'd always found it easier to get information out of firemen.

"Didn't take you long," one said, teeth flashing in the dusk. "You wanner interview me? Which way's the camera?"

"No need to comb your hair," Fay said. "It's radio."

"Oh, in that case you better talk to the chief officer. Ron!"

Firemen were always affable after it was over. "Bugger of a job getting to him," Ron said. "Right up the top, this bloody field, and the ground was all churned up after all this rain. Still, we done it. Bloody mess, though. Knackered old thing it was, that tractor. Thirty-odd years old."

"It just turned over?"

"Ah, it's not all that uncommon," said Ron. "I reckon we gets called to at least two tractor accidents every year. Usually young lads, not calculated the gradients. Never have imagined it happening to Jack Preece, though."

"*Jack* Preece?"

"Hey, now, listen, don't go putting that out till the police confirms the name, will you? No, see, I can't figure how it could've happened, Jack muster been over there coupler thousand times. Just shows, dunnit. Dangerous job, farming."

"How is he? Off the record."

"He'll live," Ron said, changing his boots. "Gets everywhere, this bloody mud. His left leg's badly smashed. I don't know . . . Still, they can work miracles these days, so I'm told."

Fay got him to say some of it again, on tape. It was 9:40, nearly dark, because of all the cloud, as she pulled out of the farmyard.

She was halfway down the track when a figure appeared in the headlights urgently waving both arms, semaphoring her to stop.

Arnold sat up on the seat and growled.

Fay wound her window down.

"Give me a lift into town, will you?"

It was too dark to see his face under the cap, but she recognized his voice at once from meetings of the town council and the occasional " 'Ow're you" in the street.

"Mr. Preece!"

Oh, Christ.

"Get in the back, Arnold," Fay hissed. As she pushed the dog into the back seat, something shocking wrenched at her mind, but she hadn't time to develop the thought before the passenger door was pulled open and the mayor collapsed into the seat next to her, gasping.

"In a hurry. Hell of a hurry."

The old man breathing heavily and apparently painfully as they crunched down the track. As she turned into the lane, Mr. Preece said, "Oh. It's you." Most unhappy about this, she could tell. "I didn't know it was you."

"I'm terribly sorry," Fay said, "about Jack. It must be . . . "

"Aye . . . " Mr. Preece broke off, turned his head, recoiled. "Mighter known! You got that . . . damn *thing* in yere!"

"The dog?"

The shocking thought of a couple of minutes ago completed itself with an ugly click. As she was pushing Arnold into the back seat she'd felt the stump of his rear left leg and heard Ron, the leading fireman, in her head, saying, *left leg's badly smashed.*

"Mr. Preece," Fay said carefully, "I'd like to come and see you. I know it's a bad time—a terrible time—but I have to know what all this is about."

He said nothing.

Fay said, "I have to know—not for the radio, for myself—why nobody keeps a dog in Crybbe."

The mayor just breathed his painful soggy breaths, never looked behind himself at what crouched in the back seat, said not a word until they moved up alongside the churchyard and entered the square.

"I'll get out yere."

"Mr. Preece . . . "

The old man scrambled out. Started to walk stiffly away. Then turned and tried to shout, voice cracking up like old brown parchment.

"You leave it alone, see . . . " He started to cough. "Leave it *alone,* you . . . "

Mr. Preece hawked and spat into the gutter.

" . . . stupid bitch," he said roughly, biting off the words as if he was trying to choke back more phlegm and a different emotion. And then, leaving the passenger door for her to close, he was off across the cobbles, limping and stumbling toward the church.

He's going to ring the curfew, Fay thought suddenly.

His son's just been mangled within an inch of his life in a terrible accident, and all he can think about is ringing the curfew.

Jonathon had been saying for months—years even—that it was time they got rid of that old tractor.

Probably this wasn't what he'd had in mind, Warren thought, standing in Top Meadow, alone with the wreckage of the thing that had crippled his Old Man, all the coppers and the firemen gone now.

The Old Man had been working on that tractor all day, giving himself something to concentrate on, take his mind off Jonathon and his problem of having nobody to hand over the farm to when he was too old and clapped out. Then he'd mumbled something about testing the bugger and lumbered off in it, up the top field, silly old bastard.

Testing it. Bloody tested it all right.

Warren had to laugh.

With the last of the light, he could more or less see what had happened, the tractor climbing toward the highest point and not making it, sliding back in the mud, out of control, tipping over, the Old Man going down with it, disappearing underneath as the bloody old antique came apart.

But Warren still couldn't figure how he'd let it happen, all the times he'd been up here on that bloody old tractor.

At least, he couldn't see *rationally,* like, how it had happened.

It was the *un*rational answer, the weird option, glittering in his head like cold stars, that wouldn't let him go home.

He followed the big tracks through the mud by the field gate,
up the pitch to the point where the tractor had started rolling
back prior to keeling over. He followed the tracks to the very
top of the rise, to where the tractor had been headed, glancing
behind himself and seeing the trees moving on top of the old
Tump half a mile away.

By the time he was on top of the pitch, he was near burning
up with excitement. It hadn't seemed like the right part of the
field at all, but that was because he'd come in by a different
gate, looking at it from a different angle.

Warren hesitated a moment and then dashed back down to the
tractor. Somebody had left behind a shovel they'd been using
to shift the mud so the firemen could get their cutting gear to
the Old Man. He snatched up the shovel, carried it back up the
pitch, prized away the top sod—knowing instinctively *exactly*
where to dig—threw off a few shovelfuls of earth, and there it
was, the old box.

The jagged thrill that went through him was like white-hot
electric wire. "Oh, fuck, oh fuck." Blinded by his power. "I
done it. Me."

His fingers were rigid with excitement as he opened the box,
just to make sure, and he almost cried out with the euphoria of
the moment.

He couldn't see proper, but it was like the hand of bones, the
Hand of Glory, in the box had bent over and become a fist.

It was curled around the Stanley knife, gripping it, and the
blade was out.

Warren shivered violently in horror and pleasure—the combination making him feel so alive it was like he was a knife
himself, sharp and savage, steely and invulnerable.

The only indestructible Preece.

eleven

At first, the figure was dressed in dark clothes so that when it filtered through the twilit trees only the soft footsteps and the rustlings told Powys anyone was coming.

He moved behind his oak tree, sure it was going to be Andy. Holding himself still, packing away the anger and the grief—an unstable mixture—because, for once, he intended to have the advantage.

What he had to do was break this guy's habitual cool. To raise the vibration rate until the bass-cello voice distorted and the lotus position collapsed in a muscular spasm.

He'd never seen Andy anything but laid-back. This, he realized, was the most impenetrable of all screens. Laid-back people were not evil. Laid-back people were wise. Evil people ranted like Hitler.

They weren't people you'd known half your life. And they were never called Andy.

But then, Powys thought, watching the figure enter the clearing and move toward the stone, the stench from a rotten egg was only apparent when the perfectly rounded, smooth, white shell was cracked.

The stone gleamed pearly gray, collecting what light remained, a ghostly obelisk. Powys watched and tried to slow his breathing. Not yet time; to get a stake into Dracula, you had to wait for daylight.

Or, in this case, until the curfew was over. The curfew was central to the Crybbe experience. The curfew was pivotal. Whatever had been building up—tension, fear, excitement—climaxed and then died with the curfew.

He'd experienced it twice, in radically different ways. The first night with Rachel, when they'd wound up in bed at the Cock so fast they hadn't even been aware of the chemicals' interacting until the chemicals had fully interacted. And then by the river, when he'd found the shotgun in his hands and come within a twitch of blowing Jonathon Preece in half.

He lifted the sleeve of his sweatshirt to expose his watch; it was too dark to be certain, but he was sure it must be ten o'clock.

Ten o'clock and no curfew?

Staggering into the church, Jimmy Preece was faced with its silent, solitary occupant, a wooden arrow pointing at the altar rails.

He stood gasping in the doorway, and there was Jonathon's smooth, mahogany coffin shining like a taunt, a pale gleam of polish in the dimness.

Mr. Preece couldn't find his breath, his legs felt like wet straw, and the urge to pray had never been as strong.

Please, God, protect us, he wanted to cry out until the words leapt into every corner of the rafters and came back at him with the illusion of strength.

And illusion was all it would be. He remembered the trouble there'd been when the old vicar was ill and the diocese had sent a replacement who'd turned out to be one of these Charismatics, some new movement in the church, this chap spouting about something he called Dynamic Prayer, shouting and quivering and making them all sing like darkies and hug each other.

No end of disturbance, until a phone call to the bishop had got rid of him. Not the border way, they told him. Not the *Crybbe* way.

Oh, Jonathon, Jonathon . . . Mr. Preece felt his chest quake in agony, and he turned away, groping for the narrow, wooden door to the belfry.

The old routine, making his painful way to the steps. But, for the first time, the routine resisted him and his foot failed to find the bottom step. Twenty-seven years he'd done it, without a break, until Jack started to take over, and now Jimmy Preece had come back and he couldn't find the blessed step.

Mr. Preece squeezed his eyes shut, dug his nails into his cheeks, raised his other foot and felt the step's worn edge slide under his shoe.

What time was it? Was he late?

His chest pumping weakly like these old brass fire-bellows his wife still kept, although the leather was holed and withered. His foot slipped on the edge of the second step.

Come on, come on, you hopeless old bugger.

He set off up the narrow stone steps, some no more than two foot wide.

Used to be . . . when he was ringing the old bell every night . . . that . . . these steps was . . . never a problem . . . even when he'd been working . . . solid on the lambing or the hay-making as was . . . bone-tired . . . because . . .

Mr. Preece paused to catch a breath, six steps up.

Because sometimes, in the old days, he'd just, like, *floated* to the top, like as if there were hands in the small of his back pushing him up the steps, and then the same hands would join his on the rope, because it was meant.

But tonight there were different hands, pressing down from above, pressing into his chest: *Go back, you poor, tired old bugger, you don't wanner do this no more.*

A son in the hospital. A grandson in his coffin.

What if you dies on the steps?

One Preece in the hospital. One in his coffin. One in a heap on the flagstones. And Warren.

Best not to think about Warren.

And a silence in the belfry.

No!

In a rage, Mr. Preece snatched out his dentures, thrust them down into a pocket of his old tweed jacket, forced some air into his broken bellows of a chest, and made it up two more steps.

He'd do it. He'd be late but he'd do it. Never been so important that he should do it.

He saw the light above him and the ropes. Never more important, now the wall around the Tump had been breached and something was in the Court.

As had been shown by the death of that woman.

But it had never been in the church. It couldn't get into the church.

No, it couldn't.

But it wasn't Andy Boulton-Trow, waiting by the stone.

It was a woman. Well, a girl.

And naked now.

She stood with her back to the stone, as if sculpted from it, her eyes closed and her mouth open, and the night sang around her.

Jesus God, Powys whispered, the voyeur behind the oak tree, stunned into immobility.

The pupil.

It was one of those nights when the thoughts were so deep you couldn't remember getting home or putting the car away. Some small thing brought you back into your body—like the tiny grind of metal in metal as your Yale key penetrated the front-door lock.

Fay could just about read her watch in what remained of the light and the glow from neighboring windows; she couldn't believe how rapidly the days had been shortening since Midsummer Day.

Mr. Preece was already a couple of minutes late with the curfew. She imagined him toiling up all those steps to the belfry, poor old sod.

Obsessive behavior. Did he really think the family might lose Percy Weale's sixteenth-century bequest if the curfew remained unrung for a single night because of a dire family crisis? Had to be more than that. Joe Powys would find out.

Oh, God, Powys, where are *you?*

One thing was sure: Jack Preece wouldn't be ringing the curfew for a long, long time—if ever again.

What does it mean, Joe?

She ought to have gone with him, even if this was something crazy between him and Boulton-Trow, something that went back twelve years or more.

It was so easy at night to believe in the other side of things, that there *was* another side. That Rachel—and Rose—had died because of a magic with its roots four centuries deep . . . or perhaps deeper, perhaps as old as the stones.

With Arnold tucked, not without some effort, under her arm, Fay went into the house. It was far too late now to send the tape for the morning news. The late-duty engineer at Offa's Dyke would be long gone. She'd have to go into the studio early in the morning again, having rung Hereford General to find out Jack's condition.

She lowered the dog to the doormat.

"I wish I could trust you, Arnold," Fay said, not quite knowing what she meant. His tail was well down; he looked no happier than she was. Jonathon Preece had set out to kill him

and had died in the river. Arnold had lost a leg, so might Jack
Preece by now . . .

If this was the seventeenth century she'd have been hanged
as a witch, Arnold stoned to death as her familiar.

Stop it, you stupid bitch.

She clenched her fists and felt her nails piercing the palms of
her hands. Everyone around her seemed to be carrying a burden
of possibly misplaced guilt. Powys for Rose and Rachel. Her
dad for Grace and for her mother. She herself . . .

Fay went down on her knees in the hall, the front door
open to the street behind her. She buried her head in Arnold's
fur. Arnold who looked no more evil than . . . than Joe Powys.
As she began quietly to sob, all the lights went out in the
neighboring homes.

Bloody electricity company. How *could* this keep happening?

Fay choked a sob in bitter anger and punched at the wall until
her knuckles hurt. Oh God, God, God, God, God.

She stood up shakily.

"Dad?"

There was no response.

She closed the front door behind her. He'd either gone to bed
or he was still over at Jean Wendle's having his treatment. Or
getting laid, if he'd got lucky. Fay sniffed and smiled. She'd
once asked the local doctor what the canon's condition meant
libido-wise. "He'll be less inhibited," the doctor had said. "By
which I mean he'll *talk* about it more often."

The canon wasn't back.

But—Arnold whimpering—somebody was.

As Fay stiffened in the darkness of the hallway, she saw a
vague yellowish light under the door of the office.

And very slowly the office door began to open.

Fay caught her breath.

It did not creak; she only knew it was opening because the
wedge of yellow light was widening, and it was not the soft and
welcoming, mellow yellow of a warm parlor at suppertime.

This was the yellow of congealing fat, the yellow of illness.

The hallway was very cold. It was a cold she remembered.

"Grace?" Fay heard herself say in a voice she didn't
recognize, a voice that seemed to come from someone else.

She felt her lips stretch tight with fear. She kicked the office
door open.

"Did she speak?" Jean Wendle had asked.

"Not a word."

Grace Legge wore a nightdress. Or a shroud. Was this what shrouds looked like?

"And she didn't move?"

"No."

Grace was standing by the window, very straight, a hand on a hip, half turned toward Fay. She was haloed in yellow light. The yellow of diseased flesh. The yellow of embalming fluid.

She was hovering six inches off the floor.

"Harmless, then."

"Grace," Fay said slowly. "Go away, Grace."

But Grace did not go away. She began to move toward Fay, not walking because her feet were bound in the shroud, which faded into vapor.

Fay backed away into the hall.

Dead eyes that were fixed, burning like small, still lamps. Burning like phosphorus.

"She can't talk to you, she can't see you; there's no brain activity there ... Blink a couple of times ... and she'll be gone."

Fay shut her eyes, screwed them tight. Stood frozen in the doorway with her eyes squeezed tight. Stood praying. Praying to her father's God for deliverance. Please make it go away, please, please, please ...

She smelled an intimate smell, sickly, soiled perfume, and felt cold breath on her face. She opened her eyes because she was more afraid not to, opened them into a fish-teethed snarl and yellow orbs alight with malice, and spindly, hooked fingers—the whole thing swirling and shimmering and coming for her, rancid and vengeful, filling the room with a rotting, spitting, incandescent yellow hatred.

Fay began to scream.

twelve

�֎ —————————————————————————————

It was fear that drew Minnie Seagrove to the window of her lounge. Fear that if she didn't look for it, it would come looking for her.

For a short while, there was a large, early moon. It wasn't a full moon, not one of those werewolf moons by any stretch, but it was lurid and bright yellow. It appeared from behind the Tump. Before it became visible, rays had projected through the trees on the top of the mound like the beams you saw seconds before the actual headlights of an oncoming car. The trees on the Tump were waving in the breeze even though the air all around Minnie's bungalow was quite still.

She'd come to associate this breeze with an appearance of the Hound.

Afterward, Mrs. Seagrove sat with her back to the window in Frank's old Parker Knoll wing chair, feeling its arms around her and hugging a glass of whiskey, the remains of Frank's last bottle of Chivas Regal malt.

Oh Lord, how she wished she hadn't looked tonight.

"I'm that cold, dear," she said, pretending she was talking to young Joe Powys or anybody who'd believe her. "I can't keep a limb still. I don't think I'll ever get warm again."

Powys knew it was on its way when the naked girl at the stone began to moan and shiver.

When the moon rose, he saw that the girl was certainly no more than twenty and might even be significantly younger, which made him uncomfortable. He wondered for a time if she was real and not some kind of vision. What kind of a girl would come alone at night into this appalling place and take off all her clothes?

Powys was not at all turned on by this.

He was afraid. Afraid, he rationalized, not only for her but *of* her.

Afraid because he suspected she knew what was coming, while he could have no conception, except of ludicrous phosphorous fur, fiery eyes and gnashing fangs, and Basil Rathbone in his deerstalker, with his pistol.

He found his fingers were tightly entwined into some creeper on the trunk of the oak tree. He squeezed it until it hurt.

The silence in the neglected wood was absolute. No night birds, no small mammals scurrying and scrabbling. If there was any sound, any indication of movement, of change, it would be the damp chatter of decay.

Max could not move. His eyes were wide open. He took his breath in savage gulps.

He lay in awe, couldn't even think.

He could smell the candles.

As if in anticipation of a power failure, the room had been ringed with them—Max half afraid they'd be black. But no, these were ordinary yellow-white candles, of beeswax or tallow, whatever tallow was. They didn't smell too good at first, kind of a rich, fatty smell.

Now the smell was as intoxicating as the sour red wine.

The mattress was laid out on the third level of the stable block, so he could lie in the dusk and take in the Tump filling the window, stealing the evening light, surrounded with candles, like a great altar.

Max lay under the black quilt, feeling like a virgin, the Great Beast–Scarlet Woman sessions with Rachel a faint and farcical memory.

For the first time in his adult life, Max was terrified.

And then, when the dark figure rose over him in the yellow, waxy glow, even more frightened—and shocked rigid, at first—by the intensity of his longing.

Warren looked up into the sky, at the night billowing in, and he *loved* the night and the black clouds and the thin wind hissing in the grass, his insides churning, his mind clotted with a rich confusion.

But the curfew was coming and the box was screaming at him to close the lid.

He slammed it down.

Then, bewildered, he started to claw at the earth with his

hands, set the box down in the hole.

Heard a rattling noise inside, the hand battering the side of the box.

It don't wanner go back in the ground.

It's done what it came for.

Now it wants to go back in the chimney.

And, sure enough, when Warren picked up the box the rattling stopped, and so he ran, holding it out in front of him like a precious gift, down from field to field until he reached the farm, where nobody else lived now, except for him and the Hand of Glory.

In the end, the curfew did come, a strained and hesitant clatter at first, and then the bell was pounding the wood like a huge, shiny ax, slicing up the night, and the girl was gone.

Joe Powys wandered blindly through the undergrowth, repeatedly smashing a fist into an open palm.

The night shimmered with images.

The bell pealed and Rose, in a pure white nightdress, threw herself from a fourth-floor window, fluttering hopelessly in the air like a moth with its wings stuck together, falling in slow motion, and he was falling after her, reaching out for her.

In the spiny dampness of the wood, Powys cried out, just once, and the curfew bell released, at last, his agony.

He staggered among the stricken, twisted trees and wept uncontrollably. He didn't *want* to control it. He wanted the tears to flow forever. He wanted the curfew bell to peal forever, each clang comet-bright in the shivering night.

The bell pealed on, and with that high, wild cry Rachel tumbled into the air, and then Rose and Rachel were falling together, intertwined.

A needle of light, like the filament of a low-wattage electric bulb, zigzagged across the eaves.

Silently, in slow motion, the rusty spike pierced the white nightdress and a geyser of hot blood sprayed into his weeping eyes.

�֎ ────────────────────────────────

thirteen

Max awoke to find himself alone, damp and smoldering, like a bonfire in the rain.

The cold deluge had been the curfew. When the curfew was gone, he realized at last, the town would be free.

He got up and shambled to the big window, wrapped in the black quilt. It was too dark to see the Tump; it didn't matter, he could *feel* the Tump. It was like the stables and maybe even the Court itself had been absorbed by the mound, so that he was, in essence, *inside* it.

No going back now, Max.

Feeling very nearly crazy, his face and hands slashed by boughs and bushes, Powys followed a dead-straight line back into Crybbe.

As if the path was lit up for him. Which perhaps it was—the bell strokes landing at his feet like bars of light. All he did was lurch toward the bell, each stroke laid on the landscape heavy as a gold ingot. And when he emerged from the wood into the churchyard, scratched and bleeding from many cuts, he just collapsed on the first grave he came to.

Its stone was of new black marble, with white lettering, and when he saw whose grave it was he started to laugh, slightly hysterically.

GRACE PETERS
1928–1992
Beloved wife of
Canon A. L. Peters

And that was all.

Powys scrambled to his feet; from what he knew of Grace she would take a dim view of somebody's dirty, battered body sprawled over her nice, clean grave.

He walked stiffly through the graveyard, out of the lych-gate, into the deserted square, his plodding footsteps marking sluggish time between peals of the curfew.

The power was off. Hardly a surprise. In four or five townhouse windows he could see the sallow light of paraffin lamps. Then, with a noise like a lawn mower puttering across the square, a generator cranked into action, bringing a pale-blue fluorescent flickering into the grimy windows of the old pub, the Cock.

Yes, Powys thought. I could use a drink. Quite badly.

It occurred to him he hadn't eaten since pushing down a polystyrene sandwich in this very pub before setting off to find his old mate, Andy Boulton-Trow. He didn't feel hungry, though. A drink was all he wanted, that illusory warmth in the gut. And then he'd decide where to go, whose night to spoil next, whose peace of mind to perforate.

He clambered up the steps and pushed open the single, scuffed swing-door to the public bar.

It was full. Faces swam out of the smoke haze, pallid in the stuttering fluorescence. The air was weighed down, it seemed to Powys, with leaden, dull dialogue and no merriment. He felt removed from it all, as though he'd fallen asleep when he walked in, and being here was a dream.

"Brandy, please," he told Denzil, the Neanderthal landlord. "A single."

Denzil didn't react at all to whatever kind of mess the wood had made of Powys's face. He didn't smile.

So where was the smile coming from? He knew somebody was smiling at him; you could feel a smile, especially when it wasn't meant to be friendly.

"Thanks," he said, and paid.

He saw the smile through the bottom of his glass. It was a small smile in a big face. It might have been chiseled neatly into the center of a whole round cheese.

Police Sergeant Wynford Wiley had sat there wearing this same tiny smile last night and early this morning while his colleagues from CID had been trying to persuade J. M. Powys to confess to the murder of his girlfriend.

"Been in a fight, is it, Mr. Powys?"

Wiley looked more than half drunk. He was sitting in a group of middle-aged men in faded tweeds or sleeveless, quilted body-warmers. Summer casual wear, Crybbe-style.

"You want the truth?" Powys swallowed some brandy but still didn't feel any warmth.

"All I ever wants is the truth, Mr. Powys." Wynford was wearing an old blue police shirt over what looked like police trousers.

"Amateur dramatics," Powys said wearily. "I've been auditioning for the Crybbe Amateur Dramatic Society. Banquo's Ghost. What do you think of the makeup?"

Wynford Wiley stopped smiling. He stood up at once, rather unsteadily. Planted himself between Powys and the door. And came out with that famous indictment of intruders from Off, those few words which Powys suddenly found so evocative of the quintessential Crybbe.

"We don't *like* clever people." Wynford stifled a burp. "Round yere."

There was that thrilled hush which the first spark of confrontation always brings to rural pubs.

Powys said, "Maybe that's why this town's dead on its feet." He finished his brandy. "Now"—placing his glass carefully on the bar top—"why don't you piss off and stop bothering me, you fat bastard."

He listened to himself saying this, as if from afar. Listened with what ought to have been a certain horrified awe. He'd done it now. Thrown down a direct public challenge to the authority of the senior representative for what passed for the law in this town. In order to retain his authority and his public credibility, Sergeant Wiley would be obliged to take prompt and decisive action.

And Sergeant Wiley was drunk.

And Powys didn't care, because tonight he'd seen the appalling thing that was known locally as Black Michael's Hound and witnessed the dark conflagration of its union with a young woman, and in terms of total black menace, Wynford Wiley just didn't figure.

"Let's slip outside, shall we, Mr. Powys?"

Wynford held open the door. To get out of here, Powys would have to step under his arm, and as soon as he was outside the door the arm would descend. He was likely to wind up in a cell. If he resisted, he would wind up hurt in a cell. If he ran away, the town would soon be teeming with coppers. Anyway, he was too knackered to run anywhere, even if there'd been anywhere to run.

"Don't make a fuss, Mr. Powys. I only wanner know 'ow you got that face."

Powys couldn't think of a way out. He stepped under Wynford's arm, and the arm, predictably, came down.

Somebody held open the door for Wynford and the big policeman followed him out, hand gripping his elbow. At that moment, as if to make things easier for the forces of the law, the power came back on, or so it seemed, and Wynford's face shone like a full moon.

Powys froze in the brightness, momentarily blinded. Wynford reeled back.

There was a figure behind the light, maybe two. The light was blasting from something attached like a miner's lamp to the top of a big video camera carried on the shoulder of a stocky man with a Beatles hairstyle (circa Hamburg '62) and an aggressive mouth.

Whom Powys recognized at once as Guy Morrison's cameraman, Larry Ember.

"You carry on, Sarge." Larry Ember moved to a lower step and crouched, the light still full on Wynford. "Just pretend we ain't here."

Wynford was squinting, mouth agape. "You switch that bloody thing off, you 'ear me? When did you 'ave permission to film yere?"

"Don't need no permission, Sarge. Public place, innit? We were just knocking off a few routine night shots. You go ahead and arrest this geezer, don't mind us, this is nice."

Wynford blocked the camera lens with a big hand and backed into the pub door, pushing it open with his shoulders. He glared at Larry Ember over the hot lamp. "I can 'ave you for obstruction. Man walks into a pub, face covered with cuts and bruises, it's my job to find out why."

"Yeah, yeah. Well, there was a very nasty accident happened up at a place called Court Farm tonight while some of us, Sergeant, were safely in the pub getting well pissed-up. As I understand it, this gentleman was up to his neck in shit and oil helping to drag some poor bleeder out from under his tractor. Fact is, he'll probably be in line for an award from the Humane Society."

Powys kept quiet, wondering what the hell Larry Ember was on about.

"Well . . . " Wynford backed off. "That case, why didn't 'e speak up, 'stead of being clever?"

"He's a very modest man, Sarge."

Wynford Wiley backed awkwardly into the pub, stabbing a defiant forefinger into the night. "All the same, you been told, Powys. Don't you leave this town."

"Dickhead," said Larry Ember, when the door closed. "Shit, I enjoyed that. Best shots I've had since we came to this dump. You all right, squire?"

"Well, not as bad as the guy under the tractor. Was that on the level?"

"Sure. We didn't go, on account of our leader was otherwise engaged, shafting his assistant."

"Well, thanks for what you did," Powys said. "I owe you one."

"Yeah, well, I was getting bored." Larry swung the camera off his shoulder, switched the lamp off. "And I figured he'd never arrest you in his state, more likely take you up that alley and beat seven shades out of you."

The cameraman, who'd obviously had a few pints himself, grabbed Powys's arm and started grinning. "Hey, listen, *you* know Morrison, don't you? Bleedin' hell, should've seen him. We shot this hypnotist geezer, taking young Catrin back through her past lives, you know this, what d'you call it . . . ?"

"Regression?"

"Right. And in one life, so called, she's this floozy back in the sixteenth century, having it away with the local sheriff, right?"

Powys stiffened. "In Crybbe?"

"That's what she said. Anyway, in real life, Catrin's this prim little Welshie piece, butter wouldn't melt. But, stone me, under the 'fluence, she's drooling at the mouth, pulling her skirt up round her waist, and Morrison—well, he can't bleedin' believe it. Soon as we get back, he says, in his most pompous voice, he says, 'Catrin and I . . . Catrin and *I*, Laurence, have a few program details to iron out.' Then he shoves her straight upstairs. Blimey, I'm not kidding, poor bleeder could hardly walk . . . "

"What time was this?"

"*Ages* ago. Well over an hour. And they ain't been seen since. Amazing, eh?"

"Not really," Powys said sadly.

*   *   *

The few oil lamps in the houses had gone out and so had the
moon. The town, what could be seen of it, was like a period
film-set after hours. An old man with a torch crossed his path
at one point; nothing else happened. Powys supposed he was
going back to the riverside cottage to sleep alone, just him and
the Bottle Stone.

He couldn't face being alone, even if it was now the right side
of the curfew and the psychic departure lounge was probably
closed for the night.

What was he going to do? He had an idea of what was
happening in Crybbe and how it touched on what had happened
to him twelve years ago. But to whom did you take such ideas?
Certainly not the police. And if what remained of the Church
was any good at this kind of thing, it wouldn't have been
allowed to fester.

He could, of course, go and see Goff and lay it all down
for him, explain in some detail why the Crybbe project should
be abandoned forthwith. But he wasn't sure he could manage
the detail or put together a coherent case that would convince
someone who might be a New Age freak but was also a very
astute businessman.

What it needed was a Henry Kettle.

Or a Dr. John Dee, come to that.

What *he* needed was to talk to Fay Morrison, but it was
unlikely she'd want to talk to him.

He passed the house he thought was Jean Wendle's. Jean
might know what to do. But that was all in darkness. Faced
with a power cut, many people just made it an early night.

As he slumped downhill toward the police station and the
river bridge, something brushed, with some intent, against his
ankles. It didn't startle him. It was probably a cat, there being
no dogs in Crybbe.

It whimpered.

Powys went down on his knees. "Arnold?"

It nuzzled him; he couldn't see it. He moved his hands down,
counted three legs.

"Christ, Arnold, what are you doing out on your own. Where's
Fay?"

He looked up and saw he'd reached the corner of Bell Street.

Sudden dread made his still-bruised stomach contract.

Not again. Please. No.

No!

He picked Arnold up and carried him down the street. If the dog had made it all the way from home, he'd done well, so soon after losing a leg. Arnold squirmed to get down and vanished through an open doorway. Powys could hear him limping and skidding on linoleum, and then the lights came back on.

Powys went in.

He couldn't take it in at first, as the shapes of things shivered and swam in the sudden brilliance. Then he saw that Arnold had nosed open the kitchen door and was skating on the blood.

part seven

�֎�֎✶✶✶✶✶✶✶══════════════

. . . but we could not bring him to human form. He was seen like a great black dog and troubled the folk in the house much and feared them.

ELIZABETHAN MANUSCRIPT, 1558

one

Max Goff said, "I came as soon as I heard."

Indeed he had. It was not yet 8 A.M. Jimmy Preece was surprised that someone like Goff should be up and about at this hour. Unhappy, too, at seeing the large man getting out of his car, waddling across the farmyard like a hungry crow.

Mr. Preece remembered the last time Goff had been to visit him alone.

This morning he'd been up since five and over at Court Farm before six to milk the few cows. He couldn't rely on Warren to do it—he hadn't even seen Warren yet. Mr. Preece was back on the farm, which he still owned but was supposed to have retired from eight years ago to make way for future generations.

Becoming a farmer again was the best way of taking his mind off what had happened to the future generations.

Everything changing too fast, too brutally. Even this Goff looked different. His suit was dark and he wore no hat. He didn't look as if he'd had much sleep. He looked serious. He looked like he cared.

But what was it he cared *about?* Was it the sudden, tragic death of Jonathon, followed by the grievous injury to Jonathon's father?

Or was it what he, Goff, might get out of all this?

Like the farm.

Mr. Preece thought of the crow again, the scavenger. He hated crows.

"Humble said you'd be here." Goff walked past him into the old, bare living room, where all that remained of Jack was a waistcoat thrown over a chair back. No photos, not even the old gun propped up in the corner anymore.

Goff said, "Reason I came so early is the meeting. It's the public meeting tonight. What I wanted to say—there's time to call it off, Mr. Mayor."

"Call 'im off?" Jimmy Preece shook his head. No, it would be an ordeal, this meeting, but it couldn't be put off. The meeting would be his best opportunity to make it clear to this Goff that he wasn't wanted in Crybbe, that this town had no sympathy with him or his ideas.

There would, however, be a great deal of sympathy—*overwhelming* sympathy—for old Jim Preece, who'd lost his grandson and whose son was now lying maimed for life in Hereford Hospital.

Goff would have realized this. Cunning devil.

No way Mr. Preece wanted that meeting called off.

"Too late now. People coming yere from all over. Never get word out in time."

"If we start now, Mr. Mayor, spread the word in town, get it out on Offa's Dyke Radio . . . "

"No, no. Very kind of you to offer, but the town council sticks to their arrangements, come fire, flood. And personal tragedy, like."

He'd be making time today to pay a final visit to each of the farmers with land around Crybbe, make sure they all understood about the need to keep the stones away. He thought they were still with him, but money could turn a farmer's head faster than a runaway bull.

"Thought I should at least make the offer, Mr. Mayor. And tell you how sorry I was."

"Aye."

There was a long silence. Mr. Preece noticed circles like bruises around Goff's eyes and his beard not as well manicured as usual.

"Well," Mr. Preece said. He might as well say it now, make it clear where they stood. "I expect you'll be wonderin' 'bout the future of this place. What's gonna happen if Jack's crippled and with Jonathon gone, like."

"It's a problem, Mr. Mayor. If there's any way I can help . . . We're neighbors, right?"

"No," Jimmy Preece said. "There's no way you can 'elp. And no I won't be sellin' the farm."

Goff spread his legs apart and rocked a bit. He didn't laugh, but he looked as if he wanted to.

"Aw, jeez, I realize you got to be in an emotional and anxious state, Mr. Mayor, but if you're thinking maybe I'm here because

I'm angling to buy the place, let me say that was about the last thing . . . I'm not a fucking property shark, Mr. Preece."

"No," Jimmy Preece said, and it might have been a question.

"This family's been here four, five centuries, yeah? Isn't there another son, young, er . . . ?"

"Warren," said Mr. Preece.

"Yeah, Warren."

"Who don't want anything to do with farming, as you well know, Mr. Goff."

"Huh?"

" 'E's gonner be a star, isn't that right?"

"I don't . . . "

"Pop guitarist, isn't it? You're gonner make the boy a millionaire. Sign 'im up, turn 'im into a big star so 'e can get his lazy arse out of Crybbe and don't need to 'ave nothing to do with us ever again . . . You ask me if there's anything you can do, Mr. Goff, I reckon you done enough."

For the first time, Murray Beech had locked the church for the night. He'd waited until the curfew was over and then walked over with the keys, surprised to find Jimmy Preece and not his son emerging from the belfry.

In an arid voice, from which all emotion had been drained, Jimmy Preece had explained why he was here, leaving Murray horrified. He'd remembered hearing the ambulance, wondering who it was for. How could lightning strike twice, so cruelly, at a single family? How could any kind of God . . . ?

Murray often wondered just how many of his colleagues in the church seriously believed anymore in a Fount of Heavenly Wisdom. Perhaps there should be a confidential survey, some sort of secret ballot within the Organization. No one could fault the basic Christian ethic, but Murray couldn't help wondering if it wasn't in the best interests of sustaining a credible, relevant, functioning clergy to have this anachronism known as God quietly phased out. God was a millstone. Three times as many people would seek clerical help with their personal problems if they didn't have to cope with God.

And without God the question of sacrilege would not arise, and nobody, he thought now, standing by the altar rail, would have to cope with . . . *this.*

The church door had not been forced last night. A window had simply been smashed in the vestry.

This morning Jonathon Preece lay apparently undisturbed, a silent sentinel, still, presumably—and Murray was not inclined to check—in his coffin, still safely supported on its bier, a slim metal trolley, only slightly more ornate than those used in hospitals. The coffin was still pointing at the altar with its white and gold cloth.

Neither the coffin nor the bier had been disturbed. Only the altar itself. In the center of the cloth, a silver dish had been heaped high with something brown and pungent.

Murray approached with trepidation and distaste to find the substance in the dish was not what he'd feared.

Next to the dish was the tin from which the brown gunge had been scraped.

It was dog food.

Murray was almost relieved.

And so puzzled by this that he failed to carry out a more detailed inspection of the church and therefore did not find out what else had been done.

Goff raised a faint smile and both hands. "I'm starting to understand, Mr. Preece. I see where you're coming from. The boy sent me a tape, right?"

"You tell me, sir, you tell me."

"Sure I'll tell you. This kid . . . "

"Warren."

"Warren, yeah. Mr. Mayor, you know how many tapes we get sent to us? Jeez, I don't even know myself—a thousand, two thousand a year. How many we do anything with? In a good year—two. Young . . . "

"Warren."

"Sure. Well, the reason he got further than ninety-nine point nine percent of the others was he sent it to the Cock and I listened to it myself. The normal thing is I pay guys to pay other guys to listen to the tapes on the slush pile, saves me a lotta grief, right? But I didn't wanna appear snobbish, big London record chief sneering at local hopefuls. So I listened to the tape and I had a letter sent back, and what it said was, this stuff isn't basically up to it, but we aren't closing the door. When you feel you've improved, try us again, we're always prepared to listen.

You know what that means? You'd like me to give you a frank and honest translation, Mr. Mayor?"

Jimmy Preece swallowed. "Yes," he said. "I'd like you to be quite frank."

"I'm always frank, Mr. Mayor, 'cept when it's gonna destroy somebody, like in the case of this tape. You ever hear your grandson's band, Mr. Preece?"

"Used to practice in the barn, till Jack turned 'em out. Hens wouldn't lay."

"Yeah, that sounds like them," said Goff, smiling now. "Crude, lyrically moronic, and musically inept. They might improve, but I wouldn't take any bets. My advice, don't let the kid give up sheep-shearing classes."

It went quiet in the living room at Court Farm. In the whole house.

"Thank you," Jimmy Preece said dully.

"No worries, Mr. Preece. Believe me. The boy'll make a farmer yet."

Behind the door, at the foot of the stairs, Warren Preece straightened up.

His face entirely without expression.

two

Jean's narrow town house had three floors and five bedrooms, only three of them with beds. In one, Alex awoke.

To his amazement he knew at once exactly who he was, where he was, and how he came to be there.

Separating his thoughts had once been like untangling single strands of spaghetti from a casserole.

Could Jean Wendle be right? Could it be that his periods of absentmindedness, of the mental mush—of wondering what day it was, even what time of his life it was—were the results not so much of a physical condition but of a reaction to his surroundings? Through living in a house disturbed by unearthly energy? A house on a ley-line.

No ley-lines passed through *this* house. Something Jean said she'd been very careful to establish before accepting the tenancy.

Why not try an experiment, Jean had suggested. Why not spend a night here? An invitation he'd entirely misunderstood at first. Wondering whether, in spite of all his talk, he'd be quite up to it.

Jean had left a message on Fay's answering machine to say Alex wouldn't be coming home tonight.

She'd shown him to this very pleasant room with a large but indisputably single bed and said good night. He might notice, she said, a difference in the morning.

And, by God, she was right.

The sun shone through a small square window over the bed and Alex lay there relishing his freedom.

For that was what it was.

And all thanks to Jean Wendle. How could he ever make it up to her?

Well, he knew how he'd *like* to make it up to her . . . Yes, this morning he certainly felt up to it.

Alex pushed back the bedclothes and swung his feet onto a floor which felt satisfyingly firm under his bare feet. He flexed his toes, stood, walked quite steadily to the door. Clad only in the Bermuda shorts he'd worn as underpants since the days when they used to give ladies a laugh, thus putting them at their ease. Under the clerical costume, a pair of orange Bermuda shorts. "I shall have them in purple, when I'm a bishop." Half the battle, Alex had found, over the years, was giving ladies a laugh.

There was the sound of a radio from downstairs.

" . . . *local news at nine o'clock from Offa's Dyke Radio, the Voice of the Marches. Here's Tim Benfield.*"

"*Good morning. A farmer is critically ill in hospital after his tractor overturned on a hillside at Crybbe. The accident happened only days after the tragic drowning of his son in the river nearby. James Barlow has the details . . .* "

Barlow? Should have been Fay, Alex thought. Why wasn't it Fay?

Alex found a robe hanging behind the door and put it on. Bit tight, but at least it wasn't frilly. In the bathroom, he splashed invigorating cold water on his face, walked briskly down the stairs, smoothing down his hair and his beard.

He found her in the kitchen, a sunny, high-ceilinged room with a refectory table and a kettle burbling on the Rayburn.

"Good morning, Alex." Standing by the window with a slim cigar in her fingers, fresh and athletic-looking in a light-green tracksuit.

"You know," Alex said, "I really think it bloody well is a good morning. All thanks to you, Jean."

Jean. It struck him that he'd persisted in calling her Wendy simply because it was something like her surname which he could never remember.

He went to the window, which had a limited view into a side street off the square. He saw a milkman. A postman. A grocer hopefully pulling out his sunshade.

Normality.

Harmless normality.

He thought about Grace. Perhaps if he left the house then, what remained of Grace would fade away. Fay had been right; there was no reason to stay here. Everything was clear from here, a different house, not two hundred yards away—but not on a spirit path.

Spirit paths. New Age nonsense.

But he couldn't remember the last time he'd felt so happy.

Hereward Newsome was seriously impressed by the painting's tonal responses, the way the diffused light was handled—shades of Rembrandt.

"How long have you been painting?"

"I've always painted," she said.

"Just that I haven't seen any of your work around."

"You will," she said.

He wanted to say, Did you really do this yourself? But that might sound insulting, might screw up the deal. And this painting was now very important, after the less-than-satisfactory buying trip to the West Country. An item to unveil to Goff with pride.

Hereward had returned the previous afternoon, terrified of facing Jocasta, with two hotel bills, a substantial drinks tab, and a mere three paintings, including a study of Silbury Hill which was little more than a miniature and had cost him in excess of twelve hundred pounds.

To his surprise, his wife had appeared almost touchingly pleased to have him home.

She'd looked tired, there were brown crescents under her eyes, and her skin seemed coarser. She'd told him of the terrible incident at the Court in which Rachel Wade had died. Hereward, who didn't think Jocasta had known Rachel Wade all that well, had been more concerned at the effect on his wife, who looked . . . well, she looked her age. For the first time in years, Hereward felt protective toward Jocasta, and, in an odd way, stimulated.

He'd shown her his miserable collection of earth-mystery paintings.

"Never mind," she'd said, astonishingly.

He'd trimmed his beard and made a tentative advance, but Jocasta felt there was a migraine hovering.

This morning they'd awoken early because of the strength of the light—the first truly sunny morning in a week. Jocasta had gone off before half past eight to open The Gallery, and Hereward had stayed at home to chop logs. On a day like this, it was good to be a countryman.

Then the young woman had telephoned about the painting and insisted on bringing it to the house, saying she didn't want to carry it through town.

He thought he'd seen her before, but not in Crybbe, surely. Dark hair, dark-eyed. Darkly glamorous and confident in an offhand way. Arrived in a blue Land Rover.

She wore a lot of makeup. Black lipstick. But she couldn't be older than early twenties, which made her mature talent quite frightening.

If indeed she'd done this herself; he didn't dare challenge her.

It was a large canvas—five feet by four. When he leaned it against the dresser it took over the room immediately. What it did was to draw the room into the scene, reducing the kitchen furniture to shadows, even in the brightness of this cheerfully sunny morning.

The painting, Hereward thought, stole the sunlight away.

He identified the front entrance of Crybbe Court, the building looking as romantically decrepit as it had last week when he'd strolled over there out of curiosity, to see how things were progressing. Broken cobbles in the yard. Weeds. A dull gray sky falling toward evening.

The main door was open, and a tall, black-bearded man, half-shadowed, stood inside. Behind the figure and around his head was a strange nimbus, a halo of yellowish, powdery vapor. The man had a still and beckoning air about him. Hereward was reminded, in a curious way, of Holman Hunt's *The Light of the World*, except there was no light about this figure, only a sort of glowing darkness.

"It's very interesting," Hereward said. "How much?"

"Three hundred pounds."

Hereward was pleased. It was, in its way, a major work, lustrous like a large icon. This girl was a significant discovery. He wanted to snatch his wallet out before she could change her mind, but caution prevailed. He kept his face impassive.

"Where do you work?"

"Here. In Crybbe."

"You're . . . a full-time, professional painter?"

"I am now," she said. "Would you like to see the preliminary sketches?"

"Very much," Hereward said.

She fetched the portfolio from the Land Rover. The sketches were in India ink and smudged charcoal—studies of the bearded face—and some color-mix experiments in acrylic on paper.

He wondered who the model was, didn't like to ask; this artist had a formidable air. Watched him, unsmiling.

And she was so *young*.

"Does it have a title?"

"It speaks for itself."

"I see," Hereward said. He didn't. "Look," he said, "I'll take a chance. I'll buy it."

She'd watched him the whole time, studying his reaction. She hadn't looked once at the painting. Most unusual for an artist; normally they couldn't keep their eyes off their own work.

"Could I buy the sketches, too?"

"You can have them," she said. "Keep them in your attic or somewhere."

"I certainly won't! I shall have them on my walls."

The girl smiled.

"One thing." She had a trace of accent. Not local. "I might be doing more. Even if it's sold, I'd like the painting in the window of your gallery for a couple of days. No card, no identification, just the picture."

"Well . . . certainly. Of course. But you really don't want your name on a card under the picture?"

Shook her head. "You don't know my name anyway."

"Aren't you going to tell me?"

She left.

It was not yet ten o'clock.

The mayor of Crybbe was seeing his youngest grandson for the first time as a man.

An unpleasant man.

He'd patrolled the farm, checking everything was all right, collected a few eggs. Then noticed that something, apart from the tractor, was missing from the vehicle shed.

When he got back to the house, he saw Warren landing hard on the settee, like he'd been doing something else, heard his granddad, and flung himself down in a hurry.

"Where's the Land Rover, Warren?"

"Lent it to a friend."

"You . . . *what?*" Mr. Preece took off his cap and began to squeeze it.

"Don't get excited, Granddad. She'll bring it back."

"She?"

"My friend," said Warren, not looking at him. He hadn't even shaved yet.

When Mr. Preece looked at Warren, he saw just how alone he was now.

"Come on, Warren, we got things to do. Jonathon's funeral tomorrow and your dad in hospital. Your gran rung yet?"

"Dunno. Has she?"

"She was gonner phone the hospital, see what kind of night Jack 'ad, see when we can visit 'im."

"I hate hospitals," said Warren.

"You're not gonner go?"

"Can't see me goin' today," said Warren, like they were talking about a football match. "I'll be busy."

Jimmy Preece began to shake. Sprawled across the settee was a hard, thin man with a head shaved close until you got right to the top, where his hair came out like a stiff shaving brush. A sneering man with an earring which had a little metal skull hanging from it. A man with flat, lizard's eyes.

Before, it had been an irritation, the way Warren was, but it didn't matter much. You looked the other way and you saw Jonathon, you saw the chairman of the Young Farmers' Club. You saw Jimmy Preece fifty years ago.

Now this . . . his only surviving grandson.

He tried. "Warren, we never talked much . . . before."

Warren's laughter was like spit. "Wasn't no reason to talk, was there? Not when there was Dad, and there was good old, reliable Jonathon."

"Don't you talk like that about . . . "

"And now you wanner talk, is it? What a fuckin' surprise this is. Fair knocks me over with the shock, that does."

Jimmy Preece squeezed his cap so tightly he felt the fabric start to rip.

This . . . *this* was the only surviving Preece, apart from himself, with two good legs to climb the stairs to the belfry.

"Now you listen to me, boy," Jimmy said. "There's things you don't know about . . . "

"Correction, Granddad." Warren uncoiled from the couch, stood up. "There's things I don't *care* about. Big difference there, see."

Jimmy Preece wanted to hit him again. But this time, Warren would be ready for it, he could tell by the way he was standing, legs apart, hands dangling loose by his sides. Wouldn't worry him one bit, beating an old man.

Jimmy Preece saw the future.

He saw himself prizing Mrs. Preece out of her retirement cottage, dragging her back to this old place. He saw himself running the farm again, such as it was these days, and ringing the old bell every night until Jack was out of hospital, and then Mrs. Preece caring for her crippled son, and what meager profits they made going on hired help as he, Jimmy Preece, got older and feebler.

He knew, from last night's ordeal, how hard it was going to get, ringing that bell. Jack must've sensed it, but he hadn't said a word. That was Jack, though, keep on, grit your teeth, do your duty. You don't have to like it, but you got to do it.

Going to be hard. Going to be a trial.

While this . . . this *thing* slinks around the place grinning and sneering.

Going to be no fallback. A feeble old man, and no fallback.

"Why don't you just let it go, Granddad," Warren said, with a shocking hint of glee. "What's it worth? Think about the winter, them cold nights when you're all stiff and the old steps is wet and slippery. Could do yourself a mischief, isn't it."

Jimmy Preece seeing his youngest grandson for the first time as a man.

A bad man.

He wanted to take what Goff had told him this morning and hurl it in Warren's thin, snidey face.

Instead, he turned his back on his sole remaining grandson and walked out of the house, across the yard.

Warren went back into the fireplace and lifted out the old box.

He set the box on the hearth and opened the lid.

The hand of bones looked to be lying palm up this morning, the Stanley knife across it, the fingers no longer closed around the knife.

Like the hand was offering the Stanley knife to Warren.

And Warren took it.

three

. . . an did bringe out hys bodie and shewde hym to the crowde with the rope about hys necke . . .

Joe Powys lay on the floor still wearing last night's sweatshirt, flecked with mud and stuff from the woods and some blood from later. He was alone; she'd slipped quietly away a few minutes ago.

The hanged man was obviously the High Sheriff, Sir Michael Wort, displayed by his frightened servants to the angry townsfolk to prove that he really was dead. So if they'd seen his body, how did the legend arise that Wort had perhaps escaped down some secret tunnel?

Only one possible answer to that.

It had been in his head almost as soon as he woke, half remembering copying out the material and half thinking it was part of some long, tortured dream. But *The Ley-Hunter's Diary 1993* was there, in his jacket by his pillow on the floor, and it was still throwing out answers. Not very credible answers.

The door was prodded open and Arnold peered around. Powys beckoned him, plunged his hands into the black and white fur. It felt warm and real. Not much else felt real.

Arnold licked his hand.

Powys looked around the room, at the dark-stained dressing table, the wardrobe like an upturned coffin, the milk-chocolate wallpaper. Not the least depressing room he'd ever slept in.

"Don't blame me for the decor."

She stood in the doorway.

She was in a red toweling bathrobe, arms by her sides, hands invisible because the sleeves were too long.

"It's certainly very Crybbe," he said.

Fay nodded. "And I'm never going to sleep here again, that's for sure."

He'd awoken several times during the night on his makeshift bed of sofa cushions laid end to end.

Once it was Arnold licking his forehead. And once with an agonizing image arising in his mind: an exquisitely defined, twilit image of Rachel's broken body, both eyes wide open in a head that lolled off-center, the perfect, pale, Pre-Raphaelite corpse, Ophelia, the Lady of Shalott . . .

Lady cast out upon a Rubbish Heap.

He'd stood up, hearing Fay moaning in the bed. "Oh God." Twisting her head on the pillow. "It hurts. It really hurts. It was just numb for a while, now it really hurts."

"Let me take you to a hospital."

"I'm not leaving this room."

"And I thought Arnold looked a mess," she said. "What's the time? There's only one reliable clock in this house, and I couldn't bear to look at it."

Powys consulted their two watches on the bedside cupboard.

"Half nine. Ten. Mine's probably right, yours is cracked. So it's ten."

"Even my watch has a cracked face." Fay smiled feebly. "I was lying there, thinking, you know, it can't be as bad as it feels, it really can't. Then I staggered to the bathroom mirror . . . And it was. It really bloody was."

The cut ran from just below the hairline to the top of the left cheek. The left eye was black, blue, orange, and half closed.

"The bitch has scarred me for life."

He remembered all the blood on the linoleum and thought she actually looked a good deal better than the quaking thing he'd found curled up on the kitchen floor, incapable, for a long time, of coherent speech.

"It's *never* going to heal," Fay said bleakly.

"It will." But she was probably right. There'd be a long-term scar. This town was good at leaving scars. He swung his legs out of bed; quite decent, still wearing his boxer shorts, but he doubted she'd have noticed if he'd been naked.

"She's back now, all right. It's her house again."

"Grace?"

"She's repossessed it." Fay shivered and held her robe together at the throat. "It's like . . . When she was alive, there was this thin veneer . . . of gentility, OK? Of politeness. Now she's dead there's no need to keep up appearances, it's all stripped away, and there's just this . . . this rotting core . . . Resentment. Hate. Just don't let anybody tell me the dead can't feel hatred."

"Maybe they can just project it. Maybe we're not even talking about the dead, as such."

Fay's right profile was all white. She turned her head with a lurid, rainbow blur and her mouth tightened with the pain.

"And don't let *anybody* tell me again that they're harmless. Joe, she flew at me. She was hovering near the floor—everywhere this icy stillness—and then she sprang. There was a perfumy smell, but it was a kind of mortuary perfume, to cover up the rotting, the decay, you know?"

Powys said helplessly, "I've never seen a ghost."

Then what did you see last night? What in Christ's name was that? The raging black horror in the wood. He was sure the girl at the stone would be killed or die of fright, but the bitch knew what she was doing.

"So I'm backing out of the office," Fay said. "Thinking, She can only exist in there. Jean Wendle said I should blink a couple of times, close my eyes and when I opened them she'd be gone, she's only a light effect, no more real than voices on quarter-inch, fragments of magnetic dust, and I hit the pause button and the voice cuts out in midsentence. So I took the advice. I closed my eyes—and I got out of the room fast because she can't exist outside there, can she? That's *her* place, right?"

Fay's fingers were white and stiff around the collar of the red robe.

"And I'm in the hall. I've closed the door behind me. I've slammed the door. In its . . . in Grace's face. And suddenly, just as I'm . . . She's there too. She's right up against me again, *in my face*. Grace has . . . had . . . *has* these awful little teeth, like fish bones. And, you know, the kitchen door's opposite the office door, and so I just *threw* myself across the hall and into the kitchen, and I . . . that's all I remember."

"You hit your head on a sharp corner of the kitchen table." She's right, he thought. She can't stay here tonight. Any more than I can spend it with the Bottle Stone. "It was too dark to see much. I thought you were . . . well, dead."

"Thanks."

"What would *you* think . . . ?"

"No, I mean . . . thanks. You keep rescuing me. That's not the way it's supposed to be anymore."

"Arnold waylaid me at the top of the street and dragged me down here with his teeth."

The dog wagged his tail, staggered to the edge of the bed, and looked down dubiously.

"Good old Arnie," said Fay. "I'd just virtually accused him of exacting some awful psychic revenge on the Preece family for trying to shoot him. Come on, I'll make some breakfast. We have to eat."

Neither of them had mentioned the Bottle Stone. He wished he could prove to her it had all happened, but he couldn't. He couldn't prove anything—yet.

"I wanted to call a doctor last night," he told her. "But you started screaming at me."

"I hate doctors."

"You ought to see one, all the same."

"Sod off. Sorry, I don't mean to be churlish, but nothing

seems to be fractured. Cuts and bruises. Anyway, look at the state of *you.*"

Powys picked Arnold up to carry him downstairs.

Fay said, "I wonder what he sees."

He thought, I think I've seen what he sees. He said, "The other time you saw this Grace thing, what time was it?"

"After midnight."

"What was it like on that occasion?"

"She didn't move. Very pale. Very still. Like a lantern slide."

At the foot of the stairs, the office door remained closed.

"Figures," Powys said. "She wouldn't be up to much after midnight. Or, more correctly, after ten—after the curfew. It probably took all her energy just to manifest. But last night, it was just minutes *before* the curfew. That's when it's strongest. That's when the whole town's really charged up. Before the curfew shatters it."

"What are you on about?" Fay shook her head, looked at the kitchen floor. "God, what a mess. Who'd have thought I had so much blood in me."

"I think . . . "

"You mention doctors or hospitals again, Joe, I'll never sleep with you again."

Fay grinned, which was the wrong thing to do because it pulled on the skin around her bruised eye.

She had to go back into the office to answer the phone. It looked, as it always did in the mornings, far too boring to be haunted.

The call was from her father, sounding wonderfully bright and happy. Last night, while she was sitting by the sink, Joe trying to bathe her eye, the phone had rung and Jean's message, amplified by the answering machine, had been relayed across the hall.

"I can't believe it," Alex said now. "I feel tremendous. I feel about . . . oh, sixty-five. Do you think I'm too old to become a New Age person?"

"You going to stay at Jean's for a while, Dad?"

"I'll probably drift back in the course of the day. Don't want to lose touch with old Doc Chi at this stage."

"Dad's shed a quarter of a century overnight," Fay told Powys. "No woman is safe."

"Well, keep him away from the Cock."

"Why?"

"It seems to have aphrodisiac properties. It turns people on."

"I don't follow you."

He told her, at last, about getting beaten up by Humble, and Rachel taking him to her and Goff's room. What had happened then, the sudden inevitability of it. "It was the right time, coming up to curfew time. I mean, Rachel was not . . . promiscuous. Nor me, come to that. I mean, lonely, sex-starved, but not . . . Anyway, I just don't think we'd ever have got together . . . if it hadn't been for the time. And the place."

"I don't understand."

"All right, think about the condoms. All those used condoms in the alley, up by the studio. In a town surrounded by open fields, doesn't it strike you as odd that so many couples should want to do it standing up in an alley?"

"I never really thought about it. Not that way."

"And last night, again at the Cock, again in the hour before the curfew, your ex-husband was suddenly overwhelmed with lust for his production assistant and whisked her upstairs."

"Catrin? Guy and *Catrin?*"

Powys nodded. "Why do they call it the Cock?" He was buttering more toast; it was, she reckoned, his fifth slice. How long since he last ate? "Is that what it's really called?"

"Certainly hasn't got a sign to that effect," Fay said.

"What do you know about Denzil, the landlord. Got many kids, for instance?"

"I don't know. He isn't married, I don't think. Somebody once told me he put it about a bit, but I mean . . . You're getting carried away, Joe."

"I'm a loony. I'm allowed." He spread the toast with about half a pot of thick-cut marmalade. "Sorry. Look, I haven't got this worked out yet. Whatever I say's going to make you think I'm even more of a loony."

"No—hang on—Joe, I . . . " Fay clasped her hands together tightly, squeezing them. "I'm sorry about yesterday. I had no right to dispute your story. Town full of ghosts, no dogs . . . I mean, Christ . . . I'm sorry."

He put a hand over both of hers. Sighed.

"Tell me," Fay said.

So he told her. He told her about the cottage and the magical Filofax and the art studio.

"Blood?" Fay touched her temple, winced. "Urine? What does it mean?"

"I don't really know. But I wouldn't have one of those paintings on *my* wall."

And then he told her about the girl at the stone, and the apparition.

"You saw it? You saw Black Michael's Hound?"

"I don't know what it was. Maybe the hound is something it suggests. Whatever it is, it's feeding off the energy which starts to build up in this town probably at dusk. And it comes in a straight line, from the Tump, through the Court and on toward the church. It's evil, it's . . . cold as the grave."

Fay shivered inside her robe. "And this girl was . . . getting off on it?"

"Something like that. When the curfew began, she'd gone. She'd done this before, knew the score."

"What does that tell us about the curfew?"

"That the curfew was established to ward something off. I think we're talking about Black Michael. Look . . . " He took from his jacket a slim black paperback, *Elizabethan Magic* by Robert Turner. "I found this in the bread oven with the Filofax. I nicked it. There's a couple of chapters on Dee, but what I was really interested in was this. The page was marked."

He opened the book at a chapter headed "Simon Foreman, Physician, Astrologer and Necromancer (1552–1611)." There was a picture of Foreman, who had a dense beard and piercing eyes.

"The book talks of a manuscript in Foreman's handwriting, evidently something he copied out, much as Andy did in his Filofax. It's the record of an attempt to summon a spirit, and . . . look . . . this bit."

He cast out much fire and kept up a wonderful ado; but we could not bring him to human form: he was seen like a great black dog and troubled the folk in the house much and feared them.

"So what it's suggesting," Powys said, "is that the black-dog image is some kind of intermediary state in the manifestation of an evil spirit. In this case, the spirit's furious at not being able to get any further, so he's coming on with the whole poltergeist bit.

There's a famous legend in Herefordshire where a dozen vicars get together to bind this spirit and all that's appeared since is a big black dog."

"So when we talk about Black Michael's Hound . . . "

"We're probably talking about the ghost of Michael himself. We know from these notes of Andy's—which I'm attributing to John Dee, for want of a more suitable candidate—that Michael Wort, while alive, appeared to have taught himself to leave his body and manifest elsewhere . . . traveling by the 'olde road,' which is presumably a reference to ley-lines. Spirit paths. And then there's this legend about him escaping by some secret passage when the peasantry arrived to lynch him. Dee, or whoever, records that Wort's body was brought out after he hanged himself, to prove he was indeed dead. So maybe he escaped *out of his body* . . . along the 'olde road,' maybe his ghost was seen—bringing a lot of black energy with it—and they managed to contain it . . . to reduce it to the black-dog stage . . . by some ritual which has at its heart the curfew."

"How does that stop it?"

"Well, making a lot of noise—banging things, bells, tin cans, whatever—was popularly supposed to be a way of frightening spirits off. Maybe by altering the vibration rate; I'm not really qualified to say."

"This is . . . " Fay held on to his hand, "seriously eerie. I mean, you're the expert, you've been here before, but Christ, it scares the hell out of me."

"No, I'm not," he said. "I'm not any kind of expert. I wrote a daft, speculative book. I'm not as qualified as most of these New Age luminaries. All I know is that Andy Boulton-Trow, with or without Goff's knowledge, is experimenting with what we have to call dark forces. He's probably been doing it for years . . . since . . . Well, never mind. Now we know why Henry Kettle was getting the bad vibes."

"Boulton-Trow put Goff onto this place?"

"Probably. Something else occurred to me, too. I don't know how much to make of it, but . . . try spelling 'Trow' backwards."

"Tr . . . ?" Her eyes widened. "Jesus."

"I mean, it could be pure coincidence."

"There are too many coincidences in Crybbe," Fay said. She stood up. "OK, what are we going to do about this?"

"I think . . . we need to get everything we can, and quickly, on Michael Wort. Any local historians you know?"

Fay smiled. "In Crybbe, Joe, a historian is somebody who can remember what it said in last week's paper."

"What about the local-authority archives? Where, for instance, would we find the transactions of the Radnorshire Society?"

"County Library, I suppose. But that's in Llandrindod Wells."

"How far?"

"Twenty-five, thirty miles."

"Let's get over there." He started to get up. "Oh God." Sat down again. "I can't. I have to go to Hereford Crematorium. It's Henry Kettle's funeral."

"You can't not go to Henry's funeral," Fay said. "Look, *I'll* go to the library. Tell me what we're looking for."

"You can't drive with that eye."

"Of course I can. And they're only country roads. What am I looking for?"

"Anything about Wort—his experiments, his hangings, his death. And the Wort family. If they're still around, if we can get hold of any of them. And John Dee. Can we establish a connection? But, I mean, don't make a big deal of it. If we meet back here at . . . what? Four o'clock?"

"OK. Joe, look . . . is there *nobody* we can go to for help?"

"What about Jean Wendle?"

"Ha." Fay put a hand up to her rainbow eye. "Her assessment of Grace wasn't up to much, was it? Harmless, eh?"

"We're on our own, then," Powys said.

four

Crybbe town hall was in a short street of its own, behind the square. An absurdly grandiose relic of better days, Colonel Colin "Col" Croston thought, strolling around the back to the small door through which members of the town council sneaked, as though ashamed of their democratic role.

Tonight, the huge Gothic double doors at the front would be thrown open for the first time in twenty years. Suspecting problems, Col Croston had brought with him this morning a small can of Three-in-One Penetrating Oil to apply to the lock and the hinges.

Col Croston let himself in and strode directly into the council chamber. The cleaner would not be here until this afternoon, and so Col made his way to the top of the room where the high-backed chairman's chair stood on its platform.

He sat down in the chair. There was a pristine green blotter on the table in front of him, and on the blotter lay a wooden gavel, unused—like the chair—since local government reorganization in 1974.

Before reorganization, the rural district authority had been based here. But "progress" had removed the seat of power to a new headquarters in a town thirty miles away. Now there was only Crybbe town council, a cursory nod to local democracy, with ten members and no staff apart from its part-time clerk, Mrs. Byford, who dealt with the correspondence and took down the minutes of its brief and largely inconsequential meetings.

The council chamber itself had even been considered too big for the old RDC, and meetings of the town council were self-conscious affairs, with eleven people hunched in a corner of the room trying to be inconspicuous. Although their meetings were public, few townsfolk were ever moved to attend.

Tonight, however, it seemed likely the chamber would actually be too small for the numbers in attendance, and the chairman would be occupying, for the first time in nearly twenty years, the official chairman's chair.

The chairman tonight would be Col Croston.

Mrs. Byford, the clerk, had telephoned him at home to pass on the mayor's apologies and request that he steer the public meeting.

"Why, surely," Col said briskly. "Can hardly expect old Jim to be there after what's happened."

"Oh, he'll be there, Colonel," Mrs. Byford said, "but he'll have to leave soon after nine-thirty to see to the bell, isn't it."

"Shouldn't have to mess about with that either, at his age. All he's got to do is say the word and I'll organize a bunch of chaps and we'll have that curfew handled on a rotation system. Makes a lot of sense, Mrs. Byford."

The clerk's tone cooled at once. "That bell is a *Preece* function, Colonel."

Oh dear, foot in it again; never mind. "All got to rally round at a time like this, Mrs. Byford. Besides, it could be the first step to getting a proper team of bell-ringers on the job. Crying shame, the way those bells are neglected."

"It's a Preece function," Mrs. Byford said from somewhere well within the Arctic Circle. "The meeting starts at eight o'clock."

Minefield of ancient protocol, this town. Col Croston often felt Goose Green had been somewhat safer.

Col was deputy mayor this year. Long army career (never mentioned the SAS but everybody seemed to know). Recommended for a Victoria Cross after the Falklands (respectfully suggested it be redirected). But still regarded becoming deputy mayor of Crybbe as his most significant single coup, on the grounds of his being the only incomer to serve on the town council long enough to achieve the honor—which virtually guaranteed that next year he'd become the first outsider to wear the chain of office.

His wife considered he was out of his mind snuggling deeper into this hotbed of small-minded prejudice and bigotry. But Col thought he was more than halfway to being accepted. And when he made mayor he was going to effect a few tiny but democratically meaningful changes to the way this little council operated—as well as altering the rather furtive atmosphere in which it conducted its affairs. He often felt that, although it gave a halfhearted welcome to new industry, anything providing local jobs, this council appeared to consider its foremost role was to protect the town against happiness.

Indeed, until being asked to chair it, he'd been rather worried about how tonight's meeting would be handled. He'd been finding out as much as he could about Max Goff's plans and had to say that the New Age people he'd met so far hadn't invariably been the sort of head-in-the-clouds idiots one had feared. If it pulled in a few tourists at last, it could be a real economic shot in the arm for this town.

So Col Croston was delighted to be directing operations.

With a mischievous little smile he lifted the gavel and gave a smart double rap.

"Silence! Silence at the back there!"

Whereupon, to his horror, Mrs. Byford materialized in the doorway with a face like a starched shirt.

"I hope, Colonel, that you're banging that thing on the blotter and not on the table."

"Oh, yes, of course, Mrs. Byford. See . . . " He gave it another rap, this time on the blotter. It sounded about half as loud. "Ha ha. Well, ah . . . your morning for the correspondence, is it?"

Mrs. Byford stalked pointedly to the corner table used for town council meetings and placed upon it the official town council attaché case.

"Glad you came in, actually," Col Croston said. "I think we ought to send an official letter of condolence to the relatives of that poor girl who had the accident at the Court."

"I see no necessity for that." Mrs. Byford began to unpack her case.

"There's no *necessity,* Mrs. B. Just think it'd be a sympathetic thing to do, don't you?"

"Not my place to give an opinion, Colonel. I should think twice, though, if I were you, about making unauthorized use of council notepaper."

Col Croston, who'd once made a disastrous attempt to form a Crybbe cricket club, estimated that if he bowled the gavel at the back of Mrs. Byford's head, there'd be a fair chance of laying the old boot out.

Just a thought.

It was Bill Davies, the butcher, who rang Jimmy Pierce to complain about the picture. "I'm sorry to 'ave to bother you at a time like this, Jim, but I think you should go and see it for yourself. I know you know more about these things than any of us, but I don't like the look of it. Several customers mentioned it, see. How *is* Jack now?"

"Jack's not good," Jimmy Preece said, and put the phone down.

He could see trouble coming, been seeing it all the morning, in the calm of the fields and the weight of the clouds.

And in the cold, gleeful eyes of his surviving grandson.

Ten minutes after talking to Bill Davies, the mayor was walking across the square toward The Gallery, traders and passersby
nodding to him sorrowfully. Nobody said " 'Ow're you." They
all knew where he was going.

Even in today's profoundly pessimistic mood, he was not
prepared for the picture in the window of The Gallery. He had
to turn away and get some control of himself.

Then, face like parchment, he pushed through the pine-paneled
door with its panes of bull's-eye glass.

The woman with too much makeup and a too-tight blouse
opened her red lips at him. "Oh. Mr. Preece, isn't it? I'm so
terribly, terribly . . . "

"Madam!" Mr. Preece, his heart wrapped in ice, had seen in
the gloating eyes of the yellow-haloed man in the picture that
the accident to Jack and the drowning of Jonathon were only
the start of it. This was what *they*'d done with their meddling
and their New Age rubbish.

"That picture in the window. Where'd 'e come from?"

"My husband brought it back from Devon. Why, is there . . . ?"

"Did 'e," Mr. Preece said heavily. "Brought it back from
Devon, is it?"

Couldn't stop himself.

"Devon . . . ? Devon . . . ?"

Saw the woman's lips make a colossal great "O" as he raised
a hand and brought it down with an almighty bang on the thick,
smoked-glass counter.

The cremation was at twelve, and Powys was late. He felt bad
about this because there were barely a dozen people there. He
spotted Henry's neighbor, Mrs. Whitney. He noted the slight,
unassuming figure of another distinguished elder statesman of
dowsing. And there was his old mate Ben Corby, now publishing director of Dolmen, newly acquired by Max Goff.

"Bloody minister never even mentioned dowsing," Ben said.

It had been a swift, efficient service. No sermon. Nothing too
religious, *nothing psychic.*

Powys said, "I don't think Henry would have wanted to be
wheeled in under an arch of hazel twigs, do you?"

"Too modest, Joe. All the bloody same, these dowsers. Look
at old Bill over there—he wouldn't do me a book either."

Powys smiled. "Henry left me his papers."

"In that case, *you* can do the book. *The Strange Life of Henry Kettle,* an official biography by his literary executor. How's that? Come and have a drink, my train back to Paddington's at ten past two."

Ben Corby. Plump and balding Yorkshireman, the original New Age hustler. They went to a pub called the Restoration and sat at a window table overlooking a traffic island with an old stone cross on it.

"*Golden Land Two,*" said Ben. "How long? A year?"

Not the time, Powys thought, to tell him there wasn't going to be a book.

"Seen Andy lately?" he asked.

"Great guy, Max," Ben said. "Best thing that could've happened to Dolmen. Been burdened for years with the wispy-beard brigade, wimps who reckon you can't be enlightened *and* make money. Give me the white suit and the checkbook any day. The New Age movement's got to seize the world by the balls."

"Andy," Powys said patiently. "You seen him recently?"

"Andy? Pain in the arse. He wouldn't write me a book either. He's always been an elitist twat. Hates the New Age movement, thinks earth mysteries are not for the masses . . . But, there you go, he knows his stuff; I gather he's giving Max good advice."

"Maybe he's just using Max."

"Everybody uses everybody, Joe. It's a holistic society."

"How did Andy get involved?"

Ben shrugged. "I know he was teaching art at one of the local secondary schools. Had a house in the area for years, apparently."

That made sense. Had he really thought Andy was living in a run-down woodland cottage with no sanitation?

But why teaching? Teaching what?

"Andy's hardly short of cash."

"Maybe he hit on hard times," said Ben. "Maybe he felt he had a duty to nurture young minds."

Young minds. Powys thought of the girl at the stone. And then a man leaned over and tapped him on the shoulder.

"Excuse me, Mr. Powys, could I have a word? Peter Jarman, Mr. Kettle's solicitor."

Peter Jarman looked about twenty-five; without his glasses he'd have looked about seventeen. He steered Powys into a corner. "Uncle Henry," he said. "We all called him Uncle Henry.

My grandfather was his solicitor for about half a century. Did you get my letter?"

Powys shook his head. "I've been away."

"No problem. I can expand on it a little now. Uncle Henry's daughter, as you may have noticed, hasn't come back from Canada for his funeral. He didn't really expect her to, which, I suspect, is why he's left his house to you."

"Bloody hell. He really did that?"

"Seems she's done quite well for herself, the daughter, over in Canada. And communicated all too rarely with Uncle Henry. He seems to have thought you might value the house more than she would. This is all rather informal, but there *are* formalities, so if you *could* make an appointment to come to the office."

"Yes," Powys said faintly. "Sure."

"In the meantime," said young Mr. Jarman, "if you want to get into the cottage at any time, Mrs. Whitney next door is authorized to let you in. Uncle Henry was very specific that you should have access to any of his books or papers at any time."

"You told me," Jocasta Newsome said, suppressing her emotions, but not very well, "that you hadn't managed to buy much in the West Country, and you proceeded to prove it with that mediocre miniature by Dufort."

Hereward nervously fingered his beard. Now that it was almost entirely gray, he'd been considering shaving the thing off. As a statement, it was no longer sufficiently emphatic.

The black beard of the dark-eyed figure in the picture seemed to mock him.

"Where did it come from, Hereward?"

"All right," he snapped, "it wasn't from the West. A local artist sold it to me."

Jocasta planted her hands on her hips. "Girl?"

"Well . . . young woman."

"Get rid of it," Jocasta said, not a request, not a suggestion.

"Don't be ridiculous."

"Take it back. Now."

"What the hell's the matter with you? It's a bloody good painting! Worth eight or nine hundred of anybody's money, and that's what Max Goff's going to pay!"

"So if Goff's going to pay the money, what's it doing in our window upsetting everybody?"

"One man!" He couldn't believe this.

"The mayor of this town, Hereward. Who was so distressed he nearly cracked my counter."

"But . . . " Hereward clutched his head. "He's the *mayor!* Not a bloody cultural arbiter! Not some official civic censor! He's just a tin-pot, small-town . . . I mean, how *dare* the old fuck come in here, complaining about a picture which isn't even . . . an erotic nude or . . . or something. What's his problem?"

"He calmed down after slapping the counter," Jocasta admitted. "He apologized. He then appealed to me very sincerely—for the future well-being of the town, he said—not to flaunt a picture which appeared to be heralding the return of someone called Black Michael, who was apparently the man who built Crybbe Court and was very unpopular in his day."

"He actually said that? In the year nineteen hundred and ninety-three, the first citizen of this town—the most senior *elected* member of the town council—seriously said *that?*"

"Words to that effect. And I agreed. I told him it would be removed immediately from the window and off these premises by tonight. I apologized and told him my husband obviously didn't realize when he purchased it—'in the West Country'—that it might cause offense."

For a moment, Hereward was speechless. When his voice returned, it was hoarse with outraged incredulity.

"How dare you? How bloody *dare* you? Black bloody Michael? What is this . . . bilge? I tell you, if this gallery is to have any artistic integrity . . . "

"Hereward, it's going," Jocasta said, bored with him. "I don't like that girl, she's a troublemaker. I don't like her weird paintings, *and I want this one out.*"

"Well, I can't help you there," Hereward said flatly. "I promised it would stay in the window until tomorrow."

Jocasta regarded him as she would something she'd scraped from her shoe. It occurred to him seriously, for the first time, that perhaps he *was* something she'd like to scrape from her shoe. In which case, the issue of his failed trip to the West, his attempt to recover ground by buying this painting on the artist's eccentric terms, all this would be used to humiliate him again and again.

She turned her back on him and as she stalked away, Hereward saw her hook the tip of one shoe behind the leg of the wooden easel on which sat the big, dark picture.

He tried to save it. As he lunged toward the toppling easel, Jocasta half turned and, seeing his hands clawing out, must have thought they were clawing at her. So she struck first. Hereward felt the nails pierce his cheek, just under his right eye.

It was instinctive. His left hand came back and he hit her so hard with his open palm that she was thrown off her feet and into a corner of the window, where she lay with her nose bleeding, snorting blood splashes onto her cream silk blouse.

There was silence.

A bunch of teenage boys just off the school bus, home early after end-of-term exams, gathered outside the window and grinned in at Jocasta.

The picture of the unsmiling man with the yellow halo in the doorway of Crybbe Court had fallen neatly and squarely in the center of the floor and was undamaged. Its darkness flooded the gallery, and Hereward Newsome knew his marriage and his plans for a successful and fashionable outlet in Crybbe were both as good as over.

Assessing his emotions, much later, he would decide he'd been not so much sad as angry and bitter at the way a seedy little town could turn a civilized man into a savage.

Jocasta didn't get up. She took a tissue from a pocket in the front of her summery skirt and dabbed carefully at her nose.

Hereward knew there was blood also on his torn cheek. He didn't touch it.

Outside, the schoolkids began to drift away. Jocasta had her back against the window, unaware of them.

Still she made no attempt to get up, only said calmly, voice nasally blocked, as if she had a cold, "I accepted some drawings from that girl a few days ago. Sale or return. Do you remember them?"

"I didn't make the connection," Hereward said quietly.

"They were drawings of an old man."

"I didn't see them."

"He was cutting his own throat."

"Yes," Hereward said dully " . . . *What?*"

"The reason I don't want this painting here is that the other night, while you were away, the figure, the likeness of this old man, the old man in the drawings, was seen in our bathroom."

Hereward said nothing.

"Not by me, of course," his wife assured him. "But the man I was sleeping with swears it was there."

Everything was completely still in The Gallery. Hereward Newsome stunned, aware of a droplet of blood about to fall from his chin. Jocasta Newsome lying quietly in the window, red splashes like rose petals on her cream silk blouse.

five

Fay had a whole pile of books and just two short names.

She was alone in the reading room of the County Library in Llandrindod Wells, nearly thirty rural miles from Crybbe, and another world: bright, spacy streets, a spa town.

Two names: Wort and Dee.

Fortunately there was an index to the dozens of volumes of transactions of the Radnorshire Society, a huge collection of many decades of articles by mainly amateur scholars, exploring aspects of the social, political, and natural history of the most sparsely populated county in southern Britain.

There were also books on Tudor history and three biographies of John Dee (1527–1608), whose family came from Radnorshire.

She read of a farmhouse, Nant-y-groes, once the Dee family home, at Pilleth, six miles from Crybbe. But it had, apparently, been demolished and rebuilt and was now unrecognizable as Elizabethan.

Dee himself had been born in the southeast of England, but had always been fascinated by his Welsh border ancestry. The name Dee, it seemed, had probably developed from the Welsh *Du*, meaning black.

History, Fay discovered, had not been overgenerous to this mathematician, astronomer, and expert on navigation—perhaps because of his principal role as astrologer to the court of Elizabeth I and his lifelong obsession with magic and spiritualism. Most schoolchildren learned about Walter Raleigh and Francis Bacon, but John Dee hardly figured on the syllabus, despite having carried out major intelligence operations in Europe, on behalf of the Queen, during periods of Spanish hostility.

Two hours superficial reading convinced Fay that John Dee was basically sound. He studied "natural magic"—a search for an intelligence behind nature. But there was no serious evidence, despite many contemporary and subsequent attempts to smear him, of any involvement in black magic.

Dee wanted to know eternal secrets, the ones he believed no human intelligence could pass on. He sought communion with spirits and "angels," for which a medium was required.

Fay read of several professed psychics, who sometimes turned out to be less well-intentioned than he was. People like the very dubious Sir Edward Kelly, who once claimed the spirits had suggested that, in order to realize their full human potential, he and Dee should swap wives.

Now *that,* Fay thought, was the kind of scam Guy might try to pull.

But there was no mention of Dee working with Sir Michael Wort in Radnorshire.

She skipped over all the weird, impenetrable stuff about Dee's so-called Angelic Conversations and went back to the Radnorshire transactions.

It emerged that while Dee himself might not have been a medium, he clearly was, like Henry Kettle, an expert dowser.

In 1574, he wrote to Elizabeth's Lord Treasurer, Lord Burghley, requesting permission to seek "hidden treasure" using a method that was scientific rather than magical (nothing psychic; Fay smiled) involving a particular type of rod.

He was also most interested in folklore and local customs, druidic lore, and landscape patterns.

OK. Speculation time.

If there were such things as ley-lines, the mounds and stones which defined them must have been far more in evidence in Dee's time.

If ley-lines had psychic properties, Dee's interest in the remains would have been of a more than antiquarian nature.

If he'd been in the area in the 1570s he could hardly have failed to run into Wort.

If Dee felt that Wort had knowledge or psychic abilities he lacked, he might have been inclined to overlook the sheriff's less savory practices.

Fay looked up Wort and found only passing references. No mention of hangings. His name was in a chronological list of high sheriffs, and that was all.

She looked up Trow and found nothing. She looked in the local telephone directories, found several Worts and several Trows, noted down numbers.

Then she simply looked up Crybbe and found surprisingly little, apart from references to the curfew, with the usual stuff about the legacy of Percy Weale, a mention of the town hall as one of the finest in the area.

Had Crybbe received so little attention because, for much of its history, it had been in England? Or was it, as she'd intimated to Powys, because local historians weren't all that common.

It was almost as though nobody *wanted* the place to have a history.

And so Fay emerged from the library with only one significant piece of information.

It came from a brief mention of Crybbe Court in an article dated 1962 about the few surviving manor houses of Radnorshire. Crybbe Court, which the writer said was in dire need of extensive restoration, had been built in the 1570s by a local landowner, Sir Michael Wort, who later served as high sheriff of the county and who lived there *until his death in the summer of 1593.*

It was precisely four centuries since the hanging of Black Michael.

"Oh, what the hell," Colonel Col Croston said. "Don't see why not."

"I'm really very grateful," Guy told him.

It was the first piece of genuine cooperation to come his way. Well, from the locals, anyway. Whether you could call this chap a local was highly debatable, but he *was* the deputy mayor.

As soon as Guy had found out that the public meeting wasn't, after all, going to be chaired by old Preece, he'd driven off by himself to the deputy's home, a partly renovated Welsh longhouse across the river, about a mile out of town on the Ludlow road.

Col Croston had turned out to be an affable, pale-eyed, sparse-haired, athletic-looking chap in his fifties. He lived quite untidily with a couple of Labradors, who rather resembled him, and a tough-looking little wife who didn't. There was a mechanical digger working on a trench fifty yards or so from the house. "Try and ignore the smell," the Colonel had greeted him breezily. "Spot of bother with the old septic tank."

What the deputy mayor had just agreed to was to let Guy shoot a few minutes of videotape in the meeting before it actually started, so there would at least be some pictures of an assembly of townsfolk and councilors. Guy would milk this opportunity for character close-ups of the taciturn, grizzled faces of Old Crybbe.

His heart lurched. He wished he hadn't thought of grizzled old faces. With bulbous noses and bulging eyes and blood fountains from severed arteries.

"And . . . er . . . Colonel," he said hurriedly. "What I'd also like, if you have no objections, is a little interview with you, possibly before and after, outlining the issues—the town's attitudes to becoming a major New Age center."

"Well, I'll do my best, Guy. But I must say, one of the things I was hoping to learn in there tonight is what exactly New Age *is.* Drink?"

"Thanks, just a small one. You like it here, Colonel?"

"Col. Name's Colin. Well, you know, got to settle somewhere. No, it's not a bad place. Once one gets used to their little peculiarities. Like the dogs—used to take these chaps into town of a morning, pick up the paper, that kind of thing. Always well-behaved, never chase anything. But a word or two was said and now I walk them in the other direction. Compromise, you see. Secret of survival in the sticks. I don't mind."

"So if I were to ask you how people here feel about Max Goff and—"

"Ho!" said Mrs. Croston, passing through, wearing stained overalls.

"Ruth's not terribly impressed with Mr. Goff," Col said. "My own feeling is it's no bad thing at all, long as it doesn't get out of hand. You've got to have an economy, and this place has ignored the possibilities of tourism and that kind of business for

too long. Agriculture's going down the chute so, on the whole,
I think we're quite fortunate to have him."

"Will you say that on camera?"

"Oh . . . why not? Long as it's clear I'm speaking personally,
not on behalf of the council."

"Super," Guy said. "Now what about all these prehistoric
stones Goff's sticking in the ground?"

"Ah well, there've been rumblings there, I have to say. Fine
by me, but country folk are incredibly superstitious. Who, after
all, got rid of the original stones? Money, however—money
does tend to overcome quite a lot, doesn't it? But I wouldn't
be at all surprised if some of them started disappearing again."

"Interesting," Guy said. "So you think there'll be fireworks
in there tonight."

Col laughed. "Will there be disagreement? Oh yes. Will there
be suspicion, resentment, resistance? Definitely. Fireworks?
Well, they'll listen very patiently to what Goff has to say,
then they'll ask one or two very polite questions before drifting
quietly away into the night. And then, just as quietly, they'll do
their best to shaft the blighter. That's how things are done in
Crybbe. If they don't like you, best to keep the removal van on
standby with the engine running."

"Doesn't sound as if it would have made very good telly, in
that case, even if we got in."

"Excruciatingly boring telly," Col confirmed. "Unless you've
got some sort of infrared equipment capable of filming under-
currents. 'Nother one?"

"No . . . no thanks." Guy covered his glass with a hand.
"Sounds like you have this place pretty well sized up, Col."

"Good Lord, no. Only been here a few years. That's just
about long enough to realize one needs to've been established
here a good six generations to even get close to it. Annoy
the hell out of me, these newcomers who profess to be like
that"—Col hooked two fingers together—"with the locals after
a month or two. I know where I stand, and I don't mind. We've
got an interesting home with about fourteen acres I'm still trying
to decide what to do with. And I'm the token outsider on the
council, which is just about as close as anyone can aspire to get.
When I'm Mr. Mayor I'll try to effect a few minor structural
changes on the council which will doubtless disappear when
the next chap takes over. Mrs. Byford will see to that—she's

the clerk. Mayors come and go; Mrs. B. doesn't."

"Is that Tessa Byford's mother?" Guy watched the colonel's eyes.

"Grandmother." No specific reaction. "The girl, Tessa, lives with them. What they call in Crybbe a problem child. Shows a lot of promise as an artist, apparently—that's not a very Crybbe thing to be, as you'll have realized. She'll leave, go to college, and never come back. They all do."

"All?"

"Anybody who doesn't want to be a farmer or a shopkeeper or some such. Sad, but that's the way it tends to be."

"Ah," said Guy, "but will she move away *now*—now there's a place for artistic types? Now Crybbe looks set to become a little melting pot for ideas and creativity?"

"Look, Guy, creativity and ideas have always been frowned upon in Crybbe—and, before you ask, no, I certainly won't say any of *that* on camera. 'Nother drink, did I ask you?"

Graham Jarrett was just too smooth, too confident. Powys didn't trust him. He'd wander down to your subconscious like he owned the fishing rights.

"I assure you," Jarrett insisted, "that this is on the level. I've checked dates, I've checked what facts I can, and . . . Now, here's something . . . the Bull. The girl said she lived at the Bull, and as you know there's no such pub in Crybbe anymore. But I've discovered the Bull was actually the original name of the Cock. And that's not a cock-and-bull story . . . " Graham Jarrett straightened his cardigan. "I have it on very reliable authority."

He'd given Powys a transcript of the Catrin tape without argument, because Graham Jarrett wanted to be in The Book, didn't he?

"OK, how many other cases have you encountered where the subject is regressed to the very same town where the regression is taking place?"

"It's been known. Very often they specifically return to a town because they feel they've been there before."

"But she didn't. She came here to work."

Jarrett opened his hands. "Stranger things . . . "

"Yeah, OK. But you've got a situation here where one personality is fading and another just forces its way in over the top, right?"

Graham Jarrett shrank back into the dark-green drapery of his consulting room. Powys was sure there must be more on the tape than there was on the transcript. Jarrett claimed he'd given the cassette to Guy, but he wouldn't have done that before making a copy.

"I know what you're going to suggest, Joe."

"Well?"

"Don't. Don't even use that word 'possession' in here."

There was a bonus for Guy in his visit to Col Croston's house. He'd raised the matter of the suicide, the old man and the razor, less inhibited about it now and less intimidated by it as time went on. There'd been no disturbance in his room at the Cock last night, unless one included Catrin's shrill moments of ecstasy. Catrin had been quite amazing. With the light out.

"No," Col Croston said. "Can't say I have." But he'd referred the question to his wife, neither of them, fortunately, seeming overcurious about Guy's interest in local suicides.

"I know," Mrs. Croston had said. "Why not ask Gomer. Gomer knows everything."

The little man working on the leaching field to the Crostons' septic tank had been only too happy to come out of his trench for a chat. There was a disgustingly ripe smell in the vicinity of the trench, and Guy found that he and Gomer Parry were very soon left alone.

"Good chap, the Colonel," Gomer said. " 'Ad this other job lined up, over to Brynglas, see, and it was postponed, last minute. Straightaway, the Colonel says, you stick around, boy, do my septic. Fills in two days perfect. Very considerate man, the Colonel."

It didn't take Guy long to get a reaction on the suicide. Unlike most people in this area, Gomer appeared to have a healthy appetite for the unpleasant.

"Handel Roberts." Gomer beamed. "Sure to be."

And who precisely was Handel Roberts?

"Copper," said Gomer. "While back now. I wasn't so old, but I remember Handel Roberts all right. Didn't Wynford tell you about this? No, I s'pose 'e wouldn't. Coppers, see. They don't gossip about their own."

Gomer broke off to wipe something revolting from his glasses with an oily rag.

He blinked at Guy. "That's better. Aye, Handel Roberts. He was station sergeant, see, like Wynford. Only there was twice as many police in them days, before there was any crime to speak of—there's logic, isn't it? Well, this was the time they'd built the new police 'ouses as part of the council estate. And it comes to Handel retiring and the County Police lets him carry on living in the old police 'ouse, nominal rent, sort of thing, everybody happy. Until—I forget the details—but some new police authority takes over and they decides the old police 'ouse is worth a bob or two so they'll sell it."

Guy could see where this was going. Old Handel Roberts, unable to afford the place, no savings, nowhere to go.

Nowhere but the bathroom.

"Ear to ear," Gomer said with a big grin. "Blood everywhere. But 'e 'ad the last laugh, the old boy did. They couldn't sell the police 'ouse after that, not for a long time. And then it was a cheap job, see. Billy Byford 'ad it for peanuts. Newly wed at the time—Nettie played 'ell, wouldn't move in till Billy stripped that bathroom back to the bare brick, put in new basin, bath, lavvy."

Guy said delicately, "And he still, er, that is, Handel Roberts was believed to haunt the place, I gather."

"Well, you're better informed than what I am," Gomer said. "Anything funny going on there, Nettie'd've been off like a rabbit. Oh hell, aye. Want me to tell you all this for the telly cameras? No problem, just gimme time to get cleaned up, like."

"No, no . . . just something I needed to check."

"Anything else you wanner know, you'll find me around most of the week. 'Ad this job lined up with the council, but it's been put back, so I'm available, see, anytime."

"That's very kind of you indeed, Gomer. I won't hesitate. Oh, there is one final thing . . . Handel Roberts, what did he look like?"

Gomer indulged in a long sniff. He seemed immune to the appalling stench from the septic tank.

"Big nose is all I remember, see. Hell of a big nose."

Powys drove to Fay's house, but there was no one in. He didn't know where else to go, so he sat there in the Mini, in Bell Street. It was two-thirty. He'd bought some chips for lunch and ended up dumping most of them in a litter bin, feeling sick.

He'd learned from Graham Jarrett that Rachel's body had
been sent for burial to her parents' home—somewhere in Essex,
Jarrett thought. He ought to find out, send flowers, with a
message.

Saying what? *I think I know why you died, Rachel. You
died because of a cat. A cat placed in the rafters to ward off
evil spirits. You died because a four-hundred-year-old dead cat
can't hurl itself from the building. Because somebody has to be
holding it and, unfortunately for you, nobody else was around
at the time.*

The Bottle Stone was no more than a sick coincidence, albeit
the kind that questioned the whole nature of coincidence.

But the cat had been part of the ritual procedure to prevent
something returning. Before the spirit could regain its occupancy, the cat had to go.

Just a little formality.

Powys took a tight hold of the steering wheel.

I am not a crank.

six

Powys waited half an hour for Fay. She didn't show. He couldn't
blame her if she'd just taken off somewhere for the night or
possibly forever, she and Arnold, battle-scarred refugees from
the Old Golden Land.

Leaving him to convince Goff that the Crybbe project was a
blueprint for a small-scale Armageddon.

On impulse, he started the car and drove slowly through the
town toward the Court.

The afternoon was dull and humid. The buildings bulged, as
though the timber frames were contracting, squeezing the bricks
into dust. And the people on the streets looked drained and

zombified, as if debilitated by some organic power failure affecting the central nervous system or the blood supply.

Which made Powys think of Fay's dad, the old canon, whose blood supply had been impeded but who now was fast becoming a symbol of the efficacy of New Age spiritual healing.

Maybe everybody here could use a prescription from Jean Wendle's Dr. Chi. Maybe, in fact, Jean, the acceptable, self-questioning face of the New Age, was the person he ought to be talking to this afternoon.

But first he would find Goff and, with any luck, Andy too. Sooner or later Andy had to resurface. It seemed very unlikely, for instance, that he wouldn't be at tonight's public meeting.

Rachel had said Goff was "besotted with Boulton-Trow." If there was indeed a sexual element, that would mean complications. But Goff wasn't stupid.

However, even as he drove into the lane beside the church he was getting cold feet about making a direct approach to Goff, and when he arrived at the Court he saw why it was useless.

Something had changed. Something with its beginnings, perhaps, in an effluvial flickering in the eaves two nights ago.

Powys drove out of the wood, between the gateposts, and, when the Court came into view, he had to stop the car.

You didn't have to be psychic to experience it.

Where, before, it had worn this air of dereliction, of crumbling neglect, of seeping decay—the atmosphere which had caused Henry Kettle to record in his journal,

. . . the Court is a dead place, no more than a shell. I can't get anything from the Court . . .

—it was now a distinct and awesome presence, as if its ancient foundations had been reinforced, its Elizabethan stonework strengthened. As if it was rising triumphantly from its hollow, the old galleon finally floating free from the mud flats.

He knew that, structurally, nothing at all had altered, that he was still looking at the building he'd first seen less than a week ago as a shambling pile of neglect.

It had simply been restored to life.

Its power supply reconnected.

Occupancy regained.

There was a glare from the rearview mirror. The Mini was stopped in the middle of the narrow drive, blocking the path of a big, black sports car. Goff's Ferrari, headlights flashing. As Powys released the handbrake, prepared to get out of the way, the Ferrari's driver's door opened and Goff squeezed out, raising a hand.

Powys switched the engine off.

"J.M.! Where ya been?"

Goff, untypically, was in a dark double-breasted suit over a white open-necked shirt. He looked strong and, for a man of his girth, buoyantly fit.

"You're a very elusive guy, J.M. I've been calling you on the phone, putting out messages. Listen, that problem with the cops . . . that's sorted out now?"

"I'd like to think so, Max."

"Fucking arsehole cops can't see further than the end of their own truncheons. They got so little real crime to amuse them in these parts, they can't accept a tragic accident for what it is."

Powys said nothing. He was pretty sure Goff must have known about him and Rachel.

"Listen," Goff said, "the reason I've been trying to track you down—I need you at the meeting tonight. I don't anticipate problems, I think the majority of people in Crybbe are only too glad to see the place get a new buzz. But . . . *but* I'm the first to recognize they might find me a little—how can I put this?—overwhelming? Larger than life? Larger than *their* lives, anyhow. You, on the other hand . . . you're a downbeat kind of guy, J.M. Nobody's gonna call you flash, nobody's gonna call you weird."

"That a compliment, Max?"

Goff laughed delightedly and clapped Powys on the shoulder. "Just be there, J.M. I might need you."

Powys nodded compliantly, then said casually, "Where's Andy these days, Max?"

Goff's little eyes went watchful. "He's around."

"Just for the record . . . this whole idea, the idea of coming to Crybbe. That was Andy's, wasn't it?"

"It was mine," Goff said coldly.

"But you did know about Andy's ancestral links with the Court?"

Dangerous ground, Powys. Watch his eyes.

Goff said, "You got a problem with that?"

"I was just intrigued that nobody talks about it."

"Maybe that's not yet something you advertise." Goff went quiet, obviously thinking something over. Then he put a hand on Powys's shoulder.

"J.M., come over here." He steered Powys into the center of the drive, to where the Court opened out before them like an enormous pop-up book. "Will you look at that? I mean really look."

Powys did, and felt, uncomfortably, that the house was looking back at him.

"J.M., this was once the finest house in the county. Not that it had much competition—this part of the border's never been a wealthy area—but it was something to be envied. You can imagine what it musta been like. This introverted, taciturn region where, by tradition, survival means keeping your head down. And this guy builds a flaming *palace*. Well, jeez—to these people, they're looking at a Tower of Babel situation. Here's a guy who takes a pride in the place he lives, who loves this countryside, who wants to make a statement about that. They couldn't get a handle on any of it, these working farmers, these ... *peasants.*"

Powys said, to get the name out, "Sir Michael Wort."

"Listen, this guy has been seriously maligned."

"He hanged people."

"Goddamn it, J.M., *all* high sheriffs hanged people."

"In the attic?"

"Arguably more humane than public execution. But, yeah, OK, that was the other thing about him they couldn't handle. He was a scientist. And a philosopher. He wanted to know where he came from and where he was going to. He wanted to find—what's that phrase?—the active force ... "

"The force above human reason which is the active principle in nature."

"Yeah."

"Definition of natural magic. John Dee."

"Yeah. I got this Oxford professor who's so eminent I don't get to name him till he comes through with it, but this guy's doing a definitive paper on the collaboration between John Dee and Wort. Has access to a whole pile of hitherto unknown correspondence."

"From the Wort side?" Powys thought of Andy's Filofax, wondered whether the professor had been given *all* the correspondence.

"Maybe. Yeah. Maybe, also, some of Dee's papers that came into Wort's possession, all authenticated material. This is heavy stuff, J.M. Point is, you can imagine how the people hereabouts reacted to it back in the sixteenth century?"

"Pretty much the way some of them are reacting to your ideas now, I should have thought." Powys wondering how Dee's private notes—if that was what they were—had fallen into Wort's hands. Unless Wort had taken steps to acquire them in order to remove any proof of the collaboration.

"They drove Wort to suicide, the people around here. A witch hunt by ignorant damn peasants, threatening to burn down the Court." Goff stood up straight, his back to his domain. "Tell you one thing, J.M. No fucker's gonna threaten to burn *me* out."

"You do have this one small advantage. You haven't hanged anybody. Yet."

Goff laughed. "You really wanna know about this hanging stuff, doncha? Listen, how many people get the opportunity to study precisely what happens when life is extinguished? When the spirit leaves the body?"

"Doctors do. Priests do."

Goff shook his head. "They got other things on their minds. The doctor's trying to save the dying person, the priest's trying to comfort him or whatever else priests do, last rites kinda stuff."

Powys saw Goff's eyes go curiously opaque.

"Only the watcher at the execution can be entirely dispassionate," Goff said. Powys could tell he was echoing someone else. "Only he can truly observe."

seven

On a helter-skelter hill road, a mile and a half out of Crybbe, there was a spot where you could park near a wicket gate with a public-footpath sign. The path, quite short, linked up with the Offa's Dyke long-distance footpath and was itself a famous viewpoint. From just the other side of the gate, you could look across about half the town. You could see the church tower and the edge of the square, with one corner of the Cock. You could see the slow, silvery river.

From up here, under a sporadic sprinkling of sunlight from a deeply textured sky, Crybbe looked venerable, self-contained, and almost dignified.

It was nearly 5 P.M.

They'd come out here because there were secrets to exchange which neither felt could be exchanged in Crybbe; there was always a feeling that the town itself would eavesdrop.

When Powys had returned to Bell Street, Fay had been in her car outside, with Arnold. "Dad's not back yet. Tried to steel myself to go in. Couldn't do it alone. Feeble woman chickens out."

"Well, if you've left anything in there that you want *me* to fetch," he said, "forget it."

"I suspect you're being indirectly patronizing there, Powys, but I'll let it go."

Her eye actually looked worse, the rainbow effect quite spectacular. Part of the healing process, no doubt. He was surprised how glad he was to see her again.

Although there must be no involvement. Not this time.

Up here the air was fresher, and a gust of wind carrying a few drops of rain hit them like a sneeze. It was unexpected and blew Arnold over; he got up again, looking disgruntled.

"I'm beginning to feel I'm part of Andy's game," Joe Powys said. "Suppose he left all that stuff in the bread oven for me to find, to give me a chance to figure it all out—while knowing there was nothing I could do about it."

"And *have* you figured it out?" Fay asked.

"Black Andy," Powys said. "I mean . . . Black Andy? How can anyone called Andy possibly be evil? Andy Hitler, Andy Capone. Andy the Hun, Andy the Ripper."

"So you're convinced now. It's Andy Wort?"

"Families often change their name if something's brought it into disrepute. Why shouldn't they simply reverse it?"

"I made some inquiries. That's why I was late. There are no Worts left in Crybbe. What remained of the family seems to have sold up everything—well, *nearly* everything—and moved down to the West Country. As for the Bottle Stone . . ."

"Please," Powys said. "Let's not . . . I think that whole episode was Andy trying out his emergent skills, weaving a fantasy around a stone, creating a black-magic ritual, seeing what happened."

"Yes, but . . ."

"Look down there," Powys said. "Goff's prehistoric theme park. The old stones back in place."

They could see a sizable megalith at a point where the river curved like a sickle.

"On that bit of tape you played me, Henry was puzzled by a standing stone he'd located because it didn't seem to be an *old* stone. He recorded the same problem in his journal. Experienced dowsers can date a stone with the pendulum, asking it questions—too complicated to explain, but it seems to work. Anyway, Henry noted that he couldn't date this particular stone back beyond 1593 . . . *when it was destroyed.*"

"After Wort's death. The townsfolk destroyed the stones after his death."

"Perhaps they were advised to . . . to stop him coming back along the spirit paths. But the point is . . . perhaps Henry couldn't date the thing earlier than 1593 *because that was also when it was erected.*"

There was another gust of wind, and the blue raincoat Fay carried under her arm billowed behind her like a wind sock.

"*Wort* erected the old stones of Crybbe. They weren't prehistoric at all. He was marking out his own spirit paths, along which he believed he could travel outside of his body."

"Are we saying here that Wort—perhaps in collaboration with John Dee—had created his own ley-lines . . . ?"

"Look," Powys said. "There's this growing perception of leys as ghost roads . . . paths reserved for the spirits . . . therefore, places where you could contact spirits. Sacred arteries linking two worlds—or two states of consciousness. New Agers say they're energy lines—in their eternal quest for something uplifting, they're discarding the obvious: leys tend to link up a number of burial sites—tumps, barrows, cemeteries, this kind of thing."

"No healing rays?"

Powys shrugged. "Whether this rules out the energy-line theory I don't know—we might just be talking about a different kind of energy. There's certainly a lot of evidence of psychic phenomena along leys or at points where they cross. And ghosts need energy to manifest, so we're told."

"And Crybbe, for some reason, has all these curious pockets of energy, fluctuations causing power cuts, all this . . . "

"I'd be interested to know how many people in Crybbe have seen a ghost or experienced something unnatural. Hundreds, I'd guess. Especially along the main line, which comes down from the Tump, through the Court, the church, the square . . . and along the passage leading to your studio. I'm surprised nothing strange has happened to you in there, with this kind of hermetically sealed broadcasting area."

"Maybe it has."

"Oh?"

"I don't think I want to talk about it," Fay said, tasting Electrovoice microphone. "Look . . . " She spread out the raincoat on the damp grass at the edge of a small escarpment overlooking the town. She patted it. They both sat down.

"Let's not mess about anymore," Fay said. "We're not kids. We've both had some distinctly unpleasant experiences in this town. Let's not be clever or pseudoscientific about this. Let's not talk about light effects or atmospheric anomalies. I've had it with all that bullshit. So. In simple, colloquial English, what's actually happening here?"

She looked down on Crybbe. The sky had run out of sunlight, and it was once again a mean, cramped little town surrounded by pleasant, rolling countryside, to which the inhabitants seemed entirely oblivious. Almost as if they were deliberately turning their backs on it all, living simple, functional lives on the lowest practical level, without joy, without beauty, without humor, without any particular faith, without . . .

"I've had a thought about the Crybbe mentality," Fay said. "But you're the expert, you go first."

"OK," Powys said. "This is what I think. I reckon Andy's got hold of a collection of family papers—may have had them years, for all I know—relating to Wort's experiments. Some of them seem to have been written by an outsider, perhaps John Dee, relating how Wort came to visit him—*in spirit*—using what he calls the 'old road.' "

"Wort was haunting him?"

"No, I think Wort was alive then. I'd guess he'd found a way . . . You said you wanted this straight . . . ?"

"Yes, yes, go on."

"OK. A way to project his spirit—that's his astral body—along the leys, in much the same way as it's suggested the old shamans used to do it, or at least *believed* they could do it."

"The psychic departure lounge," said Fay.

"Glib, but it wasn't far out. And I've seen a transcript of the so-called regression of Catrin Jones. The character assumed by Catrin seems to be suggesting that not only was the sheriff bonking her—and quite a few other women—on a fairly regular basis in his physical body, but that he was also able to observe them while not actually there in the flesh."

"Quite a bastard."

Powys nodded. "And in conclusion she says something on the lines of, 'He swears he'll never leave me . . . never.' Which suggests to me that Wort believed he would still be able to use these spirit paths, these astral thoroughfares, *after his death*. Except there's something stopping him, so he can only actually manifest as a . . . black dog or whatever."

"The curfew."

"Every night at ten o'clock somebody goes up the church tower and rings the curfew bell one hundred times, and when the bell sounds, the energy which has been gathering along the leys is released and dissipated. We know this happens, we've both experienced it."

Fay stood up, held out a hand. "Come on. I'll tell you my theory about the Crybbe mentality."

She led him a few paces along the footpath, Arnold hobbling along between them, until the town square came into view, the buildings so firmly defined under the moldering sky that she felt she could reach out and pinch slates from the roofs. They stood on the ridge and watched a school bus stop in the square. A Land Rover pulling a trailer carrying two sheep had to wait behind the bus. Traffic chaos hits Crybbe.

Fay extended an arm, like a music-hall director on the edge of a stage.

"Miserable little closed-in town, right? Sad, decrepit, morose."

"Right," said Powys, cautiously.

"The border mentality," Fay shouted into the wind. "Play your cards close to your chest. Don't take sides until you know who's going to win. Here in Crybbe the whole attitude's intensified, and it operates on every level. Particularly spiritual."

A big crow landed on the wicket gate and watched them.

Powys said, thoughtfully, "But there isn't any noticeable spirituality in Crybbe."

"Precisely. You've seen them in church, sitting there like dummies. Drives Murray mad. But they're just keeping their heads down. *Never take sides until you know who's winning.* Doesn't matter who the sides are. The Welsh or the English. Good or evil."

Fay's raincoat rose up from the ground in the wind, and the crow flew off the gate, cawing. Fay went back and scooped up the raincoat.

Powys said, "Strength in apathy?"

"Joe, look . . . being a vicar's daughter isn't all about keeping your frock clean and not pinching the cream cakes at the fête. You learn a few things. Confrontation between good and evil is high-octane stuff. The risks are high, so most people stay on the sidelines. Even vicars . . . What am I saying? . . . *Especially* vicars. But maybe it's harder to do that in Crybbe because the psychic pressure is so much greater, so they have to keep their heads even lower down."

"Neither good nor evil can thrive in a place without a soul. Who was it said that?"

"Probably you. More to the point, 'We don't like clever people round yere.' Who said *that?"*

"Wynford Wiley. The copper."

"Well, there you are. We don't like clever people. Says it all, doesn't it."

"Does it?"

"Yes ... because, for centuries, Crybbe's been avoiding making waves, disturbing the psychic ether or whatever you call it. If anybody happens to see a ghost, they keep very quiet about it until it goes away. Don't do anything to encourage them, don't give them any ... energy to play with. If they see the black dog, they try and ignore it, they don't want it to get ideas above its station. How am I doing so far?"

"Go on."

"Traditionally, dogs react to spirits, don't they? Dogs howl, right? Dogs howl when someone dies because they can see the spirit drifting away. So, in Crybbe, dogs simply get phased out. Maybe they've even forgotten *why* they don't like them, but traditions soon solidify in a place like this. The dogs, the curfew, there may be others we don't know anything about. But, anyway, suddenly ... "

"The town's flooded with clever people. Max Goff and his New Agers."

"Absolutely the worst kind of clever people," said Fay. "Dabblers in this and that."

The rain came in on the breeze. Pulling on the blue raincoat, Fay looked down into the town and saw that the air appeared motionless there; it was probably still quite humid in the shadow of the buildings.

"It's hard to believe," Powys said, "that Andy didn't know about all this when he planted on Goff the idea of establishing a New Age center in Crybbe. Especially if he's a descendant of Michael Wort. He'd know it could generate a psychic explosion down there, and maybe ... Christ ... "

He took Fay's hand and squeezed it. The hand felt cold.

" ... maybe generate enough negative energy to invoke Michael Wort in a more meaningful form. Get him beyond the black-dog stage. Of course he bloody knew."

"In just over three hours' time," Fay said, "the public meeting begins. Crybbe versus the New Age. Lots of *very* negative energy there."

part eight

❈❈❈❈❈❈❈❈❈ ═══════

Let us forget about evil. This does not exist. What does exist is imbalance, and when you are severely imbalanced, particularly in the negative direction, you can behave in very extreme and unpleasant ways.

DAVID ICKE,
Love Changes Everything

one

Even for Crybbe the night was rising early.

It rose from within the shadowed places. In the covered alleyway behind the Cock. Beneath the three arches of the river bridge. In the soured, spiny woodland which started where the churchyard ended, with a black marble gravestone identifying the place where Grace Legge, beloved wife of Canon A. L. Peters, was presumed to rest.

It filtered from the dank cellars of the buildings hunched around the square like old, morose drinking companions.

It was nurtured in the bushes at the base of the Tump.

It began to spread like a slow stain across the limp, white canopy of the sky, tinting it a deep and sorrowful gray.

And not yet seven-thirty.

"Give us a white-balance," Larry Ember said, and Catrin Jones stood in the middle of the street and held up her clipboard for him to focus on.

Guy Morrison looked at the sky. "Shoot everything you can get. I can't see it brightening up again. I think this is it."

"Wasn't forecast," Larry said. "No thunderstorms."

"And I can't see there being one in there," Guy said, glancing at the town hall. "This is probably a wasted exercise."

"What you want me to do, then, boss?"

"We've got permission to go in and grab some shots of the assembly before it starts, so shoot absolutely everything you can, plenty of tight shots of faces, expressions—I'll point out a few. Then just hang on in there till they actually ask you to leave, and then . . . well, stay outside, close to the door, and Catrin and I will try and haul out a few with opinions. Though I'll be very surprised if these yokels manage to muster a single opinion between them."

The Victorian façade of the town hall reared over the shallow street like a gloomy Gothic temple, its double doors spread

wide to expose a great cave mouth, through which the younger
townsfolk wandered like tourists. Many had probably never been
inside before; there weren't many public gatherings in Crybbe.

Guy ordered shots of their faces, shots of their feet. The
feet are probably saying more than the faces, he thought in
frustration. At least they're moving.

For the first time he began to wonder how he was going to
avoid making a stupefyingly boring documentary. He'd been
determined to keep the voice-over down to a minimum, letting
events tell their own story. But to get away with that, one needed
a pithy commentary on these events from a collection of outspoken locals. So far, the only outspoken local he'd encountered
had been Gomer Parry, who lived at least three miles outside
the town.

"What are we going to do?" he whispered despairingly to
Catrin—showing weakness to an assistant, he *never* did that.

Catrin gave his thigh a reassuring squeeze. "It'll be fine."

" . . . God's sake, Catrin, not in public!"

Catrin. How *could* he have?

This place was destroying him.

Parking his Escort XR3 in the old cattle market behind the
square, Gavin Ashpole had no fears at all about *his* story being
boring.

This was the beauty of radio. The place might *look* like a
disused cemetery, but you could make it *sound* like bloody
Beirut. Whatever happened here tonight, Gavin was going to
put down a hard-hitting voice-piece for the ten-o'clock news
describing the uproar, as beleaguered billionaire Max Goff faced
a verbal onslaught by hundreds of angry townsfolk fearing an
invasion by hippie convoys lured to the New Age Mecca.

Somebody had suggested to Gavin that perhaps he could try
out the new radio car on this one. Park right outside the meeting,
send in some live on-the-spot stuff for the nine-thirty news.

Gavin thought not; the station's only unattended studio was
not three minutes' walk from the town hall.

And he hadn't been able to drag his mind away from last
night's interrupted fantasy in that same studio. Somehow, he
had to get little Ms. Morrison in there.

Ms. Morrison who'd really screwed any chance she had of
holding down the Offa's Dyke contract. Who'd failed to provide

a report on last night's tractor accident. Who hadn't even been reachable on the phone all day.

"I'll go in live at nine-thirty," he'd told the night-shift sub, James Barlow. "And I want a full two minutes. I don't care what else happens."

He was thinking about this as he parked his car in the old livestock market. Unusually dark this evening; even the sky looked in the mood for a set-to.

Humid, though. Gavin took off his jacket, locked it in the trunk, and slung his Uher over his shoulder.

Two cars and a Land Rover followed him into the market. Half a dozen men got out. Tweed suits, caps, no chat, no smiles. Farmers, in town for the meeting, meaning business.

I like it, Gavin told himself. Everybody who was anybody in the district was going to be here tonight to listen, with varying degrees of enthusiasm or hostility, to Goff's crazy, hippie schemes. There was a small danger that if the opposition was too heavy, Goff might have second thoughts and decide to take his New Age center somewhere else—like out of Offa's Dyke's patch, which would be no use at all. But this was highly unlikely; Goff wasn't a quitter and he'd probably already invested more than Gavin could expect to earn in the next ten years, even if he did become managing editor. No, Goff had gone too far to pull out. Too many people relying on him. Danger of too much bad publicity on a national scale if he let them down.

He crossed the square and followed everybody else into the side street leading to the town hall.

Gavin quickened his pace and walked up between a couple—skinny guy with a ratty beard and a rather sultry wife. Gavin *had* to walk between the man and woman because they were so far apart, not talking to each other. Obviously had had a row.

That was what he liked to see. Acrimony and tension were the core of all the best news stories. It was building in the air.

Gavin mentally rubbed his hands.

Alex and Jean were taking tea in the drawing room.

The canon, wearing his faded Kate Bush T-shirt, was standing in front of the Chinese fire screen, legs comfortably apart, cup and saucer effortlessly balanced in hands perfectly steady.

Earlier, he'd spotted himself in a mirror and it had been like looking at an old photograph. Hair all fluffed up, the famous twinkle terrifyingly potent again. Old boy's a walking advert for the Dr. Chi New Age Clinic.

He was aware that Jean Wendle had been looking at him too, with a certain pride, and several times today they had exchanged little smiles.

"So." Jean was on the sofa, hands linked behind her head. Jolly pert little body for her age. "Shall we go? Or shall we stay in?"

Several times today she'd looked at him like that. Just a quick glance. One really was rather too old to jump to conclusions; however . . .

"Which do you think would be most, er, stimulating?"

"Och, that depends," Jean said, "on what turns you on. Perhaps your poor old brain is ready at last for the intellectual stimulus of public debate, as Max strives to present himself, gift-wrapped, to the stoical burghers of Crybbe."

"Give me strength," said Alex.

"Fay'll be there, no doubt."

"Won't want *me* in her hair."

"Or there's Grace. All alone in Bell Street. Will she be worried, perhaps, that you haven't been home for a couple of nights?"

"I thought you said she didn't exist as anything more than a light form."

"She didn't. Unfortunately, she's become a monster."

"Uh?" Alex lost his twinkle.

"Tell me," Jean said. "Have you ever performed an exorcism?"

The Cock was no brighter than a Victorian funeral parlor; Denzil, the owner, no more expressive than a resident corpse. Half past eight and only two customers—all his regulars over at the town hall.

J. M. Powys stared despairingly into his orange juice, back in his habitual state of confusion. Everything had seemed so clear on the hillside overlooking the town, when Fay was aglow with insight.

Arnold lay silently under the table. Possibly the first dog in several centuries to set foot—all three of them—in the public bar of the Cock. "We can't," Fay had warned. "Sod it," Powys had replied, following the dog up the steps. "I've had enough of this. Who's going to notice? Who's going to care?"

And, indeed, now they were inside there was nobody except Denzil to care, and Denzil didn't notice, not for a while.

Powys glanced up at Fay across the table. "It could all be crap," he said.

"There." Fay was drinking tomato juice; it was a night for clear heads. "You see . . . "

"What?"

"You're back in Crybbe. You're doubting yourself. You're thinking, what the hell, why bother? It's easy to see, isn't it, why, after four centuries, the apathy's become so ingrained."

"Except that it could, though, couldn't it? It could all be crap."

"And we're just two weirdos from Off trying to make a big deal out of something because we don't fit in."

"And if it's not—not crap—what can we do about it?"

"Excuse me, sir." Denzil was standing by their table, low-browed, heavy-jowled. He picked up their empty glasses.

"Thanks," Powys said. "We'll have a couple more of the same." Glanced at Fay. "OK?"

Fay nodded glumly.

"No you won't," Denzil said. "Not with that dog in yere you won't."

"I'm sorry?"

"Don't allow no dogs in yere."

Powys said mildly, "Where does it say that?"

"You what, sir?"

"Where does it say, 'no dogs'?"

"We never 'ad no sign, sir, because . . . "

"Because you never had no dogs before. Now, this is interesting." Powys tried to catch his eye; impossible. "We're the only customers. There's nobody else to serve. So perhaps you could spell out—in detail—what this town has against the canine species. Take your time. Give us a considered answer. We've got hours and hours."

Powys sat back and contemplated the owner, who looked away. The bar smelled of polish and the curdled essence of last night's beer.

"No hurry," Powys said. "We've got all night."

Denzil turned to him at last and Powys thought, Yes he does . . . He really does look like a malignant troll.

"Mr. Powys," Denzil said slowly. "You're a clever man . . . "

"And we . . . " said Fay, " . . . we don't like clever people round yere." And collapsed helplessly into giggles.

Denzil's expression didn't change. "No more drinks," he said. "Get out."

It was getting so dark so early that Mrs. Seagrove decided it would be as well to draw the curtains to block out that nasty old mound. Ugly as a slag heap, Frank used to say it was.

The curtains were dark-blue Dralon. Behind curtains like this, you could pretend you were living somewhere nice.

"There," she said. "That's better, isn't it, Frank?"

Frank didn't reply, just nodded as usual. He'd never had much to say, had Frank. Just sat there in his favorite easy chair, his own arms stretched along the chair arms. Great capacity for stillness, Frank had.

"I feel so much safer with you here," Mrs. Seagrove said to her late husband.

two

Like an old castle, the church was, when the light was going, with the tower and the battlements all black.

Something to *really* break into. Not like a garage or a school or a newsagent's. Magic, this was, when you got in, standing there in the great echoey space, shouting out "fuck" and "piss."

When you broke into a church, there was like an edge to it.

Sacrilege. What did it mean? What did it really mean? Religion was about being bored. They used to make him come here when he was a kid. Just you sit there, Warren, and keep it shut until they gives you a hymn to sing . . . and don't sing so bloody loud next time, you tryin' to show us up?

So when he stood here and shouted "fuck" and "piss," who was he shouting it at? His family, or the short-tempered ole God they didn't like to disturb by singing too loud?

Tonight he didn't have to break in; nobody'd bothered to lock the place after he'd done the window in the vestry, when he'd been up the belfry and then doled out this plate of dog food on the altar.

Still couldn't figure why he'd done that. Tessa's idea, she'd given him the can. Next time she'd have to explain. He was taking no more orders, not from anybody.

Warren ground his teeth and brought his foot back and slammed it into the side door, wanting to kick it in, anyway. Because it was a rotten old door that'd needed replacing years ago. Because he wanted to hear the latch splintering off its screws.

And because he wanted Jonathon to know he was coming.

Me again, Jonathon. You don't get no peace, bro, till you're in the ground.

There was a real rage in him tonight that just went on growing and growing, the more he thought about that bastard Goff and the way he'd tricked him. Warren could see right through the layers of blubber to the core of this fat phony. The *real* reason he'd had a nice letter sent back to Warren with the tape was he didn't know how Warren's granddad stood on the question of Warren's being a professional musician—for all Goff knew the old git couldn't been "supportive," as they said. And the old git was the mayor, and Goff couldn't afford to offend *him.*

Warren got out his Stanley knife, *the* Stanley knife, and swaggered up the aisle to the coffin, saw its whitish gleam from this window over the altar that used to be stained glass, only the bloody ole stained bits blew out, once, in a gale, on account the lead was mostly gone, and they filled it up with plain, frosted glass like you got in the windows of public lavs—typical, that, of the cheapo bastards who ran the Church.

Anyway, what was left of the white light shone down on reliable, steady, trustworthy ole Jonathon.

Saint Jonathon now.

He flicked out the blade, felt his lips curling back into a tight snarl as he sucked in a hissing breath and dug the point into the polished lid, dagger-style, and then wrenched it back, getting two hands to it, one over the other.

Sssccccreeeeagh!!!!!

Remember me, Jonathon?

I'm your brother. I was there when you died. Maybe you don't remember that. Wasn't a chance I could very well miss, though, was it? Not when that feller sets it up for me so nice, chucking the ole gun in the drink—couldn't go back without that, could you, bro? Couldn't face the ole man . . . steady, reliable, old Jonathon lost the bloody family-heirloom shooter.

Didn't see me, did you? Didn't see me lying under the hedge, the other side of the bank? Well, people don't, see. I'm good at that, even if I don't know nothing about farming and I'm a crap guitarist.

Always been good at not being seen and watching and listening. And you gets better at that when you know they don't give a shit for you, not any of the buggers. You learn to watch out for yourself, see.

Anyway, so there you are, wading across the river, getting closer and closer to my side. Hey, listen . . . how many times did the ole man tell us when we were kids: Never get tempted to cross the river, that ole riverbed's not stable, see, full of these gullies.

See, you might not remember this next bit, being you were in a bit of trouble at the time, like, bit of a panic, churning up the water something cruel. And, like, if you did see me, well, you might still be thinking I was trying to rescue you, brotherly love, all that shit.

Might've thought I was trying to hold your head above *the water. Well, fair play, that's an easy mistake to make when you're floundering about doing your best not to get yourself drowned.*

Anyway, you failed, Jonathon.

Gotter admit, it's not often a bloke gets the chance like that to drown his goodie-goodie, smart-arse, chairman of the Young Farmers' brother, is it?

Worth getting your old trainers soaked for any day, you ask me.

Gotter laugh, though, Jonathon. Gotter laugh.

* * *

It was quite impressive inside. Late nineteenth century perhaps. High-ceilinged, white-walled. And a white elephant, now, Guy thought, with no proper council anymore.

He was watching from the entrance at the back of the hall, while Larry Ember was doing a shot from the stage at the front. People were pointing at Larry, whispering, shuffling in their seats. Real fly-on-the-wall stuff *this* was going to be, with half the people staring straight into the lens, looking hostile.

"Make it quick, Guy, will you," Col Croston said behind a hand. "I've been approached about six times already by people objecting to your presence."

Catrin said, "Do they know who he *is?*"

"Stay out of this, Catrin," said Guy. "Col, we'll have the camera out within a couple of minutes. But as it's a public meeting, I trust nobody will try to get *me* out."

"I should sit at the back, all the same," Col said without opening his mouth.

"Look!" Larry Ember suddenly bawled out at the audience, leaping up from his camera, standing on the makeshift wooden stage, exasperated, hands on his hips. "Stop bleedin' looking at me! Stop pointing at me! You never seen a telly camera before? Stone me, it's worse than little kids screaming 'Hello, Mum.' Pretend I'm not here, can't yer?"

"Maybe you *shouldn't* be yere, then," a man shouted back.

"Sorry about this," Guy said to Col Croston. "Larry's not terribly good at public relations."

"Better get him out," Col said. "I'm sorry, Guy."

"I suspect we're all going to be sorry before the night's out," Guy said, unknowingly blessed, for the first time in his life, with the gift of prophecy.

A hush hit the hall, and Guy saw Larry swing his arms, and his camera, in a smooth arc as though he'd spotted trouble at the back of the room.

The hush came from the front left of the hall, occupied by members of the New Age community and—farther back—other comparative newcomers to the town. The other side of the hall, where the Crybbe people sat, was already as quiet as a funeral.

The hush was a response to the arrival of Max Goff. Only the

trumpet fanfare, Guy thought, was missing. Goff was accompanied. An entourage.

First came Hilary Ivory, wife of the tarotist, carrying her
snowy hair wound up on top, like a blazing white torch. Her
bony, nervy husband, Adam, was way back, behind Goff, even
behind Graham Jarrett in his pale-green safari suit. There were
some other people Guy recognized from last Friday's lunch party,
including the noted feminist astrologer with the ring through her
nose and a willowy redhead specializing in dance therapy. There
were also some accountant-looking men in John Major–style
summerweight gray suits.

Max Goff, in the familiar white double-breasted and a velvet
bow tie, looked to Guy like a superior and faintly nasty teddy
bear, the kind that wealthy American ladies kept on their beds
with a pistol inside.

Would you turn *your* town over to this man?

Guy watched Goff and his people filling the front two rows on
the left, the chamber divided by its central aisle into two distinct
factions, Old Crybbe and New Age, tweeds against talismans.

He felt almost sorry for Goff; this was going to be a historic
fiasco. But he felt more sorry for himself, because they weren't
being allowed to film it.

Alex drained his cup in a hurry and bumped it back on its saucer,
hand trembling slightly.

Exorcism. Oh God.

"Well, obviously, I was supposed to *know* about things like
that. Been a practicing clergyman for damn near three-quarters
of my life. But . . . Sometimes she was . . . in my bedroom. I'd
wake up, she'd be sitting by the bed wearing this perfectly ghastly smile. Couple of seconds, that was all, then she'd
be gone. Happened once, twice a week, I don't know. Fay
came down to stay one weekend. I was in turmoil. Looked
awful, felt awful. What did she want with me? Hadn't I done
enough?"

Jean put on her knowing look.

"Yes," Alex said, "guilt again, you see. A most destructive
emotion. Was she a product of my obsessive guilt—a lifetime
of guilt, perhaps?"

Jean nodded.

"Poor old Fay. I think she thought I'd finally slipped into alcoholism. Anyway, she sent me to the doctor's, he sent me for tests, and they discovered the artery problem. Everything explained. Poor old buffer's going off his nut. Can't be left alone. And that was how Fay and I got saddled with each other."

"And do you feel you need her now?"

"Well, I . . . No, I'm not sure I do. Wendy, this . . . this Dr. Chi business . . . Look, I don't mean to be offensive . . . "

"Of course not," said Jean solemnly.

"But this renewed, er, sprightliness of mind . . . It's just that I don't honestly feel I'm the most worthy candidate for a mira-cle cure."

Jean stood up, went over to the window, and drew the curtains on the premature dusk, bent over to put on the lamp with the parchment shade, showing him her neat little gym-mistressy ass. Came back and sat down next to him on the settee, close enough for him to discover she was wearing perfume.

"There are no miracles, Alex, surely you know that by now."

She didn't move an inch, but he felt her coming closer to him and smelled the intimacy of her perfume. He felt old stirrings he'd expected never to feel again. And yet it was somehow joyless.

"Dr. Chi and I have done almost all we can for you, Alex. You've been here more than a day. Intensive treatment."

"It seems longer."

Jean nodded. "You feel well now?"

Alex cleared his throat. "Never better," he said carefully.

"So why don't you go home?"

"Ah," said Alex.

Jean looked steadily at him in the lamplight, unsmiling.

He said, "What time is it?"

"Approaching eight. She'll be there soon, Alex."

"Will she?"

"Only one way to find out," Jean said gently. "Isn't there?"

"Oh now, Wendy, look . . . "

"Perhaps . . . " She stood up and went to lean against the mantelpiece, watching him. "Perhaps it worries you that once you leave this house, your mind will begin to deteriorate again. And when you face her once more, the guilt will return."

He squirmed a little.

"You might not be responsible for actually bringing her spirit back." Her eyes narrowed. "I think we can blame Crybbe for that. But you do seem to have made her rather more powerful in death than she was in life. You've projected upon her not only the portion of guilt which she may or may not have been due, but all the guilt due to your wife and, no doubt, many other ladies and husbands and whatnot . . . and, bearing in mind your rather poor choice of profession, perhaps your God himself. Is that not so, Alex?"

"I . . . "

"You've been feeding her energy, Alex. The way I've been feeding you. A kind of psychic saline drip. So I'm afraid it's your responsibility to deal with her."

Alex began to feel small and old and hollow.

"When you leave here . . . " Jean said regretfully. "This house, I mean. When you do leave, there's a chance you'll lapse quite soon into the old confusion, and you'll have that to contend with, too. I'm sorry."

Alex stared at her, feeling himself withering.

"No Dr. Chi?"

Jean smiled sadly. "I never did like scientific terms."

"I'm on my own, then."

"I'm afraid you let her get out of hand. Now she's become quite dangerous. She won't harm you—you're her source of energy, you feed her your guilt and she lights up. But . . . " Jean hesitated. "She doesn't like Fay one bit, does she?"

"Stop it," Alex said sharply.

"You've known that for quite a while, haven't you? You would even plead with Grace not to hurt her. It didn't work, Alex. She appeared last night to your daughter in a rather grisly fashion, and Fay fell and cut her head and almost put out an eye."

Alex jerked as though electrocuted, opened his mouth, trying to shape a question with a quivering jaw.

"She's all right. No serious damage." Jean came back and sat next to him again and put a hand on his shoulder. "Don't worry, Alex, it's OK. You don't have to do anything. I won't send you away."

Alex began quietly to cry, shoulders shaking.

"Come on," said Jean, taking her hand away. "Let's go to bed. That's what you want, isn't it? Come along, Alex."

Jean Wendle's expressionless face swam in his tears. She was offering him sex, the old refuge, when all he wanted was the cool hands.

But the cool hands were casually clasped in her lap, and he knew he was never going to feel them again.

He came slowly to his feet. He backed away from her. She didn't move. He tried to hold her eyes; she looked down into her lap, where the cool hands lay.

Alex couldn't speak. Slowly he backed out of the lamplight and, with very little hope, into the darkness.

 three

The Crybbe dusk settled around them like sediment in the bottom of an old medicine bottle.

"Thank you, Denzil," Powys said to the closed door of the Cock. "That was just what we needed. Of course it's not crap. Can't you feel it?"

He started to grin ruefully, thinking of New Age ladies in ankle-length, hand-dyed, cheesecloth dresses. *Can't you feel that energy?*

Not energy. Not life energy, anyway.

"Fay, where can we go? Quickly?"

He was aware of a picture forming in his head. Glowing oil colors on top of the drab turpentine strokes of rough sketching and underpainting. Everything starting to fit together. Coming together by design—someone else's design.

"Studio," Fay said, opening her bag, searching for the keys.

"Right."

He didn't need the gavel. Didn't need even to call for silence. In fact, he rather wished he could call for noise—few murmurs, coughs, bit of shifting about in seats.

Nothing. Not a shuffle, not even a passing " 'Ow're you"

between neighbors. Put him in mind of a remembrance service for the dead, the only difference being that when you cast an eye over this lot you could believe the dead themselves had been brought out for the occasion.

Been like this since Goff and his people had come in and the cameraman had left: bloody quiet. Sergeant Wynford Wiley, in uniform, on guard by the door as if he was expecting trouble.

No such luck, Col Croston thought. Not the Crybbe way. No wonder the cunning old devil had stuck this one on him. Thanks a lot, Mr. Mayor.

Gavin Ashpole's Uher tape recorder and its microphone lay at the front of the room, half under the chairman's table and a good sixty feet from where Gavin himself sat at the rear of the hall. The stupid, paranoid yokels had refused to accept that if he kept the machine at his feet he would not surreptitiously switch it on and record their meeting.

He saw a man from the *Hereford Times* and that snooty bastard Guy Morrison. Nobody else he recognized, and Gavin knew all the national paper reporters who covered this area.

There was no sign of Fay Morrison.

Bitch.

The Newsomes sat side by side, but there might have been a brick wall between them, with broken glass along the top.

Hereward had planned to come alone to the meeting, but Jocasta had got into the car with him without a word. The implication was that she did not want to remain alone in the house after this alleged experience (about which Hereward was more than slightly dubious). But he suspected the real reason she'd come was that she hoped to see her lover.

With this in mind, Hereward had subjected each man entering the hall to unobtrusive scrutiny and was also watching for reactions from his wife. The appalling thought occurred to him that he might be the only person in the hall who did *not* know the identity of the Other Man.

He could be a laughingstock. Or she a liar.

Col looked at the wall clock which the caretaker had obligingly plugged in for the occasion. Five minutes past eight. Off we go, then.

"Well," he said. "Thank you all for coming. I, er . . . I don't think . . . that we can underestimate the importance of tonight."

Why did he say that? Wasn't what he'd *meant* to say. The idea was to be essentially informal, take any heat out of the situation.

"Let me say, straight off, that no decisions will be made tonight. That's not what this meeting's about. It's simply an attempt to remove some of the mystery—and some of the myths, too—about developments here in Crybbe. Developments which are transpiring with what might seem to some of us to be rather, er, rather bewildering speed."

Bloody bewildering speed, by Crybbe standards.

"And let me say, first of all, that, apart from minor planning matters, the changes, the developments, introduced to Crybbe by Mr. Max Goff, are, for the most part, outside the remit of local government and require no special permission whatsoever."

"What we doin' yere, then?" a lone voice demanded. A man's voice, but so high-pitched that it was like a sudden owl hoot in a silent barn.

Nobody turned to look whose it was. Obviously the voice spoke for all of Crybbe.

Col looked up and saw Hereward Newsome staring at him. He smiled. Hereward did not.

"Can I say, from the outset," Col said, "that from here on in, only questions directed through the chair will be dealt with. However—what are we doing here? This—as it happens—was a point I was about to move on to. What *are* we doing here?"

Col tried to look at everyone in the room; only those in the New Age quarter, to his right, looked back.

"We're here tonight . . . at the instigation of Mr. Max Goff himself. We're here because Mr. Goff is aware that aspects of his project may appear somewhat curious—even disturbing—to a number of people. What's he *doing* erecting large stones in fields, even if they do happen to be his own fields? Why is he so keen to purchase property for sale in the locality?"

Col paused.

"What *is* this New Age business really all about?"

On a single page of *The Ley-Hunter's Diary 1993*, with a felt-tipped pen in a none-too-steady hand, Powys had drawn the rough outline of a man with his arms spread.

Fay thought it looked like one of those chalk marks homicide cops drew around corpses in American films.

"The Cock," Powys said breathlessly. "Why do they call it the Cock? It's self-explanatory."

"This is going to be rather tasteless, isn't it?"

"Look." Powys turned the diary around on the studio desk to face her. He marked a cross on the head of the man. "This is the Tump."

He made another cross in the center of the man's throat. "Crybbe Court."

He traced a straight line downward and put in a third cross. "The church." It was in the middle of the chest.

"And finally . . . "

Where the man's legs joined he drew in a final cross.

"The Cock," he said. "Or more precisely, I'd *guess,* the alleyway and perhaps this studio."

She looked at him uncertainly, his face soft-focus in the diffused studio lighting. "I don't understand."

"The Cock, which used to be called the Bull, occurs precisely on the genitalia. If we want to get down to details, this studio would cover the testicles, and the erect . . . er, organ would project into the square very much as the pub itself leans. I remember when I spent the night there with Rachel I was thinking the upper story hung over the square like a beer gut. Close, but . . . Anyway, we were in the room which is directly over the passage, the alley, and we're on that same line now."

"Joe, this is ridiculous."

"Not really. You ever do yoga, anything like that?"

"Never had the time."

"OK, well, Eastern mysticism—and Western magic—suggests there are various points in the human body where physical and spiritual energy gathers, and from where it can be transmitted. The chakras."

"I've heard of them. I think."

"So what we *could* be looking at here are some of the key chakras—the center of the forehead, mental power; the throat, controlling nervous impulses; the center of the breast, affecting emotions. And the sex glands, responding more or less to what you'd expect."

Fay leaned back against the tape machine. "I'm still not getting this, Joe, you're going to have to spell it out. Like, simply."

"The town . . . is the man. Is the town."

"Oh shit . . . *What* man?"

"Wort. Black Michael. In essence he's never gone away. He's fused his energy system, his spirit, with the town. I'm not putting this very well."

"No, you're not."

"This girl Jane—the character assumed by Catrin Jones—speaks of the sheriff promising he'll never leave her. He hasn't. He's left the sexual part of him here. His cock."

Fay looked down at the Electrovoice microphone, eight inches long with a bulblike head. "Jesus . . . "

"It might even be—I don't know—*buried* somewhere . . . "

"Powys, I don't want to hear this. This is very seriously creepy."

"So anybody making love—having sex, love doesn't come into it—is getting some added . . . impetus, buzz, whatever, from a four-hundred-year-old . . . "

Fay never wanted to do another voice-piece with that microphone. "Come on," she said, between her teeth, "let's get out of here before—if what you say is correct—we start ripping each other's clothes off."

Ironically—given the ragged quality of local communal singing, the absence of a trained choir or the will to form one—the church was widely known for its excellent acoustics.

And so the Reverend Murray Beech heard it all.

Standing, appalled, behind the curtain separating the side entrance from the nave, he heard everything.

The astounding confession, and then the bumps and crashes.

It was not long after eight, although dark enough to be close to ten, the churchyard outside reduced to neutral shades, the birdsong stilled, the small, swift bats gliding through the insect layer.

When Murray had first picked up the noises he'd been on his way to the public meeting at which, he rather hoped, he would be able to assume the role of mediator, while at the same time putting a few pertinent theological questions to the self-styled heralds of the New Age.

He was wearing a new sports jacket over his black shirt and clerical collar. He'd felt more relaxed than for quite some

time. Had, in fact, been looking forward to tonight; it would
be his opportunity to articulate the fears of townsfolk who
were . . . well, unpracticed, let us say, in the finer techniques
of oratory.

At least, he *had* been relaxed until he'd heard from within the
church what sounded like a wild whoop of joy. In this situation
it might, in fact, be wise to summon the police.

Or it might not. He'd look rather foolish if it turned out to
be a cry of pain from someone quite legitimately in the church
who'd, say, tripped over a hassock.

Also he hadn't reported the minor (by lay standards) acts of
vandalism of the past two nights. And if this intruder did turn
out to be the perpetrator of those sordid expressions of contempt,
a quiet chat would be more in order. This was a person with
serious emotional problems.

So Murray had hesitated before going in quietly by the side
door, noting that its latch had been torn away and was hanging loose, which rather ruled out the well-meaning but clumsy
parishioner theory.

No, sadly, this was the sick person.

"Well, well," he heard now. *"Don't* you *look cheesed-off?"*

As, behind the floor-length curtain, he could not be seen from
anywhere in the church, the remark could not have been aimed
at him.

Which meant Warren Preece was addressing his dead brother.
His—if this crazed boy was to be believed—murdered brother.

The confession had emerged in a strange intermittent fashion,
incomplete sentences punctuated by laughter, as if it was a
continuous monologue but some of it was being spoken only
in Warren's head.

It was deranged and eerie, and Murray remembered the
malevolence of Warren's face in the congregation on Sunday, the way the hate had spurted out, in shocking contrast
to the unchanging stoical expressions of his father and his
grandparents.

Murray was in no doubt that this boy at least *believed* he'd
drowned Jonathon. The hardworking, conscientious, older brother slain by the youthful wastrel. Almost like Cain and Abel in
reverse.

He ought, he supposed, to make a quiet exit, summon the
police and let them deal with it. And yet there was, in this

situation, a certain social challenge of a kind not hitherto apparent in Crybbe. The inner cities were full of disturbed youths like Warren Preece—always a valid project for the Church, although some ministers shied away.

If Warren Preece was a murderer, Murray could hardly protect him. But if there was an element of self-delusion brought about by guilt, causing a strange inversion of grief, he could perhaps help the boy reason it out.

He heard footsteps but could not be sure from which direction they came or in which direction they were moving, for these acclaimed acoustics could, he'd found, sometimes be confusing.

With three sharp clicks, the lights came on, and Murray clutched at the curtain in alarm.

"Very nice," he heard. *"Very nice indeed."*

And the perverse laughter again, invoking an image in his head of the communion chalice on the altar and what it had contained.

A sudden, white-hot sense of outrage overrode his principles, his need to understand the social and psychological background to this, and he swept the curtain angrily aside.

"All right!"

Murray entered the nave in a single great stride, surprised at his own courage but aware also of the danger of bravado, his eyes sweeping over the body of the church, the stonework lamplit pale amber and sepia, the stained-glass windows rendered blind and opaque.

And in the space between the front pews and the altar rail, the aluminum bier empty and askew like an abandoned supermarket cart.

"Stay where you are!" Murray roared.

And then realized, in a crystal moment of shimmering horror, how inappropriate this sounded. Because the only Preece in view had no choice.

The vicar wanted to be sick, and the bile was behind his voice as it rose, choking, to the rafters lost in their shadows.

"Come out! Come out at once, you . . . you *filth . . . !*"

Another slack, liquid chuckle . . . *"eeeheheh . . . "* trailing like spittle.

Murray could not move, stood there staring compulsively into the closed, yellowed eyes of Jonathon Preece.

The open coffin propped up against the pulpit like a show-case, the body sunk back like a drunk asleep in the bath, the shroud now slashed up the middle to reveal the livid line of the postmortem scar, where the organs had been put back and the torso sewn up like a potato sack.

Jonathon's corpse splayed in its coffin like a pig in the back of a butcher's van, and Murray Beech could not move.

His nose twitched in acute, involuntary distaste as the smell reached him. Otherwise, he was so stiff with shock that he didn't react at first to the swift movement, as a shadow fell across him and he heard a very small, neat, crisp sound, like a paper bag being torn along a crease.

And when he looked down and saw that his clerical shirt had come apart—a deep, vertical split down the chest and upper abdomen, so that he could see his white undershirt below turning pink, then bright red—he couldn't at first work out precisely what this meant.

four

�֍

The square was absolutely empty. Flat, dead quiet under a sky that was too dark, too early.

Powys looked up at the church tower hanging behind the serrated roofs of buildings which included the town hall. Behind him, leaning toward him, was the Cock.

They stood in the center of the square, which was where the navel would be.

"We're on the solar plexus," Powys said. "The solar plexus, I *think,* is the most significant chakra, more so than the head. It's like the center of the nervous system—I *think*—where energy can be stored and transmitted."

Fay hung on to his arm, wanting warmth, although the night was humid.

"You see, I've never gone into this too deeply. It's just things you pick up in passing. We may not even be looking at chakras at all."

Fay began to shiver. She began to see the town as something covered by a huge black shadow, man-shaped. She knew nothing about chakras, almost nothing about ley-lines, energy lines, paths of the dead . . .

"It's happening tonight," she said. "Isn't it? Black Michael's coming back."

"Yeah." Powys nodded. "I think it's possible."

It was working. From the rear of the hall—packed way beyond the limits of the fire regulations—Guy Morrison saw it all as though through the rectangle of a TV screen, and, incredibly, it was working.

In spite of his evangelical white suit, Goff was starting to convey this heavy, sober sincerity, beside which even the authoritative Col Croston looked lightweight. Col in his ornate Gothic chairman's chair, Max Goff standing next to him at the table, having vacated a far humbler seat, but oozing Presence.

Goff standing with his hands loosely clasped below waist level.

Goff, looking down at first, saying, not too loudly, "I want you to forget everything you ever heard or read about the New Age movement. I'm gonna give you the Crybbe version. I'm gonna tell you how it might relate to this town. I'm gonna make it simple, no bull."

Then slowly raising his eyes. "And the moment I cease to make sense to any one of you, I wanna know about it."

Smiling a little now, an accessible kind of smile, if not exactly warm. "I want you to stand up and stop me. Say, 'Hey, we aren't following this, Max.' Or 'Max, we don't believe you. We think you're trying to pull the wool.' "

It could have sounded patronizing. It didn't. Guy could see only the back of the heads of the two distinct factions—New Age, Old Crybbe. No heads moved on either side. They'd been expecting a showman in a white suit, but Goff had changed. Even his small eyes were compelling. Not a showman but a shaman.

"You see, what I don't want is any of you people just sitting there thinking, 'Who is this lunatic? Why are we listening to this garbage? Who's he think he's kidding?' because . . . "

Bringing his gaze down very slowly from the back rows to the front rows, taking in everybody.

" . . . because I'm *not* kidding. I *never* kid."

"I look at this town," Fay said, "and I don't see streets and buildings anymore, I only see shadows."

Powys didn't say anything. He'd been seeing shadows everywhere, for years.

"When there's a gust of wind," Fay said, "I look over my shoulder."

Maybe it's me, he thought. Maybe I've contaminated her.

"And when the lights go out . . . "

"Look," Powys said quickly, "he's always been there. Bits of him." He kept snatching breath, trying to keep his mind afloat. "Just like, behind us, along the passage there's a pool of sexual energy that fills up in the hours approaching the curfew. Accumulates in the place where the studio is. No doubt other forms of energy gather elsewhere. But it all dissipates when the curfew bell starts to ring. Each night, the ringing of the curfew frustrates the spirit's attempts to collect enough energy to activate all the power centers simultaneously."

"All right," Fay said. "So, one hundred strong, evenly spaced tolls of the bell send the black energy back to the Tump with its tail between its legs. Why do real dogs howl?"

She looked down at Arnold, lying on the bottom step in front of the Cock, panting slightly.

"I'm guessing," Powys said. "OK?"

"It's all guesswork, isn't it? Go on. This is the big one, Joe. Why—precisely—do dogs howl at the curfew?"

"Right." He sat down on the second step, and Arnold laid his chin on his shoe. "I've been thinking about this a lot. The curfew's a very powerful thing. It's like—an act of violence. It hits the half-formed spirit like a truck. And the spirit wants to scream out in rage and frustration. Now. There are two possibilities. Either, because it's at this black-dog stage, it communicates its agony to anything else in the town on the canine wavelength. Or it simply emits some kind of ultrasonic scream, like one of those dog whistles people can't hear. How's that?"

"Well," Fay conceded, "it does have a certain arcane logic."

She looked up at the church tower.

Powys pushed at his forehead with the tips of his fingers. "Somebody—let's continue to call him John Dee—saw what was happening, what Michael Wort had left behind—in essence an opening for him to return, to . . . possess Crybbe, literally, from beyond the grave. And he recommended certain steps—get rid of the stones, build a wall around the Tump, or ring the curfew every night, one hundred times. Avoid any kind of psychic spiritual activity which will be amplified in an area like this anyway and could open up another doorway. And so the rituals are absorbed into the fabric of local life and Crybbe becomes what it is today."

"Morose," Fay said. "Apathetic. Resistant to any kind of change. Every night the curfew leaves the place literally limp."

Guy Morrison was clenching his fists in frustration. This would have been terrific television. He looked around for the mayor of Crybbe—the man who, more than anybody else in the entire world, he now wanted to strangle.

Jimmy Preece was, in fact, not six yards away, on the end of a row close to the back—presumably so that he could slip away to ring his precious curfew. Guy moved forward a little to see how the mayor was taking this and discovered that, for a change, Mr. Preece's face was not without expression.

He looked very nervous. His Adam's apple bobbed in his chicken's neck and his eyes kept blinking as though the lids were attached by strings to his forehead, where new wrinkles were forming like wormcasts in sand.

The poor old reactionary's worried Max is going to win them over, Guy thought. He's afraid that, by the end of the night, this will be Max Goff's town and not his anymore.

And why not?

For Goff, indirectly, was promising them the earth. But somebody had told him about the way business was done in this locality and about the border mentality, and he was handling it accordingly. What he was telling them, in an oblique kind of way, was, I can help you—I can re-create this town, make it soar—if you cooperate with me. But I don't need you. I don't need anybody.

Goff was talking now about his dreams of expanding the sum of human knowledge and enlightenment. Speaking of the great shrines of the world, subtly mentioning Lourdes and all the thousands of good, hopeful, faithful people it attracted all year round.

Mentioning—in passing—the amount of money it made out of the good, hopeful, faithful thousands.

"But tourism's not what I'm about," Goff said. "What I'm concerned with is promoting serious research into subjects rejected by universities in Britain as . . . well, let's say as . . . insufficiently intellectual. The growth of basic human happiness, for instance, has never been something which has tended to absorb our more distinguished scholars. *Far* too simple. Life and death? The afterlife? The *before*life? The human soul? Why should university scientists and philosophers waste time pondering the imponderable? Why not simply study the psychology of the foolish people who believe in all this nonsense?"

Goff paused, with another disarming smile. "You shoulda stopped me. Tourism is an option this town can explore at its leisure. You want tourists, they can be here—tens of thousands of them. You don't want tourists, you say to me, 'Max, this is a quiet town and that's the way we like it.' And I retire behind the walls of Crybbe Court and I become so low-profile everybody soon forgets I was ever here."

Guy conceded to himself that, had he been the kind of person who admired others, he might at this moment have admired Goff. This was *very* smart—Goff saying, Of course, nobody's *forcing* this town to be exceedingly wealthy.

Laying it on the line for them: I have nothing to lose, you have everything to gain.

Not even the faintest hint of threat.

How could they resist him?

"They'll listen very patiently to what Goff has to say, then they'll ask one or two very polite questions before drifting quietly away into the night. And then, just as quietly, they'll do their best to shaft the blighter . . . "

But why should Col Croston think they'd want to? This man was offering them the earth.

"Limp. Stagnant." Powys lowered his voice, although they were alone in the square. Afraid perhaps, Fay thought, that the town itself would take offense, as if that mattered now.

Over the roofs of shops, she could see the Victorian-Italianate pinnacle of the town-hall roof, the stonework blooming for the first time in the glow from its windows. There were probably more people in there tonight than at any other time since it was built. All the people who might be on the streets, in the pubs, scattered around town.

"And then Goff arrives," Powys said. "Unwitting front man for Andy Trow, last of the Worts, a practicing magician. The heir. Crybbe is his legacy from Michael."

Fay sat next to him on the step, Arnold between them. Apart from them, the town might have been evacuated. Nobody emerged from the street leading to the town hall, nobody went in.

"OK," she said. "He's put the stones back—as many as he can. He's knocked a hole in the wall around the Tump, so that whatever it is can get into the Court—the next point on the line, right?"

"I saw its light in the eaves. I watched it spit . . . Rachel out. Along with the cat. Not much of a guardian anymore, but it was there, it had to go. The next point on the line is the church, supposedly the spiritual and emotional heart of the town, from where the curfew's rung. Jack Preece rings the curfew; Jonathon, his son, was to inherit the job. Something's weeding out Preeces."

"No wonder old Jimmy was so desperate to get to the church after Jack had his accident."

"He's a bit doddery, isn't he, the old chap?"

"Stronger than he looks, I'd guess. But, sure, at that age he could go anytime. Joe, can nobody else ring it? What about you? What about me? What about—what's his name—Warren?"

"I don't see why not. But it was a task allotted to the Preeces, and perhaps only they know how vital it is. The big family secret. The mayor's probably training this Warren to take over. He's got to, hasn't he?"

Fay was still trying to imagine taciturn, wizened old Jimmy Preece in the role of Guardian of the Gate to Hell. No more bizarre, she supposed, than the idea of Crybbe Court being looked after by a mummified cat.

"What happens," she said, "if the curfew doesn't get rung?"

Powys stood up. "Then it comes roaring and spitting out of the Tump, through the Court, through the new stone in the wood and straight into the church—*through* the church, gathering enormous energy . . . until it reaches . . . "

He began to walk across the cobbles, his footsteps hollow in the dark and the silence.

" . . . here."

He stood in the center of the square. The center of Crybbe.

"My guess is there used to be a stone or a cross on this spot, but it was taken down with all the stones. I bet if you examine Goff's plans, you'll find proposals for some kind of monument. Wouldn't matter what it was. Could be a statue of Jimmy Preece."

"The Preece Memorial," Fay said.

"Wouldn't *that* be appropriate?"

Fay was silent, aware of the seconds ticking away toward ten o'clock. Sure she could feel something swelling in the air and a rumbling in the cobbles where Arnold lay quietly, not panting now.

"So what do we do?"

"If we've got any sense," Powys said, "we pile into one of the cars and drive like hell across the border to the nearest place with lots of lights. Then we get drunk."

"And forget."

"Yeah. Forget."

Fay said, "My father's here. And Jean."

"And Mrs. Seagrove. And a few hundred other innocent people."

The rumbling grew louder. Fay was sure she could feel the cobbles quaking.

"We can't leave."

Powys said, "And Andy's here somewhere, Andy Wort. I don't even like to imagine what he's doing."

"It's too quiet."

"Much too quiet."

Except for the rumbling, and two big, white, blazing eyes on the edge of the square.

Powys said, "What the hell's that?"

The eyes went out, and now the thing was almost luminous in the dimness. A large yellow tractor with a mechanical digger on the front.

"I'm gonner park 'im yere." They saw the glow of a cigarette and two tiny points of light from small, round spectacles. "Nobody gonner mind for a few minutes."

"It's Gomer Parry," Fay said.

"Ah . . . Miss Morris, is it?"

"Hello, Gomer. Where are you off to?"

"Gonner grab me a swift pint, miss. Just finished off down the Colonel's, got a throat like a clogged-up toilet. Flush 'im out, see?"

They watched Gomer ascending the steps to the Cock, a jaunty figure, entirely oblivious of whatever was accumulating.

The commotion of the digger's arrival had, for just a short time, pushed back the dark.

Powys said, "Fay, look, we've got to start making our own waves. It'll be feeble, it probably won't do anything, but we can't drive away and we can't just stand here and watch."

"Sure," Fay said, more calmly than she felt.

"We need to try and break up that meeting well before ten. Because if they all start pouring out of the town hall and there's something . . . I don't know, something in the square . . . I don't know what might happen. We're going to have to break it up, set off the fire alarm or something."

"I doubt if they've got one, but I'll think of something."

"I didn't necessarily mean you."

"I'm the best person to do it. I've got nothing to lose. I have no credibility left. What *you* need to do—because you know all the fancy terminology—is go and see Jean, see if she's got any ideas. And make sure Dad lies low. Can you take Arnold?"

"Sure."

He looked down at her. He couldn't see her very well. She looked like an elf, if paler than the archetype. A plaster elf that fell off the production line at the painting stage, so all the colors had run into one corner of its face.

He put his arms around her and lightly kissed her lips. The lips were very dry, but they yielded. He felt her fear and hugged her.

Fay smiled up at him, or tried to. "Watch it, Joe," she said. "Remember where you are."

Have you ever performed an exorcism?

Sitting in the near-dark in Grace's parlor. Sitting awkwardly, with his elbows on the table where Fay used to keep her editing machine until . . . until somebody broke it.

And the only voices he could hear were Jean's and Murray's alternately repeating the same strange question.

Exorcism.

Well, have I?

Canon Alex Peters remembered the sunny afternoon when Murray was here—only about a week ago—the very last sunny afternoon he could remember.

Remembered exploring his memory with all the expectation of a truffle-hunter in Milton Keynes . . . finally dredging up the Suffolk business. *"Wasn't the full bell, book, and candle routine . . . more of a quickie, bless-this-house operation.*

"Actually I think I made it up as I went along."

Grace's chair waited in front of Grace's fireplace. The brass balls twisted in the see-through base of Grace's clock, catching the last of the light, pulsing with the final death throes of the day.

And now, when you really need the full bell, book, and candle routine, you haven't got the right book and the only bell in town is the bloody curfew which we don't talk about.

Candles, though. Oh yes, plenty of bloody candles. Everybody in power-starved Crybbe has a houseful of bloody candles.

Alex dipped his head into his hands and moaned.

What are you doing to me, Wendy? I can't handle this, you know I can't.

He looked at the clock. He could see the twisting balls but not the time. But it must be getting on for nine.

Nine o'clock and Alex sitting waiting for his dead wife, and frightened.

Oh yes. Coming closer to the end didn't take away the fear.

"Dear Lord," said Alex hopelessly. "Take unto Thee Thy servant, Grace. Make her welcome in Thine Heavenly Kingdom, that she should no longer dwell in the half-light of limbo. Let her not remain in this place of suffering but ascend forever into Thy holy light."

Alex paused and looked across at the mantelpiece as though it were an altar.

"Amen," he said, and lowered his chin to his chest.

He had no holy water, no vestments, no Bible, no prayer book.

An old man in faded Kate Bush T-shirt, tracksuit trousers, and an ancient, peeling pair of gym shoes, standing, head bowed in the center of the room, making it up as he went along.

What else could he do?

Certainly not this strident stuff about commanding unquiet spirits to begone. Not to Grace, a prim little lady who never even went to the post office without a hat and gloves.

"Forgive me, Grace," Alex said.

He sat down in the fireside chair, which had been hers, on those special occasions when the sitting room was in use.

"Forgive me," he said.

And fell asleep.

Fay slipped into the hall unprepared for the density of the crowd.

How could so many be so silent?

Every seat was taken and there were even more people standing, lining every spare foot of wall, two or three deep in some places.

Wynford Wiley, guardian of the main portal, turned his sweating cheese of a head as she came in, rasping at her. "Not got that tape recorder, 'ave you?"

Fay held up both hands to show she hadn't, and Wynford still looked suspicious, as if he thought she might be wired up, with a hidden microphone in her hair. For Christ's sake, what did it matter?

She stood just inside the doors and saw the impossibility of her task. There must be over three hundred people in here. Joe Powys hadn't been entirely serious, but he'd been right: the best thing they could have done was pile into the car and make a dash for civilization. And she'd been so glib: *I'll think of something.*

Fay looked among the multitude, at individual faces, each one set as firm as a cardboard mask. Except in the New Age ghetto, toward the front of the hall, to her left, where there was a variety of expressions. A permanent half-smile on the nodding features of a small man in a safari suit. A woman with an explosion of white hair, wearing a beatific expression, face upturned to the great god Goff.

Max was being politely cross-examined on behalf of the townsfolk by the chairman, craggy Colonel Croston, whom Fay knew from council meetings—the only councilor who'd ever spoken to her before the meetings.

"I think one thing that many people would like me to ask you, Mr. Goff, is about the stones. Why is it necessary to install what I suppose many people would regard as crude symbols of pagan worship?"

Goff seemed entirely at ease with the question.

"Well, you know . . . " Leaning back confidently in his chair. "I think all that pagan stuff is a concept which would raise many an eyebrow in most parts of Wales, where nearly every year a new stone circle is erected as part of the national eisteddfod. I realize the eisteddfodic tradition is not so strong here on the border anymore—if it ever was—but if you were to place these stones in the ground in Aberystwyth, or Caernarfon, or Fishguard, I doubt anyone would even notice. The point is, Mr. Chairman . . . all this is largely symbolic. It symbolizes a realization that this town was once important enough to be a place of pilgrimage—like Lourdes, perhaps. And that *it can be again.*"

Spontaneous sycophantic applause burst from the New Age quarter.

Is he blatantly lying, Fay wondered. Or does he seriously believe this bullshit?

Or are we, Joe Powys and I, grossly, insultingly, libelously wrong about everything?

But almost as soon as she thought this, she began to feel very strongly that they were not wrong.

It was ten minutes past nine, the chamber lit by wrought-iron electric chandeliers, and she just *knew* there was going to be a power cut within the next half hour.

* * *

"Come in, Joe," Jean Wendle said. "I fear we shall be losing our electricity supply before too long."

"How do you know that?"

Carrying Arnold, he followed her down the hall and into her living room, where a pleasant Victorian lamp with a pale-blue shade burned expensive aromatic oil.

"There's a sequence," Jean said, perching birdlike on a chair arm. "Tea?"

"No time, thanks. What's the sequence?"

"Well, temperature fluctuation, to begin with. Either a drop or a raising of the temperature. Coupled with a kind of tightening of the air pressure that you come to recognize. Y'see, these new trip mechanisms or whatever they use do seem to be rather more vulnerable to it than the old system. Or so it seems to me." Jean crossed her legs neatly. She was wearing purple velour trousers and white moccasins. "No time, eh? My."

He put Arnold down. "When you say 'it' . . . ?"

"It? Oh, we could be talking about anything, from the geological formation—did you know there's a fault line running up through mid-Wales and right along the border here, there've been several minor but significant earthquakes in recent years. So there's the geology, to start with . . . "

"Jean," Powys said, "we're in a lot of trouble."

"Aye," Jean Wendle said, "I know."

"So let's not talk about temperature fluctuations or rock strata, let's talk about Michael Wort."

"What about him?"

Powys sat down, gathered his thoughts, and then spent three minutes telling her, in as flat and factual a way as he could manage, his and Fay's conclusions. Ending with the shadow of Black Michael falling over Crybbe, whatever remained of his bodily power centers fused with the town's, the exchange of dark energy.

He felt Arnold pushing against his legs in the way he'd done last night in Bell Street before leading him to the blood and the semiconscious Fay. Powys reached down a hand and patted him, and Arnold began to pant. He's aware of the urgency, too, Powys thought. But then, he's a dowser's dog.

"It'll try and take the church tonight," he said. "And then . . . God knows . . . "

Jean sat and listened. When he finished she was silent for over a minute. Powys looked at his watch and then bit on a knuckle.

"That's very interesting," Jean said. "You may be right."

Arnold whined.

"Shush." Powys laid a hand on the dog's side. Arnold was breathing rapidly.

"We haven't any time to waste, Jean. I think . . . it seems to me I need to get over to the church and ensure that . . . well, that old Preece makes it to the belfry. I can't think what else I can do that's halfway meaningful, can you?"

Jean thought for a moment and then shook her head.

"What I think is . . . in fact I know . . . that you ought to go for the source."

Her eyes were very calm and sure.

Powys said, "I don't know what you mean."

"The source, Joe. Where it begins."

He thought of the great dark mound with its swaying trees and the blood of Henry Kettle on its flank.

"That's right," Jean said. "The Tump."

"I . . . " It was forbidding enough by daylight.

"Don't think you can handle that?"

"I don't see the point. I'm not a magician. I'm not a shaman. I'm just a bloody writer. Not even that anymore."

No, he might just as well have said, I don't think I *can* handle it. This was Jean Wendle he was talking to. Jean Wendle the psychic. Also Jean Wendle the barrister. The human lie-detector.

"Oh, Joe, Joe . . . You're like Alex. You won't face up to the way it is. To what has to be done. You lost the wee girl, Rose, you lost Rachel Wade."

"No." He shook his head. He didn't understand. He hadn't understood when it happened—either time—and he didn't understand now.

What am I *missing*? Suddenly he was in a mental frenzy. Why did she have to say that? Why did she have to slap him across the face with the incomprehensible horror of Rose and Rachel? And was he *missing* something?

"Don't let yourself lose this one," Jean said.

Fay?

Please . . . What can't I *see*?

"And when I get to the Tump," he asked weakly. "What am I supposed to do then?"

"You're looking for Boulton-Trow, aren't you?"

He stared at her, Arnold throbbing against his ankle.

"If Boulton-Trow has orchestrated all this, then he has to stand somewhere, has he not, with his wee conductor's baton. He has to have a podium, from which—if you really want to end all this—you must dislodge him. I'm sorry, Joe, it's never easy. You know that really, don't you? You could indeed lend Mr. Preece a supporting arm as he climbs the steps to the belfry, but are you going to be there again tomorrow night, and the night after?"

Powys stood up. His legs felt very weak. He was afraid. He gathered the trembling Arnold awkwardly into his arms, looked vaguely around. "Where's the canon?"

Jean saw him to the door. "Don't worry about Alex. He's coming to grips with his past, too." She gave his arm a sympathetic squeeze. "It's the night for it."

Col Croston was pleased and yet disappointed, too. It was going smoothly; Max Goff was making his points very cogently and even impressing *him,* as the strictly neutral chairman. And, no, he hadn't expected fireworks.

But wasn't this just a little bit *too* tame?

Hadn't once had to bang his gavel or call for silence. Just that spot of aggression toward the cameraman—minor pre-meeting nerves. And that single, reedy interruption during his introduction. All of this before he'd even called on Goff to address the meeting.

And now the fellow had been given a more than fair hearing.

"Right," Col said. "Well, I think I've put all *my* questions, but what about all of *you?* What's the general feeling? I think we at least owe it to Mr. Goff for him to be able to walk away from here tonight with some idea of how the townsfolk of Crybbe are reacting to his ideas."

Wasn't awfully surprised to get a lot of blank looks.

"Well, come on, don't be shy. This is a public meeting and you are, in fact, the public."

And when he did get a response it came, unsurprisingly, from the wrong side of the room.

The large, middle-aged woman with the white hair was on her feet.

"Yes," said Col. "Mrs. Ivory, isn't it? Go ahead."

"Mr. Chairman," Mrs. Ivory said sweetly, "I'm sure we must seem a pretty strange lot to the local people."

She paused. If she was waiting to be contradicted, Col thought, she'd be on her feet for the rest of the night.

"Well . . . " Mrs. Ivory blushed. "I suppose we all have adjustments to make, don't we. I know I got some *very* odd looks when I went into a sweetshop and said I preferred carob to chocolate, actually, and didn't mind paying the extra for a nondairy alternative."

Good grief, Col thought, is this the best you can do?

"What I mean is, Mr. Chairman, I suppose we *have* got what seem like some funny ideas, but, well, we're *harmless,* and I don't mind people thinking I'm an eccentric, as long as they accept me as a *harmless* eccentric. That's the point I want to make. We don't want to take over or impose some weird new regime. We're not like the Jehovah's Witnesses—we won't be knocking on doors or handing out pamphlets saying, 'Come and join the New Age movement.' We're gentle people, and we're not going to intrude and . . . well, that's all I have to say, really. Thank you."

"Thank *you,* Mrs. Ivory," said Col. "Well, there you are, I think that was a very, er . . . a valuable point. So. What about some local reaction? Mr. Mayor, you're down there on the floor of the meeting tonight, somewhat of a new experience for you, but what it *does* mean is you *are* entitled to speak your mind. Give us the benefit of your, er . . . "

He was going to make a little New Age sort of joke then, about the mayor's "ancient wisdom," but decided perhaps not.

" . . . years of experience."

He watched Jimmy Preece rising skeletally to his feet.

"Not expecting a sermon. Just a *few* words, Mr. Mayor."

"Well, I . . . " Jimmy Preece looked down at his boots, and then he said prosaically, "On behalf of the town, I'd like to thank Mr. Goff for coming along tonight and telling us about his plans. Very civil of 'im. I'm sure we'll all bear in mind what 'e's 'ad to say."

And the mayor sat down.

Col looked helplessly at Max Goff.

*   *   *

At the back of the room Fay Morrison looked at her watch, saw it was coming up to twenty minutes past nine, and was very much relieved. Within a couple of minutes the meeting would be wound up and all these people would go their separate ways. They'd be off the line, away from what she was slowly and less incredulously coming to think of as the death path.

"Thank you, Mr. Mayor," Goff said, rising to his feet. "Thank you, Mr. Chairman. But this is only the start of things . . . "

What?

Goff said, "I'd like you to meet at this point some of the people you'll be seeing around town. For those who wanna know more about the heritage of the area, the distinguished author J. M. Powys will be, er, with us presently. But I'd like to acquaint you, first of all, with some of the very skilled practitioners who, for an introductory period, will be making their services available entirely free of charge to anyone in Crybbe who'd like to know more about alternative health. As Hilary said a few moments ago, there'll be no proselytizing, they'll simply be around if required. So first of all I'd like you to meet . . . "

He stopped. The chairman had put a hand on his arm.

"One moment, Mr. Goff, I think we appear to have another question . . . Think I saw a hand going up at the back. Oh."

Col had recognized Fay Morrison, the radio reporter. This was a public meeting, not a media event; however, in the absence of any worthwhile response from the floor, he supposed it would be all right to let her have her say.

"Yes," he said. "Mrs. Morrison."

Goff's head spun around. "This is not a press conference, Mr. Chairman."

"Yes, I'm aware of that, Mr. Goff, but Mrs. Morrison *is* a resident of Crybbe."

"Yeah, sure, but . . . "

"And I *am* the chairman," Col said less affably.

Goff shut up, but he wasn't happy.

Col was. This was more like it.

"Go ahead, Mrs. Morrison."

"I'd like to know if Mr. Goff is going to introduce us to his chief adviser, Mr. Boulton-Trow."

"I'm afraid," Goff said coldly, "that Mr. Boulton-Trow is not able to be with us tonight."

"Why not?"

Goff dropped his voice. "Look, Mr. Chair, I've had dealings with this woman before. She's a load of trouble. She makes a practice of stirring things up. She's been fired by the local radio station for inaccuracy, she's . . . "

"Mr. Goff . . . " Thin steel in Col's voice. "This is a public meeting, and I'm the chairman. Go ahead, Mrs. Morrison, but I hope this is relevant. I don't want a slanging match."

"Thank you, Mr. Chairman," Fay said. "I've certainly no intention of being at all argumentative."

Oh God, *go for it, woman.*

"I'd simply like to ask Mr. Goff what contribution he expects will be made to the general well-being of Crybbe by employing a descendant of perhaps . . . perhaps the most hated man in the history of the town."

She paused. People were turning to look at her, especially from the Crybbe side of the room.

Goff was on his feet. "This is ridiculous . . . "

The chairman slammed down his gavel. "Please!"

"I'm referring," Fay said, raising her voice, "to the sixteenth-century sheriff known popularly, since his death, as Black Michael, and widely known at the time for unjustly hanging—"

"Mrs. Morrison," said the chairman. "With the best will in the world, I don't honestly think . . . "

"Andy Trow has, of course, reversed his real surname. He's Andy Wort, isn't he, Mr. Goff?"

There was a silence.

Oh fuck it, Fay thought. Take it all the way.

"He's also, I understand, your lover."

And the lights went out.

six

Please. Take my arm.

Better?

Good.

Do you remember when I used to offer you my arm in the street and you absolutely refused to accept it? "Not until we're married," you would say, even though you were quite poorly. Worried about your reputation, I suppose. Bit late for that.

And then, of course, when we were married it was quite impossible, with you in a wheelchair and me pushing the damn thing.

All right now, though, isn't it?

Yes. All right now.

Which way shall we go? No, you choose. Down to the river? No?

To the church! Yes, of course. Bring back some memories. Young Murray did rather well, I thought. Yes, I agree about the amendments to the vows; saved any embarrassment, didn't it? Indeed it did.

It is dark, isn't it? Careful now. Mind you don't trip over the curb or the end of your shroud.

Do tell me, won't you, if you're feeling tired.

Jolly good.

As Joe Powys drove, on full headlights, into the lane that slipped down beside the church, he formed an image of Crybbe Court as an old and poorly built house riddled with damp. Periodically, new people would move in and redecorate the rooms: bright new paint, new wallpaper, new furniture. But the wet always came through and turned the walls black and rotted the furniture.

And eventually people stopped throwing money at it and just tried to insulate themselves and their families as best they could. It wasn't much fun to live in, and the people who stayed there were the ones with few prospects and nowhere else to go.

That was the basic socioeconomic viewpoint.

Trying to explain the supernatural aspects in terms of rising damp was more complicated.

If only he could speak to the shadowy figure who, in the late 1500s, had attempted to install, just above ground level, an effective damp-proof course.

Let's assume this man was John Dee, astrologer at the court of Queen Elizabeth I.

Powys braked hard as a baby rabbit shot from the hedgerow into the center of the road and then stopped, turning pale, terrified eyes into the headlights.

He switched off the lights, and the rabbit scampered away.

Just for a moment, Powys smiled.

There's a portrait. John Dee in middle age. A thin-faced man with high cheekbones. Watchful but kindly eyes. He wears a black cap, suggesting baldness, and has a luxuriant white beard, like an ice-cream cone.

In Andy's notes, Dee (if it is he) gives only graphic descriptions of experiences, like the visit of the spirit (Wort) in the night.

Perhaps somewhere Dee has documented the action he took to contain the rampant spirit after Wort's death.

Dee never seems to have been very wealthy. Toward the end of his life he was virtually exiled to the north, as warden of Christ's College, Manchester. With Elizabeth dead and James on the throne—James who was in constant fear of Satanic plots and clamped down accordingly on all forms of occultism—the elderly Dee was forced to defend himself and his reputation as a scholar against various accusations that he practiced witchcraft. Ill-founded accusations, no doubt, but these were dangerous, paranoid times.

So what would the penurious Dee do if contacted by old friends or relatives in Crybbe with tales of hauntings and oppression by dark forces invoked by the late Sir Michael Wort?

He drove past the turning to Court Farm and could see no lights between the trees. No lights anywhere. He might, out here, be twenty miles from the nearest town. It was like driving back in time, or into another dimension.

To Percival Weale,
Merchant of Crybbe

My Dear Mr. Weale,

It was with much sorrow that I received your letter
informing me that our mutual associate, Sheriff Wort, con-
tinues to torment the town from a place beyond this life. It
has long been apparent to me that the etheric layer is so
dense upon the atmosphere along the border of Wales and
England that it may not always be so comfortable a place
of habitation . . .

And did Dee, old, impecunious, and in constant fear of arrest,
appeal to Percy Weale to make financial provision for the curfew
to be rung (so that the most dangerous hours of darkness might
remain peaceful) and to assign some long-established local family to the task?
And being unable to travel to Crybbe himself, did he vaguely
suggest that if the malignant spirit were to be controlled it was
essential for the stones to be removed, the Tump walled in, and
the spiritual energy level to remain low?

And you must warn the townspeople to continue with their
lives but not to expand the town to any great extent and,
above all, to offer no challenge to the spirit. And, as for the
hand and any other of his limbs or organs that should come
to light, no purpose will be served in their destruction. You
must take these and enclose them in separate and confined
places—I would suggest within a chimney or fireplace or
beneath a good stone floor—where they may never be
exposed to the light or the air. This is far from satisfactory,
but my knowledge does not extend to more. Forgive me.

Powys drove between the gateposts of Crybbe Court and felt
the house before he saw it, a dark and hungry maw.
He thought, *Hand? What hand? I don't know anything about
a hand.*
Get your act together, Powys.
He thought about Fay and started to worry, so he thought
about Rachel instead, and he looked up toward the house and
felt bitterly angry.

* * *

Better keep to the path, I think, my dear. Somewhat safer, in the dark.

Not that they take much care of this path, or indeed the church itself, never much in the way of civic pride in Crybbe. Poor old Murray's got his hands full.

Ah. Now. I know where we're going.

We're going to your grave, aren't we?

Now, look, before you say anything, I'm sorry it had to be down at this end—not exactly central, I realize that, another few yards, in fact, and you'd be in the wood. But it's surely shady on a warm day, and you never did like too much sun, did you? I suppose you spent most of your life in the shade, really, and . . . well, you know, I always had the impression that was how you wanted it to be.

I know, I know . . . the flowers. I keep forgetting, memory isn't what it was, as you know. You bring a few flowers with the best of intentions, and then you forget all about them and the next time you come they're all dead and forlorn and there are stalks and seedpods everywhere, all a terrible mess, and I do understand the way you feel about that, of course I do.

Hello, who's this?

Oh, Grace, look, it's young Murray.

No, don't get up, old chap.

Well, er . . . it's a lovely night, isn't it?

Yes. Indeed.

What's that?

Cain and Abel?

I'm sorry . . . I'm not quite getting your drift. What you're saying is, Abel killed Cain?

Well, not in my version, old son, but I suppose you modernists have your own ideas.

Abel killed Cain, eh?

Well, if you say so, Murray, if you say so.

Arnold was not at all happy about being left in the Mini. Joe Powys had pushed back the slide-opening driver's window several inches to give him plenty of air, and he stood up on the seat and pressed his head through the gap and whined frantically.

"I can't take you," Powys said. "Please, Arnold."

He'd left the dog a saucer of water on the back shelf. Poured from a bottle he kept in the trunk because the radiator had been known to boil dry.

Knowing full well that he was doing all this just in case, for some unknowable reason, he didn't get back.

"Good boy," he said. "Good boy."

He locked the car and moved quickly, uncomfortably away. He didn't want to be here. He *felt* he was in the wrong place, but he didn't trust his own feelings. He trusted Jean Wendle's feelings because Jean was an experienced psychic and a Wise Woman, and he was just a writer; and when it came to dealing with real life, writers didn't know shit.

The Mini was tightly parked in a semiconcealed position behind the stable block. Powys carried a hand lamp with a beam projecting a good fifty yards in front of him. It was probably a mistake; he should be more surreptitious. What was he going to do—stand amid the ruins of the wall, pinning Andy in the powerful beam as he cavorted naked in the maelstrom of black energy?

"It all sounds," he said aloud into the night, "so bloody stupid."

Earth mysteries.

Book your seats for a magical, mind-expanding excursion to the Old Golden Land.

A fun-filled New Age afternoon. A book of half-baked pseudomystical musings on your knee as you picnic by a sacred standing stone, around it a glowing aura of fascinating legend.

As he moved uncertainly across the field toward the Tump, it struck him that it was past ten o'clock and there'd been no curfew. Well, it was late last night, too. Took old Preece longer to make it to the belfry.

But he still thought, That's where I should be. Or with Fay. Not here.

Or am I just trying to put it off again, the confrontation, afraid my reasoning's all wrong and this man, with his precise, laid-back logic and his superior knowledge of the arcane, is going to hold up another dark mirror.

As was usual with these things, he didn't notice it was happening until it had been happening for quite some time.

As he climbed easily over the ruins of the wall, where somebody had taken a bulldozer for a midnight joyride, the rhythm of his breath began to change so that it was a separate thing from what he was doing, which was laboring up the side of the mound. Normally, to do this, he would be jerking the breaths in like a fireman on a steam train shoveling more and more coal on, breath as fuel. But he was conscious, in an unconcerned, dreamlike way, of the climb's being quite effortless and the breathing's fueling something else, some inner mechanism.

Each breath was a marathon breath, long, long, long, but not at all painful. When you discovered that you, after all, possessed a vast inner strength, it was a deeply pleasurable thing.

He followed what he thought was the beam from the lamp, until he realized the lamp had gone out but the beam had not, as though he was throwing a shadow, a negative shadow, which made it a shadow of light.

Out of the tufted grass and into the bushes, moving with ease, watching his legs doing the work, as legs were meant to do, tearing through the undergrowth in their eagerness to take him to the summit of the mound.

The source.

Each breath seeming to take minutes, breathing in not only air, but colors, all the colors of the night, which were colors not normally visible to underdeveloped human sight.

Moving up the side of the Tump, between bushes and tree trunks, and moving effortlessly. Effortlessly as the last time.

goes round . . . thrice . . .

goes round . . .

seven

Nobody panicked.

Well, they wouldn't, would they? Not in Crybbe. They'd be quite used to this by now. Part of everyday life. Every*night* life, anyway.

So there were no screams, no scrambles for the door. Guy Morrison knew this because he was standing only yards from the exit where the fat policeman, Wiley, was doubtless still at his post.

"Only a matter of time, wasn't it?" Col Croston called out. "Don't worry, it often happens during council meetings. Mrs. Byford's gone to switch on the generator."

It was a bloody mercy, in Guy's opinion.

The woman was completely and utterly *insane!*

For the first time, Guy was profoundly thankful he and Fay had never had children.

He hoped that by the time the lights came on she'd have had the decency to make herself scarce. The sheer *embarrassment* of it!

"Guy?"

Somebody snuggled against his chest.

"Just as well it *is* me," he whispered, and she giggled and kissed his neck.

A worrying thought struck him.

"You're not wearing lipstick, are you, Catrin?"

"Not anymore," Catrin Jones said, and Guy plunged a hand into his jacket pocket, searching frantically for a handkerchief.

"No, I'm not," Catrin said. "Honest. I'm sorry."

"Shut up, then," he hissed, conscious of the fact that nobody else appeared to be talking.

"Won't be long now," Col Croston shouted cheerfully. At least, Guy thought, it would be an opportunity for him to pretend the five minutes before the power cut had never happened.

He became aware that somebody had drawn back the curtains

at the windows, and what little light remained in the sky showed him a scene like the old black-and-white photographs he'd seen of the insides of air-raid shelters in the blitz, only even more overcrowded. All it needed was someone with rampant claustrophobia to start floundering about and there'd be total chaos.

But nobody moved and nobody spoke, and it was quite uncanny. He felt Catrin's hand moving like a mouse in one of his hip pockets. When they got back to Cardiff he'd suggest she should be transferred. Something she couldn't very well refuse—six months' attachment as an assistant trainee radio producer, or anything else that sounded vaguely like promotion.

As his eyes adjusted, Guy was able to make out individual faces. A fat farmer who hadn't taken off his cap. That cocky little radio chap trying vainly to see his watch. Jocasta Newsome and her husband—strange that she wasn't talking; perhaps they'd had a row.

The radio bloke—at least this outfit had had the good sense not to have Fay covering the meeting—was on his feet and moving to the door.

"Just a minute," Guy heard Wiley say officiously. "Where you think you're goin'?"

"Look, I've got an urgent news report to go down. Gavin Ashpole, Offa's Dyke Radio."

"Well, you can 'ang on yere. Studio won't be workin' if there's no power, is it?"

"Then I'll do it by phone. Do you mind?"

"I'm not bein' offensive, sir, but you might 'ave lifted somebody's wallet in there and be makin' off with the proceeds."

"Oh, for . . . Look, pal, I've got an expensive tape recorder on the floor under the chairman's table. You can hold it to ransom if I don't come back. Now, *please.*"

"Lucky I recognizes your voice, Mr. Ashpole," Wynford Wiley said genially, and Guy heard a bolt go back.

"Thanks."

Guy heard the door grinding open, but he didn't hear it close again. He didn't hear anything.

Had he been looking through the viewfinder of a camera, it would have seemed at first like a smear on the lens.

Then it took shape, like a sculpture in smoke, and a figure was standing in the central aisle between the two blocks of chairs. It looked lost. It moved in short steps, almost shuffling, like a

Chaplinesque tramp in an old film, but in slow motion. There was a yellowish tinge to its ill-defined features. It was a man.

His nose was large and bulbous, his eyes were pure white, and he was moving down the aisle toward Guy Morrison.

Even without his razor, Guy would have known him anywhere.

Guy screamed.

"No! Get away! Get back."

Catrin gasped and moved sharply away from him.

But ex—*very* ex—Police Sergeant Handel Roberts continued to shuffle onward as if the room were not illegally overcrowded but empty apart from Guy Morrison and himself.

"Jocasta!" Guy screamed. "Look! It's him. It's *him!*"

And closing his eyes, throwing an arm across his face, he plunged forward like someone making a desperate dash through flames to the door of a blazing room.

There was a ghastly, tingling moment of damp and penetrating cold, and then he was on his knees, his head in her lap, his hands clawing at her dress, mumbling incoherently into her thighs. He began to sob. "Oh God, Jocasta, it *is . . .* "

Jocasta Newsome didn't move. When he opened his eyes he saw there were lights in the room, but different lights, fluorescent bars high on the walls. He blinked up at her face and found it harsh and grainy in the new light and frozen into an expression of ultimate disdain.

"You filthy bastard," the thin, bearded man next to her said.

Moving like a train through the night, the track unrolling before you, a ribbon of light, straight as a torch beam. There are deep-green hills on either side—deep green because they are dense with trees—and the silver snaking river, all of this quite clearly visible, for they do not depend on sunlight or moonlight but have their own inner luminescence.

There are no buildings in this landscape, no farms or cottages or barns or stables or sheep sheds, no cars, no tractors, no gates, no fences, no hedges. In some places, the trees give way, diminishing themselves, becoming not separate, defined, organic entities but a green wash, a watercolorist's view of trees. Then they fade into fields, but with the spirit of the old woodland still coloring their aura.

It is a strange land at first, but then not so strange, for what you see is the true essence of the countryside you know. This is a country unviolated by Man.

This is the spirit landscape.

What you once presumed to call the Old Golden Land.

And the unfurling ribbon of light is what, over half a century earlier, your mentor Alfred Watkins presumed to call the Old Straight Track.

Alf. Alf Watkins, isn't it? You here too?

No answer. He isn't here. You're alone. Lying between two tall trees on top of the Tump in the heat, and moving like a fast train in the night.

Until, with no warning, the track buckles in front of you, and the night shatters into a thousand shards of black glass.

"Remember me?"

A whisper. Tumult in the hall. Nobody else heard the whisper, dry as ash.

"Who's that?"

"Oh . . . don't reckernize the voice, then, is it? Yeard it before, though, you 'ave."

"Huh?"

"Crude."

"What?"

"Lyrically . . . mor . . . onic."

"What the . . . ?"

"An' musically . . . musically *inept.*"

"Jeez, you must be . . . "

"Can't even remember my fuckin' name, can you?"

"Listen, I'll talk to you later. Tomorrow. Make an appointment."

"You're a bloody old bag of shit, you are."

"Listen, I can understand . . . "

"Don't let the kid give up sheep-shearing classes. That's what you said."

"Yeah, but . . . "

"I knows 'ow to shear sheep, already, though, see. What you do is . . . "

Gavin Ashpole was discovering that there was virtually nowhere quite as dark as a tiny, windowless, unattended radio studio during a power cut.

Belonging as it did to Offa's Dyke Radio, the Crybbe Unattended, unlike the town hall, did not have a generator. The emergency lighting amounted to an old bicycle lamp which Fay Morrison left on the table in the outer office. It took several minutes and a lot of explicit cursing for Gavin Ashpole to find it.

He knew time must be getting on as he sat down at the desk to transcribe his notes and scramble together a voice-piece. A phone call confirmed it.

"Gavin! Where've you been, man? You're on air in two minutes!"

"Huh?" Gavin aimed the bicycle lamp at his watch. It said 9:28. Shit, shit, shit.

"Much of a story, is it, Gav? We've left you a full two minutes, as instructed."

"Sod all," he said tersely. "And you're getting it down the phone—the fucking power's off. Listen, James, cut me back to one and shove it back down the bulletin. Bring me in around 9:35, OK?"

"Not sure we've got . . . "

"Just do it, eh? Take down the link now, I'll keep it tight. OK, ready? 'There's been a hostile reception tonight for billionaire businessman Max Goff at a packed public meeting to discuss his plans for a so-called New Age mystical healing center in the border town of Crybbe . . . from where Gavin Ashpole now reports.' Got that?"

Gavin hung up.

He had enough for one minute with what he'd already written. He pulled off his tie, stretched out his legs, switched off the lamp, and waited for the studio to ring.

Sodding power cut. Maybe he should have brought the radio car after all. He could have done an exclusive interview with the famous Fay Morrison.

Stupid slag. She deserved everything she was going to get. Everybody knew Max Goff was pretty well-established in shirt-lifting circles, but, unless you were seriously suicidal, you didn't bring up this issue before about three hundred witnesses including a couple of suits who looked like outriders from the Epidemic legal department.

He should sue the pants off the bitch.

pants off the bitch.

Aaaah!

Went through him like a red-hot wire. He nearly took off.

Sssssstrewth!

He wanted her.

In truth, he wanted anybody, but superbitch Fay Morrison was the one whose image was projected naked into his lap with its legs wrapped around him in the dark.

Hot.

Stifling in here, warm air jetting at him like a fan heater.

Too fucking hot.

And who was there to notice, anyway, if he took off his trousers?

The phone rang. "Gavin, news studio, can you hear this OK?"

Plugged into the news. " . . . *Major row erupted in the Commons tonight when Welsh Nationalist MP Guto Evans challenged the Government's . . . "* Then faded down, and James Barlow's voice in the earpiece. "Gavin, we'll be coming to you in about a minute and a half, and you've got fifty seconds, OK?"

"Yeah," Gavin croaked. "Yeah."

The fluorescent bars were only secondary lighting, linked to what must have been a small generator. The room was still only half lit, and the light from the walls was blue and frigid.

Fay, unmoving at the rear of the hall, knew that something had changed and the light was part of it; it altered the whole ambience of the room and better reflected the feeling of the night.

In that it was a cold, unnatural light.

She couldn't understand, for a moment, why so few people were taking in the ludicrous spectacle of her ex-husband, the sometimes almost-famous TV personality, making such an incredible prat of himself all over the appalling Jocasta Newsome.

Then she heard the silence. Silence spreading like a stain down the hall, from the people at the front who'd seen it first.

Fay looked and didn't believe, her eyes hurrying back to stupid Guy—standing in the aisle now, dusting off his trousers, mumbling, "Sorry, sorry, must have tripped."

Col Croston, up on the platform next to Max Goff, didn't see it either, at first; Goff's back was turned to him. "Ah," Col

Croston saying. "Here we are. Lights. We can continue. Splendid. Well, I think, if there are no more questions, we'll . . . Sorry?"

Max Goff's hand on his arm.

"You want to say something? Sure. Fine. Go ahead."

Fay was not aware that Goff had actually asked the Colonel anything, but now the bulky man was coming slowly, quite lazily, to his feet and opening his mouth as if to say something monumentally significant. But there was no sign of the large, even, white teeth which normally shone out when the smooth mat of red beard divided. A black hole in the beard, Goff trying to shape a word but managing only:

"Aw . . . "

And then out it all came.

He's being sick, said the sensible part of Fay's mind. He's been eating tomato chutney and thick, rich strawberry jam full of whole, ripe strawberries.

"Awk . . . "

A gob of it landed—*thoppp!*—on the blotter in front of Max Goff.

In the front row, Hilary Ivory exploded into hysterics and struggled to get out of her seat, something crimson and warm having landed in her soft, white hair.

Fay saw that Max Goff had two mouths, and one was in his neck.

He threw back his head with an eruption of spouting blood, raised both white-suited arms far above his head—like a last, proud act of worship. And then, overturning the table, he plunged massively into the well of screams.

eight

His own light was in his eyes.

"You know, Mr. Powys," Humble said, "Mr. Trow was dead right about you."

The hand lamp was tucked into the cleft between two tree roots. Humble was sitting in the grass a few feet away from the lamp.

He couldn't see Humble very well, but he could see what Humble was holding. It was a crossbow: very modern, plenty of black metal. It had a heavy-looking rifle-type butt, which was obviously what Humble had hit him with. Back of the neck, maybe between the shoulder blades. Either way, he didn't want to move.

"What he said was," Humble explained, "his actual words: 'Joe Powys is *very* obedient.' He always does what he's told. Somebody tells him to go to the Tump, he goes to the Tump."

Powys's senses were numbed.

"Well, that's how I prefer it," Humble said. *"Making* people do fings is very time-consuming. I much prefer obedience."

"Where's Andy?" Powys was surprised to discover he could still talk.

"Well, he ain't here, is he? Somebody indicate he might be?"

Humble lifted his crossbow to his shoulder, squinted at Powys. He was about ten feet away. There was a steel bolt in the crossbow.

Powys cringed.

"Pheeeeeeew," Humble said. "Straight frew your left eyeball, Mr. Powys."

Powys didn't move. You live in fear of the unknown and the unseen, and when you're facing death, death turns out to be a thug with a mousetrap mouth and a lethal weapon favored by the lower type of country-sport enthusiast.

"But it won't come to that," Humble said. "Seeing as obedience is one of your virtues. I won't say that's not a pity—I never done a human being with one of these—but if I got to postpone the experience, I got to postpone it. On your feet, please, Mr. P."

"I don't think I can. I think you broke my collarbone."

"Oh, that's where you keep your collarbone these days, is it? Don't fuck with me please, get up."

And Powys did, accepting without question that this guy would kill him if he didn't. Humble stood up, too. He was wearing a black gilet, his arms bare. Humble was a timeless figure, the hunter. He killed.

"Now, we're going to go down off the Tump, Mr. Powys, on account you can't always trust your reactions up here, as you surely know. We're going to go down, back over that wall, OK?"

"Where's Andy?" Powys said.

"I'm empowered to answer just one of your questions, and that wasn't it, I'm sorry."

Powys tripped over a root and grabbed at a bush. "Aaah." Thorns.

"Keep going, please. Don't turn round."

Powys froze. *He's going to kill me. He's going to shoot me from behind.*

Something slammed into his back and he cried out and lost his footing and crashed through the thornbush and rolled over and over.

" . . . did tell you to keep going."

As he lay in a tangle at the foot of the mound, Humble slipped down beside him, just inside the wall.

"I'll tell you the answer, shall I? Then you can work out the question at your leisure. The answer is—you ready?—the answer is . . . *his mother.* Now get on your feet, over the wall and across to the old house."

The night has gathered around Warren, and he's loving it. Earned himself a piece of it now—a piece of night to carry around with him and nibble on whenever he's hungry.

And he's still hungry, his appetite growing all the time.

He's off out of the back door of the town hall and across the square, into the alley by the Cock, the Stanley knife hot in his right hand. Only it's not *his* hand anymore; this is the Hand of Glory.

The ole box is just a box now, and what's in the box is just bones. His is the hand and his will be the fucking glory.

Felt like doing a few more while he was in there. That Colonel Croston, of the SAS. That'd have been a laugh.

Incredible, the way he just walked in the back entry and the lights had gone, dead on cue, like wherever he goes he brings the night in with him.

And he has this brilliant night vision now. Just like daylight. *Better* than daylight, 'cause *he* can see and no bugger else can.

Standing behind this fat phony, big man on a squidgy little chair, glaring white suit—you'd have to be blind *not* to see him—and all the time in the world to choose where to put it in.

Didn't need to choose. The Hand of Glory knew.

Brilliant. Thought he'd be squealing like a pig, but he never made more than a gurgle.

Brilliant.

There's someone behind Tessa in the alley. Tall guy.

"Who's this?"

Tessa laughing. "My teacher."

"How's it going, Warren?" the teacher saying. "How are you feeling?"

Warren grinning, savoring the night in his mouth, and his eyes are like lights. Headlights, yeah.

"Good lad," says the teacher.

Minnie Seagrove was not too happy with the Bourbon creams.

It was long after nine when she placed a small china plate of the long brown biscuits on one of the occasional tables and set it down by the side of Frank's chair at just the right height. Putting the camping light on the table next to the plate, still dubiously pursing up her lips. "I do hope they're all right, Frank. They're nearly a month over the sell-by date. I remember I bought them the day they took you into the General. They'd just opened that new Safeways near the station, and I thought I'd go down there from the hospital, 'cause it's not far to walk, take me mind off it, sort of thing."

Tears came into Mrs. Seagrove's eyes at the memory. "I bought a whole rainbow trout, too. I thought, He's never managed to catch one, least I can do is serve him one up for his first dinner when he comes out."

She turned away and grabbed a Scottie from the box to dab her eyes. They were Kleenex really, but Mrs. Seagrove called all tissues Scotties because it sounded more homely.

"Had to throw it in the bin, that trout. Well past its sell-by. Still, you *did* come back from the General, after all, didn't you, Frank?"

Looking at him through the tears, Mrs. Seagrove had to keep blinking and on every other blink, Frank seemed to disappear. She applied the Scottie to her eyes again and sat down opposite him. He didn't look well, she had to admit.

"Eat your Bourbons, Frank," she said. "There'll be nothing left of you if you go on like this. I know, I'll put the wireless on—you can listen to the local news."

Mrs. Seagrove kept the wireless on the sideboard. To tell the truth, it wasn't her kind of wireless at all. Justin had bought it for them last Christmas but one. It was a long black thing with dozens of switches and you could see all these speakers through the plastic grilles, big ones and little ones, all jumbled up. Why they couldn't make them with just one speaker and cover it up neatly like they used to, she'd never know.

Being that changing stations was so complicated, she had it permanently tuned to Offa's Dyke Radio. She'd have preferred Radio Two herself, that young Chris Stuart had ever such a comforting voice, but Frank said if you were living in a new place you ought to keep up with what was happening around you, even if it wasn't very interesting. Mrs. Seagrove certainly found most of it quite boring—too much about councils and sheep prices—so she put it on quite low tonight (Frank had good ears, better than hers) and she only turned it up when she heard that Max Goff mentioned.

" . . . *at a packed public meeting to discuss his plans for a so-called New Age mystical healing center in the border town of Crybbe . . . from where Gavin Ashpole now reports.*"

Gavin who? What had happened to Fay Morrison? She might have been a bit awkward about the . . . thing. But she did seem quite a nice girl when you actually met her.

" . . . *Townsfolk listened in hostile silence as Max Goff explained his plans to turn Crybbe into a kind of New Age Lourdes, bringing in thousands of tourists from all over the world and providing a massive boost for the local economy. However, he said, it would be up to the town whether it . . . Oh . . . Oh, you bitch . . . oh, you . . . oh, please . . . "*

Mrs. Seagrove recoiled from the wireless as if a wasp had flown out of one of the speakers.

"Frank, did you hear that?"

"Oh . . . oh . . . please . . . yes . . . yes, do it . . . ! CHEW IT OFF!!"

There was a long silence and then the voice of the newsreader came back.

"I'm sorry, I . . . I'm not sure what happened there. We'll try and return to that report . . . er, other news now . . . "

"Frank," said Minnie Seagrove. "Did you hear that, Frank? That's your precious Offa's Dyke Radio for you. Chris Stuart never goes to pieces like that. Did you hear . . . Frank?"

Frank's chair was empty.

All the Bourbon biscuits were still on the plate, six of them, arranged in a little semicircle.

"Frank? Frank, where are you?"

Breathing faster, Mrs. Seagrove turned and switched off the wireless and turned back to the chair and rubbed her eyes with the screwed-up tissue, but Frank was gone and the door was closed.

She started to feel very confused.

Get a grip, Minnie, get a grip.

Nothing was right. *Nothing* was right. Mrs. Seagrove went to the window and flung back the curtains. "It's you, isn't it? It's *you."*

Great, ugly slag-heap thing. She'd probably be able to see the church if it wasn't for that; always liked to see a church in the distance, even if she didn't go.

She could see the mound quite clearly tonight, even though there was no moon. It was a bit like the mound was lit up from inside, not *very* lit up, sort of a yellowish glow like a lemon jelly.

She thought she could see a shadow moving across the field.

"Is that you, Frank?" She banged on the window. "You're not going out in that wet grass this time of night!"

He was stupid sometimes, Frank, like a little boy. He'd walk down to that river and just stare at it, wondering why he never caught that many fish.

She pulled her walking shoes from under the sideboard. "You come back here, Frank Seagrove. It's not safe out there!"

✤ ————————————————————————————

nine

Fay was still seeing it like a bad home video: fuzzy, ill-lit, full of camera shake and overreaction. Women screaming, people staring at each other in shock, trying to speak, faces hard and grainy in the blue, deep-freeze light. Stricken Max Goff convulsing on the floor. Col Croston bending over him.

"Get a doctor!"

Portly man from Off shouldering his way to the front. Fay recognized him as the local GP.

Wynford Wiley—probably the last to react—moving like a sleepwalker, Fay following in his considerable wake, up the central aisle, pushing past Guy. Hilary Ivory stumbling toward them, face in a permanent contortion like that painting of Munch's—*The Scream*—etched in similar stark, nervy colors because of the stammering lights.

Hilary's hands squeezing her hair and then the hands coming out like crimson rubber gloves and Hilary's shrieks almost shredding Col's crisp command,

"Nobody move! Nobody leaves the hall!"

And then, turning to the doctor, "Bloody obvious, man. Had his throat slashed."

At which point spangled brightness burst out of the wrought-iron chandeliers—an electrical blip—and Fay saw the mayor, Councilor James Oswald Preece, standing on the edge of the raised area, holding his arms as though, with his frail frame, he could conceal the carnage.

"Silence!"

Even Wynford Wiley stopped, so suddenly that Fay almost bumped into his big blue back.

And the big lights stuttered out again, leaving the mayor with a momentary jagged aura of yellow and black.

"Listen to me!"

"Is he dying?" a woman demanded from the New Age quarter.

One of the men in suits said, "Look, I'm his legal adviser, and this is . . . "

"Is Max *dead?*"

" . . . I insist you call an ambulance."

"Is he . . . ?"

"Will . . . you . . . be . . . *quiet,* madam!"

A new and significant Jimmy Preece, Fay saw. No longer the husk of a farmer, flat-capped, monosyllabic—'ow're you, 'ow're you . . . Authority there now. Resonance.

"Now," Jimmy Preece said. "I'm not going to elaborate on this. Isn't the time. So don't none of you ask me. I'm speaking to you as your First Citizen, but I'm also speaking as a Preece, and most of you'll know what I'm saying yere."

The mayor's eyes flickered to one side. "For all the new-comers, I'd ask you to accept my word that . . . that we are all in . . . well . . . "

He stopped. His jaw quivered.

" . . . in *serious, mortal danger . . . "*

He let this sink in. Fay looked around to see how they were all taking it. Some of the Crybbe people looked at each other with anxiety and varying amounts of understanding.

"Serious. Mortal. Danger," Jimmy Preece intoned again, almost to himself, looking down at his boots.

The lawyer said, "Oh, for heaven's sake, man . . . "

"And it's more than us what's in danger. And it's more than our children and . . . and their children."

The doctor stood up, flecks of blood on his glasses.

"No!" somebody shouted. "Oh God, no!" And the New Age quarter erupted.

Jimmy Preece held up a hand. "I . . . " His voice slumped. "I'm sorry he's dead."

" . . . through the esophagus, I'd imagine," the doctor told Col Croston quietly, but not quietly enough.

"I mean it," the mayor said. "I wished 'im no harm, I only wished 'im . . . gone from yere."

Fay glanced at Guy. His face sagged. His blond hair, disar-ranged, revealed a hitherto secret bald patch. Catrin Jones was several yards away, looking past him to where Larry Ember was walking up the aisle, camera on his shoulder.

"Who let you in?" Jimmy Preece said wearily. "Switch that thing off, sir, or it'll be taken from you." Guy turned, tapped

Larry's arm, and shook his head.

To the side of Guy, the Newsomes mutely held hands.

"I'm going now," Jimmy Preece said, "to see to the bell. I urge you all—and this is *vital*—to stay absolutely calm."

" . . . come with you, Jim," somebody said.

"No you won't. You'll stay yere. You'll *all* stay yere."

"Ah, look . . . " Col Croston said, "Mr. Mayor, there's been a murder here. It's not a normal situation."

"No, Colonel, it's not normal, and that's why nobody goes from yere till I sees to the bell. I don't say this lightly. Nobody is to leave, see. Nobody."

"Who's to say," Col came close to the mayor, "whoever did this isn't still in the room?"

"No. 'E isn't yere, Colin, you can . . . "

Wynford Wiley pleaded, "Let me radio for assistance, Jim. Least let me do that."

"Leave it, Wynford. You're a local man, near enough. This is not a police matter."

"But it's a murder," Col Croston protested.

"It's a *Crybbe* matter, sir!"

"Jim," Wynford whined, "it's more than my . . . "

"Your *job?*" A blue vein throbbed in the mayor's forehead. "Your piffling little *job!* You'll take out your radio, Wynford Wiley, and you'll put 'im on that table."

Wynford stood for a moment, his small features seeming to chase each other around his Edam cheese of a face. "I can't." He hung his head, turned away, and trudged back toward the main door.

But when he reached it, he found his way barred by four large, quiet men of an unmistakable agricultural demeanor.

"Don't be a bigger fool than you look, Wynford," said the mayor, walking slowly down the aisle. "Just give me that radio."

Wynford sighed, took out the pocket radio in the black rubber case with the short rubber aerial, and placed it in Jimmy Preece's bony, outstretched hand.

"It's for the best, Wynford. Now." The mayor turned and looked around him. "Where's Mrs. Morrison?"

Oh Christ.

"I'm here, Mr. Preece."

His deeply scored lips shambled into something that might have become a smile. "You're not very big, Mrs. Morrison, but you been stirring up a lot o' trouble, isn't it?"

"What's that supposed to mean?"

One of the men opened a door for him. Another handed him a lamp, a farmer's lambing light.

"Means I don't want you left in yere," said Jimmy Preece. "Christ alone knows what old rubbish you'd be spoutin'."

He pushed her out of the door in front of himself.

Outside, it was fully dark.

It was only 9:40.

"Oh my God, my God . . . Oh . . . "

"It's only a dead body," Mr. Preece said. "It can't hurt you. Any more than that Goff can hurt anyone now."

"It's horrible," Fay said. "It's . . . perverse. You knew it was here, didn't you, like . . . like this?"

She was shaking. She couldn't help it.

"No," said the mayor. "I didn't think it was gonner be like this. But it don't surprise me."

"But, Mr. Preece, it's your own grandson. How can you bear it?"

"I can bear it, 'cause I got no choice," said Mr. Preece simply. He turned the light away from the coffin and pulled her back, but she could still see the image of Jonathon showcased like a big, grotesque Christmas doll.

Glad the power was off. Only wished somebody would disconnect the atmosphere.

Was she imagining this, or was it Jonathon she could smell, sweet corruption, bacteria stimulated by exposure to the dense, churchy air?

"Would you mind if I waited outside?"

"You'll stay yere."

"It's . . . I'm sorry, Mr. Preece, it's the smell."

"Aye. We should lay him flat and put the lid back on."

Don't ask me to help. Please don't ask me to help.

"Gonner give me a hand, then?"

No . . . ! But he was taking her arm. "We 'ave time. Ten minutes yet, see." Guiding her into the body of the church. She held fingers over her nose.

"Mr. Preece . . . "

"What?"

She took her hand away from her face. "Why me? Why'd you really bring me along?"

The question resounded from invisible walls and rafters.

"Just hold that." Giving her the lambing light.

Fay stayed where she was, well back, and shone the light on the coffin, looking away.

"Closer, girl. Shine it closer."

She felt him watching her. She moved a little closer. The smell was appalling. She imagined bloated, white maggots at work inside Jonathon Preece, although she knew that was ludicrous. Wasn't it?

Fay pushed knuckles into her mouth to stifle the rising panic.

Mr. Preece was on his knees beneath the coffin, its top end propped against the pulpit. "Never get 'im back on that trolley. Lay 'im . . . flat . . . on the ground. All we can do." He pushed at the coffin until it was almost upright and the body began to sag and belly out, like a drunk in a shop doorway.

"Jesus, Mr. Preece, he's slipping! He's going to fall out! He's going to fall on me!"

"Push him back in, girl! Put the light down."

"I can't!"

"Do it, woman!"

She did. She touched him. She pushed his chest, felt the ruched line of the postmortem scar. He was cold, but far from stiff now, and she remembered him on the riverbank, soaked and leaking, tongue out and the froth and his skin all crimped.

She closed her eyes and pretended it *was* fish and the stink was coming from elsewhere, until the coffin, with its sickening cargo, was flat on the stones and Jimmy Preece was fitting the lid on. Then she was bending over a pew, retching, nothing coming up but bile, like sour, liquid terror.

"Dead, poor boy," Jimmy Preece said.

She stood up. Wiped her mouth on her sleeve. The smell was still in the air, sweetly putrid. Would she ever get away from that smell?

Heard herself saying, "Who was it, Mr. Preece? Who did this? Who made a sideshow out of him?"

"Dead," he said. "Can't hurt you now, can 'e?" He came close. "Won't hurt that dog, neither, will 'e?"

Oh no. Something had been whispering to her that it was going to be this, but she'd kept pushing it back.

"That's why you brought me, isn't it? That's why you made me touch him."

He stood there, recovering from the exertion, his breathing like coins rattling in a biscuit tin. Max Goff stabbed to death, something unspeakably vile seeping into Crybbe, but it was the death by drowning of one Jonathon Preece, young farmer of this parish . . .

"Family thing," he said, voice as dry as wood ash. "Something I 'ave to know before I die. Jack sent Jonathon out to make away with that animal of yours."

"And why?" she said, but he didn't answer that.

"And he never came back."

"OK, I'll tell you," Fay said, in a rush. "I'll tell you what happened. OK?"

His words of a moment long ago lurched back at her . . . *Before I die? Have to know before I die.*

She didn't even want to think what he meant by this, so she told him everything. Everything except for the feelings Joe Powys had said he'd experienced on the riverbank with the gun in his hands and the urge to kill.

Mr. Preece went on breathing like a dying man. When she'd finished, he said, "There's more to it than that."

"No, there isn't, I swear."

"Jonathon was a strong boy and a good swimmer. 'E also—unlike that brother of 'is—'e had a bit o' common sense."

"I'm sorry," Fay said. "I can't tell you what happened when we'd gone. Perhaps . . . I mean, with hindsight, we should have stayed. With hindsight, we should never have thrown the gun in the river in the first place. I'm sorry. I really am desperately sorry. Mr. Preece . . . " She was aware of her voice becoming very small and a bit pathetic.

He was moving away toward the entrance, pulling out a pocket watch the size of a travel alarm clock. It had big luminous hands.

"Right," he said. "You can wait in the porch, by yere, but you don't go out. You don't open that door until the bell's finished, you understand?"

"I want to come up with you."

"We goes up alone," he snapped. "Now you remember what I said, you keep that door *shut.* Understand?"

"Yes. Look . . . Mr. Preece . . . "

"Make it quick, miss, make it very quick."

She was remembering how controlled he'd been in the town hall, how sure that the killer had left the building.

"You know who did this . . . to Jonathon, don't you? And you know who killed Max Goff when the lights were out."

He turned his back on her and mounted the first step.

"Don't you?"

He didn't look back, and a turn in the spiral staircase took the light away.

"Is *that* a Crybbe matter, as well?" she yelled. "Or is it . . . ?"

God, she thought, as the darkness in the church became, for a while, absolute, I can still smell it. Still smell Jonathon.

And she put her hands over her face.

Is it a family matter? was what she'd almost said.

Because it ought to be Warren he was bringing up here tonight. *It ought to be Warren.*

She heard the mayor stumble on the steps.

"Are you all right, Mr. Preece?"

She heard another footstep, and his ratchet breathing starting up again, like a very old lawn mower.

Quietly, she began to ascend the steps, until she could see his wavering torch beam reflecting from the curved stonework. And then the beam was no longer visible and she climbed two or three steps until the stairway curved around and she could see the weakening glimmer once more.

The footsteps above her stopped. There was a long silence, and then,

"Get *back,* you . . . "

He began to cough, and she could hear the fluid gathering in his lungs and throat, thick oil slurping in the bottom of a rusty old can.

"All right, I'm sorry, I'm going back . . . all right."

Clattering back to the foot of the stairway, thinking, If anything happens to him now, am I going to have the guts to go up there, drag him out of the way or climb over him and pull on the rope a hundred times?

Have I the strength to pull a bell rope a hundred times? (There's a kind of recoil, isn't there, like a gun, and the rope shoots back up and sometimes pulls large men off their feet.)

God almighty, will I have the strength to pull it *once?*

Leave him. He knows what he's doing. He won't stumble and break his ankle. He won't have a stroke. He won't have a heart attack. He's a Preece.

Like Jack, mangled by his own tractor, under intensive care in Hereford.

Like Jonathon, putrefying in his coffin just a few yards away.

But was there, at the heart of the Preece family, something even more putrid?

She stood at the bottom of the steps, waiting for the blessed first peal, which only a few nights ago, walking Arnold in the sad streets of this crippled town, she'd dreaded.

Presently, she saw the light hazing the stones again and heard his footsteps.

Don't understand.

He's coming down.

She heard his rattling breath, then there was a clatter and the light was all over the place and she heard the lamp rolling down from step to step.

It went out as she caught it.

"Mr. Preece . . . are you?"

He stood before her breathing roughly, breathing as though he didn't care if each breath *was* his last.

Fay flicked frantically at the switch and beat the lamp against the palm of her left hand until it hurt. It relit and she shone it on him and reeled back, almost dropping the thing in her shock, and the beam splashed across the nave.

She held the lambing light with both hands to stop it shaking and shone it at the wall to the side of Mr. Preece so it wouldn't blind him and terrify her with the obscenity of it.

It was wrapped around him like a thick snake.

"What is it?" Fay whispered, and as the whisper dried in her throat she knew.

Perhaps it was winding itself around his neck, choking out of him what little life remained.

Mr. Preece let it fall to the stone floor.

He said hoarsely, "It's the bell rope, girl. Somebody cut the bell rope."

And even Jonathon, with his putrid perfume and his post-mortem scar, hadn't scared her half so much as the stricken face of his grandfather, an electric puzzle of pulsing blood vessels, veins and furrows.

ten

GRACE PETERS
1928–1992
Beloved wife of
Canon A. L. Peters

White letters.

Cold, black marble.

Pressing his forehead against it, he thought, A. L. Peters. That's me, isn't it? But it isn't my grave. Not yet, anyway. Only one of us is dead, Grace.

What am I doing here?

He remembered now, walking in a dignified fashion through the darkened streets, arm in a crook parallel to his chest. In his best suit, of course, with his dog collar; she would not be seen out with him if he were attired in anything less.

Certainly not a faded T-shirt with the flaking remains of Kate Bush across his chest.

Peered down at it. Too dark to read the words, not white and gleaming like the letters on the grave. But he remembered the name, Kate Bush. Who the hell *was* Kate Bush, anyway?

Ought to know that.

Or maybe not. He could hear somebody, a woman, saying, *"There's a chance you'll lapse quite soon into the old confusion, and you'll have that to contend with, too. I'm sorry."*

Sorry. Well, aren't we all? Hmmph.

Cold black marble.

Cool hands.

What was all that about?

Alex shook his head.

Well, here I am, sitting on Grace's grave at the less-fashionable end of Crybbe churchyard at God knows what time of night. Haven't the faintest idea how the bloody hell I got here. Not exactly a cold night, but this is no place to spend it.

Wonder if I simply got pissed? And a bit maudlin, the way you do. Stagger along to pay your respects to the little woman. Sorry if I dislodged some of these dinky chippings that your will was so insistent we should use. No wonder old Murray had you shoved out here—probably hoping the wood would overgrow the thing. And the sooner the better. Stupid cow, no taste at all, God knows how I ever got entangled with you.

Guilty? Me? Bloody hell, you *ensnared* me, you conniving creature.

Alex clambered to his feet. Chuckled. Don't take any notice of me, old girl, I'm rambling again. *Must* have been on the sauce, I could certainly do with a pee.

He stumbled into the wood and relieved himself with much enjoyment. There were times, he thought, when a good pee could be more satisfying than sex.

Consideration for the finer feelings of his late wife, who—let's get this in proportion once and for all—*did not deserve it,* had taken him deeper into the wood than he'd intended, and it took him a while to find his way back to the blasted churchyard.

Emerging, in fact, several yards away from Grace's grave, catching a foot on something, stumbling, feeling himself going into a nosedive.

"Damn." Alex threw out both hands to break his fall. Bad news at his age, a fall, brittle bones, etc.—and, worst of all, a geriatric ward.

Something unexpectedly soft broke his fall. One hand felt cloth, a jacket perhaps.

"Oh gosh, terribly sorry." Thinking at first he must have tripped over some old tramp trying to get an early night. This was before he felt all the wet patches.

"Oh dear. Oh hell." It was all very sticky indeed, and his hands felt as if they were covered in it already. Tweedy sort of jacket. Shirt. And blood; no question of what the sticky stuff was.

"Hello. Are you all right?"

Bloody fool. Of course the chap wasn't all right. Wished he had a flashlight; couldn't see a damn thing.

Tentatively, he put out a hand and found a face. It, too, was very wet, horribly sticky and unpleasantly cold. Poor beggar must be slashed to ribbons. He lowered his head, listening for breathing. None at all.

There wasn't a clergyman in the world who didn't recognize the presence of death.

"Oh hell."

Alex's sticky fingers moved shakily down over the blood-caked lips, over the chin, down to the neck where he felt . . .

Oh God. Oh Jesus.

I've . . .

I've stumbled over my own body.

I was wrong. I *am* dead. I think I've been murdered. Grace, you stupid bitch, why didn't you tell me? Is this how it is? Is this what happens? Oh Lord, somebody get me away from here. Beam me up, God, for Christ's sake.

For the body wore a stiff clerical collar.

Crybbe Court in view again.

"Uh!"

Humble had prodded him in the small of the back, presumably with the butt of the crossbow.

They were on the edge of the Tump field, facing the court-yard. As Powys looked up at the black house, its ancient frame seemed to tense against the pressure of the night. There was a small sparking under the eaves, like the friction of flints, and the air was faintly tainted with sulfur.

Powys felt his anger rekindle.

In the moment of the sparks, he'd seen the hole in the eaves that was the prospect chamber. Below it, slivers of light had figured the edge of a piece of furniture halfway up the pile of rubbish which had broken Rachel Wade's fall and her neck.

"We're going in," Humble said, picking up the lamp from the grass.

"You might be going in," said Powys. "It's too spooky for me, quite honestly."

Humble laughed.

"You must think I'm fucking stupid," Powys said. "You want me to go up to the prospect chamber and kind of lose my balance, right?"

It would, he knew, make perfect sense to the police.

"Since you ask," Humble said. "That would be quite tidy, yeah, and it would save me a bit of trouble. But if you say no, I get to use this fing on you, which'll be a giggle anyway, so you can please yourself, mate, I ain't fussy."

"How would you get rid of the body?"

"Not a problem. Really. Trust me."

"None of this scares you?"

"None of what?"

"Like, we just saw a light flaring under the roof. It wasn't what you'd call natural . . . "

"Did we? I didn't."

Humble stood with his back to the broken wall around the Tump, a hard, skinny, sinewy, ageless man. Powys could run away and Humble would run faster. He could go for Humble, maybe try and kick him in the balls, and Humble would damage him quickly and efficiently before his shoe could connect. He could sit down and refuse to move and Humble would put a crossbow bolt into his brain.

Powys said, "You don't feel a tension in the air? A gathering in the atmosphere? I thought you were supposed to be a countryman."

Humble snorted, leaning on the butt of his crossbow.

"There are countrymen," he said, "and there are hippies. I'm fit, I've got good hearing and ace eyesight. I'm not a bad shot. I can snare rabbits and skin 'em, and I can work at night and I ain't scared. Ghosts, evil spirits, magic stones, it's all shit. If the people who employ me wanna believe in it, that's fine, no skin off my nose."

Blessed are the skeptics, Powys thought.

Rachel was a skeptic.

"And I get paid *very* well. See, I can go in that house any time of the day or night, I don't give a shit. I can piss up the side of a standing stone in the full moon. So what? Countrymen ain't hippies, Mr. Powys."

He was telling Powys indirectly who it was who'd locked the door when Rachel was in the Court. And, maybe, who'd pushed her out.

He got paid very well.

"Andy pays you," Powys realized.

Humble said, "I'm in the employ of the Epidemic Group as security consultant."

"And Andy's been paying you as well."

Humble lifted his crossbow. "Let's go."

"Where's Andy?"

"I said, let's *move!*"

"No."

"Fair enough," Humble said. "Fair enough."

He moved backward a few paces into the field until he was almost invisible against the night.

"OK, you made your decision. I got to get this over wiv in a couple of minutes, so you got a choice. You can run. Or you can turn around and walk away. Just keep walking, fast or slow as you like, and you'll never know. Some people like to run."

Oh Jesus, Powys thought. For the past twelve years he hadn't really cared too much about life and how long it would last.

"I thought you'd never shot anybody."

"Not wiv a crossbow. On the two other occasions," said Humble, "I used a gun."

Fay, Powys thought obliquely. Caught an image of the elf with the rainbow eye. I'm going to lose Fay.

"Or, of course," said Humble reasonably, "you can just stand there and watch."

He brought up the crossbow. Powys instinctively ducked, went down on his knees, his arms around his head.

Through his arms, he heard a familiar lopsided semi-scampering.

"No!" he screamed. "No, Arnold! Get back! Get away!"

He saw the black and white dog limping toward him from the darkness and, out of the corner of his eye, watched the crossbow swivel a couple of inches to the right.

"Beautiful," Humble said, and fired.

She ran at the door and snatched at the bolts, throwing one of them back before Mr. Preece grabbed her from behind and pulled her away.

She struggled frantically and vainly. He might look like a stretcher case, but his arms were like bands of iron.

She felt her feet leave the floor, and he hauled her back from the porch and set her down under the stone font. The lambing light was in her eyes, but it didn't blind her because it was losing strength, going dimmer.

"What the *fuck* are you doing, Mr. Preece? What bloody use is *this* place as protection?"

All she could hear from behind the dying light was his dreadful breathing, something out of intensive care at the chest clinic.

"There's no spirituality here anymore. All there was was the bell and now you can't reach that, there's no way you can resist . . . him . . . in this place. A church is a church only because the stones are steeped in centuries of worship . . . human hopes and dreams, all that stuff. All you've got here is a bloody *warehouse.*"

"Stay quiet," Jimmy Preece hissed. "Keep calm. Keep . . . "

"Oh, sure, keep your head down! It's what this piss-poor place is all about. Don't make waves, don't take sides, we don't want no *clever people.* Oh!" She bent her head into her arms and sobbed with anger and frustration.

Needing the rage and the bitterness, because, if you could keep them stoked, keep the heat high, it would burn out the fear.

She looked into the light—not white anymore, but yellow, her least-favorite color, the yellow of disease, of embalming fluid. The yellow of Grace Legge.

How would he come?

Would he come like Grace, flailing and writhing with white-eyed malevolence?

How would he come?

"What's going to happen, Mr. Preece?" she said. It was the small voice, and she was ashamed.

"I don't know, girl." There was a wheezing under it that she hadn't heard before. "God help me, I don't know."

She thought about her dad. At least he'd be safe. He was with Jean, and Jean was smart. Jean knew about these things.

"She can't talk to you, she can't see you, there's no brain activity there . . . Entirely harmless."

No she doesn't. She isn't smart at all. A little knowledge, a little intuition—nothing more dangerous. Jean only *thinks* she's smart.

And now Powys had gone to Jean, saying, Help us, O Wise One, get us out of this, save Crybbe, save us all.

Oh, Powys, whatever happened to the Old Golden Land?

It began with a rustling up at the front of the church near the coffin, and then the sound of something rolling on stone.

"What's that?"

But Mr. Preece just breathed at her.

She clutched at the side of the font, all the hot, healthy anger and the frustration and bitterness drenched in cold, stagnant fear.

She couldn't move. She imagined Jonathon Preece stirring in his coffin, cracking his knuckles as his hands opened out.

Washerwoman's hands.

Fay felt a pain in her chest.

"Oh, God." The nearest she could produce to a prayer. Not too wonderful, for a clergyman's daughter.

And then came the smell of burning and little flames, a row of little, yellow, smoky flames, burning in the air, four or five feet from the floor.

Fay watched, transfixed, still sitting under the font, as if both her legs were broken.

"Heeeeeeeee!" she heard. High-pitched—a *yellow* noise, flecked with insanity.

Jimmy Preece moved. He picked up the light and walked into the nave and shone what remained of the light up the aisle.

"Aye," he said, and his breathing was so loud and his voice so hoarse that they were inseparable now.

Down the aisle, into the lambing light, a feeble beam, a figure walked.

Fay saw cadaverous arms hanging from sawn-off sleeves. Eyes that were as yellow-white as the eyes of a ghost, but still—just—human eyes.

The arms hanging loosely. Something in one hand, something stubby, blue-white metal still gleaming through the red-brown stains.

Behind him the yellow flames rose higher.

A foot kicked idly at something on the stone floor and it rolled toward Fay. It was a small tin tube with a red nozzle. Lighter fuel.

Warren had opened up the Bible on its lectern and set the pages on fire.

" 'Ow're you, Granddad," Warren said.

eleven

There were too many people in here.

"Don't touch him, please," Col said. There was quite a wide semicircle around Goff's body into which nobody, apart from this girl, had been inclined to intrude. There'd be sufficient explanations to make after tonight as it was, and Col was determined nobody was going to disturb or cover up the evidence, however unpleasant it became, whatever obnoxious substances it happened to discharge.

The girl peered down, trying to see Goff's face.

"I paint," she explained casually. "I like to remember these things."

"Oh. It's Tessa, isn't it. Tessa Byford."

Col watched her with a kind of appalled admiration. So cool, so controlled. How young women had changed. He couldn't remember seeing her earlier. But then there were a few hundred people here tonight—and right now, he rather wished there hadn't been such a commendable turnout.

He was angry with himself. That he should allow someone to creep in under cover of darkness and slash the throat of the guest of honor. Obviously—OK—the last thing one would expect in a place like Crybbe. And yet rural areas were no longer immune from sudden explosions of savage violence—think of the Hungerford massacre. He should—knowing of the underlying trepidation about Goff's plans—have been ready to react to the kind of situation for which he'd been training half his life. He remembered, not too happily, telling Guy Morrison how the Crybbe audience would ask Goff a couple of polite questions before drifting quietly away.

And then, just as quietly, they'll shaft the blighter.

Shafted him, all right.

Whoever it was had come and gone through the small back door, the one the town councilors used. It had been unlocked throughout. That had been a mistake, too.

Couldn't get away from it—he'd been bloody lax. And now he was blindly following the orders of a possibly crazy old man who'd decreed that nobody was permitted to depart—which, if the police were on their way, would have been perfectly sensible. But under the circumstances . . .

He didn't even *know* the circumstances.

All he knew was that Jimmy Preece had the blind support of an appreciable number of large, uncompromising, tough-looking men and, if anybody made an attempt to leave, the situation was likely to turn ugly.

Not—looking at Max Goff sprawled in his own blood—that it was particularly attractive as things stood.

Every so often, people would wander over to Col, some angry, others quite sheepish.

"It doesn't make a lot of sense, now does it, Colonel?" Graham Jarrett argued, sweat patches having appeared under the arms of his safari suit. "A man's been murdered, and all we're doing is giving his murderer time to get clean away."

"Not if he's in this room we aren't," said Col very quickly. Jarrett's eyes widened. "That's not likely, is it?"

"Who knows, Mr. Jarrett, who knows?"

Graham Jarrett looked around nervously, as if wondering which of the two or three hundred people it might be safest to stand close to. The main exit was still guarded by large, uncommunicative farmers.

"Can't be long now, anyway," Col said. "I'd guess the mayor's already been in touch with the police."

No chance. This is a *Crybbe matter.*

Madness. It didn't even have the logic of a street riot. And Col Croston, who'd served six terms in Belfast, was beginning to detect signs of something worrying akin to sectarianism.

New Age versus Old Crybbe.

The Crybbe people scarcely moved. If they went to the toilets they went silently and returned to their seats. They did not converse among themselves. They seemed to know what this was about. Or, at least, they appeared satisfied that Jimmy Preece knew what it was about and there seemed to be this unspoken understanding that they should remain calm, restrain their emotions.

Bloody eerie. Just as they behaved in church. Admirable self-control or mindless apathy? Beggared belief, either way, and Col

Croston knew he couldn't allow the situation to continue much longer. He was under pressure from the New Age delegates who, while in a minority of about twenty to one, were making virtually all the noise. So much for relaxation techniques and meditative calm. Struck him there was a lot they might learn from the indigenous population.

A man in a suit, one of the Epidemic lawyers, said, "Look—let us out of here now and we'll say no more about it. But if this goes on, I'm warning you, you're all going to be in very serious trouble. Impeding the course of justice'll be the very least of it."

"I've found," Col told him, very clipped, "that in a situation like this, telling people what serious trouble they're going to be in is the fastest way to inflame what could be a highly combustible situation. I estimate there are more than three hundred adults in this room, and the fact that one of them happens to be dead could just turn out to be the very least of our worries. Now please sit down."

Aware of a sudden commotion by the main doors, he yelled into the New Age quarter, "Will somebody please restrain that lady!"

The feminist astrologer was threatening to damage the genitals of one of the farmers if he didn't get out of her way. It was Catrin Jones, physically stronger than the astrologer and also a woman, who was finally able to lead her back to her seat.

"They're not real, these people." The astrologer shook her spiky head. "They're bloody zombies. Everything's freaky."

The Cock being empty and Denzil looking at a bit of a loose end, Gomer Parry thought it was only reasonable to have *two* pints, aware this could conceivably put him over the limit. But what kind of copper stopped a tractor driver trundling along a country lane at thirty m.p.h.?

It was after ten when he drove out of the square in the yellow tractor with the big shovel raised up out of the way. The roads were about as quiet as you could get.

Fact everywhere was a bit on the quiet side. This Goff was obviously a big attraction. Not a soul on the streets, and with all the lights out, Crybbe looked like one of them film sets when everybody's gone home.

As he pulled out onto the Ludlow road, something else struck Gomer: he hadn't heard the bell. They *never* didn't ring that bell. Used to be said that old Jimmy Preece—well, young Jimmy Preece as he'd have been then—had even rung the curfew the day he got married. A hundred bongs on his wedding night; Mrs. Preece wouldn't be that lucky.

Poor old devil back on the night shift now, then. Talk about bad luck . . . you wouldn't credit it. Even if Jack pulled through with both legs still attached, didn't seem likely he'd be in any state to make it up them old steps for a good long while. Have to be putting the arm on that young tearaway, Warren.

Gomer was never sorry to leave Crybbe—miserable old place: miserable buildings, miserable folk—but he was never that happy about going home neither, not since his old lady had handed in her mop and bucket. He'd work every hour of daylight to put off that terrible moment when he had to get his own keys out instead of seeing the door opening as he tramped across the yard and hearing the old kettle whistling on the Rayburn.

When midsummer was past and the working days started getting shorter, Gomer's spirits started to droop, and tonight had been a freak foretaste of autumn, black clouds crowding in for a storm that never came, and dark by nine.

And now there was mist as well. That came down bloody quick. Gomer snapped on the full beams, only to discover his left headlight bulb had gone.

Bollocks. No copper'd be able to resist pulling him in to point this out, and then he'd get a good whiff of Gomer's breath . . . Mind just blowing in this yere nozzle, sir . . . Oh, dear, afraid I'll have to ask you to accompany me to the station. Well, Gomer could already see the smile cracking up the fat features of that bastard Wynford Wiley, and he couldn't stick that.

What he'd have to do then was switch off the headlights and try and get through the mist on the itsy-bitsy sidelights which were bugger-all use on these roads on the best of nights.

So he flicked off the heads and slowed down to about twenty, and it was still like skin-diving in a cesspit and he had to drop down to second gear.

Bloody Crybbe.

Didn't know why he said that, you couldn't blame *everything* on Crybbe.

Well, you *could* . . .

Gomer hit the brakes. "What the 'ell's that?"

Bloody hellfire, it's the old Tump. Where'd he come from?

Hang on a bit, boy, you done something a bit wrong yere. Isn't usual to see that thing straight up ahead, looming out of the mist so sudden like that, enough to scare the life out of you.

Hello . . . not on the road now, are we?

We surely are not!

Bloody teach you to go over the limit. Thought you could handle a couple of pints, no problem, but the thing is, you're getting older, boy, your reactions isn't what they was, see.

And now, look what you done, you gone clean off the road, over the shoulder, and you're on the bloody common now and if you keep on like this you'll be knocking down that Goff's wall for him after all and buggering up your digger like they done the bulldozer.

Gomer was about to pull up sharp when the front end took a dip and he realized that if he didn't go with it he was likely to turn this thing over. And he thought about Jack Preece . . . talk about lightning striking twice. Well, he didn't like this, not one bit.

"I can't stand it!" Hilary Ivory shrieked suddenly. "This room's so black and negative. It's oppressing me, I've got to have air. And I can't stand to look at *him* anymore!"

"Well, I'm sorry, but I'm not going to cover him up," Col told her. "Really daren't risk disturbing anything, isn't that right, Sergeant?" Wynford Wiley nodded vaguely, his cheese face sliced clean of expression; he'd given up—*he* should be directing this situation and look at him . . . jacket off, tie around his ear, glazed-eyed and sweating like a pig.

"All I can suggest is you look the other way, Mrs. Ivory, I'm sorry."

"It's *your* fault." Hilary turned furiously on her husband. "You knew it was coming. You should have warned him. What use is a seer who sees and doesn't tell?"

"Me?" Hitherto gloomily silent, Adam Ivory was stunned into speech. "You didn't want me to say a word, you bloody hypocritical cow!" Halfway out of his seat, gripping his knees. "You didn't want to throw a shadow over things. You didn't want to lose your cozy little flat in your cozy little town in . . . in . . . "

"Just a minute." Col Croston jumped down from the platform and strode over to where the couple were sitting amid Jarrett, a bunch of healers, the Newsomes, and Larry Ember standing up, smoking a cigarette, his camera held between his ankles.

"What's this about? What are you saying?"

Guy Morrison said wearily, "Adam reads tarot cards. He saw disaster looming."

"Oh," said Col, disappointed. "I see."

"No, you don't," said Guy. "Don't knock it, Col. This is a very weird setup. Guy Morrison used to think he knew everything there was to know about the supernatural, i.e., that the whole thing was a lame excuse for not milking real life for everything one could get."

Guy made a steeple out of the fingers of both hands and pushed them together, hard. "But for once," he said, "Guy Morrison was wrong."

"What d'you mean exactly?" Col looked for somewhere to sit down. There wasn't a spare chair, so he squatted, hands on thighs. "What's the score here, as you see it, Guy? I mean, Christ, I've been around. Been in some pretty odd places, among some pretty primitive people, but, well, we don't notice things under our noses, sometimes. We think it's what you might call . . . what? Rural eccentricity, I suppose."

"No. Look . . . " Guy had taken off his expensive olive leather jacket. He didn't seem to notice it was lying on the floor now, entangled in dusty shoes. "Which is Mrs. Byford? Ask her if she knows her granddaughter's some kind of witch . . . that girl, the artist. Ask her about the ex-policeman who cut his throat in her bathroom. Go on. Ask her."

Oh hell, Col Croston thought. Bit nuts. He decided not to tell Guy the girl was here, displaying an anatomical interest in the corpse.

"You think I'm crazy, don't you? Ask her!"

"Shut up," Jocasta Newsome hissed. "Just shut up, Guy. Just for once."

Guy whirled on her, eyes alight. "*You* know I'm not crazy, you of all people. You showed me the drawings. You sent me to talk to the bloody girl. You . . . uuurh."

Hereward Newsome's thin, sensitive, artistic hands were around his throat. "You . . . smooth . . . self-opinionated . . . bastard!"

Col Croston leapt up as Guy's chair crashed over into the aisle, the chair's and Guy's legs both in the air, Hereward,

teeth clenched, trying to smash Guy's head into the boarded
floor. "No wonder . . . she wanted you to . . . open the fucking . . . exhibition." Col Croston gripping Hereward's shoulder,
wrenching him off, as Catrin Jones—"Guy!"—fell down heavily
beside her producer. "Are you all right?" Lifting his head into
her lap. "Guy?" Staring up, appalled, at the madman with the
thinning hair and the graying, goatee beard, held back by his
collar like a snarling dog, hands clawing at the air.

"He's only been screwing my wife," the madman spat, and
Catrin froze—maybe he was not so mad, after all—allowing
Guy's head to fall to the floor with an audible thump.

Larry Ember was cradling his camera, ostensibly to save
it from being kicked, the lens pointed casually at the scene
below him. "One for the Christmas tape," he murmured to
Tom, his soundman. "Got to keep the old spirits up, ain'tcha?"
On the same tape were the pictures he'd surreptitiously shot of
Max Goff's body, while carrying the camera under his arm at
waist level.

"You'll put that thing away!" Sharp-featured Mrs. Byford, the
council clerk, was on her feet, back arched.

"Wasn't aware it was out, darlin'." Larry inspecting his trousers.

"Colonel!"

"Come on, old boy, please. Leave the thing under the table,
hmm?"

"I don't think so, squire." Larry raising the camera to his
shoulder, aiming it at Col, adjusting the focus.

"Guy, would you mind exerting your . . . ?"

But Guy, still sprawled half-stunned in the aisle, was staring
over the Colonel's shoulder, eyes widening. "She . . . *she's
there* . . . Jocasta . . . *tell them* . . . "

The girl stood on the edge of the platform. She wore black
jeans and a black top. Even her lipstick was black. Her skin, in
the blue fluorescence, was like a grim, cloudy day.

A small, gray-faced man, perhaps the husband, snatched ineffectually at Mrs. Byford's arm as she stepped out, screeching,
"Tessa! What you doing in yere . . . ? Get out . . . No, I . . . "

"Nobody gets out," Tessa said sweetly.

Guy was up, staggering, one hand massaging the back of his
head, the other groping for the cameraman's arm. "The girl.
Shoot her. I want the girl."

As Larry advanced slowly toward the girl, camera on his shoulder, eye hard to the projecting viewfinder, Mrs. Byford launched herself at him from behind, pummeling his back, clawing at his neck.

"Nettie!" the gray-faced man shouted. "No! Don't cause no . . . "

Col pulled her off with one hand, getting his face scratched. "Mrs. Byford! Guy, can't you stop this stupid bastard before . . . "

"So . . . " Guy was panting, "this is Mrs. Byford, is it? Perhaps she can tell us all about Handel Roberts, who offed himself in her bathroom . . . *and yet was in this room tonight!*"

"Now listen, Mr. Clever TV Man . . . " Guy turned slowly and painfully and looked into tiny, round eyes and a small, fleshy mouth set into a face too big for them.

"Handel Roberts is *dead*," said Wynford Wiley.

"*Exactly,*" said Guy.

Col's feelings about newcomers who tried to take over, assuming a more elevated intellect and an understanding of the rural psyche, were warning him to take it easy. But there was an ice ball forming in the pit of his stomach.

"Stop it!" Jocasta Newsome, rising like a Fury. "Stop it, stop it, stop it! What are you all trying to do?"

"Aye," a man's voice said. "Can't you, none of you, control yourselves?"

"At least we're not brain-dead!" The feminist astrologer with the ring through her nose. "Look at you all . . . you're fucking pathetic. Somebody tells you to sit there and you don't move again until they tell you you can stand up and leave. A man's been brutally murdered . . . You don't even react! What kind of fucking morons . . . "

A girl in her twenties, built like Catrin Jones, only more muscular, stamped across the room. "You'll shut your mouth, lady, or I'm gonner shut it for you."

"Oh yeah, we'll all shut our mouths and turn a blind eye and ask no questions. And where has that got *you* all these years? Max Goff was the only promising thing that ever happened to this shithole, and what do you do? . . . You kill him, like . . . like the bloody savages did to the missionaries. Except they weren't savages really, at least they had this ethnic . . . "

"Sit down, the pair of you!" Mrs. Byford's husband was quaking. "Can't you see, this is what it wants . . . Jimmy Preece said, be calm. He knows . . . it's what it *wants* . . . rowing and . . . and conflict, everybody all worked up, like."

"Mr. Byford is absolutely right," Col said, wondering what the hell Mr. Byford was up to. "*I'm* going to go out and find the mayor, call the police and get this . . . "

"No you're not, Colonel . . . "

"Look . . . "

And then there was a crash from the front of the hall. Larry Ember hadn't exactly *dropped* his camera—which Col suspected no self-respecting TV cameraman *ever* did, even if he'd been shot—but he'd certainly put it down quite heavily, and he was stumbling back along the center aisle, moaning in some distress, both hands over his face.

Col Croston looked up at the platform; there was no sign of Tessa Byford. "What's wrong, man, you OK?"

Guy grabbed Larry's arm; Larry shook him off, the way a child does, in a kind of frenzy. He'd abandoned the camera in the middle of the floor—unheard of in Guy's experience—and was threshing toward the entrance.

"Sorry, pal." A tweeded arm in his way.

Larry took his hands away from his face. "Oh Lord!" the man said, and Larry's knee went up into a corduroy crotch.

"Right," the cameraman shouted, "I'm out of here." Hitting the doors with his shoulder, and they burst open and the night came in, and Guy strove for the exit, followed by the Ivorys and the men in suits, and Catrin Jones was dragged along too. "Stop them!" somebody screamed. "Shut them doors!"

For just a moment, Larry Ember turned around in the doorway. Hilary Ivory screamed, and Guy nearly fell back into the room.

Larry's right eye, his viewfinder eye . . .

"Just get me away from that girl."

"I think it's a blood vessel," Guy said nervously.

"I'm going in tight on her," Larry recalled, voice unsteady. "And her eyes . . . are actually fucking *zooming* back. Giving me daggers, Guy. And then she's in the bleed'n' camera. Daggers, Guy, know what I mean?"

Larry's eye looked like a squashed tomato.

"Maybe . . . maybe several blood vessels," Guy said. "I don't know . . . Look, you get some air, I'll get Catrin to fetch your camera."

"Leave it!" Larry screamed. "I don't wanna see the bleedin' tape, all right? I wan' it destroyed . . ."

Two of the farmers on the doors were struggling to close them again, but now there was a wild crush of people fighting to get out. Larry and Guy were pushed out into the square. "Let them go!" Col shouted. "Or somebody's going to get hurt."

There was hysterical laughter from behind him. "They'll be hurt, all right, Colonel," shrilled Mrs. Byford.

And Col Croston heard what seemed at first to be a very encouraging noise; the curfew bell was ringing, the familiar, steady clangs.

"It's the mayor!" he called back into the room. "Panic over. He said it'd be OK to leave when the curfew began. Everybody just sit down for a moment and we'll file out in an orderly fashion."

"You fool," somebody said quietly.

Few among the Crybbe people had even moved.

And he knew why, quite soon, as a second bell began a hollow, discordant counterpoint, and then a third came in, and a fourth, and then they were all going.

Col stood and looked at the rows of stricken, frightened faces.

"What's going on?"

Never, in this town, had he seen such obvious reaction on so many faces.

He wanted to cover his eyes. And his ears. It was like being violently awoken in the dead of night by the sudden, shattering clangor of a roomful of alarm clocks.

Only louder. The loudest noise there'd ever been in Crybbe, a blitz of bells, hard and blindingly bright, bells to break windows, and loosen teeth and the foundations of ancient buildings, bells to burst the sky and burn up the air.

For the first time in his life, Col Croston, the only qualified bell-ringer in the town, was stilled by a most basic primitive terror, like a cold, thin wire winding around his spinal cord.

Because there was no way it could be happening. With one single exception, all the bell ropes had been taken down years and years ago.

Tonight, in some unholy celebration, the bells of Crybbe were ringing themselves.

twelve

❧ ──────────────────────────

The first bell had begun at the moment Warren Preece cut his grandfather.

"You," Mr. Preece had said, dead-voiced, as the Bible burned. No surprise there, Fay noticed. No horror at the reptilian thing prancing, white-eyed in the firelight—the thing for which Fay had at first felt only revulsion, becoming aware soon afterward that revulsion was actually one of the *lower* forms of fear.

Mr. Preece said, "I 'opened to 'eaven it wouldn't be, but at the heart of me I always knew it was."

Tipped up his brother in the coffin, slashed the shroud. Not much left in Warren Preece, Fay concluded numbly, that you could call human.

"You don't even know it all yet, Granddad." Warren grinned meaningfully. "Got a bit to learn yet, see."

" 'Ow long you been in yere, Warren?"

"Long time, Granddad." Warren put on a whining, old-man voice. "Oh, 'e was a strong boy, Jonathon. Good swimmer."

Shadows leapt with the flames from the blazing Bible. Scorched scraps of pages flew into the air; billowing black snowflakes.

"Smart boy, Jonathon," Warren said. "Bit o' sense. Not like that brother of 'is, see."

"Oh, Warren," the old man said sorrowfully. "You never once tried to . . . "

Warren smiled slyly. " 'E wasn't that good a swimmer, though, Granddad."

The Bible began to crackle.

"Not with somebody sittin' on 'is head, anyway."

Fay wanted to reach out to Mr. Preece and hold him back, but she couldn't get her body to shift, and, God knew, the poor old bloke was moving slowly enough, fragmented motion, like a battered clockwork toy winding down.

"Mr. Preece . . . don't do anything . . . " The old man was

advertising his uncontainable anger as clearly as if it were written on sandwich boards and lunging for his grandson as awkwardly as he would if he were wearing them.

"Come on, then, Granddad." Warren lounged against the carved wooden side of a back pew. "Let's get this over. Owed you one for a couple o' days. Since you knocked me down, like. Shouldn't 'ave done that, Granddad. Bad move . . . see."

Mr. Preece lurched ineffectually forward as Warren's right hand described a lazy arc. And then he stopped, unsure what had happened.

Fay's hand went to her mouth. There was another fine line on the contour map of the mayor's face, five inches long, neatly dividing the withered left cheek into two.

Then Warren was jumping back, the silver skull bouncing from his ear, the hand which held the knife leaping and twirling as though given life by the touch of fresh blood.

Oh Christ . . . Fay was barely aware of backing off. Her mind was distancing itself too, not wanting to cope with this.

"Heee!"

"You wouldn't expect, Fay thought remotely, almost callously, as the curfew bell began to toll, that Mr. Preece would bleed so normally, in such quantity, through skin like worn-out, dried-up leather.

As she watched him bleed, a question rolled into her head and lay there innocuously for a few seconds before starting to sizzle like a hot coal.

"Listen . . . " Warren Preece hissed in excitement.

Who was ringing the curfew?

"Yeah!" Warren leapt onto a pew, looking up to the rafters, both fists clenched, one around the knife, and shaking.

A droplet of Jimmy Preece's blood fell from the blade and landed on a prayer book.

And then the other bells began, and Fay clapped her hands to her ears, although it was not so loud in here—nothing to what it would be in the streets.

It just . . . *could not be happening.*

The mayor of Crybbe stood very still. He did not raise a hand to his cheek and the blood poured down his face, copious as bitter tears.

By his feet, the lambing light expired.

But the fire from the Bible was enough to show her the

crazed Warren dancing on a pew to the discordance of bells, blood glistening on the knuckles of the fist that held the knife.

The smoke made her cough, and Warren seemed to notice for the first time that he and his grandfather were not alone. He leapt—seemed to float in the smoky air—over the back of the pew, and put himself between Fay and the porch, bouncing on the balls of his feet, grinning at her, slack-jawed, vacant.

Jimmy Preece sagged against the font, unmoving. She couldn't even hear his breathing anymore.

"Who . . . who's ringing the bells?" That could *not* be her speaking. Nobody sounding like that could ever have passed a BBC voice test.

"Well, can't be me," Warren said conversationally. "An' it can't be Granddad, can it, Granddad?"

Mr. Preece, Fay thought bleakly, might have died. Heart failure. Blood pressure—a stroke, respiratory congestion.

" 'E sez no," Warren said. "Sez it's not 'im neither. An' I been in yere ages, an' nobody come in with me, see. Wonder what *that* means?"

Is that what Crybbe does? Is this the kind of "rebel" produced by a sick old town from which all unfurtive, abandoned pleasure has been bled?

"Maybe ole Jonathon . . . " Warren suggested. "Maybe 'e's come crawlin' out of 'is coffin. Bleeeaagh!"

He hunched his shoulders. Tossed the knife from the right hand to the left and then back again. "Tell you want . . . why'n't you go up an' 'ave a look, lady? Go on . . . "

When she didn't move he suddenly lurched at her, the knife creating *whing*ing sounds as he made crisscross slashes in the yellow, smoky air. "Hey, it's *you* . . . "

Fay began to back away, coughing, in the opposite direction, up the nave until she could feel the heat from the petrol-soaked Bible on her back.

Warren produced a high-pitched trumpeting noise. "This is Offa's Dyke Radio!"

He slashed the air again, twice.

"Voice of the Marches!" he said. "Yeah!"

"That's right," Fay said, cheerfully hysterical. "Voice of the Marches. That's me."

Warren stopped. Reflected a moment. "We done a good job on your ole tape recorder, didn't we?"

Oh my . . . *God.*

"Yes," she said weakly. "Very impressive."

His face went cold. Should have kept her mouth shut.

He opened the hand which held the Stanley knife, looked down at it, the hand and the knife's long metal handle both splattered with crisscross layers of blood, bright fresh blood on brown dried blood.

"Hand of Glory," Warren said. And the fingers clenched again.

As he advanced on her, up the aisle, she saw, almost hypnotized, that his eyes were altering.

She'd never seen Warren Preece close up before (only—oh my God—his spidery shape scurrying across a field at sunset), and she was sure that she wasn't seeing him now.

Something in the eyes. The eyes were no longer vacant. Someone in residence.

"Aaah." The heat at her back was acutely painful. She couldn't go any farther: fire behind her, the knife coming at her. She went rigid, looked back toward the door, saw Jimmy Preece had slipped to the floor by the font.

"Black Michael," she said, as the savage heat at her back became too much to bear and she was sure her clothing was about to catch fire. "You're Black Michael."

Warren Preece obviously took this as a huge compliment. He grinned lavishly, and the bloodstained Stanley knife trembled in his hand as he closed in.

"Say hello," he said, "to the Hand of Glory." And lunged.

Fay threw herself sideways, landing hard on the stone. Crawled, coughing wretchedly, to the top of the altar steps, where the firelight was reflected on Jonathon Preece's closed coffin. A storm of shriveled scraps of burning paper wafted from the Bible; she saw an orange core of fire eating through to the spine and the varnish bubbling on the wooden lectern as she rolled over, drew back her foot, and stabbed out once, sharply.

The lectern shook. It was made of carved oak, caked in layer upon layer of badly applied varnish, which dripped and blistered and popped. It moved when she hit it with her foot, but not enough, and she fell on her back beside the coffin, her face stinging from the heat and sparks, as Warren Preece sprang up the steps and the short, reddened blade of the Stanley knife came down at her, clasped in a fist gloved in smoke.

She curled up, and the bells clanged like wild, drunken laughter.

The bells, he thought, the bells of hell. Ringing to welcome old Alex.

He stood in the graveyard, looked up at the church tower, saw the window slits outlined in light, glowing a feeble yellow at first and then intensifying to a pure, phosphorous white as the clangor grew louder until it seemed the walls would crumble and there would only be these bright bells hanging in the night.

Welcome to hell.

No one more welcome in hell than an unfrocked priest, except . . . *except* . . . a priest who ought to have been unfrocked and escaped the dishonor through devious means.

Oh Lord, yes. *No* one more welcome in hell.

The bells rang randomly, as one might expect, a mocking parody of the joyful Sunday peal.

The bells of hell hurt his ears as they were meant to do and would continue to do, he assumed, forever and ever.

He brushed against the Bible and it set fire to the black vest he was wearing; little flames swarmed up his chest.

And he seemed absolutely delighted.

He was looking proudly down at himself, dropping down a couple of steps, grinning hugely, as the gas-soaked spine of the heavy old Bible collapsed into red-hot ash and the two halves toppled from the lectern.

Fay rammed both feet into the wooden stem.

Very slowly it began to fall toward him, and Warren didn't move.

He opened his arms wide, as the lectern fell like a tree, and he embraced it, hugging the blistering stem to his chest.

"Yeah!"

Roaring and blazing.

Fay didn't move, watched in hypnotized awe until she felt and smelled something burning, very, very close, and found a single charring page wrapped around her arm.

Book of David, she read, the page curling sepia, reminding her of the opening credits of some dreadful old American Civil War movie, and she found that her lungs were full of smoke.

thirteen

His body jerked in the grass, a convulsion. The crashing bells he accepted as the death vibrations of a brain cleaved by a steel bolt.

"Mr. Powys."

Oh Christ, he thought at once, it wasn't me, it was Arnold; he wants me to see what he's done to Arnold before he puts one into me.

He'd flung himself at the dog, just as Fay had done in the field by the river when Jonathon Preece had been strolling nonchalantly across with his gun. But Powys had missed. Arnold had kept on running, toward Humble and his crossbow, leaving Powys sprawled helplessly, arms spread, waiting for the end. The way you did.

"Mr. Powys."

He rolled very slowly onto his back, pain prodding whatever was between his shoulder blades, the place where Humble had hit him with the butt of the crossbow.

"It is you, isn't it, Joe?"

He focused on a face in the middle of a pale-colored head-scarf. He saw a woolly jumper. And below that some kind of kilt. Campbell tartan, memory told him ridiculously.

"Mmmm . . . " Couldn't get the name out.

"It's Minnie Seagrove," she said clearly. "I want you to speak to me, please. Say something. I'm ever so confused tonight. I've been seeing Frank, and now it's bells. Bells everywhere."

Powys came slowly to his feet. He didn't know about seeing Frank, but they couldn't both be hallucinating bells.

Mrs. Seagrove gazed anxiously up at him, although she looked rather calmer than he felt. Behind her the Tump swelled like a tumor that grew by night. From out of the town came the wild pealing.

Powys was disoriented. He looked rapidly from side to side and then behind him. "Where's . . . ?"

"That's another thing, I'm afraid," Minnie Seagrove said. "I think I've killed the man with the . . . what do you call it?"

"What . . . ?"

"Thank God. It's your voice. Here . . . " She pushed something into his hand—his lamp. "I can't switch it on, it's got a funny switch on it."

Powys switched it on, and the first thing it showed him on the ground was the crossbow. And then an outstretched, naked arm.

"Now just don't ask me how I got here," Mrs. Seagrove said, "because I don't know. It's been a very funny night, all told. But there you were on the ground, and this man with the thingy—crossbow—pointing it down at you—he had the lamp on—taking aim, like. I thought, Oh God, what can I do? And I came up behind him when the bells started, and it put him off, sort of thing, the bells starting up like that, so sudden. Put him off—just for a second. And I *still* wasn't sure any of it was really happening, do you understand? I thought, Well, if it's a dream, no harm done, sort of thing, so I hit him. Is he dead, Joe? Can you tell?"

"I shouldn't think so, Minnie." Powys kicked the crossbow out of the way and bent over Humble with the lamp, nervous of getting too close, ready to smash the lamp down in Humble's face if he moved.

He stood up, finally. "Er . . . what exactly was it you hit him with?"

"He's dead, isn't he, Joe? Come on now, I don't want any flimflam."

"Well, yes. He is actually."

The back of Humble's head was like soft fudge.

"Bring the light over here, please, Joe. It was like an iron bar. Only hollow. Like a pipe. I threw it down somewhere . . . Here . . . "

Powys crouched down. It was indeed a piece of pipe, with jagged rust at one end and blood at the other. He didn't touch it. It seemed likely that Humble, for all his strength and his spectacular night vision, was one of those people with a particularly thin skull.

"It isn't a dream, is it, Joe?"

"Well, not in the accepted sense, no. But really, I mean . . . don't worry about it." He put his hands on her shoulders. "You did save my life. He wasn't exactly what anybody would call a nice man. In fact, offhand, I can only think of one person who's actually nastier. No, maybe two, now."

He thought of something else and played the beam over the weapon again. Experienced a moment of pure, liquid euphoria; wanted to laugh aloud.

It looked like the tip of Henry Kettle's exhaust pipe.

He kept quiet about it, all the same. Don't tie this thing down too hard to reality. She's keeping herself together because she isn't yet fully convinced it's not part of the dream, like Frank. "Look, Minnie, you didn't see a dog, did you? He . . . he might have been hit, I don't know."

"He ran off," said Mrs. Seagrove. "He was off like the clappers, over that way."

She pointed at the gap where the stone wall had been broken down.

"The one I mean is a black and white dog," Powys said gently. "Escaped from my car. Left the window open too wide. But he couldn't have been going like the clappers, he's only got three legs now. You remember, he was shot."

"Yes, it was the same dog. Fay Morrison's dog. Joe, what's going on? What's up with the bells?"

"God knows. Be nice to think it was a few of the townsfolk up in the tower, ringing every bell they've got as a sign they've finally woken up to something after a few centuries."

He looked over his shoulder toward Crybbe Court, remembered the sparking under the eaves, like flints. Could see nothing now.

Which didn't mean a thing.

"Joe."

"Mmm?"

"What's that?"

There was a ray of light playing among the trees on the Tump, flickering erratically.

And then a dog began to bark.

"Stay here," Powys said.

"With *him?* Not likely."

The dog was barking fiercely.

Powys watched the light moving among the trees.

"Who is it, Joe?"

"I think it's one of those other people I mentioned who are even nastier than Humble."

Mrs. Seagrove said, "You're frightened, aren't you, Joe?"

* * *

Alex had remembered who Kate Bush was now.

Dark hair and sort of slinky. Seen her on TV once, a few years ago, at young Fay's flat. Made the usual comments—if I was forty years younger, etc.—and the next day Fay had presented him with this T-shirt as a bit of a joke, and he'd become quite attached to the garment, made him feel youthful, having Kate Bush next to the skin.

Even tried to listen to the music.

Going up that hill . . . make a deal with God.

Alex was going down the hill, toward the river.

He stood on the bridge and stared down at the dark water.

"Rather funny, really," he mused aloud to the river. "I thought I was dead. Can you believe that?"

Always been able to talk to rivers. Sometimes they even burbled back. Not this one, this being a Crybbe river.

"Must have gone out for a breath of air, wound up in the sodding boneyard, mooning over old Grace's plot. Went for a pee in the woods, came back and could've sworn I found my own body. No—honest to God—I remember tripping over something, about to fall flat on my face and it broke the fall. It wore a dog collar. And there was blood. Got it on my hands. Felt awfully sticky."

"Jolly convincing, really."

Alex rubbed his hands together and they felt strangely stiff. He held them out and couldn't see them at all.

You're an old humbug, Alex. Who was it said that? Not Grace, not Fay, not . . .

Wendy!

How could he have forgotten Wendy so soon. Only left her house . . . when? Was it tonight? Or was it last night? Or was it last week?

She said something like, Go back out there and you might start losing your marbles again. But you've got to do it, Alex. Got to go back.

Why? *Why* had he got to go back?

Because Wendy knows best, Wendy has cool hands.

Actually, he thought suddenly, for the first time, they're quite *cold* hands. And they all think they know best, don't they? The doctors, your relatives.

Suddenly Alex felt quite angry.

You start to lose your mind and everybody wants a bit. Even if you could get it back, it wouldn't be worth having. Shop-soiled. Messed about.

He said a civil good night to the river and began to walk back up the hill toward the square.

Deal with God. Why, after sixty years looking after His best interests, doesn't the bugger ever want to talk business with *me?*

The street had been quiet when he was walking down to the river; now he could hear people moving about, up over the brow of the hill, around the square.

Alex came to a house with a paraffin lamp burning in the window. He stopped and held up his hands.

They were covered with dried blood.

"Oh Lord," Alex said, and it didn't start out as a prayer.

Frightened?

Well, how could you not be? But it was no bad thing, most of the time. The worst thing was a belief that you were in some way protected if you did what somebody else said was right. Like walking into the Humble situation because Jean Wendle had told him he needed to go back to the source.

But he always did what he was told. Max Goff: *There's a place for you here—think about it.*

Andy Boulton-Trow: *I think Joe ought to present himself to the Earth Spirit in the time-honored fashion.*

I mean go round the Bottle Stone. Thirteen times.

Even dear old Henry Kettle: *My house is to be left to you. Consider it as a token of my confidence.*

Sod them all. But then he thought about Fay, with her rainbow eye.

"No," he told Minnie Seagrove. "I'm not frightened."

And it's too dark to see me shaking.

He was scared, for instance, to set foot on the Tump; even Humble had said you couldn't always trust your reactions up there.

So they'd stay on the ground and, where possible, outside the wall.

He'd briefly considered taking Humble's crossbow. But he didn't know how to work it, and this was no time to learn.

That was another problem: What was he going to do about Humble? There was no way this one could be suicide or an

accident. And while the police would never suspect Minnie
Seagrove, they'd be hauling Joe Powys in within half an hour
of the body being found. Minnie would, of course, explain the
circumstances, but circumstances like these would sound more
than a little suspect in court.

They began to walk around the perimeter of the Tump toward
the light.

"Quietly," Powys said. "And slowly."

The dog wasn't barking anymore. If Andy had done anything
to Arnold, he'd kill him.

OK, I'm full of shit, but I'm not going to obey instructions
anymore, not from you, not from Goff. And especially not
from Jean.

Jean, of course—it made appalling sense—was not protecting
him, she was protecting *Andy,* and Andy, typically, had wanted
him to know that before he died.

Humble had said, *I'm empowered to answer just one of your
questions . . . I'll tell you the answer, shall I? Then you can work
out the question at your leisure. The answer is—you ready?—the
answer is . . . HIS MOTHER.*

He would trace the Wort family tree later, if he ever got out
of this. Meanwhile it had a dispiriting logic, and it cleared up a
few questions about Jean that he'd never even thought to ask.
The idea of an experienced barrister giving it all up to act as
the unpaid, earthly intermediary for Dr. Chi had never sounded
too likely. Jean's professional life had been built on ambition,
power and manipulation: dark magic.

But she's *cured* people. That can't be dark magic. What about
Fay's dad?

Oh, Jesus.

"What's wrong?" Mrs. Seagrove whispered.

Fay had started pulling at Jimmy Preece's clothing and slapping
at his face and screaming at him through the smoke. "Please,
Mr. Preece, please, you *can't be* . . . "

Just a sign of life, anything, a blink, a twitch. Where did you
keep a pulse in a neck like an old, worn-out concertina? "Mr.
Preece!"

She pulled him down from the font and he collapsed on her,
deadweight, and she had to let him slide to the floor, managing to get both hands under his head before it hit the stone.

But she could do no more, because the appallingly blackened, smoke-shrouded scarecrow thing was dancing down the aisle, its clothes smoldering and its eyes all too alight. Her own eyes weeping with the smoke, with pity for Jimmy Preece and with fear for herself, she ran through the porch and began to wrestle with the bolts, throwing herself, coughing and sobbing, against the doors.

When she was out, she didn't look back, but she carried inside her head the image of the blackened monster and the scorched smell of him, knowing that if she stopped to breathe he would be on her.

She ran gasping through the churchyard and out of the lych-gate, her lungs feeling like burst balloons, the bells crashing around her like bombs. She could hear voices in the square and she ran toward them, eyes straining, looking for lights.

But the nearer she got to the square and the louder the voices became, the darker it got, as if there was not only night to contend with, but fog. She thought at first it was her eyes, damaged by the smoke, but quite soon the bells stopped and Fay began to realize there was something about the square that was unaccountably wrong.

fourteen

"First off, anybody got a torch? Yes? No?"

The bells had stopped, and the silence ought to have glistened, Col Croston thought, but it didn't. The silence after the bells was the ominous silence you could hear when the phone rang and you picked it up and there was apparently nobody on the other end but you knew there *was*.

It was too dark to see who was with him on the square, but he could guess. Or rather, he could guess who was *not* on the square, i.e., anybody born and bred within the precincts of the ancient town of Crybbe.

Graham Jarrett said, "A torch is not normally considered essential for a public meeting, even in Crybbe. Besides, even when the power's off it's not usually as dark as this."

"No. Quite."

The town-hall doors had been slammed and barred behind the last of them and then, minutes later, Col had watched as they were opened again, just briefly, and a bloated figure had emerged, stood grotesquely silhouetted between two men, and then tumbled without a word down the six steps to the pavement.

The late Max Goff had rejoined his New Age community. Col let him lie where he fell; somebody would have to explain this to the police, and he didn't see why it had to be him.

Around the square, tiny jewels of light appeared, people striking matches. But almost as soon as a match was struck it seemed to go out, as if there was a fierce wind. Which there wasn't. Not any kind of wind.

There weren't even any lamps alight in the windows of the town houses tonight.

"OK, listen," Col shouted. "We need some lights. Anybody with a house near here, would they please go home and bring us whatever torches or lamps or even candles they can find. I also need a telephone. Who lives closest?"

"We have a flat," Hilary Ivory said. "Over the Crybbe Pottery."

Hereward Newsome said, "There's a phone in The Gallery, that'd probably be quickest."

"Good. I'll come with you. Stay where you are and keep on talking, so I can find you. Mrs. Ivory, if you could find your way to your flat and bring out any torches et cetera."

"I don't think we have torches, as such. When the electricity goes out we use this rather interesting reproduction Etruscan oil lamp. Would that do?"

"I'm sure it looks most attractive, but one of those heavy-duty motoring lanterns with a light at each end might be a little more practical."

"We haven't got a car."

Col whistled tunelessly through his teeth.

"Colin, I'm over here."

"Yes, OK, got you, Hereward. Now listen everybody, I don't know any more than you do what the hell's going on here

tonight. What I do know is that none of us should attempt
to leave the scene until after the police arrive. I'm going with
Hereward to his gallery to ring headquarters and acquaint them
fully with the situation. Any questions?"

"Oh lots," Graham Jarrett said dreamily. "And I may spend
the rest of my life trying to find the answers."

"Just hurry it up," a woman said. "There's an awful smell."

"I can't smell anything."

Actually he could, but didn't want to draw attention to it. It
rather smelled as if a couple of people had lost control of their
bowels, and, frankly, that wouldn't be too surprising under the
circumstances.

"God, yes. It's vile." Sounded like the woman who ran the
craft shop, Magenta-something.

"Well, obnoxious as it might be, try not to move too far away.
Lead on, Hereward. Keep talking."

"Strange," Hereward said, "how when anyone asks you to
keep talking you can never think of anything to say . . . Good
grief, Colin, she was right about that smell. It's dreadful."

In certain periods of his SAS career, Col had been exposed
for long hours to various deeply unpleasant bodily odors, but he
had to admit—if only to himself—this was the most sickening.
It was more than simply feces, though there was certainly that.
There was also a garbage-can kind of pungency and all manner
of meaty smells—newly killed to faintly putrid.

"No power, and now the drains are blocked. You'll probably
turn on the tap when you get home, Hereward, and find the
bloody water's off, too. I really do think it's about time I put
a bomb under my esteemed colleagues on the council. Not that
they can actually *do* anything except talk about it."

"You can certainly count on *my* support. For as long as I'm
here, anyway. Look, I'm sorry about what happened in there. I
overreacted, I suppose."

"Wouldn't any of us, old chap? Some of these TV types do
tend to think they have a kind of *droit de seigneur* wherever
they happen to be hanging up their . . . Is it far, Hereward?"

"No, that is . . . I'm sorry, one gets disoriented in the dark,
especially as dark as this. I've never known it this dark, I . . . it
really should be about here, Colin. Can you feel the wall?"

"I can feel some kind of surface. Is there a timber-framed bit
next to your place?"

"Actually, there is, and it goes straight from that to the large window, but . . . "

"Maybe we're on the wrong side of the square. Pretty easy to do, even when you're on what you think of as familiar ground."

"No, I don't think . . . Oh hell, I seem to be way out."

"Isn't there a pavement in front of your gallery? Because we're still on the cobbles, you know."

"I thought there was a pavement all around the square, actually. Shows how you . . . "

A few yards away Col heard a woman scream. "It's gone. It's gone, I tell you, Hilary, the whole bloody front . . . All I can feel is this . . . urrrgh, it's filthy."

"Colonel Croston, can you help us, please? It sounds terribly stupid, but Celia's lost her Pottery."

"Look." Col took a step back. "Let's calm down and get this in proportion. Funny, how you live in a place for years but never quite notice what order the shops are in. Right . . . Between the Crybbe Pottery and The Gallery we've got the Lamb, OK, and that . . . what's it called?"

"Middle Marches Crafts," Hereward said.

"Right. And then, after the Pottery, the road starts sloping down to the bridge, and across from there, we've got the Cock. Hereward . . . " He paused, confused. "The Cock's got its own generator, hasn't it?"

"Yes, it has."

"So why isn't it on?"

"Colin . . . " A brittle panic crumbling from Hereward's voice. "Something's horribly wrong, don't you feel that?"

"It's *all* wrong . . . " Hilary's companion wailed. "Nothing's the same."

"If we only had light," Col said. "I know—cars. If somebody has a car parked on the square, they can open it up and switch on the headlights, then we can see where we're at."

"Look . . . " Hereward breathing rapidly. "I don't want to start a panic, but there were cars parked on three sides of this square when I went into the meeting. We haven't bumped into a single one, have we?"

"Well, they can't all have been nicked. Just spread the word. We're looking for anybody with a car parked on the square. Just . . . do it, Hereward, please."

Col walked to the side of the building, felt wood and some type of chalky plaster. And the cobbles, under his feet.

Knowing full well that the pavement around the square had been replaced two years ago, and there'd already been one there for years before that. And now there were cobbles. Again.

He steadied his breathing.

Face facts. It was true; everything was different. Road surface, buildings . . . even the atmosphere itself. What would it look like . . . *What would it look like if they could actually see any of it?*

Mass hallucination, Col decided logically. Some kind of gas, perhaps. Why had the townsfolk refused to come out of the town hall and, indeed, locked themselves in? Because they knew what was happening, they knew it was too dangerous to go into the square.

Were the bells some form of alarm? Had somebody actually rehung all the ropes for this occasion?

And why didn't the locals warn everybody else? Because they only suspected what it might be and were afraid of being laughed at?

Or because they *wanted* the newcomers to be exposed to it?

It was insane. Any way you looked at it, it was all utterly insane.

Concentrate. Col dug the nails of his left hand into the back of his right. Just for a few moments there, completely forgot this was not, so far, the night's most appalling development. Max Goff savagely killed in front of all of them, and *that* was no hallucination.

Something touched his arm and, such was the state of his nerves, he almost swung around and struck out with the side of his hand.

"Colonel Croston."

"Who's that?"

"It's Fay Morrison. Keep your voice down."

"Mrs. Morrison!"

"Christ, Colonel . . . "

"I'm sorry," he whispered. "Where the hell's Jimmy? You left with him, the mayor . . . "

"He's . . . he's in the church. Listen . . . I've been following you around for the last ten minutes. I couldn't approach you until you knew. At least . . . "

"I don't know anything, Mrs. Morrison. I've never been more in the dark. Excuse the humor. It isn't felt."

"But you know everything's changed. I heard you talking to Hereward. You realize this is not, in any sense, the Crybbe we know and love."

"Oh, now, look . . . !"

"I'm trying to keep calm, Colonel."

"I'm sorry. This is beyond me. Some kind of gas, I suspect."

"Colonel . . . "

"Col."

"Col. Forget about gas. Please listen. First of all, I think Mr. Preece is dead. Stroke, heart attack maybe, I don't know about these things. But I do know Max Goff was killed by *Warren* Preece, you know who I mean?"

"The grandson. Punkish type. Where is he?"

"He's hurt. He's badly burned. There was a fire. In the church."

"Are you serious?"

"Yes, I know, you can't see any flames. But you can't see anything else either, can you?"

Col gripped her arm. He wanted to feel she was real.

"Please don't," she said. "I've got a burn."

"I'm sorry, but this . . . Jesus."

"Just listen. If you think this is mad, don't say anything. Just walk away and keep it to yourself."

He tried to see her eyes, but all he could make out was the white of her face. "OK," he said.

"On this night," Fay Morrison said. "And I mean *this* night, this actual night, exactly four hundred years ago, a large number of people gathered in the square, where we are now, trying to decide what to do about the high sheriff, who'd taken to hanging men and compelling their wives to have sex with him. And there were various other alleged examples of antisocial behavior even by sixteenth-century standards that I won't go into now. But the bottom line is the people of this town decided they'd taken enough."

He would have stopped her, he was in no mood for a local history lecture, but he supposed he'd given his word he'd listen to what she had to say.

"You can imagine the scene," she said. "A bit of a rabble, not exactly organized. Not much imagination, but angry and scared,

too. Only finding courage in numbers, you know the kind of
thing. So they march on Crybbe Court, flaming torches, the full
bit. And there are a lot of them, and it really wasn't something
this sheriff would have expected. Not the border way. Keep your
heads down, right? Don't make waves. But they did—for once.
They made waves. They surrounded the Court and they said to
the servants, men-at-arms, whatever, 'You send this bastard out
or we're going to burn this place down.' Maybe they set light to
a barn or something to reinforce the threat, but, anyway, it was
pretty clear to the sheriff by now that he was in deep shit."

From somewhere close to what he imagined was the center
of the square, Col could hear Graham Jarrett, the hypnotist
guy, shouting, "You're taking absolutely the wrong attitude,
you know."

"He seems to have gone into the attic," Fay said, "and offed
himself."

"Hear him out, will you?" a woman bawled. Sounded like that
astrologer Oona Jopson, shorn head, ring through nose, who'd
threatened to emasculate the doormen.

Fay said, "What you have to remember about this particular
sheriff is that he was killed in what I'm afraid we have to call
the Black Arts. Except he thought it was science." She paused.
"Do you want me to stop?"

"I'm not laughing," Col said. "Am I?"

"I'll carry on, then. Before he hanged himself. Or while he
was hanging himself—I mean, don't think I'm an expert on
this stuff, I'm not—but, anyway, he left something of himself
behind. It's called a haunting, Col. Still with me?"

"Open mind," Col said. "Go on."

"It wasn't a spur-of-the-moment job. He'd been planning this
for a long time. Dropped hints to his women: 'Expect more of
the same when I'm gone.' "

"Look," Graham Jarrett was shouting, "if you'll all just qui-
eten down a minute, we'll do a bit of reasoning out. But I
think we've been selected as participants in a wonderful, shared
experience that's really at the core of what most of us have been
striving for over many years."

"And here we are . . . panicking!" the Jopson woman piped
up. "Well, I'm not panicking. I've never been so excited."

Guy Morrison shouted, "What about poor bloody Goff? He
didn't look too excited. He looked a bit bloody dead to me."

"Yeah, but *was* he?" Jopson. *"Is* he? I mean, how much of that was for real? How much of what we perceive is actual reality?"

Col Croston said, "Jesus Christ."

"It smells so awful," said the woman from the crafts shop, which now sold mainly greeting cards.

"It smells awful to *us,* that's all," Oona Jopson said. "Or only to you, maybe. To me, it's a wonderful smell. It smells of reality, not as it is to us these days, with our dull senses and our tired taste buds and our generally limited perception of everything. What we're feeling right now is the *essence* of this place. I mean, shit, this is . . . this is *higher consciousness."*

"And is she right?" Col asked Fay Morrison in a low voice.

"What do you think?"

"I think she's nuts."

Guy said, "Has anybody tried just walking away from here in any direction, just carrying on walking until they find an open door or somebody with a torch or a lamp?"

"My . . . " There was the sound of some struggling. "Give me some *space."* It was Jocasta Newsome. "My husband . . . he said he was going to get help. He's . . . I can't find him."

"Don't worry," Graham Jarrett said. "He'll be around. I don't think he can go anywhere, you see, I don't think anyone can. I don't think there's any light to be found."

"I think there is, Graham," a new voice said. A cool, dark voice. Lazy.

"Who's that? Is that Andy?"

Col Croston heard Fay Morrison inhale very sharply, through her mouth.

"I think," the dark voice said, "that we should consider how we can find our own light."

"Who's that?" Col whispered.

"Boulton-Trow."

"I don't think I know him."

"I mentioned him during the meeting. You haven't forgotten that, have you?"

"Oh," said Col. "That."

Her outburst. It occurred to Col that there was something personal at the back of this. That Fay Morrison had some old, probably sexual score to settle with Boulton-Trow. Anyway, it was all rather too much for a practical man to take. He had to reassemble his wits and get to a phone.

"Well, thank you, Mrs. Morrison," Col said. "You've given me a lot of food for thought."

"Col, it has to be food for action, or something unbelievably awful's going to happen."

"Look," Col said. "I'll come back to you, OK?"

"No, don't go . . . "

But he had.

"Oh, please . . . " Fay Morrison breathed into the foul-smelling dark. "Please . . . "

 fifteen

The dog was in a pool of light on the side of the Tump where the grass looked almost white, and the dog was barking nonstop.

"Wait," Joe Powys whispered to Minnie Seagrove. "Don't go any closer. Stay out of the light."

He moved quietly around the base of the Tump to see what was happening, who it was. *Don't look at me, Arnold. I'm not here. Ignore me.*

There was a single spotlight directed at the mound from the field, on the side facing the road, the side from which Henry Kettle had come on his last ride in his clapped-out old Volkswagen Variant.

The light went out. The dog stopped barking.

Powys waited.

He heard a vehicle door slam. Moved closer. Saw a match flare and then the red glow on the end of a cigarette.

"Well," a voice said, "you buggered yourself yere all right, boy."

"Gomer!" Mrs. Seagrove had appeared at Powys's side. "It's Gomer Parry!"

"Oh Christ!" they heard, and an orange firefly crash-landed in the field.

"Gomer, it's Minnie Seagrove. You replaced my drains."

"Flaming hell, woman, what you tryin' to do, scare the life out of me? Bloody dog was bad enough. Hang on a second."

Two small lights appeared in the front of what proved to be a tractor with an unwieldy digger contraption overhanging the cab. Powys had last seen it parked in the square.

He whispered, "Ask him if he's alone."

"Course I'm bloody alone. Who you got there with you, Mrs. Seagrove?"

"It's a friend of mine."

"Choose some places to bring your boyfriends, all I can say."

"You mind your manners, Gomer Parry. We're coming down."

He was scrabbling in the grass when they reached him. "Dropped my ciggy somewhere." The digger's sidelights were reflected in his glasses. "Sod it, won't set afire, grass is too bloody wet." He peered at Powys. "I seen you before, isn't it? You was with that radio lady, Mrs. Morris, hour or so ago. Put yourself about, don't you, boy?"

"Gomer!" Mrs. Seagrove snapped.

"Aye, all right. Nice lady, that Mrs. Morris. Very nice indeed."

"Pardon me for asking, Mr. Parry," Powys said, deadpan, "but somebody wouldn't by any chance be paying you to take out the rest of the wall?"

"Now just a minute! You wanner watch what you're sayin', my friend."

"Only it's, er, kind of outside normal working hours."

"Aye, well," said Gomer Parry. "Bit of an accident, like. Got a bit confused, what with the ole power bein' off, no streetlights, and I come clean off the road. Dunno what come over me, never done nothin' like that before, see, never."

"Don't worry abut it," Powys said. "Not as if you're the first."

"What's that?" said Gomer, suspicious. "Oh, bugger me . . . 'Enry Kettle! Is this where 'Enry Kettle . . . ?"

"You knew Henry?"

"Course I knew 'im. 'Enry Kettle, oh hell, aye. Wells, see. Wells. 'E'd find 'em, I'd dig 'em. Talk about a tragic loss. Friend o' yours too, was 'e?"

He nodded and put out his hand. "Joe Powys."

Gomer shook it. "Gomer Parry Plant Hire."

Powys did some rapid thinking. Gomer had gone off the road, probably at the same spot as Henry. And yet Gomer had survived.

"What happened? When you came off the road?"

"Bloody strange," Gomer said. "Thought I muster been pissed, like—sorry, Mrs. S—but I'd only 'ad a couple, see. Anyway, it was just like I'd blacked out and come round in the bloody field . . . only I never did. And then it was like . . . well, it was like goin' downhill with a hell of a strong wind up your arse—sorry, Mrs. . . . . "

"You see anything?"

"Oh er . . . " Gomer scratched his face. "Got in a bit of a panic, like, tell the truth. See all sortser things, isn't it? Thought I seen a feller one second, up there, top o' the Tump, 'mong the ole trees, like, but nat'rally I was more bothered 'bout not turnin' the old digger over, see. Best one I got, this. Customized. Fixed 'im myself, big David Brown tractor an' half of this ole JCB I got off my mate over Llandod way. Bloody cracker, this ole thing. Managed to stop 'em 'fore I reached the ole wall; if 'e 'ad gone into it, I'd've been pretty bloody sore about it, I can tell you."

"Word has it," said Powys, "that you were pretty bloody sore when somebody borrowed your bulldozer."

"Don't you talk to me 'bout that!" said Gomer in disgust. "Bloody vandals."

"You were warned off, weren't you? You could've had this wall down no problem, but they warned you off."

" 'Ow'd you know that?" demanded Gomer.

"Made sense."

"Oh aye? You know anythin' else makes sense?"

"Going back to this figure on the top of the Tump. Where exactly were you when you saw him?"

"You're askin' a lot o' questions, mister. You with the radio, too?" Although he didn't sound as if he'd mind if this were the case. "No, see, I said I *thought* I seen 'im. 'E was prob'ly another tree with the light catchin' 'im funny, like."

"Your headlights are that powerful, that you could see a man standing on top of the Tump when you're coming downhill and the lights are pointing down?"

"Light. Only got one 'eadlight workin', Joe."

"So when you said a tree caught in the light . . . "

"Aye," Gomer said thoughtfully. "You're right. Not possible, is it? See, I'll tell you what it was like. You know kids when they gets a torch and they wants to frighten other kids and they flashes it under their chin and their face lights up really weird, on account of half it's in shadow. Well, it was like that, see, only it was like his whole body was lit up that way. Scary. Only I'm strugglin' with the wheel, I thinks, get off, it's only an ole tree."

Minnie Seagrove looked at Powys. "I used to think things like that when I first saw the Hound. You do. You look for explanations, sort of thing."

"The hound?" said Gomer.

Arnold began to bark.

"Right," said Gomer, opening the door of the cab. "If there's anybody else up there I'm gonner bloody find out this time."

The single headlight spotlit the Tump again, and Powys watched as Arnold ran into the white circle.

Ran. Arnold *ran* into the light.

He'd lost a leg just a few days ago, and he was *running.*

Was this Arnold?

"Arnold!" Powys shouted. "Come on!"

The dog trotted down to the foot of the mound and ambled across. Powys bent down and the dog snuffled up at him and licked his hands. Gently, Powys slid one hand underneath. He could actually feel the stitching.

Arnold squirmed free and made off across the field toward the Tump, looking back at Powys every few yards and barking.

"He's found something," Minnie Seagrove said. "He wants to show you something."

I can't believe this, Powys thought. This is seriously weird. He isn't even limping.

Arnold's tail started to wave when he saw Powys was following him. He ran a few yards up the side of the Tump and then sat down.

He *sat* down.

The dog with only one back leg *sat down.*

Arnold barked. He turned around and put his nose into the side of the Tump and snuffled about. Then he turned around again and started to bark at Powys.

And Powys thought—the words springing into his mind in Henry Kettle's voice—*He's a dowser's dog.*

He wandered back to the digger, rubbing his forehead. "Gomer, what are the chances of you doing a spot of excavation?"

"What?" Gomer said. "In there?"

"Be a public service," Powys said. "That Tump's a liability. If it wasn't for that Tump, Henry Kettle would be alive today and locating wells."

"Protected Ancient Monument, though, isn't it?" Gomer said. "That's an offense, unauthorized excavation of a Protected Ancient Monument."

"Certainly is," said Powys.

"That's all right, then," said Gomer, glasses twinkling. "Where you want the 'ole?"

sixteen

The acoustics in the square were tight and intimate, like a studio, and the voice was deep and resonant: strong and melancholy music. Wonderful broadcasting voice, Fay thought, trying to be cynical. Radio Three, FM.

"When you think about it," the voice said, "any town center's an intensely powerful place; it's where energy gathers from all directions, thoughts and feelings pouring in. It's where we go to tap in to a town, to feel its life rhythm."

Pure radio, Fay thought. The purest radio of all, because we can't see anything. No distractions. He can design his own pictures in our minds.

"The town center is where the centuries are stored," Andy said. "Smell them. Smell the centuries."

All I can smell, Fay thought, is shit. Four hundred years of shit. And all I can hear is bullshit. Had to keep telling herself that. This was Andy Boulton-Trow, of Bottle Stone fame. Descendant of Sheriff Wort, scourge of Crybbe, black magician, the most hated man in . . .

"What you can smell," Andy Boulton-Trow said (and she felt, most uncomfortably, that he was speaking directly to *her*), "is many centuries of human life. There haven't always been sewerage systems and hot water and fresh vegetables. This town lived on the border of two often hostile countries, and it had to live within itself. It ground its own flour, killed its own meat, and kept its own counsel."

He paused. "And its secrets. It kept its secrets."

Fay thought, Drab secrets densely woven into a faded, dirty old tapestry.

Boulton-Trow's voice was the only sound in the square. The only sound in the world—for this square *was* the world. None of them could leave it, except—perhaps—by dying.

Should have been a terrifying thought. Wasn't.

She couldn't remember, for the moment, quite what he looked like, this Boulton-Trow. Only that he was tall and dark and bearded. Like Christ; that was how people saw Him.

But she couldn't see Boulton-Trow. She couldn't see anybody. You'd have thought your eyes would have adjusted by now, so that you'd be able to make out at least the shapes of men and women. But unless they were very close to you, you could see nothing. This darkness was unnatural.

Not, however, to Andy. She could feel that. He knew his way around the darkness. If anybody could lead them out of here it would be him, and that would be comforting to these people.

Perhaps it was comforting to her.

But there was no immediate comfort in Andy's message.

"And now you come here, and you want Crybbe to give up its secrets to you. To lay open its soul to you. You want to feel its spirit inside you. Isn't that right?"

"We want to help it rediscover its own spirit," someone said. "Surely that's what this is about, this experiment."

"This experiment." Andy laughed. "And who's the subject of this experiment? Is it Crybbe? Or is it us? Maybe we're here to let the town experiment on us. It's an interesting idea, isn't it? Maybe Crybbe can work its own alchemy if you're prepared to put yourselves into the crucible. Perhaps what you're experiencing now is a taster. Can you handle this? Are you strong enough?"

Talk about a captive audience, Fay thought. And it was an uneasy thought. She was a captive, too. Would she not also go along with anything this man suggested if he could lead her out of here, back into where there were lights?

"Sense of place," Andy said. "You want to feel that sense of place that finds an echo in your own hearts. You want to belong. You want to lay yourself down in a field on a summer's evening and you want the mysteries to come to you, whispered in your ears, drifting on the air and smelling of honeysuckle."

"Yes," a woman said faintly. "Yes."

Andy paused and the night held its breath.

"That's not how it works," he said. "You know that really, don't you? *This* is how it works. *This* is Sense of Place. Feel it. Smell it. Secrets come out like babies, writhing and covered in blood and slime. And all of us genteel New Age people, we turn up our noses and we start to scream. Let me out of here! I can't bear it! Give me my picturesque half-timbered cottage and my chintz sofa and my books. Give me my incense and my crystals and my immersion tank. Give me my illusions back. Yeah?"

Nobody spoke.

"I can't give you your illusions back," Andy said gently.

The silence was total.

Radio, Fay thought desperately. It's only radio. You know the techniques, you know the tricks. He's standing there at the mixing deck, the Presenter and also the Engineer, playing with the effects, adjusting the atmos.

"But if you trust me," Andy said, "I can give you the true secrets of Crybbe. Think about this. I'll be back."

And the voice was gone.

"Andy!" Jarrett shouted into the pungent night. "Don't go!"

"He can't go," Oona Jopson said. "Can he?"

"Stop!" Powys shouted.

The mechanical digger groaned.

Arnold barked.

"Take it slowly, OK? We could be coming to something."

Gomer's customized digger had an extra spotlight, mounted on the cab. It wasn't as strong as the single headlight, but at least you could focus it on the target.

Powys had been worried the wall would be a problem, but Gomer had done some skilled maneuvering, putting on a show, riding the digger like a trick-cyclist, plant-hire choreography, tapping the wall with the edge of the shovel in exactly the right places, until the stones crumbled apart like cinderblocks. Powys asking him, "Out of interest, how long would it have taken you to take this wall apart with the bulldozer?"

Gomer had leaned out of his cab, his cigarette pointing upward from his mouth so the red end was reflected in his glasses. "You what, Joe? This ole wall? Gimme hour or so, you'd never know there'd been a wall yere. Tell you what—bloody hurt me, that did, havin' to say I couldn't 'andle 'im without a bigger 'dozer."

Afterward, it had just been a question of removing enough rubble to get the digger to the Tump. And after that . . .

"Piece o' piss," Gomer said. "Sorry, Minnie."

Mrs. Seagrove sat on a broken section of the wall, dust all over her kilt, Arnold lying across her knees, watchful, both of them watching the action.

"Isn't he good, though, Joe?" she said as Gomer went into the Tump like a surgeon. "Isn't he a marvel?"

Powys smiled. She was loving it. He wondered if she remembered killing Edgar Humble, or if she still half thought that was all a dream, no more real now than Frank, her dead husband.

"Hold it a minute, Gomer, we've got . . . "

Gomer backed up, raised the shovel. Powys slid under it, lumps of earth falling on him from its great metal teeth.

"Minnie, can you pass me the hand lamp?"

It looked like an opening. No more than five feet in, and they could be into some kind of tunnel. He shone the light inside and he could see a roof of solid stone, like the capstone of a dolmen.

"Gomer, we've cracked it."

"Course we 'ave, boy. Want me to widen the 'ole?"

"OK."

He stepped back and the shovel adjusted itself, then went in again.

He couldn't believe this. They'd gone in at precisely the spot where Arnold had been sitting (*sitting*—a leg short and he was sitting) and after no more than twenty minutes they were into the heart of this thing.

Powys looked up toward the sky, black and starless.

"Henry?" he said. "Is this you, you old bugger?"

*   *   *

Fay moved among them, listening, but speaking to no one.

It was obvious by now that Col Croston was not coming back to her. Perhaps, like Hereward, he'd gone to try and find a way out of the square.

"We're not in a different time zone," Graham Jarrett was saying. "It's not as simplistic as that. We're in what you might call a timeless zone. A place where the past and present exist in the same continuum."

"What he was saying, about the town center," Adam Ivory said. "I think that's literally central to this experience. The town center's this kind of energy vortex . . ."

Fay moved on. They were creating a dream within a dream, the way New Age people tended to do, moving around scattering meaningless jargon, making themselves comfortable inside the experience.

But Jean Wendle, the most experienced of them all, was not here.

Or was she?

Fay moved around in the darkness, almost floating, coming to sense the nearness of other bodies and the emotions emanating from them: fear and exhilaration in equal quantities now. But she doubted there was one of them who would not prefer this experience in retrospect, returning to the square by daylight:

Yes, this was where it happened, just about here, yes, you can still feel the essence of it, yes, it'll never be the same again for me, this place, always be special, yes, it was like an initiation, becoming a part of this town. And now I feel I can tap in to it whenever I want to, and I can really work here effectively now because I belong, because I've felt the Spirit of Crybbe.

Fay moved on. Through the radio world.

And now he was inside the Tump.

He'd been inside them before—burial chambers, passage graves. It was suggested that many of the stone dolmens or cromlechs around the country had once been covered over, like this, with earth.

The passageway was perhaps three and a half feet wide, and was low, and he had to walk painfully bent over. He directed the beam at the walls and the ceiling; the structure appeared to be a series of cromlechs joined up, like vertebrae, wide slabs of gray-brown stone overhead, a floor of close-packed earth.

He turned around, with difficulty, and he couldn't see the entrance anymore. He wasn't naturally claustrophobic, but he shuddered briefly at the thought of the opening being sealed behind him, great bucketloads of earth dumped back and rubble from the wall heaped across so that nobody would ever know there was a passageway, so that he slowly suffocated in here and became one more well-preserved pile of bones in a forgotten Bronze Age burial chamber.

He stopped.

His chest tightened.

Gomer. Could he really trust Gomer Parry?

So many old allegiances, never spoken of, in Crybbe. And new ones, too. Could you ever know exactly who belonged to whom?

Maybe he should have asked Gomer to come with him, but he couldn't leave Mrs. Seagrove outside on her own.

Look, don't think about it, OK. Too much at stake to go back now. Concentrate on where you are, what it can tell you.

Keep going . . .

It would probably be an actual Bronze Age grave, although he doubted he was the first person since then to enter this mound. You couldn't excavate a prehistoric burial chamber in under an hour.

But was he the first to get inside since Michael Wort?

Abruptly it ended.

Out of the passage and into the chamber itself, wider, maybe eight feet in diameter, but not quite circular anymore. It was cold in here; the air smelled old and rank.

In the center of the chamber was a single flat stone.

And on the stone was a wooden box.

Powys stopped at the entrance to the chamber, put the lamp on the ground, stood blocking the entrance, head bowed.

They didn't have boxes in the Bronze Age, not carved oak boxes anyway, with iron bands and locks.

He stood staring at the box in the lamp's beam, and his breathing tightened. The box was about twelve inches deep and eighteen inches square. It sang to him, and it sang of ancient evil.

Oh, come *on* . . .

He walked across the chamber to the box, and found he couldn't touch it.

There is no evil, only degrees of negativity.

Powys started to laugh, and then, quite deliberately, he bent down and switched off the lamp.

What is this about?

Well, he couldn't see the box anymore, or the inside of the stone chamber; he could be anywhere, no visual images, no impressions coming in now.

Just me. And it. This is a *real* fairy hill, and I'm in the middle of it, and I've come here of my own free will and there's no Andy and no Jean and I'm scared. I've put out the light to induce a state of fear, and the nerve ends are bristling with it, and I'm ready.

I'm ready.

"Hereward?"

"Yes."

"Thank God."

"Why? Why are you thanking God?"

"Because I thought . . . I thought you weren't going to come back. Hereward, I'm so desperately sorry. I was only trying to get away. All I've ever wanted is to get away from here."

"And you thought Guy Morrison would take you away?"

"No . . . yes . . . Oh God, I don't know what I thought. I was just so lonely and messed up. He—Guy—was passing through, he wasn't part of Crybbe, he was going somewhere, and I was stuck fast. I was like someone just dashing outside and thumbing a lift. And he stopped. I'm sorry, that's all mixed up, I'm not very clear tonight, not very articulate."

"Don't cry."

"I'm sorry. I'm sorry about the picture, too, but you don't know what pictures can do."

"Oh, I do."

"I'm not talking about aesthetics."

"I know."

"Do you?"

"Pictures are doorways."

"Yes."

"Artists put elements of themselves into pictures, and also elements of other things. The man in that picture of Tessa's, he's her teacher, you know. He has a studio in the woods, and she's been going down there and he's been teaching her how to paint. And what to paint. How to make a picture into a doorway."

"How do you know that?"

"Because, in the picture, he's standing in a doorway, like *The Light of the World*, in reverse, because he's so dark. But darkness and light, it's all the same when you can't see, isn't it?"

"I don't . . . "

"I'm going through the doorway, Jocasta."

"Hereward?"

"It really is the only way out of here, through the doorway. The only way out for me, anyway."

"Hereward, I'm getting very scared."

"There's no need to be scared. Come here, darling. There."

"No. No, please."

"There . . . there . . . "

"Aaaugh."

"There."

Hereward felt the woman go limp, and his hands fell away from her throat. He felt himself smiling into the dark as he walked away.

The lamp was alight, and the door was ajar. When he pushed, it swung open at once, and Hereward found himself in the comfortingly familiar setting of his own workshop next to The Gallery.

A candle glowed on the workbench, where he'd made frames. *Do you know, in the early days, we used actually to make our own frames . . .*

Fragments of frames were scattered over the bench and the floor; a corner section was still wedged in the wood vise. He wouldn't need to make frames anymore; that phase was over. Perhaps he'd employ someone to do it.

"Don't suppose you'd be interested in a job, would you?" he said to the shadow sitting on the bench, next to the candle.

The shadow stopped whittling at a piece of framing wood with its Stanley knife and slipped to the floor.

Hereward saw it wasn't really a shadow; it was just black.

seventeen

Laughter in the dark.

Laughter like ice crystals forming in the air.

"Andy."

Who did you think it was going to be, Joe? Did you think you were finally about to meet Sir Michael himself?

Andy, but he wasn't here.

He was mainly gray, shimmering to nearly white at his fingertips, the extremities of him.

Andy, but he wasn't there.

Powys heard the voice in his head. He spoke aloud, but he heard the replies in his head.

He wasn't thinking about this too hard; analysis was useless. Couldn't play new games by old rules.

Don't touch him. He can't harm you.

BUT DON'T TOUCH HIM.

"The box. What's in the box, Andy?"

Why don't you open it, Joe? The lock's no big deal. Ornamental, as much as anything. Also it's very old. Pick up a stone. Break the lock.

"I don't think so."

No? You're still very much full of shit, Joe, you know that? You go to all this trouble to get into here, and you won't face up to the final challenge. What's the problem? Not got the guts, Joe? Not got the bottle? Think about this . . . think hard . . . what's it all been worth if you don't open it?

"Maybe I will," Powys said.

You'll find a couple of stones behind you, near where you left your lamp. One's narrow and thin, it used to be a spearhead. The other's chunky, like a hammer. You can slide the spearhead into the crack below the lid.

"But not here."

The eyes were white, though. The eyes were alight, incandescent.

Andy, but he wasn't here.

"I'm not going to open it here. You can piss off, mate. I'm going to pick up the box, and I'm going to take it away."

You don't want to do that, Joe. You might awaken the Guardian. You don't want that.

"No. *You* don't want that. But you can piss off."

Powys felt a trickle of euphoria, bright and slippery as mercury and, very quickly, he covered it up. Smothered it with fear. Stay frightened. At all costs, stay frightened.

A rapid pattering on the close-packed earthen floor, and something warm against his leg.

"Arnie."

Stay frightened. It might not be.

He bent down.

And the growling began.

He felt Arnold's fur stiffen and harden under his hand, and the growling went on, a hollow and penetrating sound that came from far back in the dog's throat, maybe farther back than that. Maybe much farther back. The growl was continuous and seemed to alter the vibration of the night.

"You're not growling at *me*, are you, Arnie?"

The gray thing hung in the air like an old raincoat, but he was fairly sure that Andy was not there anymore.

Powys switched on the lamp and the gray thing vanished.

He walked over to the stone in the center of the chamber and he picked up the wooden box.

Warm. Cozy. Just as before. The deep, Georgian windows, the Chinese fire screen, the Victorian lamp with the pale-blue shade burning perfumed oil.

"I wondered," she said, "if you would come back."

"Hullo, Wendy," Alex said.

She was dressed for bed.

And how.

Black nightdress, sort of a shift-thing, filigree type of pattern, so you could see through it in all the right places. Alex couldn't take his eyes off her.

"Sit down," Jean said.

"Wendy, there's something awfully funny happening out there, did you know?"

"Funny?"

"Well, I'd been down to the river and came back up the hill, and when I got to near the top, just at the entrance to the square, it all went very dark. I mean, I know it's obviously dark without the electricity supply, but this really was extra dark, as if there was a thick fog. Lots of people about the square, I could hear them talking, but I couldn't *see* any of them."

"Oh my."

"And . . . hard to explain this, but it was as if there was a sort of screen between all these people and me. Now, I know what you're going to say—the only reason there's a screen between me and the rest of the world is because I've erected it myself—but it wasn't like that. Not at all. This was really, well, physical, but not . . . How do you explain it?"

"I think you should come and sit down, Alex, and not let yourself get too worked up about this."

"That's what you think, is it?"

"I think you need to calm down."

Alex slumped into the sofa and she came down next to him, light as a bird, perching on the edge of the cushion, and the shift-thing riding up her legs. Pretty remarkable legs, had to admit that.

"And I heard Fay," Alex said. "I'd walked back—couldn't seem to make progress, you see, kept on walking and wasn't getting anywhere. You know that feeling? Happens in dreams sometimes. Anyway, I'm coming up the hill again, and this time it's Fay I can hear, talking to some chap. Telling him about how all the people had gathered in this very square, exactly four hundred years ago to the night, to get up a posse to go along and lynch old whatsisname . . . Sheriff Wort."

"I see," Jean said. She leaned over and picked up his left hand. One of her nipples was poking through the black filigree stuff.

Alex swallowed. "Then this chap she was talking to, he must have drifted away. I said, 'Listen, Fay,' I said, 'why don't you tell me—tell *me*—what all this is about . . . ?' But she couldn't hear me. Why couldn't she hear me, Wendy?"

Jean said, "What's this on your hands?"

"Blood," he said quickly. "It's Murray Beech. He's been stabbed to death. Only realized as I was walking up the hill."

"Stabbed to death," Jean said neutrally. "I see."

"Don't you believe me?"

"Alex, I believe *you* believe that Murray Beech has been stabbed to death. And what about Grace?"

"She took me to her grave. We walked together. I think we came to an agreement."

"I see."

"But you don't really believe any of this, do you, Wendy?" Jean smiled.

"Or do you?"

"Alex," said Jean, "would you like to sleep with me?"

Alex's throat went dry.

"Well?" she said gently.

"Oh gosh," Alex said. "Do you think I could manage it?"

Jean smiled. "Perhaps we should find out."

"That's what you think, is it?"

The answer burned quietly, like a kind of incense, in her eyes.

Alex stood up. He felt very calm. Calmer than ever he could remember feeling before. He did not know the meaning of the word "dementia." His heart was strong. His eyes, he knew, were twinkling quite dramatically.

The aromatic oil from the lamp was exquisite.

Jean unwound from the sofa and he took her in his arms. His breathing rate quickened at once. She tilted her face to kiss him, but he ran a hand into her soft, short hair and pressed her face to his chest, bent his head and whispered into her ear.

"You cunning bitch."

Her body went rigid, and he let her go.

What a waste, he thought. What a tragic bloody waste.

When Jean Wendle faced him from across the room, her eyes were in deep shadow, her lips were drawn back, and the inside of her mouth looked so black that she seemed, momentarily, to have no teeth at all.

The aromatic oil from the lamp smelled like the floor of a urinal.

"Oh my. You've blown it, now, Alex," Jean whispered, voice like tinder.

Alex shook his head.

"You'd had it. You were finished. You were going very rapidly into the final decline. A bed in the bottom corner of the geriatric ward, to where the naughty boys are consigned, the nurses treating you like a difficult child when you try to pinch their bottoms. Poor old man, he used to be a priest."

"Nothing more welcome in hell than an unfrocked priest," Alex mused. "Except perhaps a priest who ought to have been unfrocked but never was, because he was too damned plausible—all his life, so plausible, right up to the end, shafting old ladies."

"I brought you back," Jean said. "I fed you energy."

"But what kind of energy?"

"Ach." Jean turned away with a dismissive wave of the hand. "You blew it."

"I don't think so," Alex said. "I made a deal. I went up the hill and I made a deal."

He smiled. His heart was strong and his eyes still twinkled.

Jean Wendle turned her head and peered at him, curious. He saw in her face a pinched look, ravages, and not the ravages of years.

"Made a deal," Alex said. "After a period of protracted and considered negotiation, the Management and I formulated the basis of an agreement, nothing binding, either party retaining the right to pull out at any given time if the Second Party should happen to lose his bottle."

Alex walked out of the room. "Good night, Wendy."

Bloody waste, he thought sadly.

Joe Powys came out of the passage into the night, into a blinding light and the face of Edgar Humble.

He didn't have to force the fear.

"Hold it. Don't move."

Powys half out of the hole in the side of the Tump, the wooden box in his arms, Arnold at his ankles.

Humble's eyes were fully open, his lips apart.

"You're dead," Powys said from a throat full of hairline cracks.

"Course he's fucking dead," Gomer Parry said, leaning out of his cab. "Sorry, Minnie."

Humble lay across the jaw of the digger, quite stiff now, one arm still flung out and his crossbow on his chest. The big shovel was almost blocking the entrance to the passage.

Minnie Seagrove wasn't looking.

Gomer said, "What you got there, then, Joe?"

"Buried treasure," said Powys. "Is that thing safe?"

"Gimme a second." Gomer raised the shovel so Powys could climb out from underneath it.

"Right, then." The little man climbed out of his cab, rubbing his hands on his overalls. "We got a bit o' talkin' to do yere, Joe. First off, you finished in there? Got what you want?"

"I think so."

"Safe to block 'im up again, then."

"Don't see why not."

"Good. Mind out, then."

He climbed back into his cab, cigarette end waggling, lowered the shovel, started to tip Humble's body over the entrance of the hole.

"What the hell are you doing, Gomer?"

Minnie Seagrove turned away as Humble's remains tumbled into the soil and rock.

"Nicked that box, did you?" Gomer shouted.

"What?"

"Treasure trove, that, boy. I won't say nothin' if you don't."

"I had to tell him, Joe," Minnie Seagrove said. "I said, I'll go to the police and admit everything. And you'll speak up for me, won't you, Joe? You're a famous writer, that'll count for quite a lot. But he wouldn't hear of it."

"Bollocks," said Gomer. "Could be centuries before they finds 'im, if ever. And if they does turn 'im up, 'ow could it possibly have anythin' at all do with a sweet little old lady? Sorry, Minnie, I didn't mean old . . . "

The more Powys thought about it, the less difficult it became to fault.

"You can't leave him near the entrance."

"I shall drag 'im in just as far as 'e'll go, then I'll fill this 'ole up and pack 'im tight, see, and pile up them stones, so it looks like the wall collapsed on it, like."

"I can't stop to help you, Gomer, I'm sorry. I've got to go somewhere, and I don't think there's much time."

"No problem. I'll take Minnie 'ome."

"And could you do me another favor—take Arnold, too."

"I'll take him," Mrs. Seagrove said.

"I'll come back for him."

I hope.

Or Fay will.

"Thanks, Arnie," said Powys, putting the box down and sinking his hands into Arnold's fur, rubbing his face against the dog's encouragingly cold nose.

Arnold licked him once.

"And thank Henry for me," Powys said, "if you see him around."

He picked up the box. It was quite heavy but not too unwieldy. He balanced the lamp on top. "You're *sure* this is going to be all right? I have the awful feeling it'll look like an excavation site."

"Joe," said Gomer patiently, "this yere is Gomer Parry Plant Hire you're dealin' with. I already got the reputation of havin' fucked up once on this site—sorry, Minnie—and I'm not gonner risk 'avin' myself pulled in by that Wiley if I can 'elp it, am I?"

Gomer lit another cigarette, lowered his voice. "Wynford Wiley," he said. "Wouldn't give 'im the satisfaction. Fat bastard."

Powys nodded. "Minnie. I . . . "

"She never did nothin'," Gomer Parry said gruffly. "So you got nothin' to thank 'er for, is it? Bugger off. Good luck."

eighteen

❋

If anything, it was stronger now. She thought she'd get used to it, like when you were staying on a farm during the manure-spreading season, but this wasn't manure and it was getting stronger.

In it there was human waste and animal waste, raw meat, blood perhaps, body odors, rancid fats . . . and now smoke.

Woodsmoke? Maybe.

Or was it the church? Could she smell the fire in the church because the church was on the line linking the center of the square with the Court and the Tump?

Joe Powys would know. Or he wouldn't. Either way, it would be good to have him here. Not such a world-class crank after all, not when you listened to this bunch.

Fay walked among them, the night still alive with natural radio.

"He'll come back." Graham Jarrett.

"What if he doesn't?" Hilary Ivory.

"I tried walking." One of the lawyers, in tones of defeat. "I kept on walking, looking for a light. I kept walking, and I just felt like I was fading out . . . fading away. Losing my physical resistance to the air, becoming absorbed in the atmosphere. I mean, it was very soporific, in a way. I think it'd be good to die like that. But not yet. I got scared. I thought, I've got to go back. And when I thought that, I *was* back. Like I hadn't been anywhere."

"There's nowhere to go." Oona Jopson. "Accept it. Relish it. It's not likely to happen to you again."

"Good."

"Or maybe it will. Maybe we're being opened up to a permanent kind of cosmic consciousness, you know?"

She wondered what was happening outside the square. Was the church alight? Was Jimmy Preece alive? And what about Warren? Were the Crybbe people attending the meeting still inside the town hall? And what of their relatives in the town—had they any idea what was happening? Perhaps it had happened before, the town square sealing itself off in the past—a past which was always close to the surface of this town.

Not for the first time tonight, Fay genuinely wondered if this was some long and tortured dream. And, if it was not a dream, whether, when (if) it was over, it would have no more significance than if it had been.

Somebody was coughing very weakly, a thin scraping sound.

"Where's Colonel Croston?"

"I'm here. Who's that?"

"It's Dan Osborne, Colonel, I'm a homeopathic practitioner, but I have a medical qualification. There's a woman here in a bad way. Over here, just come toward my voice. I'm bending across her, you won't walk into her."

"OK, I'm on my way. Do you know who she is?"

"She's wearing what feels like a silk blouse and . . . a fairly tight skirt. She's got . . . thick hair, quite long, I suppose."

Guy said, "Is she wearing a thickish sort of necklet thing?"

"A torque, I think. Dear God, what's this . . . ?"

"Jocasta! What's happened? Where are you?"

"She's . . . The bloody torque's been twisted into her neck.
Please, Christ, just hold still . . . "

"OK, Mr. Osborne, I'm here. Is she OK?"

"I don't know. She didn't bloody well do this to herself, did
she? Somebody's tried to garrote her with her own . . . "

"OH GOD! GET ME OUT OF THIS!" The woman from the
crafts shop hurling herself about the Crybbe vacuum, bouncing
off people. Somebody had to crack up, sooner or later.

Have one for me, Fay thought.

Col Croston sat down on the cobbles, cross-legged, and looked
hard at the darkness. Held his own hand up in front of his face.
He could see it. Just. Could tell it was a hand, or was that
because he knew it was a hand?

The woman would live. Her throat would be a mess, but she'd
be OK. She'd tried to speak. "Who did this?" he asked, but if
she'd identified her attacker he hadn't been able to make out the
name. Wouldn't be much use anyway; how could you go after
anyone without light?

I am here, Col said silently, letting his eyes half close. I can
sense myself. I can sense my toes (flexing them and then letting
them relax), my calves (trying to tighten the muscles in his legs
and letting them relax), my thighs . . . my stomach . . .

An exercise.

As a soldier (all his family were soldiers), Col had gravitated
to the SAS not because of a need for action and physical stress,
but because he wanted to *feel* life, and for that, he'd decided,
one needed to be out on the edge of something, always within
sight of the abyss.

Rather thought he'd got over that stage now.

. . . chest (tighten, breathe in, hold it . . . relax . . .), shoulders . . .

Mind control. Expansion of the senses. Spent two weeks with
a meditation expert learning techniques for dominating the body
in tight spots. Optional course for officers; some of the chaps
thought it was all crap. Not Col. He'd actually taken it further,
after the course.

. . . neck . . . face (tensing the muscles in his cheeks and jaw, letting the tension go).

At the end of this exercise—he'd done it many times over the past twenty or thirty years—there should be a moment of pure awareness. Awareness of oneself and one's situation. And sometimes . . .

. . . back of the head . . .

. . . one emerged from it and everything looked clearer. And one knew precisely what to do next. Probably elements of yoga and meditation in there, so it was never wise to tell some of the chaps one was indulging in this sort of thing, or they'd be putting it round the Colonel talked to plants and things. Not a word to these New Age characters either, or they'd be recruiting him as an emblem.

Gradually, his breathing slowed and the voices around him in the void began to fade.

"Warm night, isn't it?"

"Hmm?"

"Stuffy. Humid."

"Yes, it is really."

Old chap in a T-shirt sitting in a doorway a few yards away.

"Colonel Croston, isn't it?"

"Col. Hey, just a minute . . . "

He could *see* this chap. It was still dark, but he could see him, could see his white beard and what it said on the front of his T-shirt. Didn't make any sense, half faded, but he could . . .

"It's Canon Peters, isn't it? Seen you in the Cock."

"Alex."

Col turned around to look at the square. He could see the shapes of buildings, very dimly; he could hear the sound of people talking and possibly screaming, although there was nothing immediate about this, no involvement; more like the sound of someone's TV set from a distance.

"Heard you talking to my daughter," the old man said. "Young Fay."

"Fay Morrison. Yes. I was. But you weren't . . . with us, were you? You weren't in . . . in . . . Look, Canon, can you help me to understand this? When you heard us talking, could you, you know, *see* us?"

"No."

Col sighed. "Thought not. Started out thinking it was some

sort of gas. Some leakage from somewhere. Or a Defense experiment, just the kind of place they'd choose. And now I'm inclined to think it's something psychological coming out. Some mass-psychosis thing. I can't begin to . . . I mean, what your daughter had to say was interesting in a purely academic sense, but not . . . Frankly, I'm lost, Canon. Where does one start . . . ?"

"Question I've been asking most of my life. Kept putting off having to answer it."

Keep cool, Col instructed himself. Keep your head. And for God's sake, don't go back in there. (In *where?* And how did I get out?)

"Canon . . . "

"Alex."

"Do you know what's happening?"

"Only the vaguest notion, old chap. But I believe I'm getting there."

"It *is* something . . . psychological, isn't it? Damned if I'm going to use that other word."

"Good Lord, no, old boy, never say that."

"Well." Col levered himself to his feet. He could actually see lamps in some of the houses on this side of the square. "You know a man's been murdered?"

"Oh yes. Murray Beech, the vicar."

"The *vicar?*"

"Stabbed to death. Lying in the churchyard. And the church is on fire. Look . . . "

Col looked up from the blackness of the square and the vague shapes of roofs, and saw the sky blooming red and orange.

"And you know the strangest thing?" said Alex. "Nobody's come out to watch."

"You've rung the fire brigade, I take it."

"No."

"Good God, man, it might burn down."

"It might. But if the fire brigade come, they'll have to go in through the square, won't they, and they might just mow down a lot of innocent people who didn't appear to see them coming. Or not be able to get through. I don't know. Don't know *what* would happen. But I think, on balance, that it's safest to let it burn, don't you? Only a bloody church."

The old chap looked gloomy, but, Col noted, entirely in

command of his faculties. The word around town had been that Canon Peters was losing his marbles.

"I think," the canon said, "that we're in the middle of what used to be known technically as A Crybbe Matter. However, on this occasion, there's been outside interference and the locals are seriously out of their depth. That's my feeling."

"Can we help?"

"That's a very interesting question," Alex Peters said.

Silly children's game, Fay thought, Hilary Ivory on one side of her, the cameraman, Larry Ember, on the other. Or perhaps only their voices. Their voices and their hands.

Silly children's game, New Age nonsense, where's the harm? No harm.

"We're all going to pool our energy." Andy's voice making soft chords in the night air. "We're going to bring down the light."

Silly children's game. No harm in it. Make a circle, everybody hold hands, dance gaily, stop, hold out hands to the sky as if in welcome. Wasn't there something like this at the end of *Close Encounters?* And something else. Wasn't it in something else?

Very silly.

"Got him?"

"Just about. Bit stiff. Bit of rigor."

Col heaved the corpse across his shoulder, fireman's lift job. Behind him, flames were coming through the church roof.

He followed Alex, the body over his shoulder. *I am here. I'm walking through a churchyard with a dead vicar over my shoulder and the church is on fire.*

This is not like Belfast, after a bomb blast. There are no spectators, no fire brigade, no police, no Army. Only the hungry flames chewing up the night.

"I trust," Alex said, "that when we get to the town hall, you'll have no difficulty getting us in."

"Count on it," Col Croston said through gritted teeth.

The box became unaccountably heavy and Joe Powys had to put it down in the courtyard.

Open it?

The Mini was still parked up by the stable block. It had been

his intention to load the box into the trunk and then drive it
out of Crybbe, but there was some uncertainty. What did you
do with these things?

Open it.

You could take it into a church—a real, functioning church,
outside of Crybbe, and place it on the altar. But you never knew,
with churches in the border country, what other forces might be
at work, what damage you might be inflicting on some other
quiet and vulnerable community while the people slept.

Or open it.

Or you could throw it into a deep lake. This had been done
in numerous legends to calm an excitable spirit, in a ceremony
normally involving about twelve priests.

He didn't have twelve priests on hand. Also this was not the
whole unquiet spirit.

Not the whole thing. But unquiet, yes. Walking back to the
Court, holding the box with both hands, the lamp balanced on
top, he'd had the illusion of something moving inside.

Open it . . .

Psychological trickery. Mind games. I'm not listening.

OPEN IT!

nineteen

Somehow they had formed a circle in the dark. When you
moved around in this formation, you couldn't, of course, see
the individual people composing the circle, but soon you began
to see the collective thing, the movement, the circle itself.

"A ring of pure golden light," Hilary Ivory breathed. "Isn't
it beautiful? And we've made it ourselves. *We've* made it."

Yes, Fay thought remotely, it *is* rather beautiful. But it's not
quite golden. More a darkish yellow. The yellow of . . . of what?

Hilary held her right hand, Larry Ember her left. Hilary
breathed and sighed, as if she was making love, while Larry

chuckled to himself, not in a cynical or ironic way, but a chuckle of pleasure. Pleasure in self-discovery.

Round and round they went in a slow circle, mindlessly, innocently round and round, like children in the schoolyard.

The air was still pungent, but the pungency was fortifying and compelling now. Tobacco could seem noxious and nauseous the first time you inhaled it, but when you were accustomed to it, it was deeply satisfying.

So it was with the scent of shit and blood and rotting vegetables, as the human circle revolved, quite slowly at first, anticlockwise, in the opposite direction to the sun, which was OK, Fay reasoned dreamily, because there was no sun, anyway, at night.

Every face was blue-lit, anxious and staring bleakly at Alex without enmity but without any hope either. A quarantine situation: nobody was to go outside, nobody from outside was to come in because of what else might enter.

But Col Croston had got them into the hall, without too much difficulty. He knew both men on the rear door—Paul Gwatkin, one of the three Gwatkin brothers who farmed Upper Cwm and Lower Cwm, and Bill Davies, the butcher. Decent chaps, both of them.

"Paul," Col had said, very reasonably, "it's essential that my friend the canon and I come in, and I have to tell you that if you don't get out of the way I may hurt you quite badly. Problem is, I was never trained to hurt people only slightly. You see my problem."

"And I hope, Colonel," said Bill Davies, standing aside, "that you might be startin' to see ours."

Col had laid a sympathetic hand on the butcher's shoulder. "We're here to help, Bill."

"Wastin' your time, I'm afraid, Colonel, it's . . . "

"I know," Col said. "A Crybbe matter."

Now, standing on the platform with its table and two empty chairs, Alex addressed the assembly, quite cordially.

"Good evening. Some of you know me, some of you don't, some of you might have seen me around. Peters, my name. For what it's worth, I appear to be the only living priest in town. And you, I take it, are what one might call the backbone of Crybbe."

He looked carefully at his audience, perhaps three hundred of them, men outnumbering women by about two to one, the majority of them older people, over fifty anyway—such was the age ratio in Crybbe. The scene reminded him of the works of some painter. Was it Stanley Spencer, those air-raid shelter scenes, people like half-wrapped mummies?

"Strange sort of evening," Alex said. "I expect you've noticed that; otherwise what are you all doing penned up like sheep left overnight in the market? Hmm?"

No response. Nobody did anything to dispel the general ambience of the stockroom at a mortuary. The blue-faced refrigerated dead.

What would it take to move these people? And, more to the point, had he got it?

As Alex stood there and watched them, he saw himself as they must be seeing him. Bumbling old cleric. Woolly-haired, woolly-headed; mind known to be increasingly on the blink.

But he'd made a Deal, if only with his inner self. He thought about the possible implications of the Deal, and a suitably dramatic quote occurred to him, from the Book of Revelations:

His head and his hairs were white like wool, as white as snow; and his eyes were as a flame of fire.

"Right," Alex said, stoking the fire, summoning it into his eyes. "If that's the way you want it. Colonel, would you ask Murray to step inside?"

"Huh?" Col Croston glanced sharply at Alex, who merely nodded. "Oh," Col said and walked out.

Alex said bluntly, "I understand Max Goff was slaughtered like a pig in here tonight."

Some of the women looked away. Nobody spoke. Alex let the silence simmer for over a minute, observing finally, "You seem to have thrown the body out. Out of sight, out of mind, I suppose. Didn't know the chap myself. However, I did know *this* poor boy."

Col Croston had returned with his arms full. Paul Gwatkin and Bill Davies didn't try to stop him, but neither seemed anxious to help him with his bloody burden.

"He's sorry he was late," Alex said. "He was obliged to stop on the way, to get murdered."

Col carried the corpse around the table, where the blotter was brown with dried blood, and curling.

Alex said, "You remember Murray? Young Murray Beech?"

Col dropped the body like a sack of coal, and it rolled over once, onto its back, a stiff, bloody hand coming to rest against the knee of a woman on the front row, Mrs. Byford, clerk to the Crybbe town council. She did not move, except to shrink back in her chair, as if retracting the essential Mrs. Byford so that the dead hand was only touching her shell.

"That's right," Alex said. "Pretend he's not there. But then, you never noticed he *was* here, did you? He was only another vicar from Off. And now he's dead. But I'll tell you one thing . . . he isn't as bloody dead as any of *you.*"

He saw Murray Beech's body, in the light, for the first time. The front of his black clerical shirt had been slashed neatly from neck to navel. The shirt was soaked and stiff.

Mrs. Byford delicately removed the hand from her knee, her mouth beginning to quiver. Murray's own mouth was widened from one corner, like a clown's. It continued almost to an ear. Or what remained of an ear.

Alex lowered himself into the chair where another body had slumped. It was sticky. He looked down into a blotter thick with blood and lumps and clots. "Talk to me," he said. "Tell me about what happened four hundred years ago when your ancestors went out to lynch this chap Wort. What had *they* got in the way of incentive that you haven't, hmm?"

He noticed the police sergeant, Wiley, near the back, in full, if disarranged, uniform. Not exactly rushing to open an investigation into the killing of Murray Beech.

Col Croston, back in the chairman's chair, next to Alex, called out, "No need for inhibition. Consider the issue thrown open to the floor."

"Well, come on," said Alex, in exasperation. "Who's the old bat in the front row trying to avoid Murray, what about *you?* Mrs. Byford, isn't it?"

Mrs. Byford spoke with brittle clarity, like an icicle cracking. "Tell this rude old gentleman, Colonel, that we have no intention of moving from yere nor of entering into any discussion on the subject."

Alex said, "Did you have much to do with Murray, Mrs. Byford? Your granddaughter did. She sought his assistance. As a priest. She wanted him to exorcise a ghost from your house."

"No!" Mrs. Byford pushed her chair back into the pair of knees behind her and stood up. Murray's hand appeared to reach for her ankle and she gave a shrill cry. "It's lies!"

"Poor old Murray was quite thrown at first," Alex said. "Not every day you're recruited to cast out a malevolent spirit. Anyhow, he came to me for advice, and I said, go along and play it by ear, old boy. Nothing lost. So off he goes to the Old Police House. Don't suppose you were around at the time, were you?"

Alex could see a number of people beginning to look worried, not least Wynford Wiley, the copper.

"And where do you think he found the evil spirit, Mrs. Byford?"

" 'E wasn't evil!" Wynford spluttered out. " 'E was . . . "

"Where do you think he found this malignant entity?"

Her back arched. "Stop this, you got no right to . . . "

"You know, don't you?"

"Keep calm, woman," an old man said from behind. "You got to keep calm, isn't it."

Alex stood up. "He found the evil, Mrs. Byford . . . He found it in her eyes. Ironic, isn't it?"

Mrs. Byford's hands, half clawed, began to tremble. She stumbled into the aisle and stood there, shaking.

"Now . . . " Alex sat down. "No, please, Mrs. Byford, I'm not trying to bully you. Look, sit in one of the empty chairs on the other side. Thank you. Right, now, did that gentleman mention the necessity of keeping calm? Keeping the low profile? Avoiding direct confrontation? Let's discuss this—but very quickly, please, time's running out. Ah. Mr. Davies."

"What can we do?" The butcher, Bill Davies, had left his post by the door and was approaching the platform, a big man with a sparse sprinkling of gray curls. "We got to live yere, isn't it."

"The mayor," said Paul Gwatkin. "Where's the mayor?"

"He's probably dead," Col Croston said flatly.

"You don't know that," said Wynford Wiley.

"And the church is on fire," Col said. "Don't suppose you know *that.*"

"Aye, we know that," the clerk's husband, little Billy Byford, said tiredly, and sighed. His wife gave him a glance like a harpoon.

"These yere hippie types," said Bill Davies. "This Goff. If they 'adn't arrived, with their experimentin' and their meddlin' . . . They think it's a wonderful game, see. They think the country-side's a great big adventure playground. Do what you like, long as you shuts the odd gate. They wouldn't think of strollin' across their motorways, climbin' all over their power stations. Oh no, you 'andles all that with care, and if you don't know nothin' about it you stays out of it."

"Sit down, Mr. Davies," said Mrs. Byford. "There's nothing to explain."

"I'm gonna say this, Nettie. City-type dangers is something they takes for granted—never questions it. But they never thinks there might be risks in the country, too, as they don't understand. Well, we don't understand 'em properly neither, but at least . . . *at least we knows there's risks."*

"The implication being," said Col, "that Crybbe is an area with a particularly high risk factor."

"You live yere," said Bill Davies, "you learn there's things you can do and things you can't do. Maybe some people's more careful than others, maybe some people takes it more serious, like. But that's same as with a lot o' things, anywhere you goes, isn't it?"

"Mr. Davies, we don't have to explain nothing," Mrs. Byford said.

Bill Davies ignored her. "And it's not like you can get 'elp, neither. Can't write to your MP about it, can you? You 'as to live with it, just like your parents and your grandparents, and you accepts the constraints, like."

The butcher sat down two seats away from Mrs. Byford, on the left of the central aisle, and crossed his legs defiant-ly.

"Thank you," said Col. "I'm very grateful to you, Bill. Can-on?"

"Yes, indeed. I think Mr. Davies has put his finger on it. I can understand entirely that there are certain prevailing phenomena in this particular town which the residents have long felt unable to discuss with outsiders. Problems which, I suspect, first, er, materialized during the reign of James I, when anyone found displaying an interest in matters of a . . . shall we say, a super-normal nature . . . was in serious danger of being strung up for witchcraft."

He looked down at the blood-spattered blotter, saw that nothing at all had changed. Outside, the church was burning, and a gullible crowd was suspended in the thrall of something even the devil-fearing James I would have been hard-pressed to envisage.

"And one can see," said Alex, "how this quite-understandable reticence would, given the comparative remoteness of the town, become, in time, more or less endemic. Yes, I can understand why it's been allowed to fester.

"But, by God . . . " Alex stood up, his hands either side of the bloodstained blotter, summoning the flames. "If you don't take some action tonight you'll regret it for the rest of your dismal little lives."

twenty

✠

The box was making a strange noise, a rolling, creaking sound, suggesting that the item inside had been dislodged from whatever secured it.

OPEN IT!

"Not a chance," Joe Powys said aloud, attempting to sound confident, in control. But for whose benefit?

The box lay in the center of the courtyard, the lamp on top of it, its beam directed at the Court, no more the derelict warehouse, the disused factory without echoes of laughter or the residue of sorrow.

Periodically, Powys would look up toward the eaves, but there were no flickerings anymore, no ignition sparks. The Court was fully alive now and crackling and hissing at him.

OPEN IT!

The appalling temptation, of course, was to break open the box to confirm that it did in fact contain what he suspected. Which was the mummified head of Sir Michael Wort, or at least a head.

But Powys was scared to look into the eyes of Black Michael, even if only the sockets remained. There was too much heavy magic here; Andy, the shaman, the heir, was projecting himself at will along the spirit path, able to manifest a disembodied presence in the Tump and probably elsewhere, while his physical body was . . . *where?*

The old ley-line, which progressed from the Tump to the square and beyond, had been reopened, a dark artery to the heart of Crybbe. Reopened for the ancestor, Black Michael.

Whose head now lay in an oak box at Powys's feet. The head was a crucial part of the process, and as long as he had the head he was part of it, too, until the pressure became unbearable.

So what am I going to do with it?

He thought, as he'd thought so many times, I could walk out of this situation, I could leave the box lying on the ground, leap into the car, and accelerate back into what passes for the Real World. I could simply stop *believing* in all of this. Because if you don't invite it into your life it simply doesn't occur.

Blessed are the skeptics.

For they shall . . .

they shall . . .

die with a broken neck on a convenient rubbish heap.

Powys closed his eyes to ambush renegade tears. You daft bastard, this is Crybbe, where normal rules don't apply. Where, once you're in the game, you have to go on playing.

Because Fay is down there in that sick little town with Jean Wendle and probably Andy Trow, and the twisted essence of something four centuries old at the door, and Fay could go—snap!—like Rachel, like Rose. But you wouldn't die, Powys, you'd go on living with the knowledge of what you failed to prevent—even though you were fully aware, at last, of what was happening—because you were scared and because you thought it expedient, at this stage of the game, to take the skeptic's way out.

All right, *all right*. I'll play. Deal me in.

He tried to envisage the layout. The Tump was the head, the church was the center of the breast, the town square was the solar plexus, and the Cock was the genitalia.

He realized he must be standing on Black Michael's throat (the throat chakra, influencing the nervous system, controlling stress, anxiety).

There came another noise from the box, like the head rolling from side to side, and his eyes were wrenched open, the breath catching in his chest like a stone.

I've got to get rid of it.

He snatched the lamp, bent down and examined the box. It was bound not with iron as he'd imagined, but with strips of lead. It occurred to him that it was probably not locked at all and all he had to do was raise the lid and . . .

No . . .

He sprang to his feet and backed away.

God help me . . . I've got the four-hundred-odd-year-old head of Michael Wort in a box, and I don't know what the hell to do with it.

The Court wanted it, he could tell that. The Court squatted in its hollow with the vengeful, violated Tump hunched over it, glowering. The Court throbbed with an ancient need, and Powys knew that it wanted him inside it so that it could digest his spirit and spit him out like poor Rachel, like Tiddles the mummified cat, which had been stuck for centuries, a tiny, constricting hairball in its throat.

The throat had been blocked. The Court had coughed and the blockage had come out of the mouth.

The open mouth was the prospect chamber.

What he had to do—the clear, bright certainty of it—went through him like a fork of cold and jagged lightning.

"I can't," he told the night. "I don't have the strength. I don't have the courage."

"I can't."

It still made no sense, of course, according to what was accepted as normal, but it answered to the logic of the place. It extended the rules of the game to put him in with a chance.

What he had to do was enter the Court and carry the box up the stone stairs to the prospect chamber. And then he had to stand in the opening, lift the box above his head, and cast it out into the night so that it fell onto the rubbish heap and smashed, symbolically, to pieces.

A ritualistic, shamanistic act which would sever the connection between Black Michael and the Court, leave a meaningful crater, a great pothole in the middle of the spirit path.

And, well . . . he knew that the ritual would be more perfect,

more complete, if *he* went out of the prospect chamber, too, his
arms wrapped around the box.

Sacrifice. Always more energy with a sacrifice. Perhaps also,
because he was hijacking Andy's ritual, he'd be releasing and
recycling the energy created by Rose's fall and Rachel's.

He stood with one foot on the box and thought about this.

It was a complete load of New Age crap.

But if he believed in it, it might work. If he was prepared to
give up his life he'd be creating so much energy that . . .

"Christ!"

He kicked the box along the cobbles. God save us from New
Age philosophy. Energy. The life force. Mother-sodding-earth.

Not got the bottle for it, Joe?

Powys gave the Court a baleful glare.

"Yeah, OK, you can play it that way, if you want," he told the
house. "You can spit me out, like Rachel and Tiddles the cat.

"But when I go . . . *he* goes."

He picked up the box, put the lamp on top, and followed the
beam toward the main door. It would, he knew, be open.

Alex simply walked out of the town hall, down the steps, and
the few yards to the end of the street leading to the square. He
glanced behind himself once at the blue light from a high window, listened to the noise of the generator from the basement,
looked above the buildings to the orange glow in the sky from
the church. Reality, or as much of it as a bumbling old cleric
might perceive.

He thought about the Deal.

If he walked into the square, he doubted he'd get out of it so
easily, if at all.

This would be it.

It was like one of those experiments you did at school in your
very first physics lesson. Fay couldn't recall the technicalities of
it, but it was all to do with making your own electricity and you
did something like turning a handle—really couldn't remember
the details, never any good at science—and this little bulb lit
up, just faintly at first, but the faster you did whatever it was
you did, the brighter the bulb became, the more sustained was
the light.

There they all were, moving around in the circle—backward,

anticlockwise—the thin golden ring (or not gold, it was yellow, the yellow of . . . of . . .)

And there it was, in the center of the circle. New Age schoolchildren dancing around a lamppost and making the lamp light up, like the bulb in the physics lesson, through the power they were helping to generate.

"Faster, please," the Teacher saying in that wonderfully smooth voice, like an old cello, and they were able, without much effort, to move faster, Fay beginning to tingle with the excitement of what they were doing—making light.

An incandescent blob in the air, yellow and fuzzed at the edges, but filaments of hard white light forming at the center, extending out like branches or veins, blood vessels—light vessels—the whole thing pulsing with it. Hilary Ivory beginning to quiver and moan, as if reaching orgasm. Larry Ember, on the other side, giggling wildly. Never heard a cameraman giggle before, dour bastards in general, this must really be something coming.

"All my life!" she heard a woman (probably that loopy Jopson woman) cry in ecstasy. "All my life I've waited for *you* . . . "

"Michael," a man—the Teacher—said. Simply that, nothing more.

And a woman said, "Yes, Michael. The Archangel Michael, slayer of dragons."

No, Fay thought, confused, not him . . . that's wrong . . .

But what did it matter?

Couldn't very well contradict them, could she, not all of them, everybody shouting in unison now, a great chant.

"Michael . . . *Michael* . . . MICHAEL . . . *MICHAEL!*"

The Being of Light was responding to the summons, the filaments forming into a complexity of vibrating muscles, pipes, and organs, rippling into arms and legs, and between the legs—bloody hell, Fay thought . . .

Realizing she was chanting, too.

"Michael . . . Michael . . . "

The bells erupted again, a huge joyful clangor, cracking the night into splinters. The sound of bells in a blazing church.

The rational explanation, Col Croston thought, was that flames had been funneled into the tower, creating a huge gas jet which exploded into the belfry.

He stood in the town-hall doorway and peered into the street. Above him the night sky was frying. If Jimmy Preece was indeed dead, this made him the First Citizen of Crybbe. An auspicious start to his year of office; at this rate he'd be mayor of a burned-out ghost town before morning.

He looked for Alex, but the end of the street still dropped off the edge of the world, and Alex was gone and Col's sorrowful feeling was that he would never see the old man again.

twenty-one

Before, the last and only time he'd been inside Crybbe Court, it had been very much Henry's *dead place;* now it was repellently alive.

It had been cold and dry; now it was warm and moist, and going into it was disturbingly, perversely sexual. The Court was a very old woman, grotesquely aroused, and she wanted him.

The main door had not been locked. He ventured quietly in, the box under his arm. Stone floor, low ceiling, and slits of windows set high in the walls. And the walls leaked.

Joe Powys ran a cautious finger along the stone and found it warm and slimy. Under the light, he saw dead insects on the walls, all of them quite recently dead, not husks. Moths, flies and bluebottles trapped in a layer of . . . fat, it smelled like fat.

Or tallow maybe, grease from candles made of animal fat.

Crybbe Court was alive and sweating.

He moved toward the stone stairs, thinking, inevitably, of Rachel. What had it taken to make her so hot and feverish and desperate to get out of here that . . . ?

But you don't know what happened, you don't *know.*

Though you'll soon find out, as you retrace her steps up these stone steps, butcher's-shop slippery now, like the walls.

Coming to the first floor—the big family living room and the bedchambers off it. In one of these, Fay had told him, Tiddles the mummified cat had slept, most recently, in a chest that was not very old. Tiddles had come down from the rafters, but had never left the house, presumably, until she and Rachel had been hurled out of the prospect chamber.

Fay.

Picturing her standing in the field overlooking Crybbe, the blue raincoat streaming from under her arm, her rainbow eye watering in the wind.

It made him so sad, this image, that he had a wild urge to dump the box and race out of the Court—filthy, clammy, raddled old hag—and run back to Crybbe to find Fay and hold her, even if they only had a few minutes before . . .

Before whatever was to happen happened.

He wore his sense of foreboding like the black bag over a condemned man's head. Yet he was still half amazed at what he was planning to do: black comedy, a bizarre piece of alternative theater. Verdict: took his own life while the balance of mind was disturbed.

The voice of the police inspector, Hughes, landed in his head. *Are you* sure *he didn't say anything to you, Mrs. Morrison, by way of a suicide note, so to speak? Or did he assume, do you think, that his method of taking his own life would be self-explanatory?*

Well, he *was* a crank, wasn't he? You only had to read his book.

He wondered if the day would ever come when an inquest would concede that the balance of mind might be affected by prevailing psychic conditions.

Bloody New Age crap.

There was a stench of rancid fat. He felt sick.

It would be good, in a way, to be out in the fresh air.

As Col turned the corner of the back street linking the town hall with the churchyard, there was an enormous splintering roar and a belch that shook the ground. And then—as if massive furnace doors had been flung wide—huge, muscular arms of flame reached out for the heavens.

"Go easy," Col said. "I think the church roof's collapsed."

There were about twenty men with him. The youngest and strongest of them, Bill Davies, the butcher, was there, and all three burly Gwatkin brothers.

"God preserve us," one of them said and then turned away, embarrassed, his face already reddened in the glare from the church.

"It's down to you now," Col said. He hoped to God the stone walls of the church would contain the fire so that it wouldn't spread into the town, but the heat was unbelievable; anything could happen. Crackling splinters—in fact, great burning brands—were being thrown off, and every so often there'd be chaotic clanging of the bells.

"What we're going to do . . . " Col said. "All over the churchyard, you'll see pieces of wood ablaze. I want six of you to get the ones you can handle at one end and bring them out. This is bloody dangerous, so be *damned* careful, but we've got to have light where we're going."

"Why can't we just go 'ome and get torches?" a young lad, seventeen or eighteen, said.

"Do as he says, boy," Bill Davies grunted. "Nobody goes out of this street. You step into that square, you'll wish you'd stayed and burned."

As a handful of men climbed over the churchyard wall, Bill Davies took Col aside. "I'm not wrong, am I, Colonel?"

"Look, be a good chap . . . "

"Tell me, Colonel. I 'ave to know, see. Is it . . . in that square . . . Oh hell, is it the year 1593 over there, or is it an illusion? Is this town living an illusion, do *you* know?"

Joe Powys went up the stairs, past a small landing with an oak door four inches thick, which was open, revealing the stairs to the attic.

Walking up the steps, toward the death chamber of Michael Wort, with what he believed to be the head of Michael Wort in a wooden box under his arm.

People like me would no more come up here alone, he remembered thinking, than pop into a working abattoir to shelter from the rain.

But you *aren't* alone, are you?

The box was heavy.

Trying to avoid touching the walls because the stone was slick with something that felt like mucus. Suspecting that if he switched off the lamp, it would glow on the stones, luminous.

And so he came, at last, to the alcove leading to the prospect chamber.

When he put down the box to open the door, he felt Rachel was standing at his side. Remembering being here with her. How two wafers of light from holes in the roof had crossed just above her head and he'd recalled her standing by the window of the room at the Cock, naked and pale and ethereal.

Now he could almost see her calm, silvery shade; they'd go hand in hand into the prospect chamber.

This . . . is the only part of the house I really like.

And together they'd take the head of Michael Wort back into the night.

He turned the metal handle and put his shoulder to the old, oak door.

New Age Heaven.

Blissful, blissful, blissful.

"I want to touch him," the woman next to her cried. "I want to bathe in him."

Michael, *Michael,* MICHAEL, *MICHAEL!*

The Being of Light lifted his head and spread his arms to embrace his town. Bright people were gathering around him, both sexes, shimmering, all shapes and sizes, from the large, smiling man in the incandescent white suit to the tiny little lady, mouth opening in delight to reveal small, sharp white teeth, like a fish's, like . . . like . . .

Couldn't remember.

But she didn't want to remember. She'd never felt so warm and yet so free. She saw herself soaring above Crybbe, and the town was decked out in ribbons of soft, colored light anchored by ice-bright, luminescent standing stones. Floating over the square, she saw the old buildings in a lambent Christmas-card glow. But some of them were not so old, their timbers looked sturdy and neatly dovetailed, especially the inn, which had a simple strength and a sign with a large, rough beast upon it; and indeed, there were farm animals in the square around a cart with wooden wheels and sacks of grain on it. There was a cow, three horses, a pig. And a dog! Black and white like . . . like . . .

Couldn't remember.

"Fay."

Who was Fay?

"Listen to me."

"Yes," she sang. "Yes, yes, yes, I'm listening."

But she had no intention of listening; this was the wrong voice. It didn't sound like a cello, it sounded old and frail, an ancient banjo, cracked and out of tune.

She laughed.

Everyone was laughing.

New Age Heaven.

"Fay," Alex said into her ear. "Listen to me, please."

"Yes, yes, yes," she sang. "But you'll have to come with me. Can you float? Can you float like me?"

She wasn't floating. She was part of a group of thirty or forty people, hands linked, slowly and gloomily moving around in an untidy, irregular circle.

Alex could see most of them now, in the spluttering amber of the blazing church.

In the center of the square, where, in many towns, there was a cross, a man stood. A tall man, stripped to the waist. He had dark, close-shaven hair and a black beard. His eyes were closed. He was sweating. His arms hung by his sides but slightly apart from his body, the palms of his hands upturned. The ragged circle of people moved around him, anticlockwise.

The old buildings seemed to be leaning out of their foundations and into the firelight, like starved tramps at a brazier. The buildings had never looked more decrepit or as close to collapse.

Similarly, the people. Alex followed Fay around, walking behind her, peering into the faces of the men and women in the circle, horrified at how weak and drained they looked, some of them obviously ill. On one side of his daughter was a stocky man with a sagging belly and one eye badly bloodshot. He was moaning faintly and saliva dribbled down his chin. Fay's other hand lay limply in a flabby hand full of rings, obviously not very expensive ones, for they looked tarnished now and the joints of the fingers were swollen around them. The woman's hair was in wild, white corkscrews; her lips were drawn back into a frozen rictus; she was breathing in spurts through clenched teeth.

Diametrically opposite this woman, Alex saw Fay's ex-husband Guy Morrison, his blond hair matt-flat, exposing a large, white bald patch; his mouth downturned, forming pouches of slack skin from his cheek to his once-proud jawline. Next to him a fat girl was sobbing inconsolably to herself as she moved sluggishly over the cobbles. On the other side of this girl, a thin woman with shorn hair was breathing with difficulty, in snorts, blood sparkling on her upper lip and around her nose, from which a small ring hung messily from a torn flap of skin, and every time she took a breath part of the ring disappeared into a nostril. She didn't seem aware of her physical distress; nor did any of the others.

"Fay," Alex whispered.

Fay's skin was taut and pallid, her green eyes frozen open, her lips stretched in anguish, which made the words issuing from them all the more pathetic.

"Flying away, high, into the light. Can't keep up with me, can you?"

He didn't even try. He stood in the shadows and watched her drift away.

He'd had to stop himself from pulling her out of the circle. He had the awful feeling that he would simply detach her body, that her mind would remain in the ring and she would never get it back, would be a vegetable.

Which was the very worst thing of all; Alex knew this.

He stood and watched her for two more circuits of the town square. A lurid flaring of amber from the dying church picked out that woman from The Gallery, ugly blue bruises around her throat, dried vomit on her chin, coughing weakly; couldn't see her husband.

Very gently he separated Fay's fingers from those of the woman next to her and slipped her small, cold right hand into his left. With his right hand he found the damp, fleshy fingers of the white-haired woman.

And so Alex slipped into the circle and began to move slowly around.

He realized at once that he'd made a terrible, terrible mistake.

His legs began to feel heavy and cumbersome. At first he felt as if he'd stepped into a pair of Wellingtons several sizes too big and was wading in them through thick, muddy water, and then the weight spread up to his thighs—he was in the middle of a river in cumbersome waders—and finally it was as though both legs had been set in concrete; how he managed to move he didn't know, but he kept on, at funereal pace, his arms feeling limp as though the blood were draining away into the other hands, his life energy passed along the chain.

Progressive torpor. This was how it happened. Initiation ceremony. They were always saying, the newcomers, how much they wanted to fit in, become part of the community.

Now here they were, all these bright, clever, New Age folk, achieving overnight what some people waited years to attain.

All moving at last to the rhythm of Crybbe.

part nine

�֍�֍✤✤✤✤✤✤✤✤✤ ═══════

In actuality, of course, dowsing as an activity is no more spiritual than riding a bicycle: spirituality is in the person . . . Compared to this rich matrix of mystery the New Age "energy" ideas are conceptually bankrupt.

PAUL DEVEREUX,
Earth Memory—The Holistic
Earth Mysteries Approach to
Decoding Ancient Sacred Sites

The digger was crunching through the wood like a rhino in heat, Gomer Parry at the wheel, grinning like a maniac, dead cigarette, burned to the filter, clenched between his teeth. Minnie Seagrove holding on to the makeshift passenger seat, which didn't have a working safety belt, a three-legged black and white dog balancing, just about, on her knee and glaring out of the window, barking away.

This had all come about after they arrived back at Minnie's bungalow and Gomer, spotting the flames coming out of the town, reckoning it had to be the church, raced to Minnie's phone to summon the fire brigade and found the bloody old phone lines were down or something.

Anyway, the phone was off and so was the one in the kiosk.

"Something bloody funny yere."

They'd climbed back into the digger, Gomer heading back toward the town, foot down, headlight blasting at the night, and then—"Oh my God, Gomer, look out!"

Bloody great wall of metal, Minnie's hands over her eyes, the dog going berserk and Gomer flattening the brakes and damn near wrenching the old wheel out of its socket.

Flaming great articulated truck had jackknifed across the road at—*precisely*—the spot Gomer himself went adrift earlier on. Was this a coincidence? Like hell it was.

No sign of the driver, no blood in the cab, couldn't have been hurt, must've buggered off for help. So Gomer did this dynamite three-point turn and they were thundering off again. "Gonna find out what the bloody 'ell's afoot, 'ang on to your knickers—sorry, Minnie, but I've 'ad enough o' this mystery. You can push Gomer Parry *just so far,* see."

"Where are we going, Gomer?"

"Back way into Crybbe. Tradesman's entrance. Never done it all the way on four wheels before."

And Gomer lit up a ciggy one-handed and spun the digger off

the road and into the field, keeping well away from the Tump this time, although he could tell it'd taken a hammering tonight, that ole thing, not got the power it had, see, just a massive great lump of ole horseshit now, sorry Minnie.

So it was round the back of the Tump, back to the Court and into the wood.

"Ole bridle path, see."

"But we can't get through here, Gomer." Minnie no doubt wondering, by this time, why he didn't drop her off home. But it wasn't safe for a woman alone tonight. Besides, he liked an audience, did Gomer Parry. Not been the same since the wife snuffed it.

"If a 'orse can make it up here," he told Minnie, "Gomer Parry can do it in the best one-off, customized digger ever built."

So now the digger was flattening bushes either side and ripping off branches. "Five minutes gets us out the back, bottom end of the churchyard, and we can see what the score is . . .

"Fuckin' Nora, what the 'ell's this?"

For the second time in ten minutes, Gomer was on top of the brakes and Minnie was pulling her nails off on the lumpy vinyl passenger seat.

The headlight'd found a bloody great stone right in the middle of the flaming road.

"Who the . . . put that thing there?" Gomer was out of his cab sizing up the stone, seven or eight feet tall but not too thick. Arnold, out of the cab, too, standing next to Gomer, barking at the stone, looking up at Gomer, barking at the stone again.

"What you reckon to this then, boy?"

Woof, Arnold went. Smart dog.

"Dead right, boy," said Gomer, looking up at the bright orange sky, like an early dawn 'cept for the sparks. "Dead right."

Back in the cab, Gomer lit up another smoke, grinned like a potentially violent mental patient, and started to lower the big shovel.

And Fay, soaring above the town, far above the opalescent stones and the soft, pastel ribbons, felt a momentary lurch of nausea as the tallest, the brightest of the stones shivered, its radiance shaken, its magnesium-white core dying back to a feebly palpitating yellow.

The yellow of . . .

" . . . *Fay* . . . "

The yellow of . . .

"Please, F . . . "

The yellow of disease.

The yellow of embalming fluid.

The yellow of pus from an infected wound.

The yellow of Grace Legge.

" . . . Fay?"

"Dad?"

She turned and saw his face, and his skin looked as white as his hair and his beard. She saw him against what looked like the flames of hell, and his old blue eyes were full of so much mute pleading that they were almost shouting down this sick, dreadful chant.

Michael . . .

Michael . . .

MICHAEL . . .

MICHAEL!!!

screamed the poor, stricken, gullible bastards in the circle, and she could see them now. She could *see* them. She was gripping her dad's hand, and she could see them all in the light of Hell, and hell was what they looked like.

Hell also was what Fay *felt* like.

Her lips were like parchment, and when she tried to wet them she found her tongue was a lump of asbestos.

Michael, she wanted to say. It's Michael *Wort.*

But she couldn't even make it to a croak.

Her eyes found the center of the square, where the Being of Light was formed, pulsing with vibrant, liquid life energy, platinum white.

Pulsing with energy, all right—*their* energy—but it was the very darkest thing she had ever seen in all of her life.

Andy Boulton-Trow, a tall, bearded man, just an ordinary man—*once*—had been fitted for a black halo; it shimmered around him like the sun in a black-and-white photo negative.

The halo was the shadow of Black Michael. There were pinpoints of it in Trow's eyes which had flicked open and were looking steadily, curiously into hers.

She put all the strength she had into squeezing her dad's hand. It felt as cold as her own.

Trow did not move, his gaze like black velvet. Playing with her. Who are you? the eyes were asking. Have we met?

The complete, charismatic, black evangelist.

Somehow, Fay had milked a little strength from her poor father, enough to observe and to make simple deductions.

You've had us all going around your Bottle Stone, haven't you. Children of the New Age. Follow anybody, won't they? Look at them now. Look at the Jopson woman, led by the ring in her nose and then—gentle tweak—you tear through her flesh, and she doesn't know or care. Look at bloody Guy—show him his own reflection in a mirror shaped like a TV screen and watch him slash his wrists. Look at Graham Jarrett, away in the ultimate hypnotic trance, lost his toupee and his nose needs wiping. Look at them. Look at what you've done.

Arteriosclerotic dementia.

You have good days. Sometimes you have two or three good days together and you realize what a hopeless old bugger you were the other day when the lift failed to make it to the penthouse.

And then, one night, along comes a very cunning lady with an amorphous Chinese blob on a lead (which, as you thought, does not exist, but why else would she be trailing a lead?). And all the time you're with her, you're fine, you're wonderful, you're on top of the situation.

Until it becomes apparent that the lady is a prominent member of the Opposition, planning a startling little coup in this dead-end backwater where surely nothing that happens can be of any significance in the Great Scheme of Things.

But old habits die hard. Once a priest . . .

Yes, all *right,* Guv, I confess, I've never exactly been up there with Mother Teresa and Pope John the Twenty-third. I've cut a few corners. I've coveted my neighbor's wife. OK, several wives of several neighbors, and it wouldn't be half so bad if it had only stopped at the coveting stage. I was weak. I used to think it was OK, as long as you left the choirboys alone, but I was never attracted to choirboys, anyway, obnoxious little sods.

Here, boss, scrap of prayer for you, this'll bring back a few memories.

Oh God, merciful Father, that despisest not the sighing of a contrite heart . . .

Got the message? I'm *sorry* . . . I really am sorry.

Listen, I know about the Sins of the Fathers. I know *all* about that.

But not Fay, please—look at her; what has she ever done to you?

Thing is—look, don't take this the wrong way, but no God of mine ever took it out on the kids. That's more *his* god's style. Can you see him there? He represents everything you're supposed to abhor. And he's winning, damn it, the bastard's winning!

OK, here's another bit, how much do you want, for Christ's sake? Listen, this . . . this is the essence of it.

Lighten our darkness, we beseech Thee, O Lord, and by Thy great mercy defend us from all perils and dangers of this night . . .

Lighten our darkness, geddit?

Come on, Guv'nor . . . we had a *deal* . . .

The stone actually broke. Cracked in two.

Split off a couple of feet from the base just as Gomer was getting underneath. Raised the shovel to ground level to have another go and gave it a bit of a clonk, accidental-like, and off it came like a thumb in a bacon slicer.

Gomer backed up, smartish, but luckily the big bugger fell the other way, straight flat across the road, whump!

"Teach me to rush the job, Minnie. 'Ang on to your, er . . . hat."

Slipping down to low gear, he drove right over the thing. Bit of a bump, but not much worse than one of them ramps they call a sleeping policeman.

"A big fat sleeping policeman." Gomer burst out laughing. "Call it Wynford Wiley."

There were big, fat tire marks across the middle of the stone. Gomer accelerated past Keeper's Cottage with one dismissive sideways glance. That could do with knocking down, too.

There was the merest tremor in Trow's gaze; enough for Fay to pull her eyes away. Turned to her father and found that Hilary Ivory, on the other side, had also turned her face, in faint confusion, toward the old man in the Kate Bush T-shirt.

Alex tried to smile. He couldn't speak.

Hilary looked at Fay, her eyes troubled. She didn't understand. The first step to recovery—the moment when, quite suddenly, you don't understand.

But Alex's hands were warm.

Dad?

A deep warmth seeped into Fay's right hand and rippled up her arm and into her breast. She could feel her heart drumming. Alex's eyes were vibrantly blue. They made the fire in the sky look cheap and lurid. He turned his head toward Hilary Ivory, and she started to smile, like people smile when they're coming out of anesthetic.

Alex's hand tightened around Fay's.

Fay grinned.

"You old bugger," she said, quite easily.

On the other side, Larry Ember, recipient of the warmth from her own left hand, demanded gruffly, "What the bleed'n' hell's this?"

Alex's lips were white. Almost as white as the beard around them. First they tried to smile, then they were trying to shape a word.

"C . . ."

His hands hot now, but his lips were white.

"Dad?"

Fay squeezed his hand, almost too hot to hold now.

She felt strong enough to risk a glance to the center of the square where Trow was no longer still, but moving within his own darkness. Squirming.

Trow screamed once,

"Michael!"

The cello grotesquely off-key.

Alex found his word.

"Colonel?" he said mildly, and the piercing blue faded from his eyes; clouds were in them now. He dropped Hilary's hand, held on to Fay's for an extra moment and then let that go too.

There was a gap now between Fay and her dad, a clear gap in the circle, and the backcloth, the screen of false reality, was torn away and the flames in the sky were no longer phantasmal but a source of savage heat and acrid fumes.

"Now." Col Croston's crisp voice, and the Crybbe hordes poured through the gap, bearing their flaming torches, farmers in tweed trousers and sleeveless body-warmers over their under-shirts, Bill Davies incongruously clad in his butcher's apron, Wynford Wiley ludicrously wielding his truncheon. Faces she'd seen on the streets—" 'Ow're you, 'ow're you"—now hard with determination below the blazing brands. The circle in disarray. Lights appearing in windows. From somewhere in the innards of the Cock, the sound of a generator starting up.

Col Croston, bringing up the rear, scanning the square.

"Over there! That's the man. The sheriff! Don't let him . . . " The sheriff?

"Right!" Fay was screaming. "The sheriff! He's in the cen . . . "

But she couldn't, in fact, see the man they were looking for. Andy Boulton-Trow had gone from the square.

He's taken his darkness back into the night.

"Larry! Camera!"

Guy was in a mess. He'd lost his jacket, lost his cool, lost his hair. "Larry, we have to get this . . . "

"Piss off, Guy," Larry Ember shouted happily from some-where.

Fay found she was giggling. Hysterics. Absurd.

"Dad?"

Alex managed a smile.

"Dad . . . We did it! *You* did it."

Alex touched her arm, stumbled. Sat down quietly on the cobbles. Fay went down beside him, taking his hand.

Which was not so hot anymore, not very hot at all. The blue in his eyes had drifted away. Far away. Gently and discreetly, Alex slid over onto his side. He was breathing. Just. Hilary Ivory crouched down next to Fay. "Is he OK? I used to be a . . . a nurse . . . Well, sort of alternative nurse, really."

Fay didn't reply. She pulled off her cotton top, rolled it into a ball, slid it between Alex's head and the cobbles.

"Dad?" Softly.

Fairly sure he couldn't hear her.

She picked up his hand; very little warmth remained. Alex's lips moved and she put an ear to his mouth. One word came out intact.

"Deal," he said.

Alex's breathing ended almost imperceptibly.

Fay sat for a long time on the cobbles, holding her father's cooling hand under the hot red sky.

two

A single candle burned in the attic at Crybbe Court. It was two inches thick and sat in a blackened pewter candle-holder with a tray, laid on the topmost stone step. It was a tallow candle and it stank; it filled the space with a pungent organic stench; it reeked, somehow, of death.

Or perhaps this was because of the wan and waxy aura it gave to the rope.

The old, frayed rope which had hung from the central joist in the attic was gone. Its replacement was probably just as old, but was oily and strong. An inch thick, it dangled four feet from the apex of the roof, and at the end was a noose, a very traditional hangman's noose secured with ten rings of rope.

It was into this noose that Andy Boulton-Trow fitted his head.

He had, it would emerge, studied hanging.

The original short-drop method, with the rope only a few feet long and the condemned person's feet almost touching the ground, resulted in a rather prolonged death by slow strangulation. Whereas the long-drop system, introduced in Britain in the late nineteenth century, by which the subject fell about ten feet, perhaps through a trapdoor, brought about a swifter and more merciful death by fracturing neck vertebrae. In the sixteenth century, it appeared, Sir Michael Wort had experimented with both techniques and others besides.

A trapdoor had been constructed in the attic floor, originally to dispose of bodies after execution by dropping them into a narrow, windowless, well-like chamber directly underneath.

In later years, more squeamish owners of the house had boarded over the trapdoor space, but the floor remained weak at this point, the boards had rotted, there were cracks. When Andy Boulton-Trow stood on the beam, nearly two feet thick, from which the executees—and Sir Michael himself—had taken a final step, he could see a few jagged black holes below his feet.

First, he had taken off his shoes and his trousers, so that he stood naked now in the candlelight with the noose loosely around his neck.

For the purposes of magical projection, a modification of the short-drop method was the most appropriate. That it had worked, to a significant extent, for Michael had been amply demonstrated to Andy tonight. Andy, who had spent twice as many years as Michael in study and preparation, was warm after his sprint through the wood, still angry at the damage to the stone and the debacle in the square. But the night was churning with chaos, and out of chaos . . .

There was little time to waste. He was hot inside, with excitement and anticipation.

To make sure everything was still in working order, he and Humble had once hanged a fisherman Humble had chanced upon, casting alone into the upper reaches of the river. It had not really been necessary, but Humble had enjoyed it.

Just as Humble would enjoy watching Andy hang. So why wasn't he here?

Perhaps he was. Humble could be quite discreet.

Andy put both hands behind his head and tightened and adjusted the noose under his chin. It was so easy to make a mistake.

He stood on the floor joist in the candlelight and began to visualize, to bring himself to the necessary state of arousal.

He visualized the woman who'd looked at him across the square, telling him with her eyes that she was slipping out of the enchantment. Andy smiled; he would return for her one night, quite soon perhaps.

A small wind drifted through the holes in the slates; there was no wind tonight.

"Good evening, Michael," Andy said. "Again."

He closed his eyes, and Michael was within him once more, a now-familiar sensation. In his solar plexus he felt a stillness which was also a stirring, and there was the familiar small tug at the base of his spine.

In time, the walls of the Court evaporated, and he saw the town at his feet. He held back, and the vapors rose within him. He felt the blazing chaos that was Crybbe, the dissolution of barriers, the merging of the layers, one with another, the lower levels open to the higher levels, the atmosphere awash with spirit.

He felt his destination.

And when the time was right, he stepped lightly from the beam.

There was a bright light, a widening carpet of light, and something rolling along it, toward him.

This was the first thing he was really aware of after he stepped into space and the noose tightened on his Adam's apple.

There was no pain, only darkness and then the carpet of light and the thing that was rolling.

Rolling very slowly at first, but its momentum was increasing. And then he was staring into the face of Michael Wort.

The eyes had gone. The lips had gone. There was some hair, but not much; most of the beard had disappeared. There were gaps in the ghastly brown and yellow grin; few people in Michael's day had kept their teeth beyond middle age.

"Michael," he said eventually.

The noose was still around his neck, but it was slack. There was no pain in speech.

Behind the lamp, he saw a pair of sneakers and legs in muddy jeans.

"He came with me," Joe Powys said. "He couldn't manage the steps on his own."

Andy had smashed through the floor, spinning and twisting. He'd screamed once, but it had sounded more like triumph than terror, suggesting he was unaware of anything having gone wrong.

Well, you wouldn't be, if this was the first time you'd hanged yourself.

The way he was lying in the center of the windowless, stone chamber was bent, unnatural. Powys said, with little concern, "Can you move?"

"I don't know," Andy said, his feelings sheathed. "What did you do?"

"I saved your life."

"Thanks," Andy said. "You fucker."

Powys said nothing. He was shaking.

"Humble," Andy said after a while. "He was supposed to have killed you."

"Yeah?"

"He will."

"Can't see it," Powys said, "somehow."

He had the feeling both of them were in shock. He put a hand out to the wall; it was dry again, and dusty. The Court was a dead place again. The room was narrow enough for there to be an enforced intimacy, and yet there was a distance, too, because the Court was dead.

"I nearly killed *myself,* though," he said, still appalled enough at what might have happened to want to hear himself talking about it. "Seems absolutely bloody insane when I look back, but I had this idea that the only way I could straighten things out was to take the head up to the prospect chamber and hurl us both out. I couldn't have been thinking straight. Well, obviously. But you don't, do you, in these situations?"

"And what stopped you," Andy asked him, "from killing yourself?"

Powys smiled weakly. "Couldn't get in. The door in the alcove was locked, and there was a sign that said: 'Danger. Keep Out.' "

The final bitter irony. Rachel had saved his life. He'd stood outside the door, on the greasy stairs, and felt her there again, cool and silvery. *You really can do better than this, J.M.*

"So then I saw the light in the attic. Thought maybe you were up there, but there was only one rope. Hate nooses. Went back outside and broke into the stable block, through a window, with a brick. I pinched a bread knife. Brought it up to the attic and sawed through most of the rope until it was just hanging together by a few threads. Where I'd cut it, I covered it up with the coils of the noose."

He saw that Andy was thinking very hard, the muscles in his face working.

"I figured it out," Powys said. "It came clear. When I saw the noose. You were going to do"—he pointed a foot at the head—"what he did. On the four-hundredth anniversary of his death. I couldn't believe it at first. I can't understand that level of obsession."

"Of course you can't." Andy glanced up at him, eyes heavy with contempt. "You puny little cunt."

"We're talking sex magic, aren't we? I was once at a signing session for *Golden Land.* Some regional book fair, and one of the other writers there was this retired pathologist. He said, apropos of something, that a remarkable number of hangings which look like suicide are actually accidents. Blokes—or teenage kids in a lot of cases—trying for this uniquely mindblowing sexual buzz you're supposed to get from hanging by the neck. Like, when the rope jerks, you jerk off down there, too. That it?"

Andy said nothing. Powys could see him trying surreptitiously to move different muscles.

"And with sex magic, you use the buildup of sexual tension to harden and focus your will. And then, at the moment of orgasm . . . whoosh. Max Goff used to play about with it. Who taught him? You?"

Andy was stretching his neck, easing it from side to side.

"Sex and death. Hell of a powerful combination. This was how Black Michael pro—"

"Don't call him that," Andy snapped.

"This was how Sir Michael Wort . . . Bloody hell, Joe Powys always does what he's told . . . ! This was how *Black fucking Michael* projected himself into Crybbe, fused his spirit with the spirit of the town so that the town is the man is the town is the . . . "

Andy stopped trying to flex muscles and stared at Powys in the electric lamplight, and his eyes were so strange that Powys wasn't sure anymore which of them he was talking to, Andy or Michael. But, clearly, the stage Andy had been striving to reach was something that went beyond personalities.

"What did it really mean, though?" Powys said. "Was it simply a quest for eternal power? Some kind of semiphysical immortality?"

You have to fracture the cool, he remembered telling himself. To damage this guy, you have to tip his balance, dislodge him from his mental lotus position. Even lying there, with unknown injuries, he can, maybe, still take you unawares.

"Or is it," Powys said casually, "just the ultimate ego-trip? Get yours from beyond the grave?"

He had to look away. The blackness from Andy's eyes came out like iron spikes.

Iron spikes. Images of Rose cruelly speared his own cool, and he stared back into the eyes of the thing that had so dispassionately manipulated their fate.

"I can't move," Andy said suddenly, the first sign of human panic. "I can't fucking move, Joe. I can't move my arms or my legs. I'm fucking paralyzed."

"What I think . . . " Powys remembered conversations with Barry the osteopath, his neighbor in the Trackways building. " . . . is your back was broken in the fall. You can obviously move your neck. What about your shoulders? Try shrugging your shoulders."

Andy's shoulders convulsed. There was a sudden sheen of sweat on his body.

"How's your breathing?"

"I can breathe."

"In that case," Powys said slowly and callously, "you'll probably be what's known as a tetraplegic. It won't be much fun, but no doubt a lot of innocent people'll be saved a lot of grief by your confinement in Stoke Mandeville or wherever you wind up."

"You're a worthless piece of shit, Joe."

"Me? *I'm* shit?"

"You couldn't even kill me."

"You're safer like this. Dead, you could be a problem."

Andy turned his head and looked into the eye sockets of Black Michael. As an exercise in mummification, Powys thought, Michael had turned out to be rather less impressive than Tiddles.

He said, "Where are the other bits buried?"

"Why should I tell you that?"

"The head, naturally, was in the Tump. Did you ever go into the Tump? Physically, I mean."

"No."

"And the genitals are under the Cock. Walled up somewhere in the cellars. I'd guess somewhere directly beneath that passageway leading to this studio. The heart under the church—is there a crypt?"

Andy didn't reply.

"And who would have buried your bits, Andy, after the hanging? Humble?"

"Where is Humble?" Occurring to Andy, perhaps, that there might be more wrong than he knew.

Powys said, "What's happening down in the town? What's on fire?"

"Not my problem," Andy said.

"You're beyond me." He was getting impatient. And nervous. He was face-to-face with the man who'd smashed his life and all he wanted to do was get out of here. Call an ambulance, anonymously. Man with a broken back. Tried to hang himself. Take him away.

Yet there were things he had to know.

"Look . . . I mean . . . For Christ's sake, *why?* Is your mother behind this?"

"What?"

"Jean Wendle."

Andy laughed. It wasn't a very strong laugh, suggesting his breathing was not, after all, unaffected. "There's no blood link between Jean and me. She's my spiritual mother, if you like. It's a concept you wouldn't understand."

"Which of you is the descendant, then?"

"Listen . . . Jean had been studying Wort for years, right? There's almost . . . this kind of Michael Wort Society. Very exclusive, Joe. Not for the New Age morons. Not for the wankers. Not for the . . . authors of popular trash books. Not for the . . . the fucking *popularizers*. For the Few. And now . . . "

Andy began to cough.

"I can't feel that," he said. "I can't feel it in my guts, you know?"

"And now . . . what?"

"The New Age." He gave a short wheeze of a laugh. "Suddenly this . . . worldwide movement dedicated to throwing esoteric knowledge at the masses. Max Goff—millions of pounds to . . . "

"So you hijacked Goff."

"Well put. Yeah, I hijacked Goff. He loved me. In all kinds of ways."

"To provide the money and the psychic energy you needed to condition Crybbe for the Second Coming of Black Michael."

Andy grimaced. "Let's get this right, there was no Second Coming. We were just completing Michael's plan. I've had access to all his papers since I was sixteen, and to the people who could explain what it all meant. And then it got to the stage where I knew more than any of them. We were completing the plan. Patching up the damage John Dee did. Also, removing the Preece problem and altering the psychic climate."

"Stirring things up. Emotional conflict. Anger, bitterness, confusion."

"We awoke the place," Andy said, "from centuries of sleep. An unhealthy, drugged sort of sleep. Psychic Mogadon, self-administered. I've been planting little time bombs, like . . . OK, I took a job for a few months, teaching art at the local high school. I wanted a girl. I wanted to take a girl living in Crybbe and *turn* her. There was a perfect one—I mean, this happens, Joe, there's always somebody there who fits, and she was entirely perfect. I worked with this kid over a year. I taught her to paint, I mean *really* paint . . . "

"In your studio. In the wood."

"Sure. I taught her the arts. The real ẚrts. You give them a little at that age, they become quite insatiable. She was a natural. She can make paintings that become doorways . . . But that's something else. Also, I used her . . . to penetrate the Preece clan. And in the heart of the Crybbe household, I—well, Michael and I—we created *the most wonderful* little monster, a creature entirely without heart, dedicated to destruction. In the heart of the Preece household. Again, ripe for it. Warren Preece. Maybe you'll meet him. Everybody ought to meet Warren."

"You're a scumbag, Andy," Powys said.

"So kill me," Andy said quietly.

There was silence in the little well-like cell, its ceiling jaggedly open to the attic.

"You still got that bread knife? Kill me. Cut my throat. It's easy. Even Warren managed to cut Max Goff's throat tonight, with a Stanley knife."

"What?"

"You didn't know about Max? He was killed in the public meeting during a power cut. It was quite beautiful. And perhaps the most beautiful thing of all is that when this is all over, who's going to get the blame for this orgy of destruction? The New Age movement. You've got to laugh. Warren says that. Got to laugh."

Powys said coldly, "You're insane. Your brains have turned to shit. I'll get you an ambulance."

"No, you'll kill me, Joe."

"Like I said, I wouldn't trust you dead."

"You'll kill me. Look, you're squeamish about knives, use the rope. Strangle me. No hassle. I'm weak, I'll go easy. It'll just look like I hanged myself and the rope broke."

He'd almost forgotten the noose still hanging loosely around Andy's neck. Hesitantly, he walked across, began to remove the rope, trying not to touch Andy's skin. "Just in case you're lying about not being able to move your arms. Hate you to try and do it yourself."

Andy grinned, white teeth exploding through the beard.

"Do it!"

"No."

"OK, something you didn't know. Rose, right? Poor spiked little Rosie. And the baby was spiked, too, yeah? Your baby, Joe?"

Powys shook his head. "I've got past that. I don't want to kill you for that. I'm happy you're going to be a paraplegic or a tetraplegic. I hope your breathing degenerates; you'll be even safer in an iron lung."

"It wasn't your baby, Joe."

His hands froze on the rope.

"I'd been fucking Rose quite intensively for several months. I've always found I can get any woman, any man . . . I want. Part of the Wort legacy, if you will. Also, it was my understanding that, come bedtime, the great visionary writer's creative imagination would tend to go into abeyance, and so . . . "

Powys wrenched down the noose, jerked Andy's head back, slammed the knot tight into the back of the neck. Andy grinned up at him; even the whites of his eyes were almost black.

Abruptly, Joe Powys let the rope go slack and pulled the noose over Andy's head.

"I'll get you an ambulance," he said.

three

Gomer couldn't get near the church, least not within thirty yards. Not much he could have done, though, anyway. Be a long time before that ole place saw another service. If ever. Roof mostly gone, windows long gone. Still some flames—plenty of wood in the nave, pews and stuff, to keep them well-nourished for some hours yet—but the worst was over. The stone walls would stay up, and so would the tower, even if it wasn't much more than a thick chimney by now.

"Bugger-all use fetchin' the fire brigade," Gomer concluded. "Burned 'imself out, see." He turned to his companion; no way of hedging around any of this. "Pardon me askin' this, but your Jonathon—was 'e gonner be cremated anyway, like? 'Cause, if 'e 'ad to . . ."

"Gonner be buried. And he still will be, whatever's left."

They'd come upon Jimmy Preece sitting on the low part of the churchyard wall watching the fire. The digger had crunched out of the wood and there the old feller was, hunched up, knotted and frazzled like a rotting tree stump, sounding like it was gonner take Dyno-Rod to clear his lungs. And it was clear straight off to Gomer that nothing happening tonight would have been a mystery to Jimmy Preece.

"Who done this, Jim?" he asked bluntly. "And don't give me no bull."

Arnold the dog limped over to Jimmy Preece and stood there, watchful. Jimmy Preece leaned down, hesitated for several seconds, and then patted him. Arnold wagged his tail, only twice and just as hesitantly, and then plodded off. Gomer had the feeling this was a very strange thing, momentous-like, and patting a dog was only part of what it was about.

"I'm glad," the mayor said to nobody in particular. "Wish I was dead, but I'm glad. Couldn't go on, see."

"What couldn't?"

"You're not a Crybbe man, Gomer, is the problem."

"Well, hell, Jim, I'm only a few miles up the valley, born an' bred."

"Not a Crybbe man," Jimmy Preece said firmly. Gomer was near fuming.

"Who done it, Jim? Too late for all that ole crap. Just bloody spit it out."

Something gave. Jim's grimy face wobbled and what had looked like a smear of thick oil down one side of it gleamed in the firelight and didn't look like oil anymore. When he opened his mouth the words oozed out in a steady stream.

"Same one as run your bulldozer in the wall, same one as slashed my face, same one as left me to suffocate, same one as . . . as done for Jonathon."

The mayor looked away. "Pretended I was dead, see—didn't take a lot o' pretendin'. Wanted to close the old door to the tower, keep the fire out, last duty, see. Then I was gonner lie down. Next to Jonathon."

Gomer saw Minnie Seagrove trying to climb out of the digger and held up a hand to tell her to stay where she was.

"Couldn't do it," Jimmy Preece said, studying his boots now. "Not got the guts. Fire too hot. Old body sayin', get me out o' yere. Ole body allus wins."

"Where is 'e, Jim?" Gomer had no doubts who they were talking about anymore. "Where is 'e? Dead?"

"That's all I got left to hope for," said Jimmy Preece. "But I reckon we've long ago given up all rights to hope. In Crybbe."

"Jim . . ." Gomer feeling sorry for him now, town falling apart, family collapsing around his ears. "I'd like to 'elp."

The mayor stared for a long time into the ruined church before he replied.

"You really wanner do some'ing, Gomer?"

"What I said."

"Then get rid of all these bloody stones for me. Do it before morning, make it like they was never yere, know what I'm askin'?"

"Tall order," said Gomer. "Still . . . Only I don't know where they all are. Seen a couple around, like."

"I'll tell you where they are. Every one of 'em."

"Might mean goin' on people's property, though, isn't it? Trespassin'."

"Depends on what you thinks of as other people's property, isn't it?"

"Course, if it was an official council contract, like . . . "

"Consider it an official council contract," said Jimmy Preece, wearily.

They carried Alex into The Gallery, Joe Powys and the capable-looking guy who'd introduced himself as Col Croston.

He was quite a weight.

"Obviously too much for his heart," Col said. "And it was a hell of a big heart. How old was he?"

"Old," Fay said distantly. "Pushing ninety." She sniffed. "Pushed too hard."

Alex had still been lying on the cobbles when Powys had stumbled uncertainly into the square, seemingly bringing the lights with him—the power was back. He'd walked past Wynford Wiley and Wiley had hardly glanced at him. Guy Morrison had nodded and said nothing. He'd gone directly to where Fay sat, close to the steps of the Cock, guarding her father's body like a mute terrier. "I thought you were going to be dead, too," was all she'd said, and then had laughed—unnaturally, he thought, and he wasn't entirely surprised.

They put Alex on the only flat, raised surface in The Gallery, the display window, under mini-spotlights. He looked peaceful, laid out with pictures. "He'd hate that," Fay mumbled. "Looking peaceful."

"Don't suppose," Col Croston said, "that there's much I can say, is there? The awful thing is, nobody will ever know what he achieved in the last few minutes of his life. Even I can't begin to explain it, and I was there. And I know . . . " He broke off, looking uncharacteristically lost. "I don't know *what* I know, really. I'm sorry."

"He won't mind," Fay said. "It was quick, and he never became a vegetable, did he? That was all he was scared of. The geriatric ward. He might have done something silly. Like half a bottle of malt whiskey and some pills, or a last train to Soho or somewhere, with a view to departing in the arms of some . . . aging harlot."

She's rambling, Powys thought. She's blocking it out. Her body's producing natural Valium. Everybody has a breaking point.

From behind them, a small, raw cry.

After letting them in, the woman who ran The Gallery, Mrs. Newsome, had remained silently in the doorway, leaving Powys wondering about the weals and bruising on her throat.

Now she was pointing at a door to the left of the glass counter. It was a white door, but there were marks and smears all over it now, in red.

Col saw the blood, flung out an arm to hold everyone back, snapped, "What's behind there?"

"He . . . " It wasn't easy for her to talk, and her voice, when it emerged, was like a crow's. "Hereward's workroom."

"Anybody in there," Col called out harshly, "will get back against the wall and keep very still. Understood?"

The marks on the door included smeared fingerprints and one whole palmprint.

"Mrs. Newsome, have you any idea . . . ?"

The act of shaking her head looked as painful as talking.

Col shrugged and nodded. "Everybody keep back, then," he said and hit the door with a hard, flat foot, directly under the handle. Powys wondered why he didn't simply open it. Shock value, he supposed, as the door splintered open and Col jumped back and went into a crouch.

"Oh, Christ." Powys stared into the shadowed face of the man he'd left fifteen minutes earlier lying crippled in the center of a little stone chamber.

Remembered thinking as he'd run out of the Court that Andy might not be so badly injured as he appeared. That someone practiced in yoga and similar disciplines might be able to contort his body sufficiently to stimulate a broken spine.

But Powys hadn't gone back. He'd kept on running all the way to the car and then driven to the phone booth on the edge of town. Which worked, thank God. "Ambulance, yes. And . . . police, I suppose. And the fire brigade. In fact, send the lot. Jesus. In force."

"God in heaven," Col Croston was saying. "Don't come in, Mrs. Newsome."

It wasn't the face. The face, Powys saw with short-lived relief, was only in a very large painting—Andy dressed in the kind of somber clothing Michael Wort might have worn, standing by a door meaningfully ajar. Powys remembered Andy talking about a girl, the artist, who could "create doorways." With that in mind, he didn't look at it again. But what was beneath it was worse.

The unframed canvas was hanging on the wall above a wooden workbench with sections of frames strewn across it and, fastened to the side, a large wood vise with a metal handle and wooden jaws.

The vise would hold a piece of soft timber firmly, without damaging it, unless you really leaned on the handle, in which case it would probably squash anything softer than iron.

Powys nearly choked. He didn't go in. Blood was still dripping to the sawdusted floor and there were deltas down the walls made by high-pressure crimson jets.

The dead man was on his knees, the jaws of the vise clamped like the hands of a faith healer either side of this giant red pepper, his head, once.

Powys's stomach lurched like a car doing an emergency stop.

Col Croston emerged expressionless, pulling the door closed behind him. "Mrs. Newsome . . . Let's get some air, shall we?"

Her face began to warp. Col Croston took her arm and steered her into the square. Powys quickly closed the door behind them and stood with his back to it; he didn't want to hear this.

"What's in there?" Fay said from far away.

"A body."

"Is it Hereward? Hereward Newsome?"

"Hard to say, he's been . . . damaged. And I don't know him. And if I did, it wouldn't help. Look, Fay, can we . . . ?"

"Warren Preece," Fay said, as if this explained everything. "I expect Warren Preece did it."

She took a last disbelieving look at her dad and watched Powys flick off the lights. She didn't move. He took her hand and towed her into the street. She went with him easily, like one of those toy dogs on wheels. From down the hill, across the river, blue emergency beacons were strobing toward the town with a warble of sirens.

Powys pulled Fay into a side street. "It'd be a bit daft to leave town, but I'd rather not be the first in line to make a police statement, would you?"

"Where shall we go?"

"My cottage?" They were in a street of narrow terraces and no lights. "Or your house?"

"I suppose it is my house now," Fay said, still sounding completely disconnected. "Unless Dad's left it to some mysterious woman. I mean . . . I don't want it. I'll take the cats, but I'm not having Grace. Can you give a house to charity?"

He took hold of her upper arms, gently. "Fay, please."

She looked at him in mild inquiry, her green eyes calm as rock pools at low tide.

"I need you," Powys said, and he hadn't meant to say that.

Fay said, "Do you?" from several miles away.

He nodded. They seemed to have been through years of experience together in about two days.

He'd tried to explain briefly what had happened. About the Tump, the head in the box. About Andy. Not about Jean Wendle; it wasn't the time.

What he wanted to tell her now was that something had been resolved. He wanted to say reassuring things about her dad.

But as he reached out for her he felt his body breaking up into awful, seismic shivers. It's not over—the words squeezed into his brain like the fragmented skull of the man in the vise—*it's not over.*

four

Joe had left the candle behind.

Taken the lamp but brought the candle down from the attic and left it on the floor in the open doorway, well out of the reach of Andy Boulton-Trow.

The candlelight would guide the paramedics with their stretcher to the room where Andy lay, feeling no pain, only a frigid fury which he knew he had to contain if he were to preserve the legacy.

And fancied he could hear distant sirens; didn't have much time. He picked up the head of Michael Wort and held it above him—oh, yes, he could use his arms, he'd lied about that. But not his legs; he couldn't feel his legs or his lower body, only the bubbling acid of rage which he would have to control and channel.

"Michael," he hissed, and his lungs felt very small and also oddly detached, as though they were part of some ancillary organism.

The head of Michael Wort had no eyes, its remaining teeth were bare, its skin reduced to pickled brown flakes. But the skull was hard.

Andy looked deep into the dark sockets and summoned the spirit of the man who, four hundred years ago this night, had dared to seize the Infinite.

"Dewch," he whispered, *"Tyrd i lawr,* Michael." He lay back and—balancing the head on his solar plexus—closed his eyes, slowed his breathing, began to visualize with an intensity he'd never known. *"Tyrd i lawr."*

The first police car arrived as they approached the bridge. Joe didn't want to cross at first, in case they were stopped. Joe was a worrier. Fay didn't see any problem.

And the car didn't stop.

As the police car warbled away, she remembered something. "Where's Arnold?"

"Mrs. Seagrove's looking after him. He's . . . Well, I'll tell you. Sometime."

Sometime? Fay looked at him curiously. Then said to herself, *My father's dead.* Every time she thought of something else, she was going to make herself repeat this, with emphasis. What she wanted was to be suddenly overcome with immeasurable grief, to sob bitterly, throw a fit in the street.

No parents at all anymore. No barrier. In the firing line now. Stand up, Fay Morrison. Bang.

Bang.

Bang!

Fay stopped. *My DAD'S DEAD.*

Yes. But that wasn't the whole point. This was Crybbe. In Crybbe, death wasn't necessarily the worst thing that could happen to you. He'd looked peaceful under the gallery spotlights, with the paintings. But *was* he at peace, or was he going to hang around, like Grace, as some kind of psychic detritus?

Was this the destiny of the dead of Crybbe, to molder on, like the town?

"Psychic pollution," she said suddenly. "What can you do about psychic pollution?"

She peered over the bridge parapet, down to where the dark water loitered indolently around the stone buttresses.

"Nuclear waste you can just about bury," she said. "Hundreds of feet underground in immovable granite. And, maybe, after four hundred years . . . " She straightened up. "You know, I really underestimated the . . . the *toxicity* of this town. It's a *really unhealthy place.*"

Joe was staring at her. *I need you,* he'd said, the words sounding strange. Probably because nobody had actually said that to her before. Not her dad, not Offa's Dyke Radio, not even her old boss at Radio Four. Certainly not Guy. (We could be good for each other, Fay.) No. Nobody.

She looked at Joe in the light of the street lamp at the end of the bridge. She thought he was a nice guy. She could, in better circumstances, be quite seriously attached to him.

He still looked sort of wary, though.

"Maybe they were right," he was saying, "with their curfew and their Crybbe mentality. Maybe it was the best they could do. Maybe they just hadn't got the knowledge or the resources to handle it."

"Handle what exactly, Joe?"

"I don't know. I don't suppose we'll ever know. Whatever . . . properties it has. To amplify things. The Old Golden Land. Where psychic doorways are easy to open."

"And pretty near impossible to close."

"John Dee knew it," Joe said. "Wort knew it. Just goes a lot deeper than either of them probably imagined. When you think about it, the great Michael Wort was probably just another loony. Like Andy. He didn't know what the fuck he was doing either."

They were approaching the cottage which overlooked the river.

Fay said, without thinking about it, "Is that the Bottle Stone I can hear?"

"What?"

"Thin drone, like the hum from a pylon."

"I can't hear anything."

"Probably nothing."

"Probably," he said uncertainly. "Funny, isn't it? We build up this big theory about Black Michael, and because he was four hundred years ago we think he's some kind of god. But he was just another . . . just another pollutant."

Out of the night came a slow clapping of hands. Ironic, essentially mocking applause.

"Persuasively argued, Joe," Jean Wendle said.

Joe Powys froze.

Jean Wendle was leaning against the cottage wall. She was wearing a pink velour tracksuit. She looked elegant and relaxed.

Two police cars went rapidly past, followed by a fire engine.

And Joe Powys froze, and Fay sensed it wasn't because of the police cars, not this time.

"But quite wrong," said Jean. "And you know it."

He didn't say anything.

"Michael Wort," said Jean, "had one of the finest of the Renaissance minds. Scientist, philosopher . . . these terms simply cannot encompass Michael's abilities. We no longer like to use words like magus, but that's what he was, and the reason he isn't as famous as Francis Bacon and Giordano Bruno and even—God forbid—John Dee . . . is that he realized the futility of books and so never wrote any. And also, of course, he lived not in Florence or Rome, or even London. But in Crybbe."

Fay could see Joe trying to say something, trying to frame words.

"If he never wrote anything," she said, "how do you know he was so great?"

"Because," said Jean, "like all great teachers, he passed on his knowledge through training and through experience."

Another police car went past, followed by another fire engine.

"There's a Michael Wort tradition," Jean said. "It began with his own family, and then was passed to selected scholars."

"What kind of tradition?"

"Fascinating stuff," Jean said. "All to do with the spirit land-scape, and the interpretation of planes. Knowledge we are only now beginning to approach."

"They called him Black Michael," Fay said.

"As they would. In Crybbe."

"He hanged people."

"He studied death, and he utilized his period as high sheriff to pursue that study. That was all."

How bizarre, Fay thought. All hell breaking loose up in the town and here we are, three uncommitted observers from Off, calmly discussing the background as if it's a piece of theater.

"Knowledge," said Jean, "isn't evil."

"And what about what happened on the square? What about the killing of Max Goff? What about . . . ?"

"You know as well as I do, my dear, that there are some very misguided and unbalanced people in Crybbe, and there always have been. People Michael was trying to help."

"I didn't know," Fay said, "that you knew so much about Michael Wort."

"You didn't ask," said Jean. Her short gray hair shone like a helmet in the street light.

"Fay . . . " Joe said.

"Joe's trying to tell you to come away," Jean said. "He doesn't want to end what he began."

"Which is?"

"The Bottle Stone," Jean said gently. "Come and see the Bottle Stone."

"No!" Joe backed away.

"He blames it for everything," Jean said. "For all his problems, all his failed relationships. The deaths of his women."

"Fay." Joe sounded suddenly alarmed. "I don't know what she's doing, but don't fall for it. I meant to tell you. Jean and Andy are in this together. She sent me up to the Tump tonight, she set me up for Humble . . . "

"Did he tell you," said Jean, "how the Bottle Stone followed him here?"

"Yes," Fay said, her throat suddenly quite dry. "He told me that."

"Come and see the Bottle Stone, Fay. Come on."

"Fay."

"Come along," said Jean.

She rose from the wall and picked her way carefully to the gate of the cottage. "Come *on!*"

Fay glanced at Joe. "Don't," he said quietly. "Please."

I meant to tell you.

She turned and followed Jean Wendle.

They went around the side of the cottage and across the damp lawn to the piece of land at the rear. Jean had produced a small torch and they followed its thin beam. Fay could hear the river idly fumbling at its banks.

Jean stopped. She directed the beam a short way across the grass until it found the thick, gray base of a standing stone. Then Jean casually flipped the torch up so that they could see the top of the stone.

"It doesn't look awfully like a bottle, does it?" Jean said.

The stone appeared no more than three and a half feet tall. It was fairly wide, but slim, like a blade.

Fay said, "It doesn't look *anything* like a bottle."

Andy Boulton-Trow lay on his back, holding the head above himself with both hands. The hands didn't ache now.

"Michael," he said, "forgive me. It was a shambles. I was using weak, stupid people. I failed you."

In the doorway, the candle was burning very low. He'd thought he could hear sirens a while back. He couldn't hear anything now.

Joe Powys hadn't rung for an ambulance.

Joe Powys had lied.

five

❖ ⸻⸻⸻⸻⸻⸻⸻⸻⸻⸻⸻⸻⸻⸻⸻⸻⸻

"One more, I make it," Gomer said, a short trail of recumbent stones in his destructive wake. "Then that's the lot."

"You know, Gomer," Minnie Seagrove said, sitting quite placidly next to him in the cab, the three-legged dog on her lap. "You've surprised me tonight."

"Surprised myself," Gomer said gruffly. "I'll be very surprised if I collect a penny for all this."

"No, what I mean is . . . Well, I'd come to the conclusion—and I'm sorry if this sounds insulting—I'd come to the conclusion that there weren't any really decent men in Crybbe. Like, men we used to say would do *anything* for you. Nothing too much trouble, sort of thing . . . if it was the *right* thing."

"Done a few bloody wrong things tonight, Minnie, my love," Gomer said, plunging the digger halfway down the riverbank. "That's for certain."

"No they wasn't. They wasn't wrong things at all. You've saved me from being arrested for murder, you're working overtime at a minute's notice to help that poor old chap who looks like he's on his last legs. And you've been no end of help to young Joe . . ."

Gomer plowed through an unstable-looking fence and up into the field that served as a narrow floodplain for the river.

"I got no regrets about gettin' you out of a bit o' bother," he said. "An' I'd stand up in court an' say so. But that Joe—well, I'd like to think that young feller'll keep 'is mouth shut, see, that's all. You know much about 'im?"

"Not a lot," said Minnie. "But I'm sure he's all right."

"It's rather sad, really," Jean said. "They're all bottle stones to Joe."

Fay started to feel faint. To pull herself together, she said—screamed it out inside her head, like biting on something hard, to fight extreme pain,

MY FATHER IS DEAD.

And wondered if Jean knew about that yet. Jean, who'd given him a new lease on life. Which he'd expended in what appeared at this moment to be a distressingly futile way.

Fay felt sick.

"I don't know precisely what happened," Jean was saying. "Over this girl of Joe's. Rose, I mean. Whether it was an accident, or suicide, or . . ."

"Or what?"

Jean put a hand on Fay's arm. "Look, my dear, it's over. It's all in the past. Whatever happened, there's nothing we can change now. Nobody we can bring back to life."

"No," Fay said numbly.

Something white in places caught her eye, over to the right of the Bottle Stone. Joe Powys's muddy T-shirt. He was standing on the other side of the perimeter wall, watching them silently, like an abandoned scarecrow.

"About Andy," Jean said. "Andy's not a bad boy. A little wild, perhaps, in his younger days, a little headstrong. His lineage is not a direct one to Michael, but he developed a very strong interest in the Tradition from his early teens. And, give him his due, he didn't deviate in his resolve to discover things for himself."

"And the Bottle Stone ritual?"

"Exists not at all," said Jean sadly, "outside the head of J. M. Powys."

"He showed me the field," Fay said. "Where it happened."

"And was there a Bottle Stone there? And a fairy mound? With a fairy on it?"

"What about Henry Kettle? He was there too. There was nothing wrong with Henry Kettle."

"Oh? Henry told you, did he? He said he was there?"

A police car howled a long way away.

"No," Fay said bleakly.

"Oh, my dear . . . "

Fay was bent over, gripping her thighs with both hands. She felt a stabbing stomach cramp coming on.

"Oh God," she breathed. "Oh God."

And as Andy's breathing, shallow as it was, began to regulate, he looked into the dark sockets and saw within them pinpricks of distant light.

He watched the lights as they came closer—or, rather, as he moved closer to *them,* his consciousness was focused and drawn into the sockets, now as wide as caverns.

He felt the familiar tug at the base of his spine, and never before had it felt so good, so strong, so positive, so indicative of freedom. For, while imprisoned within his twisted body, Andy could no longer feel anything at all at the base of his spine.

When it happened—and he'd been far from certain that it would under such conditions—there was an enormous burst of raw energy (O Michael! O Mother!) and he was out of his body and soaring toward the lights.

"It's a shame about Crybbe," Jean said. "But it's no different in any of these places. You ask the ordinary man in the street in Glastonbury how he feels about the Holy Grail. How many miracles he's seen. They're not the least bit interested and indeed often quite antagonistic."

Looking beyond the stone, Fay could no longer see Joe. Perhaps he'd crept away.

"So you can imagine how they reacted in Crybbe," Jean went on. "A place so remote and yet so conducive to psychic activity. Can one blame the peasantry? I don't know. The knowledge has always been for the Few. Not everyone has the spiritual metabolism to absorb it. Not everyone has the will to see through the dark barriers to the light."

All at once, as if to illustrate Jean's point, the stone which bore no resemblance at all to a bottle was lit up from its grassy base to its sharp, fanglike tip.

"Goodness," Jean said. "Whatever's that?"

Beyond the stone, there was a kind of parapet overlooking the river, and to one side, dropping down to the floodplain, a narrow, muddy track, its entire width now taken up by a crawling, grunting monster with its single bright eye focused on the stone.

Fay saw a wiry figure leap from the creature and advance upon the stone. Jean flashed her torch at it and the light was reflected in a pair of old-fashioned wire-rimmed National Health glasses.

"Evening, ladies. Gomer Parry Plant Hire. I realize it's a bit late, like, but I got official instructions to remove that stone, see."

Jean stiffened. "I *do* beg your pardon."

"Official council operation."

"Now why is it," Jean asked smoothly, "that I rather doubt that?"

"Madam, I got special authorization yere from the town mayor 'isself."

"Oh, Gomer," Fay blurted out. "The mayor's dead."

"Miss Morris?"

"Isn't it sad?" said Jean. "Isn't it primitive? There was once a notorious farmer, you know, in Wiltshire, known as Stonebreaker Robinson, who devoted his energies to eradicating megalithic remains from the face of the countryside. It's been popularly thought that such Philistine ignorance was dead."

She turned to Gomer Parry. "Do yourself a big favor, little man. Go home to bed."

"Do *me* a favor." Joe Powys scrambled down from the perimeter wall. "Flatten the bloody thing." He stood next to Gomer.

Jean switched off her torch. Now both Gomer and Powys existed only as wavy silhouettes in the headlight's blast.

But the stone was fully illuminated.

"What are you afraid of, Joe? Afraid of what you'll do to Fay?"

He didn't say anything. He seemed to be shaking his head.

"I shouldn't worry, my dear," Jean said to Fay. "You can stay at my house tonight."

"Flatten it," Powys said.

"Lay one finger on that stone, little man," said Jean, "and, I promise you, you'll regret it for what passes for the rest of your life."

"It's not an old stone, Gomer," Powys said. "If it was a genuine prehistoric monument, *I* wouldn't let you touch it."

There was a flurrying then in the track of the headlight. It was so fast that Fay thought at first it was an owl until it veered out of the light. At which point it ought to have disappeared, but it didn't. It carried its own luminescence, something of the will-o'-the-wisp.

"Oh my G . . . " Fay gasped as, with a small, delighted whimper, it landed on her feet.

"Arnold!"

The dog jumped up at her; she felt his tongue on her legs.

"Oh God, Arnold." She pushed her hands deep into his fur.

And felt him stiffen.

The air above the standing stone seemed to contract, and to draw into it the headlight beam. The headlamp itself grew dim, fading to a bleary yellow.

The yellow of . . .

Fay felt Arnold's hackles rise under her hands. He growled from so far back in his throat that it seemed to come not from him at all but from somewhere behind him.

Like from her.

"Bloody battery!" Gomer Parry ran for his cab.

. . . of disease.

Embalming fluid.

Grace Legge.

The stone glowed feebly at its base, rising in intensity until its tip was lit with a magnesium radiance, and Fay felt an intense cold emanating from it, a cold that you could almost see, like steam from a deep freeze.

The yellow, and the cold. And the aura of steam around the stone formed into an unmistakable shape of a beer bottle.

But it was the one word that did it.

"Yesssss." Drawn from Jean Wendle's throat like a pale ribbon of gauze.

And Fay flew at her.

She smashed her open palm so hard into Jean's face that Jean, caught unawares, was thrown back, off her feet, and Fay heard a small crack and felt wetness in her hand and pain too, as if it had been broken. Heard Joe Powys crying, *"Gomer . . . Go for it . . . Now . . . "* Saw the lights in the stone shiver and shrink and the digger's lone headlight brighten and the metal beast heaving about, its shovel raised high like a wrecking hammer.

For several icy-white, agonizing seconds, Andy Boulton-Trow once again experienced his whole body . . . a savage, searing sensation, a long, physical scream.

The experience came as the lights exploded and he was tossed contemptuously back into his body like a roll of old carpet.

He was still staring, from a place beyond the boundaries of despair, into the sockets in the head of Michael Wort. The sockets were just as black but no longer empty. The eyes of Michael Wort swirled like oil. The smile made by the exposed, chipped, brown teeth was malign.

The head felt heavy.

Gomer was not proud of what happened. There was no control, no precision . . . no *finesse*.

With a wild, hydraulic wrench, the cast-iron shovel came down several feet too quickly and simply smashed in the top of the stone.

He leaned out of his cab and heard the uppity Scotch woman shrieking.

There was a sudden, unnatural strength in Andy's arms.

He raised the head. He brought it down.

The skull smashed into his own.

Michael.

He felt his nose shatter in a cloud of blood.

Michael.

He felt his teeth splinter into fragments.

He raised the head again, his fingers splayed around shriveled skin and wisps of hair.

Michael
   Michael
     Michael . . .

The blows continued, with a vengeful intensity, long after Andy was dead.

From the doorway, Warren Preece looked on, fascinated by the head clutched in the two hands, the arms moving ferociously up and down until the other head on the floor was red pulp.

The old candle was near burnt to nothing when Warren picked it up.

But then, so was Warren. Stripped to the waist, and his chest was black, like charcoal. He could smell his own scorched skin. He figured his lips had been burnt away, too, so that his teeth were stuck in this permanent grin, like the head that was now rolling across the dusty, boarded floor toward him.

"Got to laugh."

He didn't have to tell the head. The ole head was laughing already at what it'd done.

Warren picked it up and stuck it under his arm, like one of them ghosts.

Two heads are better than one.

Got to laugh.

With his other hand he picked up the candle, just melted wax now, but he picked it up, squeezed it tight, so the boiling hot wax bubbled up between his fingers, feeling painful as hell. Feeling good.

He held up his hand, and there was wax dripping down the clenched fist, so it was like the hand had become the candle, the wick sticking up through his knuckles with a little white flame on the end.

Hand of Glory.

He went over to the Teacher, brought his hand down to get some light on the face. The face looked good, all smashed, one eye hanging out. Wished he could take this head too, bung it under his other arm, but cutting off a head with a Stanley knife would take too long. Thought about it with the other feller, before deciding on the vise.

Never mind.

Warren walked out of the room, by the light of his own hand. He felt really full of power now, like he'd just done a one-man gig in front of thousands of his fans.

With the head under his arm, he walked down the ole steps in a sprightly kind of way. Felt like he owned the place. Probably did. Least, he owned the farm now, with every bugger else dead or crippled, like.

Strolled through the old baronial hall–type place straight to the front door, his hand held out before him. He could smell the skin smoldering now. Pretty soon it'd all start frizzling off and there'd be nothing left but wax and bones.

The real thing. The authentic Hand of Glory.

The front door of Crybbe Court was open wide, and Warren Preece walked out into the spotlights.

Just like he'd always known it'd be, one day.

The courtyard was lined with people, silent, awestruck-like. Warren recognized a few of them, local farmers and shopkeepers and such. But also there were two ambulances and . . . FIVE cop cars. All the headlights trained on the door he'd just come out of.

"All right?" Warren yelled.

Didn't seem much point to the candle, with all these spotlights, so he squashed it out between his legs. Then he held up the head with both hands, way up over his own head, like the Football Association cup.

"Yeah!" Warren screeched.

About half a dozen coppers were coming toward him in a semicircle. Warren stuck the head under his arm and fished out his Stanley knife.

"Come on, son," one of the coppers said. "Let's not do this the hard way."

Warren flicked out the blade and grinned.

" 'Ow're you, Wynford," he said.

six

"I always imagined," said Fay, "leaving Crybbe for the last time and driving off into the sunset."

There was a peach-colored glow in the eastern sky, over the English side of Offa's Dyke.

"But it must be better," she said, "driving into the dawn."

Powys drove. They were in his Mini.

All of them. Arnold half asleep on her knee. Two resentful black cats with Russian names in a laundry basket on the back seat.

Fay would probably have brought her dad as well, if the body would've fitted in the trunk. But she'd get him out. He wasn't going to be planted in Crybbe.

Once they'd crossed the town boundary, past the signpost at the top of the hill, Joe stopped the car. He took her hand—the other one, not the one that was nearly broken rupturing Jean Wendle's nose—and led her out to the famous viewpoint, near the stile.

Below them, Crybbe was a somber, smoky little town which had sometimes been in Wales and sometimes in England but had never belonged to either.

The real owners of Crybbe were hidden in its own shadows and weren't apparent at dawn, for Crybbe's time, as Fay had long ago realized, was dusk.

She could see smoke still rising from the ruins of the church. The nave had collapsed, but the bell tower remained, Col Croston had told her a few minutes ago. And one bell still hung—the seventh bell.

"Which I intend to ring myself," Col said. "Every night, in the ruins. These picturesque old traditions," he said with a tight smile, "shouldn't be allowed to lapse."

When the stone was down they hadn't even looked for Jean Wendle. What could they do about her anyway? She'd committed no crimes.

Nobody had seen her since.

"I didn't believe her, of course," Fay said now.

"You bloody did," said Joe.

"She had me going for a while," Fay said. "However—as I *did* try to tell you at one point yesterday—I checked out the Bottle Stone. It *was* in that field in Radnor Forest and it *was* shaped like a bottle and he *did* take it away."

Powys reeled.

"I *am* a reporter," Fay said. "I came back that way from the library and went to the nearest farm. Took a while—you know what farmers are—but I got it out of them. That land—about eighteen acres—still belongs to the Trows. It was funny, the farmer actually called them Worts, sort of contemptuously. He rents the grazing, but they wouldn't sell the land."

"Andy?"

"Andy showed up there—about ten years ago, the guy said, but it was probably twelve—with a stone on the back of a truck, and he had the stone planted in the middle of the field, which annoyed the farmer, but he couldn't do anything about it. Andy promised to come back and take it away, and he did—last week."

"Why didn't you . . . ?"

"You kept saying you didn't want to talk about the Bottle Stone, and anyway . . . "

"And there was I, thinking you had faith in me."

"Oh, I did, Joe. That's the point—I didn't need to have the Bottle Stone bit confirmed. It was . . . a formality."

Powys said, "Your eye looks better."

"Let's not start lying to each other at this stage," Fay said.

"Of course . . . " Chief Inspector Hughes, hands in pockets, was pacing the square. "There are still things we *don't* understand."

"Really?" Col Croston was trying to sound surprised. A slow, dawn drizzle glazed the square. There was the acrid, dispiriting smell of fire and water.

"Oh, I've got *most* of it," Hughes said quickly. "And I think I grasp the social pressures which caused it."

Col had forgotten that Hughes was one of the "new" policemen with a degree in something appropriate.

"You look at the background," Hughes said. "The kid's stifled by it. Rural decline, brought up in this crumbling farm. And let's face it, this town's a good half-century behind every-where else."

"At least," said Col.

"So young Preece listens to rock music and he dreams . . . without much hope. And then along comes Salvation with a capital S, in the shape of our late friend Mr. Goff. He sends Goff a tape of his band, and Goff, no doubt conscious of the politics of the situation, responds favorably."

"How do you know this?"

"Letter from Epidemic in Warren's pocket. Charred, but read-able. We can only assume he made another approach to Goff and Goff told him to clear off. I'm telling you all this, Colonel, in the hope you can throw a bit of light . . . "

"All new to me, Chief Inspector."

"So we're assuming this is what pushed Warren over the edge. Given all the other pressures—losing his only brother and then his father's tractor accident. The boy seems to be of limited intel-lect—must have thought the whole world was against him."

"Psychiatrists will have a field day," said Col. "Where is he now?"

"Hospital. I'd like to think he was going to be fit to plead one day, but I wouldn't put money on it. He took most of Wiley's nose off with that Stanley knife before we disarmed him."

"Lovable little chap. I'm furious with myself. I was just yards away when he killed Goff."

"Who would have expected it?"

"I was *trained* to expect the unexpected, for God's sake. Do you know how many he's killed? I make it four—Goff, the vicar, poor old Hereward Newsome . . . and of course that chap Trow."

"Tie things up nicely if he put his hand up to the Rachel Wade business, too—her signature was on the letter suggesting Warren's music wasn't half bad. But what I was going to ask you, Colonel . . . the Trow killing's somewhat different in style. I can't go into details, but Warren seems to have finished him off by bludgeoning him with this other skull. We thought we had another murder when he came out of the old house with that thing, but it's obviously of some age. So where did it come from? Have any graves been disturbed locally?"

Col thought this over. "Well, he was obviously in the church, and there are a couple of tombs in there. Might be worth sifting through the ruins."

"Oh, we'll do that, all right. Obviously, it's not a major issue, but it's something we have to clear up."

"Well, I have to congratulate you, Chief Inspector. You seem to be putting it all together very nicely."

Hughes nodded. "Open and shut, really," he said.

Fay said, "I could be making a fortune at this very moment. There'll be a hundred reporters here before breakfast, like a flock of pigeons scrabbling for crumbs. Even poor bloody Ashpole seems to have missed it all."

"And what are they all going to say?"

"Hard to say precisely *how* they'll work it, but I can guarantee that, by tonight, Warren Preece will be very famous."

"And Michael Wort?"

"Who's Michael Wort?" said Fay.

More to the point, Joe Powys thought, *where* is Michael Wort? Back—hopefully—in his own carefully constructed limbo. He was still unsure what had happened over the Bottle Stone—whether it had been installed at the riverside cottage and then replaced with another stone, or whether the power of suggestion had made him *see* the Bottle Stone in the tense, burgeoning atmosphere before Rachel's death. In that case, where was the original Bottle Stone now?

Powys looked over his shoulder, half expecting to see the thing sprouting from the earth behind him.

Fay said, "I have to say it didn't occur to me for quite a while that what she . . . what Jean was doing at the stone was trying to generate—in *me*—enough negative energy for him—Andy, Wort, whatever—to make some kind of final leap. To save himself . . . itself."

"It occurred to me," Powys said.

"Well, it would, wouldn't it. You're a clever person. And you know what we thinks about clever people yereabouts."

Arnold limped toward them and fell over. He stood again and shook himself, exasperated.

Fay Morrison and Joe Powys looked at each other. Eyebrows were raised.

Neither of them had said a word about Arnold's remarkable turns of speed at critical moments. One day, Fay thought, she'd dare to mention that strange, glowing, phantom *fourth leg*. But not yet.

"He's a dowser's dog," Joe said laconically.

As she bent down to pick up the dog, a disturbing thought struck her. "What about the girl . . . Tessa?"

"She should really be taken away," Joe said, "and put through some kind of psychic readjustment program. Except they probably don't exist, so she'll go on causing minor havoc, until she grows up and turns into something even nastier. Like Jean."

"Is there nothing anyone can do?"

"World's full of them," Powys said. "Crybbe'll always attract them, and sometimes it'll manufacture its own."

"We can't just leave it."

"We bloody can."

"Yes," Fay said. "I suppose we can."

And she turned her back on the town, albeit with an uncomfortable feeling that one day they might feel they had to come back.

They got into the car. They were going to Titley, to Henry Kettle's cottage, which Joe had said was the best sanctuary he could think of. For a few weeks at least, he said, there'd be a danger of residual nasties from Crybbe clinging to them. Grace-type things.

Fay said, "Can we handle that?"

"Count on it," Joe Powys said grimly.

From the back seat, Rasputin the cat mewed in protest at his confinement in the laundry basket.

Fay said, "When you said you, er, needed me . . . what did you mean exactly?"

"I don't know. It just came out. Heat of the moment."

He turned on the engine.

"However . . . " Joe said, looking straight ahead through the windshield. "I know what I'd mean if I were to say it now."

Fay smiled. "What did the police say to you?"

"They said, 'Don't leave town.' "

Joe Powys grinned and floored the accelerator.